Aim above morality.
Be not simply good, be good for something¹.
~Henry David Thoreau

Fiction by Susan McGeown:

A Well Behaved Woman's Life

A Garden Walled Around Trilogy:
Call Me Bear
Call Me Elle
Call Me Survivor

Recipe for Disaster
Rules for Survival

The Butler Did It

Joining The Club

Nonfiction by Susan McGeown:

Biblical Women and Who They Hooked Up With

A

GARDEN

WALLED

AROUND

By Susan McGeown

Faith Inspired Books

Published Faith Inspired Books
3 Kathleen Place, Bridgewater, New Jersey 08807
www.FaithInspiredBooks.com

Footnote credits appear at the end of this work.

Call Me Bear:
To My Husband, David
(My very own Bright Feather)
"Always with breathless anticipation…"
Hebrews 10:24

Call Me Elle:
To My Parents
Marylynn and Herb
My Faith is because of them and the examples they set…
Hebrews 11:1

Call Me Survivor:
To My Children
Ian, Gracie, and Luke
My Greatest Treasures
3 John 1:4

A Note From The Author:

A Garden Walled Around was my very first foray into writing. Encouraged (or depending on your point of view: discouraged) by numerous agents, I divided the book up into the more manageable *A Garden Walled Around Trilogy* that it has been published as: *Call Me Bear, Call Me Elle, and Call Me Survivor.*

But I always meant for it to be one book. So, just because I can, I've put it back together. Here is Elle's story – in its entirety – as I always intended it to be: one monstrously long book.

Enjoy.

Table of Contents

Rattlesnake, bear, and owl show this man the center,
where their voices rise as smoke from blue mountain.[2]

~Gladys Cardiff

Captive

Bare feet in grass soggy with the earliest of spring rains can cause a chill in a body so fierce it can be hard even to move. As I peer into the first rays of the morning sun just breaking over the ridge, I do a silent battle with the morning shivers. Once I get busy with my chores I warm up a fair bit, but having risen from a warm spot in a corner of Old Woman's hut, gathering water from the stream first thing in the morning is always a sore trial for me. The trees look almost as cold as I do, me with steam coming out of my teeth-chattering mouth and them with steam rising off their rain soaked bark. I try not to think about having to step in the freezing cold river to fill my deerskin buckets, afraid that the shivers will just take me over completely. A vision of me, frozen solid just outside the hut's door, could have almost made me laugh out loud were it not for my *present circumstances*. I've been in this village a few weeks now. I'm many things.

I'm a white captive.

I'm a fourteen year old girl.

I'm alone.

I'm frightened.

I'm no better than a slave.

But I'm not a red savage.

My family lives on a homestead in the state of Virginia. There's my Pa, my little brother Eli, and my older brother Henry. Ma died when Eli was born. We settled there after the second Great War with Britain in the year of our Lord, 1817. I suspect the choice of where we settled was Pa's decision. I don't ever recall Ma saying a word about it one way or the other. Pa told me once that he was bound and determined to get as far away as possible once and for all from any body – Royalist, Colonist, British or French – who had war thoughts on his mind. Said he'd spent his whole life surrounded by war. He'd survived fighting in one, and he was damn certain he was not going to try his luck a second time. Furthermore, he didn't for one moment believe that any people who even had so many as ten rifles between them would be peaceful for long.

Our homestead is beautiful. Looking off the front porch, the sight of the mountains rising in their blue mist often causes a body to stop and stare at the wonder of it. But I suspect Pa chose it mostly cause it was the farthest piece of land he was able to get. Away from wars and hatred and killing and such. We were right happy there for a time. When I think of happy thoughts, I think of those early days building and planting and laughing. Then Ma died and much of the happiness went with her. I worry about Eli the most. I was the only Ma he knew and now I'm gone. It's a wonder to me how a life, as comfortable as an old shoe, can disappear in just the blink of an eye.

The red savages come one evening just before nightfall. They whoop and holler and sound terrible fierce. Pa grabs Eli and shouts to me, "Run, Elle!! RUN!!" I hear the great fear in his voice, and it's almost more frightening than the savages' screams. Then I see their black painted faces and I see their eyes that are so filled with hate and I change right quick what makes me scared. I try to run to the forest, but my skirts trip me and I fall. As I struggle to get up a savage grabs me by the back of my dress and hauls me across the front of him like I'm a sack of potatoes. I'm so frightened I wet myself. I'm so frightened that I can't move. I lie there across that horse certain my heart will beat right out of my chest and fall on the ground just like my pee does.

We ride and ride those first days and nights only taking time to rest the horses, I suspect. Riding face down on a horse is downright uncomfortable, but I'm not in a position to complain. My head and stomach ache something fierce. I look at a foot that's red, bare and filthy and my nose twitches at the smell of my captor. He's as close to naked as a body can be without showing the important parts.

By the start of the third day, I drag my feet some and struggle as I get hauled up once again onto the horse. I've had nothing to eat and only managed to drink some water from the stream. My stomach especially tells me enough is enough. My captors no longer have black painted faces, but red is just as terrifying as angry savage words are said, and I'm pulled roughly by my hair and dress back into place: face down, staring at that same dirty, red foot. I can't help it as my stomach empties in one great gush. *There,* I think, *at least I gave your foot a wash.*

I end up flat on my back trying to catch my breath. As I struggle to sit up Dirty Feet gives me a hard kick in the side, and I lie back down. I stare at the eyes of my captor as he ties a rope around my neck like a pet dog. I decide to keep my mouth shut and my head down. No need to court more trouble than I'm already in. As I walk alongside Dirty Feet it seems that my head and stomach will get a rest, but that might not make my bare feet so happy. Two times I end up face down in the dirt because I don't move fast enough. Dirty Feet holds my rope and watches as I haul myself up to standing. He doesn't even give me time to catch my breath or spit out the dirt in my mouth. I try real hard to pay a bit more attention to things so that I don't give Dirty Feet another chance to have fun with my rope.

The days that I travel with the savages are full of darkness and worry. We travel up into the misty blue mountains, up and over and then past some even bigger mountains still. Even in my fearful state there are times that I just have to catch my breath at the beauty of it all. I'm pretty sure we travel mostly south because I watch the sun. Maybe west a bit, too, I can't exactly say. I walk all that day and for the first time we rest for the night. Good thing my feet are tough and strong. Being barefoot is something I'm used to. I spend most of my time working to keep my mind as blank as the faces of the savages I travel with. Whoever would have thought that it's nigh onto impossible to think of nothing instead of something?

Those worry thoughts are like a jigger under my skin. I think about running away back home which will be a might difficult as I seem to have become Dirty Feet's newest pet. There's not one moment when my rope is free. Besides, how would I manage to get away? How can I out run the savages in their own woods when I couldn't manage it in my own yard? And which way would I go? I decide running is not something I should forget, but something I need to wait a bit on.

I wish I knew if Pa and Eli were safe. My heart says they must be safe while my head says, *Can Pa run faster than an angry red savage on a horse?* I make my head be quiet and let my heart sing its song. I'm fair certain that Henry is all right. He'd driven the wagon into town the day before the savages came to get seed for early spring planting and was not expected back for another day or so. Being almost eighteen, Pa said he could handle such a grown up chore, although I think he was a bit scared to be going off by himself like that for the first time.

I think and think about where they are taking me. And why me? Would they not have taken Eli, a strong boy of six, if they took me? Could they have killed a six-year-old boy? Could Pa have stopped them? Will someone come for me? Is there even a body that will miss me? When my head gets to aching from asking all these questions, I work hard on thinking of nothing again.

Three days of walking finds me limping something fierce and eating more dirt than I care to mention. Finally, even Dirty Feet looses interest in his rope game, and I find myself staring at his bare back, more than a might scared that I'm going to be dragged by my neck rope the rest of the way if I fall from the savage's horse. When we break into a gallop I'm forced to hold on to Dirty Feet, my face pressed to his body. Even with my eyes tight shut, my nose will not let me forget where I am and who I'm with. I'd rather eat dirt again.

The savage's village we finally arrive at is twelve full days from my homestead. There are more than thirty huts, some shaped round and squat and some shaped long and tall. Some are big enough to house large families and some seem to be for just one person. As we ride down into the clearing, I think the village looks a little like a wagon wheel with the biggest hut in the center and the others stretching out in all directions.

Dirty Feet brings me to a hut almost right in the middle of the village and dumps me at an old woman's feet, rope and all. There were so many sights and sounds that first day I can't remember them all. I remember seeing lots of naked children running around – boys and girls! – and thinking that maybe Eli would like it here. He always loved the summer because that was the only time Pa would let him run naked by the pond and go skinny-dipping. I remember lots and lots of barking dogs and was afraid I'd get bit. Dogs don't like strangers, do they? And I sure look strange compared to everyone else as far as the eye could see.

These are not the first red savages I've seen. I've seen pictures drawn in a newsprint once. Twice on the trail when we moved to our homestead we saw them watching us go by. Once at Cooper's General Store I saw one up close. And three times that I know of they passed through our homestead rather than go around as they should have, and Pa had to scare them off with the rifle. But each of those times it was always with my Pa close by, never by myself, lying in the dirt filled with too many feelings for one body to figure out in a lifetime. I look for something familiar to help me stop this spinning terror that's slowly pulling me under. But there's nothing I recognize. Not even the thoughts inside my head.

I'm not sure that anyone is happy with Dirty Feet's gift of me. There's not one smile or even a nod. No one gives him a pat on the back or shakes his hand. In fact, no one says much at all. Do savages even smile or laugh or sing or hug? I sure have never seen such. They all gather around and look silently at my sorry self sitting in a heap, lost and alone. I try hard not be rude and stare, even if they don't seem inclined to follow the same example. Finally, even the dogs stop barking.

The old woman of the hut has a face more wrinkled then a winter's dried apple. She dresses entirely in deerskin, with decorated moccasins on her feet. At first I think she has paint on her face, like the savages did the day they took me. Old Woman has lines and dots between her eyes and up across her forehead. But after a week or so I'm sure it isn't paint; it doesn't wash off, and I never see her redraw it. Somehow it's on her face for good. She isn't mean to me, but she isn't what you'd call kind either. She shows me what chores I'm expected to do, and if I don't do them fast enough or the right way she gives me a fair slap or kick. I learn right quick I'm never to touch the herbs and things she has hanging and stored all around her hut. I think she might be a healer. She puts a funny smelling salve on my neck when the rope is finally taken off. But once I get the rhythm of the work, she almost pretends that I don't even exist. She feeds me funny gruel made with grains and a bit of meat. It fills my stomach, which always seems to be growling and unhappy. I sleep in the corner of her hut and even have a few furs to keep me warm on these cold early spring nights.

Twelve days away from Pa, Henry, and Eli, I think over and over. Twelve days, and only three of them I walked. I can't get my head to figure how I'd manage to get back home. I'd get lost. I'd be hungry. I'd be frightened. I'd not be able to defend myself against dangerous animals or furious red savages coming after me ready to teach me a powerful lesson. I get angry at myself when I realize that the person I am is what makes me a prisoner more than the place where I stand. With that thought I feel like I've finally lost a big fight that I hadn't even realized I was in. Even though I'm no longer tied up, I'm a prisoner just the same, and there's nothing I can do about it. Running, I now know, is something I need to forget.

I think I take to most things quick. I watch and learn. Pa always said I'd have been a fast learner at school had I ever gone. Ma taught me my letters, and I took to reading and writing right swift. I don't have so much a memory of how I did the learning; it seemed to just make sense and flow into my head like learning a song. I do remember Henry being angry at how I could keep up with him in most of the lessons. Pa made sure all of us practiced our reading from the big Bible each night even after Ma died. Already Eli at six can spell his name and do some easy figuring. I could keep house by the time I was eight, which was when my Ma died. I cooked and cleaned and sewed and cared for Pa, Henry, and Eli from the moment it was clear Ma never would again. *Who cares for them now?*

I struggle most with the quandary that I can't understand a word anyone says. It just sounds like foolishness to me. On the trail, traveling with the savages when they first took me, they made hand motions when they said something to me. Sometimes I understood, like when I was to sit against the tree and get tied at night or mount up on the horse to ride the next day. Sometimes I didn't though, and they'd give me a hard cuff to the head letting me know just how stupid they thought I was. I'm not stupid though, I just don't understand their talking, that's all.

If I were forced to choose, I'd have to say that I like days better than nights. Days I can keep so busy I scarce have time to think of Pa, Henry, and Eli. Each and every day is the same, filled with chores for Old Woman or any one else who might be inclined to take the trouble to get me to understand what they want done. I gather sticks for firewood, I grind corn, I fetch water, I stir the cooking pot. Old Woman only notices me if I'm too slow. I work very hard not to be slow.

Nights, lying in my corner, I try real hard to fall asleep quick. But it seems no matter how hard I try and no matter how tired I am, I can't get my head to shut down fast enough and just think of nothing. Sometimes the ache to see Pa, Henry, or Eli is so great I fear that I'll just shatter into a million sobbing pieces and mess up Old Woman's hut something fierce.

Even though Ma died more than six years ago, I remember some things. She told me that to pray was to talk to God personal like, just as if He was close enough to whisper to. One of my strongest memories of Ma was nighttime prayers and me whispering in God's ear about all manner of things. When she died, I wondered whether the whispering had done any good. I did not whisper in God's ear about Ma's dying or living; was it my fault she died? Those late nights as I sat up with Pa helping to care for screaming baby Eli, I found myself thinking did Ma take God's ear with her? Can He still hear me or has He moved on? Pa still does prayers each night, but there's a different feeling to them, almost like seeing the maple syrup jug but knowing it's finally empty. Not until the savages came to take me do I try to whisper in God's ear again. Lying in my corner trying to sleep, I make deals with God. "If You let Pa and Eli get away then I'll stay here in this village and not ask for one thing else, God." Or, how about, "I'll bide my time quiet like and wait until Pa comes to get me from here." I even try, "I'll never complain or ask for anything else if I can just go home, soon. Please."

But sometimes the strangeness of it all, the worry of who I am and the terror of where I am gets so big I can't catch a breath. There are some nights that nothing – not weariness or prayers - can make my head be quiet or get my heart to sing, and I'm bone weary when the sun comes up. For the truth is this: I'm a captive of the savages. I'm a white and they are red. It makes no matter how hard I work, how fast I move, how small I try to make myself; the difference will always be right there on the skin of my hands and face.

Another week passes and I find myself thinking more and more about skin and the colors it comes in. I remember when Pa caught me trying to get a look at myself one time in the water trough and teased me for a day or two. Told me about a poem he had read one time that said, *'And all the carnal beauty of my wife, is but skin-deep[3].'* But not until I was the only one with different color skin did I really start to think about what is *underneath* it all. Does the color on the outside make a body different on the inside? I always thought that was so. Black skin makes a nigger slave, red skin makes a savage, and white skin makes a person like a farmer or a soldier. Ain't that the way it is always so? Never once, until my sorry situation, did it occur to me that maybe, *just maybe*, skin color's got nothing to do with it.

Squatting outside Old Woman's hut, stirring the venison stew for dinner, I look at my white hands and realize I have to puzzle this through a bit more. For the only one with white skin in this village is a slave. And those with red skin are the farmers and the soldiers and the healers and the children. The only real savages I've met so far are Dirty Feet and his three companions. But something tells me it has nothing to do with red skin and everything to do with heart. *Maybe*, my head thinks, *it's what's underneath it all that's the only thing that counts*. I'll have to ponder this some more.

The little ones in the village are the only ones that make me smile sometimes. The babies don't care who I am or what color my skin is; they just want to see a friendly face and I'm happy to oblige. Mothers wrap their babies in blankets around a board that they either strap to their backs or hang from a tree branch. Each babyboard looks different, and I find I remember the babies more by how the carrier looks than the baby! Some are decorated with embroidery and porcupine quills, some have shades built over the top, and others have some of the funniest objects dangling in front for the baby to look at: bird skulls, feathers, and animal claws. Those babies go all over with their mothers, when they're tending the gardens, washing by the stream, foraging in the woods or preparing meals. There's something peaceful about watching the babies swinging in the branches fast asleep. Watching all this, I learn that savages do laugh, cry, and love. I find it mighty surprising.

The older boys, eleven or twelve or so, the ones that wear clothes, are the meanest. Scuttling down to the river to fetch the day's first water I look down at myself. They must have a good chuckle over my clothes, since the way they look now deserves a good laugh; torn, dirty, with all manner of smells and stains on them! They throw rocks and sticks at me like I'm a moving target. They try to trip me when I'm hauling wood and think nothing's more funny than seeing me sprawl in the dirt covered in sticks and dust. They spy on me when I'm trying to have a private moment in the woods. They make me tired. They make me mad. Were I to have the right words and were I to be in a different place, I'd tell them a thing or two. But I work to stay small. It's easier. It's safer.

The older girls, around my age I suspect, work almost as hard as me but stay away from me. I'm so different. I feel their stares all the time. Pa always taught us it was rude to stare. It made no matter how interesting the sight was you were wishing to see. There was red savage girl at Cooper's General Store one time. She was tied by the waist and roped to a trapper's belt, more dirty and worse for wear than I ever saw a body to be. Even at my worst time with the savages so far I don't think I've ever had the look she had in her eyes. She was a dead body that just hadn't laid down yet. But I did not stare. No sir. I waited to ask questions until we were in our wagon and on our way back home. That was when Pa explained the way of things to me before I even had a chance to open my mouth.

"Mind your own business, Elle. Worry about your own troubles. Keep your head down and your mouth shut. Most battles in this world come about when people stop following that rule."

I pondered that for a while and then felt obliged to ask. "Doesn't that mean that the strongest always get their way?"

Pa took so long to answer that Eli had time to crawl into the back of the wagon and fall asleep leaning against a sack of grain. But finally he said, "There are a pile of things in this life that are stronger than you, Elle. Always will be, too. War is stronger. Hatred is stronger. Death is stronger. Some you can avoid ... hide from." I remember the look on Pa's face that day and the shadow of sorrow that settled there like a dark cloud as he thought of Ma. *"And some things will find you no matter what you do to hide from them."*

"So that savage girl ..." I'd tried to ask.

Pa interrupted me, hoping to end things quick like. "Is none of our business, Elle. The savages had their time. Their present circumstances are not our concern. Our homestead is on what used to be the red savage's land. Bought by the government with cash money and signed away by the savages free and clear. Made available to families like ours. Those savages have made choices how to live just like we have made choices. My choice was to live separate. Apart. Where no one could bother us or interfere or force us to fight a battle or choose a side." He'd looked at me. "I will not choose sides anymore, Elle. I just want to be left in peace! No more wars for me, no more debates. I have moved my whole family – everyone I care about - far, far away. I am an honest, law abiding, and God – fearing man. If I see something I don't agree with and it has nothing directly to do with me and mine then I just keep my head down, my mouth shut, and I mind my own business! It is the right path to take. The only path to take! You hear me?" He was fair shouting at me. Eli stirred at the sound of Pa's raised voice.

"I heard you, Pa," I say out loud to myself and my memories. But now I know something else that can be stronger than hatred or death or war: fear. I think about that savage girl tied to the trapper's belt, and I touch my neck that still has a healing rope burn. I suspect Pa never thought I'd be a captive in a red savage village. Would he have wanted someone who saw me tripping and stumbling and eating dirt with a rope tied 'round my neck to 'keep his head down and mind his own business'? It would appear to me that life tends to change a body's way of viewing the world, that's for darn sure.

It takes me almost two weeks in the savages' village before I notice that there are not too many men around. Young men I should say. There are lots of mothers and children and old ladies. There are many old men, too. But there seems to be only a few fathers. I think to myself that Pa would be disappointed in my slowness. He used to say to me, *"Elle Girl, you make a body more tired with your questions than a full day's plowing does!"* But I really just haven't been myself. It took a long time to notice the lack of men, but less time to figure out why. They must be raiding, attacking other places, just like the savages who took me. Or hunting, I guess. Even Dirty Feet and his companions were gone the very next day.

I sense a change in the village just a few days after I figure out the men are gone. Maybe it's just me seeing something new, like when you walk the same path in the woods everyday and then one day spot an owl's nest. Each time after that you always check to see if you can see the owl; the walk is just different. Old Woman works me close to death these days. I carry wood, grind grain, gather herbs and plants in the woods with her sometimes, work in the big garden doing all manner of things, and prepare fish the young boys catch. I just never seem to stop! By the second day, I'm stumbling around stupid with tiredness. Old Woman slaps me three times that day. She didn't hit me that much even in the first days. When I spill an entire bowl of ground corn I'd just finished she looks mad enough to kill me. She does almost worse, she sends me to my bed corner without dinner.

I lay there in the dark with my stomach cursing me and my clumsiness. I think about Pa, Henry and Eli. I think about our dinners together, sitting inside if the weather's poor or outside on the porch if the weather's warm and the bugs are cooperative. I think about me making dumplings and venison stew. I can almost smell it cooking. I can see Eli grinning at me because he just loved my dumplings and venison stew. I see Henry hunched over his bowl shoveling it in almost faster than an eye can see. I hear Pa saying, *"Why don't you just swallow the whole thing, bowl and all, Henry?"* and us laughing and laughing at the thought. I feel myself finally drifting off to sleep just when the screams and whoops and shouts erupt. It could almost be funny; here I am in a red savage village being terrified by the same sounds that terrified me at home with Pa, Henry and Eli!

I creep to the opening of Old Woman's hut and see a sight that chills my blood almost to a stop. Red savage men, more than I can count, mounted on horses, painted and armed, galloping and whooping through camp. I hear a strange whimpering in the tent and look around surprised because I think I'm alone. It takes a moment to realize that *I am alone*; the sound's coming from my own throat. And then I see a sight still stranger, a savage woman, long dark hair loose and blowing out behind her, running fast as lightning, not *away* from the fierce savages but *towards* them. One savage separates himself out from the terrifying band and lets out a piercing yell, one that sends goose skin up my arms. I watch, unable to look away, knowing that the woman is seconds from death. In one quick move the savage leans low over to one side of his horse, reaches down, and hauls the woman up behind him. It's almost like a dance to watch the two of them; her yipping and screaming and laughing holding on to the back of him while he wheels his horse around and charges back into the chaotic mass. And then I know. The village men are home.

Celebrations go on all night: shouts and screams, laughter and shrieks. The smell of roasting meat makes me weak with hunger while the sounds make me weak with fear. The world outside, which had only begun to feel safe, is strange again. I look down at my torn and ragged clothes, filthy bare feet, and cracked and broken nails. I touch my hair, knotted and tangled and limp with dirt and grease. I know how horrible I look, yet I know I'm no longer as safe as I'd been yesterday. I'm unfamiliar with the ways of men and women but not stupid. The enemy is here now, right outside my door, and I'm all alone. *Keep your head down. Keep your mouth shut. Mind your own business. Worry about your own troubles. Prisoner, captive, slave. White ... red ... savage ...* Somehow, Pa's advice doesn't seem to work so well anymore. Why does that make me feel even more alone?

Towards dawn, as the sounds quiet, I drift off to sleep only to be roughly kicked awake by Old Woman before the sun has even fully lit the sky. She makes a motion with her hand, *Get on with your chores as usual,* and stumbles to her pallet exhausted from a night of celebrating. Weakness from hunger and tiredness is not the only reason I hesitate leaving Old Woman's hut. I'll never be able to make myself small enough or red enough not to be seen.

Had Old Woman stayed awake I'd have received a hard kick for taking so long to get busy. But she's already snoring on her pallet, twitching in her dreams. Can I hide in the hut all day? At last, I finally ask myself just who do I fear more, the Old Woman or the unknown men outside? I step outside the hut and head to the creek to get water, shivering *this* morning with the cold, as well as fear, tiredness and hunger. You don't need to be a red savage with a painted black face to cause a body to tremble, just a face as wrinkled as a dry apple with a nasty temper to match.

My fears are without cause in these early morning hours. The entire village including many of the children is exhausted from a night of celebrating, and I go about my chores with less bother than usual. I even manage to eat a hearty bowl of leftover stew that I find from the night before. My stomach at last is happy ... for the moment. During the later part of the day the village begins to stir to life, but it's slow and I'm able to go largely unnoticed until dinner.

By dinner, Old Woman has stirred and grunted her approval at me for having done all my chores without her watching. I'm fixing the evening meal when I hear footsteps coming. My head is down, but I'm able to recognize the visitor right quick: Dirty Feet. I hear his voice and his companions' laughter. He grabs me by the hair and roughly pulls me to my feet. I struggle to stay on my feet and not cry out with the pain. He points to the stain on the front of my skirt and the laughter gets louder. Part of me wants to curl up in a ball and disappear, but part of me wants to put them in their place. *Is it my fault that I'm in this state?* Angry thoughts growl in my head. *Have I done something to deserve all this?* My hatred boils up like a cook pot.

When he lets go of my hair, I find myself raising my head. I'm fair certain that there's nothing I can do that can keep this unwanted attention off me. I look into Dirty Feet's mocking eyes and let my eyes say what my slow tongue can't. I feel my fear alive and kicking, tightening my chest, stopping my breath. But then I feel something else. It's hatred. *I hate you, red savage, for who you are and what you've done to me and mine.* I understand now why Pa said hatred could be strong as I feel it fill me and push aside a bit of my fear, making room for me to draw a shaky breath. I work hard to hate Dirty Feet more than I fear him.

Even though I can't speak I'm fair certain that Dirty Feet gets my message loud and clear. Pa often used to say, *"Why waste your breath over something unworthy?"* After a moment or two one of his companions mutters something under his breath and shoves Dirty Feet who stumbles. Everyone laughs but the mood has changed. Old Woman chooses this time to make an appearance, and she speaks to the men in the same tone she uses with the big boys when their teasing of me gets in the way of her needs. As Dirty Feet and his companions leave, I'm still standing staring at their backs. I turn to look at Old Woman, and she looks at me for a long moment and seems to *see* me for the first time since I've been there. *You watch yourself, Old Woman,* I think to myself, *I suspect I can find enough hate for you, too, should I be so inclined.* She says something to me and then snorts with laughter and walks into her hut. It takes me a moment to realize that she's not cuffed me for standing still for such a long time.

There are more celebrations that night. This time, I'm expected to serve and fetch and carry and *work*. At least there's plenty to eat even if my bones ache with tiredness and lack of sleep. I fear I'll not last the night. Finally, late in the evening, I know that no one is paying me any mind and creep toward Old Woman's hut to collapse. The risk of a beating for leaving seems worth a bit of sleep. For once I believe that I'll fall asleep without thoughts of Pa, Henry and Eli.

In the darkness outside Old Woman's hut, I'm roughly grabbed from behind. Tiredness makes me slow and weak but I kick and struggle anyway. I'm slapped hard across the side of my mouth when I begin to scream, and I taste blood. Instructions are hissed in my ear. Meaningless as they are to me, I know what they mean, *Shut up*. I continue to struggle but feel the last of my strength seeping out of me. *Maybe,* a small voice says in my head quite clear like, *maybe you will die now.* I'm so terrible tired that the idea is no longer something to be scared of, it's a relief. I stop struggling and just go limp. My attacker is not prepared for this and we both end up tumbling to the ground. As he scrambles to stand and I lay in the dirt, my tired mind is not surprised to realize who my attacker is: Dirty Feet.

Grabbing my arm, Dirty Feet pulls with all his might to get me to stand, causing me to cry out. A white-hot pain burns through my shoulder and my arm falls useless to my side. Furious, he bends down, scoops me up, and throws me over his shoulder. A loud scream is ripped from my throat as my arm and shoulder are again moved; then everything goes black.

I awake in an unfamiliar hut. It's one of the larger huts that contains a large family group. Bigger than Old Woman's hut and shaped like a rectangle, its sides are open to let summer heat out and cool evening breezes in. I lay there for a moment and take stock of my hurts. My shoulder and arm are right painful and tightly wrapped against my body making it awkward to sit up, but I finally manage. The side of my face is swollen, and I still taste blood in my mouth. I can feel a tooth loose as my tongue wanders. My head aches. My stomach growls. I roll my eyes. It seems some things never change. I make my way out of the tent to find some privacy and deal with the awkwardness of being one armed when two are needed.

It's near night, and I assume I've slept the night and day away. Do I feel better for sleep? I shake my head "No" to myself and then groan at the pain of it. No, I don't feel better at all. I begin to make my way back to Old Woman's hut, worried to have missed a full day of chores. What will she do to me? I head toward the center of the camp knowing that I can get my bearings once I'm near the great main meeting area. My head aches as I try to concentrate on the layout of the village as I remember it. As I get close, I begin to have second thoughts. It seems the whole village is present. Murmurs run through the crowd as all eyes seem to notice me. I wish for a hole to hide in. Before I can disappear, hands roughly grab hold of me, and I'm brought to the center near the great fire. There stands Dirty Feet, Old Woman, and the man I have always thought to be the Chief. He wears necklaces of animal claws; bear and cougar are two I recognize. He's naked aside from his breechcloth as all men in camp are. Across his face and chest are patterns in stripes and dots. On his shoulders is a cape made of glorious feathers of every color a head can imagine. The first time I saw it, I wondered how it would feel to touch it, but he's terrifying to look at. Beside him, wearing the pieces of a bright red coat of a British officer, sits a woman. Strung around her neck are buttons of gold, more than one army coat could ever have. She, too, wears marks on her face that I suspect won't wash off. Tied in her hair is one dark feather that seems as much a part of her as her dark black eyes. She looks as peaceful and calm as a fully alert rattlesnake, and in many ways Red Coat is more frightening than the man I call Chief. I'm seated next to Red Coat.

The Chief is talking back and forth with Dirty Feet and Old Woman. Dirty Feet seems to be angry when he speaks. Old Woman seems to be put out. Both look often at me. There's no doubt that I'm the topic of discussion. I hear a sound often. Is that their name for me? At last the Chief speaks, and another young woman steps forward. Although she's a red savage, she's a slave I'm certain, but puzzle over how I know for a time. I finally decide it's because she has the same fearful look in her eyes as I know mine have. Her clothes are a mixture of savage and white; tattered cloth skirt and dirty buckskin top. The Chief speaks without emotion although he makes an effort to be persuasive and respectful I think. He motions to me and touches his right arm, the same arm that I've hurt. He runs his hand down his arm lightly touching his skin and touches the captive savage girl's skin. The meaning is obvious even to me. Why would Old Woman want a broken white girl when she can have a whole savage? No one would be so foolish as to turn down such an offer. Old Woman is no fool. With a brief comment and a nod of her head the red savage captive's ownership is transferred. Dirty Feet's look to me says, *You are mine!*

The Chief turns to address Dirty Feet. He speaks in the same tone he has addressed Old Woman, without emotion. I close my eyes and listen to the sound of his voice flow up and down in a calm, rhythmic flow. Dirty Feet's voice is angry and loud. I open my eyes to see him shouting and waving his hands, spittle flying from his mouth. The Chief does not respond to Dirty Feet's speech; clearly his decision had been made. He has spoken. Dirty Feet stalks away into the dark night. I take a deep breath. Now what?

The Chief turns and looks at me and seems to have the same thought. *Now what do I do with you?* It's an obvious question. I stare back at him, aching all over, inside and out. I'm tired. I'm hurting. At least I'm no longer afraid. That makes me sit up straight and think. *When did I stop being afraid*, I wonder? I try to think but my head hurts too much. And then I remember: it was the moment I thought that death would be a relief. That's when the fear left me.

At last the Chief speaks. A red savage man steps forward. His long dark hair is decorated to one side with bright feathers in the colors of yellow, red, and blue, and he too has permanent marks on his face. Beside the feathers in his hair, the marks on his face, and the knife at his waist, the savage wears no other decorations. The Chief speaks in short, clipped, phrases to the savage who stands tall and quiet before him. His face does not let you know any of his feelings. The savage never speaks to the Chief, but he does speak directly to me before turning and disappearing into the dark night. Although I don't understand a word he says, I know what he means. *Follow me.*

I scramble to stand and follow after this savage I'll call Bright Feather. He never once looks back to see if I follow; he never once slows his pace. When he finally stops outside a single hut like Old Woman's on the edge of the village, I'm winded from the pace and from all of my hurts. Bright Feather motions to the hut and speaks briefly to me and then turns and leaves me alone in the dark. What should I do? With no place else to go, I crawl into the hut, which is similar in many ways to Old Woman's without the herbs and the smells that go with them. There are furs neatly piled in the corner. I fall into an exhausted sleep in the same corner where I've always slept in Old Woman's hut. Still a captive. Still alone. Still lost. I sigh. But maybe not so much afraid anymore.

I wake before dawn at the time I usually start chores with Old Woman, and Bright Feather is nowhere to be seen. I get up and step outside to greet the morning. All my aches and pains sing hello, some more loudly than others. I've noticed most men are part of a larger family unit: being sons, husbands or fathers. From what I've seen few live alone, but those that do seem to receive a share of the crops and are cared for by neighboring women or distant relatives. A majority of the huts in the village are large enough to sleep mothers, fathers, children, grandparents, aunts, and even uncles as best as I can tell. Old Woman has received the same kind of care from one nearby hut, and I often did work for those people as well as for Old Woman. As I stand in the cold dawn a savage woman with a babyboard on her back appears out of the morning mists. I think she's very pretty with her hair loose and her deerskin dress decorated with small fringed edges at the sleeve and hem. The straps of the babyboard show detailed stitches of decoration, too.

She seems surprised to see me, although she makes great effort not to let me know. It's something about her kind eyes I think that give away her shock. She holds a basket in her hand; Bright Feather's breakfast? For a moment we stare at each other and then she motions to my arm. I touch it protectively. *No, you can't touch it, it hurts too much*, I will her to understand.

She places the basket down near the fire and then approaches me slowly. I back away just as slow. Then Bright Feather appears and a long talk starts. He looks at me without speaking. *Sit down*, his look says. *Let her look at your shoulder*. I sit. She unwraps the bandage and the ache makes me just about swoon. I look into the eyes of the baby peeking at me from the babyboard as it leans against a tree. She wraps my shoulder up again. There's a lot more talking between Bright Feather and Kind Eyes.

Bright Feather goes into his hut. He comes out with his weapons and other things I don't know about. He hands Kind Eyes a bundle of furs, beautiful in their shades of brown and gold. He unhobbles his horse, mounts and rides off without looking back. Kind Eyes touches my arm, motions and smiles. *Follow me.*

I'm clean! I've washed my body! Kind Eyes has given me a soft leather dress that reaches to below my knees and leggings that lace up to the top of my calves. I've washed my hair. It's clean and combed and bound with pieces of leather. *I'm clean!!* Kind Eyes helped me wash myself, she was gentle with my shoulder, but even still I fairly died whenever it was moved. I think, though, if I had to do it all over again – pain and all – I'd do it just to feel this good about being clean! The savage women wash near a bend in the river. It's a place not chosen so much for privacy but for ease and speed. *Never is there so much white skin for all to see as bathing at the river*, I think as I strip and scrub. The water runs swift but is not too deep, and there's plenty of fine sand for scrubbing. Kind Eyes has herbs that she rubs in my hair that smell clean and make a kind of suds. Oh, it's heaven to be clean!

From that day on a pattern happens. I sleep every night in Bright Feather's hut, although it's many, many nights before I see him again. That first night I go to prepare a meal for Bright Feather, but Kind Eyes stills my hand and shakes her head. *He will not be here to eat dinner.* Every morning I rise before the sun and make my way to Kind Eyes' hut and it's there that I start my chores, helping her do things that need to be done. Most of the chores are the same I did for Old Woman with one exception: I get to help care for Kind Eyes' baby. In my head I call him "Owl", always peeking out from his babyboard with those big, wide, dark eyes. I find out right quick he's a boy. I try to take all my loneliness and miss-you feelings for Eli and give it to Owl. Beside Kind Eyes and Owl there's also Kind Eyes' husband who I call 'Coon. He's quiet and fierce looking, and I give him his name for the raccoon tail that swings from his hair.

I'm taught how to plant the savage way, it being spring. A huge garden is prepared by all the women that's for the entire village. There's the turning of the earth, preparing the soil, planting the seeds: corn, beans (that they will have grow up the cornstalks), squash, sunflowers, pumpkins, and others I'm not sure of. The small children and old women mind the birds, shooing them away should they be mistaken and think there's an easy meal nearby. Hampered with my arm, I spend a lot of time amusing and caring for the many small children who are always present wherever the women go. I still do all my other chores as well, such as hauling water, collecting wood for fires, grinding corn (that was tricky, but I manage to hold the bowl 'tween my legs), and helping prepare meals. I'm clumsier seeing it's my right arm that's hurt, and it's my right arm that I'm more inclined to use.

Kind Eyes always works to include me in everything and makes sure I'm doing what needs to be done the way it needs to be done. I'm right pleased that the women trust me with their children. Pa used to say, *"Don't always listen for the words, Elle, watch for the actions."* In fact, as the weeks pass, I take it as a downright compliment that so many of the women allow me to care for their children while they work in the garden doing the heavy work of hoeing, digging, and planting.

As the days and weeks progress, it's with Kind Eyes that I finally begin to understand my first few savage words. They come very slowly. Pa may have thought I was quick with some things, but not with this. I begin to hear sounds that I put with things; words like "fire", "wood", "grain", "corn", "sit", "go", and "baby", although I'm not sure if the word I think is "baby" is just Kind Eyes' name for her child. I'll have to listen and see if the other mothers call their babies by the same sound. But mostly it all just sounds like a jumble of sounds to me, like a pile of mush on a plate. Every once in a while I recognize a sound that I hear and if I work real hard finally I seem to piece it together with what I know. I've never once tried to speak it though! That's nigh on impossible.

I have to be shown how to prepare the meat and the skins as it's not something I know how to do. It's also powerful hard work, and with my arm the way it is, I'm little use. Although it's better, it still pains me, especially if I do heavy lifting or hauling (which is often) but I no longer keep it wrapped, and I'm happy to say that the tooth that was loose from being hit is solid again in my mouth. So I watch careful as Kind Eyes works the hides so that when I'm able I can do it on my own. From start to finish it can take a full week of hard, hard work to do a hide proper. I look around me in the village at all the moccasins and pants and dresses and I see weeks and weeks of hard break-your-back work. *No wonder so many go around just about naked.*

I travel daily with the women to collect herbs and learn about many new ones. Kind Eyes always takes the time to try to explain what each plant does – for stomach ills, lady cramps, tooth aches, and skin rashes. If we are not working in the garden we are gathering in the forest. The men may do the hunting, but it's the women who seem to do everything else. I suspect Bright Feather notices the strings of herbs hanging to dry from the roof of the hut when he is in the village, but he says nothing as usual. I enjoy a treat of maple syrup drops one day, and I look forward to that chore in the fall!

From Kind Eyes I learn the rhythm of the camp. Some ways are powerful familiar, like the way they tend their clothes by the river and the way they love their children. The children near to Eli's age seem to spend their days full of laughter and fun and play. Little ones are well loved by the grown-ups here, spoiled and teased and cared for with as much attention as I cared for Eli. I watch two old men sitting outside their huts give a group of troublesome boys a dressing down and I remember Old Mr. Hobson sitting at Cooper's General Store in the corner by the checkerboard frowning and giving me the evil eye for something Eli had done. I puzzle over that. Savage and white the same? Until my time here I'd not have even thought to ponder such a thing, let alone believe it to be so.

I see the way two savage girls giggle and laugh and whisper like they are friends, and I'm stunned to realize that I wish to be a part of that. I smile at 'Coon as he teases and tickles little Owl, and I think of Pa singing to Eli at night as we all drift off to sleep, and I long for that closeness with a body, too. My head stretches and creeks a bit like an old house as it shifts to make room for this new way of thinking and looking at the people I'm living with. For the first time I'm not so sure that 'savage' is a word that fits them all. For maybe they are all more like me than I care to admit.

But then there are many things that are so downright strange it would be like if you were to try to go through your day walking on your hands instead of your feet. I still struggle mightily with this savage language which I suspect I never will fit in my thick head. And it seems to me that no one thinks much of possessions or ownership or property much like Ma did about her fancy china dishes and Pa did about his gold pocket watch. Then there's the fact that everyone here lives together so close, and all Pa wanted to be was away from *everyone*.

As the spring flows into summer, my life with the savages takes on a pattern as regular as my life at home. I cook, I clean, I work in the garden, and I care for children. Sometimes I laugh at the antics of the children. Sometimes I share a smile with Kind Eyes. I'm not so sad, I'm not so fearful, but I still struggle with the fact that I'm a stranger, still a captive white girl in a borrowed buckskin dress that can't even manage the simplest of talk.

I still miss Pa, Henry, and Eli but the ache's like my arm that's slowly healing. Even the worst of injuries, if it doesn't kill, finally begins to heal. Nights are not so hard for me anymore. It isn't that I don't think of my family, but it's more like I've decided to carefully put them to rest in my mind like some treasured item in Ma's chest.

Ma had a big cedar box that Pa called her Hope Chest. Sometimes he'd let me and Eli look through it, and it was full with all manner of treasured things: clothes, letters, locks of hair (Pa said they were Henry's), a beautiful colored quilt, and even some pieces of jewelry. My memories of

Ma have been put away for a long time. There are so very few and they are shadowy like the way things look in the early morning mists that come down from the mountains. Pa told me I look like Ma with my long brown hair and green eyes. I suppose many of things I do around the house reminded him of her, but I can't remember what she looked like. It upset me at first that I could not remember her face clearly after a time, but I treasure the memories of her hands. They were good hands. I can see them more clearly in my memories than her face. I see them covered with flour kneading bread, and doing other chores that have to do with cooking. I feel her hands smoothing my back and stroking my face in comfort over something Henry has done to tease me. I remember her hands combing and braiding my hair each morning and teaching me how to lace up my shoes. I see her hands clasped in prayer at night by my bedside and listening to me whisper into God's ear. Looking through that chest and smelling the special smells, I can almost conjure up Ma's face in my head and almost hear her voice. Henry never wanted to look in the Hope Chest, I suspect for the same reason. Odd how that is, I think; I'd get comfort and Henry'd get upset from the same thing: memories. Eli couldn't remember Ma, of course, but I'd tell him what I remembered.

So my memories of Pa, and Henry and Eli and Ma I keep now neatly stored in a private place in my mind, 'cause I for certain have no Hope Chest. I take them out whenever I like, but they no longer tear at me like a festering wound. I let different things fill my head as I lay on my pallet at night waiting for sleep to come: new words I'm trying to remember, herbs I'm trying to recall, and the cute way Owl looks at me when I play peek-a-boo with him.

Bright Feather is often gone three or four weeks at a time. He never stays in the village for long, no more than four or five nights. He returns with meat (deer, turkey, rabbit, and once even a goose) and furs in many rich shades. Does he set traps? Pa used to do that. I wonder how it's different and how it's the same. He makes no move to talk with me. It's just like living with Old Woman 'cept he doesn't hit or kick me. Not even once. A few times Kind Eyes takes time to show me how to do things that I suspect Bright Feather told her I'm doing wrong. He speaks with her just now and then. I cook for him and he eats it, so I suspect that's a victory. Once I learn the way of using their birch bark containers I manage quite well. They are sturdy enough to boil water by dropping hot stones into them and can even be set directly on the fire, but once that's done I've discovered it's not much use to you after that! I don't fear him, I'm glad to say. Course I do my best to have everything just as I should, and even with my bad arm I try to be quick with my chores.

When Bright Feather is in the village, most evenings are spent at the main hut where the Chief and Red Coat can be found. Many of the men spend their evenings there, and some of the women, too. It's not a place for me, and I make every effort to avoid meeting times there. I'm happy to stay out of sight at Bright Feather's hut.

I continue to struggle mightily to learn the language and try to get more words each day. I make an effort to pick up two or three new words a day, but some days I can't even do that. Still, after nearly four months, I've yet to utter a single savage word fearful that I'll do it wrong. I now know the name for Kind Eyes and her baby, even the name for Bright Feather, but I don't understand the meaning so I continue to call them the names I know them by in my head. I know "fire" and "fish" and "stick" and "river" and "corn" and even "no", "yes", and what I imagine to be "Go! Get out of here!", which comes from spending so much time with the mothers and the young children. I know the word that you are supposed to yell at the birds when they try to steal the seed, like my "Shoo!" although they don't sound anything alike. Kind Eyes has taken to talking with me at night like we can really talk with each other. I concentrate so hard to understand and hear the different sounds that my head aches something fierce, and I've come to almost dread these times. I don't know if Kind Eyes ever gets fed up with me, but she's always patient and never gives up trying. I've no idea what 'Coon thinks about me.

I come to realize as I go about my days that the only thing that now keeps me apart from everyone in this village are just three things of my very own doing: my slow tongue, my white skin, and my thoughts of what is savage and what is not. For I'm almost always treated with kindness and respect, curiosity and teasing, and a regular dose of laughing wonder, none of which, as far as I can see, is that bad at all. Once again, being the only different one in a place has a powerful way of changing a body's thoughts about what is … right and wrong … *savage and not*. The more I ponder what truly makes a body a savage and what does not, the more tangled my thoughts become.

One hot summer day when we are all bathing at the river, I realize for the first time what everyone assumes about Bright Feather and me. As we wade into the wonderfully cool waters, splashing ourselves and rubbing our skin with the fine sand, one of the savage woman touches my flat, white stomach and the meaning is clear. *How come no baby?* I'm sure I blush right down to my ankles, and for long moments for once all of us are redskins. Kind Eyes looks at me for a moment then looks at the other women and shakes her head "no". There then begins a long conversation in which I hear Bright Feather's name mentioned many times. I would have done just about anything to understand what was being said. Even going back to being dirty.

When I say living with Bright Feather is just like living with Old Woman, I mean it. *That* aspect never even occurred to me, but it seems it has to others. Again, Pa, it seems I ain't so quick. For many nights after that day I worry about this new idea in my head. My sleep is filled with dreams in which I'm chasing something just beyond my sight and just when I'm too tired to go any further I realize that I must run because something terrible is chasing *me*. I wake with my heart pounding and my breath coming out in gasps. I lie there on my fur pallet and think about the savage woman's red hand on my bare white belly and think, is this what is expected of me? Of us? There are many young women in the village, some not much older than me I'm sure, that seem to … be … with a man in more ways than I'm with Bright Feather. Has he just been polite? Have I been just plain stupid again? Is he waiting for a sign from me that I'm so inclined? My gut clenches in a wave of panic that I've not felt in many months. Again I feel an anger with myself. If I could learn this language, I'd at least know what people say and think and expect of me. But no, not only am I a prisoner here because I can't help myself to escape, I'm also powerful stupid because I still can't speak, or even seem to learn the words I need to talk with my captors. I decide I'll try to watch Bright Feather more closely the next time he's in the village. *And,* my head says to me, *what will you do if you see what you are afraid is expected of you?* I've no answer for myself.

I'm going on a hunting trip with a group from the village, and Bright Feather is back and will go along, too. I suspect I was chosen to go because I've no child and they know I work hard. Some women are going along on the hunt who do have very small children, but most are young men and older boys and girls. Kind Eyes has tried mightily to explain, but she has finally just gone around and begun to make a pile of things that I should bring. She smiles a lot and nods her head. I think I'm supposed to be excited about going, but I'm frightened. Strange as it seems, I feel safe in the village now. Will I have to be with others I don't know? Will others take the time to be patient to show me what needs to be done like Kind Eyes does for me? Then other thoughts creep into my head: Will I be days closer to my home? What if Pa comes for me while I'm away? Kind Eyes smiles while I worry.

There are five men, ten women, and fifteen older boys and girls. Most of the men, including Bright Feather, are mounted on horses carrying supplies, while the rest of us carry light packs of supplies on our backs. Two of the men carry infants in babyboards hooked to their saddles. I delight in the cute faces staring solemnly out at the world flowing by. I know things'll be much heavier coming back. It being late summer, I know whatever we can kill will be important to feed us in the winter. Pa and Henry would be busy hunting whenever they weren't tending to the crops, too.

Bright Feather keeps to himself even within a group of his own people. He responds to questions or conversations when needed, but otherwise is a man apart. Even when we settle in the temporary hunting site, the lean-to we erect is farthest from the rest of the group. The other men seem respectful of him and keep their distance as well. As they laugh and joke amongst themselves, Bright Feather watches just like I do. He's a man apart and when he sees me watching him, he goes off into the woods.

The hunting party divides, leaving the women and girls to prepare and wait. Some go in pairs, but I'm not surprised that Bright Feather shows every sign of going off by himself. I'm stunned when he hands me my pack and motions to follow. We head out on foot. He seems familiar with these woods, and I'm not surprised when we stop at a ready-made lean-to where we set up our things. Bright Feather has been here before.

We sit almost all day silent and still in the forest. Even with me sitting just a small distance from Bright Feather, he blends in with the woods so well that I must concentrate to find him sometimes. It's the first opportunity in all these months for me to study him. The feathers I name him for belong to birds I'm familiar with: red for the cardinal, yellow for the goldfinch and blue for the bluejay. They are twined in his waist-length black hair that for this hunting trek is bound tightly with leather strips like a long tail down his back, just as I wear mine. I don't know how old he is nor can I even try to guess. His skin is smooth and unlined, but darkly tan from the sun like the polished wood of Pa's rifle. He wears permanent marks on his face like Old Woman, but of different designs, three lines across each check and down his chin. He's lean and muscular, but all savages seem to be. He never seems to smile, laugh, or show any feeling really. Maybe I should have called him Living Rock, I think, as I watch him sit unmoving hour after hour. Is this how he spends his days away from camp?

With a start I realize that Bright Feather is exactly like I expected all savages to be before being brought as a captive to this village. Unfeeling. Strong. Silent. Separate. Frightening. Not really a person. He fits the pictures I've seen in books, the glimpses I've seen with my own eyes. With Bright Feather I can still do what Pa told me to do: *keep my head down, keep my mouth shut, and mind my own business.* I study him in the dappled summer shade and ponder what would make a body wish to be so far removed from life. Bright Feather seems to want and need no one. Why, even 'Coon, for all his work to look and act fierce can make Kind Eyes blush with just a word and Owl giggle with a look.

The truth is I can no longer fit the people of the village to the picture of red savages I have in my head. They are mothers and fathers, grandmothers and toddlers. They laugh and cry, yell and sing, play games and give comfort when it's needed. Yes, they all have red skin, but I can't always fit together the words 'red' and 'savage' anymore. Those words must be kept separate and only joined if they're earned. Dirty Feet and those that traveled with him have earned them. And finally, I come to the conclusion as I sit and sit and sit that it's not Bright Feather's red skin that makes him savage. No, with great certainty I know that something else has made him this man who seems to enjoy no one's company ... not even his own.

A forest is a noisy place, but I never notice it until I sit that day with Bright Feather. First there's silence as every living creature with any sense scatters at your appearance. Then, if you sit still enough, long enough, gradually you are forgotten and the creatures with their noises return: birds and mice, rabbits and deer, squirrels and foxes. I sit and study the animal village we visit that day and wait and wonder just who Bright Feather is expecting. Just before dusk an elk of enormous size wanders into the clearing. I don't see him move, but all of a sudden Bright Feather has an arrow notched and ready and sits motionless again. I hold my breath as the elk moves closer, closer and closer still to us. ZING! The arrow flies through the air, the elk drops to the ground, and I hear Bright Feather say words quietly under his breath. We have just enough time before dark to quickly gut the animal and string the carcass up high to keep other interested predators away. We share a meal of fresh roasted meat in the light of the almost full moon.

A sound wakes us both late in the night. Bright Feather reaches out, and for the first time ever touches me, placing his hand on my bare arm. *Be silent. Be still*, the hand says. Soundlessly, knife drawn, Bright Feather creeps out from our sleeping spot. I can't resist and shift ever so slightly so that I can see who wants our elk. It's a bear! A large black bear, so intent on our elk hanging just out of reach that he pays no mind to the promise of death that's creeping up silently behind him. The bear is almost as big as Bright Feather, standing on its hind legs and grunting in frustration as he swipes at the dangling hoof of the elk. In one silent leap, Bright Feather jumps on the bear's back and reaches around and slits the bear's throat. The bear has only time to grunt in surprise and lower itself to all fours before it begins to stagger. I've time to think, *Can a bear be afraid?* as I hear Bright Feather again repeating words quietly under his breath.

If I could speak to Bright Feather, I might suggest we just sit here for a week or two and collect enough meat to feed the entire village for the whole winter! When I make motions to begin helping him deal with the bear he grunts and shakes his head no. So much meat, we can be careless it seems. The work can wait until morning. He goes and washes briefly at the stream down the slope and then returns to the lean-to. In moments we are both asleep. I dream of a great bear who comes and sits beside me. He talks in the savage language, and I tell him that I'm sorry but I can't understand him. "It's no matter," he says right conversationally, and gets up and lumbers away.

We work hard the next day; skinning, wrapping, and packaging the carcasses. It's hot, dirty, messy work. It seems funny to me that we spend all one whole day sitting doing nothing and then fair kill ourselves the next day doing enough work for five days. As we kneel exhausted at the stream at the end of the day and wash as best we can, I must chuckle out loud at the thought of it, for all of a sudden Bright Feather stops what he's doing to look at me. I look back, not sure what to do and certain with nothing to say. We are close enough to touch, and he reaches across to me. I'm motionless, not knowing what to expect, as he reaches up to my head, hands dripping water, and delicately takes something from my tangled mess of hair. I see it's a feather, a robin's I think, long and dark gray brown. He hands it to me as he stands to go back to the lean-to. I look at the feather resting in my clean, wet hand.

Thoughts of Eli, Henry and Pa no longer keep me awake at night, but sometimes, on nights when I'm tired to the bone, they invade my dreams. I never can remember the dreams, but they must be sad, for I almost always wake up knowing I've been crying. In the lean-to that night with Bright Feather I must be having one of those dreams and awaken him with my crying. I open my eyes to find him leaning over me and the bright moon shining behind his head. I know right away where I am, but can't understand what's wrong. He reaches out and touches my cheeks, and his fingertips glisten in the moonlight with wetness. *Oh*, I think, *a sad dream*. I sit up and scrub my face with the hem of my tunic. "It's no matter," I hear myself saying, startling us both with the sound of my voice. Nothing compares with the look of stunned surprise on Bright Feather's face. I've spoken to him in his own language.

We go back to the camp for strong backs to help carry out all the meat. The other hunters have been successful, too, but not as much as us. Great exclamations are said over the elk and the bear. Bright Feather stands stoic and silent; I stand dumb and stupid. What a pair we are.

Back in the village, Kind Eyes and I set to work to cure the bearskin and the elk hide. My arm reminds me how hard the work is and how much it still must heal. We spend days and days working, but I sense that Kind Eyes is glad for the help and the company even if I'm still as silent as a stone. Bright Feather has told Kind Eyes of my sad dream and my speaking to him, I can tell. I can see it in Kind Eyes' expressions when she talks to me and I concentrate hard to understand. I find that I feel more comfortable trying out some savage words and phrases with the little ones. "No." "Sit." "Stay." "Come here!" "Stop!" I know these words are clear because they work. I whisper endearing terms in the ears of the babies. Words that I hear the mothers' say with a tone of love and guess them to be "You'll be fine," "My sweet baby," "Don't cry," and "I'm here."

Fall is just beginning to add a smell to the air the morning I wake and make my way to Kind Eyes' hut as usual. Bright Feather has been gone for more than two weeks again, but not before giving me the bear pelt from the hunt for my own. Aside from the clothes on my back, the moccasins on my feet, and the robin's feather in my hair, it's the only thing I can call mine. I listen to the sounds of the forest and the village as I make my way - sounds of different families, dogs, horses, the sounds through the trees when the wind is rising up, and the sound of the summer bugs - some get louder with the heat and some get softer. The noise I hear as I walk to Kind Eyes hut that morning is different, and at first I don't notice. But gradually, it's the silence of the forest that makes me turn and squint into the dim dawn light and the cool morning mists.

For those brief few moments I think that perhaps I'm really just asleep curled up on my furs in Bright Feather's hut having another funny bear dream. My eyes say, now can you really, truly be seeing a bear sitting on a horse? I stop in my tracks, bare toes curling in the cool wet grass and work hard to focus my eyes through the haze. And as I stand there, the bear and his horse move forward. It's the smell that makes me realize that it's no dream. I was very close to a bear a few weeks back, and a real one doesn't smell so bad. The vision grins at me then, a wide toothless grin through his tangled mass of dirty beard. It isn't a bear, my mind finally understands, but a man! Not a savage man, my head says to me, what's different about him? How long has it been since I've seen one? For he's a white man, wearing a filthy matted cape of an old bearskin and a fur cap stuck on his head. Two more white men slowly come out of the forest and rein in their horses.

My heart begins to pound as I squint closely through the mist at the three white faces before me. Could it be Pa or someone who has come looking for me at last?!

"It's a white woman," I hear one drawl in absolute wonder, and the words sound just as strange in my ears as the sights do to my eyes.

I take two steps back and the bear one starts to move his horse toward me with purpose. "Need some rescuing, girly?" he grins toothlessly at me.

Suddenly I hear Pa's voice in my head clear as if he was standing right next to me and we were still in Cooper's General Store more than three years back, *"That be Bear John, Elle. Don't look at him or talk to him. He's trouble wherever he turns up. As bad as he smells is as bad as he is."* Then I remember the bite of Dirty Feet's rope around my neck and the red savage girl I last saw tied to Bear John's belt more dead than alive.

White skin. Red skin.

Savage. Man.

Fear. Safety.

Good. Bad.

Right. Wrong.

Home…

My world is tilting and changing, making no sense. Who am I? Where am I? What do I want? What do I do? Who do I ask for help? Who do I need? My feet don't move while my head sees one thing and my heart feels another. A prickling rush of fear starts in my belly and begins to travel through my body and finally reaches my stuck feet. I step backwards one step. Then two. Bear John is close enough to me that he begins to lean down out of his saddle and reach toward me. My mind, fair to bursting already, notices the bits of food stuck in his filthy matted beard as he smiles at me. The bulge of his belly peeks out from underneath his bearskin cape as he stretches out to grab me. "Ain't you just a pretty bit of a thing?" he says with absolute hunger in his voice.

I turn and run. I scream savage words I know that mean danger but don't necessarily fit the picture: DANGER! FIRE! STOP! BEAR! HORSE! NO! COME! FIRE!

It's natural for me to run towards Kind Eyes' hut, but too late I realize I've brought danger right to her. I turn towards the center of the camp, yelling my savage words. But Kind Eyes has already stepped from her hut at my noise. She has a puzzled expression as if to say, *What foolishness are you saying girl, the first time you decide to speak to us?* The change of her expression tells me how close the danger is. She starts to run toward the forest, stopping first to scoop up Owl in his babyboard resting against the hut.

Bear John's companions are laughing and shouting to each other, "Head west!"

"Don't go too far into the village!"

"Don't see no men! You were right, John!"

I can smell Bear John behind me. Kind Eyes begins to sob as Owl's babyboard sticks on a root. I turn to run to help and hear horse hooves slow and his raspy voice laugh, "Here, let me help you get that loosed." NO! Not Owl!

Kind Eyes screams as he leans down to grab the babyboard. My head doesn't think, I just grab a burning stick from the fire and swing. I miss, but the pass of the flame startles the horse, and it whinnies and screams and rears up. Bear John, leaning out of the saddle is unseated and falls hard on the ground winded and stunned. I step forward and hit him hard with the burning stick, once, twice, three times. His great bear cape and beard catch on fire, and he begins to scream.

The smell of burning hair and skin and fur mix with the stink Bear John has already brought with him. He rolls on the ground, screaming and swatting at the flames, but in his panic he rolls right into the fire that I've gotten the stick from. I turn and run after Kind Eyes and Owl who are almost to the woods now, with the screams of Bear John, the other white men, and the village rising up behind us. Owl's screams are the loudest of all. As soon as we stop, Kind Eyes puts Owl to her breast to hush his cries and keep him silent. Bear John and the other men are wrong; though a large party has gone out hunting just the day before there are men in the village. We can hear whoops and shouts and then silence.

I don't know how long we hide in the woods. My stomach knows the time better than me cause it starts complaining pretty loudly after a while. When we finally hear the sounds of hooves approaching, the sun is well in the sky. It's a savage pony that's for sure, as there's no sound of metal or creak of leather. Kind Eyes sobs with relief to see her husband 'Coon. He takes the sleeping Owl up before him and hoists her up on the horse behind him. I walk quiet beside as Kind Eyes talks and talks. Coon answers questions and asks some himself. Three times I can feel his eyes on me. Bear John is gone, but you can see which way he's been dragged, and his smell is still with us some when we get back.

There's much talking the rest of the day. Runners are sent out to find the hunting parties and Kind Eyes is questioned by the Chief. They talk to me, too, or try to. They show me Bear John's body and two of his men who've also been killed. All of their possessions are spread out on the ground, each having been touched and studied. Standing there looking at the bodies and smelling the awful smells my knees get to shaking so much that I finally just have to sit down in the dust.

Many in the village come to stare at me over the rest of the day while I try my best to act like nothing much has changed. The day is just the same as any other.

Except for the fact that I've killed a man.

A white man.

Men, women, boys, girls, and even a few curious dogs all troop by to have a look-see at the murderous captive white girl grinding corn and keeping watch over her birch bark bowl stewing over the fire calm as you please. I try my best to ignore the stares and whispers just like I always have. And it's impossible, just like always.

They give me Bear John's horse! What will Bright Feather think when he comes back and sees a white man's horse hobbled next to his hut? I hope Kind Eyes is nearby to explain, since all I can probably say is "Bear, John, fire, hot, no, run!" Too bad I can't say "stink." I'll just hold my nose. The poor horse appears to be better cared for than Bear John cared for himself, and certainly that savage girl I saw him with so long ago. *Life is sure strange me being in this savage village now and so far away from Pa, Henry and Eli,* I think to myself more than once.

Many of the men are back, and more than a few have come by to stare at me and Bear Johns' horse. Maybe I'll get used to all this attention after all, I think. I decide to call the horse Willow because her dark brown mane and tail flow like the willow tree's branches near the stream. I like the bright white socks on her legs. She seems like a gentle mare, although I haven't ridden her yet. I don't have much practice riding astride a saddle, let alone bareback. They didn't give me the saddle. I've brushed and fed her, and she seems happy with all the care.

Kind Eyes is in a state, brushing my hair and checking my clothes. I keep trying to do the usual chores that need to be done, and she keeps shooing me back and looking impatient. She finally takes my face in her hands and says words real slow like, willing them to seep into my thick skull. I concentrate hard and repeat the ones I understand: "Night", "Fire", "Chief", and the word that means me.

We eat no evening meal at the hut, but as night falls make our way to the center of the village. I'm not happy to be seated next to the Chief where all eyes are able to see me. Kind Eyes does not have kind eyes when I make a move to go someplace else. Her look is plain. *You sit right there and don't you move.* I sigh. I sit.

My head aches with the strain of trying to listen and understand. The Chief, Red Coat, and even Old Woman speak for a time. *When will I understand this speaking?* I think to myself, angry like. Most of the men and all of the women and children from the village are gathered. I don't see Bright Feather, but that's not a surprise. He has only been gone two weeks. We eat dinner, and my stomach is happy. Sweet venison, corn, squash, late strawberries and blackberries; my lips and fingers are shiny and bright with my eating. No wonder the men meet here each night when they are home, I think!

Someone begins to play a drum, and there's dancing and shouting and singing. Someone acts out a bear hunt, another acts out a battle with an enemy. I see a flash of color, and I recognize Bright Feather's red, yellow and blue colors in the dark on the edge of the circle. Had a log not slipped and exploded into a short bright flame I'd never have known he was there. I feel eyes on me as the drums play, but no one else steps forward, and then from the shadows I can see a shape emerging, a bear. I gasp in fear and the Chief reaches and touches my arm. He looks at me and back at the shape, then back at me and out to the crowd. *Tell your story,* his look says, *They want to hear your story.* How do I tell him that telling my story in front of all these faces is almost more terrifying than facing the real Bear John? How do I tell him that I can still smell him in my nose and hear his screams in my head?

I stand up and smooth my tunic; I'm barefoot and my hair is tied back like it was that morning. I realize I look just like I did on my way to Kind Eyes' hut: just like I'm supposed to. I try to ignore the fire and the crowd, shut my eyes and let the drums creep into my head and my heart and through my blood. It's calming because the drumbeat is slower than my scared heart is pounding, and I feel things inside me start to slow, start to quiet. I open my eyes and imagine walking to Kind Eyes' hut. I turn my head; what's that change in the forest's sounds?

I feel the terror and a sob of sheer remembry rips through me. I make them laugh shouting the savage words I know in warning. They slap their thighs, hold their sides, and wipe away tears from laughing so hard. Kind Eyes joins me in front of the fire and we do a dance almost remembering how things went. We even have Owl's babyboard – with a cornhusk doll inside instead. At the end, I break the tension again by holding my nose; remembering the stink of the burning bear man. Then with Owl's babyboard, Kind Eyes and I run off into the dark edges of the firelight.

They like my show. I want to wander off to Bright Feather's hut and curl up on my pallet and go to sleep, but that isn't how it's to be. Kind Eyes fair drags me back to the light and then, instead of letting me sit down and do my best to disappear, the Chief stands and begins to talk to me and the village. I hear Bright Feather's name, and Kind Eyes, even Owl's and Old Woman's. I hear "bear", "fire", and I'm fair certain I hear the name they call me which I don't know what it means. Then the Chief speaks just to me. He places his two big, warm hands on my shoulders and speaks like he talked to Dirty Feet, Old Woman, and Bright Feather that night so long ago - respectful and without emotion. He takes a necklace strung with bear claws and shells from around his neck and places it around mine. Old Woman stands and speaks quick like. She does not look at me once but speaks only to the Chief. I see others look at me though, as she speaks and I think, *Now what?*, but I don't know the answer for I can't understand her words. Red Coat steps forward, her gold button necklace flashing in the firelight, and ties a belt with a knife sheath around my waist. I'm handed Bear John's knife, and even I knew its value, for it's real metal and not flint.

Then the Chief turns me to face the village and says one last thing. He calls me 'Bear'. And the village cheers.

As the cheering quiets, the crowd parts and makes room for a man I immediately recognize to be Bright Feather. He leads Willow, who whinnies nervously from all the unfamiliar sights, smells and sounds. She's no longer bareback but has a beautiful thick woven savage blanket thrown over her back and a savage rope harness around her head. I recognize my very few possessions: moccasins, bear skin, plus some splendid pelts I know Bright Feather has kept carefully aside from all the others he has used and traded. He walks through the firelight to stand in front of me and reaches for my hand, in which he places Willow's reins. He bows his head every so slightly and says simply, "Bear," and turns and walks away.

I'm not sure of anything. But I think I'm a member of this tribe now, no longer a slave. I think I'm called Bear. And I think I'm without a place to sleep.

Bear

Autumn is heading quick to winter and there are many surprises and just as many discoveries for me. Right quick after I'm given my name Bear and begin to sleep in Kind Eyes and Coon's hut, I begin to dream in the Indian language of the village. It's powerful strange not to understand what's said around me day *and* night. Then POP! one day it seems that regular small talk I hear walking past huts or over the fire at dinner makes sense in my head. I hear Raccoon call Kind Eyes by the name he has always used for her, and I know that her true name is Otter. I hear Otter call Owl "Little Bird" and I understand. One day as we hike through the forest collecting pine cones and firewood, almost knee deep sometimes in fallen autumn leaves, I ask Otter in her language, "Is Bright Feather your brother?"

She stops in front of me, Little Bird's piercing stare and drooling mouth swings out of my line of vision and I see a pair of surprised, kind eyes instead. She takes one step, then two towards me and asks me, "Who is Bright Feather?" But she knows. She just wants to hear me talk.

"The one who wears three colored feathers in his hair. The one who's hut I kept. The one who is never here."

She stares at me for a moment and then grins a great wide grin. "At *last*," she says and turns to continue walking, nodding as she says, "Yes, he is."

I feel her excitement and her desire to talk and talk and talk. But she waits, letting me take things at my own pace. "What does his name mean?" I ask, and I say the confusing long string of sounds.

"His name means 'One Who Is Always Alone', but I like 'Bright Feather' better. Long ago he was called Hawk because he was such a great hunter."

At the evening meal, seated around our small fire, Raccoon is eating. I'm shy around him and hesitant to speak. He thinks nothing of my silence. Otter is like a little child with a surprise she has trouble keeping. He notices her mood and teases her. "Impatient to get to our furs tonight?" She blushes furious and so do I, but Raccoon does not see. She looks at me finally with a stare, *Either you say something or I will!*

I stir up my little bit of courage and ask, "Raccoon, will you teach me to ride my horse, Willow?" Raccoon chokes on the bit of meat he's eating and coughs and sputters while Otter laughs and laughs, pounding him on his back. I wait hopefully for his answer yes.

He looks at me real fierce. The permanent marks on his face, across his forehead and down his nose make him look even more frightening. But I know what a good man he is, I've seen him with Otter and Little Bird. I'm not afraid of him even a small bit. I look back at him and finally have to smile. His look softens at last and with a slow smile he nods, "Yes, I will teach you how to ride your horse." Then he looks at Otter and says, "You said you thought the words would come soon." She looks smug because she was right.

Otter and I spend days and days talking. It's like we're best friends who have been apart for months trying to tell each other all the things that have happened over our whole lives. Raccoon puts bits of fur in his ears to drown out our voices that never seem to rest. I've never had a real friend, I realize. It was always just Pa, Henry and Eli when I lived in Virginia. Our homestead was the farthest west of any that I knew of from the nearest town known as Ward's Mill. The closest families to us had no children my age and were more than a day and a half ride by horse. The few times we went to town, excited as I was, what time was there for me to make acquaintance, first with a baby, then a toddler, and finally a spirited boy in tow?

I learn that they call themselves The Real People and they believe the center of the world rests right here where we live and walk and breathe. They believe that as long as the world is in balance that life is good; good crops, good health, good weather. It's The Real People's job to make sure the world is always good. This particular area of The Real People's land is called The Maple Forest.

The Center of the World. A mighty far cry from the red savage village you once thought it to be, my head says to itself.

"Even within our lives," Otter explains, "we try for balance: women farm, men hunt. At the Green Corn Ceremony late each summer we clean out our homes and council circle, we throw away broken pottery and baskets, start new fires, end unhappy marriages, and forgive old wrongs. We celebrate by eating newly grown foods we pick from our gardens. We start fresh each year to make the world a better place than it was the year before."

One day as we speak more about this idea of balance and harmony and the center of the world, I feel I must make a point or two. Little Bird is sitting happily in Otter's lap chewing on her finger. A big puddle of drool is collecting in the dirt in front of them. Now I can see that Otter's, and Raccoon's, and Little Bird's lives seem mighty happy and balanced. They are together and strong and healthy. I look across the fire out into the village and, I suppose, the center of the world moving quite smoothly as far as the eye can see as it goes about its evening chores and prepares to bed down for the night. Things seem calm and peaceful if always a bit busy.

"I don't suspect," I feel compelled to say with a careful tone, "that my Pa would agree that The Real People have made his world particularly good. Or balanced. Or filled with harmony."

It's a measure of our friendship that I feel comfortable enough to say such a thing and that Otter stays calm enough to hear it. Even more so, that she takes the time to try and say a bit more to help me understand. "Bear, a wrong must always be made right, a bad deed must always be punished and a slight must always be revenged." She pauses for a moment and then says in a rush, "Even your presence here in this village was an attempt to right a wrong and restore balance."

That's mighty surprising to me, and I say so. "What could have happened that would cause me to be brought here?!" I sputter with confusion. "What did my Pa or Eli or Henry or I do?!" But Otter purses her lips and suddenly will not answer my question.

I feel compelled to say one more thing as Raccoon joins us, scooping up a squealing Little Bird. "Perhaps," I say with just as much care as I did before, "the problem is deciding who has the say who is right and who is wrong, what is in balance and what is not ..."

Raccoon looks at Otter's tense face and then at my careful one. "There has always been a sacred trust between The Real People and the world," he explains quietly. "We honor the animals, and it is with great respect that a hunter apologizes to the spirit of each animal he kills." I think of Bright Feather and the words he said as he killed the elk and the bear, and I realize he was talking to their spirits. "We are careful with the land, and it is with great thanksgiving that we harvest the gifts that the earth gives us each fall." He takes the time to tickle a giggle out of Little Bird and then looks at me directly, "Does that sound right or wrong to you?"

I open my mouth and then I close it, gathering my thoughts.

"We have learned," he continues, "that the words the white men say are not to be trusted, that they honor the things they own or wish to have more than harmony, and that they can be vengeful without a wrong being done to them. They have taken our land through trickery. They have brought sickness to our people that has made entire villages disappear. The desire for white man's guns and metal have made some of our people greedy; at one time there was no such thing. There are some Real People who say that the white men will destroy us, that there will be a time when The Real People are no more. Tell me, who will keep the world in balance then?" he asks me. This time it's me who purses my lips with no answer to give.

Otter encourages me to go and sit in the evenings at the council fire where much of the village gathers to talk. When I say I wish to stay behind she says, "You have earned the trust of The Real People, Bear. Learn what you are now a part of. You are no longer the captive, scurrying from one place to another hoping not to be seen or caught. You are now Bear, of The Real People of The Maple Forest."

Am I? my ever confused head says in a quiet voice that only I can hear. I smile and nod and follow along behind Raccoon, Otter and Little Bird. To look at me you would see that I travel with the women and no longer need to be shown the right and wrong ways to do things. I can laugh and visit and talk with anyone I wish. The children still seek me out because, I suspect, no matter how I dress or sound I'm still an oddity in this village with my white skin and my ability to kill bad white trapper men with flaming sticks. I sigh. In some ways I feel more lost and alone then ever now that the village has claimed me as one of their own. *Shouldn't I feel happy?* I think to myself. *Peaceful at last?* But I feel none of these things.

I think about Pa, Henry, and Eli and I look at Raccoon, Otter, and Little Bird. I still don't feel like I fit in this village and suspect I never will. But the more terrifying thought is that I don't know if I'd fit any better at my homestead anymore. I'm a white girl who has lived with the *red savages*. Even worse, I've killed a white man to protect those *red savages*. I'm for sure not the same girl I was many months ago making Pa's favorite cornbread and wiping Eli's runny nose.

The Chief in this village is called Great Elk, and I learn there are many villages throughout the land of The Real People like this one in The Maple Forest. They trade with, support, and defend each other. It's not uncommon for different villages to socialize at times and to become connected through the joining of a man and a woman.

On the nights I sit at the council fire and listen to the conversations back and forth, I study the faces that I've come to know and listen to the words I've come to understand. There's talk about weather and crops, debates about hunting and fishing techniques and stories about the antics of old and young alike. I never speak, just watch and listen. Different nights bring different people and different moods. I sit and learn about The Real People of The Maple Forest and this center of the world.

The woman I called Red Coat is really called War Woman. She's almost as silent as me at the Council Fire, but I begin to find it mighty disturbing that her favorite thing to watch each evening seems to be me. She's the head of the women in this village and has great influence even in the surrounding villages. Even though Otter continues to try to set my mind at ease, War Woman's stare still reminds me of that rattlesnake waiting for me to make a wrong move.

"Why does War Woman stare at me so much?" I grumble one night as we make our way back to our hut.

Otter looks thoughtful. "Have you spoken with her?" she finally asks.

I shake my head. Why would I think to talk to her? Getting stared at by her all the time is bad enough.

"She does not think too much of whites," Raccoon seems inclined to mention as he carries a sleeping Little Bird over to his spot in the hut.

Otter gives Raccoon a look and then turns back to me. "Perhaps you should make an effort to speak with her, Bear," she tells me and I wish I'd had the smarts to keep my mouth shut in the first place.

"The feather she wears in her hair distinguishes her as a *warrior*, victorious in battle," Raccoon makes a point to tell me. He turns to Otter and asks casual like, "How many redcoat soldiers did she kill when she was just a young girl? I think it was fifteen?"

Otter rolls her eyes at Raccoon and walks over to me and takes my hands. "You are Bear, of The Real People, of The Maple Forest," she says softly to me. "You are a part of this hearth now. This worry and uncertainty you carry with you *is all your own.* No one can help you set it aside but yourself."

Otter turns to glare at Raccoon, who is busy making himself comfortable on their pallet, working hard to look like he's already dozing off to sleep. "War Woman is wise and kind," she says. "One of the many things she does in this village is to offer support, encouragement and advice to any who seek it. *You have no reason to fear her.*"

"I think she slit the soldiers' throats as they slept," Raccoon says out loud without bothering to open his eyes. "It is a painless way to die, I am told."

I look at Otter's face by the flickering bear-fat lamp. She looks me right in the eye and says, "You need to decide who you trust, Bear. No one can do that for you but yourself."

As I do the hard work of curing a hide the next day, I hear someone say my name and turn. I try hard to keep my face casual like as I look into War Woman's stern, unsmiling eyes and say, "Welcome. Shall I find Otter for you?"

She folds herself into a sitting position and says, "I am here for you. Otter says you wish to speak with me."

I take the time to set my tools down and wash my hands in a container of water we keep for such purposes. My thoughts are whirling around in my head like a pile of angry bees. I join War Woman, keeping myself busy stirring up the cook fire and adding some sticks. "I don't know why Otter sent you to me."

War Woman just looks at me like she has done so many nights before. I puzzle over the idea that she never seems to blink.

Finally, I feel compelled to say, "You watch me nights at the council fire." When that gets me nothing, I add with a shrug, "Raccoon says you do not like whites."

"Are you white?" she asks me.

I frown at her and hold out my hand. "You can't tell?"

At last, War Woman blinks. I know because I see her do it. She says patient like to me, "We have welcomed you at the Council Fire. You speak the language of The Real People. You wear the clothes of The Real People. You answer to a name given to you by The Real People. Maybe you need to answer that question for yourself."

I shake my head and look down at my hands now clasped tightly in my lap and feel a strong need to speak the truth, even though I suspect it will not stop her from staring at me any time soon. "I don't know what I am anymore. I will never be red. But I don't feel so white anymore."

War Woman sighs. "I watch you because I try to see how you are coping with the blood on your hands. It is not an easy thing to become accustomed to."

White hands that can never be washed clean. *Oh.* Now I see why I'm so all fire interesting to watch. Bear John. The man I've killed. I hear his screams in my head and can almost still smell the smell of him burning. My stomach roils at the memory. I close my eyes and try to take a deep breath.

"I killed six men before I turned sixteen summers," she says quietly, and I look up at her with stunned eyes, hearing all the things that Raccoon said last night again in my head. "They were white men," she says matter of fact, "soldiers who fought for the British army. Did you know that some of our people fought in your wars - The Great War with the British and others, too?"

I shake my head 'no' because I'm not so sure my voice will cooperate.

War Woman nods slightly. "We supported the people we had made treaties with, even though they did not keep all of the promises that they made. When they came and told us of this great battle that was to come and the need for our people to help, it was decided that it was the right thing to support their cause. We had given our word to support and defend the people called The British, and so we were obligated to do so. But, once again, they did not stay true to their words. Those we fought with did not treat us as equals. They did not provide us with the same food and supplies as the white soldiers were given. When the white enemies of The British attacked our villages because our braves had fought alongside The British, no one came forward to protect our women and children." She spoke quietly and with great sorrow. "Many of The Real People died in The Great War whether they were warriors in battle or just women and children waiting home in their villages. In the end, it seemed as if we fought alongside no one, and all white men were our enemy.

"I was just a young girl traveling with the braves who fought with the British during The Great War." She shrugs. "It was not a very important job. I was to provide them with food and care for them as they needed. I thought it would be a great adventure when I was told that I could go…" She looks at me then, and I let her see in my eyes exactly what she's showing me in hers: my despair, my confusion, and my horror.

War Woman sighs a deep, weary sound and nods in understanding. "I saw when a Real People's village was attacked by the white enemy. The white soldiers we were with did nothing to defend the village and would not allow our braves to do anything that would reveal our position. Some of the soldiers even laughed as they watched women and children being killed." War Woman is quiet for long moments. "It was then that I realized that all of those men in their bright red coats with their shiny brass buttons were just as much the enemy, if not more so. So, in the night, when they all were asleep, I killed the soldier who would not defend those innocent women and children and his comrades who laughed at the slaughter." She fingers the buttons that hang around her neck, enough for six coats I now know. "I restored the harmony that had been unbalanced and was honored for my deed by being given the name War Woman."

War Woman extends both her hands out in front of her. They are red, strong, capable hands. "Even though those men deserved to die, I struggled with what I had done." She shakes her head. "In the heat of the moment, I did not take the time to think it all through, but afterwards…" A long silence stretches out between us, both of us lost in our own thoughts.

"I am not sorry for killing Bear John," I say at last. "Otter and Little Bird's lives are worth the trade." I swallow. "I have trouble with the differences it is making inside of me, though. I … do not think that I fit … home, with my Pa … anymore."

She nods, seeming to understand exactly what I'm fighting to say, and stands in one graceful, fluid movement. She surprises me when she says, "I never went back to my village after I became War Woman. My life has always pulled me forward faster than I feel ready for. Only much later in my life did I realize what was happening to me." War Woman turns and begins to stride away.

"What was it that was happening to you?" I call to her back, mighty curious to know.

Her long bound hair, filled with much gray but still some black, swings as she turns and looks at me over her shoulder. "I was becoming a wise and powerful woman instead of a girl," she says. "It is the same journey that you are on."

I make sure to tell Raccoon as soon as he returns to the hearth that night that War Woman killed *six* white soldiers, not fifteen. And he doesn't seem happy to hear that I've told War Woman what he said her thoughts about whites were. I promise Raccoon that the next time War Woman and I talk I'll make sure to find out how she killed the soldiers, and I want to know is there anything else he wishes me to ask her? He says no, that I've certainly done enough already.

Otter has spoken before about this 'powerful woman' business. I like the sound of it I must admit, for I for certain am not one. *A wise and powerful woman.* I roll the phrase around in my mouth and test it out. *Not a girl.* Now that sounds even better.

"War Woman is not the only one of power in this village. Each and every woman you see has much power about all that she does: her life, her family, the village." Otter gives Raccoon a sweet smile as we sit around our hearth eating the evening meal. "Even who she chooses to join with."

"Who you marry – *join with* - is the woman's choice?" I ask in a surprised voice.

Otter nods. "When a man joins with a woman, he goes to live with her people, he becomes part of her clan, and the children they have trace their history through their mother's people. Should they cease to live together as a couple it is the woman who keeps the children and all the possessions."

Within a Real People village, families are divided by clans, like our families at home, I imagine. There's the wolf clan, the turkey clan, the otter clan and so on. Otter says with great pride, "I am Otter, of the Wolf clan, of The Real People of The Maple Forest, and through our joining so is Raccoon, and because he is my son, so is Little Bird."

"My white name is Elle Graves," I tell her. "My Pa's name is Andrew Graves and my Ma's name was Elizabeth Graves." I explain how it's just the opposite with white names and all. I tell them a bit about Henry and Eli. Otter and I laugh about what a struggle it can be to have brothers.

But Otter saves the best part for last. Perhaps the most amazing thing is that she tells me that all this now applies to *me*. I'm Bear, of this village. *You are a woman who has great power, too,* Otters tells me.

Me? Powerful? Twice in one day two women have used that word to describe me and not meant to be funny.

I ponder this new way of thinking. It's like peering into a looking glass and learning to do things opposite. I feel like a flower bud opening up to the warm spring sunshine. The wonder of it all... All of a sudden *I* can make choices about my life instead of everyone else doing it for me? Where, who, what, how… all those questions are just up to me?!

"I can learn to ride Willow?"

"I can learn to shoot a bow and arrow?"

"I can learn to hunt?" I ask.

Each time Otter smiles and nods her head, *Yes*. "And you can choose who you wish to join with, too," she's inclined to add. Otter looks down at the basket of dried apples and pretends to look hard for the perfect one. She picks up one and makes a face and tosses it aside. She picks up another, looks closely at it, sniffs it, makes another face, and tosses it aside. She picks up a third apple, turns it all around carefully, sniffs it, smiles, and hands it to me with a nod.

But she's stunned by my next question. "Can I choose not to marry?"

"Why would you do that?" she sputters. "You, who love children more than anyone! What would you wish to do instead?"

I think about my whole life. All fifteen years, for a birthday has happened for me sometime in the late part of autumn. I think about not so much the bad parts or the good parts but about the wonderment of having the chance to make a choice. I think about my time with Pa, Henry, and Eli and my caring for them and all that I did. I can't remember a time that I was able to get out of my bed and not have a list of things that I knew had to be done, and no one to do them but me. I think about Dirty Feet and Old Woman and Bright Feather and how I came to be here. I think about my days being filled with the weight of listening and watching and learning and doing.

There has been no real time that I can remember since I was a young child that I had a choice in what I wanted to do or be. I think about this center of the world, this Maple Forest where I sit. Being able to pick and choose and do something all because that's the direction *I* choose to put my foot, now *that's* an amazing thing to ponder. How can I explain this to Otter so that she will understand? I pick my words extra careful. "I would wish to do it because I *can*. I would wish to do … *just a little bit of everything*."

As the fall is just beginning to fade away and winter begins to blow its cold breath, Raccoon at last finds time to teach me how to ride Willow. It's a new experience for both my horse and me. Willow is a white man's horse that is to learn to be an Indian pony. I'm a white girl who has to learn to ride like an Indian. White people's horses are taught to listen to their riders with their mouths. Indian ponies are taught to listen to their rider's knees. I think if I were a horse, I'd prefer the Indian way.

First, Raccoon teaches Willow. She's a very smart horse, I decide. She's cautious with strange men, which Raccoon certainly is. I talk to Willow and try to explain that the marks on Raccoon's face and the raccoon tail in his hair are just a special way of making him stand out like her beautiful brown tail and mane and the bright white socks on her legs. "Isn't that so?" I ask Raccoon. He gives me one of his fierce looks which I point out will only make him stranger to Willow.

"Do you have special words that you say to a horse before you ride one," I ask, "words that will help the horse understand the balance and harmony of being ridden?"

He stares at me while I stroke Willow's nose and let her taste my tunic as I wait patiently for him to answer. He finally tells me that no, there are no special words. "Is there a special ceremony that makes a white horse officially an Indian pony, then?" I ask.

He stares at me again for long moments and finally tells me no there's no special ceremony.

"I think that until Willow feels comfortable with all these changes, that you are going to have a difficult time," I feel inclined to caution Raccoon.

He tells me what a good rider and horseman he is, and that he was training horses since before I was able to stand up on my own two legs. With a sudden leap he's on Willow's bare back, and with a sudden hop and back kick Willow has him on the leaf-covered ground staring up at the almost bare trees. I look down at Raccoon and say, "I think Willow is unwilling to change her mind about things until she's shown that the new way is better." Willow and Raccoon don't want any company for a couple of weeks until they work out all their problems.

Finally, it's time for Raccoon to teach me. Raccoon mounts Willow and shows me how to talk with my legs and body so that Willow will listen. Willow is a very good listener. I ask, "What special things have you said and done so that Willow is now happy to have you as a rider? I want to make sure that I can do as good a job as you are doing."

Raccoon sighs and says, "As long as you have done the riding ceremony, any Indian horse will accept you."

"I have not done the riding ceremony," I say with a bit of worry in my voice.

He looks mighty surprised. "How can that be?" Raccoon shakes his head. "I cannot teach you to ride until you have completed the riding ceremony," he says with regret as he slips down off Willow's back. "Come," he says leading Willow by her halter and walking deeper into the woods. "First, we will do the riding ceremony. *Then*, I will teach you how to ride."

The riding ceremony takes us all afternoon. I must be silent and not say one word or Raccoon says it will not take. I must do everything he tells me to do, which means I stand silent beside my horse watching the sun move across the sky for a very, *very* long time. I can't move. I can't ask even one question. Finally, Raccoon says that we can go back to the village now that the ceremony is over.

When we get back to our hearth, Otter asks me how my first riding lesson went, and I tell her about the riding ceremony. "Bear," Otter says after she glares at her husband as he's playing with Little Bird, "there is no such thing as a riding ceremony."

Raccoon looks up at me and gives me a slow wink, although he does manage not to smile. *So that's how it will be*, I think to myself suddenly much wiser. I look at my friend Otter and say, "Actually, then, the first riding lesson has taught me much more than I ever thought it would."

My riding lessons continue, with me much the wiser. Most every day if I can find time outside my chores, Willow and I practice the new things we have been taught by Raccoon. It's as I'm riding through the woods one of these days that a thought comes into my head that stops me still. I look down at Willow and out into the woods and I think, clear as day, *twelve days - twelve days ride from home and Pa, Henry, and Eli.*

For moments I can't catch a breath. My heart pounds and I wait for someone, *anyone* from the village to come rushing toward me to grab and hold me back from leaving. Then Willow knickers and stomps her feet to ask what she should do next, and a bluejay reminds me to move on and leave him be.

Not only have I been given a name by The Real People of The Maple Forest, but I have been given a horse. *And a knife*, my head reminds me. I'm the powerful woman, Bear, who has many choices. I realize that I've everything I need to go back home - *should I choose to.*

Suddenly, everything's different.

The only thing that keeps me here is myself. I've a horse I've only just learned how to ride. I've a knife that's as much decoration as the robin's feather in my hair and, I'm forced to admit, just as dangerous since I've no skills to use it. I'd get lost. I'd be hungry. I'd be frightened all on my own. I'm as trapped as ever.

Actually, nothing's different.

I sigh. I'm stuck, I realize. I live as a member of this village but still feel separate. Otter says I'm now a powerful woman, but I still act like a confused girl. There are many wonderful choices to be made, but I stand still with the confusion of it all. *So?* my head says. *Now what will you do?*

Maybe, my head thinks, it's time you make some choices and see how it will feel. Maybe, making just one choice will help you make another.

At home, Eli and I never liked winter as much as the other seasons. I suspect Pa and Henry felt the same, having to do so many outdoor chores in the bitter cold, but I don't recall them saying. For me and Eli, it was too cold, it got dark too quick, we were stuck inside too much. We had a puzzle that Pa said was a gift to him and Ma when they were married. It was a map of countries far across the ocean. Pa called it *Europe*. Eli and I did that puzzle more times than I could count. We would hide a piece and play a game: who would be the first to figure out what piece was missing? It was always fascinating to me to watch all those little bits slowly join together. Separate, each piece was alone and seemed useless, but once the entire puzzle was joined a whole picture could be seen. The loss of one piece could ruin the whole puzzle by making the picture incomplete. Pa said a puzzle was a lot like life.

But winter in an Indian village, to me, means freedom. No garden to tend, no herbs to gather, no fish to prepare, no meat or hides to cure. There are still meals to cook and firewood to find, and a whole passel of other things to do, but there's time to ride Willow, too. I take to riding at noontime after morning chores and before the evening meal is to be prepared. I ride Willow out into the forest and gather firewood and listen to the world around me full of harmony. In the privacy of the woods, me and Willow get to know each other, and we discover that we like one another quite a bit. Once Raccoon is satisfied with my skill, sometimes I ride out with Little Bird on my back to show him the sights of the winter forest.

"You know," I say one night at the dinner fire with Otter and Raccoon, "I was thinking that if I knew how to shoot a bow and arrow when I went out riding on Willow, maybe I could do some hunting." Little Bird crawls and plays in the furs and snow falls quietly outside.

Sometimes I think Raccoon can't wait until Little Bird is Big Bird and he does not have to be alone in a hut full of powerful women. "I am not so sure I have my strength back from teaching you how to ride," Raccoon says in a tired voice. Otter told me that Raccoon said he never met a person who asked as many questions as me. But how's a body to learn something they don't already know? I'm not discouraged by Raccoon.

"Who do you think would be strong enough, then?" I ask respectfully and Otter claps her hand over her mouth so not to laugh out loud.

Raccoon is in a spot because whoever he says, he knows I'll seek out, and whoever I seek out, he knows they will know that he sent them. He thinks and thinks and then sits up straight. "Cloud!" he says with certainty. "Cloud is the one to teach you!" Otter's look is not so certain.

Cloud must be one hundred years old, I think, when I go to see him for the first time. He's the oldest person I've ever seen, let alone talked to. He has hair as white as snow, and it flows loose down his back like a frozen waterfall. He's blind and he's almost deaf and his joints ache him so that he usually stays wrapped in furs by his fire. His hands, though wrinkled with age and crippled with pain, still move and dance as he speaks for Cloud loves to talk. He seems to enjoy answering my questions that he can hear and says he would be delighted to teach me how to shoot.

Bows I learn are best made in the spring when the sap is running new and the trees are coming alive for the summer. Hickory, ash, white oak, or cedar are the best wood. I fear I'm out of luck until Cloud lends me his bow on the promise that I'll return it when I've made my own. It's beautiful and smooth and shiny in my hand and heavier than I thought it would be. Unstrung, it rises almost to my waist from the ground. I must learn how to care for the bow, for even though he's no longer able to travel and to hunt, Cloud cares for his bow each and every day. When not in use it's unstrung, the deer sinew unnotched from one end and carefully wrapped around the other. I learn that nettle woven into a strong fiber or, best of all, snapping turtle skin are used for the bowstring. He shows me how to oil and rub the bow to protect it from moisture and keep it in best working order. It's always stored and carried in its bow sack which is strapped across the back underneath a quiver of arrows. Boys, he explains, are taught to make bows from the time they are young. He looks at me with sightless eyes that twinkle just the same, "And sometimes young curious women, too, it seems." For a time, after he was no longer able to hunt, he was the one to whom everyone came to make and repair their bows if they wanted the best work possible. "But now," he says sadly holding up his hands that look like carved wooden bear claws, "these old hands can no longer even do that."

He spends a full day explaining the shape and size and texture of the branches I need to make arrows and then sends me off. There's a tree that's perfect for arrow shafts, and it's called arrowwood! Dogwood, too, is good he says. "A fine piece of wood can be straightened if necessary," he tells me but he's hopeful that I'll be able to find a collection in the woods that's workable without that extra effort. Willow and I search for three days until I've a good assortment. Cloud examines, sniffs, and even tastes each one. Of the thirty I've brought him, he rejects seven, and I add them to the fire. By the end of two weeks I've twenty-three arrows with various tips. Some are sharpened to a point, some are blunt on one end (Cloud says to shoot small birds with). Each has feathers split in half and trimmed and tied to the shaft with deer sinew. "Animal glue or spruce gum will hold the feathers on, too," he tells me, and I file it away in my head carefully. The feathers are important, I learn, because they make the arrow fly true. "A good arrow wants to do its job but does not understand that each end has a different job. Feathers at one end remind a good arrow which end does the killing and which end does the guiding."

We examine his arrows, and I learn that there are still more kinds to make and use but not for me yet. He has arrows in his quiver that are tipped with sharpened flint stone, with bone, horn, shell, and even copper. "Learn to shoot with these first," he says touching my precious collection of twenty three, "and then you can move on to these," he says motioning to his various tipped ones. To hold them, we make a quiver out of buckskin with a piece of wood inside to keep it stiff. "Some braves like to decorate these," he says in a tone that says he does not think much of the idea. "Let your shooting speak for you not the designs on your quiver." His quiver is well cared for but plain. It takes more than two weeks, but finally, I stand with one bow in its bow sack strapped to my back and twenty-three arrows – some blunt and some sharpened to a point – in my plain quiver. The bow is only borrowed, but Cloud says to call it mine for now. The bow and quiver lie across my back peeking over my left shoulder and down past my right hip.

He has who I believe to be his great, great grandson, Red Fox, show me how to hold and shoot the arrows – under his supervision. I think Red Fox must be my age or maybe a bit older. Red Fox is shy but patient with my fumbling first attempts as Cloud shouts out instructions to both of us: where to put my feet, how to hold my bow and arrow, where to look with my eyes, the angle my head should be tilted. I think Red Fox is very kind in not laughing at my shots, and I make sure that Raccoon hears of his patience. We practice two full weeks out in the cold, with Cloud wrapped in all his furs making comments, and our noses growing red, and our fingers becoming numb. I try not to get discouraged, but it seems like I'll never master all the things I need to know and still hit the target. Finally, a day comes when I'm able to hit the target not once but seven times. Cloud tells me to go into the woods away from laughing eyes and practice. My lessons seem to be done.

Riding Willow becomes a time to go off on my own, learn the forest, gather firewood, find more sticks for arrows, and practice my shooting. With no one else to give comments, except Willow who tends to keep all of her opinions to herself, I learn the feel of the bow and arrow with my fingers. Some days Red Fox offers to come along, and I find I like his company. He has good suggestions and never laughs at my shooting as I know Raccoon would. We tramp through the cold snowy wood, often on foot, for he does not have a horse as I do, and find good places where we set up targets to shoot at. He shimmies up a tree just like a squirrel to put a target up high and blushes when I tell him that he should be called Quick Squirrel instead of Red Fox. I think he's happy to help me learn to shoot better because he shares in the teaching of it.

Red Fox can shoot from a horse for he often borrows Cloud's. I'm happy to return some of the many kindnesses he has shown me and offer to let him ride Willow so that we can both practice riding and shooting. Willow is patient and willing to help out, too. Maybe she hopes Red Fox will do better at this bow and arrow business than me, which isn't saying much. Even though Red Fox does not have a horse of his own, he's a better rider than me and there's nothing for me to teach him. We have a lot of laughter running and riding around in the cold winter woods taking turns being the hunter or the hunted. We use the bird arrows that have no sharp tips, but there's no reason to worry since we never seem to hit anything anyway.

I do discover one thing right quick: learning to shoot an arrow from a *moving horse* is just like learning to shoot an arrow standing still for the very first time. There are so many things to think of; steer your horse, find your arrow, load the bow, sight your target, aim your shot ... *Watch for low branches! Watch for uneven ground! Watch for rocks! Watch for streams!* It seems to me that just when I think I've got everything in order a new piece gets thrown in that I must remember. After a time, even Willow starts making snorts of disgust about my mistakes and failures. I realize that I may be able to hit a target while everything is stock still, but I don't expect much otherwise. I begin to think as the weeks go by first, that I'll never get this and second, that I'm glad Raccoon is nowhere near to see me and make fun.

Red Fox is full of good advice. "Cloud says always to remember one thing; it wasn't the loss of his sight that caused him to lose his ability to shoot his bow and arrow true. It was the loss of his feel because of his joint aches. Even sightless, he would listen and smell the wind, notch his bow and the moment a deer would start to run it would find an arrow in its throat. I saw."

He tells me wonderful stories of hunting trips he has been on. Tales of black bears larger than a man sitting on a horse, and of elk antlers too large to be carried by one person. But the story I find most interesting is of the 'lord of the forest', a large cat that hides up in trees and is bigger than a full grown man. Red Fox has traveled far into the forest surrounding the village and beyond, and I hear stories of places and adventures that fill my head with excitement.

"Are these real stories?" I finally need to ask him, and at Red Fox's hurt expression I take some time to explain the riding ceremony Raccoon made me do.

"Ahhh," he nods in understanding. He takes the time to look at me serious like for a moment and then says, "I promise, Bear, I will *always* tell you the truth. You can always count on my words."

As we stand there in the cold and the snow with our steamy breath making clouds around our faces, I make the same promise back to Red Fox. I smile at him, for it seems I've another friend to add to my list.

I tell him about my one trip helping Bright Feather and about the elk and the bear. I even tell him about my bear dream. My story is not as exciting as Red Fox's, and yet he seems happy enough to walk beside me and listen.

He tells me with sadness how there are fewer and fewer animals in the forest, and that there are some winters when The Real People of The Maple Forest are hungry. "The Real People believe that everything is equal and that all are kin to one another. No one is better than the next. No one is more important." We are sitting quiet on a hill in the forest in the shelter of a big rock overhang that protects us from the winter winds. "I am no better than the earthworm, the bear is no more important then the tiny goldfinch. Our only reason for being here is to help Mother Earth care for the rest of creation. We are all part of the Great Circle. Respect for life is so important that one would rather starve than take another life without permission, without asking the spirit of the animal for food and fur for warmth. This balance and harmony in our life has been kept for many, many years." He's quiet for a while.

"But things have been different lately. The balance and harmony in our life has been disrupted. The white men do not think as we do. The need for balance in Mother Earth is not something they seem to care about. They hunt and trap and prepare the earth for farming without a thought of others. They wish to take things from the forest for others besides themselves without respect or thoughts for those who remain. Too many animals are hunted and trapped, too much land is taken for farming, and those of us who live by these things become hungry, lose our homes, grow weak," Red Fox looks at me with eyes that seem all of a sudden older, "and frightened. The way is changing, and there is nothing The Real People can do about it."

He talks to me as if I'm not white, I realize. I wonder, *What does he see when he looks at me?* I'm wear fur - lined moccasins and pants underneath my tunic and wear my bearskin as a cape. My hair is wrapped and tucked inside my tunic and my robin's feather whips about my head in the brisk winter wind. Aside from the tips of my nose and fingers I'm toasty warm. I still have white skin. And green eyes. *Does he see all these things or just some of them?*

I think about the way of things with my life and how until just recently there was nothing I could do about it. *Is that what life is?* I think to myself. *Do we all just hang on as we drift down the river like a dry autumn leaf?* I've no answer for myself and no words to comfort Red Fox.

Raccoon tells me that he thinks my name should be Dog because once I grab onto something I won't let go like a starving dog with a juicy bone. That's because I want him to take me winter hunting with him, and he says no. Each time I ask him in another way, polite and kind, he says no. After he makes the Dog comment I tie three dog bones to his horse, but I do stop asking. He comes in holding the bones and looks at Otter and me who have innocent eyes. "Bear," he says finally to me, "would you like to come hunting with me today?" I'm ready to go before Raccoon is.

I try real hard to stay quiet on that first hunting trip with Raccoon. I ask no questions – not one; just watch and try to remember everything we see and do. Perhaps Raccoon thought I *couldn't* be quiet or *couldn't* be still. He hadn't gone with me when Bright Feather and I'd hunted so he didn't truly know. We sit in a spot for most of that winter's day, me never more thankful for my furs. I remember that summer day with Bright Feather and go through my mind about all the things that have changed since then besides the temperature. I conclude that aside from the robin's feather still stuck in my hair there's not one thing that's the same.

I think about what Otter has told me about Bright Feather (she calls him that now, too, in the private walls of the hut). He's always gone all winter. He leaves during the first sign of frost and returns at the first thaw. He hunts and traps the whole mountainside and brings back many furs that he then takes to trade. I now know that he had a mate and they had a son. Otter said that it was a time five summers ago that Hawk became known as One Who Is Always Alone. I want the missing pieces to this puzzle something fierce, I realize. But I learn right quick that Indians don't like to talk of the dead, and so since no one will speak of them, that leads me to obvious conclusions. It wouldn't be right to say that I miss Bright Feather, but I think I'd like to be able to show him how I can ride Willow now and how I can shoot my bow and arrow, and perhaps thank him proper for my bearskin.

I think all these things sitting with Raccoon that afternoon. Twice I catch him looking at me in wonder at my silence, I suspect. The second time I show my teeth and growl like a camp dog. He can't help but chuckle and shake his head at that. Finally, into the clearing comes a buck. Raccoon said later that he was very, very old, lame, half starved, and probably deaf *and* blind, but I shoot it! I'm so proud I nearly burst. Raccoon teaches me the right words to thank the spirit of the deer for the gift of his life and in the quiet of the forest I repeat them with great respect. I've learned working side-by-side from Bright Feather how to gut and skin and prepare the carcass. Raccoon and I are quickly ready to go back to the village. Raccoon has me ride right to the council circle and Great Elk's hut. I give Great Elk the buck's heart and War Woman the liver (Raccoon said such would be expected), but to Cloud I give the antlers and he whoops and laughs with pride like he'd done the kill himself. I'll make something special with the hide.

Sometimes the men allow me to come along on their short day hunting trips after that first hunting time with Raccoon. I never get to shoot much, and so I never kill anything, and I suspect that I'm only allowed because of Raccoon, but I'm happy just the same. I study how the other men hold their bows and ride their horses. If I forget myself and start asking too many questions on these trips, Raccoon tends very casual like to stuff anything he can find in his ears – leaves, sticks, even pieces of dried venison one time - to muffle the sound of my voice. It's another thing I learn: watch others to see how your acting makes them act.

On these occasional trips, one brave named Beaver is always most patient with me and takes the time to point out things in the forest that I don't notice. I learn to tell the scat from a deer from the scat from an elk from the scat from a fox. I learn the shape of footprints in the snow and what animals they go to and to watch certain kinds of rough tree bark for bits of fur. Beaver is always most serious, and even Raccoon behaves when I'm with him. Often he takes so much time to teach me what I need to know that the others we are traveling with wander off and leave us all on our own.

Beaver is older than Red Fox, not because he looks it so much, but mostly because he acts it. Always serious no matter how many summers he is, he's inside an old soul as Pa would have said. Being taught by Beaver leaves no time for teasing like with Raccoon and no time for laughter like with Red Fox. Learning with Beaver is all business, and I best pay attention to not miss a thing.

When Beaver finds out that I can't start a fire on my own, he takes the time to show me how to start one from a fire kit he carries with him *at all times*. Right there in the cold winter woods, in the shelter of a fallen tree with nothing around us but the snow and the wind and the two of us and our horses, Beaver sets out to make a fire. The others once again ride off without a backward glance, I suspect glad to be rid of the one who doesn't know enough and perhaps the one who knows too much.

I watch Beaver's face, solemn and sure, as he reaches down and clears a spot and scans the area for things he needs. His voice is deep and mellow, smooth a little like slow moving molasses. "The ceremony of life begins with the origin of the first fire," Beaver says, and I look forward to the magic he weaves with his words. He's full of stories of The Real People and is always happy to tell one. His hands, red and strong and sure, snap the kindling sticks he has found around us and make a careful pile. "In the beginning there is darkness and no fire. The Great One sent the Thunder Beings to bring life to Mother Earth. The new Earth is cold, and Sun had just started to heat the land during what we now know as day. Still, the nights are cold, as Moon's task is to protect us and to slowly start the germination of seeds for trees and plants on this new island called Mother Earth. One of the sacred trees to come to this new land is Sycamore; many others, such as Oak and Pine will come later. Some of the trees, such as Redbud and Cherry Tree, are eager to come to this new land, but they have to wait because they need much light to bloom and to create fruit for the animals.

"The Thunder Beings send their lightning to put fire at the bottom of a sycamore tree that is on a small island in the water by itself. All the animals see the smoke, but they are not sure how to bring the fire back to their tribal council. The animals meet in council and decide that all the animals that can swim or fly will go and bring the fire back to council. First to make the trip is Raven. He is a beautiful large bird with white feathers until he flies over the sycamore tree where fire and smoke rise high in the sky. Raven cannot land on the tree, and his feathers become scorched and black. He returns without the fire. The same thing happens to Owl, who gets his eyes blackened with the hot smoke as he looks into a hollow part of the tree. To this day, members of the Owl tribe have rings around their eyes, and they have trouble seeing except at night."

Beaver has made a small pile of sticks, as dry as can be found, and from his fire kit he takes out more bits of kindling and what looks like cat tail down. He stops his story and takes time to explain all this down to the placement of the sticks, the amount of kindling that is just right, and the need for there to be air space for the new fire to catch a breath. When he is certain I've all this information stored away in my very empty head, he continues with his story.

"It is decided that the Snake tribe would swim to the island. First is little Racer Snake who got close to the burning fire. He is blinded by the hot ashes, and his body is scorched black. Ever since, the racer snake darts back and forth as if trying to get away from the fires. The same thing happens to Blacksnake.

"Finally, little Water Spider says that she will quickly move across the water and weave a bowl to carry a hot coal on her back. The council agrees. Thus, Water Spider brought the fire to the First Council on Mother

Earth, and she is always honored in ceremonies that recall that first fire. Fire is held sacred by The Real People, and it is always in the center of the Sacred Circle in ceremonies."

He takes his fire rocks and strikes once, twice, and sparks fly. Leaning over he blows carefully into the small, smoking bits, and like magic small orange flames spring to life. Carefully, slowly, he feeds in more bits of his precious kindling, explaining all the time exactly what he's doing. Finally, the fire is dancing brightly before us, and I put out my hands to enjoy the warmth. He makes it all look easy, but I make sure to be on my own the first time I try to do this and be sure Raccoon isn't around to watch. It's another thing I must practice *on my own away from laughing eyes.*

Beaver looks at me with his stern face and says, "Fire is the reminder that we must always go back to the center and celebrate life as our main focus in our thoughts and actions. *Fire is life.*"

"Can a person loose her center?" I ask watching the firelight cast dancing light across Beaver's face.

He nods his head. "Yes, that happens when there is nothing in your center strong enough to draw you back."

"What if it is not so much that there is nothing in your center but *too much?*" I think about my red and white self dancing and crowding each other in my center making it impossible for me to be still and peaceful.

Beaver takes out a piece of dried venison from his pack and hands me a piece. I take out a dried corn cake and share a bit with him. We munch in silence. "You struggle with the two worlds you have walked in," he says after a time. "It is a struggle that The Real People have been fighting for many more years than you have."

"How is that so?!" I ask with surprise.

He shrugs, and his long black hair slips forward and shadows part of his face. "The Real People struggle with the life that the white man wishes us to lead. In many ways, just as *you* have been forced to lead the life of *the savage Indian,*" and I wince as the words sound foul and wrong coming from his mouth, "we, for many, many years have been forced to change to the life of the white man. No more hunting, learn to be farmers and raise cows and chickens. No more migrating to suit the seasons and the land, learn to set down roots in one spot, and never move like an old oak tree. No more honor and trust, instead sign papers and take *things* to prove a trade. Learn to want instead of give and learn to force instead of allow."

His serious face is full of sorrow as he looks at me across the crackling fire. "You say, 'yes' and you say, 'no'. You must decide who you wish to trust, and honor, and ... love ... most of all and put them in the center of your life. Then you must be forceful with what you allow in and what you keep out. Maintaining your center is a job that only you can do, Bear. For it is *your center,* and no one else's."

"So I must decide if I have a white center or if I have a red center," I say with a voice filled with defeat, for I'm right back where I have always been.

"No," Beaver says, "that is not what I have said. "I do not believe that you, Bear, can ever be only white or red. Why should that be? What I *said* was you have to decide who you will trust, and honor, and love." He begins the process of putting out the fire, pushing snow across the embers, and I listen to the hiss and steam of it all. "If you choose the right things from both parts of your life, then you will have the best and brightest center of us all."

"The best of my red and white self ..." I say quietly and I get goose skin up my arms.

It's late winter and I've traveled with the men quite a few times when a herd of winter elk is spotted not more than a half-day's distance from the village. It's hoped that two or three animals may be brought down, and I'm invited to go! It's the largest hunting party I've ever been with - eight braves and me. Red Fox is along, too, riding on Cloud's horse. I think he's as excited as me, but he tries very hard not to let it show. So do I. I'm excited because maybe, *just maybe,* I'll be able to do some real hunting.

I think that I see some signs that spring will be coming soon. My favorite places show very small signs that the earth may be waking up from its long winter's sleep. Following behind the men on this day, I see bare patches of ground where snow has been. The brown, bare trees look like they are ready to pop with color. I see some robins hunting like we are. Everywhere I look, squirrels are chasing each other across the forest floor and up the tallest trees.

At the top of a ridge we spot the herd of maybe fifty animals. The men discuss the wind and the land and who goes where and who does what. I'm paired with Raccoon, a curse he regularly bears with silence. As we head toward the spot we are to take charge of he says casual like over his shoulder, "How's your shooting coming along on a moving horse?" I realize that he has seen my practicing with Willow. I'm embarrassed and a little mad.

"Better than my hearing is for strange people in the woods," I say with what Pa would have called a smart lip.

He laughs out loud. He doesn't turn around so I can't see, but I hear a smile in his voice. "You learn quick, Dog," he says. Sometimes he calls me that when he's trying to be funny, although I never laugh as I feel it's best not to encourage him.

"Woof," I say.

I've never hunted in a large group like this. Raccoon for once must do more talking than me to explain how things must be done. Some of the men travel all the way down to the farthest part of the herd. The rest of us are in spots along the way where we know the herd will run once they are startled. Each of us, hidden along the way, will have a few brief moments to shoot at the passing herd as it runs terrified past us trying to escape.

"So," says Raccoon, "you let off your first arrows seated still on your horse as the herd comes towards you. Once the herd gets alongside you, you begin to ride and shoot more as it passes. If you see a wounded one, try to kill it with your knife - if you can get close enough." He grins at me. "So you can have practice with being still and moving. Maybe there will be a very, very old, lame, deaf, blind *elk* you can kill this time." For once I choose just to be quiet and say not a word.

We wait. I practice over in my head all the things I need to remember when I'm moving, the horse is moving and my prey is moving. I think of the times that I've practiced on my own and with Red Fox. Of course Raccoon has added a new piece I've now got to consider, the jumping off your horse and using your knife part. Will there ever be a time when I've got all the pieces in one place, I wonder?

We hear the whoops and shouts and the pounding elk's hooves before we see anything. But what a sight when it all comes into view! The largest animals can easy look me square in the eye, and the bucks with their antlers are taller than Willow. I see Beaver and Red Fox whooping and shouting and following behind the herd. I realize it's hard to keep yourself still, let alone your horse, when you see a sight like that pounding toward you stampeding wild with fear. I fix my sights on the biggest, tallest animal, because my thinking is it's the easiest to hit. I see it's eyes wild with fear, and I let one arrow fly and am pleased that I've time to let a second arrow fly before it's time for me to start practicing my shooting while on a moving horse. I don't know where Raccoon or any of the other men are, but I can hear shouts and whoops as Willow and I take off at a run towards the edge of the herd. I load my arrow and take aim, watching the trees and watching the ground and watching the herd. I pick the closest animal and let an arrow fly. My arrow goes wild as Willow jumps over a fallen tree trunk. I load another arrow and aim at another animal. I shoot and am amazed to watch the creature stumble and fall to the ground my arrow piercing the lower side of its stomach. It's a young male with small antler stubs just peeking through his skull. His eyes are wild as he jumps and bucks and tries to rise and run away from me. Willow is trained well and stands still behind me where I get off, and I find myself talking softly to the animal that's dying right in front of me. I know the terror it's feeling, and I pull out my knife and cut it's throat so it will stop its struggling and escape from its fear. I say the words of thanks I know are right to say that Red Fox has told me, and whisper with great respect, "Thank you, spirit of this elk, for the food and hide you will provide us." Then I stand and look. The herd is no longer to be seen, but there's still a distant rumble like thunder as they continue to stampede away.

I'm standing proudly by my buck with my knife still in my hand and Willow munching grass behind me as Raccoon rides his horse over to me. I grin a huge grin, "WOOF!" I say, "He does not look very, very old, or lame, or deaf or blind. And we were both *moving*," I feel that that's important to add.

Raccoon dismounts and looks very intently at the buck. He examines where my arrow hit and how I cut the animal's throat and then looks at me and says very serious like, "But he looks very, very dumb I am thinking."

All in all we take down five elk. Beaver and Red Fox have taken down a large buck whose antlers alone I can't lift! We take the major portions of meat and leave the carcass for the wolves and other scavengers. On the way back, we see Bright Feather coming through the trees. Just as Otter has said, he returns with the first thaw. Greetings are exchanged and information is shared. I can see from the back of the group where I'm mounted, that not only does he have his own horse but a pack horse as well, loaded high with beautiful pelts. I see fox, beaver, and otter. I never knew that brown can be such a rich and glorious color. All the pelts glint in the fading sunlight. I know that winter trapping rarely gets you more than the meat you need to eat, the furs are the treasure you hope for.

Bright Feather asks polite questions about the success of the hunt. It's Raccoon who seems happy to point out that one of the five elk was brought down by *Bear*. I watch Bright Feather's face and enjoy seeing him look through the group of nine before his eyes settle on me. I sit straight and tall on Willow, who moves not a muscle just like I've taught her. I think how I must look to all of them with my white skin and red cheeks, my bear cape and bow and arrows peeking over my shoulder. Bright Feather does not speak to me but looks at Raccoon and says, "Can she understand our spoken word yet?"

Raccoon has his back to me, and I can just imagine the face he must make to this question, and all of a sudden I'm not happy about being talked about like I'm a deaf and dumb piece of rock. "Welcome back, One Who Is Always Alone. It would seem that your trapping has been successful this winter," I say loud and clear in the silence of the forest.

He turns to me and studies my face for a long time, it feels. "So it has been, Bear," he says.

We return together as a group to the village in high spirits. I try not to gloat too much over my elk and speak only when spoken to. Otter has saved us all portions from the evening meal and Bright Feather, Otter, and Raccoon talk about the success of the hunt and his winter trapping. Bright Feather talks of his travels, and reports on animal as well as people movement he has seen or not seen. There's a discussion as to when he will travel to trade his furs and what the village can use in the way of supplies, but I fall into an exhausted sleep on my pallet to the murmur of voices still speaking over the nearby fire and don't hear the answers.

I dream of my bear again, but this time I'm home with Pa, Henry, and Eli. I'm busy in the barn milking our cow, Two-Bit, and my bear peeks in to wave at me.

"Come inside, to the warmth of the barn," I say all friendly like.

But he shakes his head sadly and will not come in.

"Why not? Two-Bit will not mind."

"I cannot," he says, "for I am not dressed proper."

"What?!" I say with a laugh. "You look just fine with your thick, dark coat and shiny black eyes. You look more smartly dressed than I do for this weather." I look down at myself and stick my foot out to prove a point. Underneath my skirt and all my petticoats are my fur lined leggings and moccasins.

"That's what I came to tell you," he says, just as sad. "You should not be in here either. Your Pa just came and told me that you have got to go, too."

In the morning, I prepare breakfast for Bright Feather like I've always done although now the silence between us is strange, I think. I'm shy now with my talking, worried that Raccoon has told Bright Feather all of my bad points. He has teased me that while *he* thinks I'd better be named Dog, there are many in the village who think an even better name for me would be Never Stops Asking Questions. So I work hard to stay quiet.

It's Bright Feather who makes the first effort to speak as I prepare his breakfast over the fire. "What is your horse like?" he finally asks.

And so I tell him how I call her Willow because of the way her mane and tail look like the willow branches to me. I tell him how smart she is and how Raccoon helped me train her and what a good Indian pony she is now. I tell him she's fast and obedient. I tell him she's gentle but brave.

He asks if I've trained her to sounds, and I don't know what he means and say so. He explains, "You can teach a horse to listen to special sounds that come just from you like a whistle or a hoot that works in a time when your knees are not close enough to talk," he explains.

Questions boil up in my head. *Oh no*, I think. "Has Raccoon told you that I ask more questions than any person he knows, and that I make him more tired with my talking than a full day's ride does?" I ask Bright Feather.

He stares at me for a moment or two and then finally nods his head. "Yes."

I look at him right in the eye and say, "I don't want to tire you out either," and go back to fixing the food.

He chews on his stew, thinking about what I've just told him. I feel him watching me closely, and I hope he realizes I've given him an honest warning from a powerful woman. "Ask your questions," he finally says. "I will go away when I get tired."

So I do. I take a deep breath, and out they pour: "Is it difficult to train a horse to sounds? How long does it take? Are there special sounds or can they be any old sounds? Are some sounds easier to teach than others? Can all horses learn or only extra smart ones? What kind of things can you train your horse to do?" I pause to take a breath and he has stopped chewing to sit and stare and listen. He blinks but says nothing, so I add in a rush, fearful that he's already tired and planning on going away,

"Could you help me see if we could train Willow? And, if yes, how soon can we start?"

Bright Feather finishes the last bite of stew, sets his bowl down and rubs the side of his smooth, brown cheek. I wait, certain he's going to stand up and run to his horse to get away. I should have only asked one question, I think. Or maybe two.

He takes a deep breath and begins to tell me how he trained his horse and says, if my horse is as smart as I say, that he can certainly teach me how to train Willow. He answers each and every question, patient and slow, and then promises to help me during the time I tell him I usually practice riding and shooting. I rush off to get my chores done.

Otter teases me as I hurry through my chores to get them finished. "Are you off to play with Red Fox in the wood," she grins at me over her shoulder as she wrestles with Little Bird, trying dress him in some warm furs, "or has Beaver thought of something new he needs to teach you besides hunting tips and starting fires?"

I shake my head. "I am going to teach Willow some new things, and Bright Feather said he would help me."

She stops and turns to stare at me. "One Who Is Always Alone wishes to help you train Willow?" she asks her voice filled with surprise.

I nod. "Even though he says Raccoon warned him about how tired I can make a person, he still says he will help me." I feel compelled to add, "He said that when he gets tired he will just go away again."

"Is that so," she says in a very thoughtful tone. She studies me as I bustle around, frowning in thought. "Did you ask him to help you?"

I stop and look at her and nod. "He asked me about Willow when I brought him his breakfast this morning, and we got to talking."

"*You 'got to talking'?*" she asks me now with more wonder than surprise.

"Yes," I say slow like for she seems to have trouble understanding my talking today. "It is the first time we have really spoken; when he was here last I was as talkative as a stone. At first I was a bit shy, but you should make sure that Raccoon knows that *Bright Feather asked me the first question.*"

"He asked the first question…," she repeats to me still sitting, looking at me while Little Bird has managed to escape her and is now digging through one of our storage baskets with great delight.

"Are you all right, my friend?" I feel compelled to ask.

She suddenly notices Little Bird and snatches him back to finish the job of dressing him. "Yes, I am fine," she says. After a moment or two, Otter says, "Training a horse to sound is not as easy as you think. Bright Feather's horse is the only one in the village that I know of that has learned the skill. It takes a lot of patience ... and time to succeed."

"Willow is as smart as Bright Feather's horse," I say with certainty.

Otter nods her head. "No doubt," she says.

Later that day, Bright Feather and I ride out to a spot not too far from the village. I tell Bright Feather about how I've learned and practiced all winter to be able to ride and shoot. I tell him all about learning about the forest and describe to him some of my favorite places that I'm sure he knows about already. He nods his head a lot. I do most of the talking. "Am I making you tired?" I finally ask him.

He's ahead of me on the trail. He shakes his head "no." "Not yet," he says. I'm relieved.

Bright Feather calls his horse Companion. At first I think it's a mighty odd name for a horse. But then I think, for a man who is on his own all the time, it makes perfect sense.

We come to a clearing we both know of and dismount. Bright Feather says to me, "Otter says you have a name that you call me. I would like to know it."

I swallow. Names are special things, much more so than white man's names like Henry, Eli, or Elle. I was told in no uncertain terms that I was *never* to call Old Woman "Old Woman" to her face. Her name is One Who Knows, and she holds a position in the village of great honor, almost as great as War Woman. She's the village healer and wise in the way of sickness, births, and wounds. Otter speaks of her with great respect and even some fear, I think. "She can explain your dreams, and sometimes she knows the future. When you have a question or a concern, she's the one to seek out," Otter tells me with great seriousness. Nor am I to call Dirty Feet "Dirty Feet", for his name is Weasel. I commented to Otter that I didn't think that 'Weasel' was much better than 'Dirty Feet', but Otter didn't laugh. In fact, the subject of Weasel seems to make her uncomfortable, and it's soon changed. When I try to ask more questions, she ends up silent, just looking at me. Her silence speaks of death, I think. At last I say to Bright Feather as he stands silent and patient in the winter woods, "I call you Bright Feather because of the feathers in your hair," and watch his face real close to see if I see anything at all.

"Do you know the birds they are from?" he asks me after a brief moment.

"Yes," I say. "Red for cardinal, yellow for goldfinch, blue for bluejay."

He nods his head and scratches Companion's ear. I'm correct. "The cardinal," he begins to explain as he looks into the forest, "is a beautiful but hearty bird that stays put even during the harshest weather of the winter and survives. The bluejay is distant and unfriendly to strangers of all kinds and often to its own breed as well. The goldfinch is hard to see even in the best of seasons. You can search all summer and hardly catch a glimpse of him." He looks at me then and I think, *All of those birds are a little bit like you.*

He hesitates a moment and then says, "I had a name for you, too, but it does not fit anymore."

I'm powerful curious. "What name was that?" I ask.

"Mouse," he says, "for the way you scuttled around all the time doing your chores, trying not to be noticed and moving so quick you did not notice much yourself."

I think for a moment, and I remember my early time in the village with One Who Knows and Bright Feather. I think about how all I wanted to do was get my chores done, get back in the hut to safety and stay small. I was just like a mouse.

"Raccoon sometimes calls me 'Dog' and people in the village say that I could also have the name 'Never Stops Asking Questions'."

"Names are windows to the heart, Bear. What people call you are what they see and think of you. A wise person watches and listens and learns more about himself through watching how others behave when they are with him." He turns and strokes Companion's neck. "That way, if a person feels inclined to change, he knows where to start." He shrugs and says, "You may call me Bright Feather if you wish."

I think about the window of my heart that I show people. I can be a bear, a mouse, a dog, and always asking more questions than most people want to hear. Even my window shows how mixed up inside I still am, I realize.

"It is a good thing that you became Bear," he says quietly interrupting my thoughts. "Now why don't you show me how smart this horse of yours is?

Companion comes when Bright Feather whistles, trotting right up to Bright Feather's outstretched hand. He stops when Bright Feather clicks his tongue and does about five other things just by sounds alone. "Can you whistle?" Bright Feather asks me. I nod my head "yes." He motions towards Companion. *Try and call him.*

I whistle and whistle. Companion never even raises his head from cropping the grass he's eating. "*That's* the hard part," he says to me finally.

I decide that the first sound I want Willow to learn is to come when I call. Bright Feather stands with Willow at one side of the clearing, and I hold in my hand some sweet clover that Willow loves. I whistle and she keeps eating the grass right in front of her. I take two steps closer and whistle again. This time she looks up but still does not move. I take two steps closer and whistle again. Two more. Finally I'm close enough that when she lifts her head when I whistle if she stretches her neck as far as she can she can just grab the clover with her lips. Who would say she's not smart? This is going to take a long time I think.

We practice until it's close to dark and until Willow couldn't care less what I feed her because her belly is full. "Show me how you shoot," Bright Feather says to me when it's clear that Willow's lesson is over for the day.

I take out my bow and arrows and quiver, and I tell him all about Cloud and Red Fox and my practicing when I *thought* I was on my own. He listens as I talk about Red Fox and how helpful he has been teaching and helping me learn to shoot even better and better. He nods when I speak of Raccoon and how I pestered him to take me hunting. Bright Feather grunts when I get to the part about the very old, very lame, deaf and blind first deer I killed. I explain all I know about tracking an animal from what Beaver has taught me, and I'm proud to be able to tell Bright Feather that I can start a fire on my own from my fire kit.

He examines every arrow and my quiver. I tell him how my bow is really Cloud's but he said I can call it mine until I make my own. "This is good work," he finally says, looking at my arrows and quiver closely. I show him how I shoot. He watches and tells me to change my footing just a little and lift my elbow just a bit higher. He watches me until I've emptied my entire quiver. As I go to retrieve my arrows he says, "Keep practicing." I guess he's more impressed with my arrows than my shooting which I must admit is not a surprise.

As we ride back to the village I ask him about his traps and the woods farther from here than I've ever been. He tells me just a little bit about his travels, and says traps are easier to explain when they are in front of you to see.

As we get to the village and dismount and are walking our horses, I say, "Do you ever go into Virginia?" That's all I ask, but we both know that there's a lot more hanging in the air. He stops, so I stop and he looks down at me.

"No, I always go west, Bear. I never cross over the mountains unless it is to trade, and then there is only one place I know that is safe to go to," he says. He looks around at the village with all the activity around us. "No one in this village ever goes east."

"Except Weasel," I can't keep myself from saying it, and get quiet. I've talked very little with Otter about Dirty Feet, who is called Weasel, and that time almost a full year ago. Mostly it's because she seems to not want to speak of it, but also because it's still a part of me that causes the most pain and sorrow. Why all of a sudden do I feel comfortable bringing this up to Bright Feather?

Because he carries a sadness and a loss around him just like you, my head says as soon as I ask the question. Because there's no one in the village that seems as lost and as confused as you but him.

"I think I will say that I am tired now, Bear," he says quietly, but he stops and waits, and I must tilt my head up to look at him. It's very small, but I think I see a sadness in his face he works hard to push back inside. "But that doesn't mean you can not ask me that question again another time. When Willow learns to come when you whistle, let me know, and we will work on a new sound." With that, he and Companion begin to walk away. I think of something and call to Bright Feather. He stops and turns and waits for me and Willow to catch up with him.

"I never thanked you proper for the bear skin," I say, looking back at it thrown across Willow's back. "I could not have done half of the things this winter had I not had it to keep out the cold."

Nodding, he says, "That makes me happy to hear," and turns and walks away toward his hut.

Otter says that spring is well and truly here, and much to her delight it seems that there are some with mating on their minds. Raccoon, working on a new set of arrows, says, "Good thing you are becoming such a wise and powerful woman, Bear. It seems as if you will have to do some choosing soon." He looks like a camp dog that has stolen a choice piece of meat from the fire.

I've learned always to take what Raccoon says with a great bit of care. I look to Otter and her grinning face and ask, "What do you know that I do not?" Raccoon snorts and shakes his head.

"Red Fox came looking for you a while back," Otter grins at me. "Says he wishes to have a word with you."

"Or perhaps an entire, *long* conversation somewhere *far away* out in the forest where it will be *just the two of you alone*," Raccoon says without looking up because he's busy tying feathers carefully on the end of his arrow shafts.

"It seems that Red Fox enjoys your company very much, Bear," Otter says carefully. "More than any other young woman in this village."

Otter seems to think that Red Fox has begun to think of me in ways other than *I* thought possible. Raccoon seems to think that this is just what he needs as a new and interesting way to tease me. I sigh and think, *Just what I need: more confusing thoughts to muddle up my head.*

With Red Fox, we have spent enough time hunting with each other that an easy friendship has happened. I enjoy our times together and have greatly improved my shooting, too. The fact that I have Willow to share makes me feel that for once I can give back some of the kindnesses someone else has given me. When I'm in the woods hunting and shooting and laughing with Red Fox, it seems to be the only time I'm peaceful with myself and who I've become so far. We joke and talk and share and things are just *easy*.

But I tell Otter she has ruined all that for me now that she has pointed out how Red Fox seems *always* to be around, even when we are not hunting together. Raccoon suspects Red Fox never sleeps. Since he spends all of the daylight time following me around, he must be doing all of his chores throughout the night. It's like finding out that the horse you have been riding for many weeks is really a bird; once someone points it out to you, you can't miss it, but until then you were just busy enjoying the ride. Red Fox is there when I'm gathering firewood, he's there when I'm working on the early chores of the garden, he's there, just by accident, when I'm going out to ride or practice shooting whether I go right after my chores are done or just before the evening meal is set to be eaten. I think, *What do you do with your day Red Fox, except keep track of me and where I am?*

That same evening, just after I realize the truth of Otter's words about Red Fox, as Raccoon and Otter and Little Bird and I sit and enjoy each other's company by the fire finishing our meal, who should join us but Beaver. He sits down at the fire and talks and visits with us like he has done this every evening since I've been in this village. He talks about the weather and asks how my shooting is going. He and Raccoon discuss the techniques of fire starting, and I'm glad that that's something I've finally mastered. He talks with Raccoon about different concerns regarding boundaries being violated by white settlers to the east. He talks and plays with Little Bird. Otter looks like she's fair ready to burst making the effort to behave like everything is just like it always is. Her look to me says, *Spring is well and truly here now, Bear.*

Raccoon seems just delighted with Beaver's visit and invites him to come and share our hearth with us whenever we are not at the council fire. His eyes twinkle with positive joy as he finds it important to mention all the times that I've gone hunting with Red Fox over the winter, causing Beaver to offer to take me out and give me lessons on how to shoot while riding Willow. Raccoon then finds it important to mention to me how much better Beaver would be at teaching me to hunt from horseback *since Beaver owns a horse* while Red Fox does not. Raccoon grins at me across the fire while I glare at him to make him shut his mouth.

Raccoon mentions what an important skill knife fighting is, and Otter smiles and points out what a quick learner I am. Beaver wants to know if I've learned to handle my knife for anything other than gutting a deer or skinning an elk? When I say no, I've not, he says he will teach me that, too, and he offers to take me out tomorrow to begin the lessons.

"That sounds like a good idea, does it not, Bear?" Otter says with delight.

"Yes," I say looking right at Raccoon. "I would very much like to become deadly with a knife."

As we sit around the fire that night, I answer the questions and talk polite like but I'm thinking how I can make Raccoon as powerful uncomfortable as I am at this moment and enjoy it just as much as he seems to? I think of stinger ants and scratch ivy and places I can put them. Raccoon says he thinks that Red Fox and I are planning to go hunting tomorrow, and perhaps Beaver can go along and give us both tips on hunting and such. Perhaps Red Fox needs some tips on knife throwing, too? Beaver says he thinks that would be a fine idea. I decide where I'll put the scratch ivy.

So my knife lessons begin with Beaver. It's like a deadly dance, I think, slipping and sliding, whirling and turning. It may be hard to understand, but Beaver is beautiful to watch as he works to show me what to do. Always serious, he teaches me how to stand, how to move and how to hold and throw my knife. If I want to be good at this, he says the knife must be as comfortable at the end of my arm as my hand is. That's mighty comfortable. Many times we practice, sometimes just us two and sometimes with Red Fox. Occasionally, even Raccoon makes an appearance and feels compelled to add a comment or two. I suspect he just wants to see how springtime is coming along.

As the last few signs of winter slip away and spring wins the final battle, I'm one busy powerful woman between my knife practicing with Beaver, my bow and arrow practicing with Red Fox, and my horse training on my own with Willow. Of them all, I enjoy the quiet time with Willow most, although in order for it to be truly *private and alone* I often have to sneak out of the village without Red Fox seeing me.

One day as Willow and I are walking back from a quiet time in the woods, I think how deadly I'm becoming thanks to the attentions of all these kind men. I think about all the things that have kept me here in this Indian village and all the changes in me. I have a horse for the twelve days ride, I can shoot a bow and arrow so I can hunt, I can start a fire from nothing, and now, should you rile me enough, I can stick a knife in your throat from at least fifteen paces. *Sometimes.* When the wind is right. When you're standing stock still. When my hand is steady and I'm not shaking with fright.

I ponder this change in me. Over the course of one years' time, I for certain don't feel like a terrified young girl anymore. *At least on the outside*, my annoying head seems inclined to whisper. *Inside, you still seem mighty cowardly to anyone who'd care to take a second glance.* I sigh for it's true. I'm still afraid, still too uncertain to choose what I'm going to allow in my center of who I really am.

Am I Bear? Am I Elle? How white am I still? How red have I become?

I think about Pa, Henry and Eli and how much I still miss them. I open up my Hope Chest and let the thoughts swirl around me like a wind storm. The feel of Eli's arms as he hugs me around the waist, the sound of Henry's laughter over the silliness of life, the look of Pa's sad but loving eyes as he stares at me in the kitchen doing chores.

But then I add to those memories the joy of having a real, true friend such as Otter, the delight of Little Bird crawling into my furs with me in the morning and the teasing fun of living with a man such as Raccoon. I think of Cloud's whoop of pride when I brought him the elk antler's and War Woman telling me about being on the path to becoming a wise and powerful woman. I can't forget the blushing grins on Red Fox's face when we race through the forest playing hunter and hunted, the strong emotions Beaver shows when he speaks about The Real People of The Maple Forest, or even the quiet loneliness that Bright Feather has in his walk through life.

Swirling into the mix comes my joy of learning to ride Willow, the satisfaction of learning to shoot and hunt, the triumph of going from a scared, lonely, captive white girl to this ... person I now am.

I stand in the cool spring shower, for it has begun to rain as I'm making my way back to the village with Willow and an armload of firewood. Cold wet raindrops fall down on me from the sky and from the brand new leaves just opening up on the trees. Like a whirlwind, my thoughts swirl round and round me and suddenly – just like that! - I know what is in my center.

"I have been thinking the wrong way all along," I say in wonder out loud to myself, Willow, and the raindrops. In being Elle and in being Bear, I realize, I've not been *two people*. I've been *one changing one*. Elle Graves was a white fourteen year old girl. But Bear is not, and never will, be a red savage; she's a mix of all I *was* and all I'm *becoming*. And even though looks may be confusing, I'm still the same person deep down inside.

What did War Woman say? Life has always pulled me forward faster than I felt ready for.

And then I know. I can't ever, ever go back. Life won't let me. It'd be like trying to put a small sapling tree back into the seed pod it started out from. "Bear," I shout out loud to myself and the woods, "is Elle Graves made into a wise and powerful woman!"

For the truth is, I'd miss someone else far more than Pa or Otter or even Willow were I to loose it.

I'd miss the person I've become.

I'd miss, Bear, of The Real People of The Maple Forest.

I sigh.

I smile.

Welcome to the center of my world.

Powerful Woman

My name is Bear. I've a beautiful brown horse named Willow. I sleep in the hut of Otter and her husband, Raccoon, and their son, Little Bird. I'm happy here in this Indian village even though to look at me you would see that I've white skin. If I've a chance to go back to my old home in Virginia, it would be just to say, "Hello" and see how Pa, Henry, and Eli are and give them a hug and kiss, for I still miss them fiercely. And maybe to take a remembry back with me from Ma's Hope Chest. But this place in The Maple Forest is where I call home now.

It's very early spring and those who knew me when I lived my life with Pa, Henry and Eli would scarce recognize me. Even I can hardly keep up with all the changes sometimes, but that's the way of life I'm told. A body might even have trouble seeing me were they to come across me in the forest. My long brown hair is tied back with leather strips and has my brown robin's feather tied to the side. I wear a heavy black bear skin as a cloak and long fur lined leggings and fur lined moccasin boots under my tunic. They are the warmest things I've ever had in my life. Around my waist I wear a knife that's from a white man I killed named Bear John. On my back are my bow and arrows I've made myself. Sitting positively still on Willow in the forest that's just waking up from its winter sleep, where the only color but brown is the occasional evergreen tree, do you think you could find me? *I don't think so.*

But as the business of spring begins for certain, days spent on my own with just Willow for company fade into my memory. Practicing my skills of riding, shooting, and knife throwing must now take second place to more important chores. The earth is waking up from its winter sleep, and the job of preparing the village garden is the job of every woman and child in the village. It's a group effort filled with laughter and sharing and a powerful dose of hard work.

At the council fire on the night of the new moon, we celebrate the ceremony of life. It's a time when The Real People try to make a fresh start, setting things right that may be wrong, and celebrate friendships and life itself. I've sat through this ceremony quite a number of times now, but with my new peacefulness over who I am and what I'm doing and where I'm planning to be, I let it's meaning seep into my bones and it makes my toes curl. *I'm a part of all this now*, my head thinks, *this is where life has pulled me.*

If we are not at the council fire, in keeping up with these rules of spring that Otter and Raccoon find so amusing, Beaver joins us at our hearth after meals almost every night. Raccoon teases me and says that it's the only time Red Fox is not busy watching me, when he's busy eating his evening meal.

Beaver is more serious and adult than Red Fox. I can't imagine running around in the woods laughing and taking turns being hunter and hunted. I don't know how old Beaver is; his ways make him seem old, but I think he's younger than he behaves. Sometimes he tells us stories that I'm sure Otter and Raccoon have heard many times, but for me they are new and exciting. His love of his people and their way of life is a powerful draw for me, and I find I enjoy Beaver's company quite a lot.

On the evening after the new moon Beaver says to all of us around the hearth fire, but I suppose to me in particular, "When we share warmth and energy with others, we establish and maintain the right relationships in the Great Circle of Life." He looks at only me and says, "That is why I have begun these visits to this hearth. I enjoy sharing this time with all of you and *establishing* and *maintaining* these *new* relationships."

After Beaver leaves, I put my head in my hands and moan. Otter is like a proud mother, though she's barely much older than me, and says I should be pleased, because both Red Fox and Beaver are from good families and are well respected in the village. Otter says that I should make sure to look real close at these apples before I toss them away because maybe the basket is not as full as I think. For the first time ever, I think I know how Raccoon feels and want to stuff something in my own ears.

"Why must I even be considering these things?" I ask Otter in frustration, hands on my hips. "What's the rush? Did you not tell me that it's the woman who makes the choice?"

Raccoon must add his words. "A woman pursued by a man has some space to make choices. A *man* pursued by a *woman* has no hope at all." He shakes his head in mock defeat. "Just ask any one of us."

Otter laughs at Raccoon, but then frowns at my mood. "But Bear, is it not good to know who you have to choose from? Red Fox has never shown an interest in any young woman in the village until you. Do you realize how special that makes you? And no one is more serious than Beaver in regard to what is right and best for The Real People. It is *such an honor* that he would choose to let you know that he is interested in you as well. Why don't you spend some *more* time with them and get to know them a bit *better,*" she says with a twinkle in her eye.

I look blank at her for a moment because she's giving me that look that says whatever she's saying is meaning something else. Then it dawns on me, and I blush as red as a dangerous red summer sun. Otter's words make Raccoon laugh out loud as he sets down the knife he's sharpening and watches me close for my answer. "*No,*" I say firmly to both of them, "my choice is *no.*"

I've done all my chores including helping prepare the garden for planting. I've gathered wood. I've done all the things needed to make dinner. I've fetched water. I've finished sewing a new tunic I've made for myself from the skin of a deer I've killed. I've worked on Bright Feather's pelts from his winter's trapping. Then I see Red Fox heading purposely towards our hut. Suddenly, I'm so tired! "I am going to ride Willow, I have not had a chance in two days," I say to Otter and jump on Willow's back and off we ride before she has a chance to say anything. I escape to my quiet place high up on the hill.

Already I'm tired of this mating business, and Otter tells me it has only just begun. Maybe there are not so many choices here as I think. Maybe when you scratch down past the surface of things, there really is no difference at all. If that's true it would make me mighty sad I realize. I think and think and think. There's no woman in the village who is not with a man, unless she's old and done with that. There's no woman who has an interest in traveling with the hunting parties. (I go only sometimes, but I think that it's just so they have someone to put up with their teasing.) I'm a good cook and quite like all the chores that are part of a woman's life in the village. Some of my best times in the village, besides being with Willow and learning how to shoot and hunt, have been with the children and the women. I ask myself real serious like, "What do you really want?"

My head flashes a million different pictures. I think about becoming a wiser and more powerful woman. I like that the women speak up just as much as the men at the council circle. What would that be like, I wonder, to have wise enough words that others would want to hear them? I think about the joy and freedom that I have here choosing to change the person I am. Now I'm a hunter, a fighter, and a tracker. What other things have I yet to learn? Fishing? Bow making? Trapping? The ways of healing and herbs? All of these seem exciting and interesting. There's a part of me who wants to see things I've not seen, places of wild beauty that Red Fox has told me of and that I suspect Bright Feather is already right familiar with. I can't begin to tell them all.

So I ask myself, "What don't you really want?" The only thing I know is that I just don't want to have to make any choice yet that will take away any other choices I can still have. My head knows one day I will, but right now I just don't want to. I say out loud, "A powerful woman makes her own choices and decides when, too." And I'm determined to become a more powerful woman with each and every day.

All of a sudden I know that I'm not alone. I hear the snap of a twig and the quieting of the birds, and two squirrels that were playful nearby me are now nowhere to be seen. I imagine my ears pricking up like Willow's do when she hears a sound and I look over very slowly to her and she's no longer cropping grass but has her head up, her ears perked and is chewing slowly. She's looking in the direction of the snapping twig. I've just a moment to feel proud at myself for finally knowing when I'm not alone when I'm expecting to be when my world goes black.

It's not the kind of blackness when I hurt my arm. It's the kind of blackness when your head is covered, and the sun is blocked from view. I fight like a wild thing this time for I'm not hurt, I'm not tired, I'm not weak, and I'm no longer a white girl. I'm Bear. Without even thinking I grab my knife, and I hear one of my captors grunt in pain when it finds a place to bite.

"She has a knife!" someone yells in Indian, although the sounds are a tiny bit different. My wrist is caught and twisted painfully and my knife drops to the ground. My arms are roped to my side but my legs are still free, and I kick and scream and fight with all my might. For a moment the bright sunlight blinds me and then a rag is stuffed in my mouth and darkness returns. When my legs are finally tied I'm hauled across a horse.

I think, *this shouldn't happen one time in my life, let alone two!* I hear Willow whinny, and I know they have taken my horse, too. Maybe that's good and maybe that's bad. I try to concentrate on directions and don't struggle anymore. I need to save my strength. I concentrate this time. *This time* I push my fear all the way down to my toes and I listen and I remember. I ride all day across the front of the horse tied, gagged and in blackness. I concentrate on the warmth from the sun, and I know that we travel south and west a bit, too. *I'm different,* I keep telling myself over and over, *so this time things'll be different.* It becomes a song I sing in my head over and over.

When we stop for the night I'm given one brief sip of water, one small piece of dried meat to chew, one brief very unprivate moment, and then I'm tied, gagged, and blindfolded just as before. We leave before the sun is up and ride south again all day.

It's not until the third night that my gag is removed for good, and I'm allowed to see the sky. The meaning is obvious; we are too far away for anyone to hear my shouts. There are four braves, none that I know. They are all Indian and dress in a similar style to what I know, although I see some white things that I've not seen in a long time: rifles, a cloth button shirt, a felt brimmed hat. I'm glad to see Willow. She seems all right.

We ride southwest for nine whole days before we get to a village. We are so far south that the snow that has just about disappeared by our village is gone completely here, and the trees are in full bloom. My hands are never untied, although by the third day they allow me to ride astride with one of the men. The rawhide strips make sores around my wrists which hurt something fierce. Willow is here, but they don't let me ride her.

By the time we arrive, I've made some plans. I eat whenever they feed me to keep up my strength, and I no longer fight or show any sign of anger. I've never spoken again after my first shouts so they are unsure of what I understand. I try real hard to keep my face still so that it doesn't do any talking like my mouth. The Indian braves talk little between themselves; just basic discussions about when and where to camp and comments on the weather and, aside from a few odd phrases, I understand all they say. I ask myself so many questions that I tire myself out. Why me? Why have they taken me? Where are they taking me? Have they chosen me special or would they have taken anyone? What will our village think? Will they look for me? How will I get free? The scariest questions I choose not to ask more than once. Will they hurt me? Will I ever get back? *Is this life pulling me faster, once again, than I'm ready for?*

The village is larger than ours and looks nothing like I'd have expected. We pass through enormous cultivated fields larger than the ones in our village, and more like some of the great plantations I remember from long, long ago in my travels out west to settle in Virginia.. But it isn't the size of the village or even the odd feelings I get as we ride in that are the most frightening. No, most frightening is the white men I see, some dressed in buckskins and furs and some dressed in clothes Pa would wear. They walk casual like among the Indians and that makes me truly become scared. The Indians of the village wear a mixture of Indian clothing and white clothing in any number of ways. Everywhere I look I see things that remind me of my time living with Pa, Henry, and Eli. These are people accustomed to each other's company.

The Indian homes are different here than at ours. Not so many are squat and round. Now they are all long. Some must have at least six families living in them. It's warmer here, so they have already shifted into the summer style of huts with sides open and just a straw roof across the top to protect a body from rains. I'm stunned to see two white-men style homes off to one side of the village surrounded by traditional Indian ones. As we ride slowly into camp, I see another building far too big to be a home, and evidence of still another building being built. I push the fear that has begun to creep up my legs into the pit of my stomach back down to my toes and say to myself, proud like Otter says her name, "I am Bear of Great Elk's village of The Real People of The Maple Forest" over and over. I sit straight and tall as we ride in. I look directly ahead and look in no one's eyes, but make an effort to remember everything I see. *Pay attention, Elle, you never know what you can learn from just looking,* I hear Pa tell me.

I'm taken to the large structure and finally my hands are untied. It feels good to move them. The sores are raw, and I try not to touch them much for they hurt. We sit on sturdy chairs and there are tables, too. There's a group of men who make attempts to speak to me, but I choose not to talk. *No need to rush,* I think to myself. There's another white language here that I don't know. It can almost be funny that I understand the Indians better than I understand some of the white men. I've had enough trouble learning the Indian language let alone a new white one! While some of the words are different that the Indians speak here, most are familiar. I'm happy to keep them guessing, and in front of me they discuss if I can understand the languages. *Maybe I'll learn something,* I think further. Even more reason to keep my mouth shut.

The white men speak the Indian language almost as comfortably as the Indians speak the English. Even the children respond to both. Beside the man I think to be chief there are two others of Indian blood and two whites who sit around the table in chairs that first day. One white man, all in buckskins, reminds me greatly of Bear John in his dress. He tries to talk to me in a white language I don't know. The other white man wears a black Sunday suit, although it has seen better days - I can tell by the careful mending I see in many places. He speaks to me in English. They ask me questions in voices that I'm to think are friendly. What's my name? Where am I from? Who is my family? How old am I? How long have I been in the Indian village of Great Elk's in The Maple Forest? I do my best to look like I used to before I understood everything at Great Elk's village.

I learn that the chief is called Dark Cloud and the white man in the buckskins is called Martin. I study Dark Cloud and I think, do I know him? I look at his face and his mannerisms and the sound of his voice and a part of my head says yes, and a part of my head says no. It's a puzzle. I study Martin careful like, too, and decide one thing right quick about him; he may not smell like Bear John, but he has the same look in his eye when he looks at me as Bear John did, and I'll not trust him, not one single bit. I watch as he speaks to Dark Cloud, and even though I can't understand some of his white words I know he lies because I can see it in his eyes. He's small, just a bit taller than me with dark hair and eyes that are shifty like a rat. I know what his Indian name would be.

"Perhaps the young woman has been so severely traumatized by her time with the savages that she has lost the ability to speak and think on her own," says the white man in the old suit. "God only knows just what she has gone through over the course of the past months or years." He studies me close like, and it's very hard to keep my face like a dumb piece of rock. I feel him try to probe deep into my head and see if there's anything worth rescuing. After a bit he looks away, I hope he does not see much.

"Your concerns are without merit, Reverend Wilder," Dark Cloud says, also studying me intently as I look back at him and struggle to keep my look blank. *Reverend? What would a preacher be doing here?* "I understand she fought like a wild thing when she was first taken and even used a knife to defend herself. She was alone, unescorted in the woods when she was found. She also spoke extensively in Indian." The look he gives me says, *I'm not fooled one bit.* I think, *Why do I think I know you?*

"Would not anyone defend herself in the face of such a brutal abduction?" Reverend Wilder counters with great emotion. "It is conceivable that this young woman has now been abducted not once, *but twice* by Indians! How did your braves come upon her? Where exactly was she taken from? Why was she taken and brought here by force? Look at her wrists! She has been forcibly tied for days!"

I'm desperate to hear the answers but Dark Cloud is still watching me like a hungry hawk. I try not to think mouse thoughts. "I will be happy to discuss these things later with you, Reverend. In the meantime, let us get this poor young woman settled and offer her some of our hospitality."

"I insist that she stay with Rebecca and me. I will not have her subject to further brutalities at the hands of strangers," Reverend Wilder says.

Dark Cloud looks at me, and I struggle to keep my dumb rock look. "I speak to you in the language of The Real People, for that is what I understand you spoke clearly. I also suspect that you understand English." He looks at Martin and then back at me and he puzzles for a moment, "But maybe not the *Francois*."

"You have two choices while you are here in this village. You can be treated like a prisoner, or you can be treated like a guest. In either capacity, *you may not leave.* You will have noticed that there is extensive presence in this area by Indian and white. This is the center point of The Nation of The Real People, with heavy traffic at all times by both whites and natives. I can assure you of your safety within the walls of this village but outside it I offer no such promise. I will let you stay with the Reverend Wilder and his wife, Rebecca, as a *guest.* Should you try to escape, you will be then treated as a prisoner. Do you understand my meaning?" He gives me a look of great menace, and it takes all my thinking power not to respond or change my face. I think of the last time I rode Willow and the smell of the forest as it wakes up in the early spring…

"Two Killers," Dark Cloud says without moving his eyes from me. He speaks to the brave sitting at the table with us still, and who I recognize as one who took me from Great Elk's village. "Maybe the Reverend Wilder and Miss Rebecca will offer you their hospitality as well." As the Reverend Wilder helps me to my feet, exclaiming in concern over my pitiful state, Two Killers follows the Reverend and me out into the bright sunshine.

The Reverend's a short, squat man, balding, and with a constant flush like he has been running for a while. He walks as if he's always late, and I follow at a quick pace alongside of him. He chatters to me, "We must have Rebecca see to those wrists of yours. I cannot believe they would keep you tied for such a long period of time if at all! What were they thinking? What were they afraid of in such a young slip of a girl?"

He points to the building being constructed that we hurry past, "*That* will be the mission school that will complement the church. Right now, we use the church as a place of worship, schooling, and council meetings. The United States Government and The American Missionary Board have been very generous in their efforts to civilize the red savages. Dark Cloud has been very willing to have us come and educate the youth and the adults who show interest. He recognizes the positive potential for a solid education built on a Christian foundation. I have been provided with implements of husbandry, stock animals for farming, five plows, ten hoes, ten axes, as well as money and materials to establish this church and eventually the mission school here. The men have shown great enthusiasm over the merits of farming, and we have had excellent crops these past few years. I have spinning and weaving equipment for the women so they may be industrious and productive as well, and the products that they make show great promise. I've already, of course, begun to preach out in the open air, and Rebecca has been schooling the children, but we have grander hopes! Eventually, I would like to build a large dormitory to house a hundred Indian youth that we would then educate and send out to save others from all over this territory! It has been a Calling From God since I was a small boy, and the Good Lord has sent Rebecca to help me fulfill this dream."

He stops abruptly and looks at me, and I recognize the expression as one that Otter used to have with me before she was certain I understood her yet desperate for it to be so. "These savage people," he sweeps his hand out in a wide arch and I glance at Two Killers standing silent and blank a few steps back, "must be civilized. Christianity and civilization always go hand in hand. These sons of the forest must understand that they must be moralized or they will be exterminated." We resume the fast pace and I roll the words 'moralized' and 'exterminated' around in my head. I'm not sure what they mean, but something tells me that they aren't good.

The Wilders live in one of the white homes, and I'm surprised to learn that Dark Cloud and his family live in the other. Miss Rebecca falls upon me as I enter the cabin like I'm her long lost daughter. She's almost a full head shorter than me, as round as she's wide, and speaks with the same breathless speed that the Reverend does. She sheds real tears as she exclaims over my wrists and my general savage appearance. Like her husband, she keeps up a running commentary, and she seems to care not whether I understand or answer. Within a very short period of time my wrists are washed and dressed with clean bandages, and my hands and face and feet are washed with strong, harsh smelling soap. When she makes a move to take my clothes I take a step back and without speaking give her a look that says, *That's far enough, thank you.* We stand there for a moment in the silence of the cabin with Two Killers sitting silent and still in the corner on a straight back chair watching. "Well, dear," she reaches up and gentle like touches my hair in an effort to calm me, I suspect, and says, "I don't suppose that I have anything that would fit you, anyway. We must work on getting it clean though…"

It's funny to sit on chairs again, eat off tables with spoons and plates, and sleep in a straw and feather tick bed, but I manage to do all of them. My sleep that first night is filled with busy dreams that keep startling me awake, although I can't remember them. I'm tired in the morning. I miss my own place.

Unlike my early time at Great Elk's village, I'm allowed no time when I'm unwatched. They expect me to run away the first chance I get, and I have to understand that they are not stupid. Someone is always with me, if it's not Reverend Wilder or Miss Rebecca then it's Two Killers or another Indian brave. Someone is always awake, for even in the middle of the night as I make my way to the necessary house out back I hear footsteps not far away, and I know I'm watched. I'm eager to run, but I understand I must choose the time careful like. I don't need a whole village of red and white men running after me, especially if I'm on foot. I've not seen Willow since I arrived.

I realize, with a start, that I'm already learning new things here. I'm learning to bide my time and working hard at becoming wiser by the moment. I say a quick whisper prayer to God and ask if that might be all I have to learn so that I can get back to The Maple Forest and home.

I spend much of my time those first days in Dark Cloud's village thinking and watching. Every day I'm brought to the church council building and asked the same questions over and over about who I am and how I came to be in Great Elk's village. Sometimes there are a few people present – white and red – and sometimes there are many. It suits me to keep them guessing and to keep them annoyed, and I speak to absolutely no one. They might as well have as many unanswered questions as me. Why do they care who I am? Why bring me nine days south to find out my name when they could have heard the story with a lot less time and trouble in Great Elk's village? I know there are pieces missing. I listen to Reverend Wilder and Miss Rebecca talk, and I know that they puzzle over why I'm here also.

As the days go by, I study what directions people come and go. I know where the white men camp and live and where the horses are kept. I remember what braves seem to spend the most time with Dark Cloud in the church council building and have decided who are the leaders. I know where the women go to bathe and gather wood. I know where the small village garden is as well as the massive gardens that the men are in charge of farming. I know the hut in which the women do their "industrious and productive" weaving. I even learn the sounds that they make to the dogs of the village to tell them to hush. I try not to miss anything that can help me when I run.

On the sixth day of my time at Dark Cloud's village as I enter the council church building to hear more of the same questions, there's a face sitting at the table I know, and all things make more sense. Seated to Dark Cloud's right is Weasel. As they both sit looking at me waiting for my reaction, I see what I've missed; Dark Cloud is Weasel's father. The same look that struggles not to say anything but says a lot. The same dark mean eyes and the same thin, tall body. I feel an anger that wipes away all my fear, and I think two times in my life I've been taken away from places I felt safe and from people I cared about, and both times he's the cause. There's no doubt in my mind that even though he was not part of the group that brought me here, he was the one who caused it. The anger grows white hot in my belly and grows and grows. It feeds on the fear I keep in my toes and the tears I've packed behind my eyes and the aches I keep in my heart, and it explodes in a blinding flash. I'm not held or tied, and I dive across the space between me and Weasel and I think, *I'll kill you before they will kill me.*

There are screams and shouts and an "Oh My Dear Lord!" from the Reverend Wilder, and by the time three braves have me held a distance away from Weasel all eyes are on me as I spit out of my mouth clearly for all to hear, "Weasel! I called you Dirty Feet! But I should call you Bear John because your insides stink now more than his ever did, even now! You watch your back and all you hold dear because the first chance I get I will cause you sorrow you cannot begin to imagine." I've nothing to throw, nothing to kick, nothing to hit, so I spit at him, and he must move his leg quick to make sure I miss him.

All around me are different kinds of faces. The Reverend Wilder looks like he's just about ready to explode with shock. Weasel has a look of such intense hatred it flows out of his eyes like smoke from a fire. And Dark Cloud looks triumphant. *I knew it*, his eyes say to me with something that almost seems like pleasure.

The brave holding my hair lets go, but the two holding my arms make me sit in a chair in front of Dark Cloud and Weasel and Martin and the still shocked Reverend Wilder and some others I don't know. The braves sit close to me on either side, tense and ready, but let go of my arms. I see women in the background who are often present serving and caring for the needs of the men, scurrying around cleaning up cups and pitchers and baskets with food in them that have been spilled and glancing scared eyes at me. The children who often peer into the windows when they question me make every effort to get as good a viewing spot as possible to see what I'll do next. It's almost funny to see one by one new black heads appearing in the windows. Dark Cloud asks me questions again and I refuse to answer any question he will already have the answer to from Weasel. At last he asks me, "Why do you not talk to us?"

"You have not asked me a question that you truly need the answer for yet," I say.

"I knew that after the length of time you were in Great Elk's village that you must understand the language by now," he says in a satisfied voice, and I realize, of course, the last time I saw Weasel was a very long while ago. He wouldn't have been able to assure them that I could speak the language, and that would have been one of their problems. I think about the last time I saw Weasel, and I know that he has not been in the village since the night I was given to Bright Feather, and I realize that there are many things he does not know about me *white* or *red*.

"Do you know that there are those who are looking for you?" *Who does he mean*, I think. *White or Indian?*

"Have them talk to *Dirty Feet*," and it makes me happy to see him bothered by the name I call him. "All who seek me, *red and white*, can get the answers from him," I spit out with much hate. I don't talk or look at Weasel, only to Dark Cloud. "Why have you brought me here?" I ask. Now it's my turn to ask a question.

Dark Cloud looks angered that a woman, a captive, should ask him a question. The women in the background look my way, tense and frightened. I don't think there are so many powerful women in this village, and they are surprised, too, it seems. Why are there no women sitting in the church council building, I wonder? Weasel leans over and he and Dark Cloud speak in quiet voices.

At last Dark Cloud says, "You were brought here at the request of your village. There is a danger for them in having you there since there are white people who search for you. It is dangerous for any village to have you present."

I think about this for a moment. I think about Great Elk and Otter and Raccoon and Cloud and Red Fox and Beaver and all the others who have welcomed me and made me a part of their village. As far as I know I'm the only white captive Great Elk's village has ever had, and aside from Bear John and his two companions, there has never been mentioned any other white faces within their boundaries. Would they have made this decision without speaking with me? Would they have caused me this great terror once again? Would they have left this in the hands of Weasel? *No, they wouldn't.*

I say very quietly, "And what will you do in *this village* with the danger you have with me *here?*" Both Dark Cloud and Weasel are shocked by my threat. The white man called Martin is surprised, too. The look he gives me says, *You are much more than I thought at first.* The look of hate I give him says, *Maybe you should also watch your back for you are in danger from me, too.*

"Why is Weasel here in this village?" I ask although I think I know some of the reasons.

"Weasel is a son of this village," Dark Cloud answers after a moment. "He became a son of the hut of One Who Knows in Great Elk's village of The Maple Forest for a time. He has come back to live with us now."

I realize the words not said speak of those that are dead and never mentioned - One Who Knows' daughter. Things about my first capture make more sense. Why I was taken, why I was brought to One Who Knows' tent, why Weasel thought his attentions towards me would have been allowed, and even, my mind thinks, why One Who Knows was happy to see me put Weasel in his place that one night when I was still a slave.

"What village will you try to get to take him next?" I ask slow and polite like although my eyes say different. Martin laughs out loud at this. Weasel tenses and gives us both dark looks. *Watch your back,* I think again as I look at him.

"My dear," says Reverend Wilder. "Tell us please what your name is. Tell us who you are so that we may return you to your family; those that love and miss you and must surely be still searching for you after all this time." I know he speaks of Pa, Henry, and Eli but I look at Martin and Dark Cloud and Weasel. Their faces don't show the same concern that Reverend Wilder's does. With a flash I know that what Reverend Wilder believes to be so is not the truth or the way things ever will be. *They* know of my hatred for them, *they* know of the dangers from Pa should I tell him who these Indians are that are returning me. They will never trust me or risk their lives to *return* me when it's because of them *I'm here now.* I'll never be returned to Pa, Henry, or Eli by the same Indians that took me in the first place. Never. *They* know that, and *I* know that now, too.

"I am Bear, of the village of Great Elk, of The Real People of The Maple Forest," I say loud and clear and strong.

"But my dear...!" Reverend Wilder begins, but he's silenced by Dark Cloud.

"Perhaps you are right, Reverend. Perhaps her time in The Maple Forest has damaged her in ways we cannot understand. We are not equipped for something of this nature here in our village. Martin will take you back to his people, the *Francois*. They will have connections with people who know of those poor unfortunate children who have been tragically taken from their homes. From there it can be determined who you are in the white world and then you will be taken back to your own people to heal and become whole again. We are happy to aid in the return of you to your true family," Dark Cloud tells me kind like although his eyes tell a different story I can't quite understand.

"I will bring my horse with me," I say like it's already decided. "If you plan to do this *kindness*," I say with eyes and tone that mean different than the word, "then you must be certain that all of my things are returned to me." Dark Cloud hesitates, unhappy to be called almost a thief. He glances at a puzzled - looking Reverend Wilder and at last he nods that it will be so.

I say nothing else but I know pieces are still missing. I think I'll be patient and wait until I'm free of this too big village with its too many whites and Indians and wait until I'm with this little white man called Martin. And I've one more wish, I realize, as Reverend Wilder helps me to stand and guides me out into the bright spring sunshine.

I hope Weasel comes along on the trip so that I've a chance to put my knife in his back. Balance and harmony. Righting wrongs. It's the way of The Real People here at the center of the world.

I've been at Dark Cloud's village for more than four weeks, and I feel like a bow that has been strung too long without a chance to rest. I'm told there are many reasons for the wait. First, they say it's the weather. I tell them I'm not afraid of snow or rain and that they shouldn't worry; I don't melt. Then I'm told that there's the need to find two braves beside Martin and Weasel to travel with us. I'm just one small girl, I say sweetly, why do you need any others? After the first week, they will not answer my questions about the wait, and I just keep to myself.

They would like me to be more afraid I think. I'm happy to disappoint them. I don't talk to anyone, man or woman, white or red unless it suits me. I help the women in the huts when they will let me for it makes the day go quicker, but in most cases they seem happier to stay away from me. I play with the children who are brave enough to come close; once again they are the ones I find the most joy in. I help Miss Rebecca with her chores as well, and there are many days that I sit with her while she teaches and translate her words or needs to her students into the Real People's words. She seems to struggle with the Indian language even more than I did although the Reverend seems to know it well enough.

After watching the Reverend Wilder and Miss Rebecca over these weeks, I decide after much thought that they mean no harm. They seem to have a true love of the Indians and a sincere desire to help them, although I'm not so sure that I agree with their way.

I struggle with their great efforts to change The Real People from "savage" to "civilized". I remember my way of thinking when I first came to The Maple Forest and how I thought that black skin meant slave, red skin meant savage, and white skin meant all the rest. It was spending time with those in The Maple Forest that I came to see that it's the inside of a person that makes them what they are. Skin has nothing to do with it all.

But while the Wilders are quick to use the word "savage" whenever they speak of The Real People, they seem to already know what I spent the last year learning. And that's what bothers me. For, as far as I can figure, the Wilders seem to think that it's the *inside* that needs the changing. It's just as Beaver tried to explain to me so many weeks ago, *The Real People struggle with the life that the white man wishes us to lead. In many ways, just as you have been forced to lead the life of the savage Indian we, for many, many years have been forced to change to a life of the white man.*

Women don't need to be powerful and wise, they need to be "industrious and productive". They need to learn skills not like hunting and knife fighting, but weaving and raising children "proper" with school and church and such. Housekeeping should no longer be in deer-skin huts with birch-bark containers to cook in, but be more like a home where I grew up in with Pa that has wood floors and metal pots.

Men need not hunt but should instead farm cows and chickens. Farm enough to sell to others to earn money so that things can be bought. There's no need to train to be warriors, instead they should learn "diplomacy" and "forbearance". I think about my time as Mouse in The Maple Forest and realize I already know a lot about diplomacy and forbearance.

I realize that what upsets me something fierce about the Wilders is they seem to want to change The Real People's centers.

I think about myself in my now clean Indian tunic and hear Miss Rebecca call me *Bear*, and I wonder what they must think about me in particular. Have I gone from civilized to *savage*? At one time I'd have thought that to be true, but now I know I'm more wise than before. *Forget about my outsides*, I think, *I'm wiser than I've ever been in my life.*

Living with Miss Rebecca causes flashes in my mind of Ma: a certain way she sounds swooshing around in her great skirts, the smell of the baking bread in the oven and the way she comes by at night when she thinks I'm already asleep to adjust my covers and smooth my hair. I've many dreams, sleeping on my straw and feather tick bed, of times at home in Virginia that are mixed up with birch bark containers and War Woman sitting in my Pa's rocking chair.

The Wilders don't press me to find out any more about my white family. They make it clear they are powerful concerned about my welfare and especially my soul but have no desire to upset me by making me talk about things I choose not to. They are loving and kind to me and seem glad for my company. I find myself explaining to them my understanding of the ways of The Real People, and more than once Miss Rebecca takes me along into the women's places of gathering and asks me to translate while she struggles to sit in the dirt with them while they weave or grind or cook or just talk. She seems to have an honest wish to really know them. I'm amazed that these two white people seem to really *love* The Real People without understanding them at all. When I say something about that they both look surprised.

Rebecca says, "Our Dear Lord Jesus did not just stay with those He called family or those He thought acceptable, nor did He go to places that were always safe or always clean or always what He knew. He did all of this, knowing what unappreciative, violent, hateful, *awful* people we were simply because He had such a Great Love for us He could not abandon us." She grabs my hand and holds it tight to make her point. *"He loved us so much that He chose to die to save us rather than to live without us.* We are guaranteed to live forever if we just make the choice to believe that we are all sinners, that Jesus is the Son of God, and accept Him as the center point of our life. *The Real People* as you call them do not know of this Great Love, of this Great Savior, of this Great Promise, and James and I cannot sleep with the burden that we feel to tell of it."

While I don't say anything, I sit up straighter when Miss Rebecca starts to talk about centers and life. I find it mighty amazing to hear talk about centers with the Son of God in them when I have spent so much of the last year trying to sort out my own center and what to put in it. Another thing to puzzle over when my mind is not so cluttered with the business of my life…

"God has been so good to bring us both together," she says, and Reverend Wilder smiles tenderly at her as they exchange glances across the room, "both with the same passion and desire. I can tell that you do not like us to use words like *civilize* and *savages*. James and I have talked about that, and we realize that you may be right. Words like those are not complimentary and they imply that we disapprove of the Indian and that way of life. It is not correct to say that we *disapprove*, but it is correct to say that we *fear* for the Indian."

"Fear!" I say in surprise and confusion. "You *fear* for The Real People? I do not see that. I see only that you wish to make them white. You wish to change them from one thing into another."

Miss Rebecca sighs and stops to rearrange her thoughts, I suspect. "We fear for them because we see how the whites are taking advantage of the kind and unselfish way of the Indians. The whites have not been fair with business dealings, and in many instances the Indians have suffered greatly because of it. James and I believe that if we can educate the Indians with white words and white customs, perhaps they will be better prepared to deal with the whites in the future."

"It is not so much that we approve or disapprove of the white or Indian way, Bear," Reverend Wilder tries to explain. "More accurately, the Indian way is disappearing. No longer are there enough animals left in the wild to feed an entire village. No longer is there land enough to spare so that whole villages can migrate and move at the whim of the seasons and the migration of the animals they follow. And like it or not, more whites are coming each day. Here. To this place. They are gobbling up all available land, and guess where they will go once all of the available *white land* is taken?" He does not wait for me to answer, but looks sad and says, "They will come here to Dark Cloud's village and, eventually, to your village in The Maple Forest as well. And if The Real People are not equipped to deal with the whites properly, they will simply loose more and more of what is rightfully theirs."

"I had not thought of such a thing …" I say and then hear my Pa saying, *The savages had their time. Their present circumstances are not our concern.* Our homestead is on what used to be the red savage's land. Bought by the government with cash and signed away by the savages free and clear. Made available to families like ours. Suddenly I've a powerful sick feeling in my gut.

"Take you for instance," Reverend Wilder says smiling, "you have not told us how you came to be in an Indian village, wearing Indian clothes, and talking the Indian tongue. Yet, at some point you had to decide whether you were going to adapt – *go along with things* – or not. You could have refused to cooperate or change, could you not have?"

I nod my head and think of Old Woman and her fury should I have tried such a thing.

"Your life would have been even more difficult as a result, correct?" Reverend Wilder continues.

I nod again.

"You adapted, Bear. Changed to fit your circumstances. Reinvented yourself to survive. Rebecca and I are not saying that one was good or one was bad, we are simply saying what you did was a wise choice." Reverend Wilder looks at me, I suspect, to see if what he says is sinking into my thick skull.

I sit up straight at the "wise choice" words for I for sure would like to be thought of that way.

Miss Rebecca waits for a moment or two and then touches my arm so that I look at her. "But there is something else that is even more important that brings us here, Bear. Yes, we love The Real People and yes, we want them to be better prepared to deal with the white man and their immediate futures. But more importantly than all of that, we fear for the Indians because we know that they have not heard of the Truth and the Love of Jesus Christ and *not been given the opportunity to choose.* It is primarily because of this Truth and this Love that we are here. Perhaps we can teach *The Real People*," she smiles at me hopeful that she has used the proper term, "how to survive in a white world *and* teach *The Real People* of God's Great Love and Faithfulness."

I decide, as I think about what the Wilders have told me, that I believe *them* and what they say is their reasons for coming. But that's because I've seen their insides, they have shared with me their centers. I'll give Miss Rebecca and Reverend Wilder my trust about what they say being true. Their words match their actions, which is just how those in The Maple Forest proved to me the same thing.

Over each meal we bow our heads, and I listen to the Reverend Wilder pray to God. He speaks loud and strong and sure and I think, those times I whispered, could God even hear me? I ask about this and tell them how Ma told me about whispering close and personal to God. They exchange looks across the table, and it's Reverend Wilder who says, "God can be so close and so personal Bear that He can be *right inside you* and even hear your thoughts. You can talk just in your head and heart and He will hear you as loud and clear as I am talking to you now."

I'm glad about that for I'd like to be sure that the things I've whispered have been heard, as many or as few as they have been. "What do you pray for, Dear?" Miss Rebecca asks quiet like.

I'm careful with how much I tell, but I can see that they want only to know of my concerns and are not interested in learning things I still wish to keep secret. "I pray sometimes that my white family is safe and healthy and that the braves who took me did them no harm." The words said out loud make my heart pound and my stomach clench with the worry of it. It's more fearful said out loud for some reason. "I pray that they know that I'm happy and strong and healthy and safe."

"Why is it that you will not tell us who you are so that we can return you to this white family that you are concerned about?" Reverend Wilder finally asks.

I sigh and look down at my dinner plate with my fork held tightly in my tan, white hand. Despite Miss Rebecca's best tries I've refused to change out of my Indian clothes. I must always be ready to go. When I look up at them both sitting, patient like, waiting for me to answer, I must give them a bit of a smile. I decide that I like these two people. *Always look for the good in a dark situation,* I hear Pa say to me. *Here it is, Pa. I've found it.* I look at each of their troubled faces. "The only people I feel I can trust here are those I eat with now. And you do not hold the power in this village, others do." That's all I'll say.

The weeks creep slowly on, and the questions in my head never stop. Why do I need guards if they are just worried about getting me home? Why all the delays? What are the secret pieces that I don't understand? How does Weasel fit into all of this? Why can't they find two men to travel and take me back in a village this size? Where are 'Martin's people' located, and why must I go to the French rather than an American outpost? *Where are they really taking me?*

I pose some of these questions to the Wilders, but they are as in the dark as I am about my situation. And probably a great deal more, I realize. Their great fault, I think, is that they are too trusting. They accept kindnesses without taking the time to understand or even see where it comes from and why. It's with some shock that I realize that they are in perhaps more danger than I am! When I try to voice these concerns they smile their sweet smiles, and Miss Rebecca gives me a hug. "Aren't you sweet, child, worrying about us! We have always followed God's lead and trust that He will keep us safe as we forge ahead to do His Will. *Though I walk through the valley of the shadow of death, I will fear no evil…6,*" she quotes to me, and Ma comes flying into my head in a memory of the Bible words.

"Psalm twenty-three," I say to Miss Rebecca. "My Ma liked that, too."

At long last, the morning comes for me to finally leave. Miss Rebecca has shed many tears over my departure. She does not fear for my safety I think as much as for my soul. I realize, I, too, will miss these two people. I struggle with a powerful sense of loss that I've not remembered since Ma's death. It's different from the fear of both takings by the Indians, it's more like a careful scraping of all my soft insides like when we gut an animal we have killed. It's not a fear so much as a terrible empty loneliness. I work to not shed any tears, but find I don't have the hate and hardness ready for these two and it's powerful difficult to stay strong. As I mount up on Willow, Mrs. Wilder rushes out in the bright sunshine and takes my hand as the tears slide down her plump, flushed cheeks. "I will pray for you, Bear. I will pray that God becomes close and personal inside you. I will pray that you still continue to whisper in God's ear and listen for His answering voice. You must trust that the Lord loves you and that He cares for you and watches over you in all you do.

'For I know the thoughts that I think toward you,' saith the Lord, 'thoughts of peace, and not of evil, to give you an expected end.

Then shall ye call upon me, and ye shall go and pray unto me,
and I will hearken unto you.
And ye shall seek me, and find me,
when ye shall search for me with all your heart.
And I will be found of you,' saith the Lord:
'and I will turn away your captivity,
and I will gather you from all the nations,
and from all the places whither I have driven you,' saith the Lord;
'and I will bring you again into the place
whence I caused you to be carried away captive.'"

She carefully wraps a faded pink ribbon around my wrist, smiles through her tears and ties it in a bow. "You are no longer white. You will never be red. I think you are just a beautiful shade of pink."

I look down at the pink ribbon tied carefully tied around my wrist, and I feel a wave of love for these two people. How did they know? For I'm no longer white; I will *never* be red. It makes me happy that they were able to understand, and I smile through the few tears that blur my eyes. They have given my center a color: pink. I look back only once as we leave Dark Cloud's village to see the Reverend Wilder with his arm around Miss Rebecca as she sobs against his shoulder. He raises his arm in a farewell salute.

At last we are on the trail. There's Martin and Weasel, me, and two braves named Running Feet and Two Doves. As soon as I see Running Feet and Two Doves I understand the wait; they are the same ones that took me the first time from Pa, Henry, and Eli. If they are not brothers of Weasel, they should be. The first time I see them I look at them from the top of their heads to the tip of their toes as I sit on Willow and Miss Rebecca sobs in the background. Then I look them right in the eye and say nothing, but I think many unkind things. Very slow - like I fan the anger in my belly just to make sure the coals are ready when I need them. They look away first and turn to Weasel. Before they can say any thing, he says sharp like, "It is time to leave." He heads toward his horse and mounts up.

It's so good to be riding Willow. Me and my horse have not had a chance to be together in many, many weeks. I could only view her from a distance in the herd kept outside the village and heavily guarded by white soldiers. In her own horse way she seems as glad to see me as I am to see her.

On the trail I'm always watched with someone ahead of me and Weasel is always behind. I note that we are traveling south, a direction that brings me still farther away from everything I know or care about. In Dark Cloud's village, Weasel kept his distance from me, but on the trail all that has changed. He's always the one that's with me, guarding and watching. It's he who I am tied to at night as we sleep. It's he who takes me for my not so private moments in the woods. And it's he who insists after the first day on the trail that my hands must be permanently tied again as I ride, and even as I sleep. This makes it necessary for someone to help me onto and off of Willow, which Weasel does as well, too. I look down at the rawhide strips over my pink ribbon and think about me and the much more "savage" than "civilized" thoughts running through my head. It seems as if each time he must touch me he becomes more brave and bold. I find his eyes on me at all times; they bore into my back as we ride and they are the last and first things I see each day. It makes my skin feel scratchy and my stomach feel sick.

My anger for him is savage and hot, but I keep it tucked away careful like for when I'll need it most. I think, *A person is what they are inside,* and I feel my center fill with a hate that's almost too big for me to keep inside. There are things to fear on this trek to Martin's people that I realize are fears I put away long ago in Great Elk's village and have had too many things on my mind these past weeks to truly think about until now. Weasel is not the only one I have this fear about. *Remember, it's spring,* I think. Then I look at Martin and Running Feet and Two Doves, and I realize that I shouldn't be fast to dismiss anyone. Weasel watches me like a man watches a woman besides like a captor watches his prisoner.

On the third day of the trail we stop at noon near a stream to water the horses and ourselves. As Weasel helps me off Willow his hand touches my breast and this time it stays there. He smiles a lazy smile and gives me a look that says, *Who's in danger now?* I work hard not to let him see fear in my eyes but my heart feels like it might burst right out of my chest. I think of that night that he took me from Pa and how I wet myself. I take a deep breath to calm my shaky breathing.

I'm not Elle. I'm Bear. I'm wiser. And more powerful.

I don't have my knife. I don't have my bow and arrow. I look him right in the eye and spit in his face. He lets out a howl of anger and, grabbing me by the back of my hair, hauls me off towards the woods. He shouts instructions over his shoulder as Martin and the braves look in our direction. "Leave us be!"

He drags me kicking and fighting and shouting into the woods. I call him Dirty Feet and remind him how his mother hides her head in shame and all who know him laugh at the joke of what his is. I tell him of my hate for him and my hopes and dreams of burying my knife in his back or his neck or his heart. The words that pour out of my mouth help me forget my terror as he drags me deeper into the woods, and I wonder what he has in mind.

Weasel finally gets tired of my words and reaches down and grabs a handful of moss that he shoves deep in my mouth. I choke and gag as bits of dirt trickle down my throat, but I'm quiet now. We walk a good long distance from the others, and he shoves me to the ground and I fall hard, unable to catch myself with my hands tied.

I curl up in a ball in case he plans to kick me, but he rolls me on my back and with a flash of delight on his face pushes my tied hands up over my head and hooks them on a tree root sticking out of the ground. Then he sits on my stomach and with a Woof! the air leaves my lungs. I gasp for breath from my nose and choke and cough at the moss in my mouth and now trickling down my throat.

The "Woof" sound makes me think for a flash of Raccoon and the smile on his face when he came to me standing over my elk. Raccoon makes me think of Otter and Little Bird and Red Fox and Cloud and even Bright Feather, and I blink my eyes to keep from crying. I let my white hot hate swim up behind my eyes and eat my tears.

He waits until my breathing slows a bit and then he gets real close to my face and starts speaking. "You are good for *nothing*," he says, "nothing but *this*. You are not a good white woman, you are not a good Indian squaw. You have caused me nothing but grief since I first saw you. It is because of you I had to leave Great Elks' village and return to Dark Cloud in shame. I should have killed you just like we killed your father and your brother," he sneers.

His words rip me wide apart with a sorrow so awful that I forget all but what he says to me.

"We used our knives," he says so close to my face that I feel his spittle rain down on me, "but made sure that what we did to them made them die slow and painful. Do not worry, Bear," he grinds out my Indian name, "I will give you a small taste of what we did so that you will have no doubt."

I look at him desperate like and search his eyes to see if what he says is true or if I can see he's lying to me. He looks smug and like he's the winner of a fight. The white hot anger has more tears to feed on and bigger aches in my heart than I ever thought there could be. "We take you to the

Francois to *sell* you," he says. "At last there will be something good from you. A white woman trained to be an Indian squaw can bring much gold. Enough to make Dark Cloud happy, enough to make Martin happy," here he gets so close to my face I can only see the hate in his eyes, "but not enough to make me happy."

With a smile, he takes out his knife and cuts open my tunic to my waist and touches my bare breasts with his hands and with his knife. He laughs low when I try to struggle, and cough and choke on more moss as it trickles down my throat. He lowers himself down my legs and then I feel his mouth on my breasts and then his teeth. I feel a terrible pain as his teeth close on my breast as he bites down hard. The white hot anger has more to feed on as it works on the pain of his teeth and his knife.

A blackness comes down on me, different from the blackness of the hurt of my arm, different from the blackness of my last capture. This blackness is the kind that happens to a house late at night when you know a terrible storm is coming; you close the shutters tight, you blow out all the lanterns and you crawl deep under the covers to escape it all. I feel my shutters close, and I feel my lanterns get blown out. The last bit of darkness comes over me like my favorite heavy quilt I remember at my house with Pa, Henry, and Eli. *Elle, will you sleep with me tonight? I'm scared of the thunder* ... I hear Eli ask me. I leave Weasel outside like a mad wolf that no one has had the fortune to kill yet.

I don't hear anyone approach. And I don't hear anyone shout or yell. And I don't even feel Weasel move away. All of sudden my hands are free, and I feel my tunic painfully pulled over my breasts and I'm lifted and carried away. I feel the moss scraped out of my mouth and for a moment things stop while I cough and retch at my feet. It's not until I hear a familiar whistle that I peek my head out from my blackness. I'm passed up to someone on a horse and wrapped in a rough blanket, and I open my eyes just quick enough to see a raccoon tail dangling from a dark shiny head.

We ride and ride and ride for a long while before we stop. I hear splashes in water and then finally we stop on the far edge of a stream. I'm lifted down and feel two strong warm hands on either side of my face, and I hear someone say very soft like, "Bear."

I open my eyes and I see three stripes on each brown cheek and three stripes drawn down the chin, and I see three bright feathers, one red, one blue, one yellow, and I say with the last bits of strength I have, "What took you so long?" The dark eyes that stare back at me are filled with worry.

"We will take a moment to see to your wounds," Bright Feather says as he reaches for his pack of supplies. I sit still as he opens my torn tunic wide, and I stare straight ahead into the wild forest, afraid to look down and see what he's looking at. I feel a wetness trailing down my belly and know that I bleed in many spots. I look once at his face, but he's too good at showing nothing.

Bright Feather quickly but carefully washes the bites and cuts. With great tenderness, he puts a strong smelling salve on each spot, and even though I still do not look, I count eleven in all on my breasts and stomach. He also takes the time to wash the new sores on my wrists. I'm too tired to make a sound even though the pain is something fierce. He helps me take the top of my cut tunic off my arms, and then from his pack he pulls a soft leather shirt over my head that I recognize as Otter's. Then we pull my torn tunic back over the clean shirt. I watch the pink ribbon float down the stream, a small bit of color covered in blood and dirt and sweat.

Bright Feather takes my face in both his hands and looks at me real serious like. "That is all there is time for now," he says and I nod. He gives me water to drink and dried venison to chew. He looks over my shoulder, and for the first time I realize that Raccoon must be standing directly behind us tending to the horse. Waiting. Watching.

Bright Feather looks at me again. "We must keep riding."

I nod my head. "I know."

He studies my face for a moment, touches my cheek softly with one finger, and then says the strangest thing. "Can you whistle?" I take another sip of water and then let out a piercing sound. I hear hoof beats and a familiar whinny. I look at him with surprised eyes. Willow! "Good thing she never learned to listen to *only* your whistle," he says.

Bright Feather stands and talks low with Raccoon. They will split up to confuse anyone that might follow. They talk about directions and each reminds the other of things along the trail. Then Raccoon is bending down in front of me looking more serious than I've ever seen him before. And he can look powerful fierce when he wants to. He works to soften his look and then says, "Don't make him too tired now, Bear. You both need all your strength for a while."

We look at each other for a moment or two. I manage a quiet, "Woof."

That seems to be exactly what he wants to hear for he gives me a small smile. And then he's gone.

Bright Feather lifts me up on Companion, and I make noise about riding on Willow. He shakes his head, looking up at me. "There is not time to argue or ask questions. We will travel for a long way the rest of today and for a time tonight, Bear. You do not have the strength. Willow will follow us." He looks as movable as a mountain.

But I have to ask just one question. "How far are those that will follow Willow?"

He looks up at me for a moment seated on Companion's back. I can look mighty fierce, too. He sighs. "Our trail will be very cold by the time anyone from Dark Cloud's village begins to follow us – if they ever do," he says. I understand what he does not say. *There's no one in the woods here alive that will follow us today.*

He mounts up behind me, pulling a woven Indian blanket across my lap and carefully wrapping his arm around my waist so as to not cause me anymore pain. I nod in answer when he asks if I'm warm and comfortable. *Funny,* I think as I feel my eyelids droop shut, *this is the most comfortable I've been in many weeks.* And then I'm asleep.

We travel all the rest of that day and long into the night until the moon sets, and it's too dark for us to ride safely. We camp by a fallen log without a fire. I look down at myself and Otter's shirt is soaked through with my blood. Bright Feather must help me remove it to wash things more proper like and seems to know that I cannot bring myself to look down again just yet. I sit on a log by a fast moving stream, and he once again takes care to wash and clean each and every spot. From his pack he gently applies an ointment to each and every cut and bite. It smells something awful but makes some of the sting less. "This ointment is from One Who Knows," he says to fill the silence, I suspect. "She told me that should you be injured each and every cut must be carefully cleaned and then to put this salve on." He looks up into my eyes, no smile of course, but I seem to sense some humor, "I hope it is as good at healing as it is at smelling."

As I sit there like an honest to goodness bump on a log, he rinses Otter's top and lays it careful across a low branch to dry. Again he fills the silence with his own words, "Otter packed most of these things for you. She was very afraid for you."

I feel the questions bubble up in my head but am just too tired to get the words out. Bright Feather helps me put my torn tunic back up on my shoulders. "Can you sit here while I get camp ready?" he asks and I nod, feeling dumb and useless.

In a short time he's back, helping me stand and guiding me back away from the river bank, hidden behind some brush, near the horses. "We will share a pallet," he says. "One Who Knows said that you might get a fever and that I am to watch closely for that. I am to not let you catch a chill either, and to keep you warm at night. Since we can not risk a fire, this seems like the best way to stay warm."

I look at him and blink slow. If he thinks I'm inclined to fight or argue or ask questions he's wrong. I curl up on the pallet he has made, and he slips in behind me drawing the blanket over us. He slips his arm under my head for a pillow and wraps his other arm careful like around me, pulling me close against him. He's like laying with a pile of hot coals. I'm asleep, in moments, warm and safe.

We travel north and west the next day, I'm riding in front of Bright Feather with Willow following behind. She seems just as happy to be free as me. Bright Feather says it's north because it's away from the Dark Cloud's village, west because it brings us further away from the whites. We will not travel closer to Great Elk's village and The Maple Forest until we have gone a number of days of just traveling *away*.

"Dark Cloud told me that there has been talk about the search for a white girl who was taken captive. He also said that it was those of The Maple Forest who wanted me to be taken away because they were afraid my presence would cause trouble."

"What did you think of those things when you heard them?" he asks me quietly from behind.

"I decided that even if there was a concern in the village, they would not have had Weasel take me a second time."

Bright Feather, I learn, never talks quick. He always takes a thoughtful moment before he decides to speak. "You are right," he says after a moment or two, "Great Elk would never have allowed you to be taken like that." He pauses and then says almost as if he doesn't want to, "I have heard talk about the search for a white, captive girl. But there is no one in The Maple Forest that has fear because of that."

"Why was I taken again, I wonder…"

"Greed causes people to do frightening things, Bear. Things that are dark and terrible and … hard to imagine sometimes. Maybe you were to be traded for guns or gold."

"Who would they trade with?" I say in a voice that's small and scared at the thought of it all. There's a place where you can trade a girl for a gun?

I feel Bright Feather shrug. "The French, other tribes, ... trappers. There is much greed in the world, Bear. Some people will do anything to get what they want."

"Does all of this have something to do with the time Weasel lived in One Who Knows' hut?" I ask.

Bright Feather rides in silence behind for a time, and I've learned that I must wait and see if I will hear an answer. Finally, I hear his voice above my head, "Yes. Dark Cloud's son," he says, unwilling to call him by name, "brought you to One Who Knows' hut to end a debt that can never be paid. He was angry that things he thought should be easy for people to forget were still there to haunt him whenever he was in the village. He spent the first half of his life making mistakes and the last part of his life running from them."

I think about what Weasel has done to my life. "It would seem that Weasel has debts with many people that can never be paid." I decide that the hard topic of Weasel is best not talked about anymore for a bit.

I'm surprised when long, long moments later Bright Feather says, "Yes, Dark Cloud's son has many debts with many people that can never be paid. Even from the grave."

We stop for lunch, I suspect more for me than for Bright Feather, and we sit by a stream and eat from supplies that Bright Feather carries with him. When I make moves to start the fire and get the meal going, Bright Feather pushes me down to sitting.

"I do not need you to cook for me," I say. I'm a powerful woman after all.

He does not look up at me as he starts a fire with sure hands and begins the process of setting out the meal. "I cook for myself," he says matter of fact. "You are welcome to join me if you wish." Then he glances up at me. "After you go to the stream," he gestures to the left, "and clean your wounds." He hands me the special salve in a small pottery bowl. I stare down at his bent head and think that for someone who is always alone and almost always silent he has sure become bossy all of a sudden.

I walk to the water, wading into the stream to sit on a rock by the fastest moving part. I've changed my torn tunic to a deerskin skirt and top that Otter has sent me. I slowly take off the top and stare down at the mess that's my body. It's the first time I've really, truly looked. Eleven bite and cut marks, some still bleeding, all terrible sore. *We used our knives but made sure that what we did to them made them die slow and painful.*

I suddenly feel so cold I start to shiver. Did Pa get cut like this? A moan crawls out my throat as I think, *and my Eli...?* I can't stop shivering and I wrap my arms around my bare self and rock and moan and cry with the cold that's more inside me than out. I can't get warm. I can't... I never will...

I don't know how long I sit, shaking and crying but suddenly strong warm arms scoop me up, and I'm no longer sitting on a rock but in Bright Feather's warm lap. I can't stop my sobs, no matter how I try, and Bright Feather sits right there with me in the middle of the stream and holds me like a baby. "You are safe now, Bear," he says over and over in a soft voice in my ear. He copies my movements and soon we are both rocking back and forth. "You are safe, Bear. I will see to it. The wounds will heal. The scars will not be noticeable. You are safe from those who took you. Never again," he whispers sing-song like over and over, "never again."

For long moments, I let him think I cry for my sorry state, and once again take advantage of the warmth of him. He does not know what Weasel has said of Pa and Eli, I realize, and I try and try but can't get the words out to tell. They are so awful just in my head, what will they be like said out loud by my mouth?

"Weasel ..." I manage and he leans in close to hear my words. I swallow, suddenly feeling sick as well as sore. "Weasel .... told me of Pa ..." I start to rock and cry and moan again but I manage to get out, "and Eli ..."

"Ahh," he says rocking and holding me tight. "You carry more wounds *inside* than out. And we do not have a salve to put on them, hmmm?" He tucks my head under his chin, cuddles me close in his arms, and we sit on the rock in the middle of the stream for so long that the shade and the sun patterns change around us.

"These inside wounds," he says finally as if no time has passed at all, "they cause more hurt than any knife can. I know. They will, with time, heal a bit, but these inside scars ..." he sighs, "sometimes show more than the outside ones."

He's One Who Is Always Alone, I realize, because all of *his* inside scars have made him so. *At a time long ago he was called Hawk because he was such a great hunter,* I hear Otter tell me.

At last Bright Feather helps me clean my eleven wounds, careful and easy. Out comes the bad smelling salve and I wrinkle my nose at the stench of it. "It seems to smell worse and worse with each day," I grumble as we dab it on all my sores. He keeps silent, and I wonder at his mood. Have I stirred up his sorrow and pain now with all of my tears? "I suspect you will be happy when I can ride on Willow instead of with you on Companion." Nothing. So I add, "Behind you. Down wind." He does not look up from his work but he grunts at me. Not only do I tear at his old inside scars but I also smell worse than a bad piece of meat. "I could ride on Willow until we stop for the evening meal, if you wish," I suggest.

It's then that he looks up at me with eyes so sharp that I lean back a bit at their force. "I would have you riding in front of me on Companion smelling twice as bad and talking twice as much," he grinds out and I'm stunned to see what might be a tear in his eye. He stands and I look up at him standing in the swift flowing stream. "I have no room inside for more scars, Bear. I am very glad that you are here. Come, dinner is ready." And he wades to shore without a backwards glance.

He would like me smelling twice as bad?!

And, an even bigger thought to ponder. He wouldn't mind me talking *twice as much?!*

I shake my head in amazement. He's one mighty strong warrior to be able to handle such things.

"How did Weasel of Dark Cloud's village come to be at One Who Knows hearth in The Maple Forest?" I ask Bright Feather as we ride once again, both on Companion, after we have eaten and rested a bit.

"At one time, the villages of Dark Cloud and Great Elk were closer together. Hunting and trapping areas were shared, braves married and lived in the hearths with their mates and there was a strength in the harmony that the two villages shared.

"The white man brought more changes than just what you can see with your eyes," he explains. "For some Real People, the opportunity to own white man's rifles and other possessions they considered of value began to interfere with the way things had always been. There were disagreements among The Real People over how things should be. Should we make changes that will make the white man happy? Should we fight to stay the same? Should we sign another treaty and give up still more hunting and trapping areas? Should we allow ourselves to be moved to unfamiliar places? Who knows the right path? Who should be listened to? Suddenly the way we had always done things, to talk and come to an agreement could not help us solve some of these concerns. For who knew if just one person was right and all the rest were wrong?"

We ride in silence for a time, and I think about the hard choices The Real People had to face. It was hard, Pa told me once, to move our whole family out to the Virginia homestead. What would it have been like had Pa tried to convince an entire town to move with him?

We talk about the neighboring Indian tribes. I'm surprised to learn that there are many reasons why the Indian's regret the white man's arrival. Distrust and even battles between The Real People and their neighbors have been a sorry result. "You fight amongst yourselves?" I say in surprise. I remember the words about harmony and balance and the center of the world needing to be right.

"Some tribes are eager to gain white man's possessions," Bright Feather tells me, "guns, metal pots and pans, and," he says as though he has dirt in his mouth, "*liquor.* Some tribes do not agree. Disagreements lead to fights. As you have seen with Dark Cloud's village and Great Elk's village, it has reached the point that we even disagree among ourselves."

I tell him what I know about liquor. I remember a corner in Cooper's General Store and the jugs and how the men would crowd around and laugh and talk and drink. I remember Pa again saying, *"It burns your belly when you drink it, but it's your brain that carries the scars."* I tell Bright Feather.

"He was a wise man," he says, and I wonder just how wise Pa really was and what he would have thought of Bright Feather. Would he have been able to see past the skin and the feathers and the permanent lines on his face and be able to see what a good man he is — *red or white?* Would he think only savage?

The savages had their time. Their present circumstances are not our concern. That sounds as if Pa knew about the things that Beaver and the Wilders and now Bright Feather are telling me and the hard way of things for The Real People. Then I wonder, does minding your own business and keeping your head down and your mouth shut stop you from learning new things? Keep you from seeing the truth? I suspect it does. For it's only since I've made the effort to pick my head up, pay attention, ask questions and make hard choices that I've gotten to be this wise and powerful.

From my memories of Pa, he seemed fair and true. But he did not let much into his life and worked hard to stay as far away from the world as he could. He was loving and kind and true to his family. But only his family. *Would that extend to his daughter mated with an Indian brave?* I wonder. That's a question I can't truly answer.

Bright Feather does not know my thoughts and continues to explain that while the Indians desire white men's possessions, the white men desire the Indian's furs. I ponder this for a bit, and then must finally say that it sounds like an easy matter of barter and fair trade.

I feel him shake his head 'no'. "These woods and the animals in it are a good supply for the people who live here, but not for a whole world across the ocean which is where many of the furs go. Already the whites come further west to hunt, because the forests to the east are empty."

I think about Pa, Ma, Henry, Eli, and I and try to recall us traveling to the place I remember that used to be my home – Ward's Mill, Virginia. The memories are small and few, tiny flashes of moments; a white wagon, a bear and Ma's frightened screams, Henry holding a small baby rabbit he found in the woods. "Pa was a white man, but in some ways he lived like an Indian," I say after a while. "He had no desire to become rich or to hurt or kill. He just wanted to be left alone to live a life with his wife and children on a piece of land he could call his own." Memories of how things changed after Ma's death are clearer for they are more recent. "When Ma died it seemed that Pa lived only for each day. There was little talk of times before nor was there any talk of future dreams." I realize that made him even more like an Indian.

"Dark Cloud argued very strongly in those early times that we should accept the white man's offers," Bright Feather explains. "He traveled to see the land they offered to give us if we would move from the forests, and he said that the land was fertile, the forests full of animals, and the rivers jumping with fish. He embraced many of the white man's ways, had already agreed to move to the village you saw, and was happy to accept many gifts that were offered to him: guns, clothing, cooking utensils, seed for planting. Great Elk felt less certain about the decision. He counseled with those in his village he respected: Cloud, War Woman, One Who Knows, and many others I cannot name. No one from Dark Cloud's village had seen what War Woman had seen in The Great War. No one felt that a move would bring us balance or harmony. We already knew the woods and the mountains, the streams and the animals. Our ancestors' spirits roamed the land and guided and protected us. Great Elk decided to stay in The Maple Forest, and so the villages became two places great distances apart rather then two places a day's quick ride away."

I feel Bright Feather shrug as I lean against him. "Great effort was made to maintain contact, but the differences became greater with each passing season. The white men had great hunger for the deer hides and furs that our forests provided, and Dark Cloud and his people began to hunt for more than just themselves. They forgot, I think, about the important role a hunter plays in the forest. They no longer respected and appreciated the animal for the gifts it gave us, but saw it only as a way to acquire more things." He shook his head and said almost to himself, "There is no balance in a life that lives to only get more things.

"In a final effort to keep the contact between the villages, it was decided that braves from each village should be encouraged to marry women in the opposite villages. It was something that had always been done in the past, but with the great distance it had not happened in many seasons. There was a great outcry from both places, I understand, neither wanting to move to the other's village." Very quietly I hear him say, "Maybe they were right...." He offers no more information, and I'm left to guess and sort out ghosts that neither one of us can name.

Finally I say, "Dark Cloud's village did not have the same feeling as The Maple Forest. When I was there I felt ... mixed up. It was like before I found my center and decided what I would be. Only it was a whole village of people like that."

We ride in silence for a bit, and I wait. At last Bright Feather says, "The Maple Forest fights to keep the harmony and balance that we know is so right. But it is very hard to find harmony and balance anywhere else."

I begin to doze to the rhythm and sway and warmth of the ride. "And what is in your center, Bear?" Bright Feather asks me as his arm tightens around my waist and Companion works his way careful down the sloping path.

I realize that I've let some things into my center that I shouldn't have. Weasel's cruel words for one. I'll have to work hard to get them all cleaned out. I think about the Wilders' words and about this soul of mine that they seemed so powerful worried about. Perhaps I should put that in my center to protect it, too. I'll ponder that. "Me," I finally say to Bright Feather. "A wise and powerful woman named Bear. She loves to learn, and she is working hard to keep only the good things in and the all the bad things out." I turn to look at him behind me. "And she has a color. She is not white. She will never be red. She is pink."

"Pink," he says and grunts.

By the second full day on the trail, I insist that I'm strong enough to ride Willow. I suspect Bright Feather travels slower and stops more often than he would if he was alone, but I don't say anything. My cuts and bites have stopped bleeding and some have begun to heal. There are two bites, one on my left breast and one high on my right hip that cause me much pain and show signs of festering. At each stop Bright Feather makes certain I go and clean all of my wounds carefully, and I continue to spread the ointment on them. It's bear grease, he suspects, with special herbs that One Who Knows mixed up before he and Raccoon set out in search of me.

I'm surprised to hear that there are some in Great Elk's village who thought at first that I'd made a run to go back to Virginia and Pa, Henry, and Eli. It's Otter and Raccoon, and most surprising to me, One Who Knows, who steps forward and say no to this, but precious time was lost in the arguing. Bright Feather and Raccoon found the place in the woods where I fought and understood the truth of things. Red Fox and Beaver wished to come along to search as well, but Great Elk had them stay in case the village needed to be protected. I'm amazed to learn that all those weeks I waited in Dark Cloud's village Raccoon and Bright Feather were camped no more than a day's ride away waiting and watching patiently for a good time to rescue me.

"Raccoon was certain that you would escape, and we only needed to wait for you to show up," Bright Feather said. He studies me for a moment. "You may make him tired with all your questions, but he thinks greatly of you."

"What do you think of me?" I ask, and then wish I can suck the words back in my mouth before they reach Bright Feather's ears. What made me ask such a thing I wonder?

We have finally stopped for the night, and I'm tired and sore from a full day of riding, even if we are going at a slow pace. He stirs up the fire that we have started to cook the rabbit he has caught. The sparks shoot up into the night and look like stars in the night sky. When I look at him he's watching me, "You are someone who despite all the things that have happened to you can still find joy in life. You change people who are close to you with the person that you are. That makes you very strong. When I am with you, I feel like my name is Bright Feather instead of One Who Is Always Alone." I've no more questions to ask and nothing to say.

Towards the end of the third day on the trail, I find myself achy and tired. The bites on my hip and breast pain me, and I'm looking forward to getting down off Willow and washing in a cool stream. Bright Feather startles me by saying, "I can take you back to Virginia if you wish."

I'm so stunned that Willow and I just stop on the trail while Bright Feather and Companion continue on ahead of us. He knows I've stopped following him, but he continues on a bit before he has Companion stop. With his back still to me he says, "Great Elk said I was to do as you wished if I found you."

My precious box with memories of Pa, Henry and Eli bursts open, and they fly all around me like the bees around a flower. I've trouble remembering their faces I find, but I remember Pa's laugh and the silky feel of Eli's brown hair. I can feel Henry's strong arms around me as he hauls me up over his shoulder and dumps me – clothes and all! - into the stream. I can see one of Henry's rare smiles as I sputter and try to stand in my clumsy wet skirts and splash him. I can see our cabin in the woods and the flower garden that Ma planted and that Pa and I worked hard to keep alive. I see Eli's big blue eyes and those eyes float up before me, and they become the dark eyes of Little Bird and Pa's laugh becomes Otter's as we giggle over something silly. I see Cloud sitting in the warm sunshine with my Elk's antlers tied to the front of his hut. And I remember the night Elle went away and I became Bear, a powerful woman, and how the village cheered a welcome. I think of Miss Rebecca and her words to me, *You are no longer white. You will never be red. I think you are just a beautiful shade of pink.* I come back to the here and now, and Bright Feather is still sitting on Companion with his back to me waiting patient as ever to hear if he will get an answer.

My knees tell Willow to move up the trail until I'm alongside Bright Feather who is staring straight ahead at the tree line in front of us. He looks tense to me, like he's ready to go into battle. I reach out to touch him and hesitate. I realize I've never touched him before. *He* had touched *me*, but never the other way around. I suddenly have such a powerful strong urge to do just that that my fingers twitch, and so I do.

His arm is warm and solid, a deep reddish brown compared to my white, tan hand. I feel the muscles in his arm jump, and he turns to look at me. I loose my words and my thoughts as we stare at each other in the late afternoon sunshine. As usual, his face is careful to show nothing, but I wonder what mine shows. *I like this Bright Feather I'm learning to know,* I think loud and clear in my head. Bright Feather looks down at my hand still resting on his arm and then back to my face.

I take a moment to find my voice and then say, "I was happy when I lived in Virginia with Pa, Henry, and Eli. My life with them was not easier or harder, it was just different. I was happy in Great Elk's village, too. I found a person that I didn't know I could be." *I'm pink now,* I think to myself. "I don't think I can go back to being Elle. You cannot put a plant back into its seed. I like the person that I have become in Great Elk's village. I like this powerful woman, Bear. I think I want to keep watching and see what else she will do." He has a moment where I can almost say he looks pleased, and then he frowns at me, suddenly furious it seems. His hand reaches across and covers mine that's still on his arm. His touch is wonderfully cool.

"Bear …" he begins and makes hasty moves to get off Companion and come around beside me still seated on Willow. I puzzle over his sudden change in mood. "Bear, you are very hot," he says with real concern in his voice. He reaches up, and I protest as he makes a move to help me down.

"Don't!" I shout, afraid he will touch my sore hip or breast.

He hesitates just a moment and then turns into a stubborn mountain right before my eyes. "I will," he says. His strong hands reach up and lift me gently down with only a brief twinge of pain. He leads me to a spot of shade, has me sit down, and then squats before me. "Let me see," he says fiercely, and I know not to argue.

The two wounds are wet and oozing and have stuck to the soft buckskin of Otter's shirt. As the fabric separates from the skin, I feel a sticky wetness trickle from both places and a bad smell rises up from them that has nothing to do with One Who Knows' salve. "Bear," he says in a very angry tone, "you told me that they were healing!"

I feel angry a little and tired a lot. "Most of them are!" I say strong like back to him. "Except these two," I say a little less strong.

He makes a moaning sound in the back of his throat and makes quick moves to set up camp and get a fire going. When I try to help he shouts at me, "Sit and stay!" like I'm an annoying child. I glare at him for a bit, but he takes no notice. I doze, lying on a blanket as he moves about the camp. I'm far too hot to cover myself, and the cool evening air feels good on my burning skin.

When Bright Feather comes to squat beside me and cover me I throw the covers off. "It's too hot," I grumble. If he treats me like a child, I decide, I'll act like one.

He makes me drink from a water skin. "I go to find some more water," he says. "We have not camped close to a stream."

"You chose this spot, not me," I say, fanning myself with my hand. "Why did you start a fire? It is *so hot*."

He touches my neck with his wonderful cool hand and moans again in the back of his throat. "Stay here, Bear. On your pallet. Do not move. Do not get up. Do you hear me?"

I give him an angry look. "No wonder you are always alone," I say with a smart lip as I close my eyes. "It is because you are so bossy, no one can be bothered with you."

He grunts and stands up holding our water skins.

I don't know when he returns, but when I next open my eyes he's squatting by the fire tending to our birch bark bowl we carry for cooking. *He's a handsome man,* my head thinks as I watch him working. Then he turns to look at me and gives me a fierce frown. I sigh and close my eyes again.

I struggle mightily with Bright Feather when he comes to clean my wounds. "I can do it myself," I insist, but he's back to his silent self and ignores my words as if I've not even spoken.

He sits besides me grimly with a birch bark bowl and a deerskin cloth. "I must work to clean the bites that are the most sore, Bear. You will not like me for a time."

I can't help but say, "What makes you think I like you at all?" but then I smile a bit. As usual he does not think I'm funny. *I miss Raccoon,* I think sudden like. At least he teases me back.

Finally he says, "I will work as quickly as I can, but you must let me do what I must do? All right, Bear?" When I just stare at him without answering, because my words are a bit confused in my head, he leans down and looks into my eyes, "Did you know that all powerful women each have their own special war cry?"

I blink at him, and try to focus, but the heat that's rising off of me is making things blurry. I shake my head 'no'.

He nods as he puts down his bowl and dips the rag into the liquid. I see that it's steaming too, with heat. "Yes," he says and takes a deep breath. "Powerful women scream their war cry when they are most angry, most sad, and most hurt." He touches my cheek with one cool finger. "Tonight you will find your war cry, hmm?"

Despite the fire Bright Feather builds, by the time it's dark I'm so cold I can't stop shivering. My throat and voice, sore and tired from my war cry, moan at the pain that the shivering causes to the rest of my hurts. *How can a body be so hot one moment and so cold the next?* I think in my misery, along with, *I'll never, ever be warm again.* Finally, a very hot body and strong arms surround me and hold me tight and share a warmth that my body can't make on its own.

I have busy dreams that mix up my lives and make them one: Bright Feather trying to pull a blanket over my head and take me away from where I want to be. Pa and Raccoon hunting. Eli tied on Little Bird's cradleboard and swinging on a tree hung by a pink ribbon. Henry teaching me how to shoot a bow and arrow and looking close in my face and speaking *Francois.* Bear John with a burning stick that he touches to my hip and to my breast and me screaming with the pain of it. My Ma comes to me and she cradles me in her arms and sings to me a lullaby in the language of The Real People. Sometimes Bright Feather is there in my dreams forcing me to drink cool water, but sometimes it is Weasel and I fight powerful hard to get away. I hear Miss Rebecca's words over and over, *For I know the plans I have for you, to give you a future and a hope.*

I open my eyes, and they focus on Bright Feather who is sitting against the opening of a small cave, his long legs stretched out in front of him. A small fire smolders just at the cave's opening and sputters now and then as drops of rain hit it. His eyes are closed and his breathing peaceful, yet he has an alertness about him that makes me know he's not full asleep. It's pouring rain outside; a mighty thunder of water crashing down all around us. Inside this little place we are warm and dry. I study his face and I think he looks mighty tired. I make the slightest move and his eyes snap open and he looks at me. He looks close at my face, and I see him relax a bit. He draws one leg up and leans his arm across it. "How do you feel?" he says quiet like.

I shift a bit and feel a little like the time I fell off Willow when Raccoon was first teaching me to ride and tell him so. "You have been sick for a while," he says.

I struggle to sit up, and it takes great effort and my head swims round and round like pieces are loose inside. He comes to me and squats down. With both hands on my shoulders he steadies me. He seems to know not to let me go or I'll fall right over. "How long have I been sick?"

"You have been with fever for three days," he says.

"Three days!" I shout. He grunts.

He shifts and moves so that he's behind me, and I'm leaning against his chest, sitting between his legs. I hear him yawn, and he reaches up a hand to rub his face a bit. "Raccoon knew what he was talking about when he said you could make a body more tired then anyone else he knew." I turn to see his face, and he bends down so I can look at him. His dark hair and colorful feathers swing loose behind his shoulder. His eyes are so dark brown you can't really see the black centers in the light of the cave. *Here is a good man,* I think loud and clear and strong in my head. I reach up to touch a yellow feather. *The goldfinch is hard to see even in the best of seasons. You can search all summer and hardly catch a glimpse of him.* Bright Feather has dark circles under his eyes. "Are you hungry?" he asks quiet like.

My stomach rumbles loud enough to be heard over the rain, and before I can speak he reaches across to hand me a bowl of warm rabbit stew. I hold it in my lap and take a small taste. It's delicious, and I gobble it all down. "Sleep some more," he finally says after sitting quiet behind me while I eat. As he moves away and I lay down again, he sounds very far away to me. "Tomorrow we must move from here to stay safe." My last thought before I fall asleep is, *I always feel safe with you.*

I feel much better in the morning and with Bright Feather's help I'm able to wash at the stream. Both bites look much better and no longer ooze or smell. There's a good scab over the top of both and some of the other knife cuts and bites itch something terrible. Bright Feather says that's good, too.

I once again ride in front of Bright Feather, too weak to ride far on Willow on my own. I notice we travel east, the first time we have gone in that direction since we have left Raccoon, and say so.

"Unless you tell me different, we return to Great Elk's village. We will be there in five days at a fast pace, six otherwise." He rides silent behind me while I once again think about what he has said about taking me home to Virginia.

"It would be dangerous for you to take me back to Ward's Mill," I say.

"It can be done," is all he says back to me.

"I have been gone a long time," I feel inclined to point out.

"Not so long," Mr. Talkative answers back.

"Do you think I should go back?" I ask, powerful curious to hear what he will say.

"No one can choose your own life path but you."

"Weasel did," I say with a bit of anger.

"Did he?" Bright Feather asks, "Or did he just bring you to another place to start making new choices once again?"

I think back to the time when I knew that the only thing keeping me in The Maple Forest was my own self and what I couldn't or wouldn't do. I keep quiet because Bright Feather is right about Weasel. My thoughts of The Maple Forest make me excited to see Otter and Little Bird and Cloud and even, maybe, One Who Knows, and I know I won't tell Bright Feather different. I think then of Red Fox and Beaver, and I feel tired again. I must make a sound like a sigh. "You are not happy we return to the village?" Bright Feather asks.

I tell him about spring and mating and Red Fox and Beaver. I tell him about Otter and the basket of apples. I tell him about sitting up on my quiet spot the day they came and took me, and why I'd gone there that day, and that I was thinking about all the choices I have as a powerful Indian woman. I wait to hear what he has to say, and I think about how much I like to talk to Bright Feather, because he always seems to listen and tries to understand.

"All I wanted when I was a boy was to be a great hunter," he says after a time.

"It seems you got your wish."

He shrugs his shoulders. "When you are young you are stupid, too. You don't always know the best things to wish for."

"I never even knew I *could* wish for anything," I tell him. "For almost all of my life I have done what was needed or expected. There was not a time ever, until I became Bear, that I was told I could decide what I wanted to do with my life. *Having choices!* There is a magic in just that, you know ... More than I thought I could even dream of."

He thinks on this for a while. I can tell I've given him a new taste to try in his mind. "So what choices are there for a powerful woman to consider?" he asks. I know he's not teasing me.

"That's part of the fun. I don't even know them all yet." I say. "All of a sudden I am no longer the mule, I am the driver. Who knows where I can go or what I can do? I guess the only choice I must make right now is when do I stop looking at the choices and start making some?"

"Choices are a little bit like weeds," he says at last. "Some left to grow can have beautiful flowers. Others might be important for healing. But if you aren't careful and choose some to pull out now and then, they'll take over your whole garden and you won't have any crops to harvest come fall. You'll die from starvation. You never have to *stop looking* for choices, but always, at the same time, you must never *stop making* them. That's life."

We ride in silence for a very long time as I think about all the choices I've to consider. "When we get back to Great Elk's village," he says as the sun begins to set, "you must choose a mate. Otter is right."

"That's the one choice I don't want to make yet!" I shout, and his arm goes tight around me to keep me from jumping off Companion and moving away from his words.

With his arm tight around my waist and his mouth close against my ear he says, "The only way you can keep your other choices is to make this one. Choose a mate who will let you keep looking for other choices *or* the choice you've made of staying with The Real People may be taken from you instead."

I twist in the saddle to look at him and feel the pull of the scabs at my hip and my breast but I don't care. "Why do you say that?" I shout.

"Because," he says calm and quiet like, "you will always be more tempting to be rescued and brought back should you remain on your own. Remember, they look to rescue a 'captive white girl'. Once you take a mate and establish a family and blood ties, things will be much more difficult to unravel. You may think you are Bear, and to many of us you are, but you must realize that to some - red *and* white - you will always be *Elle.*" My white name sounds funny in his mouth.

I'm more quiet than ever as we set up camp for the night and prepare the evening meal. Bright Feather leaves me alone with my thoughts, and we work and eat in silence. My brain works and works to put all my choices in a pile, and I sort through them one by one trying to make everything fit just like I want. No matter how many times I try, it always comes back to the same way of thinking; Bright Feather and Otter saw what I did not. If I'm a mate of an Indian brave and a mother of Indian children, there will be many more strong reasons for me to stay where I want to stay than if I stay Bear, a powerful woman on her own. The Indians might understand this way of thinking but white folk never ever will. As I fall asleep under the stars I make a choice that really is no choice; I understand that I must choose a mate.

I spend the whole next day riding on Willow lost in more choices. I don't see the beautiful forests, I don't hear the conversations of the birds, I don't taste the cold venison we chew for lunch, and I don't notice the place we choose to stop for the night. I think about Red Fox and his kindness and patience as he taught me to shoot a bow under Cloud's directions. I think about his shy smile when I ask many questions and his willingness to answer and explain everything I ask to know. I think about us taking turns being the hunter and the hunted and the laughter and fun we have together. I think about his offers to take me hunting, to go riding with me. I remember discovering through Otter that I seem to be the only thing in the village he watches closely, and how she said that I was the first girl in the village that Red Fox has ever seemed interested in.

I think of Beaver, tall and sure and proud. He's War Woman's son. For the first time I think, is he Great Elk's son, too? I compare the two and realize they are the same height, they have the same muscular build, and they have the same proud bearing. Yes, they are of the same blood, I conclude, and another piece to the puzzle of life in the village slips into place. I'm amazed that of all the young women in camp, Beaver has looked at *me*. I can become the mate of one of the most powerful men in the village it seems. I think about him and his patience on our hunts, teaching me how to track animals and tell one apart from another just by what they leave behind. I think about him working patiently to teach me how to light a fire. I think about his sitting with Otter and Raccoon and me the many nights he visited our hearth and talked. I think about the wonderful stories he tells that bring the way of The Real People to life in my mind.

The silence between Bright Feather and I is comfortable. He seems as comfortable with my silence as he does with my questions. After almost two weeks on the trail with only each other for company, we have found an easy rhythm. He's not at all surprised it seems, after almost a full day of silence between us, when I finally ask over our evening meal, "How does a woman choose a mate?"

"She begins to spend time with him, she accepts gifts from him and does kindnesses for him in return, and at some point they choose to set up a hearth together."

"White folks have to have a preacher – a special man of God - say special words before you call yourself joined," I volunteer.

"Is that so?" he says. "There is often a celebration in the village at the time, but there is no other person that says 'yes' or 'no" to the joining. It is the couple's choice, and often they live together for a time to see if the choice is right."

"What happens if a baby comes?" I ask.

He looks surprised at the question, "Babies are always considered a wonderful thing." I realize I still have many thoughts in my head that are white.

"What happens if a woman is interested in a man who doesn't seem interested in her?"

He shrugs. "She makes her interest known, and he must decide what his thoughts are."

I sigh. "I am certain Pa married Ma 'cause he loved her," I say remembering. I see flashes of laughter and smiles between the two of them. I hear him calling her "Lizzie" sometimes instead of her proper name, Elizabeth. I know for sure that the only times I ever heard Pa laugh was when Ma was around to cause it. I can hear her voice say with soft love, "Oh, Andrew," over something he has said or done that I can't remember. I remember a sadness in Pa that never went away after she died. He became a different person. I look at Bright Feather and think, *Pa would have changed his name after Ma died had that been our custom, too.* But Pa had me, Henry, and Eli, and he couldn't become One Who Is Always Alone. A wave of missing Pa washes over me that I haven't felt in a long time. I work hard to close my memory box.

"There are many reasons to join with another, Bear," Bright Feather says after a time. "Some join for love, some to make tribes and families stronger – like Great Elk and Dark Cloud's villages, some to gain more respect in the village," he looks to me, "and some for security and wise choices for the future."

I make a face at him. "That is an old song I have heard too much of these past days."

He shrugs his shoulders and becomes silent again, eating the last of his meal. I study him and remember. Bright Feather, the hunter, sitting silent, alone and nigh on invisible in the woods, waiting. Bright Feather the night he brings me Willow in the council circle and calls me "Bear". Bright Feather helping me train Willow and answering question after question I ask. Bright Feather holding my face right after my dark time with Weasel and saying my name and the look in his eyes. Bright Feather holding and rocking me as I talked about my inside scars. Bright Feather sitting in the cave tired and exhausted from caring for me while I was sick. I have a thought, and I decide to speak real quick before I change my mind, like jumping into a pond you know will be ice cold so you do it fast to get it over with. "I have spent time with you and have received gifts from you and have done kindnesses for you in return, and I have even kept a hut with you."

"So you have, Bear," he says, and he waits patient like, his brown eyes staring at my face and the breeze blowing his colorful feathers and loose flowing hair around his head.

"And you will let me keep looking for choices even while I keep making them," I say quiet like, almost at a whisper.

"So I will, Bear," he says, and still he keeps looking at me with nothing moving but his hair and feathers.

"And you don't seem to get as tired as Raccoon when you are with me, and you seem willing to answer my questions and teach me things that I still need to know to become a more powerful woman," I say in a whisper that's hardly louder than the breeze.

"So I do, Bear," he says.

I feel the tears pool in the corners of my eyes and begin to wander down my cheeks as I look into his face, and I see things that he has never, ever let me see before: caring, loneliness, need... There's no hate to eat these tears I realize, and I can't stop them. He reaches across the fire to catch one tear with his finger, and I speak again so quiet he must lean forward to hear me. "And I think," I say almost more to myself than to him for he must surely know the answer already, "you must like me just some small, small bit."

"A powerful woman is good company for One Who Is Always Alone," he says, and he takes me in his arms and holds me very tight.

Mate

"I think," I say to Bright Feather much later on as I watch him add more wood to the fire, "that this mating thing is much more complicated than I ever dreamed."

"How is that, Bear?" he asks as he comes back beside me, lying on his side, propped up on one elbow with his silky dark hair collecting on the pallet behind him.

"Well," I say, "I just had no idea that you mate with your head and your heart as well as your …" I clear my throat and suspect I blush a bit, "well you know what I mean."

"No," he says serious like, "I don't. Try to explain."

I start to open my mouth and explain, and I catch Bright Feather's look. I sit up and study him for a moment in the firelight as he looks right back at me. "You're teasing me!" I say in absolute wonder, for as best as I can recall he has never done or said anything but serious things for as long as I've known him. He grunts a sound that I suddenly realize is as close to a laugh as he can manage. He reaches out to me and runs a finger from the top of my forehead, down my nose, slow across my lips and then down my neck between my breasts to my belly and beyond. I feel my nipples tighten and my stomach clench and goose skin runs wild all over my body, and I decide to stop talking for a while again. I suspect I need to learn a lot more about this mating business before I'll be able to explain anything.

Nine days later, we enter Great Elk's village of The Maple Forest amid great shouts of welcome. It seems we have traveled slower than even Bright Feather planned. Otter and Raccoon stand outside their hut with grins that just about split their faces apart. Toddling at their feet is Little Bird, walking on two very fat, sturdy legs. There's great commotion in the village, and after we care for our horses we are fair rushed to the council circle before we have time to even wash, eat, or drink.

Seated in the bright spring sunshine are many faces I'm familiar with; Great Elk, War Woman, Raccoon, One Who Knows, and Beaver among them. But I'm stunned to see a white man dressed in some Indian style and some white, sitting comfortably next to Great Elk, laughing and talking with much ease. I feel my steps slow and fear shoot like lightning all through me. I hear Bright Feather's words of delight from a distance further than where he truly stands, "Deer! My brother! At last you have found time to return to your home!"

The white man stands, wraps his arms tightly around Bright Feather, and says in perfect Indian words, "One Who Is Always Alone! What are you doing here? You should be out hiding by yourself in the woods like I hear you always do!" There's much back-slapping and good natured shoving, and Bright Feather shows a joy that I've seen only in the last few weeks.

I stay silent and apart during this time, but Bright Feather finally turns to me and says, "Bear! Come meet my brother, Deer. He has been away from us for a long time, and it is good to have him back!"

I step forward, awkward and fearful, but somewhat better having watched Bright Feather's mood. *Would he not have a worry if there is one?* I think. "Welcome, Deer, brother of One Who Is Always Alone. I am glad to know you," I say carefully.

"No you are not!" he laughs good-naturedly. "You look terrified! Has anyone not told this child of me?" he shouts to the crowd as he reaches out to grasp my hand and hold it firm and sure.

I feel my back go up like an angry camp dog. "I am not a child," I hear myself growl, furious at the first thoughts I've caused in his head. I stand tall and push the fear away, reminding myself that I am a powerful woman. "I am Bear, of Great Elk's village, of The Maple Forest of The Real People. I have earned the name and the right to say that." I firmly remove my stiff hand from his warm one.

"Whoa-ho!" he shouts with delight, and makes a motion to count all the fingers on his hand to see if I've bitten one off. He turns to Raccoon and says, "You were right about her! She is much more than she first appears." I glare angry eyes at Raccoon who gives me his innocent look. Deer bows respectfully towards me, but his eyes as he lifts them to look at me twinkle with mischief and delight. "Please, accept my apologies if I have caused you offense, Bear, of Great Elk's village, of The Maple Forest of The Real People. You must know that all Raccoon has learned about the seriousness of life and all that One Who Is Always Alone has learned about the dealings between others, they have me to thank for."

I can't stay angry but also can't keep myself from saying with a flip tongue, "Then I add another man to my list of who I must retrain." But I smile at him just the same.

"I look forward to the opportunity," he says with a wink.

I've many, *many* questions boiling in my head for Bright Feather, but they must wait. Questions are directed to me and Bright Feather instead about our travels and time away. Much information is exchanged, and I'm surprised to hear Bright Feather report on what seems to be the borders of Great Elk's territory. It has not occurred to me that he would be expected to do such a thing. Could I have been so complete with my descriptions had they asked me the same questions? I disappoint myself because I know the answer is 'no'. They ask him questions about animal patterns and human activity and finally a few brief questions about Dark Cloud's village. Weasel is never mentioned. *They must have talked with Raccoon just like they talk with us now*, I realize.

They ask me questions, too. How large is Dark Cloud's village? How many braves? How many whites? How many soldiers? How many huts? How many horses? Do the people look healthy and strong and well fed? Did I see any sickness? What did I hear and see that I think is important for them to know? I try very hard to tell them as much as I can remember.

I tell them how there's a different feeling in Dark Cloud's village. People behave differently with each other, the men to the women, the women to the men, the adults to the children. I try hard to explain but it's difficult. "There is more secrecy, more fear, more distrust it seems between everyone. Every face works hard to tell a different story than what really is."

When I speak of the white men who seem so comfortable in Dark Cloud's village there's great interest. I'm able to answer their questions in most cases. How many white men? What kind of weapons did I see? I tell them of guns and metal pots and pans for cooking. I tell them of the white clothing on the Indian people and even how the white men have places to sleep in the village. I tell them of two white men style homes, one for the preacher and one for Dark Cloud, and the large building that's used as a church, school, and council meeting place with chairs and tables. I talk of more building that's planned and how I understand it's to be for a large school.

They hear about Reverend Wilder and his wife, Miss Rebecca, and their plans for a mission school as well as the farming and weaving projects. I remember that they spoke of money from the Government of the United States and from the American Mission Board. "I believe that Reverend Wilder and Miss Rebecca are filled with good intentions." I tell them. "They seemed at all times to have nothing but good thoughts for The Real People who they help and teach. But they are the only white people I saw there that I can say that about. I have fear for the Wilders for they seemed to be in as much danger as I was."

I tell them of the French that I heard spoken and how I understood the Indians better than some of the whites when they spoke. I tell them how it seemed that both languages fit in the village, and it seemed to be only me who couldn't speak the French white words.

Finally, War Woman addresses me. "One Who Is Always Alone spoke with you and the choice you had to return to Virginia." It's a statement, not a question with an odd accent on the English word.

I nod my head yes. "One Who Is Always Alone told me of this offer," I say. "But I am eager to get to know more of this powerful woman that's called Bear who I now am. I choose to stay here in Great Elk's village in The Maple Forest."

"It is possible that your presence can bring trouble to this village," she says, and I feel my heart begin to pound loudly in my chest and in my ears. This is what Dark Cloud had said as well. Will they make me leave now that I've chosen to stay? I glance at the faces around the circle and look longer at the new face of Deer than any of the others. I think, why has he not been spoken of before? Has he brought news that I'm the only one who does not know? He looks back at me with an Indian face; it tells me nothing.

War Woman and I look at each other across the council fire. *Are you white?* I hear her ask me. I choose my words careful like and speak with great respect, "It would seem you speak only of my skin color because I have made my best effort to be a powerful woman of The Real People in every way but that," I begin, stopping for a bit to let my words sink in. I try to calm my pounding heart by remembering her kind words so many months ago. *I watch you because I try to see how you are coping with the blood on your hands. It is not an easy thing to become accustomed to.*

No one speaks. I swallow and continue. "But there have been others in this village who I will not speak of who have had the right skin color and yet seem to have brought more trouble and sorrow than I can even think of.

"I was taken from my home in Virginia by force. Over this past year, I have struggled with who I am and where is home. I look at my skin and I think, "Am I red? Am I white? Is one right? Is one wrong? At one time in my life I would have called you all red savages." I look at each of the serious faces watching and listening to me speak here at the council fire. I remember wanting to have wise enough words so that others would want to hear them. I swallow with worry. When does a body know when that time has come? I for sure don't. But I will tell them the truth of the thoughts in my head and let them decide for themselves. "That was all that my head knew about skin color: black was slave, red was savage and white was everything else." I shake my head. "It was not much to know, that is for sure."

I sit up straight. Proud. Tall. "But I am older, now. And wiser. And more powerful because of it. I know that the color of my skin has nothing to do with whether I am a slave or a savage or anything else. It has everything to do with what is inside my head and my heart. It has everything to do with what I choose to make my center."

I look at War Woman. "You told me once that life has always pulled you forward faster than you felt ready for." She does not nod, but she blinks. "It seems that will be the way for me, too. This past year has not been easy, but I am better for it. And that is why I wish to stay here in The Maple Forest. I would see what else this place can teach me and help me to become.

"One Who Is Always Alone has shared with me the dangers this village faces in having me live here with you. Even Dark Cloud spoke of it to me. But tell me this: should I leave, will this village cease to face dangers? Who is to say that as the white man comes further west – and we all must believe that he will – that I will not be a help to this village; a woman who has lived in both worlds?" I've a flash of Rebecca Wilder and realize that I, too, love these people now and want them to succeed, just like she and her husband do. *They are my people now, and I want to be theirs.*

I put my hands out in front of me, palms up, where they are the whitest even with my summer brown skin. *Let them look and see,* I think, *one last time and let this all be over – who is white and who is red.* "Is this all you see of me?" I ask quiet like. "I have learned that there is so much more to a person than just what your eyes can see." My gut clenches with the need for them to understand this as I do now. *"I am so much more, you know,"* I say to them with pleading eyes.

I glance at Bright Feather sitting silent and still. The look he sends gives me strength to finish. I clench both my hands into fists and rest them in my lap. "There are dangers at all times in life! Let me tell you the story of my life so far to prove my point! I have learned that life is filled with choices, some of them very hard to make. I have made the choice to stay here. I am ready to become a part of this village and all that that means."

I stop and am quiet for a moment. I look at Great Elk, War Woman, One Who Knows, Raccoon, and Beaver. I make my eyes meet each one of the people that sit around the circle. "But should this village wish for me to leave because they feel that it is a better choice for all, then I will go, for I want only what's best for this place I now call home." I take a breath to calm my stomach, head, and heart, and look down at the hands in my lap that I'm now holding tightly together. "Thank you for listening to my words," I say quiet like, full of worry that I've said too much. Or not enough. "I have finished speaking."

Bright Feather reaches out and places his hand on my tightly clasped ones, warm and strong. It's a motion that stuns even me for it's not his way to even speak, much less to show how he feels with a touch in front of all. I look up at him in surprise, but he's looking at those around the council fire. "And should you ask her to leave, I will go with her," he says, quietly but firmly to all.

I catch Raccoon's look of wonderment that says, *Otter was right again.*

I feel a warmth seep from mine and Bright Feather's hands right through my body to my heart. *Pay attention to all of us wise and powerful women!* my look says back to Raccoon when he glances my way. I take another deep breath and get ready to hear what else will be said this day.

There's much silence around the council circle as everyone chews on the words I've said, sprinkled at the last with Bright Feather's surprise. Finally, Great Elk speaks to me. "You are well spoken, Bear. For one that struggled so long to learn our language it is obvious that you no longer have trouble."

I look at Raccoon who has made a small sound in his throat but has an innocent look on his face as he meets my glance. "It is surprising that you speak of the white man coming further west," Great Elk continues in his deep, smooth voice. "Deer has only arrived this morning and is here to tell us more of what he has learned about the white man's plans regarding where he wants to put his foot next. It would seem that there is talk of still another treaty and another attempt to gain more land from us. He feels that very soon we will be asked to attend a great council to discuss this. Speak to us Deer and tell us what you know."

Deer addresses the council circle in serious tones. "I hear many things at the trading post when I walk in my white life as William Holland Thomas. Some things I know to ignore for I consider the source, and some I know to follow through on. I am most fortunate to have some powerful friends in the white world some through the accident of my birth and others through the course of my schooling in the law. Some share my passion for The Real People," here he shrugs, "and some do not. But it is always wise to know what your enemy is thinking as well as your friend. I am known throughout the area as one who sides regularly with what is in the best interests of The Real People."

White life? School of Law? Accidents of birth? My head whirls with all that's being said while Deer, or *William Holland Thomas*, continues to speak to us. Oh, the questions I want to ask!

"I speak to you today as a full a son of War Woman's hearth, of the Wolf Clan, of The Maple Forest of The Real People. Brother to a precious few," he looks around the circle and makes eye contact with Beaver, Bright Feather, and Otter, "and your chosen eyes, ears and mouth in the white world. I will remind all of you of things as they were and as they are, for there are some who do not know and some who may need to be reminded. It is always important not to forget the good as well as the bad. That keeps us wiser.

"The last treaty between the government of the United States of America and The Nation of The Real People was one that gave more than half of the tribal lands to the whites in exchange for money and other lands across the Mississippi River."

Deer draws a circle in the dirt. "If we were to divide all of The Real People into three equal pieces," he cuts the circle into three big pieces of pie, "one piece would be to the west of the Mississippi and two pieces would still remain in the east on the small piece of land that the United States Government allows us to call our own. As you know, a delegation of representatives from The Nation of The Real People traveled out west of the Mississippi River at the time that this treaty was being considered and selected lands they agreed to accept in trade for what they planned to give up here. Many promises were made by the United States Government to help make the move and the trade favorable and profitable for The Real People."

I look around the council fire at those sitting listening to Deer talk, and they wear the same sad face that Deer wears. "We now know that many of these promises have not been faithfully kept."

Deer looks right at me when he says, "This 'Nation of The Real People' that the United States Government deals with and talks to is different from what you know here in The Maple Forest, Bear. When I speak of 'The Nation of The Real People', you must understand that I am not speaking of people in The Maple Forest."

I frown my confusion and work powerful hard to keep my questions to myself. In the council circle it's not proper to interrupt speakers until they are finished. "Those who support The Nation of The Real People argue strongly that the only way to survive the encroachment of the whites is to adopt their white ways. But in an effort to gain recognition by the United States government, the ways they have adopted are greatly contrary to the way things have always been, our *Old Ways*. It is as if they wish for The Nation of The Real People to be like the white world in every way but skin color."

Deer looks at War Woman and One Who Knows and then back to me. "In The Nation of The Real People, the advice of powerful and wise women such as War Woman and One Who Knows is no longer welcomed in important decisions nor is their counsel sought or listened to. They are no longer allowed to express opinions nor are they allowed to help choose the men who go to the treaty councils to represent them."

He looks at the entire council group and gestures wide with his arms, "This council circle here in The Maple Forest no longer holds power in The Nation of The Real People as it once did. They no longer wish to hear our words of advice or caution. They wish our children to be schooled in the ways of white children: they wish us to worship their God and to learn their language. They wish to encourage all men to become farmers, not hunters, for farmers need less land than hunters do. The government of The Nation of The Real People accepts and welcomes these changes while here in The Maple Forest we do not."

Deer looks at me again. "Bear has seen this in Dark Cloud's village. She has just spoken of it. Many of these 'new' ways have been a fact for so long that youth do not even know there has been a change or another way.

"In this last treaty I spoke of, The Nation of The Real People conducted a census – a count – of all of their people. The Government of the United States needed to know our numbers, they needed to know how many of us wished to go across the Mississippi and how many of us wished to stay.

"Besides the many promises and land trades they offered, the Government of the United States offered all The Real People who were displaced by the changing boundaries an amazing thing: *citizenship*. They said to you, 'If you are not happy with these promises and land trades, then we will offer you something else instead. We will give all of you the chance to become citizens of the United States of America. Should you do this, you would no longer be a part of The Nation of The Real People; you would be a part of the United States of America. And you would be entitled to all the rights and privileges that go with that title. Any new citizens were promised land, each household – six hundred and forty acres!'"

Deer shook his head. "When I first heard of this offer, I did not believe it. It could not be possible. I insisted that the person who told me of this show me proof, and he did. I saw the treaty and read the words that made these promises to all of you. I spent much time thinking and asked many people their opinions – those I considered my friends and those I considered my enemies."

Suddenly, Deer looks older, more tired. He sighs and says quietly, "In the end, I encouraged you to accept the offer of citizenship. Weapons and might no longer will win this fight, so I wanted us to put a wall of words around us as protection. I know that there were many of you in this village who were unsure of this advice. 'How could separating ourselves from our own people make us safer?' you asked me. But in the end you trusted me and my words. I am greatly honored that you thought about and then listened to my suggestions." Deer takes the time to look at every person sitting around the circle and nod respectfully to each of them.

With a bitter laugh, Deer asks, "Who could believe that leaving The Nation of The Real People and becoming citizens of the United States of America would allow you more of a chance to continue your Old Ways than had you stayed? But it is so. Sitting here in The Maple Forest and hearing about the way things are in Dark Cloud's village in New Echota is proof."

Leaning forward, his face fierce, Deer says, "You chose to accept the citizenship offered to you by the United States Government in an effort to keep your heritage, your land and your Old Ways. You did not take the white man's money, possessions, and promises. You understood what was the most precious thing."

I can't believe what I'm hearing! I look around at the faces sitting silent and unhappy around the council circle, and my head says with amazement, *You are all citizens of the United States?! Just like me and Pa, Henry, and Eli?!* And then I have another thought. *You left your own nation so that you could keep living the way you felt was true and right.* I hear Beaver saying to me, *"It is a struggle that The Real People have been fighting with for many more years than you have."* And then I look at Beaver and the look on his face has nothing to do with sorrow. He looks angry. Angry enough to kill.

"The Maple Forest," Deer continues speaking to this silent group all wrapped in sorrow and bright bits of anger as well, "where you have always lived and where our ancestors who have gone before us still walk, is on land that is now part of the state of North Carolina."

He laughs another bitter laugh and shakes his head, looking down for a moment at the ground and then back up at the group. *Does he look ashamed?* I puzzle. "The United States made the offer of six hundred and forty acres and citizenship in the treaty, and you accepted it. It was only later, after the treaty was signed, and after all agreements were made, that the *State of North Carolina* told the United States government that there was no land to give you, whether there was a treaty or not, whether you were a citizen or not, and whether you were homeless or not.

"This land that we sit on, that you made such hard, hard choices to keep, had already been put up for sale to be bought by white settlers. There was no land in North Carolina free for the giving, not *six hundred and forty acres* for each family, not even *one tree*."

As I look around the circle, I see many different feelings on the faces. I see no surprise on Great Elk's and War Woman's faces and I think, *They know this already.* I look at the dark look One Who Knows shows, and I know it's not a surprise for her either. But Beaver's face shows an expression of such anger, such *fury* that for a moment I can only stare and watch the emotion grow as Deer keeps on speaking. "It was in this last treaty, the Treaty of 1819, you also appointed me your agent. You officially told everyone that I was your spokesperson in the white world. I have been doing *much talking.* I have talked with the Government of the United States in Washington, and I have talked with the Government of the State of

North Carolina. I have talked loudly and fiercely and at great length. I will not be stopped. I will not be made silent. I will not surrender this fight of paper words and broken promises.

"I have used my family money and profits from my trading post, and I have been buying land as it becomes available for sale. I have finally secured an agreement with both governments, that the Treaty of 1819 is *binding*. That means that they cannot go back and change what has been said and written. *They must honor it.* It has been agreed that the land offered to you, your 640 acres, was *fair*. North Carolina, admits its mistake in not having land to give you and has offered to give you money instead." Deer sighs. "I have accepted on your behalf the offer of this money in lieu of land. I have received several large payments towards this debt North Carolina owes you."

Deer looks at Beaver, and I know that he has seen the anger that's pouring off him like a raging fire. "Beaver, you wish to speak?"

Beaver struggles to keep his voice calm as he speaks to Deer, "What good is white money?! What good are these Treaties?! What good is this *citizenship?!*" he spits the word out of his mouth just like I remember Bright Feather saying the word *liquor*. "What has it brought us but separation from our brothers and sisters and a hatred from all people both red and white?"

Beaver looks at Great Elk and War Woman, his voice strained. "You said you trusted Deer! You said you believed this was the way to choose; to go against all that we have ever stood for and side with the *whites* against our own people! Do you still believe that we have made a better choice? Do you still believe we should sit here quietly and wait for the white settlers who *purchased our land with their white money* to move in and tell us to get off their white property? Do you think that severing ties with our nation and our people has given us a strength now when we find that there is *still no land for us?*"

Beaver looks around at all those sitting at the council fire wearing faces that show no thoughts, giving nothing of their inside feelings away. "Our brothers and sisters still at least have land to call their own! I cannot believe that the whites will *ever* treat us fairly, that we will *ever* be given the respect that we deserve. There is no harmony in these choices! I believe we need to return to our people and stand firm beside them in this *fight*." The word "fight" is thrown down into the council circle, just like Beaver has taught me to throw my knife. Beaver looks at Deer, and through teeth gritted in anger says, "I have finished speaking."

Deer waits in the silence of the circle for a time. He seems to me to be gathering his thoughts and carefully arranging his words so that each one that's spoken is perfect. He looks at the group and says at last, slowly and softly, "After these many seasons, *over seven summers*, I still think you have made the right choice. When I step into this village, I see the Old Ways everywhere I look. I sit within this circle and am honored to accept the wise counsel of *all* elders in this village. I am pleased to feel harmony and balance with all those that walk in this center of the world."

Deer looks at Beaver, still steaming his fury. "While I know that there are some at this council circle who are not happy with the advice and the choices that have been given, I must tell you that the part of The Real People who live west of the Mississippi are in a sorrowful condition. I tell you these things so that you can understand that your choices, as hard as they may have been, were the right ones." He runs his hand through his hair, a very white movement I think, and looks at each one of us in the circle, including me. "The Real People west of the Mississippi live on lands that are part of the Territory of Arkansas. Even that far away, they fight with the whites for the land that they were promised and battle with the other Indian tribes that were there before them. They are suffering great degradation and misery and have already sought relief from the Government of the United States. They request money, better lands, protection, and the fulfillment of promises made but never kept."

I feel the sorrow travel around the circle even as I ponder the fact that these *savages* as Miss Rebecca and Reverend Wilder called them *are citizens of the United States of America* just as I am! But looking at the faces around the council circle and listening to Deer and Beaver's words, I know there is little comfort in that.

"As for those of The Nation of The Real People here east of the Mississippi," Deer says, "I do not like the talk I hear at the trading post and beyond. I fear for the safety and security of the two parts that remain. I fear that the land they claim to be theirs will be something the whites will want. I believe that soon The Nation of The Real People will be approached once again with another treaty and more promises in exchange for the land they still claim as theirs. This is the land south of here, at Dark Cloud's village and beyond, in New Echota, in the white state known as Georgia.

"I have come here to you, having traveled many miles, having spoken many words, and having spent much time trying to stay ahead of what is coming this way to The Maple Forest. I will not betray your trust.

You must be prepared. You must be informed. Hard times are coming for The Nation and for The Maple Forest. I cannot stop it, but I will be here right alongside you as we *deal with this together.*" Bowing his head, Deer says, "I have finished speaking."

"I cannot believe that even Dark Cloud would settle for less land again," Great Elk says with great certainty. Many others around the circle nod in agreement.

Deer looks powerful sad when he says, "Then the United States Government may use force to help him make the choice that the Government wants."

"What are you saying?" Beaver says, the anger in him sparking and crackling now like a log exploding on the fire.

"I am saying," Deer says slowly and carefully, "that there has been little bloodshed over these past years because an agreement has always been reached between the United States and The Nation of The Real People. But should an agreement prove impossible this time, it does not mean that the Government of the United States would not use force. I do not for one moment believe that the Government of the United States will accept 'no' as an answer from The Nation of The Real People."

"And we would just sit here while this happens?" Beaver shouts to Great Elk. "You would allow soldiers to come in and remove our people by force and you would not step forward to help?!"

With a tired voice, Great Elk says to Beaver, "The Nation of The Real People separated from *us,* long before we made the choice to accept citizenship with The United States. These choices we made here in this village were not ones that we made over night quickly just to keep our land. We sought to save our *entire way of life:* the Old Ways that continue to honor our ancestors and those spirits that have gone before us."

Great Elk uses the same quiet voice he always uses no matter the feeling surrounding him. But he holds out his hand to Beaver, reaching out it seems to calm him. "My son, when a village is viciously attacked by an enemy, you seek to gather those closest and dearest to you and try to save a *small few.* It is only a fool who thinks he can save a whole village all by himself."

I think of Bear John the morning he came to our village and how I only had care to save just one small baby I called Owl.

Beaver stands no less angry and no more calmed by Great Elk's words. "It is thoughts like that, I believe, that have divided our people. You are right to say that only a fool thinks he can save a whole village all by himself, but it is also a fool who puts himself in the position to be *alone* rather than in a trusted group. I will gather my things and return to The Nation of The Real People. I will not be a fool who is alone, but a warrior who is with my brothers." In the silence of night, I hear the noise of the crackling fire, the breeze blowing the leaves above our head, and the footsteps of Beaver walking away from The Council Circle.

No one speaks for a time. I think of the important things I know are at Beaver's center. I remember his serious ways and how much I learned about The Real People because of all of the wonderful stories he shared with me. Much of the peace I carry in the center of who I am and what I've become and where I plan to go is thanks to Beaver and his wise words.

I wish I could give him some words of peace or calm back, but I'm at a loss.

Deer says at last, "I respect Beaver's opinion. I too have great fear for The Real People of The Maple Forest, for I know that our walls of safety are not as strong as I would like them to be. The United States Government cannot be trusted to deal fairly when the prize is the land they want so desperately. It will lie, it will cheat, and, finally I'm afraid, it will steal.

"But I still believe that The Real People's only way to be victorious in this battle is to fight and *win* with the white weapons of words and laws. I cannot agree with Beaver. Our chance of victory through might and warfare is long, long gone. I have been buying up land with my profits from the trading post as I said, and I have been using the money I have received in the capacity as your agent to purchase even more land. This land we sit on I have already purchased; it is *in my name* and is already owned *by us*. Every chance I get, every penny I receive, I buy more precious land. Each family head within this village, because he has not received the promised allotment of six hundred and forty acres of land is receiving money instead. All the money that I receive, I immediately use to purchase more land in my name for this village. We will fight this fight quietly and carefully and win in the end with the weapons the United States Government has given us. While we cannot ever claim land with confidence that we have been promised in *any* treaty, we *can* claim land that we have purchased outright, legal and proper, with *real white money.*"

Great Elk nods in agreement as does War Woman and a number of people sitting around the council fire. War Woman finally says, "We have worked in this village to remain separate from the white world even though we are now legally a part of it. We have worked in this village to remain separate from The Nation of The Real People even though we will always be linked with it through our heritage and our history. We must do a careful dance between both of these worlds and watch over the careful barrier of words that Deer has put around us to always see what is coming towards us, be it with red or white skin."

Deer smiles a smile that's more fierce than friendly. "What I hear makes me have concerns and urges me to ready all those white weapons we have to protect us. Only this time I fear that both The Nation of The Real People and The Government of the United States will have to be carefully watched." He looks at each face within the circle. "I owe you my life." He touches his chest with a closed fist. "The person I am is because of you. *I will not forsake you even from my grave. I will make sure that you are taken care of.* You are my people and my family. Again, I am finished speaking."

Great Elk looks at the council circle. "Your words are not a surprise to many of us, Deer. And I have long been aware of Beaver's opinions of the choices we have made as a village. It is right that children listen and learn and develop their own beliefs and opinions. He knows that whether he lives in this village or elsewhere he is always a son of this hearth, and we are always happy to welcome him. Maybe it is good for him to go and see what Bear has seen." He looks at me for a moment. "Sometimes words cannot do justice to what our eyes must see and our heart must experience.

"We do not need to be One Who Knows to understand the way of things with the white people and their constant desire to have more and more land. What is more distressing to many of us is this division within The Real People that could not be avoided. I feared the response that we have seen with Beaver. Those that are young still believe things can be solved with might and weapons while those of us with gray hair know they cannot."

He turns to Deer, "You are a treasured friend and son of this hearth, and your concern for us is a weapon that the whites cannot match. We will take your words to heart and look forward to more words that you can send our way or bring us yourself."

Great Elk looks at War Woman who nods her head ever so slightly. War Woman looks at me. I sit up straight and realize that me and my white skin have not been forgotten. She begins to speak. "Although you are young, you are clever with your mind and with your words, Bear," she says. "You watch and listen and learn. You are quick to see the way of things."

With her head, War Woman motions to One Who Knows and I look at her. Her dark eyes stare out at me from her dried apple face. I remember my time in her hut and how I was Mouse, always scurrying to do my chores hoping no one would notice me. While I'm still looking and lost in memories, War Woman says, "One Who Knows feels strongly that you bring brightness to this village rather than dark." I look at War Woman in surprise and shock. *One Who Knows thinks good things of me?* I shake my head. Surely I must not have heard correctly. When I look at her she gives me a look I've seen many times before: it's impatience at my stupidness.

War Woman's words draw me back, "It would seem, Bear, since you *are* a member of this village and you *are* one of only a few able to speak both the white man's and our language, that you are indeed very important to us. We of The Maple Forest would be foolish to think that we would be better off without you here. And when the time comes to go and talk with the white men and our brothers and sisters in The Nation of The Real People about a new treaty," here War Woman stops and looks at all those sitting around the council circle, "and we all know that time will come soon," her stare finally rests on me, "you will be one who will go as a voice of The Real People of The Maple Forest."

I feel a flush of pure joy rip through my body. It heats my face and neck and arms and body. *I'm truly a part of this place,* my heart sings. *I've known it for a time now, but they seem to know it, too!* I look at this collection of people sitting and looking at me, and I'm speechless with the wonder of what is being said.

Then my heart begins to jump and pound as what they are telling me sinks into my slow head. They wish me to speak for them?! They trust me to do such a thing?! *I can't!* my terrified head says in a scream, *I'm just a* . . .

And then I stop myself from saying what my head is going to say. I push any of those 'I can't' thoughts out of my center and make Bear sit up straight and tall in the council circle. *I'm Bear,* I force myself to think, *of The Real People of The Maple Forest. I'll do what needs to be done. And do it well.* I look up into the unsmiling, wrinkled face of One Who Knows, who now has the same satisfied face that she did that night I stared down Weasel and his friends.

Great Elk turns to Bright Feather, "And it will also seem, One Who Is Always Alone, that since you are inclined to go with her – even were she to be put out of this village," he pauses and waits for Bright Feather to nod that that's so, "then you will not be alone so much anymore." I catch a brief movement from Deer; he winks across the circle to Bright Feather. Or was it to me?

Later that night, Bright Feather and I lie close in our hut, and I ask some of my many questions. I struggle with what to ask first.

I learn right off that he thinks little of the citizenship. "Deer felt it was the right choice, and we trusted him in the end. We were having such a difficult time trying to maintain connections with Dark Cloud's village with all of the changes they were embracing and encouraging us to embrace as well. Dark Cloud eagerly accepted the money, gifts, and promises that the white man offered The Real People. He willingly moved his entire village within the new boundaries drawn in that last treaty and assumed a position of power within the leadership of the Nation of The Real People that was recognized in the white world as well. We talked among ourselves and realized that to align ourselves with Dark Cloud was not any more appealing than aligning ourselves with the white man's government.

"It was One Who Knows again who agreed with Deer and spoke out to follow his advice." He shrugs his shoulders. "She said there was no choice really, and she was right. We chose to keep the land of our ancestors where their spirits still walk and where we can still practice the Old Way that we know brings harmony and peace. The offer of money, white man's things, and different land to live on did not interest us. In the end, we became separate from both worlds by our choice. We are the better for it."

After a moment's pause, he adds, "I hope that Beaver will find a peace," and I feel his sorrow.

The topic of Deer takes much longer to explain. Deer has not been to Great Elk's village in many seasons, but that does not mean that some in the village do not see him regular, I come to find out, including Bright Feather. "We all know that things are very serious if Deer left his family and the trading post to come out here to speak with us.

"Why was he never spoken of?" I finally ask.

Bright Feather looks at me in the darkness of our hut. "I am sure he was. You just never thought of a white man's face when you heard his Indian name spoken." He touches the white skin on my neck below my ear with a gentle finger.

"How did he go from being *William Holland Thomas* to Deer?"

He grunts. "The better question is how did he go from being Deer to *William Holland Thomas*. He was found in the woods by a hunting party from the village many years ago when he was just a boy. Back then there were fewer whites and more land claimed by The Real People. Yet it was still impossible for them to bring the boy back to his people. What white man would believe that no harm had been meant? He was a pitiful, scrawny, frightened white boy, found terrified and lost in the woods. Because we spoke different words, he could offer no information to the puzzle of who he was and how he came to be where they found him. The village welcomed him, and he became a son of War Woman's hearth. Yet even after he became able to speak and understand our language, he was never able to remember what brought him to be in the forest alone and so full of fear. He could not even remember who he was were he to go back to the white world." Bright Feather's silent for a time, lost in thought I suspect, fiddling with my hair and touching me here and there.

"He had flashes of memory," Bright Feather explains, speaking softly against the top of my head, and I can hear his voice rumble quiet like in his chest. "He described it to me once like keeping your eyes tightly shut all the time and then, very briefly opening them up quickly to take just a peek of what might be there to see." He sighs. "But there are no memories of anything that will answer the questions he always wonders most about. He became known as Deer for he was a swift runner, and just like the white tail deer that can give brief flashes of whiteness now and then, so does he. He is a member of The Real People of The Maple Forest through and through. He, Raccoon, and I grew up together, best of friends, inseparable.

"But as Deer grew older, the curiosity of who he was in the white world began to eat at him. Who was his white family? Where were they? Was there a need for revenge? Were the answers to these many questions only to be found in the white people's towns? Would there be family or people that knew him? I think," Bright Feather says in the quiet darkness of our hut, "that even though his mind could not remember what truly happened in the forest and before, his spirit could and that was why he could not find peace.

"The village encouraged him to search for answers recognizing the need for him to balance both sides of who he was. So he was taken back to where he had been found in the woods, and Raccoon and I traveled with him as far as The Real People's territorial land to the east. There were still those in The Maple Forest who remembered the old territorial hunting grounds and were able to give guidance as to what direction he should head once Deer was on his own." Bright Feather sighs. "I missed him so once he was gone.

"He was gone for almost a season, and we had great concern for him," Bright Feather says. "I, being young and foolish and quite full of myself, wanted to cross territorial lines and go looking for him, but even Raccoon would not support me much as I tried to convince him. At last, late one summer evening he rode into camp on his Indian pony dressed in white man's clothes. 'Have I missed the Green Corn Celebration?' he asked like nothing was different and no time had passed."

Bright Feather grunts at the memory. "We sat around the council circle fire that first night he was back, Raccoon wearing Deer's white man's pants, me wearing his white man's shirt, Otter wearing his fancy hat and even Beaver stumbling around in his white man's shoes while Deer sat there in his breechcloth looking much more like we remembered him."

Turning on his side to look at me, he fingers my robin's feather. "He was never able to find out about the death of his parents or how he came to be alone and lost in the woods, but he did discover who he was in the white world: William Holland Thomas. The last information his white family had had of him, according to the slaves his family kept, was that his father, a prosperous farmer and landowner, had traveled to seek out some business interests and had taken William and his mother along on the trip. A sister of his mother welcomed him back with great enthusiasm. Even more surprising, he discovered that there was family property he was entitled to and quite a bit of family money that was due him. In the white world, it seems, he was quite a wealthy man.

"But he returned to his true family, The Real People of The Maple Forest, to seek their guidance," Bright Feather says, his voice filled with approval. "He was still filled with indecision. Should he stay in the white world or the red? The sister of his mother offered him the opportunity for some white schooling. Should he accept and live with them and learn their ways?" Bright Feather says with real sympathy, "After spending time in the white world, he seemed almost more eaten up with the way of things when he returned to us than before he had left.

"It was One Who Knows who stepped forward and told him what to do. I remember that night as she stood there and told him that he was forever destined to be a person with two spirits that would never be at peace with each other. 'You are Deer to us and always will be. You know him as well as do we. But you must go home to your white family now and become *William Holland Thomas*, for you will always be that, too, and you need to know him better.'"

"I know some of what he struggled with," I say quietly after a time. "That wondering of the choosing." I hold up one hand in the dark, "Should I chose this?" and I lift my other hand, "Or this? Which is the way to go? Which is the way to leave?"

"But you were able to weave your two selves together," Bright Feather points out. "Like a twisted piece of rope, you bound them tightly together and became stronger because of it. Deer could never seem to do that. He has always been two pieces that cannot be joined together."

"Maybe because he couldn't remember."

Bright Feather nods. "Yes, I believe that to be so. He was always more haunted with what he did not know, than what he did." He cups my face and says, "Your strength is in your remembering and in your ability to take the best of both lives and use them to be the powerful woman you now are." He kisses me once, twice, three times in the dark.

He lays back down on his back pulling me beside him, and I feel him shrug. "So Deer listened to One Who Knows. He put on his pants and his shoes and his shirt and his hat, and he left the next morning to find *William Holland Thomas*. He visited us regularly and often, but he never lived with us again." In the silence of the hut, I hear Bright Feather's breathing grow slow and steady, and I know he's falling asleep. Questions are still crashing around in my head like the children outside playing at first light. I'm not tired at all. Not one bit.

"Do you know," I say in the silence of the night as I lay snuggled against his side with my head on his shoulder, "that there are some in the village who would like to call me 'Never Stops Asking Questions?'"

I listen to his breathing, and it does not change, not one bit but at last he says, "Besides being a powerful woman, I was warned by a number of others that that was so."

"You told me that you never go east into Virginia and white territory. If he hasn't been here to this village in so long, how is it that you see him at times?"

He begins to trace slow lazy circles along the plane of my face as he speaks. "Just like Great Elk recognizes your value to the village in your ability to fit in both worlds, the whites recognized his value as a white man who can speak with The Real People and travel between the two worlds. On more than one occasion he has been asked to interpret council sessions between The Real People and the white settlers. Over the years he has become a prosperous trader on property near the red and white border on his family's original land which the whites call *North Carolina*. He is faithful and fair to all Indians who deal with him. It is to Deer that almost all those of Great Elk's village – and many other villages of The Real People - go whenever there are furs to trade or goods to be bought - me included. His is the only place I go to to trade my furs and get supplies. I trust no other and deal with no other." It turns out that Bright Feather and Deer have contact at least once each season.

His hand continues to caress my face and then begins to trace the outline of my lips and the lines of my eyes and angle of my jaw and the bend of my ear. I struggle in my head to recall the wide awake questions that only moments ago were running wild in my head, but they have all of a sudden slipped far, far away. He gently eases my head down on the pallet and raises himself on his arm to look down at me, his hand still making their lazy travels. It's pitch black now in the hut, and I can't see anything, despite the fact that I feel like every single piece of me is straining to pay attention. I feel and smell and hear him bend down over me, and his hair tickles my bare shoulder and pools at my neck. I feel his lips brush against my forehead, not in a kiss so much as just in a feel, and I hear him breathe deep the smell of me. His hand moves down and rests firm and sure in the curve of my waist and the heat of it is almost – but not quite – enough to distract me from his mouth that has felt its way down the bridge of my nose to stop just above my lips, untouching. Every single piece of me is aware of him hovering like a hawk silent above me in the dark, watching and waiting. I barely breathe; waiting, waiting…

"Your questions are wonderful to me," he says oh so quiet, and I feel the heat from the breath of his speaking, "because they come from this mouth of yours that is *so sweet* to taste." At last I stop asking questions.

Deer joins us at Otter and Raccoon's hut the following evening for dinner, and I listen to many stories as they talk and reminisce far into the night. I begin to draw a picture in my head of what Bright Feather was before he was One Who Was Alone, when he was known as Hawk.

"He was always the most serious," Deer moans with Raccoon nodding in pained agreement. "Always the voice of common sense. Always concentrating on the hunt or the trapping or the faster way to ride or the quicker way to shoot or the more accurate way to shoot. The first to hunt all night alone, the first to make a kill, " Deer looks at me with great seriousness as he holds out his hand, keeping count of all the firsts, "the first to master trapping, the first to own a horse. He was never any fun at all." Raccoon nods again.

Bright Feather listens to most of the stories and comments as I expect him to; in silence. But he has a casual air about him as he leans back against a tree with me sitting close by listening. Maybe not casual, maybe peaceful is a better word - and content.

After a time, I have to finally ask the question and no one seems particularly surprised when I do. "Have you heard of me? Of my family that lives in Virginia? If you have a trading post then you must surely see people from all over. It has been said that there is talk of a missing white girl from Virginia … named Elle … ?"

I find there are times as Deer talks to us, and in particular to me, that I realize he puts on his white face that speaks sometimes when his mouth is quiet. But at other times, as now, he puts on his Indian face; the one that doesn't talk at all. "I have heard word at my place of the search for a white girl who was taken captive some time ago. But you are not the only captive, Bear, so this is not necessarily about you."

I study him for a bit looking close at his face and think, *Why has he put his Indian face on if he has nothing to hide?* Surely the search for a white girl – whichever girl they're searching for - will be careful to give details so to tell each captive white girl from the next – if there are so many of us. Then I realize, if there were details about me specific like, there were probably details about my Pa and Eli, too. Pieces of another puzzle slip into place, and I know all of a sudden that he knows things of Pa and Eli. I know this even though when I stare into his eyes I see only blueness like the skies. I think of Weasel and what he told me in the forest outside of Dark Cloud's village. I remember his eyes as he spoke to me close to my face with such great anger, and I remember I saw no sign of lying. I swallow for I know all of a sudden that what I must hear is what I wished never to hear.

I look at him serious with *my* Indian face and I say, "I will have you tell me what you know. I will hear the truth of the way things are. I wish to hear *all* the words you have in your head, not just the ones you think are those that I can swallow easy."

Raccoon snorts loudly. "Watch and learn quickly, Deer. The most powerful asset we may have in this village is that little *girl* sitting across from you who has got a mind sharper and quicker than a rattlesnake's bite."

Deer begins to speak and my mind struggles to keep up as my heart gallops in my chest. "In the late spring of last year, word was sent out around the surrounding territory, in particular to trading posts like mine in Forest City that have a great deal to do with the Indian trade. The words spoke about a white girl who had been taken captive in the early spring and who answered to the name *Elle*."

I sit and wait in the silence that wraps around us just like the darkness of the night. I know there's more. Besides my white name, there had to be other things the "words" spoke of. I finally lift my tired green eyes up to meet his unblinking blue ones and let them talk to him, for all of a sudden I'm far too tired to speak with my mouth. *And???*, my eyes say to him, *what else must you tell me that my ears must hear?*

Deer sighs deeply and finally says, "The actual description, if I recall it properly, was," here he speaks in white words that sound hard and rough to my pink ears, "'*Orphaned white girl whose mother has died and father and brothers have been murdered by marauding Indians, who answers to the name of Elle.*'"

The only sounds around us are the sounds of the night forest and the crackling of the fire before us. No one speaks. At first I feel the ache grow and the tears burn behind my eyes and I think, *Hurry hate, get busy with those tears!* But who is there to hate now? Weasel is dead and so are the other two braves who took me that night, Bright Feather and Raccoon have seen to that. Whatever one killed my Pa and Eli and … Henry, is gone now.

I stare at the fire, and I remember Pa looking so terrible tired sitting by the fire; I understand all of a sudden that the look was *powerful sadness* over the passing of Ma not tiredness at all. I see Henry working so hard in the barn that his face is flushed beet red and the sweat is dripping off his nose, and all of a sudden I know, *that was tears*, not hard work. I feel Eli's dirty, sticky, sweaty hand in mine as we walk out to the field to bring Pa and Henry their lunch and all of a sudden I'm certain, *that was true love.*

I think sudden like, *What happened to Ma's Hope Chest?* and that's the silly thought that makes the tears spill down my cheeks. I make a deep, deep sigh; it seems to come all the way from the darkest bottom of myself, and I'm all of a sudden so powerful tired that I can't sit up any longer. At that very moment I feel Bright Feather stand, bend over, and scoop me up like I'm a tiny child rather than a powerful woman of The Real People. I bury my face in his neck and try to escape my sadness with the good smell of him. Sometimes, it seems that a powerful woman must yell her war cry *or* shed many a tear.

Bright Feather and I ride out very early the next morning in silence. He seems to know my need to be away from the village to think and to mourn proper, and then with a start I realize, *Of course, he's One Who Is Always Alone.* He knows all I feel and maybe a pile more. I think about his first mate and child and wish I could ask him questions, but the dead are never spoken of. Then I think about Pa and Henry and Eli and I'm brought up short. Can I no longer speak of them? I'll not like that.

"Why do the Indians not speak of their dead?" I ask as we crest the first hill and all signs of Great Elk's village slip away behind us.

"The Real People believe that the spirit world is the next place we go on this journey of life," Bright Feather explains. "It is a nearby place much like this one, and those who become spirits are much more powerful than those of us who are living persons. Spirits of the dead can return and have been seen in times of great good and in times of great bad. Their presence in this world can create great disharmony or great peace. It is believed that to mention the name of someone who has passed on to the spirit world calls them back here to this place. It can cause the spirit to become lost and confused to see the world he or she once knew rather than the new world where he or she now belongs. It is always best to allow those in the spirit world to make choices to return to us on their own rather than with our interference."

How many times have I mentioned Pa and Eli and Henry to those of the living? I think about my time since I've been here in Great Elk's village – and farther - and how many times I've heard Pa's voice in my head like he was standing right next to me. Each time it has happened it has brought me great comfort or good advice and never has it been bad. Has Pa been a spirit with me all this time as I continue my walk here in living? Have Henry and Eli also spoken to me quiet like with their remembrances I often have of them in my head? In my speaking their names have I caused them confusion or for them to become lost?

Bright Feather knows my thoughts. "Whether their names are mentioned or not, sometimes the spirits of those we love and care about choose to watch over us and follow us and guide us all the while we are here in this place of the living." I follow him through the beautiful green forests bursting with summer life wondering if I'll always fill this gaping hole of sadness. "They wait quiet and patient for us to join them in the spirit world so that the walk can be continued on together." He reins in Companion and waits until Willow and I ride up to be beside him, and he looks over at me. "Or sometimes they wait just long enough until they are certain that those of us left behind are safe and secure and headed on a path that they know to be right."

We sit side by side on our horses looking at the beautiful valley stretched out before us. As far as the eye can see are green tree covered hills. I think of what Miss Rebecca and Reverend Wilder have told me about God and prayer and living forever depending on the choices that are made about believing things or not. I tell Bright Feather about this Jesus and God and how they say He's so close that he can hear words that are in your head before you let them out of your mouth. "Miss Rebecca told me to always talk to God for He's always ready to listen and help. She called Him *personal*."

"What do you think of that?" Bright Feather asks, and I think again how much I like to talk to him.

I let my Hope Chest of memories open up and think on what I remember. "When I lived with Pa, we read from The Bible, a great big book that was filled with the wise words from this God. Ma's favorite verse she used to say to Henry and I when we were scared of something was, *'Thou preparest a table before me in the presence of mine enemies: thou anointest my head with oil; my cup runneth over. Surely goodness and mercy shall follow me all the days of my life: and I will dwell in the house of the Lord for ever.'*"

I smile at Bright Feather, "I remember Henry saying, 'Who'd want to eat dinner with an enemy, Ma? That sounds like powerful foolishness to me."

"What did your Ma say?" Bright Feather asked quiet and thoughtful.

"She said, 'Well, there can't be much fear in you if you can sit down and enjoy a meal with someone, now can there?' I liked the 'goodness and mercy' part following me all my days best." I laugh a little. "Henry used to say to me, even after Ma died, when we were scared of something, *'Shall we start cooking dinner, Elle?'* to make me laugh and stop me from being frightened. I wonder if it helped him, too…" I ride for a few moments in quiet and then finally say, "I'd forgotten that until now…."

We ride again in silence, deep in thought. Then I finally say, "I think maybe I like the idea of this Personal God always willing to listen and hear what we think and say. I like the idea of putting Him in my center where He will always be close."

Bright Feather looks at me with great seriousness, "Maybe I do too, then."

We ride for a long while in silence, taking in the sights and sounds and smells of the forest: chirping birds, rustling breezes, deep green ferns curling in the shade, and the rich scent of damp earth. At the top of a ridge we stop in a spot of the forest where I don't think I've ever come before. I realize that we have been riding most of the morning as I look at the sun. We are quite a distance from the village. *No matter how loud your thoughts are Elle girl, you should always be sure to listen and know about the things around you. That's called "survival,"* I hear Pa say in my head. *I'm still not so good at that one yet, Pa,* I think to myself.

"I have spoken often of my Pa since I have been away from him. And Eli and Henry, too. I hear his voice in my head, and I talk back to him, too. His words are always wise and good and kind," I tell Bright Feather and search his face for his thoughts, for I'm worried that I should no longer speak of Pa or mention him in the way of The Real People.

He's quiet for a long time, and we watch a hawk soar high above the trees down in the valley below swooping and diving in the warm air. He does not look at me, but stares straight ahead for a long time before he finally says, "I have a quiet voice that speaks to me in my head, too." He sighs and looks down at his hands holding Companion's reins. "It, too, speaks of good things. But sometimes," he makes a slight face, "it shouts at me to do things other than to live up to my name of One Who Is Always Alone." He looks at me then, searching my face and says at last, "It speaks a lot of you."

"Me?!" I say in puzzlement and great surprise. "What does the voice say about *me?*"

He reaches across and cups my cheek in his palm. His thumb strokes me soft and sweet. "It says to love you," he says, and he gives me a look of such great tenderness that it melts away large pieces of my grief and pain. "And so I do."

Two nights later there's a celebration in the village. I remember a time over a year ago when I was terrified of the whoops and screams and shouts of joy from the returning hunters and how I was just like a mouse scurrying around in the shadows trying hard to go unnoticed. Now it seems I'm right in the center of it, for the celebration is for our return and, more than a little bit, I suspect for the joining of me and Bright Feather and for the visit of Deer.

I'm given a new tunic to wear. It's of soft deerskin and decorated along the hem and the sleeves with the tails of an animal whose fur is so soft it feels like warm butter. I ask the name of the animal but can't recall ever having heard of it before when Otter tells me its Indian name. I try on the tunic and the tails swish against my bare arms and legs in a way that reminds me of Bright Feather's softest touches. Ten bear claws shiny and black are carefully sewn around the neck. Down the front in a "V" pattern to my waist and all around the hem are detailed stitches that as I look closely I see are a robin's tracks. "The tunic is from One Who Knows," Otter tells me, "she made it just for you." She hands me matching moccasins, each one decorated with two bear claws and robin's feet stitches. For the third time I'm taken aback and puzzle over One Who Knows and her thoughts of me.

I run my hand over the detailed stitching that would have taken even the fastest person many, many days to do. As I look at Otter, my head is so full of questions that I screw up my face to decide which one to ask first. Otter bursts out laughing, "Well, first off," she starts, guessing already my first question, "that is how she got her name!"

"Why these great kindnesses to me?" I ask in wonder. "First, she speaks up for me when I am taken, then I learn she has told Great Elk and War Woman that she believes I will bring brightness to the village, and now this," I hold my arms out and look down at my beautiful tunic and moccasins.

Otter ponders this. "I think for many reasons," she begins. "First, she wants to make a point with you and the entire village that she thinks highly of you despite how things first started out between the two of you. Second, she has always known things that the rest of us do not. And last, I think she wants to send a message to Bright Feather that she is happy for him and gives him her blessing."

I look puzzled. "What's between One Who Knows and Bright Feather?"

"Bright Feather was a son of her hearth for a time," Otter says quietly.

My head spins this information around slowly and then faster and faster as I see the bigger picture. Bright Feather's mate was One Who Knows' daughter … Weasel was also a son of One Who Knows hearth for a time … So One Who Knows has lost at least two daughters and at least one grandson … "Such sadness she has known," I say finally.

"Yes," Otter says, "more than most people can bear."

We hear a crashing sound as a basket is tipped over, and Otter jumps up. "Little Bird!" she scolds, "put those down! They are special!" Big eyes begin to drip enormous tears. "Well," she says, "then bring them to Bear as your gift to her." Flat, wide, brown feet pad happily to me, and I take from each tight fist some feathers. One big gray brown robin's feather, "To replace the one you lost," Otter explains and two small dark red feathers – also a robin's. "New ones to add," she says with a smile, "two because there are two of you now." She helps me comb out my hair which has gotten quite long – almost to my waist – and we wrap it with deerskin strips in a tight tail down the back. One Who Knows has sent two more tails of the same soft fur to the tunic to decorate my hair, and we add the feathers at the side in the same style that Bright Feather wears his. Otter surveys her handiwork and claps, "Perfect!"

I find Bright Feather near a clearing you can see from the hut where Willow and Companion are hobbled. Both horses knicker a greeting, and I take time to scratch Willow in the favorite place behind her ears and to rub Companion's soft muzzle and blow my scent up his nose. Bright Feather is looking at me with the silent look that I've already come to know is a look of great caring. I smile shyly at him and touch the beautiful new tunic that I wear.

"This is a gift from One Who Knows," I say, still with wonder in my voice.

He takes in all the details, touching the bear claws, fur tails, and robin's feet stitches. He touches the feathers in my hair and the tails that hang there, too. "It is fine work," he says, but his eyes look at me, and I realize he speaks of me and not so much my clothes. I sigh a great sigh and lean against him and his arms go around me. I breathe deep his wonderful smell of the outdoors, and wood smoke, and Companion, and sweet sweat.

"I do not know the animal that has fur as soft as this," I say after a time touching one of the tails.

"White men call it *mink*," he says. "Those both white and red who trade with each other do not always know many of each others' words, but they almost always know the word for *mink*."

I search my mind for words to say because I feel a sadness in him as well as a happiness. Does he think of other times and One Who Knows' daughter that he joined with? Does he have a voice in his head that speaks to him today? I struggle with what to say that's just right.

It's finally Bright Feather who speaks first. "One Who Knows thinks like I do of a time just as this long ago. She remembers the joy and the excitement and the dreams of good things to come. She must know better than we do of the happiness you and I have and the great things that are to come for us. She knows that it is good that I am no longer One Who Is Always Alone and am instead Bright Feather." He takes my chin in his hand and bends down and kisses me on the mouth, soft at first like the brush of a bird's feather and then again a little harder. I wrap my arms around him and feel the mink tails swish against my arms and legs as he scoops me up and carries me to a more quiet spot in the woods.

Before the celebration begins that night I make my way to One Who Knows' hut. She's waiting outside in the last rays of the setting sun as if she has been expecting me. The girl who took my place, Turtle, is working carefully on a hide stretched out on cross poles. All around One Who Knows are her precious herbs, some newly gathered, some dried and carefully tied together, and still others in the process of being carefully ground into small bits. I sit down beside her and am at a loss for words. I take a deep breath and remember the smells of her hut; memories of my first months in the village creep through my head along with the smells that creep through my nose.

"Thank you," I begin, "for many things."

She's silent, staring straight ahead. I can't help but think of my time with her when I knew her as Old Woman, and I force myself to remember that things are different now, that I'm a powerful woman, the mate of Bright Feather, and no longer called Mouse. "Thank you for speaking up for me more than once during important times," I say, and for once words seem to be missing from my head and from my mouth.

One Who Knows grunts and says, "I am far too old to worry about what people will think of me or my words. I speak only truth, and those who hear can decide to listen or not," she says. "I saw your destiny in this village the night you stood outside my hut filthy and tired yet strong and proud enough to stare down those who meant you harm. I knew the truth of things, then."

My mind goes back to the night with Weasel and his companions as they laughed and made fun of me. I murmur, "My Pa used to say, *Why waste your breath on something unworthy?* I'm not quiet often, but there are times when silence speaks more than words, I think."

She looks at me then and studies my eyes and my face and I stare back at her and all of a sudden I realize I'm right comfortable sitting with this woman who has a face as lined as a dried apple. "And the older you get," she says at last, "the quieter you will become." I think I see a twinkle of fun in her eyes.

"Thank you for my tunic. One Who Is Always Alone says that you know of the happiness he and I have and the good things that are to come," I look down and trace the robin tracks along the hem.

"You are tiny to look at but strong like a stone inside. One Who Is Always Alone is strong to look at but with many cracks inside his heart that make him weak." She looks at me, and I feel goose skin go up my bare arms. "There is much difficulty as well as joy to come for both of you, but," here she weaves her old and narrow fingers together in her lap making a sturdy bridge, "together you will be unstoppable."

I stand to go, and she motions for me to help her up. The bony hands grip my arms with a strength that's surprising, and she holds on tightly to me even after she's standing. "Your first place when you came to this village was my hearth, as hard as it was for you. Despite the things that have happened to you, you have remained strong and good and true. Never think that what happens to you is by chance, for your destiny began with your start in your mother's womb. You embrace our ways here with The Real People of The Maple Forest because you say they have made you a powerful woman. But," she says pointing a bony finger at me as she bends very close to me so that I see deep into her dark brown eyes, *"you were always a powerful woman even before you knew it.* I was proud to claim you as a daughter of this hearth many months ago," she says and then turns and goes inside her hut.

Daughter?! She claimed me as daughter months ago? Bear. Daughter of One Who Knows. Of The Elk Clan. Of The Maple Forest. Of The Real People.

I stand there in the evening twilight outside One Who Knows' hut for a long time watching the movement of the village, listening to the voices and sounds, smelling the smells. I feel a connection here that's so strong that for a time I imagine I'm rooted to the ground like a great tree with roots that extend under all I see and branches that tower over and shade each and every hut. *My village,* I think, *my people, my life, my choice!* I hear steps behind me, and I know they are Bright Feather's. He does not disturb me but waits until I turn and look at him and I can't help myself as I give him the brightest of smiles even as tears make fast trails down my face. We search each other's eyes for long moments and then he nods and gives me a gift I'd never thought to expect. He smiles, a quiet, beautiful smile that fills me with a rush of warmth.

I *know*, his smile says, *I know*.

There are food and games and laughter and story telling late into the evening. We are given gifts to celebrate our joining. Raccoon gives me my knife that was lost to me almost two months ago. "Found it in the woods," is all that he will say, but I see it's cleaned and sharpened and polished, and it's in a beautiful new sheath belt to wear around my waist. He gives Bright Feather two very small balls of black fur that we all puzzle over for a time. "For your ears," Raccoon finally volunteers, making motions as if to block out sound, "I am certain you will need them." Bright Feather grunts and the village howls with laughter. I try to look angry but can't keep the face for long.

Red Fox steps forward, shy and awkward, but also with a gift for me. It's a beautiful new bow, quiver, and thirty arrows. "I know your others were taken," he begins. "I made the quiver and arrows, but the bow is a gift from another." I search the crowd for Cloud and it's Bright Feather who reaches out and places his hand on my back gentle and firm. *He's not here anymore*, the hand says. I feel my eyes fill with tears. "Thank you, Red Fox, for your kindness," I say. I rub my hand along the smooth lines of the beautiful new bow and think of the old and crippled hands that made it. I touch the quiver, with no outer decoration but beautiful in its own way, and hear Cloud's voice, *Let your shooting speak for you, not the designs on your quiver.* Arrows peek out from the top, and from the weight I know there are arrows with special tips and new things for me to learn of now. "The time I spent at your hearth last winter learning all I know about shooting was one of the happiest times I've had in this village." I make a point to meet his eyes with my tear filled ones. "I will hear wise words in my head each time I prepare to draw my bow." He looks happy at my words.

As he turns to step away, I say, "Red Fox, I am thankful for this friendship that we have that I treasure more than this gift."

He smiles a sweet smile at me, "As I treasure it too, Bear."

War Woman stands to speak and even children's voices hush. "There are many reasons we celebrate tonight. We celebrate the return of our daughter, Bear, who was taken from us by force and returned to us by choice. We celebrate her joining with One Who Is Always Alone who now we shall call Bright Feather. We celebrate the time we have with our son, Deer, who spends so much time away from us." She looks out at the crowd, and despite the large number of people – young and old – there's a strong feeling that each one is noted. "Let us all realize the power of choices good and bad and make every effort to always be wise."

She turns to look at us, "Bear, daughter of One Who Knows of the Elk clan and Bright Feather of the Wolf clan and son of my hearth, The Real People of Great Elk's village of The Maple Forest look eagerly toward the future and the good that you will bring us." The people shout and cheer and laugh and talk and the noise around us rises up like the heat of a great fire that has just caught.

I look at Bright Feather as he speaks and nods to well-wishers who have crowded forward. *I'm the mate of the son of War Woman,* I think in wonderment, for in all this time I did not know who Bright Feather's mother was. *I've joined with the chief's son. I've joined with the brother of Beaver.* My head tries to fit these new pieces in my mind, but I realize that they are far too large, and I'll have to clear a powerful bit of space up there before they fit right comfortable. *Not so quick again, Pa,* is my last quiet thought to myself before I'm caught up in the celebrations.

With the first morning light the questions begin for Bright Feather, who seems not at all bothered to open his eyes and find me sitting waiting to ask. "The position of chief is traced through blood," Bright Feather explains as we ride out to do some hunting in the company of Deer. Strapped across my back is my new bow and arrows and my fingers itch to try them out. "While a child's heritage is traced through the family line of its mother," he tells me, "the position of chief is always traced through the line of the chief through his sons."

The fact that he's the *oldest* son of Great Elk and War Woman's hearth does not mean he must be chief. "It is a decision the entire council makes since it affects the entire village," he explains. "Over these past years when I was called One Who Is Always Alone, more and more often people looked to Beaver and consider whether he would be chief. But Great Elk has many years of leadership ahead of him. The time to decide is not yet." He does not speak of his feelings or desires. I remember his words, *All I wanted when I was a boy was to be a great hunter.*

"I, too, am a son of Great Elk," Deer says in seriousness. "I was adopted into their clan and welcomed into their hearth in the same way that One Who Knows now claims you as her daughter. Remember, Bright Feather first introduced me as his *brother*."

I do remember our first meeting and realize that I'd thought the term "brother" to be only a kindness and say so. Bright Feather nods, "Yes, that is done, but Deer speaks the truth; he is my full brother just as Beaver is. He has every right to be considered for the position of chief as I do."

"It is not my calling," he says quickly, and I turn back to look at him and see him use his white face to make a silly look. "Everyone knows that I struggle with who I am even today – White? Red? A chief must be certain of many things, including who they think they are. Of that I am quite certain."

"So," I say after thinking quite a while and trying to arrange these very large pieces in my head that feels smaller by the moment, "if you should become chief and we should have a son…" My voice trails off with the huge understanding of it all.

"Were I to become chief, it will be my sons who will follow in that path." Bright Feather voices my thoughts out loud.

I've more pieces to add to the puzzle. I think about War Woman's questioning of me and the answers I gave her when we returned from Dark Cloud's village. I think that this Indian village has willingly accepted me and welcomed me as a daughter even after Bright Feather chose me for a mate. I think about One Who Knows and what she said to the village about me and what she told me in private. I see her bony fingers weaving together to make a strong bridge. *There is much difficulty as well as joy to come for both of you, together you will be unstoppable.*

"Will there be a time when I know all the things I need to know?" I ask out loud to anyone in particular after my head grows weary from trying to make sense of all this.

"No," Bright Feather and Deer say both at once without hesitation. *I didn't think so,* I think to myself.

Before Deer leaves he speaks to us both privately. Looking at Bright Feather he says, "Learn the white man's language. Have Bear teach it to you. Do not tell anyone even in this village that you know it, or even that you are practicing. It will be a hidden weapon that will always be ready and can only mean good things for The Real People of The Maple Forest. Bear and I may not always be available to help, and your only true chance at winning future battles in the council tent over the treaty table is for you to understand and know how the white man thinks and plans. Learning his language is the first step."

He looks at me, "Can you read?" When I nod 'yes', he looks relieved. "Good. Many things are often written that are never spoken of, and once a treaty is signed in the white man's world that is all they care about. Do not let *anyone* sign *anything* until you are certain you have read and understood everything that is written. And if this one," he gestures his head toward Bright Feather, "shows that he might have the skill for it, teach him to read the white man's word, too. But that is really too much for me to hope for."

He looks again to Bright Feather, "You may be surprised and disbelieving, but there are *some* whites who are speaking out about the poor and unfair treatment of the Indians. There are some who feel that what has happened has been nothing short of theft. With the new government of *The United States of America*, there may be hope that things will be different." He looks to the eastern horizon and squints his blue eyes against the rising sun. "But it will be like walking barefoot through a nest of ground bees; *possible,* but highly unlikely that we might not get stung at some place along the way. *We just don't want to be stung to death, that's all,"* he mumbles almost to himself. He meets our serious stares with his own. "Both of you are the brightest hope for this village," he says. *"It just may be possible* we will be able to get through this to the other side with only a few stings to show for it."

It's a good summer for me. I work hard, learn much and smile most all of the time.

I help with the village chores, in particular the garden, and delight in watching it grow to wonderful summer fullness. I spend much more time at Great Elk's and War Woman's hut in the circle of leaders each evening. I wish to become familiar with the workings of the village and maybe more so, understand the many thoughts and beliefs and ideas that make up the face of this place. I listen to the wise words and interesting discussions, no topic more talked about than what Deer has told us about the white man, the census, the new treaties to come, and *citizenship*. Debates range far and wide. There are some in the circle who hate the white man and believe he should be destroyed. There are some who don't believe that the white man is as great a threat as others believe, and can't possibly succeed for their lack of harmony in their life and with the world around them. Stories are told of mysterious powerful white magic that has killed whole villages in a moon's time. I watch the faces of those around the circle as the white man is discussed and see fear, anger, disbelief; each face shows different thoughts.

In the privacy of our tent, Bright Feather tells me that such stories are true. "There were great tribes in the north and east that shared the woods with my people's ancestors, and they are no more."

I learn many things about The Real People and their history. We hear nothing specific from Beaver, but from others who travel to Dark Cloud's village for trade and business we do get small bits of news We know he has settled there and has a position of authority in the council circle. I miss his stories.

Many summer nights are spent listening to stories of bravery told at the council fire. The Real People have been part of this land for longer than my brain can understand. But some stories are from times even before they lived in this place and are filled with adventures of travel and ice and great mountains and rivers the likes of which I've never thought of. And there are stories that go back farther still to the beginning of the earth and what was before.

I discover that there is a greater story teller in the village than Beaver; it is One Who Knows. While she does not speak often at the council fire, when she decides to the gathering always is its largest. "In the beginning of time," One Who Knows tells us one evening as we sit around the council fire, "Mother Earth was a celestial body floating in the universe among the stars, like a great island floating in a sea of water. The island was suspended by invisible cords at four places or directions in the sky vault and was a solid rock that had special energy and power. The old ones tell of the cords being delicate, and they feared that one day these cords would break and the island would sink into the ocean of the universe and become part of the flow of water energy for all time."

"All spirits were in the sky vault in a place called The Father's Place. During one of the councils with the Great One, the animal spirits asked for more room, since it was getting crowded in The Father's Place.

"Water Beetle was the first to go see what was below. Because she was Beaver's grandchild, the animal spirits thought she would be able to fly and land on a surface in the water. She flew and flew but found no place to land. Finally, she dove into the water to discover that it was mud which clung to her as she moved back to the surface. The animals were so excited that they provided what we know as gut string to tie the dried mud in the four directions to provide balance to Mother Earth.

"Great Buzzard, one of the Bird tribe, was sent to find a place suitable for each of the tribes to locate. When he flew over the area, he found that the mud was still very soft. Being tired, he let one of his wings dip into the mud which created valleys and mountains. Today, we know that as the place of The Real People because of the beautiful mountains that seem to always smoke and the other beautiful mountains that always have a blue misty haze across their ridges. There are still places in the valley called Buzzard's Place.

"At last it was time for the four-legged ones, the winged ones, and all of the Great One's creations to come down from The Father's Place to this new place in the sky vault called Mother Earth. The Great One sent the Thunder Beings to give a special life energy to Mother Earth. He also asked Sun to be the father over this new land knowing that the Great One was very busy with everything in the Universal Circle. Also, the land was dark until The Sun and Grandmother Moon agreed to watch by day and night.

"While this was the beginning for Mother Earth, the early Real People knew that there were other worlds out there in the Universal Circle, and others such as the Sun, the Moon, and Thunder beings oversaw those worlds.

"All living things on Mother Earth were to be brothers and sisters to one another. As there was opposite energy, so there would be balance and equality for all. The wisdom of The Real People and all the tribes would protect that balance so that all creatures on Mother Earth and in the Universal Circle could live in harmony.

"And so it is that all the animals and creatures, big and small, would live in peace on Mother Earth."

I think about *all living creatures* living *in harmony* on Mother Earth. I've a powerful strong understanding of why The Real People have such a distrust and fear of the white man. I know that for many white people *harmony* is not the first thought of the day.

I hunt with Bright Feather and become so familiar with my bow that I can feel it even in my sleep. I work on my shooting with a variety of new arrow tips, and Bright Feather encourages me to determine the kind I like best and forget the rest. We both agree after a time that I'm best with the plain arrows fashioned to a sharp point; I just don't have the arm strength to handle the heavier ones and make them fly true. We practice my shooting from Willow as she runs, and I try to hit a moving target. We both know my skill still needs much work, but it doesn't need to be spoke out loud. I'm happy that Red Fox joins us on these times and after many weeks have fun teasing him for I see he watches Turtle now with as much care as he watched me at one time. It's hard to see it, but I'm certain that he blushes now and then from my teasing.

I become a teacher, and Bright Feather becomes my student. I'm surprised at how many white man's words he does know, even if they are all related to hunting, trapping, animals and trade. It's a starting point, and we work each free moment we have away from the village. He has a good mind for the language, and more than once I'm surprised at how quick he is to pick it up and remember it. With the ending of summer and the excitement of the fall harvest, I'm amazed that Bright Feather and I can spend an entire day hunting in the forest and speak only white words if we choose. One late summer afternoon he says to me, "I think it is time that we go visit Deer and see if we can find out any news about things." He has spoken in perfect English.

But lastly, as the summer heat slips into brief catches of autumn's cool, my most favorite parts of the summer are those times I work on this way of being a mate. I grow to love and cherish the man that less than one and a half years ago I'd have called a *red savage* just as Miss Rebecca and Reverend Wilder did. And I ponder sometimes the knowledge that all who knew me as *Elle* still would call him *red savage*.

I enjoy this role of mate and of knowing things about him that no one else knows. I treasure our time together as we learn what it is like to be two who work as one. I delight in the skill we seem to have of being able to talk to each other without too many words but with just simple looks or gestures. I'm well and truly honored that just as *I* chose him, *he* chose me. I realize that while I was a Powerful Woman before I met him, I'm more powerful now that I'm loved by him.

I hear One Who Knows' words, *Together you will be unstoppable.* And it causes me to smile.

When you were born,
you cried and the world rejoiced.
Live your life so that when you die,
the world cries and you rejoice.[10]

Cherokee Expression

Listener

The trees slip into their bright autumn colors and just as Bright Feather said, we head out for Deer's trading post, also known as *Forest City, North Carolina.* Our trip to Deer and Forest City is in a very roundabout way. Bright Feather explains it's to make sure we don't travel on any white settler's lands.

"But isn't this the land of The Real People?" I ask, confused.

"Yes," is all he says. I'm left to conclude obvious answers.

We travel for five days, and I'm jumpy and nervous the whole time despite Bright Feather's best efforts to calm me. Is it safe for me to travel? Is Bright Feather safe *with me?* What will people think if they see us together and with me dressed as I am? Will they shoot first and ask questions later? Mouse thoughts crowd my head. I miss the feeling of safety that I have in my village and at my hearth. Those feelings of fear that I had leaving The Maple Forest on the way to Dark Cloud's village bubble to the surface. More than once I think that I want to go back to where I know I'm safe. More than once Bright Feather reminds me that we are traveling to a *trading post,* and many people of all kinds come and go with safety. But that does not make me feel much better.

Some powerful woman I am, I think with a big dose of disgust. How am I expected to be a voice for The Maple Forest at a great council circle if I can't overcome my jitters about traveling to a trading post owned by friends?

My first thoughts riding into the cleared space in the woods that is Deer's trading post is just one surprise after another. It looks more like Cooper's Store back in Ward's Mill, Virginia, than I'd expected. Then, as Deer steps out grinning from ear to ear to welcome us, I think he looks nothing like Deer and everything like William Thomas dressed from head to toe in white man's clothes: boots, button fly trousers, white shirt, suspenders and all. Then he greets us with the words of greeting of The Real People, and I relax a bit.

I meet Deer's mate, and she introduces herself to me as "Possum of the Turkey clan of The Real People of The Maple Forest, but you can also call me Mary," she finishes with a laugh. "It does not matter," she says serious like but quiet just to me, "as long as they speak polite and respectful to me." She's shorter than me with bright dark eyes and long, long dark hair. She, too, is dressed in white clothes, including an apron dusted with flour. I see bare feet peeking out beneath her skirt.

We are welcomed with great enthusiasm into their sturdy wood-frame home that sits separate but within a few quick steps from the trading post. Sipping on cool apple cider and eating warm corn fritters dipped in maple syrup, I struggle with the strangeness of it all. The wood plank floors and the sturdy chairs and tables are not what I'm accustomed to anymore. Looking at Bright Feather sitting casually talking to Deer, I realize how silly it is that he seems more at ease than I do.

Bright Feather and Deer go outside to examine the hides and furs and other items we have brought for trade. Deer is happy to hear that aside from the usual things, we have had an excellent season in the garden and have even brought along many seeds good for next year's planting. He's eager to examine them, too.

I smile at Possum as she gives me more than one shy smile. I think we will have fun talking on this visit! Before we have time to speak in burst three children of different ages.

"Is One Who Is Always Alone here yet?" says the oldest boy.

Possum smiles the same smile I see Otter give Little Bird. "Bear, this is our oldest boy, James, *Red Bird.* He is seven." Possum puts her arm around a girl looking at me with wide, interested eyes. "This is Eliza, *Sleeping Rabbit.* She is five. And," peeking out from behind Eliza's skirts is another small boy that Possum grins at, "and this is my smallest bit of trouble, Richard, *Small Turtle.*"

Richard holds up a filthy hand. "I'm thwee," he says with no small bit of pride.

I study them, an amazing mix of white and red, and see my future staring right back at me with dark Indian eyes and hair, yet fairer skin. They greet me with Indian faces and polite Indian words, yet within moments are shouting white words and greetings to Bright Feather and their father outside in front of the trading post. The boys eagerly follow Bright Feather, asking if he has brought his bow and arrows and can they ride Companion and will he take them hunting? Possum looks at me and rolls her eyes as I giggle.

Eliza can't seem to take her eyes off me. She's keenly interested in my dress, for I'm in full Indian clothes, including my weapons still strapped to my back and waist. She's in full white clothes. In no time she's close enough to me that I can see the freckles sprinkled across her nose. I recognize a kindred spirit, for the questions just bubble up and never seem to stop coming. "Are these real bear claws?" she asks as she fingers my necklace from Great Elk. "Did you kill the bear yourself? Is that why they call you 'Bear'? Pa's teaching me how to shoot a rifle. Can you shoot? What kind of knife is that? Pa says I'm too young to learn to throw a knife. Is that really your very own bow and arrows? Will you let me try? What is your horse's name? Can I have a ride on her? How long are you staying?"

Oh, how I remember! A time before Ma died, when I was just a little girl running wild with Henry, everything and anything I saw or did always led to a question. Or three. Or ten. I grin at Eliza and work hard to answer every question she can dream up.

Finally, Possum can stand it no more and shoos her out the door. "The questions never stop!" she says in mock frustration as Eliza makes her way outside, but on slow and not so happy feet. "And she's the most opinionated child you'd ever want to deal with!" She sighs and takes a sip of apple cider. "It is good to finally meet you. I am so happy that you came. Deer said that he thought you would come with *Bright Feather*," she tries to hide a grin as she makes an effort to call him by the new name, "when he came to trade next time." Possum studies me and seems to see what she likes, for finally she says, "Only the most special of women could have caused the change I see in him. He has been alone for so long, I feared that he would never find a new path."

She asks of the village and the people and is quite happy to hear any and all things I can remember. She's familiar with many people, and we laugh over things that never seem to change. I finally ask her how long she has been away from The Maple Forest, the mate of Deer.

She answers after thinking for a bit. "Close to nine summers," She smiles and shakes her head slowly in memory. "My family was not happy when I told them I wished to come with Deer to this place so far away from them and so close to the white world," she says. She sits up straight and tall in her chair and grins a wide, mischief-filled grin. "But they could not stop me!" She leans forward and whispers, "I was the most opinionated child you'd ever want to deal with!" and then laughs with me at her joke.

Possum shakes her head at the memory of it all. "I had my eye on that man from the moment I knew to look. He would visit for the summer and for a week or two in the spring and fall. As a child I would follow him around like a puppy and was a sheer annoyance. As a young woman on the hunt for the man of her choice, I completely terrified him." That made me laugh out loud and Possum grinned again, nodding. "Poor Deer, he always wanted so to do all things right and proper, especially once he began living in the white world and only came to The Maple Forest for short stays. He was so respectful and helpful, always listening, offering suggestions, making promises about what he could try to do when he was with the whites.

"His life made it impossible to do as it was always done when two people mate: join with my clan, set up a hut in my village, provide honor and protection to the village. How could he do such things, he argued, when he planned to live in the white territory as William Thomas and establish a trading business? It was the same fight each and every time."

"Didn't you ever think of giving up? Of choosing another?"

Possum laughed and shook her head no. "Oh, my family agreed with Deer and told me to choose another. So I just started a new argument and said I would go with him to live in the white world and help him with his trading business. That made Deer even more crazed. He said he feared for my safety and refused to even consider bringing me with him to live.

Possum smiles a sweet smile and looks at me. "Do you know, every single time we argued about whether or not to join, he *never* told me he did not want me for a mate, he *never* said I should choose another. He only ever gave me arguments why it would not be proper or why it would be dangerous." She nods with certainty. "He loved me."

She shrugs. "Despite what my family thought and despite what Deer said was right and proper, I was bound and determined to go with him. He had come to the village to tell Great Elk and the others that he was finally to a point where he was opening up this trading post and how he hoped they would come where they knew they would be treated fairly. He spent a week with us that time and on the morning he got ready to leave I was seated on my pony packed and ready to go! I had made my choice, and there was no one who could stop me."

She sighs a deep, deep sigh. "I was young and foolish and had no idea what to expect. *Deer knew*, he'd tried to tell me, but I was in love and that was all I could see." She smiles at me sadly. "It was terrible hard for me those first few years. James came along and then Eliza… Things were better by the time Richard was born. I had grown accustomed to the life of a white trader." She looks at me for a moment and says quietly. "Perhaps you know a little of what I felt…"

We stare at each other and seem to speak without words for a time. Finally, I say, "The Indian way is easier, better …" I shake my head in annoyance for I can't find the right word. "I chose the Indian way," but I look out the window and see Bright Feather helping Richard up onto the back of Companion as he squeals with delight.

I turn back to meet Possum's eyes again, "I made that choice, though, before things were the way they are now with Bright Feather and me. I know, now, I will follow him anywhere he needs to go and wouldn't think twice about it."

"Ahh, so you do know," she says with a smile and a nod. "That is called *the path of love,* and it can be as difficult as the path of war!" She shrugs, "I adjusted slowly to the life here. Deer was good; he tried so hard to help. The children kept me busy and gradually I began to feel confident with the language and the people and the business. Slowly I found my place here. Now, I am happy. Now, I fit. I can be Possum of the Turkey Clan of The Real People of The Maple Forest one moment and turn around and be Mary Thomas, of William Holland Thomas Trading Post of Forest City, North Carolina the next. *Just as long as they speak polite and treat me with respect*, everything is just fine."

She stands and begins making preparations to cook dinner. "Can I help?" I ask. "At one time I made a pretty tasty venison stew with dumplings…"

Possum turns to me. "Now I am *really* glad you are here!" she says with a laugh.

I learn that the trading post is not on the family land that Deer discovered he owned as a result of being William Thomas, and while the trading post is on land that's close to Indian boundaries, it's carefully placed in white territory. The family land, I gather, is sizeable, as it's supported by the work of black slaves. Profits from this land helped to purchase the land for the trading post. "Deer's aunt and her husband have been seeing to it from the time of his disappearance, and when he returned, it really was not something he felt he wanted to take over," Possum explained. "He wanted to keep contact with the Indians and this," she gestures with the sweep of her hand, "offered that chance.

"This trading post helps him hear new things that will impact The Real People. He takes his job as their agent in the white world very serious and listening to all of the folks that wander through is a perfect way to hear what needs to be heard. Through his law schooling he knows people in government here in the state of North Carolina and even in the United States Government. Now that James is older he helps quite a bit at the trading post. The last time Deer had to go to Washington to discuss business about citizenship and such, James and I were able to handle things here all on our own." There is great pride in her voice when she tells me this.

The trading post is a busy place with a steady flow of people – red and white – coming by. I have fun wandering around the place; looking at the bolts of colorful cloth, stacks of furs and hides, tools and pots and pans, sacks of grain and seed and jars of fruits and vegetables stacked neatly on the shelves. It's a family effort and all are involved, large and small. I help Possum with the various chores of sorting and cataloging and organizing. I listen to the steady flow of conversations, some white, some Indian, and despite reassurances of my safety, try very hard to remember my life as Mouse whenever strangers come in to do business.

Something makes me work especially hard to be invisible on our second day there when I hear a group of people enter. By the sounds of their sturdy boots I know it to be white men, and it's not just their skin color but their numbers that make me skittish. I'm a powerful woman, but I've already learned two good lessons in my life about being *powerless*. With my back to the group I know I look like an Indian squaw, and I concentrate on the containers of thread and buttons and needles in front of me making a show of great interest.

"William," a voice says in way of greeting, and I try hard to determine how many pairs of feet I hear. Four? Maybe Five?

"Samuel," I hear Deer say in a cordial response. "What a surprise. It's been quite a while since you and your men've been by this a-ways."

"Got orders to do some patrolling of the western perimeter. Seems the Injuns have taken offense to some of the new settlers west of here. No violence yet but there's been reports of stolen horses and such, and Nancy Jamison of Pine Ridge claims Injuns broke in to her home and stole a ham right out of her oven!"

"Is that so?" I hear Deer respond. "Seems like settlers who make a point to set up a homestead on Indian land are only asking for trouble, wouldn't you think?"

Samuel snorts at this comment. "Should know better than to discuss this with you, now, shouldn't I, William, being how we all know how you feel about Injuns and all."

I try so hard not to move or breathe. White men are one thing but soldiers, too! I'm certain that Deer and Bright Feather may not have concerns about any others visiting the trading post and seeing me, but *soldiers* are a mighty different story. My heart pounds so loud I know that it must be heard by everyone. I make myself breathe deep and concentrate on calm thoughts rather than panic. I realize I've been holding a spool of blue thread for longer than it will take to make it, and I put it down with a clump louder than I'd like and look up at the shelves in front of me.

"Better keep an eye on your goods," I hear Samuel say. "The squaw's awful quiet over there and might be helping herself while you're distracted with me. Those Injuns are a thievin' lot, you know."

"I thank you for your concern; I'll be sure to keep a watch," Deer says. "Can I help you with anything?"

"Have you heard or seen anything that we should know?" Samuel says, and I hear other footsteps of the men in his party beginning to wander around the store. *Think*, my head says to me. *What should you do now? What will you do if they notice you are not as much an Indian squaw as they think you are?* I look up at the rows of trinkets on the shelves, and at the end of the shelves are papers and bits tacked to the rough wood of the wall. Good ideas escape me, and trying to look calm instead of a frozen Indian statue, I wander a few steps further into the darkness of the corner and start reading the faded scraps of paper, some yellow with age. I think tiny mouse thoughts in my head.

"It's been quiet," Deer says, "although John Henry from up the river brought me the best damn ham steak I've had in months a few days back."

"John Henry?" Samuel puzzles aloud. "Ham steak...?" and then he gets the joke and laughs uproariously. "Oh! I see! Did he steal it from Nancy Jamison's oven do you think? Ha! Ha! Ha! That's why I always like to stop by here William, even if you are confused in some of your political opinions. I always get a good laugh!"

I hear Deer chuckle as casual like as possible. "Actually, got some excellent apple cider that Mary's just made, cold and sweet outside hanging in the cistern if you'd like a cup. She might even have some of her apple pie, too. I think I remember your men liking it last time they were here..."

The wandering boots stop and make a hasty return back to the center of the store. "That would be right kind of you, William," I hear Samuel say. "The men and I have been a long way aways from good cooking and treats of such like for quite a few weeks."

The thought of fresh apple pie is enough to make them even forget about me. In the cool dark of the trading post, I feel my heart begin to slow and find it's natural rhythm. My eyes focus on the edge of an old paper peeking out beneath some new notices that have been tacked over it and I see the words, "- of Ward's Mill, Virginia." I reach up pulling the newer papers away to see the old page beneath, and I see a rough sketch of a white girl with "ELLE GRAVES" written in big letters below. My heart begins to pound again as I take the paper down to read it.

"On the evening of TUESDAY, the 22nd of March in the year of Our Lord 1828, the peaceful homestead of Andrew Graves, Esq. of Ward's Mill, Virginia was violently and savagely attacked by a marauding band of blood thirsty Indians. No surviving witnesses were found to provide an accurate account, however it is with the Utmost Hope and Desire that the person of Mistress Elle Graves might still be Alive and with the Most Extreme Care and Speed be found and returned post haste. All leniency will be afforded to those cooperating with authorities in the positive outcome to this tragic occurrence. April 10, 1828, Cornelius Cooper of Ward's Mill, Virginia." Beneath the writing is my picture, roughly drawn with the description: "Orphaned white girl whose mother has died and father and brothers have been murdered by marauding Indians, who answers to the name of Elle.."

"Don't suppose even if you held that up right next to you, they'd recognize you, you've changed so much," Deer says quietly behind me making me jump almost high enough to bump my head on the ceiling. "Bright Feather said to tell you to stay quiet and out of sight for a bit until the soldiers are long gone. He's gone off to follow them to make sure we know what direction they're choosing to follow."

I turn around to search his face, "Will he be safe doing that?"

"No one has ever seen Bright Feather — on foot or horse — unless he chooses it to be so. And a whole passel of white soldiers, talking and clanking and crashing through the woods are not going to notice one quiet Indian trailing them from behind. Yes, I'm sure he will be safe." He shows me his white face and lets me search it thorough until I'm satisfied.

I touch the picture of me on the yellowed paper. "It would be better if they thought I died with my Pa…" I say quietly. "I don't want to bring any harm to Great Elk's village, for they had nothing to do with it."

Deer looks at me for long moments and then sighs. "Ah, but there you're wrong, Bear, for it was under Great Elk's instructions that you were taken."

The look I give Deer seems to alarm him, and he reaches out to take my arm and steady me. "I'm sorry, Bear," Deer says to me with real concern. "I did not mean to have that come out as blunt as it did. I have a reputation of being frank and forthright in all of my business negotiations, but that does not always work so well on the personal level." He rolled his eyes. "Just ask Possum."

"Here," he says, "walk with me a while, and I will tell you a long story." I notice his son, James, in the shadows by the counter busy with his ever present whittling. "Can you handle things for a bit, son?" he asks. James flashes him a quick smile and gives him a nod. "Fetch your Ma if anyone comes, hear?" And we walk out the back of the store into the cool shade of the bright autumn forest.

"First off, for reasons that will be clear very quickly, I speak to you as William Thomas, not as Deer. Possum and I spoke for a long time about whether I should tell you things *I* know that Bright Feather never will. At last she made the wise suggestions that I speak with Bright Feather and ask *him* whether I should tell you or not." He sighs and looks at me serious, "Last night I spoke with him about telling you things you should know that he will not speak of. I speak to you because he said I could.

"To understand how you came to be in Great Elk's village you must go back many years even before I came to be a son of War Woman's hearth, and I must speak of people who are no longer alive," he says. I feel a prickle of goose flesh up my arms as we walk into the forest full of bright reds and golds and oranges. I struggle to slow my head and my heart down and just listen and take it all in. "I ask *you* before I go on with any more of the story. Do you want to hear what I have to tell you?"

The pieces to the puzzle that I'd never thought to see, I think as I look into Deer's serious face. *The chance to understand all the whys.* There are so many pieces to the puzzle that are missing. Had I lived my whole life in Great Elk's village there would be more understanding. Do I want to know the whole picture? I must admit that I do. "I think that I must trust you and

Possum and Bright Feather and hear what you have to say," I answer, but my voice is quiet and unsure.

"Weasel was the son of Dark Cloud and would have been one of three sons who would be considered for chief." Deer shrugs his shoulders, "It is easy knowing the things we know *now* to think that Weasel would have *never* been selected to be chief, but at the time I speak of, there was no such certainty. Some sons of chiefs do not have a great desire to take their father's place. They look at the job as something they must face should the time come." He looks at me certain that I know, "Bright Feather is one such as that." He looks away and continues, "Other sons hunger for it like a starving man hungers for a warm bowl of tasty stew. Weasel was one such as *that*.

"It was during the time when Great Elk's village and Dark Cloud's village were still struggling to maintain a bond. They wanted to remain close in spirit even though they were no longer close in distance. Marriages were arranged, between the two villages in the hopes of keeping the bond tied with blood. I do not know how Weasel's village came to choose him to come to Great Elk's village and join with One Who Knows' oldest daughter, Raven. I do know that Raven considered it an honor, for she told me, but in fairness she was not traveling to a new village, and the two braves that traveled to Dark Cloud's village from The Maple Forest were not overly happy about the move.

"For you see, by then already there were difficult feelings between the two villages about the white man and how much involvement we should have with him. Those differences had made each place a very different world to live in." We stop by a peaceful spot that I sense he comes to at times, and he motions for us both to sit down on a massive tree trunk covered in moss. Deer searches my face, "Bright Feather has told me that you have talked about these things," and I nod my head 'yes'.

"Weasel arrived in Great Elk's village angry, and he stayed angry for as long as I knew him. He disagreed with those who sat around the council circle on almost everything that was discussed, and he challenged those who had differing opinions rather than trying to understand their thoughts.

"One of his greatest continual battles was over the decision of whether The Real People should go west of the Mississippi, stay east on smaller tribal territory, or accept the offer of citizenship. Weasel married Raven in the spring of 1818 the year after the treaty was signed that commissioned the census of The Nation of The Real People. The census was begun in the summer of 1818, and it was during the census that one was to be counted *and declare their intentions* about what they wished to do. The Treaty of 1819 contained a list of those who requested citizenship. Weasel was present for the census in Great Elk's village that summer of 1818 and I made a point to be there when the agents for The Nation of The Real People and the representatives of the United States Government arrived." He looks at me with a sorrowful and serious face. "I so feared the outcome with Weasel there. I did not know how he would react.

"Weasel supported the views of his father, Dark Cloud, and was passionately vocal about it. His arguments fell on deaf ears, for there was no one seated at Great Elk's council circle that had any desire for the white man's money or the white man's possessions. Weasel simply could not understand that.

"He made great efforts to discredit those of us who were sons of Great Elk, and at every opportunity sought to show that he was better, faster, smarter and wiser than we were. Bright Feather, Beaver and I chose not to respond to him, for all knew it was useless to argue with a person who could only see one side of things. As more and more people felt that the path of citizenship was the right one, Weasel had more and more people to challenge and argue with. He succeeded only in making all those who dealt with him unhappy, none more so than One Who Knows' daughter, Raven." He sighs and runs his hand through his hair, and I realize that try as he may to be speaking only as William Thomas, the man that's called Deer is there, too. "There was no harmony in Great Elk's village from the moment Weasel arrived.

"Many people were at the council circle that night when The Real People Agents and the United States Government Representatives arrived. Great Elk spoke as did War Woman. I think he made every effort to explain the facts fairly the way he understood them to be. Great Elk said, 'I do not tell you all these things to upset you or to make you angry. I tell you all this *so that you know the way of things*. There are many different people who believe they have only the best interests for The Real People at heart, and there are many different choices we are faced with. Some will choose differently than our neighbors or our friends or even our brothers.' He said his greatest fear was the eventual division of The Real People.

"War Woman explained about the census," and Deer smiles with the memory. "She was harsher and made less of an effort to speak in the middle. She said, 'Why does the United States of America want to know our numbers? My first thought is it is always best to know the size of your enemy.'" Deer chuckles. "I can still see the nervous faces on those United States Government Representatives.

"She told all about the offer of citizenship and what she understood it to mean. It meant that they would not be considered part of The Nation of The Real People anymore but would instead be considered part of the United States of America. She said that with the promise of citizenship came the promise of land – six hundred and forty acres for each household."

Deer smiles at me. "War Woman also reminded everyone of promises that were never kept fully in the past and others that had been outright broken. And she also reminded them about the fact that The Nation of The Real People *no longer recognized* anything that they decided within the council circle but instead depended solely on the decisions made by Dark Cloud and his village of advisors.

"The hardest thing she tells them, though, is that the land they are sitting on, the land they have always considered theirs, was not part of the new tribal boundaries that would be drawn. She said, 'The Maple Forest is not within the new boundaries of The Nation of The Real People. Your choice is this: stay with The Nation of The Real People and loose the ancestral land that has always been ours or leave The Nation of The Real People and claim citizenship with the nation we have always considered our enemy ... and the right to land that we are *told* comes with us.'" Deer looks at me. "It was not much of a choice, was it?" It's easy to admit that it was not.

Deer pauses and lets the many words he has said slowly seep in. "I sat there in the firelight with all of the people whom I considered my brothers and my sisters, and even though I knew everything that was going to be said, to hear Great Elk and War Woman say them aloud was devastating. There were many who sat there in that circle that night crying silently for they knew, *they knew* much of the Old Ways were disappearing right before their eyes."

He shrugs his shoulders. "So, the Government Representatives stayed and counted each and every person in the village. Everyone stepped forward and made the decision whether they would move and stay with The Nation of The Real People or not move and become citizens of the nation they considered their enemy; the nation they did not trust.

"Weasel went just about mad as they all made their decisions, and he was counted as one who wished to stay in the east as part of The Nation of The Real People and accept money and goods in trade. He was the only man in the village who did not request citizenship," he pauses for a moment in memory and deep thought, "although I wondered for a time whether Beaver would decide to go with The Nation of The Real People rather than stay in Great Elk's village." He looks me right in the eye, "And Raven is the only woman who is counted as wishing to stay with The Nation of The Real People for he forbade her to go against his wishes.

"Raven was a good woman: strong, independent, smart, and loving," and for long moments he's quiet with his memories. "She was full of life and mischief. She could charm you to do just about anything that suited her. All the braves were in love with her at least just a little," he smiles a bit shy like. *Including you*, I think and know it to be true when I look into his eyes. "She was proud to be chosen, and she entered into the joining with Weasel willingly; not for love of a man but for love of her people. *Braves fight*, she said to me the night before he arrived, *women love.*" He laughs an embarrassed laugh. "I tried to convince her to leave the village with me rather than join with Weasel. There was no one else like her," he said with just a whisper and then looks at me. "Except her younger sister, Black Fox." *Black Fox*, my heart jumps at the sound of the name. I feel a shiver run up my spine, Bright Feather's mate when he was called Hawk and the mother of his son was Black Fox.

"Weasel was cruel to Raven in his manner and his speech and his behavior. He showed her no respect, he did not recognize her goodness and he was quick with his hands in his anger. One Who Knows and Black Fox," he snorts with bitter humor, "never ones to be quiet in the face of difficult situations *ever* were silent about Weasel. It *had* to be at Raven's insistence; nothing else could have kept them still. She was quiet and tried to do everything he demanded. She never spoke ill of him nor did she do anything to discredit him. It soon became apparent that he was destroying her spirit, and as they entered their second winter together all in the village wished that come the Green Corn Ceremony of the summer she would end the union."

He stands and begins to pace about in the small area where we are; the memories of it all make him restless. "That would be good for her, but bad for him, for he would have to return back to his village in a less than favored status, while she would be free of his anger and frustration to start fresh." Deer pauses, quiet for a while, and I can almost see him sorting through the words he will say to me and those he will not.

"Weasel convinced her to visit his village at the end of the winter just before the trees began to bud. It was not unusual to visit other villages, and Dark Cloud's village was certainly one we traveled to often yet One Who Knows was insistent that she not go. She spoke with great passion at a number of council circles against the visit - I was present at some of them - but Raven was determined to go. By then Hawk had joined with Black Fox, and they were expecting their first child. They, too, tried to convince Raven not to go, but Raven would not listen to anyone.

"The morning they left, One Who Knows tore at her clothes, painted her face black, and cut her arms in mourning as though Raven was already dead. I was leaving to go back to the white territory and can still remember standing there watching Raven and Weasel leave while One Who Knows wailed her sorrow."

He shook his head. "I never spoke to Raven about it. I never asked her. No one has ever shared with me her thoughts. Many times I have wondered, *Why?* Why did she feel so strongly about going, especially with One Who Knows' objections?" His sorrow sits with us like another person in the forest, huge and big.

We are there in the silence of the forest for a bit, pondering the reasons that we can never really know. "Maybe she just wanted to have a piece of the puzzle that might help her understand Weasel," I say at last. "Maybe she thought if she met his people and saw his village, she could understand his anger better. Maybe she cared for him one small bit. Maybe she thought she could see goodness in him where others couldn't. Maybe she wanted the joining to work for the sake of her people."

He nods his head and shrugs. "Those are as good reasons as any, I suppose."

He sighs. "No one ever saw her again. Weasel returned to the village a full month later without her with a story none of us ever believed. He claimed he had been set upon by a group of white trappers who had beaten him and left him for dead, and that they had taken Raven as a captive. He claimed to have traveled to Dark Cloud's village first because it was closer to seek their help, and despite their best efforts they were unable to find any trace of her or the trappers." He looks at me, his eyes showing great pain. "Why didn't they send riders to our village so that we could join the search?

"Hawk came to me here at the trading post that first night he heard Weasel's story. We searched the forest and surrounding areas based on where Weasel told us everything happened, and we found nothing either. We notice that Weasel's story seems to change with every telling. We sent riders to Dark Cloud's village to speak with the braves who had come from our village, as well as others. There were different versions of his story from almost everyone we talked to. We heard everything from he showed up alone flashing a new rifle to he showed up bleeding and almost dead barely able to speak." He shrugs, "But the only thing that was certain was there was no Raven. We searched for almost three weeks for her."

He comes and sits back down by me and his speaking has gotten so quiet that I catch myself leaning in closer and straining with all my might to hear. "When we returned to Great Elk's village, Hawk and I, it was with great sorrow because we had nothing to show and nothing to tell for all of our weeks away. We arrived to a village in full mourning, for Black Fox, in her grief over her sister, had gone into labor early and both she and the baby – a son – had died. One Who Knows who's entire life had been healing and guiding had done her best and yet had been unable to prevent either of her daughter's deaths. We thought she mourned only Raven's death that day she left with Weasel, but One Who Knows knew even more sorrow was to come.

"Hawk was inconsolable after Black Fox's death. He blamed himself for so much … He said more than once he should have traveled with Weasel and Raven when they first set out, yet he had not wanted to leave Black Fox, who had not done well in her pregnancy from the start. He knew how upset Black Fox had been when he left to search with me, and yet even she had encouraged him to go and look as best he could. Hawk blamed himself for much of the sadness that came into the village but there was, of course, no one to blame but Weasel."

He looks at his hands clenched tight in front of him, "The village was such a sorrowful place that even I found many reasons not to visit after a time. The business at the trading post became the best excuse. Hawk became One Who Is Always Alone and was hardly there either. Even Weasel was more unhappy than ever, but pride made him stay rather then go home to Dark Cloud's village for a long while."

I have a thought all of a sudden in my head and must make a sound in my throat for he looks at me. "I, I think I saw Raven once …" I say.

He studies me for a moment. "Bear John," he says finally. "Yes, I know. *I knew him*, believe it or not. He used to come here to do business, and it would take a week to clear out the stench."

The last pieces to the puzzle begin to fall into place. "You never found any trace of her because she was with Bear John, and he was in Virginia," I say quiet like. "He must have headed north into white territory as soon as he got her from Weasel." My head is full of memories of her and me standing safe and sound with my Pa, Henry, and Eli at Cooper's Store.

Deer nods his head sadly. "I heard much talk once we gave up searching, and I got back to the trading post. Mostly from the white trappers and hunters – not the homesteaders that have one spot and stay there - but the ones who were temporary and had no place they called home. They spoke of Bear John and laughed over his 'Injun squaw'. They thought it was funny how he kept her on a rope like a dog. Each one said the same thing; he'd brought her proper like from her 'Injun brave' who traded her for a brand new rifle. Those stories made more sense than Weasel's story to most of us. Selling captive Indian enemies to the whites was something that had been going on for many years. Whites would think nothing of an Indian slave any more than a black one." He extends his hands out in front of him, "What could we do? I made many inquiries as to Bear John's whereabouts, but there was nothing solid for us ever to act on. It was not until you killed him that we had any idea for certain where he was."

He stands again and paces, "There was a scrap of deerskin cloth they found in his saddle bag after you killed him, you know," he says, and he stops and looks at me. "Bear John used to clean his rifle with it apparently. It was from Raven's tunic. One Who Knows recognized the stitching and decorations even through all the filth. After she died, he used her clothes to keep his rifle clean." I remember after Bear John's death how his possessions and all of his companion's possessions had been carefully examined and looked through.

"In those months after Weasel returned without Raven, and Hawk became One Who Is Always Alone, I think Weasel actually began to believe his own stories. He talked at length of revenge and was angrier and more filled with hate than ever before. He never tired of the debate about the bad choices the village had made and the good choices Dark Cloud's village did. Council circles at Great Elk's village were filled with Weasel's condemnations of those elders who had steered the people falsely and his grand talk of vengeance for the wrongs that had been done him. One Who Knows sat there silent and accusing, never speaking a word. Finally, Great Elk challenged Weasel to seek out his own revenge if he was so certain he deserved it, but War Woman refused to allow him to take anyone from the village with him. She told him that revenge must be a personal thing, and she would not have the village dragged into something that it had no part of. It was then that Weasel knew there was no one sitting in the council circle who did not blame him for all that had happened in the village."

Deer comes over to me and kneels down in front of me and looks at me with sorrowful eyes. "That's how you come to be sitting here with me today. I think the village hoped that Weasel would just go, and for quite a while he did. There was word that he went back to Dark Cloud's village for a time, but he did not stay. How he came to be in Ward's Mill, Virginia," he points to the paper I realize is still clutched in my hand, "on March 22nd, 1828, on the property of Andrew Graves, Esquire I will never know."

He reaches out and grasps my hand tightly, further crumpling the notice and speaks with great emotion, "Weasel brought you to Great Elk's village and in many ways he restored the harmony there, whether he intended to or not. I need only to sit around the council circle and see the changes in every face as a result of your presence. *That* is why One Who Knows speaks of your brightness, *that* is why One Who Is Always Alone is now *Bright Feather,* and that is why you are no longer Elle but *Bear.*" He laughs a strange laugh, "You have made so many choices on your own with your good heart unaware of the tangled mess of broken hearts and spirits around you, and *all your choices have been fine ones.*"

I hear Bright Feather's words in my head as we rode back from my time in Dark Cloud's village. Choices are a little bit like weeds. Some left to grow can have beautiful flowers. Others might be important for healing. You never have to stop looking for choices, but you must always at the same time never stop making them. That's life.

Deer stands in front of me and pulls me to my feet. He takes his hat off his head and bows a formal bow to me in the forest amid the bright autumn leaves and bustling animals scurrying to prepare for winter. "It is a privilege to know you, Bear, daughter of One Who Knows, of The Maple Forest, of The Real People," he says solemnly. "I count myself honored to call you friend." My eyes fill with tears from his words, and I can't find any words in my mouth. He steps forward and puts his arm around my shoulders and turns me to head back to the trading post.

And now I have a puzzle I can see the whole picture of.

Bright Feather is in the courtyard of the trading post showing James how to hold his bow and shoot when we walk into the clearing. He stands and walks toward us as we come out of the forest, Deer and I, and his eyes search my face for a brief moment. *I know the name of the spirit who speaks to you in your head,* my head says. *Her name is Black Fox.* He touches my cheek gentle like, and I smile at him, my heart full of sorrow and tenderness and love all rolled into one. "The soldiers go north," he says to both of us. "That is the direction I would have picked if I could have." He looks at the two of us, "Did you have a good walk?"

"Can you believe it, brother?" Deer says in wonderment. "She barely asked one question!"

Later that night Bright Feather lies next to me in our private space in the back storage room of the trading post which is lit by flickering lantern light. "I have a gift for you," he says and reaches over beside him and hands me the parcel.

I feel like a child as I unwrap the deerskin and am flooded with curiosity. I sit up with excitement when I realize what it is. A book! *"Hymns and Spiritual Songs,"* I read aloud and touch the fine black leather cover aged but still sturdy, *"by Isaac Watts, 1707."* I look at Bright Feather in great wonder. "Why? Where?"

"Deer was very pleased with how well I am speaking the white language," he explains. "He thinks maybe *my* thick skull might be able to begin to read it now. This was the only book he had, and he thought we can practice my reading *and* maybe save my soul as well. I'm not so sure about the soul part, but the reading should be something we can work on."

I open the book and read aloud by the flickering lamp, "Teach me the measure of my days, thou maker of my frame, I would survey life's narrow space, and learn how frail I am. A span is all that we can boast, an inch or two of time; man is but vanity and dust in all his flower and prime[11]." The book feels strange in my hand, for aside from the great family Bible we used to read at home with Pa, I've never held one, let alone owned one. "White people consider books to be very precious," I say after a time. "We had a family Bible that we would read from – me and Henry – each night to practice. It had many names of our family who had been born and died from before they even came here to the Colonies. Ma's mother gave it to her when she and Pa married. Pa let me write Eli's name in it when he was born and Pa wrote of Ma's death…" My head is full of memories of sitting by the firelight listening to Pa's strong confident voice reading the hard words out loud, then Henry and finally me reading through the verses and struggling with the understanding of it all.

"We would read once Eli was in bed, and he would slowly drift off to the sounds of our voices. There were many times I had trouble understanding what it all meant. But there was one verse I remember I liked the sound of 'cause it was so hopeful." I whirl the white words around in my head trying to change them to Indian and keep them sounding good. *"It is of the Lord's mercies that we are not consumed, because His compassions fail not. The Lord is my portion, saith my soul; therefore I will hope in Him. The Lord is good unto them that wait for him, to the soul that seeketh him*[12]*.* That is from the book of *Lamentations*, third chapter, verses twenty two to twenty five."

For many moments I feel powerful like I'm back home in the cabin in Ward's Mill, Virginia, and I expect to hear Pa's voice any moment say, *Well done, Elle, and can you tell us what your understanding is of 'mercies'?* "Pa would have us read verses, some we'd just open up to, some he'd make us find and then we'd talk about the meanings of the words and the meanings of the verses. He always was patient and kind, although he must have been powerful tired by then, for I knew for sure I was. Most nights I just wanted to curl up in bed with Eli and fall fast asleep. I remember Henry and me many nights complaining and wanting to skip lessons. *What good will this book learning ever do for us, Pa?* I can still hear Henry saying in a voice filled with tiredness. Pa would insist we practice, and it was a quiet time I must admit has a powerful good memory tied to it now."

"What is my 'soul' that Deer speaks of needing to be 'saved'?" Bright Feather asks quietly.

"Pa said the soul was the part of us that never died. He said that our bodies can last just only so long, but the soul goes on forever. Once the body is gone, the soul moves on to the next special place where God intends it to be. In those early times after Ma died, I used to think that maybe Ma's soul was in Eli and her things around the house, like her Hope Chest. Now I think about what The Real People believe and how the spirit world is the next place we go on this journey of life. I think about how I hear Pa's voice in my head and about your voice," I look across to him in the lantern light, and he looks back at me with dark thoughtful eyes. "I think about those we love who are not with us anymore, and I think about a time in the future when you and I will be separated like that. I hear the word *destiny* quiet like in my ear, and I know as sure as you are sitting here close enough to touch," I reach out and touch the warm, alive, bare skin of his thigh glowing gold and orange and beautiful brown in the flickering light, "and I *know* there is another life after this one where we will all surely be together as well.

"Reverend Walker and Miss Rebecca talked about a God that loved us so very, very much that He sent His son to die for us and take the blame for our wrongs," I tell Bright Feather. "I've pondered what they have told me, and I understand it to mean that He allowed His death to bring Harmony back in exchange for all the wrongs that we have done.

"What is truly amazing to me is that Miss Rebecca said that God's son, Jesus, loved us so much that he chose to die rather than to live without us."

Bright Feather stretches out and puts his head in my lap. "That is an amazing love," he says after a time. "I would like to ask many more questions." He gives me a tender look. "Do you think I am learning that from you?" He places his hand at the top of my head and follows my long wrapped tail of hair down my back. He wraps his arm around my back and says, "Read me more of this *Isaac Watts* and then let us make some powerful good memories of our own."

I open the book and begin to read, "We are a garden walled around, chosen and made peculiar ground; a little spot enclosed by grace out of the world's wide wilderness. Like trees of myrrh and spice we stand, planted by God the Father's hand; and all his springs in Zion flow, to make the young plantation grow[13]," I read aloud with the book resting on Bright Feather's bare chest and my hand stroking his hair as it lays like some shiny blanket thrown careless over my crossed legs. Nice new memories to mix with the old, I think in my head with a happy sigh.

"What is 'peculiar'?" Bright Feather asks.

I roll the word around in my head, and I hear Pa trying one of my dinners and saying, *This has a mighty peculiar taste, Elle...* Then I hear Eli say, *We put honey in it, Pa! Honey,* Pa says thoughtful like, *honey and trout. Now that's a new pairing I'd not thought of...*

I say, "Peculiar means, I think, different, not what you'd expect."

"I like that one," he says after a moment. "'*We are a garden walled around, chosen and made peculiar ground...*' that's just how The Real People of The Maple Forest are; surrounded by the whites and the reds, '*a little spot enclosed by grace out of the world's wide wilderness.*'" He picks up one of my hands and kisses it, settling it against his heart. "Read that one again," he says. And I do.

On our third and last day, Deer speaks with both Bright Feather and me as Possum fusses about the kitchen. "I must speak to you of what news I have heard. And none of it is good. There is great trouble on the horizon for The Nation of The Real People. I have heard even more talk since I last visited The Maple Forest. It is not good that Andrew Jackson has been elected President of the United States. He will not look towards the direction of what is right, but will instead, always look towards the direction of who shouts the loudest." Deer looks at both of us serious like, "And the white man always shouts the loudest."

He smiles at Possum as she pours him some hot black coffee, and takes a careful sip. "Already the state of Georgia has asked for permission to enter Real People lands to mine for gold that has been found in the northern part of the state. Georgia has never recognized the tribal boundaries and for many, many years has sought to have the piece of paper giving rights to The Nation of The Real People destroyed. They have tried things legally, and they have tried things outside the law. I do not believe they will stop until they get what they want: the land." Deer shakes his head. "Should Georgia decide to act on its own without the Government's permission, I do not believe anyone will try to stop them. In fact, I suspect all will watch carefully and see how successful they are at getting what they want. I speak to you plainly: there will be Real People lives lost, and the land will be taken by theft."

Deer sighs and Possum sits down next to him, putting her hand on his shoulder. "For a time, the Government and the states will look toward the largest pieces of land that are held by The Nation of The Real People. They will set their hungry eyes and hands on where they can get the most with the least effort. But they *will come* to The Maple Forest. You must believe that. No matter what we do or hope. We must be ready."

Deer has a look of such powerful sadness, I feel my throat get tight with tears. My heart beats fast and furious and I look at Bright Feather's solemn face and Possum's fearful one, and I know I am not alone with my great worries. "For many of us," Deer says, "it will be a fight to the death whether we go to a war with weapons or not. Words on paper sometimes can kill more than a rifle shot can. Our greatest defense in The Maple Forest is to be ready and to continue to collect all those weapons – paper ones, wisdom ones, and" he looks at me, "people ones.

"I told you last I saw you in The Maple Forest that I thought that you two were a great asset to your village. Watch, listen, learn, and *think*. Always think.

"We must believe that it will be our *difference* that will give us our greatest strength. We have made ourselves separate and apart. We are citizens of the United States with all the rights and privileges that affords us. I have worked long and hard to sew all these paper piece walls together to protect us when the time comes. Though it will not keep us from the battle that is coming, it *must* make us victorious in the end."

The Maple Forest is chosen and made peculiar ground, I think, and I look at Bright Feather. He looks back at me, and I suspect the worry he sees in my face makes him reach for my hand. *Enclose us in grace*, I whisper prayer to God, *please*!

I'm quiet that evening of the last day at Deer and Possum's trading post as I think about all the things I have learned in these three short days to Forest City, North Carolina. Names swirl through my head: Raven, Black Fox, Bear John, Weasel, ... Hawk. Are the spirits restless for the talking that was done about them? I think about Bright Feather and the great sorrow he must have felt to have lost both a mate and a son. *Truly he does know how sorrowful a heart can be.*

I think about Cornelius Cooper of Ward's Mill, Virginia, and the notice he posted about my missing. If Pa, Henry, and Eli are all gone, why should he care about me and my circumstances? Why would he go to such trouble to have a 'positive outcome' to such a 'tragic occurrence'. Is he after all this time still looking for me? Still wishing for my return? I find that thought upsetting for he has no reason to have concern about my safety.

I help Possum bake bread and work on a gift I'm making for One Who Knows. Eliza and I go for a ride together on Willow, and I let her talk herself dry. As I brush down Willow later that afternoon I think about our "garden walled around" in The Maple Forest and am so glad for it and have a yearning suddenly to get back there. I ponder over this man who is President, Andrew Jackson, who will listen to those who shout the loudest rather than those who are the wisest. *Why can't things just stay quiet and still and peaceful for just a bit?* I wonder.

Night has fallen and I enjoy the quiet moment sitting on Deer and Possum's front porch swing. I sigh and put my head on Bright Feather's shoulder. I decide to show Bright Feather the crumpled notice about my missing. I've kept it to myself for a day, but now the pile of worry I'm keeping inside me is too much for just one body to hold. I can't worry about Andrew Jackson *and* Cornelius Cooper all by myself.

He searches my face as I hold it out to him. "Read to me what it says," he says softly against my ear after pulling me into his arms. I decide to make it a sort of reading lesson saying each word slow and careful like. It takes us a while because whenever I say a white word he doesn't know he makes me stop and explain it. It takes me quite a while to realize that he's choosing the big ones I sometimes stumble on on purpose. "Mind yourself, young man," I say in the best stern white Pa voice I can manage. He grunts. White folks furniture comes in handy sometimes I think as we swing, and I enjoy the heat of his body burning through the sides of my tunic.

"The picture is not you," he says after studying it for a while.

"Deer said the same thing, just about. He said if I held the picture right next to my face those soldiers would not have been able to see the likeness."

"Your eyes are more almond shaped and your mouth turns up in the corners all the time so that you always look like you're just about smiling even when you are trying to be serious." He hesitates and then says, "I have seen this before."

I sit up and turn to look at him. "When? When did you see this?"

"Well, that's a mighty long story," he drawls out in his best white person words.

I sigh and snuggle back up against him and put my head on his shoulder. "This trip seems to be all about stories."

He waits a moment and says, "That first night when Great Elk took you from One Who Knows, I had just gotten back from visiting Deer and Possum. I had returned earlier in the day and the village was in an uproar over what had happened to you. I kept thinking, '*White girl? What white girl? Here?*' When I ask finally, all One Who Knows will say is, 'Watch and see.' Before I know it, Great Elk has given you to me to care for my needs. More than once I think I should have waited *just one more day* before I returned." I pull away and look at him with a fierce stare. "I am not always as quick to see the good in things," he says by way of apology.

"I took you hunting," he says with a deep sigh, "at Otter's insistence. 'I hunt alone' I told her over and over, but she would not hear me. I planned to leave you with the women at the hunting camp, but you looked so uncertain. You sat quiet with me that whole day and then worked so hard the next. And you still had the energy to laugh at something as we washed in the stream at the end of that day. I looked at you and you had the robin's feather stuck in your hair, and I thought, *There is something special about this girl.*

"The next time I visited Deer, it was just about this time last year, autumn time. That was when I saw this picture hanging on Deer's wall. He thought it was important I take note of it once I mentioned that there is a white captive in the village. He read to me the words, too, so I knew what they said." He felt compelled to add, "You did a good job at explaining the big words. Deer explained them almost the same way," and hugs me tight and finally gives me a kiss when I pretend to try to give him a good shove.

"But I did not know for sure it was you. I realized I had never really even spoken with you. I had every intention of finding out your white name when I returned to the village. I made a point to remember *Elle Graves* so that I could say it to you when I got back to Great Elk's village. I arrived to another big gathering, and again you seemed to be in the center of it all. I watched you sitting by War Woman that night and trying so hard to be a Mouse. I saw Otter speak sternly to you when you tried to get up and scurry and hide in the shadows like you preferred to do. I knew then as I looked at you that the drawing was not very good, but that you were the young girl in the picture, and I sorrowed for you and your loss even though you were unaware of it.

"I went and I got Willow and your things and was ready to come forward at the end of the celebration to bring you home to *Cornelius Cooper of Ward's Mill, Virginia.* I watched you tell your story with Otter to those around the council fire. I knew Deer has talked to you, so you can imagine my shock to hear *who* you killed. The very man Deer, Raccoon and I had searched so long and so hard for but never found. Then I heard Great Elk call you a daughter of One Who Knows and name you Bear, and I knew that you had a family again and One Who Knows had a daughter again. I realized that your place most certainly was now with The Real People of The Maple Forest. So instead of taking you home to sorrow and grief, I brought you your horse and acknowledged you before the village and gave you your freedom from any obligations to me.

"I worried that whole winter that I had made the wrong choice. What if you were unhappy? What if you had more family to go to? What if you felt just as much a prisoner in Otter and Raccoon's home as you had with One Who Knows or me? I returned from my winter trapping determined again to speak to you and offer you the chance to go home to your own people. And what do I find on my return? I find a beautiful and powerful Indian woman sitting proudly on her Indian pony with her bow and her arrows, wrapped in her furs, her face flushed with victory over a kill, who put me smack in my place when I failed to address her properly and with respect. I can still see Raccoon sitting on his horse grinning like a fool at my confusion.

"That was the first time we talked. We talked about horses and shooting and the forest. When I left again to hunt, it was the first time in many years that I felt that my name did not fit me so well anymore, for as I rode into the woods the only thing I wanted to do was to come back and answer many more questions for you. I made myself stay away. I argued with the voice in my head that I was best off with the trees and the animals and Companion. I made myself do all the things that I had always done, and I made myself remember the pain and the sorrow and the tears of loosing someone. I stayed away as long as I could stand it and then rode back to the village telling myself that I was going to just be the way I had always been. But I had plans about what I would show you, and things I wished to teach you and places I thought you might like to ride to, and the voice in my head teased me about lying to myself as well as others. I returned to find the village in turmoil for you had disappeared not two days before.

"While they argued over whether you had gone on your own or not, Raccoon and I searched the woods. He knew some of the places you liked to go, but it turned out that you had shown me still others. It was at your quiet place that we saw the signs of the fight and even found your knife with blood on it. We rode back to the village to get supplies and tell them what we were doing." He shook his head, "Some were still arguing about what to do when we rode out.

"As we followed the trail, all I could think of was how could I be doing this again? Looking for someone I cared about who I was certain was in danger. It was on the trail and the wait outside Dark Cloud's village that I had to be honest with myself that you made me not want to be alone anymore." He grunts. "By then Raccoon had told me that Beaver and Red Fox had made their interests in you known. I did not want to interfere with your choices, and again told myself lies that I would bring you home and leave you again so that you could make the decisions you needed to make." He shakes his head. "I even knew I would make the offer to you about going back to Ward's Mill, Virginia, as Great Elk had instructed me to, and worried if I would have to tell you what I knew to be true about your family."

I turn to him on the swing, and I take his face in my hands and cover his mouth with mine to make him be quiet. It's a long, sweet, slow kiss that seems to go on and on and on. I finish kissing his strong mouth and kiss his eyes and his cheeks and his forehead, and he breathes a loud sigh and finally wraps his arms tight around me. He pulls me across his lap and holds me so tight I'm not sure he will ever let go, and still we kiss again for a very long time. Finally, we stop and both take a long shaky breath.

"I will not let Cornelius Cooper have you," he says after a time, and I feel my worry bow release about that very thing.

"I do not need to fear that he will come searching for me," I say without a question.

His arms tightened around me, and he pulls me close, almost across his lap. "No, you do not need to fear."

I ponder how he knows this to be so but decide I no longer wish to ask questions about this worry. "You know," I say to him, "different places, different languages, different *worlds*, and still," I can't help myself, and I draw him down to me and kiss him again longer and slower, "we found each other. What do you think that means?"

He's grown tired of the talking at last, I can tell, and he's more interested in the kissing. He has me cradled in his arms, and he kisses my neck while he touches my breasts both slow and careful like; he's in no hurry at all. "It means," he says, "we are each other's *destiny*. No person, no situation, no thing will stop this that we have." He holds my face with his hand and leans over to whisper in my ear, "And that makes me *so glad*."

I'm up with the very first rays of the sun on the day we're to leave Deer and Possum's trading post. I walk out into the cool, autumn dawn and wander through the forest alive with colors of red and gold and orange. I walk as far as Deer's thinking rock where we sat just two days before as he filled in all the puzzle pieces I'd been missing for so long. Now I must think of Bright Feather's new puzzle pieces of life. My head is just too busy to sleep. I must take some time by myself to look at this new picture that's been made. Sitting on the rock, I shiver a bit at the coolness; sleeping beside a hot furnace body night after night causes a body to become less accustomed to the coldness of being on its own.

I feel a heaviness pressing down on me this morning. It's in my head and in my heart. My head worries about my people and those that I now consider my family and friends. The more I learn about the world, the more I fret about what's ahead. Will we win this battle that's to come of words and paper and selfishness and greed? Will the world invade our garden walled around and destroy it? Will I be able to do more for anyone than I did for Pa, Henry, and Eli? My head can't imagine how I could.

Part of this heaviness is about what my future has in store for me. Will I get pulled ahead faster once again than I'm ready for? How many times does a body have to face such a thing? I think about Bright Feather and all he told me last night sitting on Deer's swing. My heart swells big with love for him.

I realize that I've much more to loose now than when I was a white girl named Elle Graves! As Bear of The Maple Forest I've become a powerful woman, mate, sister, daughter, and friend. It'd seem that being all these wonderful things also means that I've just that much more to fear losing. Could I carry on after the loss of all those precious to me a second time? My heart beats fast with terror. I don't see how my heart could survive such a thing.

I look down at my hands tightly clenched with worry. My white hands. But I know better about such things now. With that thought my heart begins to slow and my head begins to calm. For I now know that the color of my skin's not what makes me the person that I am. There's much more power in what's *inside* a body than what's outside. I can fit in two worlds instead of one. I have a strong pink color. It's better than only white, better than only red. Suddenly, I realize that this makes me stronger than the most powerful warrior in the village.

I think of my pink center and what it holds. Standing proud and tall is a young woman named Bear, who's a part of all she's met along the path of her life: some have made her wiser and some have made her stronger. I think about this God I whisper to and decide right then and there to let Him stand beside me in my center and invite Him to put His arm around me, full of this special love that seems to know no boundaries. I feel a strong sense that I'm no longer alone in this battle for those I love and hold so dear.

I let the strength of my center push the heaviness away and I decide that I'll look forward to the future. I've made it this far, haven't I? Surely, with all I have inside me and all I have surrounding me, I'll succeed again. *How can I not?*

There're so many things that I am. But, I suspect, more importantly are the things that I *am not.* I have been a captive and an orphan. I have been alone, frightened and helpless. At one time, my only thoughts were ones about what I didn't know and what I couldn't do.

Though I hear no sound I suddenly know that I'm no longer alone sitting here on Deer's thinking rock. Looking up, I stare into the concerned eyes of Bright Feather who stands silently on the edge of the clearing patiently watching me ... Waiting ... Loving ...

I stand and make my way toward him. With each step I think about what I am now.

I'm capable!

I'm smart!

I'm brave!

I'm strong!

I'm eager!

I'm a partner!

I'm a friend!

I'm a daughter!

I'm a sister!

As strong arms enfold me I know that these thoughts are those of a wise and powerful woman.

Call me Bear.

May the paths from every direction
recognize each other.[14]

From a Cherokee Sacred Formula

Elle Graves

The fierce Indian brave walks towards me strong and sure. He's naked except for his breechclout and bright feathers tied in his hair. He doesn't smile or laugh or make any motion 'cept to walk toward me in an easy, long legged stride. When he gets close enough to me he stops, raises his hand and touches my cheek. "Are you ready to go, my mate?" he asks in his best white person words that I've taught him.

Before I can answer, the door behind us opens and out comes our friend, Deer, looking a bit sheepish. "Got any more room on those packhorses? Seems as if Possum has found still *more* things to send back to the village with you …" He rolls his eyes like he can't believe what his mate has done.

"There would be *plenty* of room still on those horses if you had not insisted on sending those sacks of new fangled seed you want the village to try planting," comes an impatient voice directly behind him. Possum, Deer's mate, comes into view holding a basket, covered carefully with a piece of muslin cloth.

Deer and Possum are the mirror images of Bright Feather and me, he with his white face and she with her Indian one. Of all of us today, only Deer looks truly white instead of his Indian self, choosing to look like the proper white trader known as William Holland Thomas with his homespun shirt, tan trousers and cloth suspenders. For you see, even though Possum wears the clothes of a white person, no one would be able to mistake her for one with her dark snapping eyes, beautiful long black hair and red Indian skin. She is Possum, of the Turkey clan of The Real People of The Maple Forest. But you can call her Mary. She'll answer to either name as long as you speak to her proper like, with respect.

Which is the problem, you see. For many a white person would call her a savage no matter what she wore or how she behaved because they can't see past the red skin. I was like that for a time. Until I was taken from my white home. Until I was made a slave even with my proper white skin and all. Until I had to realize that it wasn't the skin color that made you a slave or a savage or anything else. It was what was *inside* that made you the person you *chose* to be. I have white skin, I wear savage clothes, I love an Indian brave, and I call The Maple Forest of The Real People my home. I'm not white anymore. I'll never be red. If you need to say a color, you best call me pink.

I grin at Possum. "I've still got some room, but you'll have to help me fit it on Willow's pack." As Possum and I start to walk to the horses, I realize that even Possum looks more white than I do from behind at least with her proper cloth skirt and blouse.

We are almost ready to leave with our pack horses piled high and final shouts of best wishes from Deer and Possum's three children: James, *Red Bird,* Eliza, *Sleeping Rabbit,* and Richard, *Small Turtle.* This being my first trip to white territory since Bright Feather and I have joined together, I was powerful worried about just about everything. Would I be safe? Would Bright Feather be safe with me? What if we met others besides Deer and his family at the trading post? What should I say? How could I explain my circumstances? Do I have the right words to tell my story? All of my worries are needless in the end. Even with soldiers showing up unexpectedly at the trading post, by keeping quiet and in the shadows they thought I was nothing more than a "thievin' Injun squaw" I think is how they put it.

In the end, this trip to Deer and Possum's has filled in a powerful large hole in my puzzle of life. Things I'd wondered about, like why I was taken in the first place from my home in Ward's Mill, Virginia, to Great Elk's village in The Maple Forest.

And then there are the things I never thought to consider. I glance at Bright Feather as he talks quiet like to Deer. I had no idea that so many of my choices had been so right. I had no idea how my presence has brought healing to so many.

Bright Feather stops talking to Deer and turns to look at me across the hard packed dirt of the yard. For a moment there is no Deer or Possum, no horses stomping and flicking away annoying flies with their tails, no Eliza, *Sleeping Rabbit,* pulling on my arm and asking me the last few one hundred questions she needs to ask before I leave. There is just me and Bright Feather. Standing separate and yet joined so strong I feel as if he is touching me, can smell his manly scent, can hear his thought whisper in my ear, *Are you alright, my mate?* I sigh and give him a brief nod and a small smile. *Yes, I am fine, my husband.* He turns back to finish speaking with Deer.

I have promised Deer and Possum's daughter, Sleeping Rabbit, for that is how Eliza now insists on being called, that perhaps in the coming summer she will travel back to Great Elk's village with us and stay for a bit. Their son, James, already had the chance this past summer I am surprised to learn and Sleeping Rabbit feels that she is ready now, too.

"Think *long* and *hard* before you make the final decision about her coming," Possum says to me in pointed words while rolling her eyes as Sleeping Rabbit shouts her last few questions to me as Bright Feather joins me and we mount up on our horses in the chilly morning mists.

I feel adult and grown up but look at Possum and smile thinking back to me and my endless questions. "I remember," I say to her as I turn to answer Sleeping Rabbit's latest question, "When I come to visit Great Elk's village and stay with you, can I have a tunic to wear made just like yours?"

"Perhaps," I say to Sleeping Rabbit with a smile, "we can make you a tunic that is decorated with rabbit fur. What do you think of that?" She claps her hands in excitement.

"I will remember your words," I tell Possum for she has asked me to send greetings to a number of family and friends in the village. "Thank you for everything."

"*Thank you, too,*" she says and she looks up with meaning at Bright Feather as he guides his horse, Companion, near me and says, "Are you ready to go now?" Possum must grin a wide grin every time she calls Bright Feather "Bright Feather" instead of the name she has known him by for so many years – One Who Is Always Alone.

Because of me, the name no longer fits him, you see.

That makes me smile a bright smile as I cast a glance back at the trading post at Forest City, North Carolina, and wave to the family of red and white skin that has made three beautiful pink children. It is a peek at my future that I hope sometime soon will come true.

The journey back seems much faster than the journey there. I have nothing to worry about and many stories to remember and sort through. I think about all the pieces to the puzzle of my life and am amazed at how large the puzzle truly is! I ponder over why I came to be taken from my white home in Ward's Mill, Virginia, and all the heartache and sorrow that went along with it. I now know the gift Bright Feather gives me in choosing to love again for I have learned of the heartache and sorrow that brought him to be called One Who Is Always Alone for so long. I now know that the choices I made were wise ones.

I think in particular about the times that Bright Feather came so close to bringing me back to Virginia. I wonder what I would have done with the chance had he offered it and how much I would have missed about finding out about me as a powerful woman. I think about the flier telling others about my capture and pleading for my safe return. I think about Cornelius Cooper of Cooper's General Store and wonder just what he would have done with me had I shown up on his doorstep at any one of those times? Just what would he have done with an orphaned white girl who had lived for a time with the *wild Injun savages*. I remember his face and his store and his kind, plump wife who I only knew to call *Mrs. Cooper*. I can't recall any children although they were both older so perhaps their children were married and gone. Would they have adopted me like One Who Knows has done in The Maple Forest and would I have become their daughter and learned all about their store and married some white settler and gone on with my white life just as I have here in this Indian life? I look at Bright Feather's straight back in front of me Companion and I think, *Would I have even missed you? Would you have even missed me?* A wave of sorrow deep and sharp cuts through me at the thought of being without him. It's different from the sorrow of losing Pa, Henry and Eli. This sorrow feels like all of my insides are being carved out and thrown on the ground to be trampled and left to rot. It's a pain so strong I decide maybe not to think on this subject anymore and make an effort to turn my thoughts away.

But then I hear Bright Feather's words in my ears from last night when we talked about different places, different languages and different words and how we still found each other and what it meant. In between his kisses, Bright Feather had whispered to me, *It means we are each other's destiny. No person, no situation, no thing will stop this that we have,* and I feel certain that at some point even if had I become the adopted daughter of Mr. and Mrs. Cooper of Ward's Mill, Virginia, a tall handsome Indian brave with bright feathers in his hair would have crossed my path somehow. *Destiny.*

The village of The Maple Forest is glad to see us and is happy to receive the many, many things that we have brought. I tease Bright Feather that now I understand why everyone always seems so glad to see him when he returns each time. I thought it was just because they missed him. He pretends he does not hear me.

As soon as I have finished kissing and cuddling Little Bird and answering my friend Otter's many questions, I make my way into the village to deliver Possum's words and gifts. Possum, I have come to learn, has a sister and an aunt in the village who are happy to receive all the things I bring with me. It was here that James spent his summer last year while I struggled with the unexpected directions my life had taken through no fault of my own. I answer their polite questions and tell them of Sleeping Rabbit's hope to visit next summer. I laugh in understanding when they seem to hesitate (Sleeping Rabbit has quite a gift at making a body tired with all the questions that she asks) and things become more comfortable after that.

My final stop before I return to our hut is to One Who Knows. My adopted mother. A woman who at first I was a slave to and now I am a daughter to. One Who Knows is as her name replies: she is a healer and she can sometimes tell directions for the future. She is also old and mighty crabby. Age has made her impatient with stupid questions, annoying people, and, well, most things in general.

Turtle, the young Indian woman that lives with her, is preparing the evening meal and tells me that One Who Knows is somewhere out in the forest gathering her precious herbs. I smile at Turtle and ask if she is ever allowed to help prepare the herbs. For sure I never was. She gives me a horrified look and says, "Oh No! The worst slap I ever received was when I accidentally ruined some of the herbs she had drying in the sun. I am *never ever* to touch *or even look at* the herbs she uses for healing."

"I suppose she told me that too, many times, but I couldn't understand her words then."

A sharp voice behind me says, "That is true. When you were with me you were more of a trial than Turtle ever was, as slow as she is. Head as thick as rock, you have. How was I ever supposed to get anything done with a fool white girl that always seemed to draw trouble to her quicker than ants to a tasty crumb?" Turtle scurries to get back to work and I remember the fear I see in her eyes.

I turn as she is speaking and her expression is as hard and dark as how I recall it to be when I was in Turtle's place, only called Mouse. But I know many things now as I stand there in the late afternoon shadows and I know that there are many differences from when I was Mouse and now: I am unafraid, I am Bear, and *I am her daughter by her choice.*

"I come to wish you well, *Mother*, and inquire how things are with you. I bring greetings to you of Possum of the Turkey Clan of the Real People of the Maple Forest."

She snorts through her nose and rolls her eyes. "Help me with these things, *Daughter*," and she says the title with not the same kind meaning as I meant mine, "they are heavy and anyone polite will have done it without being asked." I remove her precious gathering basket from her back and am amazed at how heavy it really is.

"Tell me," I say politely and with great respect, "when I was Mouse here in this hut with you, did you speak to me like this even when I did not understand you?"

She looks at me for a beat and then I see the twinkle in the eye. "I speak to *everyone* this way and that was one of my greatest frustrations with you. How can I cause you to jump with fear at threats you cannot understand?" She sighs as she settles on her furs at the opening of her hut. "I was well rid of you."

"You claimed me for your daughter the night I was named Bear. I did not know that until Bright Feather told me. I thought you claimed me as your daughter the night we celebrated my joining with Bright Feather."

She begins to sort through her basket and hands me some herb I don't know. "Goat's Beard," she says. "Good for poultices for bee stings and to be brewed as a tea to stop bleeding after childbirth." She whispers quietly to me, "I like to soak my swollen feet in it at times, too." I watch her speed and skill as she works. "Best picked right before the end of the growing season. You must immediately break off the roots and hang it in a bunch in a dry, dark place or it loses much of its power. Here." She thrusts a pile of the plant in my hand and I watch as she works to prepare it for hanging. I am pleased to be allowed to help and carefully begin to follow her directions. "Bright Feather has a big mouth," is all she will finally say about my comments.

"If you claimed me for your daughter, why did I not go back to live with you in your hut?"

She looks at me and I sense impatience. "Do you ask questions of me because you like the sound of my voice? I have some songs I can sing you that might be more interesting than just repeating things you already know."

I look down at the herbs and study them closely while I think. At last I say, "If I were to come back to your hut, without understanding the language well enough, I would have just thought that I was going back to being your slave again."

She nods ever so slightly. "And Otter needed companionship. And Raccoon needed someone to stir him up a bit. And One Who Is Always Alone needed someone to make him remember he was a *man* not some solitary creature of the forest. And I needed someone I can threaten more with my words." She smiles a sweet innocent smile at me that can almost be more frightening then her dark looks and I can't help it; I burst out laughing.

"I have brought you a gift," I say finally and I hand her a package wrapped in an old seed sack and tied with twine. "Two, actually."

She puts down her herbs and for a flash seems almost like a child as she unties the twine (and carefully wraps it up for future use) and opens the seed bag and draws out what I have brought her. "It is a collecting bag," I say all of a sudden worried that it is a foolish thing to give a woman who has been gathering herbs for longer than three of my lifetimes – at least. "The whites use them when they are planting and it is used for carrying large quantities of seed." I stand up and demonstrate, "It sits comfortable like at your shoulder like this – see the padding here? – and then drapes across your body to rest at your hip. They are not usually decorated like this but Possum showed me some stitches and gave me some thread and so I added some decorations on it so it didn't look so plain." In the face of her silence at the gift I add, "If you prefer your basket, then you can always use it for something else ..." She examines it with quiet concentration; the fabric, the stitching, and the decorations. But remains silent.

"And this," I draw out the other thing that I have brought her from the seed sack, "Deer tells me is called a *mortar and pestle* by white doctors and such. It's heavy because he says it's carved out of a kind of rock! I think it will be easier to grind your herbs with it. White folks use it for the same thing." This too she examines with great interest, turning it over in her hands.

"I have no use for two gathering containers," she says at last, "and lately the gathering has gotten to be harder with these tired old legs." I feel the disappointment in me well up almost like tears and then she says. "But to have company sometimes along for the walk to talk and listen and that I can share things with, now that might just give me a new passion for things.

You would have to be content with that old basket though for I am not inclined to share this new gathering bag with *anyone*. And I am not inclined to say things more than once, well maybe twice, so you are going to have to carve a hole in that thick skull of yours to quick catch all the things I would be teaching you. You are far too old to learn to be a healer, but there is a skill in just knowing the herbs that you can probably master in time."

I grin at her a great wide grin. "I will be back again tomorrow. Is this time of the day good?"

"Of course not! I am just about done for the day. Come as soon as you can and it will still be too late." She picks up her herbs and starts working on them, but not before she carefully folds the seed bag and places it by the rolled up twine.

"Good night, Mother," I say to her as I walk away.

"Good night to you, too, Daughter." She says it with no sharp words or tones. I think she liked my gifts.

I tell Bright Feather that I have given One Who Knows her gifts and of her reactions and words to me. In my excitement over the gifts it's not occurred to me that he has made no comments during the preparation of the gathering bag nor my plans to give One who Knows the gifts. "I am happy that she is pleased," he says at last.

I sit down next to him and look at his face. "I did not ask you about the gifts, should I have?" I ask for all of a sudden I think I'd like to hear his thoughts.

He shrugs. "One Who Knows is difficult to understand," he begins carefully and I can't help but laugh quietly at his way of description. "There has been no one in many years that has helped her in any way with her gathering and healing. At one time, many sought her out to learn her thoughts and seek her advice about important things in their lives. These past years she has kept most of her thoughts to herself except when it suits her to hurl them at you almost like a sharp rock. At one time, she anticipated people's needs and wants and almost knew before you did when you needed a special herb or other special care. These past years if you needed her you knew where she is. She rarely ventures out among the village except to sit at council circles. And often even then she is silent and unwilling to voice her thoughts.

"I did not know how she would react to your gifts, especially since they had to do with her healing arts. I think it is best that you did not speak to me about my thoughts before you gave them to her for I would have had to tell you these things that I just did. Then maybe you would not have chosen to give her your gifts and things would be unchanged.

I spend the rest of the fall tramping through the forest with One Who Knows trying my best to crack open my thick skull and shove as much knowledge as I can inside. More than once I feel that I'm hopeless and should just give up. Very soon, she tells me, there'll be nothing to look for until the spring comes. Today I'm walking in the forest with One Who Knows, she with her new gathering bag and me with her old gathering basket. I feel much the way I did when I struggled to learn the Indian language and the words always seemed to come and go too fast for me to keep them in my head. One Who Knows seems to me to be made entirely of knowledge about the forest and its plants and the more time I spend with her the more I begin to realize that I'll never, ever know all she knows about these things. I tell her that finally in frustration when she scolds me for not remembering correctly the uses and care of an herb I *do* remember she tried to teach me about the first or second day we began gathering together.

"I was not so quick with learning these things, either," she finally tells me as we walk slowly back to the village. "I was young and beautiful and smart but was more interested in other things than the silly dried herbs I had grown up with hanging from the roof of my hut and smelling in the baskets around my head while I slept."

"What was more interesting to you?" I have to ask and wait for a sharp word for asking such a question.

"Boys," she says, "quite a few of them," and she giggles the most wonderful giggle I've ever heard. It sounds like happy water in a quick flowing brook.

I grin at her. It's hard to imagine at first the stooped, gray haired old lady walking slowly and carefully beside me as a beautiful Indian maid chasing boys, but the giggle manages to paint a good picture in my mind. "I never, ever thought of boys much," I say to her in all honesty, "until Bright Feather."

"You had survival on your mind," she says quickly. "The mind is very wise and works on important things one step at a time. You do not make plans to build a hut to live in while you are still a baby in a cradle board. Once you do decide to build a hut, you make sure each step is sound: choice of location, choice of materials, care of construction. Who wants to live in a house that is unsafe? Who wants to rest each night in a house that threatens to collapse in on you with the first stiff breeze? Life is filled with hard choices that correctly made lead to an existence of harmony and peace. But it can take a long time to get there.

"You will not learn all I know about the herbs and the plants around you. Do not frustrate yourself over the things your brain will not have the time to do in this lifetime. Concentrate on the things you know you can do. Learn one piece at a time, just like you learned our language." She mimics me shouting, *DANGER! FIRE! STOP! BEAR! HORSE! NO! COME! FIRE!* the day that Bear John came to attack our village. I remember the fear in my heart as I struggled to decide what I should do and how I could make my slow tongue explain it to those I cared about. I remember the look of puzzlement on Otter's face at my shouts and screams and then the terror when she realized what was coming fast behind me. I remember the feeling of power that poured through my arms as I picked up the burning stick and killed a white man to save my red friend and her baby …

One Who Knows grunts and shakes her head in disgust at the obvious shortcomings of my brain bringing me back to my present difficulties. "Maybe, walking through the forest with me pointing out things is too much for your thick skull. We will do it differently in the spring. We will start with the herbs you already know and I will tell you all the things I know about just them. Then, I will send you out on your own for these old legs are just not what they used to be anymore and I cannot do this every day, and you can bring me back things you find and I will tell you what I know. How does that sound?"

I worry that she is disappointed with me. "I want you to be pleased with what I learn from you. I want you to understand that I am doing my best and trying my hardest," I say to her with great emotion.

She dismisses my words with a wave of her gnarled, old hand. "You are foolish to worry about such things. Mothers always understand that about their daughters." She looks at me and I have learned to watch for the brief twinkle of fun that flashes very quickly now and then. "No matter how stupid they appear sometimes."

Sometimes she says things to me that I have no answer for. We fall into an easy silence as we walk through the beautiful forest not unlike my times hunting and riding with Bright Feather. My mind wanders and I think of Otter and Raccoon and Little Bird. "Otter is expecting another baby," I say to One Who Knows after a time. "She says the baby will come in the late summer."

"You worry about not one but two things," she says to me casual like and I feel the goose skin run up my arms across my neck and into my hair even for she is right.

Her bent old legs carry her with purpose through the forest as she says to me over her shoulder, "They call me One Who Knows because I know more than most people but I don't know everything. Sometimes it is a terrible thing to see only parts of the future, not enough to know anything for sure, only enough to be afraid." She is quiet in her thoughts and I know she must think of her daughters Raven and Black Fox that she could not save from an early death. And perhaps even Weasel and how she could not keep his evil from those she loved and cared about. She shrugs. "But I see good things, too, like the brightness I spoke about seeing where you are concerned.

"You worry first about whether you will have a child with Bright Feather for it has been some months since you first mated." She turns and smiles a rare, sweet smile at me. "You do not need to be One Who Knows to know of that concern for it is something almost every young woman thinks of – I am sure white *or* red – if a baby does not come with the first time you are together with a man.

"But a bigger fear you have still is that you worry that you *will* have a child with Bright Feather. That," she says with certainty, "is another fear that one does not need to have special skills to know about. All women worry of such things for all women know of those who have gone on to the spirit world during the hard battle of childbirth."

I am silent just as she is lost in memories. We walk for long moments, she with thoughts of her daughter Black Fox, Bright Feather's first mate, and the grandson that never lived to see a sunset. Me with thoughts of Ma and how Eli knew only ever me as his Ma even though I was just a girl of eight. I wonder, what do I dread more? Do I fret that I never will have a child with Bright Feather or that I will? I can't decide which path is more filled with worry.

We walk for a bit more and I know we are close to the village. "Men worry about such things, too, but their worries show in different ways. Maybe the baby I know you will have with Bright Feather waits until it knows the worry of *wanting* a child will become greater than the worry of *having* a child – for both of you." I had not thought of Bright Feather worrying about me and the dangers of childbirth. It was the death of Black

Fox and his son that caused him to go from being the great hunter known as Hawk to the man I first met known as One Who Is Always Alone. I sigh and shake my head at the tiny hole I peek through to view my world. I realize I must work more on seeing how others think and feel than just my selfish self.

She touches my arm. "When the worry gets great about the *having*, look around you at every single living being you see and know that the *wanting* usually wins out eventually." She snorts loudly at her own joke. "And have fun with the practicing in the mean time."

We enter the village with her hand still on my arm and I'm certain my face is red with the thoughts of the 'practicing fun' to make a baby with Bright Feather. As we get towards the center where the council circles are held, her hand tightens on mine in caution and warning. "Watch and listen carefully for the brightness, my daughter, for darkness is here in this village again." I raise my head in concern to see a strange Indian brave talking with our village chief, Great Elk and War Woman, his mate. He wears the clothes of a white man but it does not change who he is. But the darkness One Who Knows speaks of, I realize, is more probably in the form of the white soldier standing stiff and surprised and looking right at me.

One Who Knows stumbles and I stop to catch and steady her. "Are you alright? Shall I take you back to your hut?" I ask quick with concern. My mind scrambles to still the millions of thoughts buzzing around in my head like an angry hornet's nest. My heart thumps and thumps. *Don't forget me too!*, it seems to say with a panicked shout.

She places her hand on top of my hand and looks deep into my eyes calm and unconcerned. "I am fine. *So are you.* Remember who you are and what you have learned and where you choose to go. You have handled many situations much more difficult than talking to a white man here in your own village." I realize she has stumbled on purpose to give us a moment for *me* to gather my thoughts.

I grin at her serious eyes. "I am Bear, daughter of One Who Knows, of the Elk clan of the Real People of the Maple Forest and the mate of Bright Feather, son of War Woman of the Wolf clan and Great Elk, chief of the Real People of the Maple Forest. I am a Powerful Woman."

She nods her head satisfied. "*Now*, you can take me home. We will meet these men tonight I am certain."

I realize something about myself as we walk casual past the strangers in our village. I feel my heart slow and my thoughts still and my eyes take stock of who is present and who is not and my senses register the feelings around the council circle group. I realize I do particularly well in unexpected situations; my brain and heart get the sudden shock – like getting struck by a bolt of lightning I suspect – and then everything settles into a hum of high alert. *Experience is the best teacher, Elle,* I hear Pa say loud and clear in my head. Lord knows I've had some experience with unexpected situations! Kidnapped by Indians not once, but twice. Responsible for the death of one white man and pleased about the death of at least three red ones. All before I turned sixteen years. I sigh and shake my head at the passel full of experience that I've been educated by as One Who Knows and I make our way to her hut. *Proper schooling would have been a might easier I suspect,* I think with a quiet chuckle to myself. *Oh well...*

By the time I have the council fire area to my back, I already know that these strangers have just arrived for they are not seated nor have their horses been tended to. I see that Great Elk and War Woman are alert yet do not appear overly threatened. I see a number of others who sit regularly in council circles making their way towards the council area. I am certain that the brave has white blood in him. And I know that the soldier is powerful curious about me for he follows me with his eyes like no other.

I leave One Who Knows at her hut and am glad to see that Turtle has begun the evening meal. She gives me a shy smile and then gets back to her work. At our hut, I have not even finished the preparations of our meal before Bright Feather, Raccoon and Red Fox show up; Red Fox has obviously gone and got them. I stand as they approach and see the concern in their eyes. "They have seen me," I tell them, "and they are powerful curious who I am." Then I tell them what I have seen and know.

As it is with almost every night in the village, after the evening meal is completed many travel to the council circle to talk and hear the way of things. Tonight has a different feel to it as Bright Feather and me make our way through the dark and light spots of the village to join the evening's discussions. Just before we enter the bright spot of the council circle fire, Bright Feather pulls me into the shadows for a long embrace. I feel his tension and know his desire to protect me; it is a good feeling. But there is something more I realize as I reach up and touch his face and kiss his mouth and smell the wonderful smell of him. I realize with a start that I am right calm about things. I reach up and touch my husband's face and smooth my fingers through the three colorful feathers tied in his hair – red for cardinal, yellow for goldfinch and blue for blue jay. In the darkness and shadow the flickering firelight flashes brightly on his long dark hair. "These people were once my people," I say to him quiet like in the safety of the shadows. "I know *both worlds*. More than anything, I remember what One Who Knows and Great Elk have said that I bring brightness to this village. I think this village is much better off with me here than without. I think that much of what has happened to me so far is to make sure I am right in this spot right now. So let us go see just what I can hear and understand about these people who think they still *are* my people." I draw him down for a long and lovely kiss.

When the kiss is finished, Bright Feather takes long moments to search my face, in no hurry to go into the light. Then he grunts, the closest I have ever heard him come to outright laughter. He's apparently satisfied with what he sees. "Do you think this soldier is afraid? I think maybe he should be." He kisses me again holding my face between his two big red hands and then takes my white hand and leads me to the brightness of the council circle.

The white soldier seated in the council circle cannot conceal his surprise as Bright Feather and I arrive hand in hand. It is Bright Feather's way of making a statement to these strangers, I know, as we rarely show affection to each other within the village and never in the council circle. The Indian brave that has traveled with the soldier shows no expression whatsoever but watches us both just the same. Seated with the newcomers are War Woman, Great Elk, One Who Knows, and Raccoon. I realize that this group is specially called for others that regularly join the council circle are not here. All wear their serious faces, even Raccoon who enjoys nothing more than to cause me problems and confusion with his teasing.

"My name is Major Alexander Everett and this is my interpreter, George Maw," the soldier with fair hair and blue eyes says to me. He looks strange among the ring of dark faces and dark hair and I realize that with my brown hair and tan skin I go more with the dark than light. Even his partner has dark brown hair and brown eyes. "I am a member of the Second United States Calvary, Division of the Army, Company A. Our unit is presently based in Virginia, and we work with Ninth Virginia Cavalry, Company D out of Fort Winston, Virginia, of which George Maw regularly works." He looks at me seated across from him sitting between Bright Feather and Raccoon.

"I am here because of a communication I have received regarding one," here he searches through his pack and takes out a letter which he begins to read aloud to the group. He speaks in English and I translate to all those in the circle ignoring George Maw.

"- poor young woman of obvious gentle breeding for her manner and way was most kind and solicitous to all she came in contact with when treated with care and compassion.   She was brought to this Indian settlement as a rescued captive and spent approximately six weeks with us this April last, 1829, however, it was our understanding that prior to her arrival she had spent a considerable amount of time north of here in the Indian village that is frequently referred to as "Indiantown" for want of a better name. Upon her arrival here, she was fully acclimated to the Indian way of life and was fluent in the language and customs to the point where she was unwilling to reveal her white name or history. She departed with three Indian braves, one being the eldest son of Chief Dark Cloud, and one French trader by the name of Martin DuBois with the destination I understand to be the hopes of returning her to her white relations. None in the party have been seen or heard of since. The Cherokee Nation has made every effort to cooperate and become a civilized partner with the United States of America. The United States Government has been supportive and eager to encourage a solid alliance with the Cherokee nation. It seems to be an easy matter to join these two like mannered forces and to inquire into the safety and well being of this young woman whom my wife and I have embraced and taken to heart as if she were our own daughter. We would be most appreciative to any assistance you could afford us in securing information regarding this young woman's whereabouts and health. Your Humble and Sincere Servant who in His Holy Name I entrust my soul and safety, Reverend James Francis Wilder, New Echota, Georgia, July 15th, 1829"

His blue eyes meet my green ones and I feel the silence stretch across the fire growing longer and longer. At last he says, "Are you the young woman Reverend Wilder refers to in this letter?"

"Yes, I am," I say but I answer not in English but in the language of the Real People. George Maw translates to Major Everett and when he finishes I explain, "I will speak to you in the language of The Real People as that is the language of this council circle."

"I understand," Major Everett says politely, "and I will trust that you will continue to translate my words as carefully as George Maw does yours." I nod my head.

He reaches into his pack and takes out another paper, one that I recognize before he hands it across to me for I have seen the likeness drawn on it. "Have you seen this?" he asks, and I translate his words and then read aloud the words about me and my capture to the council circle:

"On the evening of TUESDAY, the 22nd of March in the year of Our Lord 1828, the peaceful homestead of Andrew Graves, Esq. of Ward's Mill, Virginia was violently and savagely attacked by a marauding band of blood thirsty Indians. No surviving witnesses were found to provide an accurate account, however, it is with the Utmost Hope and Desire that the person of Mistress Elle Graves might still be Alive and with the Most Extreme Care and Speed be found and returned post haste. All leniency will be afforded to those cooperating with authorities in the positive outcome to this tragic occurrence. April 10, 1828, Cornelius Cooper of Ward's Mill, Virginia." Beneath the writing is my picture, roughly drawn with the description: "Orphaned white girl whose mother has died and father and brothers have been murdered by marauding Indians, who answers to the name of Elle.."

I look up when I have finished reading and translating and look and Major Everett. "Yes, I have seen this," I answer, "I saw it just this past month in the trading post of our friend and brother, Deer, also known as William Holland Thomas, in Forest City, North Carolina." I hand the paper back to him.

"Are you Elle Graves?" he asks, taking the paper and holding it casual like in his hand.

"No, I am not," I answer strong and sure and I meet his eyes. I try not to even blink. "I am Bear, of the Elk Clan, daughter of One Who Knows, mate of Bright Feather, son of War Woman of the Wolf Clan and son of Great Elk, chief of The Real People of the Maple Forest."

"I see," he says, after listening to the translations and carefully studying each blank Indian face in the council circle. "I had suspected that you would say that. You understand that there are those that still search for this Elle Graves and wish for her safe and speedy return?"

After I translate, at first I am silent. But then finally I say, "Yes, I can see that there are those that search for her. But none of them are her family it seems."

He looks down at the flier and I see him read through the final bits and see *Cornelius Cooper*. He puzzles for a moment and then he finally says, "Often the proprietors of general stores or trading posts are listed as the point of contact as they are more easy to find and more well known. She might have other family members besides the ones that are spoken of." His answer from all is silence.

Major Everett looks at all of those around the council circle but then settles on me and finally he asks, "How is it that you sit here in Indiantown when last you were seen on the trail with four men charged with the assignment of returning you to your white relatives? Are those men here and we do not know it?"

"You have been misled if you think that I am not where I wish to be." I tell him. "You were also misled if you believe that *the four men charged with the assignment of returning me to my white relatives* had anything such as that planned. I am not a prisoner here, I have never been tied nor have I ever been attacked or brutalized here. The only time that I have ever been hurt by anyone was under the *care* of Dark Cloud's son of whom I refuse to speak for his name is dirt in my mouth. I carry scars from him and his treatment on my arms," and I hold up my hands that show wrists forever marked by rope burns, "and on my body," here I open my tunic to show the scar that is still pink and new over my breast. "I carry more wounds such as this made from a knife and from teeth – eleven in all, do you wish to see more?"

Major Everett swallows and appears even paler than before. He does not need the translations I think from the sound of my voice as I speak, the scars I show on my body and the anger I flash in my eyes. "No, I do not need to see more," he finally manages to say.

I continue. "As for the whereabouts of these men, I do not know and I have never known. I am back here where I want to be in the village of The Real People of the Maple Forest. I know only that I was taken by force by this son of Dark Cloud and held against my will at that village. The only people who showed real concern for my safety were the Reverend Wilder and his wife, Miss Rebecca. They were unwilling to believe anything less than what they were told by those in charge and I was never in a position to convince them otherwise. I am grateful for their concern over my health and safety. Please assure then that I am fine, wish them well, and," I smile a little smile, "I am still saying my prayers."

Major Everett is smart enough to realize that to discuss my white life will not benefit him much in this council circle and the talk finally turns to other things. Food is brought and enjoyed and I feel the tension up my back start to ease just a slight bit. I learn that Major Everett has been part of the 2nd Division of the United States Calvary for more than fifteen years. George Maw has been many times to Dark Cloud's village, but always in the capacity of the cavalry's need for a translator. Both soldiers agree that the opportunities within the cavalry cannot be equaled anywhere else within the military. "There is an independence that cannot be equaled in riding your own horse, scouting new and different places and viewing the world from a higher place than most," Major Everett says with a shy smile.

Bright Feather and I decide the next morning to have me ride out early on Willow and avoid any more contact with either Major Everett or George Maw. Bright Feather will stay in the village and watch the way of things. Willow is glad to see me and dances in excitement as I ready her to ride out. "That's a beautiful horse you have," a white voice says to me and I turn around startled to see Major Everett leaning against a large oak.

I take a deep breath to still my jumping heart and stroke Willow's soft silky side. "She's white and learned to be an Indian, just like me," I say. "Miss Rebecca Wilder said that I couldn't go back to being white but would never be red and that perhaps I was more closely pink. Willow's the same way."

"I know you are Elle Graves," he says in the quiet of the forest as I mount up onto Willow as fast but as casual as I can. "The picture is not a good likeness, but the age fits and Dark Cloud was able to share with me when he knows you came to be a part of this village and where he suspects your family is from."

"Seems powerful interesting to me how much he seems to know about me considering I never had the *pleasure* of knowing him until a few months ago and even then I told him *nothing* of myself," I say, and I remember how very, very much I hate him and his dead son.

Major Everett surprises me with a laugh. "Do you know, that is exactly what I said to him." He looks at me, "Considering the Wilders insisted that you never revealed anything about your white past to them, I found it hard to believe that you would have chosen to tell Dark Cloud anything of a personal nature and I said so to him. He told me that in his capacity for leadership he had many connections and had heard information about you from a number of sources." His face tells me that he finds those words hard to believe. "You have nothing to fear of me. I am not here because of Dark Cloud but because of the Wilders. Rebecca is my aunt, you see."

I don't know what to say to him but I search his eyes and think, *Why would he lie to me?* I can't think of a reason.

"They are tenderhearted, the two of them." He smiles shyly at me and sighs. "I'm glad that God watches over them for they need all the help they can get."

I remember my time at Dark Cloud's village and the danger I feared for them more than for myself. "Almost nothing is as it seems in that place," I finally say. "Yet, whenever they spoke, I knew that their words meant just what they said and had no hidden meanings. There was never a time that I didn't believe that they were truly worried for my safety and my well being." He smiles a smile of gratitude for the way I think of his aunt and uncle.

I will him to go away. Far away. Away from me and my life here, leaving me safe and sound and where I want to be. He looks at me with concern and kindness. And a fair bit of stubbornness, too, I realize with regret. Finally I say, "The flier says that Elle Graves' father and brothers were killed and that her mother was already dead. She's called an orphan. Seems to me that there isn't much for her to go back to."

He sighs and walks away from the oak to mingle among the other horses and view the beauty of the autumn forest with its floor of golds and reds and yellows. "Indiantown is an aberration. Do you know what that means, Bear?" he asks me and I shake my head 'no'. "It means that it is a place unlike any other place that people know of." *A Garden Walled Around ... chosen and made peculiar ground*, I think of the words of the Isaac Watts song. "It is an Indian village that has barely any signs of the white world in it. That alone is stunning in this day and time. It is like going back in time to before the whites' arrival before the sicknesses, before the lies, before the Old Ways were called the 'old ways.' But this is not an Indian town, is it?" He laughs and sweeps his arm out towards the sounds of the stirring village. "This is a *United States of America town* full of *citizens* of that country. Here is the problem which you might find surprising, but unfortunately you probably won't: *No one wants this place or knows what to do with it.* The United States of America doesn't really want it. The State of North Carolina certainly doesn't want it. And here is the saddest thing: The Nation of The Real People don't want it anymore either. They would *all* just like this Indiantown to *go away.* Disappear. Cease to exist. Never have happened. Every single one of those powerful institutions would like you all to just vanish and they would love to find a reason to make it happen."

He walks over to stand next to me and I look down at him from Willow's back and he gazes up at me. The last remaining fall leaves drift down around us like colorful snowflakes. "*You* could be an excellent reason to make trouble for this place called Indiantown. *You* could be a reason for the United States of America to reconsider the citizenship status of this village of *red savages. You* could be a reason for the State of North Carolina to reconsider its *magnanimous* offer of money in replacement of the land reservations they promised but could not give. *You* could be the reason that The Nation of The Real People does not step forward in defense of this place for they have done everything in their power to secure your freedom and have even had blood shed over it. *You are exactly what all these powerful institutions are all looking for.* The unanswerable questions that surround you and the voices that call you still from the white world could be music to the ears of those who wish this place serious harm."

Major Everett's words are awful words to hear. I want to throw my hands up over my ears and keep them from getting into my head and heart. I feel like I have so often felt in my life that there are no choices for me, just action I must do. "So what do you tell me to do? For it seems to me whether I am this Elle Graves or not, just the fact that I am a white woman in this Indian village seems to be a problem. I have heard that from Dark Cloud already and even from Great Elk and War Woman."

"Seems to me that you have only one choice," he begins to say but I interrupt him.

"Choosing between two things is a choice," I say with bitter words, "choosing between one thing is not a choice at all."

I really think he is sorrowful for me as he says the next words, "You must go back to Virginia and tell them what has happened to the young woman named Elle Graves." I feel the fear and the tears begin to build and turn Willow into the forest so that Major Everett will not see either feeling. As I ride into the woods I hear him say to me, "We will wait another day before we leave. We would be a good escort for you should you wish it." I want the black fur earplugs that Raccoon gave Bright Feather to shut out Major Everett's words but I know it is already too late for they are colliding around in my brain sucking my life right away.

I ride the whole day alone on Willow feeling powerful sorry for myself. My heart is full of sorrowful questions that tear me apart. What is it about me I think? Why does disaster seem to be the course of my life whether I live in the white world or the red? Does everyone have a life like mine and face choices that are no choices? I listen in my head for wise words from Pa and try to remember important things I have learned from Bright Feather and One Who Knows but my thoughts are silent. Then quietly, I hear Miss Rebecca's words, *Then shall ye call upon Me, and ye shall go and pray unto Me, and I will hearken unto you. And ye shall seek Me, and find Me, when ye shall search for Me with all your heart.* So I try praying to this God that is supposed to be so loving and I am told cares so much about me and I ask Him, *Why? Why must I do this thing? Why must I leave those I love to go back to a life that has nothing for me? Why?!*

And then the answer comes to me like the start of a soft breeze that grows and builds with force until it becomes a blasting force that whips your hair across your face and tears the branches off of trees. *For Love*, the answer says. *Only for Love.*

I ride into the village that evening just before the evening meal, and as I expected with guests in the village, many including Bright Feather, Otter, and Raccoon are seated around the council circle eating and talking. Bright Feather stands as Willow and I walk into the flickering firelight. I have returned as planned and I can see just passing concern for me as he walks towards me. He touches my cheek and murmurs for only me to hear, "I missed you, my mate, but I hope your day was a good one. Things have been quiet and easy here in the village today."

I smile at him - a sad smile - and he stops short for he can tell that tears are close and that is powerful unusual for me. "Are you well?" he asks in concern and I nod my head 'yes' but choose not to speak for I am uncertain if my voice will work.

"Will you join us to eat?" I hear Otter call from the circle with her usual bright smile and she rises to get a bowl for me. I can see all eyes are on me. I slip my hand in Bright Feather's and still concerned he grasps it tightly. Together we walk closer to the group. I see Major Everett and George Maw seated amongst the group relaxed and at ease.

At the edge of the circle, I look at Major Everett and his eyes tell me he knows I have made a choice that really is no choice at all. I struggle on the words that I manage to push out of my mouth as I look at Major Everett and clutch onto Bright Feather's hand. "My white name is Elle Graves, late of Ward's Mill, Virginia," I say to him in English and the words just about choke me. Bright Feather, of course can understand what I say although no one else in the village can. He looks at me and then to Major Everett and back at me again and I look at him and think how much I love this man. The feeling bursts from the very center of me and is greater than any sorrow or hurt or loneliness I have ever felt or imagined. As I look in Bright Feather's very troubled eyes, I say clearly to Major Alexander Everett of the Second United States Cavalry Division, Company A, "I am the girl you are looking for and the one that must be returned to her people in Virginia."

I've never seen Bright Feather angry I discover right quick. The talk around the circle swirls around me as I stare at the uneaten bowl of rabbit stew that Otter has placed in front of me. For once, it seems, my stomach is not hungry. George Maw is hard pressed to do all the translating back and forth for I'm not inclined to do any talking and he must do the part I did last night. Major Everett explains the same things he has explained to me. Bright Feather, Raccoon and even some others around the circle argue that there are other ways around these things. They're all ways I have thought of over the course of my long, terrible day alone with me and my sorry thoughts and there are still a few more I've considered that they haven't gotten to yet.

It's One Who Knows who at last speaks and causes the arguments to stop. "My daughter, Bear, is right. She must return to the whites just as our brother Deer had to return although for different reasons." She looks at me fiercely but it sends me love and strength just the same. "Bear knows who she is, Deer was uncertain. Bear knows where she belongs. Deer could not decide. Things must always be done in the proper order. *Life is filled with hard choices that correctly made lead to an existence of harmony and peace. But it can take a long time to get there.* This village must gain strength and prepare for fierce battles that are coming. That involves fixing things inside our borders *and outside.* Deer has warned us; only but the greatest fool would deny that great battles are still ahead. Bear must return and carefully put out all fires that could spread to this village and threaten its existence of peace and harmony. But she will return to us for she is no longer *Elle Graves* and though many will force her to look for her, she will not be able to find her."

"I will travel back with my mate," Bright Feather finally says in a tone that asks no permission and denies any discussion.

"No, you will not," I say to him for I've prepared myself for this argument that I knew would come. His look tells me that he's prepared to argue with anyone but me. "They will not understand that you are my husband, even if we say it is so. You can be blamed for my taking and for the killings that happened at the homestead. It would be your word and mine – a foolish young girl who's been kept with red *savages* for nigh onto two years – against an angry group of homesteaders powerful hungry for revenge. You will not go, you will stay safe here. Major Everett will travel back with me."

It's War Woman who speaks, but many nod in agreement. "She is right, my son, you cannot travel with her."

"In fact," I turn to Major Everett, "I do not want them to know where I was found. Is that possible?"

"I see no reason why we need to be specific about the location of your *rescue*," he says after thinking for a moment. He looks at George Maw who shrugs his shoulders.

It's Raccoon who speaks next. "It is obvious that Bear feels that she can trust you, Major Everett. I mean no disrespect when I question the character of Mr. George Maw. Tell me, what is your opinion on the way of things here in this village and beyond its borders?"

George Maw finishes the translating of Raccoon's question and then answers for himself. "My mother is full Cherokee," he says, "and my father is full white. I was raised with a strong taste of both worlds. I grew up away from the lands of the Real People but returned each summer to spend time with my mother's family and learn their ways. When land was taken again in the Treaty of 1819, most of my mother's family chose to travel west of the Mississippi. I am a translator because I can do it and do it fairly." He looks across the fire at me and smiles a small smile, "Major Everett has told me what his aunt has said to you. I am a different shade of pink than you, but I am pink just the same."

In our hut that night the silence continues from me. I've nothing to say and am tired to the bone. And for sure there is nothing that anyone can say that will make me feel any better. I lay down on the furs and curl up into a tight ball willing my thoughts and worries and tears to go away and leave me in peace but that doesn't work. Bright Feather seems unable to settle down, too, and finally walks out into the night leaving me to my own sorrows. I understand his helplessness, I think. I lay there tense and miserable wishing I could just escape to a place with no sorrow or pain or worry. But there is no where to go.

Time passes but I don't sleep. My mind struggles to remember pictures to carry with me that will help me once I'm away from this wonderful place. I must keep my memories sharp and not let them grow cloudy. I listen to the noises of the village and the woods and try my hardest to remember every speck of it. I listen to the nightingale sing and hear Companion and Willow stomping and snorting in their place nearby.

Then I realize that the nightingale sings a powerful lonely song, one that I'm unfamiliar with and I know that it is no nightingale at all.

I step out into the dark night and follow the song for I know all of a sudden that it is Bright Feather. He's seated in a clearing that's so bright that there are shadows of the trees on the ground cast by the light of the full moon. I sit down next to him and rest my tired, sorrowful head against his shoulder. He makes no move to touch me and for the first time in many, many months I remember how he was when he was called One Who Is Always Alone.

"It was a choice that was no choice," I begin. "It was not something I could discuss with you for it was my decision to make and not one that you could have helped me with. You said one time to me, *The only way you can keep your other choices is to make this one.* This was just like that, Bright Feather. I had to make the choice to go back for otherwise I could lose these other choices that mean so much to me: you, the Indian way, this village. A wrong choice could mean that it could all be lost." I weave my arm underneath his and find his hands clenched in tight balls. "I will come back. I will go back and say, 'Here I am: Elle Graves, but I am no longer her. I am healthy, strong, happy and smart. I am Bear. I am the mate of Bright Feather. I wish to go back and live with them always. Where is my horse? Thank you, good bye.' I will be back before the first flower buds."

He is silent for a moment and then he grunts and shakes his head. "That is a ridiculous plan but you are the only one I know who might be able to succeed with it." His tight fists open and he wraps his big warm hands around my one small one. "As soon as you leave here I ride to Deer. I will tell him what has happened and ask him what we should do." He lets go of my hand and turns and grabs my face and holds it tight, almost too tight, and says fiercely, "If you have trouble, *any trouble* you send word to Deer's trading post by letter or a messenger you trust. As soon as you can, you go there to his place and I will come to get you there."

"I promise," I say. "I will do as you ask. Now it is my turn to ask a promise of you."

His hands release my face and he lays back on the grass, throwing his arm across his eyes. "What," he says in a tired voice and I realize that he is as day weary as me. "What would you have me promise?"

"No matter what you hear or what concerns you have, you will not leave Indian territory to come for me. I cannot have that fear tied around my neck forever worrying that you will risk your life for me."

Still without looking at me he sighs and says with angry words, "And tell me, Bear, how that is different from what you are doing now."

It is my turn to be angry for I realize the importance of this promise. "There is a great difference and you know it! I can never be in as much danger as you would be just by crossing a border." I lean over and pull his arm from across his face and his dark eyes look at mine hovering over his. "Give me your word," I demand.

In a flash I am flipped on my back and he is above me, looming in the dark night. "I promise ... that I will not lose you. I promise ... that we will be together again. I promise ... that I will always love you. I promise ... that I will not put myself in danger unless it is the only way to help you. Those are the only things I will promise you, *ever.*" The fierceness of his look tells me I know I must settle for that.

I touch his face and try to smooth away the fierce look and the lines of worry I see around his eyes. "You must remember, I am much more than I was the last time they saw Elle Graves. I am a powerful Indian woman with much knowledge and ... only a little fear. I will watch, and listen, and learn, and be very patient. And then I will come home to you," and I pull him down to kiss him.

"You seem to be in some danger now," he says quietly after a time, but I laugh at the threat.

"If I could only be in this kind of danger for the rest of my life," I say and I sigh a wonderful sigh as he kisses the hollow between my neck and shoulder and I feel his warm breath send shivers up my back. I force the fears and worries away as I wrap my arms and legs around him and try with all my might to draw him right inside of me.

"I love you, *Elle Graves*," he says to me in my ear.

The chill of the autumn night finally forces us back to our hearth and the warmth of the furs. A full moon's brightness does not warm like the sun. Still neither of us wishes to sleep. I stir up the fire and add a few sticks to the red coals. By the time Bright Feather has dragged out two big wraps, the fire is warm and inviting.

"Tell me how you got your permanent marks," I ask him suddenly as I stare at his face in the firelight and will myself to remember every single speck that I see.

He shrugs. "It is a little bit like names for you often get them to celebrate an important part of your life. For me, I received them when I received the name of Hawk. Three lines for the three claw marks a hawk often leaves on its prey. Great Elk did them for me."

"I would like some," I say all of a sudden before I can change my mind. "One Who Knows has them. I wish to have some so that no matter what clothes or skin color I have, people when they look at me will know that I am more red inside than white."

He looks at me for a moment, pondering my face as an artist would. "And what would you have?" he finally asks. I think as an afterthought he adds, "It is painful, you know."

I shiver but it is not from the cold. I draw my bearskin around me and Bright Feather moves closer to me. "I do not know," I say. "I do know that I have many marks on my body from my times since I left Ward's Mill, Virginia. There are few people who see them, but I know they are there just the same. I would have some marks on my body that speak of other times that I would choose to remember with love and happiness."

He reaches over and studies my face and his hands touch the smoothness of my forehead and my cheeks and my chin. He is like an artist searching for the right place to do a design I realize and I shiver again. He takes his knife out and places it in the hot coals of the fire. "Do you know of the four sacred directions?" he asks me finally.

"No," I say concentrating hard to stop the shivering nervousness that seems to be slowly creeping through all parts of my body. I shut my eyes and concentrate on the gentle rhythm of his voice.

"Well," he says, "the direction in which the sun rises from is called *The Direction of Beginnings*. It speaks of family, togetherness, sharing, and spiritually-same thoughts. Within a family or group of friends there is a certain freedom that comes with that sense of belonging and unity." As I listen to his voice my shivering slowly stills and I close my eyes and remember my family here in this village and I know exactly of that sense of freedom that comes with that feeling of belonging. "This first mark on your chin," he takes the knife from the coals and I hear the sizzle of it being cooled in the birch bark container we keep nearby to drink from, "is for the *Direction of Beginnings* and I feel a sharp pain as he cuts my chin and a greater sting as he rubs the wound with ashes from the fire.

He puts his knife back into the coals. "The direction in which summer comes earlier and winter comes later is called *The Direction of the Natural*," he says in a quiet soothing voice. He blows a cool breath on my stinging chin. "It speaks of the natural way of life and the boundaries that must be kept in place to make all things harmonize. It reminds us of respect for Mother Earth and the importance we have in protecting her. It is rooted in innocence, play, and the respect of learning." I think of the contrast of the way of life between the whites and what I have learned here in the Maple Forest. I think of love of my Pa and how I think he was more Indian than he was white with the way he wanted to live his life. I think of all that I have learned to love and respect in my time here in the Maple Forest. I hear the sizzle hiss of the hot knife cooling just before feel the second sharp cut in my chin.

"The direction in which the sun sets," Bright Feather continues, "is called *The Direction of Introspection.*" This time he blows warm breath and follows that with a light feather kiss on my trembling lips. I work to concentrate on his words and not the pain that screams so loudly on my face. "Our strength, our will, and our self-awareness comes from this direction. Belief in one's abilities and the understanding of what should be valued and what should be forgotten is a part of this direction, too." I think of the changes that came about in me when I realized what a Powerful Woman I am. When I realized that I was no longer white and could never go back to the frightened white girl I once was. I think that perhaps this Direction of Introspection is one that has grown the most in me. I feel the third cut get made and the sting of the ashes as they are rubbed into the wound.

With my eyes squeezed closed I am held in place only by Bright Feather's words and touch. I take short quick breaths to forget about the pain as Bright Feather blows, then kisses and then finally, this time, trails hot, wet kisses down my neck. He bites me careful where my neck and shoulder meet and I jump and for a moment I forget just about everything else but his mouth.

At last he says to me, "The final direction is called *The Direction of Sharing* and it comes where it is always coldest." He places his knife in the fire and I feel him kiss my mouth gentle and careful one more time but I still do not open my eyes. "This direction is a quiet one for it comes on the whisper of the winds. It speaks of generosity and sharing like the deer who is gentle and kind and Mother Earth who is generous with all nature has to offer. It is my direction for it is like when I used to be alone all of the winter and it is yours, too, for it is from you that I have learned of the *sharing of love.*" And he kisses me again just before he makes the fourth cut and then does the final piece of smoothing in the ash.

The shivering starts again and it is not from chill I realize but from the thoughts of being far away from this man I love so fiercely and fear of being on my own with strangers who do not know me and do not care and I feel the tears building up behind my eyes and slipping out from my still shut eyes. *"Remember me, and I will always be there[15],"* he whispers soft into my ear and gathers me close on his lap and wipes my face of tears and just a little blood I think. Silently we sit there, the two of us as one dark shadow, rocking back and forth, sharing our love and sorrow and fear. *"Destiny,"* he whispers then, *"remember destiny,"* he reminds me of our pledge on Deer and Possum's porch not so long ago, "no person, no situation, no thing will stop this that we have." And he loves me again in the warmth of our hut and furs and I try hard to remember every single moment and believe that I will be back here before the first flower blooms.

"I love you, Bear," is the last thing I remember him say before I finally fall fast asleep.

'Twas in the watches of the night, I thought upon thy power,
I kept thy lovely face in sight, amidst the darkest hour.[16]

~Isaac Watts

Guest

The next morning Bright Feather and I say our final goodbyes in the privacy of our hut. We speak less with words and more with looks and touches. Words can't tell what we both feel deep inside.

"Remember you are not One Who Is Always Alone anymore," I say as I move to walk outside our hut.

"Remember you are not Elle Graves anymore," Bright Feather says back to me with a fierce growl.

We prepare to ride out me, Major Everett and George Maw. I sit on Willow and feel like the last lone autumn leaf on a tree that's been battered by storms all night. My mind is foggy and slow from the nervous shivers that I still feel now and then and the near sleepless night I've had. And let's not talk about the pain of the permanent marks that I now have on my chin.

Otter reminds me of Miss Rebecca sobbing quietly next to Raccoon who has his most menacing look on. I can't work up the notion to say a word to either of them.

One Who Knows approaches me and I see the twinkle in her eye as she looks at the very sore cuts on my face. "Hurt something terrible do they not?" she says. "I regretted mine for days after. You should have asked me." She studies me a moment and then says, "But maybe the pain will give you something else to think about, eh?"

"I've a gift for you," she says in the same way I had spoken to her just a few weeks back and she hands me her old gathering basket to place in among all my things. "I've filled it with important herbs that will be no good to you if your thick skull can't remember what to do with them. At least most of them will smell good when you are sick."

She studies my sorrowful face that can't fight the tears that now and then escape. "I am proud to call you my daughter. He," she gestures her head to Bright Feather who I see is in a serious conversation with Major Everett, "is proud to call you his mate. And all of us," she gestures around her and I see what must be the entire village standing quietly watching, "are all proud to call you *ours*. Remember," and she holds both of her old hands up and weaves them together, "You are destined for great things but I have told you once: *There is much difficulty as well as joy to come for both of you*. You do not need to be close enough to hold hands to still be together. Now is a time for the difficult, but there is still more joy to come." She smiles a rare smile. "Joy never comes without a bit of work to get it." As she walks to stand beside War Woman and Great Elk, I hear in my head what she has told me before, *You were always a powerful woman even before you knew it*.

Bright Feather comes and stands beside me as I sit on Willow. He rests his warm hand on my thigh and says, "See you before the first spring flower buds." He smiles at me and quotes Isaac Watts, *"Were I in heav'n without my God, 'Twould be no joy to me; And whilst this earth is my abode, I long for none but thee[17]."* He mounts up on Companion and rides out of the village without looking back at me. As he has promised, he leaves for Deer's place to learn what should be done.

Major Everett, George Maw and I travel that whole first day with no conversation and set up camp in a place I take no note of. I work hard to feel nothing for otherwise I will just die from the pain of it I think. I have no thoughts or words in my head. I just work at being empty.

I sleep like the dead that night making up from exhaustion in my head, my heart and my body. The morning dawns bright, shiny and cold and we travel out after a quick meal that I don't taste. As we stop for a moment's rest in the middle of the day, Major Everett at last breaks the silence and asks me, "What are your plans?"

I stare at him for a moment, with a dumb look I'm sure, and think, *Why are you talking to me? Can't you see I'm not alive anymore?* But he continues to stare at me with his polite, interested look and I struggle to spark some life in me.

"I don't understand what you are asking me," I finally say.

He gives me a sideways smile and looks at George Maw. "First off, you might be better received if you switch over to English for a time." I don't even realize. I repeat my question in English.

"Well, as a first point," he says. "How will you behave? Will you be cordial or hostile? Will you be polite and helpful or will you be silent and withdrawn? Will you make every effort to be Bear or will you be Elle Graves?"

I realize that I've not thought a moment past the leaving of my people and have no answers for them and say so.

"Can I make some suggestions?" George Maw asks polite like. I look at him but don't speak. He continues in the length of my silence. "Looking at you here, now, you appear remarkably *savage*; the bow and arrow, the knife, the tattoos, the dress. You are going to walk into that general store and the whole world is just about going to stop and take note. You can behave like a *savage* and prove many people's first impressions correct or you can behave *civilized* and shock them right down to their toes." He shrugs. "The first way will make a strong point but will gain you little in the way of support. The second way will confuse even the greatest critics and may win over a few sitting on the fence."

I mull over his words in my tired, slow, sorrowful mind. "I thank you for your suggestions," I say in my politest English I can manage. I look at Major Everett. "What did Bright Feather speak to you about before we left?"

He takes off his hat and scratches his scalp and chuckles a little quietly to himself at the memory. "Well, we had a right polite conversation, him and I." He looks at me pointed. "In perfect English I might add," and I work to hide a little smile at the fun Bright Feather must have had. "He spoke at length about the *Real People's* belief in balance and harmony and how *the only purpose for The Real People of the Maple Forest* here on earth was to keep the way of things correct here within the bounds of Mother Earth and all those things that she holds dear." I nod my head, for I know this to be true. "Then he very politely told me that if anything were to happen to you before you are returned to him he would hold me personally responsible and hunt me down and kill me in the most painful way he could come up with." I don't have anything to say about that but I hear his voice in my head, *Remember me, and I will always be there* and for a brief moment I can almost smell his smell and feel him sitting next to me. It's a good moment.

The ride to Cornelius Cooper's store, of Ward's Mill, Virginia, takes us fourteen days. I remember that with Weasel the trip took less time, but we're not running from anything and I suspect Major Everett and George Maw think I need a slower pace. Maybe I do for by the time we have arrived I've at least been able to do some planning and make some decisions.

In my whole life, I've been to Cornelius Cooper's store five maybe six times, I think. That's the best my memory serves me. It was always just a two day trip with Pa and there was so much to see and take in all the while caring for Eli that it was usually more than my brain could take in completely. I can conjure up the image of plump Mrs. Cooper for she always gave Eli and me some sweets that tasted right delicious. I can remember her kind smile and voice. Mr. Cooper I remember being a big man with a huge white apron that I think Ma could have used for a tablecloth had it not been so filthy. He was always busy bustling with the customers and I don't recall ever having spoken one word to him.

Ward's Mill, Virginia, as best as I can recall has a blacksmith and stable, Cooper's General Store and the mill. Cornelius Cooper has owned the mill along with the store for as long as I've known. I can remember at harvest time traveling sometimes with Pa and Eli and Henry and waiting with the other farmers for their turn to have their grain ground. The rule was always "whoever came the farthest goes first" so there were times that we camped a night or two or three waiting for our turn. During harvest time the mill runs day and night, but I know it'll be silent now in the late part of autumn, early part of winter. That's all that I can remember but as we ride into town it causes my heart to pound practically right out of my chest because it is so *white civilized* and I am, after all so *red savage* inside now.

"Perhaps I should go in and prepare them," Major Everett says as we sit there on our horses and hear laughter and conversation spilling out from the store. "No need putting you into any more awkward of a situation then there already is," he says as he dismounts. "George, you wait with her."

We sit on our horses and almost immediately as Major Everett walks in, a man walks out. He stares at me like his brain can't believe what his eyes are seeing. "Well, well," he says after a time. "Lookit what we've got here." He steps down into the dirt by me and Willow and I sense that Mr. George Maw has gotten almost as tense as I am. "It's a pretty Injun squaw." He takes his hat off and squints at me and begins to walk slow around Willow. "No … no … it's a pretty white maid all done up like an Injun squaw. Now that's something we haven't seen around here in … I don't think forever. Why don't you come on in and enjoy the hospitality of Cooper's? Here, I'll help you down …"

"I appreciate the welcome and the invitation," George Maw says and the man seems to see him for the very first time. "But Major Everett has gone in to speak with the Coopers and we were told to wait outside here for the moment."

The two men eye each other, and I am reminded of two male dogs at Great Elk's village that were always fighting amongst themselves. "Is that so," the man says. "Well, I'd be a fool to carry on home and miss all of this, now wouldn't I?" He turns and steps back up into the store and disappears inside.

Major Everett comes out a few moments later and looks at me, "Are you ready?"

I think it is a powerful foolish question and choose not to answer. But I dismount just the same. I am Bear, of the Elk Clan, daughter of One Who Knows, mate of Bright Feather of the Wolf Clan, son of War Woman and Great Elk chief of The Real People of the Maple Forest. The look I give Major Everett says, Let's go.

Cooper's General Store is absolutely stone quiet when I walk in. There's not a sound as I step into the darkness of the inside. I feel eyes on me taking in everything there is to see and I hear George Maw's voice saying, *Looking at you here, now, you appear remarkably savage; the bow and arrow, the knife, the tattoos, the dress.* That suits me just fine I realize and I stand and let them all drink their fill of me while my eyes adjust to the dim light.

It's Major Everett who must speak first for it seems that all present are stunned into silence. "Mr. and Mrs. Cooper, may I reintroduce to you Miss Elle Graves, late of this town and who we have been searching for nigh onto two years."

My eyes can now see the couple I remember to be Mr. and Mrs. Cooper and the looks they have on their faces tell me that they never, ever, *ever* thought to see me standing in their store being reintroduced to them. I step forward and extend my hand, "It's good to see you again and I'm right grateful for your offer of hospitality."

"Well, well," I hear the same voice from outside, "seems like the Injuns didn't change her manners none," and there's some laughter.

Mrs. Cooper finally manages to make herself come to life instead of being carved out of wood and she says, "My dear, Elle, welcome home ..." But her voice fades away. She doesn't know what to do with me, I realize. And she never takes my hand.

Mr. Cooper steps forward and he's as big as I remember and his apron's as stained as I recall, too. I look at him and he says, "Where've ya been all this time?"

Major Everett speaks before I can even form thoughts. "She was brought into the Cherokee town of New Echota down in Georgia. My aunt and uncle are missionaries down there and so I was contacted and asked to escort her home as my company is currently stationed in Virginia and I was heading back north anyway." I am impressed with his words, for they are not lies actually, they just don't tell the whole story.

Major Everett looks at the Coopers and must finally ask, "Do you have accommodations for this young woman? Or are there nearby relatives I should escort her to?"

"Her Pa's dead," Cornelius Cooper says and he talks in front of me as if I cannot understand his language.

Major Everett looks a bit annoyed. "We are aware of *all* the sorry details of Miss Graves immediate family." He reaches into his coat pocket and withdraws the notice that speaks of my disappearance and has my likeness drawn on it. "We are here first because of this flier that has been circulated. Am I correct in bringing her here or should I take her someplace else?"

For a brief moment I have a rush of hope that is so overpowering I am afraid it will knock me over. *Please say you do not want me* I will him to speak with every speck of me. *Please say there is no place for me here.* My mind plays mean tricks of me riding happily into Great Elk's village and enjoying a welcome embrace from Bright Feather. "Oh, of course we have a place for her," I hear Mrs. Cooper say. "We have a bedroom in the back that would be just perfect for her. Come dear, let's get you settled and, er, cleaned up a bit," she says.

"I have a horse that needs to be cared for," I say, "and things I need to carry in."

"I'll not have no bug infested Injun things in my home," Cornelius Cooper says quick like and I hear a snicker from the background audience of nameless people.

"Cornelius!" Mrs. Cooper says in a shocked tone. She turns nervous eyes on Major Everett and George Maw and then finally on me. "Benny, will you help Miss Graves stable her horse round back and find a safe place to store her things *in the barn?*"

"Sure, Miz Cooper," I hear from behind me. "I've already offered once to assist *Miss Graves* and I'm more than happy to help now." There's more snickering behind me. "Come along, *Miss Graves.*"

I turn to follow Benny out as I hear voices begin to start up again as everyone talks at once. Willow's waiting quiet and calm outside and I work real hard to be just like her. Benny says, "This a ways ..." He walks around the store towards a small barn and I lead Willow around back to it. There's space for four horses although only two are in use. As I care for Willow and carefully stack my things in the corner of the stall, I feel Benny's eyes on me. Finally, he says, "I just can't believe you're still alive. We'd all taken you for dead long ago."

What do you say to something like that? I wonder to myself. *Surprise!* Or *I'm sorry to disappoint you.* Or, *Let's just pretend that I am,* and ride away. I sort through the stuff I want to bring inside and the things I can settle to leave outside for a bit. I settle on my book from Bright Feather and my basket of herbs from One Who Knows. I smile to myself, *I can always smell them to get some comfort since I probably can't remember what they're good for!*

"Cornelius said he didn't want any bug infested things in his home," Benny observes as I walk out of the stall carrying my bits.

"There's no bugs, I checked," I say matter of fact and walk past him but not before I see him puzzle over how I could have done such a thing.

Major Everett and George Maw are waiting outside as I come around the corner. Major Everett looks powerful uncertain about everything and I can't help myself. I look at George Maw and say in Indian, "Seems like he worries for his life a small bit," remembering Bright Feather's threat.

"Hey! No speaking Injun in this town!" Benny shouts and looks as if I've just shot his pet dog.

"I remember listening to a private conversation was rude. Have things changed since I've been gone?" I ask him in clear English.

He looks mighty put out and mounts his horse. "Welcome home, Miss Graves," he says in a voice that means no such thing and rides off.

I know Major Everett and George Maw can't stay no matter how welcome or unwelcome I am. They know that too. "Where is the Second United States Calvary, Division of the Army, Company A that is presently based with the Ninth Virginia Cavalry, Company D located?" I ask matter of fact. "Just in case it suits me to stop by," I add but they know what I am saying. If things are difficult for me here, they're much closer than Deer's trading post in North Carolina.

George Maw spends time with me explaining the route to Fort Winston, Virginia. North of Ward's Mill by a bit, it would take me two days to reach by fast horse riding he tells me. I work hard to remember all the details and then repeat them back to him. He nods his head that I've spoken correctly.

"We will come through here anytime we pass by. We will be happy to carry messages then too," Major Everett says. "Will you be alright?"

I study him and think it's kind that he has concern for me. I think it's genuine and not just because of Bright Feather's threat. I tell him, "This is the third time in my life that I have been brought to a place that caused me fear. So far, each time I have become stronger. Each time I learn good things about myself. I trust One Who Knows' words that there will be joy again in my life and that I just need to go through some difficult times to get there."

But I don't tell him I will be alright, because even I don't know that.

I watch Major Everett and George Maw ride out of Ward's Mill, Virginia, and when I cannot see them anymore, I go back into Cooper's Store. "Here you are, dear," Mrs. Cooper says to me. "Come let me show you where you can sleep." She starts towards the back of the store to what seems to be a back room behind the main counter.

"Hang on there, girly," I hear Mr. Cooper say to me. "I told you no Injun things with bugs in them in my house." Mrs. Cooper looks nervous but says nothing.

"I'm sure they've no bugs," I start to say.

"What's this?" he says and the basket of herbs is taken from my hands. "Looks like a lot of weeds and such. This is best left in the barn. Anything gonna have bugs, this is sure it. And what's this? A book!?"

I clutch it to my heart and will my voice to stay calm and my heart to beat slow and steady. "It's a book of Christian hymns," I say.

"Surely she can keep *that* with her, Cornelius," I hear Mrs. Cooper say. He walks away without answering and I take it to mean *yes*.

After I have brought the basket of herbs back to the stable, Mrs. Cooper takes me to my room which is no more than a storage closet with a cot and pitcher and bowl for washing in between the sacks of grain and other bits of store supplies. There's a looking glass hung on the wall and after she leaves me, I study my face in the mirror. Even at Pa's there was no looking glass and I find it amazing what I see for I do look like a wild Injun savage! I study my permanent marks proper healed now and no longer painful and I touch the robin's feathers in my hair. My green eyes stare out at me from my tanned face and I touch the bear claw necklace that hangs around my neck. "I am Bear," I say to my face looking back at me and I decide that I like very much what I see.

I wash my hands and face and put my book down on my bed. I sit on the edge of the cot for a moment and I think, *Now what?* and a huge wave of loneliness just about swallows me up. I press my hand to my mouth to stifle the moans that boil in my throat and begin to rock myself back and forth for I feel the panic and the shivering coming over me something terrible. "I want to go home," I hear myself moan and I rock and rock and try to comfort myself in the quiet of the tiny cramped closet.

"You are our guest, my dear," Mrs. Cooper says to me the next morning over breakfast. I hear Mr. Cooper call her *Naomi.* They are both horrified to discover that the marks on my chin will not wash off no matter how hard you scrub them and no matter how strong the soap is. They've a habit of discussing me as if I'm not there or at least as if I don't have a brain in my head to understand what they say.

"Can you imagine doing such a thing, Cornelius?" Mrs. Cooper says in shocked tones when I tell her the lines are forever.

"Injun savages do all kinds of horrible things, Naomi," Mr. Cooper says in a voice filled with great knowledge. "I know for a fact that they eat the hearts of their enemies right on the field of battle, that they sometimes sacrifice their own children to gods that they worship, and they sometimes have three, four, even five wives at a time."

"NO!" Mrs. Cooper says, and clutches her hand to her chest as if to still her shocked heart. It never occurs to either one of them to ask me if these things are so, so I remain quiet. She does eventually look at me as if to see if any of those evil possibilities are lurking across the breakfast table in the form of one Injun-looking white girl. I try not to blink.

"We must do something about your clothes and your hair, dear," she says. "You cannot be seen around town looking as you do. You'll put a scare into everyone." *That would suit me just fine,* I realize but again I keep quiet with my thoughts.

"Anything she takes from the store she'll be required to work to pay off the expense," Mr. Cooper says. "This ain't no charity place and never will be. If she's to be a *guest,* she will be a *paying guest.*"

"I'd be happy to help around the store in anyway you can see fit," I say polite like and they both look startled that I speak civil and proper. *George Maw was right,* I think. I will win more battles being civilized than savage.

I forget how cumbersome white clothes are once I'm dressed a week later in button down chemise and over blouse, skirts and petticoats, stockings and shoes, and a bonnet for my head when I go out. I stand in front of the looking glass in my room and I can hear Raccoon laughing all the way back in the Maple Forest. For the first time I think, *Perhaps it's best that no one's here to see me* as I smile too at how silly I look. I'm careful to store away all of my clothes in a secret spot I've found out in the woods aways from the general store. Once again, in front of me, the Coopers have discussed burning all my bug infested things and the next morning I search for a safe place to put everything to stop them.

Mr. Cooper keeps a tally of all the monies I owe him as a result of staying with them. He charges me for rent of room and meals and for the materials I used to sew the clothes on my back. He charges me for the stabling of Willow and for her food as well. He regularly reminds me of the debt I owe him and that it must be repaid. I think back to my imaginings of becoming the adopted daughter of Mr. and Mrs. Cornelius Cooper of Ward's Mill, Virginia, and how wrong the thinking was. I work hard and am willing to do anything they ask of me. I try to be very polite and kind and never voice the unkind thoughts about the Coopers and what I think of them that regularly roll around in my head like big stone boulders down a steep hill.

Mr. Cooper jokes that I've been good for business, for word has spread throughout the surrounding areas that I'm here and there's always a steady stream of curious people coming into the store to have a look at me. I, once again, am polite and respectful despite the fact that they discuss me like I am a stabled horse they've come to check out rather than a living, breathing person. The women in many cases are worse than the men.

"Can you *imagine* what it would have been like to live with *savages* for almost two years?" they say with voices filled with horror.

"What do you suppose she had to do while she lived there to stay alive?" they say as they whisper loudly behind their hands as I work at counting stock.

"Even dressed in proper clothes she has a vicious streak about her, don't you think?" one of the old biddies says to her friend and I think, *And you don't even know about the knife strapped to my thigh from the white man I killed.*

"I hear that white women when they are captured often have to immediately be married off to a brave." I walk away when I hear that conversation begin for I can't manage to think of Bright Feather without tears and moans and I *will not* do such a thing in front of mean - spirited, curious eyes.

"How do you suppose she got those marks on her face? I'd never be able to go out in public if that were me." I lift my head with pride and straighten my back as I sweep the floor.

"Have you seen her wrists? She's got scars from being *tied up!*" My head thinks of Weasel for a few moments and how full of harmony my life is now that he is dead.

I keep a running conversation of things I'd like to say to these mean spirited women. These thoughts running around in my head sometimes get funny enough that I have to fight to keep the laughter down. *I've got a mighty big scar on my left breast when Weasel bit me there. Shall I show you? Or, I suspect that I am capable enough with my knife to fight all of you women and a few of your men. Would you care to try? Or, I suspect I'd be less inclined to appear in public missing my two front teeth like you are, Mrs. Bekeman. I'll take my permanent marks any day. And Mrs. Jamesway, about your powerful body odor …?* The men, particularly the ones who visit the liquor corner of the store, seem more harmless than hurtful.

"I hear Injun squaws are better wives than white women."

"I hear Injun women are responsible for torturing and killing prisoners during war time."

"I hear Injun women fight right along side the men and some can even handle knives and bows and arrows just as well."

I have a big chuckle to myself when I think of the looks on all their faces when I imagine telling them that all of *these* comments are actually quite true. Now *that* would be worth all the commotion it would cause, I suspect.

I have little time to ride Willow but I visit with her every day and try to walk her a bit to get some exercise. I brush her and talk to her and bring her treats I sneak from the root cellar. I care for my bow and arrow which I have hidden in my secret spot in the woods every day, too. My knife strapped to my leg under my skirts is kept sharp and well cared for, too. (That was the only time I was thankful for all the foolish layers.)

By the end of the third week with the Coopers, I know the way of the store enough to wait on customers that will allow it (some won't even talk to me) and have a regular routine of chores I do. I become familiar with some of the faces that come into the store and there are even a few that stir vague memories from the occasional times I might have met them on a visit with Pa.

Old Mr. Hobson comes in once a week, every Friday. He says it's for supplies, but I suspect - since he spends most of his time in the liquor corner - that there are only certain specific supplies he's looking for. Benny Stokes is the blacksmith and it's my opinion that it's unfortunate he lives within walking distance of the store. He's married to Emily who's one of the people who'll not allow me to wait on her nor will she talk to me. She just stands there looking right past me to a spot on the wall waiting for Mr. or Mrs. Cooper to come and serve her. She and Mrs. Cooper spend time each visit whispering quietly in the corner somewhere out of earshot of me. They glance at me often and I am the obvious topic of discussion.

Jane and Ezekiel West live on the nearest homestead and are kind of shy and unsure around me. She smiles kindly which is more than I can say for many. She's expecting what I learn to be her first baby and whenever she visits, there's much talk about babies and birthing and pregnancy and such. I hear One Who Knows saying to me, *It is something almost every young woman thinks of – I am sure white or red – if a baby does not come with the first time you are together with a man.*

I ask the Coopers one time what I get paid for all the work that I do, since I'm always reminded of how much I *owe* and I'm told that figures and figuring are not something any lady should concern herself with, *ever*. And that came from Mrs. Cooper not Mr. How will I ever be able to settle a debt if I can't worry my "ladylike head" over figures?

I learn that the Coopers have a son named Johnny but it's a sad topic that often makes Mrs. Cooper cry and Mr. Cooper look angry. I take it that there's been disagreement over "sweet Johnny" as Mrs. Cooper calls him and *"that boy"* as Mr. Cooper calls him for years and years. Mrs. Cooper tells quiet bits at times about him how he loved horses and loved to travel in the forest and she has me taste "sweet Johnny's favorite candy" but she does it mostly out of earshot of Mr. Cooper.

I find by the end of my first month with the Coopers that I feel sorry for the both of them at times because neither of them seem happy ever. *Life is what you make of it, Elle*, I hear Pa say in my head and I realize that he's right. For me, the first month's best described as wandering through a strange forest that's thick with fog. My brain's slow and I'm often tired. Like my first days in Great Elk's village my nights are filled with thoughts of those I love but now the faces are white *and* red. I dream busy dreams that make me wake in the morning more tired than ever but I can never remember them. I work hard over the course of each day to stay busy and preoccupied, even welcoming the distractions of unkind and nosy customers rather than face the chance to be alone with my thoughts. I'm happy to just have something – *anything* – to fill in the huge hole of loneliness that I feel constantly in my stomach, making it ache and roll and pitch with the sickness of my sadness.

One night, over dinner, as the first serious snow fall blows outside, I finally feel comfortable enough to ask the Coopers why they felt inclined to put the flier out about me not knowing me too well and all. They look at each other in a puzzled fashion for a moment and then Mrs. Cooper finally says. "Why my dear, we didn't put that flier out about your disappearance. Your brother, Henry, did." A loud whining starts in my ears like a hundred tiny mosquitoes all buzzing at the same pitch at the same time. It interferes with what Mrs. Cooper's still saying to me and I hear only snatches like, "I thought you knew … Asked our permission … Been searching since that terrible day … Sent word out to him but haven't heard anything yet …" and then the buzzing's so loud in my ears I can no longer hear her words. For the third time in my life a blackness descends on me and the lights begin to dim and everything at last is dark and quiet.

When light returns and I open my eyes, I'm lying on the floor with Mr. and Mrs. Cornelius Cooper looking down at me like some kind of spill they don't quite know how to go about cleaning up. Both look shocked but neither make any move to help me to sit up and eventually I seat myself back in my chair. My forehead stings and I reach up to find my fingers wet with blood. I stare stupid like at my bloody fingers all the while my thoughts whirl around in my head. *Henry's alive? Henry's been here? Henry's put out the flier?*

A large hand pushes a rag into my hand. "Why would you have thought that we would've put out the notice?" Cornelius Cooper says in a tone that lets me know he knew I was an idiot and now this proves it. "We hardly knew your Pa, let alone you." I've no answer and just look at him.

"Major Everett said that first day you arrived that you 'were aware of *all* the sorry details of your immediate family,'" Mrs. Cooper says, "So we rightly assumed that you knew all about Henry's posting the note." She thinks of something. "Do you mean that Major Everett has made no effort to contact your brother? Does that mean you have been here all this time and Henry has not been informed?!" She looks at Mr. Cooper. "Dear me …"

Mr. Cooper's angry. "That Major Everett assured us that all involved parties had been informed and taken care of! He said that there was *no need* to make any further inquiries into 'the situation known as *Elle Graves' Kidnapping and Abduction.'* He said that you had been returned safe and sound and that he'd taken care of everything that needed taking care of!" Mr. Cooper's voice gets louder and louder as he speaks until he is shouting. "DO YOU MEAN TO TELL ME THAT YOU'VE BEEN HERE ALL THESE WEEKS TAKING ADVANTAGE OF OUR KINDNESS AND HOSPITALITY AND NO ONE'S COMING TO TAKE YOU AND SETTLE THESE DEBTS?!? DO YOU MEAN THAT YOU ARE PROBABLY HERE FOR THE ENTIRE WINTER??!"

My thoughts swirl as I try to unsort this big tangle of things that all of a sudden I've tripped over. I've a brief moment of thought wondering if all of this had been said in the language of the Real People if there would be so much confusion? I understand what Major Everett was trying to do in those first few moments of my arrival here. He meant to settle any swirling dust and cover all tracks that would have led back to The Maple Forest. Just like I asked him to. I sigh a deep sigh as I dab my head.

"The flier said that my father and *brothers* had been killed ..." I say looking back and forth at Mr. and Mrs. Cooper in confusion. "I ... thought ..." I frown with puzzlement. *What did I think?*

"Fool printer made an error," Mr. Cooper mumbled. "No sense spending money to print the thing again."

Except for the fact that I thought my brother was dead and he isn't, I think. I work to form words. "What was your understanding from Henry," and it feels *so strange* to say his name and realize he is alive somewhere out there, "that you should do if I showed up on your doorstep?" I ask finally.

Mr. Cooper walks over to a jug of liquor he keeps for "family and medicinal use" and pours himself a cupful. He takes a long swallow. He looks at me with great anger and spits out, "Your fool brother paid cash money for me to allow him to put my name on the fliers. He told me that he would satisfy any debt that you incurred if you should show up and that we should keep a running record until he came and got you. That was *over a year and a half ago*, you little idiot! *No one* thought you'd turn up after all this time." He takes another long swallow. "Henry went off and joined the Army," he looks at Mrs. Cooper, "how long ago?"

"Oh, I'd think it was early last year at least ..." Mrs. Cooper says thoughtful like.

Mr. Cooper looks at me and I realize that he has worked very hard to conceal a hatred and disgust that he no longer makes any effort to disguise. The only reason he's tolerated my savage self is for the money he was certain he would get from Henry. Money he now realizes he's not so sure he's going to get now after all this time.

He's the only businessman in the area, Elle, I hear Pa say to me in a tired voice as we ride into town that very last time. Anyone who deals with Cornelius Cooper knows that he follows every penny in and out of that store.

"We've tolerated your stinkin', bug infested, Injun presence here in this store because I plan to collect a tidy sum for all the trouble you've put us through. And that's *the only reason*. I have a *signed piece of paper* that says that should you arrive that he will pay me *cash money* for all expense that you incur. It's called a *Promissory Note* and I can have him *or you* locked up if you do not settle this debt as *promised. Just watch me!* Anyone who's associated with *red savages* for nigh onto two years, whose *lived with them*, and *eaten with them*, and *God knows what else with them*, is not welcome in this town let alone this house. If your fool brother wants you, *he can have you.*" The wind rises up and the snow sounds like it has turned to hail as it pelts against the outside of the house. "And by Christ, he'll have a *hell of a bill* when he finally shows up, too."

"Now Cornelius, things have worked out so far …" Mrs. Cooper starts to say.

"*Shut up, Naomi,*" Mr. Cooper says. "You don't think for one moment I'm going to listen to you *again*, do you? You don't for one minute think that *your opinion* is ever something I want to hear, do you? Just like I listened to you over your "precious little Johnny?" Mrs. Cooper gets the look she usually does when she knows that Mr. Cooper is going to speak ill of their son. It is a look that makes me think of a cowering dog in a way. "How can you defend this," he waves his hand at me like he can't think of a word that's low enough to mean me, "this *Injun lover* when you know what the Injuns did to your *precious little Johnny*? You made excuses for him his whole life even though we know he was more stupid than a mule. Couldn't learn to even count bales of hay in the back let alone money to help me run this store! So stupid he couldn't remember to do the basic things in life like *take a bath* or even learn to *not piss in his own bed* for Christ's sake!" Mrs. Cooper has begun to cry and puts her hands up over her ears to block out the words her husband's throwing at her. "You would've allowed him to stay here forever even when the stench of his presence became so bad that customers wouldn't even come to the store because of it!!"

Mr. Cooper has worked himself in to a state of fury that I've never seen in my whole life. I watch him take another long, long swallow of the whiskey as he paces around the small dinner table. He glances at me before he continues shouting at his wife. "And you would have loved him, *your precious Johnny, even after he brought his stinkin' self and A STINKIN' INJUN WHORE* home, wouldn't you have? Would you have ignored *him and his Injun slut* just like you ignored everything else, Naomi? Huh? Would You?

"Where is he now? We heard those blood-thirsty savages *murdered him*, remember Naomi? We heard they hunted him down and killed him. I heard they *scalped him* and *ate his heart for revenge*. And you can sit here and feel any sympathy for this, this ... *red and white whore?!*"

He looks at me and I feel my stomach clutch and tuck and roll and I think, *Oh no, I think I'm going to be sick* ...

Mr. Cooper is not done for he turns to me with fire in his eyes and disgust on his lips. "I hated the Injuns from the start because that is *the proper way of things*! I tolerated the idiot son we had because Naomi said it was the proper way of things, too, for a father to tolerate his son no matter what. But even Naomi knew that we were done with *precious Johnny* when he showed up with his squaw tied at the end of a rope like a pet dog! Grinning like an idiot, wasn't he Naomi. 'Look what I got, Ma!' he said to you like he'd brought you a bunch of *damned flowers!!* Even you couldn't swallow your *precious Johnny* being an Injun lover. Could you, Naomi? Could you?"

Mrs. Cooper is sobbing and sobbing. Her head is cradled in her arms while her hair half lays in the remains of her dinner plate. The shouting stops and aside from Mrs. Coopers crying there is no sound except the storm that is blowing and blowing outside. My thoughts are clear as a bell for once.

So, these are Bear John's parents.

I have Bear John's knife strapped to my leg.

I have Bear John's horse out in the stable.

I'm the one who killed your 'precious Johnny'.

And then a more curious thought enters my head. *Am I sleeping in Bear John's bed?* I add another sound to the wailing cries of Mrs. Cooper and the blowing of the winter storm outside as I vomit on the floor in front of me.

Things are different with the Coopers after that night. Mr. Cooper can hardly stand the sight of me and makes that plain to me every day. Mrs. Cooper's quiet and withdrawn and it becomes obvious to me right quick that she thinks little of me, too, aside from what money I'll bring in when Henry arrives to claim me and pay the bill. Outside it's a winter unlike any winter I've ever remembered for it snows and snows and snows. Aside from the brave customer that surprises us every now and then (Ezekiel West comes occasionally searching for something for Jane, but even Old Mr. Hobson misses a few Fridays) there's little business at the General Store. Mr. Cooper spends much time in the evening drinking his 'medicinal liquor' and watching me with dark looks. I try to go about and do my chores as quick as possible, trapped by the weather and by my own circumstance. Mr. Cooper talks aloud for me to hear sometimes about Injun squaws and what they're good for and what they're not. I realize I'm only good for the money Mr. Cooper hopes to collect from Henry and a small fear begins to grow in me when I think *What if Henry never comes? How long until things become different yet again and I become a paying guest who can never pay?*

This winter with the Coopers offers me little joy trapped with people who hate me and with no place I can go. I remember the winter learning to ride Willow with Raccoon and to shoot with Cloud and Red Fox and must think of it only in tiny bits for it makes me powerful lonely and sad. I remember talking and talking and talking with Otter that whole first winter and having a friend for the first time and I again must put those thoughts away for I find that tears come too easy try as I might to keep them hidden behind my eyes. I can't, under any circumstances, think of Bright Feather unless I'm in the quiet of the room I sleep in (which I find *was* Bear John's) for it brings about a misery so complete that I often lose whatever was the last meal I managed to choke down. I sometimes try to read my book of songs that Bright Feather gave me but more often than not I end up just curled up in a ball rocking myself back and forth and trying to make the loneliness find another place to stay.

One snowy cold day, Ezekiel West braves the weather once again for something for Miss Jane. He smiles shyly at me and asks, "Do you have any jarred peaches still available? Jane has a powerful hunger for it that just can't seem to be satisfied."

I search the shelves and find just one carefully preserved and labeled jar. I ask how Miss Jane's feeling. "She's been told she's doing better than most. Her main complaints are that she's powerful tired and hungry, although nothing much appeals to her to eat." He looks at the peaches on the counter and smiles at me. "Except peaches it seems. Put them on my account, will you?" He says. He puts his hat back on his head and tucks the precious peaches inside his snow covered coat. "She's been told by some ladies that they were sick to the point of vomiting sometimes in the morning and sometimes all day!" He blushes something fierce. "Having a baby's more complicated than I imagined." Taking a deep breath to prepare himself as he ventures back outside he gives me a kind smile and says, "Much obliged."

That night as I lay on my cot I think about Ezekiel and Jane West and the complications of having a baby. I think about Otter and wonder how she's doing and try to imagine Little Bird and how much he's talking now. All of a sudden my head thinks, *When was the last time you had your monthly?* and I realize I have no recollection of having had them ever here with the Coopers. And I've been here more than two full months. Suddenly, the sickness and the tears and the tiredness and even the time I had blackness happen to me the awful night when things changed here at the Coopers makes more sense to me. I reach down in wonder at my stomach and think, *Is there a baby in there?* I've a brief moment where I'm flooding with warmth from the top of my head to the tip of my toes like one great Whoosh. *Bright Feather's and my baby,* I think in delighted wonder. *Remember me and I will be there.*

Gradually, however, the thought of all the things that I'll have to face with *that* new bit of information causes me to run to the basin and throw up again. As I stand there in the dark, the way of things for me seems more than I can handle. On my own, with no one I can depend on, trapped by the weather, and now, *with a baby on the way.* I feel the easy tears begin to flow again and all of a sudden I think with a pile full of disgust, *Is this how a powerful woman behaves?* My mind looks hard at myself and aside from the permanent marks on my chin, there's nothing to see of the powerful woman that I'd become. These past weeks and months seem to have sucked all the power out of me and I feel like I'm in a big deep dark pit that has no way out. That fills me with great sorrow. *I've got to find this Powerful Woman again soon,* I think, *before she fades away forever.*

"Help," I hear me say quiet and whisper like in the dark and I realize that it's a prayer. "I need to find some help." I remember Ma saying, *Thou preparest a table before me in the presence of mine enemies:*[18] and later on Henry saying, *Shall we start cooking dinner, Elle?* I realize I need to find someone I can cook with.

In the morning I make some decisions. I do my chores and then inform Mrs. Cooper that I'm taking Willow for a ride. I don't ask her, I tell her and she seems to not know just what to say. I leave before she can think of something. Riding Willow in white clothes is not something either of us likes. I do my best to tuck my skirts and petticoats down about my legs so that their flapping in the wind does not spook Willow too much. It's not snowed since Ezekiel West's visit yesterday and I'm able to follow his tracks and within a bit of time I find myself looking at their small cabin thinking, *What am I doing?* But my head also tells me plain and clear that of all the people I've met since my return to Ward's Mill, Virginia, these two are the only ones who seemed to show me true kindness. I hear Deer's mate Possum say to me, *It does not matter what they call me as long as they speak polite and respectful to me.* I tie Willow near a tree that's sheltered from the wind, gather up my courage and knock at the front door and wait.

Miss Jane opens the door and she looks as pale as the snow that I'm standing in. "Why Miss Graves!" she says in a mighty surprised voice and she makes a motion to smooth her hair and straightens her clothes. After a moment's hesitation she says, "Won't you come in?"

It's a small but tidy cabin and I can tell right away that she's still been in bed for the place is cool and the covers on the bed are thrown back and rumpled. "May I offer you some tea?" she asks, but she seems at a loss as to what to do first.

"I'd be much obliged," I say. "Can I help you stir up the fire?"

"Oh, yes, please, that would be a help. Ezekiel got it going before he left but I must have dozed off for a bit…" She sets out two cups and a tea pot and I stir up the fire and swing the iron kettle over the flames to heat the water.

Tucked in the pocket of my skirt I draw out another jar of peaches and place it on the table. "I found another jar on the shelf this morning while I was doing my chores and I thought you might appreciate these," I say.

She picks the jar up like it is a most precious thing and looks at me real grateful. "Thank you, *so much*," she says and she hugs the jar tight. "I've had a terrible craving for these for about a week now and it's driving me fair crazy. This isn't exactly the best time to hunger for fresh peaches," she says as the wind picks up and moans outside. She looks at me, "Won't you have a seat?"

I sit at the table and look around the place. It's neat and tidy and she's made an effort to make it look homey. There are curtains on the window and a fresh clean tablecloth on the table. I spy a drawing hanging on the wall and am moved to look at it. It's a beautiful sketch of man staring thoughtful and intent at something in the distance. His hair is tousled and there's a slight shadow of a beard. Even though it's only a pencil sketch, it's alive and breathing almost. You can sense the man's intensity and almost find yourself straining to hear what he's listening to. It's Ezekiel West.

"That was the first time I saw Ezekiel," I hear shy like behind me. "At the town meeting in Richmond concerning the availability of newly available homestead lots. I was there with my Ma and Pa for the same reason. I was bored and started sketching things." She laughs a quiet laugh. "He was the most interesting subject."

"You have a fine talent," I tell her and she looks pleased. The kettle boils and she makes the tea. We sit in silence for a bit.

"How are you doing?" she asks me but her look says she already knows.

I take a deep breath. "That's why I am here. I've no one to talk to or ask questions and I hope you'll not think I am a bother. Please tell me if that's so and I'll just go."

"No, no, I'm glad you're here. Ezekiel's told me of the general opinion of folks from what he's heard and seen. We would've made more of an effort to welcome you but I've just been so tired with this baby coming and all. Next week I start my fifth month, so I'm hoping that things will improve." She looks a bit unsure. "They told me things would get better after the third month, though."

I start to talk. "I'm not sure where to begin or just what to tell you for I don't want to cause you upset. Perhaps I'll just ask you how you knew you were pregnant and what were the symptoms and what you know about it all." She studies me across the table and I look direct back at her. "Or maybe I should tell you a little about myself first and where I've been ..."

She puts her teacup down, folds her hands in her lap and says, "Well, I was hoping to become pregnant so I'd been watching for signs. I think the first thing that happened was my breasts got terrible tender. Then of course, I missed my monthly. Then came the tiredness unlike anything I've ever felt and it seems no matter how much I sleep I'm still exhausted."

She points to the peaches. "The cravings are something new. Up until then, I felt hungry but never really wanted to eat anything. Some of the ladies I've seen at the store have told me horrible stories about constant sickness and dizziness and even passing out. I'm glad I haven't felt any of that though." She blushes. "And there's one thing else, and I'll tell you since you've asked. Ezekiel says I have a funny dark line that travels from my belly button downwards..." She blushes an even darker shade of red. "He says that's new since I've been pregnant." She picks up her teacup and tries to hide behind it as she takes a sip.

"I've not had my monthly for going on three months," I tell her. "I've had passing tiredness, and I've had the sickness – often late at night, and I did collapse one time and wake up moments later. And I've cried more in these past two months than I think I've cried in my whole life."

She stares at me for a moment and then the blush returns full force. "Of course," Miss Jane says to me, "you know that you must be, er, well, *intimate* with a man, right?"

I wait a moment and then finally say, "I am Bear, of the Wolf Clan, daughter of One Who Knows, *mate* of Bright Feather, son of War Woman and Great Elk chief of The Real People of the Maple Forest."

She stares at me for the longest time with her teacup in her hand midway between her mouth and the table. Finally she sets the teacup down and stares at me for a while longer. At last, she licks her lips, clears her throat, smiles a tiny smile and extends her hand. "How do you do, Bear. It's a pleasure to meet you. My name's Jane West. Please call me Jane."

I burst into tears.

At that very moment, Ezekiel West blows in. "Jane ...?" he says, his voice full of concern. "Are you all right? There's a strange horse outside ..." He takes in the picture before him. "Oh. How do you do, Miss Graves?"

"Not too well, as you can see, Ezekiel," Jane says as she hands me a clean cloth to wipe my face and nose. Her look at me asks, *Can I tell him?* I nod my head to her. "It would seem that things are much more complicated than they would appear for ..." she hesitates and I see she struggles with what name to call me.

"I don't care what you call me as long as you speak to me polite and with respect," I say to her in all seriousness.

"... Elle," she settles on, "seems to be in the same condition as I am," and she gestures to the peaches.

"She's got cravings for the peaches?" He says in confusion and he looks back and forth between me and my tear stained face and his wife's pale tired one. "She wants the ones back I bought yesterday? I thought you ate all those already?!"

Jane looks first at me and then at him and then at me again and we both can't help it, we burst out laughing. And we laugh and laugh and laugh until the tears roll down both our faces and we're gasping for breath. "Glad I'm so powerful entertaining," he finally says as we struggle to pull ourselves together.

"No, Ezekiel," Jane finally manages to say to her husband as she wipes her face on her apron. "It would seem that Elle is *pregnant* just like *I* am."

"Oh ..." he says and then as he thinks it all through his brain and I watch him slowly fit all the pieces together, he looks at me and says, "*OH*," more loudly.

"Elle informs me that she is married to an Indian brave named," she looks at me to correct her if she's wrong, "*Bright Feather*," and I nod, "who happens to be the *chief's son* of the tribe in which she's been living these past years."

"Oh ..." is all Ezekiel can say again, but he's moved to pull up a stool and sit down.

Jane gets up and refills the kettle and swings it over the flame. She adds more wood to the fire and goes to the cupboard and takes out some biscuits and a bit of jam in a dish. "You'd better tell us the whole story as to *why you're here* instead of *there.*"

So I tell them all I know, except I leave out the Bear John part of the story. I bring them right up to the point where I'm with the Coopers and how I'm am no longer such a *welcome paying guest* because there's now a concern as to whether Henry'll ever be found to pay my bill. I tell them how the mood has changed in the house and how I don't know how they will react when they find out I'm with child.

"Well no one says you have to tell them about the baby right away," is the first thing Jane says. She stands up, turns sideways and beneath her skirts and apron there's just a hint of a bump. "You can easily hide things for another few months I'd say so the child part is not a primary concern. As long as they are not suspecting, it's probably the last thing on their minds. Do you agree, Ezekiel?"

Poor Ezekiel. He has a look of stunned confusion like he's stepped bare foot into hot horse dung and not sure where to go next. He looks at his wife, "I suspect so, Jane," he says finally.

Jane looks at me with fear in her eyes, "You are in danger, however, should Cornelius come to the conclusion that your brother Henry will never come, claim you, and pay your bill. And don't for one minute think that Naomi will lift a hand against him to help you. She is quieter and less obvious, but they are the same those two. Do you agree, Ezekiel?"

Ezekiel seems to finally spark to life. "Cornelius Cooper of Ward's Mill, Virginia, is ruthless," Ezekiel says with feeling. "He keeps careful records and charges heavy interest when you're late in paying. He has no desire to hear any excuses, he just wants the money that's due him." He looks at me serious like. "He was not the original owner of the mill. Seems Jonathan Ward, who could not read or write, signed a loan agreement that stated that should he ever be late with his bill to the general store or reach a certain level of debt, he'd give the ownership of the mill over to Cornelius as payment. When he reached a point where he owed so much and was indeed late for a bit on his payments, Cornelius took the mill." Ezekiel looks at me, "Debt and uncertainty is the way of life when you make your living farming, you know."

"Jonathan Ward was my father," Jane says quiet like. "He was a good man, a loving man. Always ready with a smile or a moment to stop what he was doing should I stop by to see him. He was fair, too, never ever cheated a soul out of even a grain of wheat. When in doubt he gave more than less." She looks down fondly at Ezekiel and smoothes back his hair that is damp from the melting snow. "Maybe that was his downfall, he just didn't believe that there were people who could be so evil and cruel."

Ezekiel reaches up and puts his arm around her waist as she stands next to him at the table and says, "Jonathan Ward took his family back to Richmond, where they both had family. He still owned some property here in Ward's Mill and so when Jane and I married, I staked a Homestead Claim that bordered on the Ward Property. It's a sizeable piece that we have to offer our children, now, but without the mill."

Jane smiles a sad smile. "My mother died just before we married. I was determined not to let Cornelius and Naomi Cooper keep me from my father's inheritance. Our success," she says as she looks at Ezekiel, "is their defeat."

Ezekiel says, "He owns Old Man Hobson's place, too, you know. Reached a point where the bill was so great he forced Hobson to hand over his deed. Charges him *rent* now, plus takes most of the crops that are grown over there by Hobson to sell them for his own profit and to "settle Hobson's continuing debt." Only allows Hobson to live there because he's just like slave labor." He studies me for a moment and then decides to tell me. "He owns the property that once was yours, too. When your Pa was killed," he swallows and looks at me, "I'm sorry," he says, "your Pa had just ordered and received a full season's worth of seed, plus he owed some money for other things needed for the season. Cornelius claimed he was due payment and I understand that Henry finally gave the property over to him when it became obvious he couldn't pay and couldn't handle the place all by himself. Henry went into the army because there wasn't much else left for him to do."

I stare at my empty teacup and then at the sorrowful faces of Jane and Ezekiel West. I'd not realized that there were so many puzzles to life. Here's a new one that truth be told I would have been happy to just leave undone. At last I say, "Thank you for your hospitality," and I stand to leave.

"Wait! Where are you going?!" They both say together.

"It's getting dark. I need to get back. I need to think." I look at them with very serious eyes. "Thank you for listening to me. Thank you for talking to me."

Jane comes to me and puts both hands on my shoulders. She's a small bit shorter than me, but not by much. "Our door is always open to you, Elle," Jane says as I wrap my shawl around me and pull on my wool mittens. "Should you have trouble, need a place to stay ..."

Willow and I travel back to the store and it's dark and freezing cold when we get home. My stomach rumbles in hunger and a bit of nerves, too, I think. What a mess I'm in. Here I am, back in the white world to put *out* any fires that could burn problems towards The Maple Forest and I've probably started more than ever now. If Henry sold the homestead to Cornelius Cooper because he didn't have the funds to pay what he owed, how will he ever be able to settle any bill that I add to each day with simply sleeping, eating and breathing *now*? And if I try to sneak away without paying what I owe, suppose Henry shows up sometime after that? Would he be arrested? What do they do to people who don't pay their bills and have nothing to give in trade? And how many months do I have before everyone in the world knows that I'm pregnant *with an Indian baby*. I do figuring in my head and think maybe three months more, *at the most*. It's almost the end of February. That brings me to May. Right after the first spring flowers bud. *Bright Feather,* I think with a sob, *I miss you.* I work hard to put Bright Feather thoughts away.

I stable and rub down Willow and come in through the back door, not the main front one. The front one is for customers, the back one enters the space that the Coopers consider their home. I'm cold and tired and powerful hungry, but my terrible big problem is what causes me the greatest thought.

"WHERE THE HELL HAVE YOU BEEN?!" I hear roared at me as I step into the house and before I know it I am lying on the floor with a bloody lip and a ringing head. Cornelius Cooper towers over me just about purple with anger. "YOU HAVE BEEN GONE <u>ALL DAY</u>. WHAT RIGHT DO YOU HAVE TRAIPSING ALL OVER CONDUCTING SOCIAL CALLS? YOU HAD WORK HERE TO DO!"

I stand up and dab my dripping mouth and growing fat lip with the edge of my icy shawl. "I did my chores this morning."

"You did *morning chores,*" I hear an angry female voice say and to Cornelius Cooper's left appears Naomi Cooper and she is just a few shades lighter in anger then her husband. "You have *afternoon* and *evening* chores that you're responsible for that because you chose to disappear I was stuck doing."

I take a deep breath. "I apologize," I say. "I meant to cause you no trouble." It's just about the hardest thing I've ever had to say.

Cornelius Cooper's hand shoots out and closes around my throat. I feel my feet lifted off the ground so that only my toes can barely touch and I struggle and grab at his hand to loosen it and let some air in to breath. "You don't leave here without permission. Do you understand?," He says real close to my face. I nod my head as best as I can 'yes'. "And forget about dinner, you're not around to prepare it, you're not entitled to eat it. What do you have to say about that?" He sneers as he releases my throat and I sag against the door gasping for breath.

I struggle to get breath into my lungs and I look at him and her and this time *I* make no effort to conceal what I think about either one of them. "Just make sure you don't charge me for it," I say cold and flip and I brush past them into my closet room.

The next morning I do my best to get on with my chores and avoid the two of them as much as is possible in a smallish place with no where to escape. When I finally do manage to go outside for a brief moment to feed and care for Willow like I always do, I stand for a few moments unable to understand why I'm looking at an empty stable. A wave of terror washes over me and I go running inside as fast as the snow will allow. As soon as I come in, huffing and panting from the run, I realize what I missed this morning as I went about my business trying to avoid the two of them. They appear happy as they both look up at me, pretending curiousness at my state.

"Problem?" Cornelius Cooper says cordial like to me.

"Where's my horse," I say from gritted teeth and I feel the cold blade of the knife strapped to my leg and I think about who and where I would like to stick it in first.

"*Your horse?*" Mr. Cooper says. "I find it mighty strange that someone in your *position* would claim to own *anything*. Your bills are more than three months past due as of today. I sold *your horse*," he says with a quiet chuckle at the foolishness of it all, "to get some much needed payment towards the bill that you continue to mount. The gentleman that bought her, saw no need for all the bug infested bits that went with her so I burned them. At least now, your bill will only reflect the care and feeding of you and not *your horse* as well." I struggle with the words he's said to me that feel just as painful as his punch and choking of last night. Maybe worse I realize as the misery of the loss of Willow seems to grow and grow. The pain of Willow's loss will still be there long after my bruised lip and throat have healed. *Do not cry. Do not cry.* I'll not give them the satisfaction. I clench my hands into a fist and feel the knife through my skirt and concentrate on my breathing. *Think, think…*

"Elle, I need you to help with the noon meal," I hear Mrs. Cooper say from behind me as if nothing is unusual or out of place. I turn to look at her and she gives me a bright, friendly smile like my first few days here. *I guess her friendliness depends on the size of my bill*, I realize and I feel a calmness grow slowly in me as I take stock of my situation and what I can and cannot do. I look back at Mr. Cooper and he gives me a look that says, *Go ahead, I dare you.*

I think of Bright Feather then as I stand there and rather than make me cry as it has done in the past months I feel strong and powerful and not alone all of a sudden. *Remember me and I will be there.* I think of the baby nestled in my stomach and that there are *two* of us here now. I feel my brain snapping and crackling like a just caught log on fire and feel a wave of relief like finding something you thought you'd lost for good. I feel, all of a sudden, more like Bear of The Real People of the Maple Forest than I have felt in a very long time.

I think about my pink horse and all that she has meant to me. She's been with me longer even than Bright Feather. She's filled empty spaces made by my separation from Pa, Henry, Eli, Otter, Raccoon and Bright Feather over that past two years. I think about Bright Feather calling his horse Companion and understand now clearly the way of things between a person and their horse.

My awakening brain says loud and clear to me, *You are free. Willow's sale has settled your bill.* And then, what did Jane say? *They told me things would get better after the third month.* I've been here three months so that must mean that I'm three months pregnant then. *Guess I'm feeling better,* I think.

I walk real slow over to where Cornelius Cooper is standing and he watches me approach with a guarded look. "How much did you get for my horse?" I ask quiet like.

"Enough to pay your bill and give you a few more weeks of grace, before you start owing us again," he says flip back to me. "Course that's just for food and housing. It doesn't pay what you owe for all the clothes and such. You still owe us for those things we've been kind enough to provide you with."

"Did you keep a list of all those things as well?" I ask.

"Sure did," he says smug like. He reaches underneath the counter where he keeps his ledger book and flips through the pages and says, "Here it is …" and proceeds to read every stitch of cloth and thread and button that I've been given. He finishes with, "one pair of stockings with garters – dark black, one pair of boots and one bonnet." I can see neat little columns of figures listed on the page that says 'Graves, Elle'. One column has many, many numbers, while the other column appears to have only one lone entry. *Willow's sale.*

He looks at me with hate and I return the feeling. I begin to unbutton all of the tiny buttons down the front of my overblouse, which I take off and drop to the floor. I unhook my skirt and that drops in a heap at my ankles, followed by one petticoat, two petticoats, and finally my chemise. I hear "Oh my God!" behind me as Mrs. Cooper watches me disrobe before the two of them. Cornelius Cooper can't believe what's happening before his very eyes. I see him take in my scars of Weasel's treatment of me, the bite and knife scars that are long healed by now but still show. I bend over and unfasten my boots and stockings until all that's left on me is my knife strapped high on my right thigh. I'm glad for my still flat belly; no one would suspect that there are two of us bare naked in this room! "Make sure you mark down in that book of yours that I gave it all back," I say low and quiet. "Make sure you make note that I left here with *nothing* on my body that you were *kind* enough to give me." He's stunned by my nakedness. Perhaps by my knife strapped to my leg as well, I think as an afterthought. He just sits there and stares and stares unable to move as I turn to look at Mrs. Cooper.

Mrs. Cooper has her mouth hanging open in a big, wide stunned "O". Sometimes it flaps in an effort to form words but she cannot manage it it seems. She too, takes in my scars and my knife, but she's the one that sees the hate in my eyes when I say to her, for I cannot resist, *"Precious Johnny's knife,"* as I pat my thigh. I turn and walk to my closet room where I pick up my book of Isaac Watts hymns and then walk out the back door into the freezing snow. The shock of the cold's not something I care to describe. Not ten steps into the snow and I can't feel my feet but that's good for the pain of the cold's bitter. I start to shiver and realize that I must move fast before I die from this crazy foolishness. I can hear the back door creak open just as I begin to run into the forest trying to keep my head calm as I search for my hidden place of Indian clothes and my bow and arrow and other bits. I've never, ever walked there in a direct route always fearful that I was being watched and they would find my secret place. As I run through the woods I feel the cold gradually rob the feeling from my body. My feet go numb first, followed by my fingertips and my nipples. I stumble twice and try to be more careful with my frozen feet. I don't think I'd be able to feel enough things to get up should I fall. The snot in my nose freezes as I run and it runs. I see the large fir tree that I chose - green all year round despite the season - and I must stop just once to look back and make sure that a purple faced monster's not following me. I'm alone, I see, just me and my baby freezing quickly to death. I crawl under the fir tree and dig through the layers and layers of evergreen needles that make a prickly floor for me to kneel on. Out comes my bear cape, my fur lined trousers and boots, my long leather tunic and even my beautiful dress and matching shoes One Who Knows made me and that I wore a lifetime ago when the village celebrated my joining with Bright Feather. I put it all on but am so cold that the shivering doesn't seem to know that I'm not naked anymore.

It takes the last bit of my strength to make me step out in the biting cold and wind and stomp my feet and wave my arms like Raccoon has taught me in those early days of teaching me how to ride Willow. I feel my feet begin to prickle and my fingers begin to sting and worst of all is my nipples that feel like they are on fire. But the pain is good I know. When I finally feel more warm than cold, I crawl back under the fir tree, hunker down out of the wind and wait for night. And think. Always think.

What is an Indian?
Is he not formed of the same materials with yourself?
For "of one blood God created all the nations that dwell on the face of the earth." 19
~Elias Boudinot

Journeywoman

Every night like clockwork, Mr. Cornelius Cooper of Ward's Mill, Virginia, drinks exactly three cupfuls of 'medicinal' liquor. At the completion of the third cup, with steps unsteady, he lumbers outside to the necessary house, does his business and then buttons the house down for the night bolting both doors front and back.

I figure, given the excitement of this day in particular, perhaps Mr. Cornelius Cooper will have four cupfuls of medicinal liquor tonight which can only work in my favor. I wait quiet in Willow's empty stall in the dark of the night waiting for the necessary stop and sure enough out he stumbles just as expected. While he does his business, I sneak into the store and hide quiet like behind the counter and the last two sacks of flour he's still hopeful to sell. I'd forgotten how wonderfully quiet a body can be dressed in comfortable Indian dress. I hold my knife in my hand just in case.

I hear Mr. Cooper stumble in through the back door and place the bolt in. Three or four times since I've been there he's forgotten to do this and he and Mrs. Cooper have had an argument in the morning when it's discovered. He'll think he's forgotten in the morning once again. The dim glow of the one lit candle flickers and dances as he carries it into the bedroom and I can hear Mrs. Cooper's snores get louder for a brief moment as the door's opened and then shut. I hear the creak of the bed ropes and the rustle of the cornhusk and hay mattress. I hear three loud farts. I wait and finally I hear the start of thunderous snoring that joins in horrible tune with Mrs. Cooper's. I'm all alone until morning.

Slowly my eyes grow accustomed to the darkness so that I can see dim shadows. There's no moon or stars for the sky is heavy with snow clouds. I'm not stealing, I tell myself, for I still have some money *on account for a few weeks of grace* just as Mr. Cooper has said. I must be wise with what I take for I can only carry what I can fit in One Who Knows' gathering basket and I'll be on foot. I can hunt for meat, but there are other things that I should bring along. I go to their family store of food and take what's left of day old bread and the biscuits that I baked early that morning. I wrap in an old cloth the remains of the salt pork that we've been eating for a few days. There are three apples from the root cellar. While I think, I sit on the floor and eat an entire jar of strawberry preserves for they would be far too heavy to carry. They taste mighty good. I decide to eat a biscuit with some of the butter I find, the remains of a wedge of goat cheese, and finally one of the apples. There's a pitcher of milk and I drink that, too. Finally, my belly is happy. I take nothing from the store supplies and only a few things to keep me for the walk I plan to make to the West's. I know I'll not be fast enough to escape an angry purple man on a horse in the snow should he decide to follow and I don't want to have anything great to be guilty for should I be caught.

As I head for the door, something makes me stop and go into the store once more to behind the counter where I know Mr. Cooper keeps his precious ledger book. I think about my Willow and how it was the only thing that Mr. Cooper could take from me that would cause me grief and pain. I look at that ledger book and finally after a moment put it in my basket. I'm a powerful woman settling a score that needs to be settled. I suspect I need to restore a bit of balance and harmony, too.

It's begun to snow again. That's good and that's bad I know as I head out in the direction of the West's cabin. Good because any tracks I may have made'll be gone by morning and good because believe it or not it feels warmer than it did this afternoon with the bitter wind and cold. Bad because I'd thought that if I could find Willow's tracks in the snow perhaps I would follow them and see where they lead. That'll be impossible now.

I walk a large portion of the night. Things are slower because I'm on foot and because of the snow. I also decide to take a more round about route because I'd like to avoid getting found by Mr. Cooper for at least a day or two. Will he come looking for me? Would he bother? Perhaps not when I ran naked into the snow and he thought I would be frozen dead inside a few brief moments, but once he realizes that I've been in his home he'll be angry. And once he finds the ledger book gone he'll want to kill me. I have a brief thought of perhaps I should've left it, and then I shrug. No chance to go back now.

At the West's cabin I wait out in the cold in the same place where I tied Willow only the day before. I wait until I hear sounds from inside the cabin and I know the Wests are awake. I pluck up my courage and knock on their door for the second time in three days.

Ezekiel opens the door this time and if he looked surprised to see me the other day sitting in his kitchen he looks absolutely stunned to see me in full Indian dress standing at his doorstep at the crack of dawn. "Miss Graves!" he says in startled tones.

"Ezekiel?" I hear a sleepy voice from the corner where I know the bed is. "Who is it Ezekiel?"

He grabs me by the arm and pulls me in and I blow in with wind and snow and cold. "We have a visitor, Jane."

"Elle! Are you well?" she says with true concern in her voice struggling with the covers to get out of bed.

"I am," I say, "although I'd appreciate if I could sit down. I'm a bit tired from walking."

"You walked out here in the storm?!" Ezekiel explodes. "Are you out of your mind?"

I tell them what has happened since they saw me last and I remember as I speak the big bruise by my mouth, the split lip and the bruises around my throat. As I talk Ezekiel insists that Jane stay in bed while he works at preparing breakfast. I grow weak from hunger and tiredness at the smell of the frying potatoes and onions, eggs and bacon and hot biscuits baking in the oven pan. I sip on hot tea which dribbles a bit down my chin because of my lip.

Once my belly is full from Ezekiel's mighty fine cooking there is nothing else I can possibly consider doing but sleeping. I refuse the kind offer of Jane and Ezekiel's bed and curl up on a quilt on the floor. I don't even remember putting my head on the pillow, sleep takes me away so quick.

It's dark when I wake and I've slept the day away. The smell of more food cooking is what rouses me and I try not to look at the large pot simmering on the fire. "How are you feeling?" Jane asks and I'm handed another cup of hot, steaming tea.

"Better," I say with a smile. "Thank you for your continued kindness."

"Ezekiel and I've talked all day about what you'll do." She looks frustrated and worried. "We can't think of any good solutions. You're welcome to stay here but he and I do not think you'll be safe here for very long."

I shake my head as she's talking. "No, I can't stay here. It'd not be safe for me but it'd also be dangerous for you. You two will live here in Ward's Mill forever and you don't want to be on the wrong side of Mr. Cooper. I came here last night only because I knew that no one would be able to follow my tracks." I smile a kind of smile. "Snow can be a good thing, you know."

"Then what will you do?" Ezekiel asks with concern.

"I'll go to Major Everett and the Ninth Virginia Cavalry, Company D and ask that he escort me back to William Holland Thomas' trading post in Forest City, North Carolina. George Maw said that it would take two days by horse to get to Fort Winston, so I figure I can get there in four maybe five days on foot."

"You plan to walk there?" Ezekiel says.

I look at him serious for a moment. "I've no other choice. I cannot stay here. I must get there. As difficult as it'll be for *me* to get there, it'll be just as hard for anyone to follow me." I try to reassure him. "I've traveled and lived outside in the winter time. I can start a fire and make a shelter. I can track and hunt. I'll be okay." I smile at him and then must stop real quick for I feel my lip start to split again. "I'll be much better off than as a guest at Mr. and Mrs. Cooper's home."

He's nothing to say to me and at the mention of their names I remember the ledger. I stand up and my muscles remind me that they've not had so much walking experience these past many months. I go to my basket and take out Mr. Cooper's precious ledger book. "I took only one thing that I was not entitled to," I say to the Wests, by way of preparing them. "It was a fair exchange for them taking Willow." I put the ledger book on the table.

It's Ezekiel who touches it first and he draws it towards him. "His ledger book?!" he says to me in wonder. "You took his *ledger book?*" I shrug my shoulders but deep inside me my heart does a few leaps with worry. Ezekiel understands that Mr. Cooper's anger over this would be a great and deadly thing towards me.

He opens up to the page that says, "West, Ezekiel/Jane" at the top and scans down the columns. He frowns and turns the pages and looks at other entries of other customers. "Why that bastard ..." he finally mutters under his breath.

"Ezekiel!" Jane says shocked.

"He has us buying more seed than we bought, for prices higher than he's charged others. He's charged you," he looks at me, "ridiculous amounts for the cost of your clothes and for your room and board. And the amount he sold Willow for," he shakes his head in disgust, "you should have gotten twice that."

"Does it say who the buyer was?" Jane asks and I think with excitement, *Good question.*

But Ezekiel shakes his head 'no'. "What's this?" he says at the piece of loose paper that has slipped out from the back. He opens the paper and Jane and I both peer over his shoulder to read:

Land Property Deed

29 Dec. 1815

Homestead Property Sale to Daniel and Francis Hobson, 320 acres Wards Mill, Virginia, west side of Reedy River, northern line between said John Benson and his father Charles Benson's old tract mentioned in said Charles Benson's will, south side by Bridges and Sammon's corner, Robert Duncan's old corner and line, Brock's corner.

Witnessed Isaac Bradley, signature, Dennis Chairis, signature;

Daniel Hobson signature

Francis Hobson signature

Received and acknowledged 22 April 1816.

"Old Man Hobson's deed to his property," Ezekiel says in wonder. He searches in the back of the ledger and finds more papers including the deed to the mill and the general store property. The third piece of paper which he opens we see:

Land Property Deed

15 March 1817

Homestead Property Sale to Andrew Graves and Elizabeth Graves, 320 acres Wards Mill, Virginia, west side of Buckhorn corner, on south bank of Weirs Creek, to Bruce's line.

Witnessed John W. Wood signature, Jeremiah Forrest his mark (X).

Received and acknowledged 3 August 1817.

Andrew Graves signature

Elizabeth Graves signature

Looking at the paper with my Ma and Pa's names written with their own hands causes me to sit down with a thump in the chair. "Are you alright, Elle?" I hear Jane say from far away. I can't imagine that Ma or Pa could have ever imagined what could happen to our family in just a few short years.

Ezekiel says in an excited voice, "Elle! Do you realize what these papers mean?"

I look at him in silence because I don't.

"Once a Land Title Deed is made, that piece of land can travel through many different hands. But the Land Title Deed just gets longer and longer with the additions and changes written on it. There is nothing added to these! That means that Cooper never went to the trouble to have the deeds officially changed over into his name! He would have had to travel to the nearest land office." He stops and thinks. "Why, that's probably all the way back to Richmond! He couldn't be bothered. Must of figured he had plenty of time to do all that." He waves the deed at me. "*Forget the ledger, Elle. Here is your revenge.*" He hands me the deed to my parent's land. "It belongs to Henry or you as the surviving children."

I take the paper in my hand and think, What good is this to me? What could I ever do with this land? And then the little voice in my head says, No, that's not the point. Cornelius Cooper doesn't have it anymore. That's the point. I reach into my basket and pull out my Isaac Watts book of hymns. I touch the faded leather cover, open the book and carefully put the deed inside. Who knows what I will ever do with it? I wonder to myself.

The last piece of paper we draw out is the Promissory Note that Henry signed for Cornelius Cooper. It promises to pay all bills *incurred by Miss Elle Graves while housed at Cornelius and Naomi Cooper's on the event of her return.* It is signed *Henry Graves, Esq. April 10, 1828.* I reach over and pick up the ledger and the Promissory Note and walk to the fire with it. Just as I go to throw them in, Jane shouts, "WAIT!"

I turn and look at her and all of a sudden I'm tired again and look forward to my quilt bed on the floor. I feel as if many ghosts are surrounding us in this tiny cabin all of them unhappy. They pound at my head and my heart and I feel like I am not much use to anyone at all. What good am I? I can not even keep my own self safe and out of danger. She walks towards me and takes the ledger from my hands. "Maybe it wouldn't be wise to burn that just yet," she says. Ezekiel looks at her and so do I.

"I can't take it with me," I say and look at them. "It's too dangerous for you to be caught with it."

She shrugs her shoulders. "Who'd suspect us to have it?" She walks over to the bed. She kneels down on the floor and wrestles with the bedclothes for a moment. We hear a brief tearing sound and then a crunching of hay and corn husks as she shoves the book deep inside the mattress. "A few quick stitches and no one will be the wiser. We can always burn it later if it seems the smart thing to do." She walks back over to me and takes the Promissory Note from my hand and tosses it in the fire. "*That* should have been burned long ago, though."

Moments later we're all in our beds. I've only a few brief moments wondering if I'll be able to sleep after having slept the day away before I collapse with exhaustion.

The morning dawns bright, clear and crispy cold with the sun casting a blinding glare on the snow. I eat a hearty breakfast and joke that I better leave before I eat their pantry bare. Ezekiel listens to the directions I remember George Maw giving me and agrees with the path. He adds important details like where he thinks will be safe places for me to stop and sleep for the night: a cave he knows at the top of the one ridge that he found hunting one day, Old Man Hobson's barn, and two other barns along the way that he knows of that he figures I can sleep in without being detected. We're unsure what Cornelius Cooper'll do but want my trail away to be as cold and hard to follow as possible. As a result, though it's possible I could request the hospitality of people along the way, we decide it'd not be wise to have anyone see me if possible. "Our greatest hope is that he thinks you froze to death and are buried somewhere under the latest snowfall," Ezekiel says. Neither of us discuss the possibility of that still happening over the next few days to come as I travel on foot through some mighty dangerous circumstances.

Getting word to Deer seems nigh on to impossible until I reach Major Everett and winter has ended. "I'll keep an eye out should someone come into town and is traveling south but until the snow stops and winter breaks there'll be little opportunity," Ezekiel says. "Even with the spring rains, there's the struggle with muddy roads that get so terrible that wagons can sink all the way up over their wheels." I know that if the opportunity arises, he'll send word and I must be satisfied with that.

"I promised Bright Feather I would return by the start of spring," I say. All three of us are silent, realizing that by then I'll be far along with my pregnancy and rough travel probably will be unwise for both me and the baby. "I tried to get him to promise not to put himself in danger by coming this far into white territory ..."

Ezekiel snorts his disbelief. "I'm sure he refused," he says.

"He did," I say and I sigh a deep sigh of frustration.

Jane adds some foodstuffs to my basket even though I try to tell her no. "It's not open for discussion," she says firmly and embraces me.

"I'm sorry it's only some tea and cheese … I'll keep you in my prayers," she says quietly in my ear. I remember my prayer of help and my request to find someone to cook with and I smile. "I prayed for someone just like you two just the other night." I look at the remains of breakfast still around the room. "Even down to the cooking," I hold my split lip together as I laugh at my own joke. I look at them and say, "I've been told that God loves us greatly and can hear even our most quietest whisper. You two are proof of that." I must remember, as I look at their worried faces, that even when things seem so dark and bleak, when you look careful, you can always find a shiny, good spot.

I leave by way of the footsteps that Ezekiel makes to their barn and hen house not wishing a trail of lone Indian footprints to shout any clues. He walks me as far as the forest edge and dumps a load of refuse to attract further footprints and confusion. "Until we meet again," he says to me with a smile. "Both *families* probably by that time."

"I look forward to that," I say in all seriousness. "Thank you for seeing the inside of me instead of just the outside."

The going's far more slow and difficult than I ever imagined. Sometimes the snow's over my knees and I'm ready to drop by the time I reach the crest of the ridge that Ezekiel has said to follow. I watch for the cave he's described and fight down times of tiredness that go into real fear. Can I do this? If I can't make it to the first stop, how can I make it the rest of the way? I talk to myself and the baby at the same time about what it's like to be a powerful woman, why I am one, and how tough things were to help me earn the title. That makes me keep going. At last I see the three large boulders that Ezekiel said hides the mouth of the cave and I begin to breathe slower and a little easier. I must work on this worry thing and right quick for I've a long way to go and have no spare energy to waste on foolishness.

Sure enough, it's a cave large enough for a full size man to crawl into so just perfect for me and my baby. *Isn't it amazing*, my head thinks. *I never feel alone anymore.* I put my basket down and take a moment to sit and look at my surroundings. My first order of business is to start a fire. I carry bits of kindling and dry straw to start a fire, although I'll need to find some wood that's close to dry to keep the fire going. Inside the cave are some small branches that look like they were washed inside by an old rainstorm. Every little bit helps I think. With my bow and arrow ready, but my pack safe in the cave, I stomp through the snow in search of sticks and food. I find a good supply of almost dry wood in the hollow of some more boulders. No sign of anything to eat though and I'm thankful for what I have in my basket.

As I work at starting the fire, I think about Beaver, for it is from him that I learned this skill. As I feel myself begin to warm up with the energy of the work, I think about how serious Beaver was when he taught me. "Being able to light a fire can mean the difference between life and death," he explained to me. "Always carry a hearthstone, always carry some small kindling or dried grass, and always carry your drill and fire bow." He had looked at me and said, "Those things are as important as your bow and your knife." I believed him when he spoke those words. Now, as I crouch in my cave and work up a sweat starting the fire I feel a rush of thankfulness for him.

Where is he now? I wonder to myself. The last I saw him he was stalking off into the night angry with the decisions that Great Elk and the rest of the council members had made regarding The Maple Forest. Beaver did not agree with joining the village with the United States Government and accepting their offer of citizenship while at the same time separating from The Nation of The Real People and all of the changes it was embracing. As I work at the starting of my fire, I remember Beaver and his passion for his people. A passion that was strong enough to make him leave all he knew and loved to fight for what he believed was the right thing to do. *Just like I have done*, my head feels inclined to point out. I snort out loud in my little cave. "I sure hope he's a sight more successful with what he's doing than I am," I say to me and my baby.

Learning to start a fire was almost as difficult as learning to ride Willow or learning to shoot my bow. Raccoon always made a point to be around when I began to practice all of those things so that he could be insured a laugh or two or ten. A wave of loneliness washes over me for all of those I hold dear and I put my head down and concentrate on the task at hand.

The hearthstone is a small flat rock with a small dip in the center. The drill is a stick that fits in the dip and the bow is just like a bow except the deer sinew is wrapped once around the drill. You pile a small bit of dried grass (I had straw with me) at the place where the drill meets the hearthstone and then you start the work. It's funny how much body heat you can work up just by trying to start a fire! Beaver explained that starting a fire was just like riding a horse. Everyone does it just about the same way, but everyone has their own special style that works just right for them. "I can only tell you what you need to have and do and show you how to put it all together. Whether you ever learn to start a fire on your own, though, will depend on if you practice and find your own special way of doing it."

As I squat, tired and hungry in the cave, working on my style of fire lighting I'm never so happy for Beaver and all those times he made me practice and finally master the art of lighting a fire. The smell of the smoke and the final glow of the small flame does more for my spirits that first night than I can put into words. In my basket I find some tea leaves carefully wrapped in cloth and placed in a battered tin cup. I think of Jane and drinking tea in her cozy little cottage. I melt some snow and float some precious tea leaves in the hot water. Sitting warm and snug in the cave sipping hot tea as I chew on the cold pork and the dry, hard biscuit I've taken from the Coopers by the light of my crackling fire, I catch myself almost smiling. *I will be okay,* I think. *I am a powerful woman on her own.*

The dawn of the next morning, I'm sore from leg, shoulder and back muscles that say to me, *Are you sure you know what you are doing?* But what concerns me more is the slight cramping I feel which reminds me of what I sometimes have when my monthly flows. I put my hand on my belly and hear myself say out loud to my baby, "Hush now, it will be just fine. You rest today and so will I." *What is the rush?* I think. I hurry to another white place that'll look at me with curious eyes. I can only guess at my welcome and am quite happy to take my time receiving it. I spend the day checking out the area by the cave. I stay alert. If Ezekiel found this place hunting, then that tells me I might be lucky with my bow and arrow. I finally shoot a rabbit, but it takes me two tries. I'm out of practice and am glad to be certain that Raccoon's not spying on me to tease me about my poor aim.

That night I dream of Bright Feather. He never speaks but he searches my face with fierce eyes that will me to tell him the truth, *Are you okay?* In my dreams I smile back at him, so glad to see him and to touch him and to smell him. *Yes I am okay,* I tell him although in my dream my mouth never speaks either. *I am warm and safe and dry and am remembering all the things I have learned that have made me a powerful woman. And I have wonderful news,* I tell him as he searches my face and touches my cheek gentle like he does, and I so much want the fierce look to go away. *We are to have a baby! I guess the wanting a baby finally got stronger than the fear of having one for both of us...* In my dream I kiss him deep and long and I delight in watching the fierceness fade away and the look of relief and joy replace it. *Come, I say to him, get warm with me in the furs and love me for it has been too long since I have known you that way* ... He kisses me fierce and it reminds me that I'm his and he's mine and the powerful love that there is between us that has made this baby in my belly.

I wake that second morning in the cave and I turn to look at Bright Feather's face to see it once again. I can't understand why he is not here with me and search the tiny cave with my eyes and my senses to find him. As I realize that it was a dream, I try with all my might to go back to sleep to find it, but it's no use. It's powerful hard to dwell on the delight of the dream rather than the reality of the day.

I'm anxious to move all of a sudden. I remember as Bright Feather and I traveled from Dark Cloud's village this past summer and the happy decisions we made between us to join. My muscles are still sore. *Let's get moving,* my body says. I let my remembrys of my pink horse keep me company as my baby and me get on the way.

The first thing I notice is that the snow is different as I work through it along the ridge, following the path of George Maw, with added bits from Ezekiel West. It seems heavier, damper and I realize that the air is slightly warmer, too. So spring is fighting the battle with winter to arrive at last. It'll be a tough battle I think for Winter has enjoyed her time here this year.

My next stop is Old Man Hobson's place. I think about *Life is what you make of it*, as Pa has told me. I think about all the pieces to the puzzle of my life and wonder if they ever will connect and make one great picture that makes sense *and* show more joy than sorrow. For the time being it seems that there is a bit more sorrow than I'd care to put up with. I worry about the pieces that connect my white life with my red. What will the picture show?

I stop on the ridge that overlooks Old Man Hobson's place in the late afternoon and look at the tiny cabin and small barn in the back. I study the place for a while to be certain that the only person at Old Man Hobson's is Old Man Hobson. I'm glad I wait for who do I see step out of the cabin but Cornelius Cooper followed by Old Man Hobson. Mr. Cooper seems to do most of the talking, as is the custom with everyone I realize. Except maybe Mrs. Cooper, I think after a time though. He points and has what seems to be angry gestures. Then he mounts up on his horse and rides away. Old Man Hobson stands in front of his cabin for a space of time and then finally walks back toward the barn and disappears inside. A few minutes later I see him go back into his small cabin and all is quiet.

I look at the sun. It's low on the horizon and soon it'll be more dark then light. I decide to wait until full darkness before I decide to settle down in the barn for the night. I chew on some of Jane West's cheese and the last of the bread and biscuits from the Coopers which is just as well for if I wait another day to eat them I'm sure I'll break some teeth. As the sun sets, I walk along the ridge until I'm directly behind the barn and I study the best way to walk down and leave the least amount of tracks in the snow. I decide to come down nearer to the necessary house for it's closer to the wood's edge than the barn. Then I'll just walk from there to the barn and hope that no one will notice two kinds of tracks rather than one.

It's a slight fingernail moon to enjoy once the sun sets that lights up the nighttime world a bit, reflecting off the snow and making things twinkly. I open the barn door just wide enough to slip in and give my eyes a moment to adjust. I hear the snort and stomp of horses and the familiar smell of hay and dung.

The first horse I recognize is Old Man Hobson's battered old mare. So old and so battered that I bet that it's the only thing that Old Man Hobson still owns since it's worthless to even Cornelius Cooper. I pat her muzzle and say quiet like, "Hello. Can I sleep here with you tonight in your barn?" She nods her head and snorts her welcome. But it's the second horse that gives me the greatest welcome, for it's none other than Willow! The rush of pleasure I feel as I stand there looking at her warms me from head to toe and I cannot help myself and I start to cry.

"Willow!" I say as I sniffle and touch her muzzle in wonder and she knickers her greeting to me that says, "And just where have you been all these days?"

My head thinks and I realize that of course Mr. Cornelius Cooper would have kept my horse and of course he would have hid her at Old Man Hobson's. How can a brain be quick one moment and slow another? *Some things just make more sense viewed from behind,* I hear Pa say. Willow's happy to share her stall with me and I bed down in the not so fresh straw while I think the choices I now face.

I am only here, free of Cornelius and Naomi Cooper because my debts with them were paid by Willow's sale. Before that time I feared for Henry should I have left with a large debt written in Mr. Cooper's ledger book. I think about the thing he called a *Promissory Note* and it even sounds bad just saying it in my head. But now I know things that I didn't know before. I know that besides being ruthless and heartless, Mr. Cooper is also a liar, a cheat, and a thief. I think about my working done at Cooper's

General Store and how I never got paid for any of that. There's not one note recorded in the ledger book of all the *morning, afternoon, and evening* chores I did *every single day I was there*. I think how Ezekiel West said that the amount Cornelius Cooper charged me was much more than was fair for room and board of both my horse and me. And I think about the Promissory Note burning in the West's fire. I look at Willow standing over me munching on some hay and she looks at me. "I think," I say to her in the quiet of the barn, "that just like the land Ma and Pa originally had was still mine and Henry's, you are still mine, too." The choice is made. Willow leaves with me in the morning.

A soft horse muzzle shoves me awake the following morning and I open my eyes to the barrel of a shotgun aimed at my head. "Morning," Old Man Hobson says to me in a neighborly like tone despite the tone the gun speaks with.

"Good morning, Mr. Hobson," I say as I struggle to sit up and clear my foggy brain.

"Cornelius said I was to watch out for you. Seems he hopes you're dead but isn't foolish to believe it until he sees it. My visit to the necessary house this mornin' showed an odd set of tracks. Got my shotgun and followed them right to you."

I stare at him at a loss for words. *Now what?* my head says to me.

"I travel to Fort Winston to find Major Everett," I say.

"Cornelius says you stole goods – a whole side of pork - from the store and that you attacked him and Naomi with a knife you keep strapped to your leg. He's says that the time you've spent with the Injuns has made you crazy and that you should not be trusted for a minute. He says Naomi's so terrified by your attack that he's not sure she'll ever recover and that she's insisting that he keep the doors and windows to the house and store barred at all times." While he's telling me all these things he's watching me closely to see my reaction.

"He told me that you're a fool drunk and that your worthless mare has more brains then you do," I say back at him sitting there in the straw and leaning against the wall.

He snorts. "I'm sure he did." He gestures with his gun, "Git up." When I stand he says, "Make your way to the house." I pick up my basket and things and he follows behind me.

The hut's dark and glum and smells of unwashed body, dirty clothes and filthy bed linen. There is a tin mug and plate and spoon on the table with the last evening's meal still sitting cold and clotted on the plate.

My stomach remembers it's empty, it *was* hungry, and how it's been mighty temperamental these past months. I swallow and try not to breath too deep. Mr. Hobson enters into the cabin behind me and shuts the door. He seems to see the place for a moment with my eyes.

"At one time, it was a right cozy place," he says almost to himself. He nudges me in the back gentle with the gun. "Have a seat."

I sit in the chair closest to me and farthest away from the plate of old food. "I want my horse back," I finally say as he walks over and settles himself in the other chair. He lays the rifle across his lap and before my disbelieving eyes picks up a bone from the plate and chews some of the old meat and grizzle off of the end. I swallow again.

"I suspect you do," he says. "However, Cornelius made it quite clear that the horse belongs to *him* now, in payment of the debts you owe." He looks at me intently for a moment. "Cornelius Cooper is not my favorite person, but I would take his word over the word of an *Injun lover* any day."

My head says, *Oh, so that's the way it will be.* My mouth says, "Just like this farm belongs to Cornelius Cooper in payment of the debts *you owed him.*"

"How is it you know of that?" he says, alert now like a rattler thinking about a strike.

I think and am careful how much I say for I don't want to get the Wests into any trouble of any kind. "I've heard talk about these things."

"Gossiping sons a bitches," he mumbles under his breath as he searches the plate in front him for something else to eat.

"How about we make a deal?" I say to him. He looks at me with eyes that tell me he'd just as soon eat horse manure. *Stop thinking of food and eating!,* my stomach says firmly as it flips and flops as Old Man Hobson crunches on the bone and grizzle off the second bone on the plate. I swallow and try not to breathe.

"Just what do you have to make a deal with?" he says and his look says there's absolutely nothing he sees that he could possibly want from me.

"I can get you your farm back," I say with a voice I hope sounds strong and sure.

He stops crunching on the bone and finally sets it down on the plate in front of him. He wipes his greasy fingers on his shirt front and very carefully and slowly picks up the shotgun and levels it again at my face. "What the hell do you mean?" he says at last.

"You gave Cornelius Cooper the deed to this farm as payment of your debts. I don't know how long ago that was but I know you did it because I've seen your deed. Only here's the important part. Mr. Cooper never traveled to Richmond to formally change the claim title. You're still legal owner. And there's more. Cornelius Cooper was dishonest in his business dealings with you. You probably never were in as great debt as you thought you were. You probably never had to give him the farm in the first place had he been fair about things."

He looks at me and I see him struggle to hear and understand and finally sort through what he thinks is true and what he thinks is not. "You're a lying Injun lover," he finally spits out making his decision plain as day.

I'm calm. I'm not frightened. I'm a powerful woman on her own. I know for a fact that he may have a shotgun but he's not going to shoot me when he's still not exactly sure what he should believe. I look him right in the eye when I say, "I'm an Indian lover who knows that your wife's name is Frances, yours is Daniel, and an Isaac Bradley was one of the witnesses who signed the deed."

He looks at me over the long barrel of the shotgun. "Isaac Bradley was my brother in law," he says almost to himself. "Francis' older brother …" He looks at me and takes aim with the gun. "Where's the deed now?"

I say absolutely nothing. My eyes though say to him, *Maybe it's time to put the gun away.* We sit like that for a good few long minutes until finally he lowers the gun. He gets up and walks to the window and peers out through the grimy pane of glass. In putting his back to me, he's saying he's giving up this game. I relax a might.

Without turning around to look at me he says in a voice filled with defeat, "The day a teeny tiny Injun lovin' girl terrorizes Cornelius and Naomi Cooper is the day that pigs will fly. Take your goddamn horse. I've no use for it."

I look at him and feel a great wave of pity. He's not as old as I first thought. He's old because he acts old and defeated and he's given up trying to live anymore. I stand and swing my basket on my back. I'll leave quickly before he changes his mind or Cornelius Cooper stops by to pay another visit.

"Thank you," I say as I stand at the door.

"Git out," he says low still without looking at me.

"If you're ever in the area, Mr. and Mrs. Ezekiel West make a powerful good cup of tea," I say just before I step out into the bright morning sun. "It would be worth your wile to make the effort to stop by for a visit." I stand there looking at him for one beat, then for two. He never once looks at me.

It's wonderful to be back on Willow again and I munch the last of the salt pork from the Coopers and the last of the cheese from the Wests as I ride as fast and as far as I can. Willow and I even ride for a time into the night for the moonlight reflected off the snow is bright enough to make the traveling safe. Late into the night, after the moon has traveled most of it's path across the evening sky, Willow and I bed down for the night in a natural shelter made by a huge fallen oak. If I am right with my directions, I hope to be at Fort Winston by noon time tomorrow. I make no fire for I'm too tired and sleep wrapped in my bearskin with the sounds of Willow only an arm's reach away.

Fort Winston is nothing like I expected. What did you expect? my brain asks me and I snort to myself. I expected to never have to come here and see it so I never even thought of it. I expected to be on my way back to Bright Feather to see him before the first flowers of spring. I expected to ... But I get distracted from my thoughts as I look at the sight before me.

Fort Winston's not a fort yet. I see two walls, standing tall and sturdy amidst the cleared forest. Walls made of huge tree trunks straight and tall, cleared of their branches sunk deep into the ground and lashed together with rope. One sentry tower rises above the highest part of the wall and I can see a lone soldier watching the business below him. Along the shelter of the two standing walls are a number of buildings that show all kinds of activity from the smoke that pours from some of their chimneys to the dirty snow and mud I see trampled all around them. Willow and I watch from the shelter of trees and I'm able to gradually figure out the stable, the long low building that must be sleeping quarters for the soldiers and then three other buildings that must be officer quarters or homes. I see two women, no children, and about twenty-five soldiers during the time I sit and watch. I'm too far away to see if one of the soldiers is Major Everett or George Maw.

It's hunger that finally makes me venture down into this new white world. I've not eaten since the pork and cheese the day before and have been unsuccessful at hunting. My stomach rumbles with its need to be fed and I feel dizzy and lightheaded from tiredness. I cannot see where is the best place to enter, through the door that stands open on one of the standing walls or just right down into the open living place of the fort. I choose to follow what appears to be the most traveled route; right up and to the main open door.

Willow and I ride slow and steady out of the forest and join the well traveled path of mud and snow towards the fort. The walls and the tower are much higher standing looking up, I think. I see the soldier in the tower look and then look again at me and then finally shout to someone down below. It's at that point that Willow and I just stop and wait and watch to see what happens next.

A mounted patrol of cavalry soldiers, four in all, ride out almost immediately from the fort at the shout from the tower soldier. They're too prepared and equipped to have been sent out just for me I think as they ride toward me with great purpose. It's almost fun to watch the expressions on the faces of the four men as they get close enough to me to see that I'm white and I'm a woman. At least two of the men scan the surrounding forests with nervous eyes to make certain I really am alone. I choose to be silent and just wait.

"Do you have business at the fort?" one of the soldiers finally asks me as we five sit silent and examining of each other.

"I seek Major Alexander Everett or Mr. George Maw," I say.

"Both of those men have traveled to Washington. They're not expected back for another few week's time." He looks up at the sky trying to determine the way of the weather. "Especially with the way the weather's been this past winter."

I'm at a loss and my face must show it. It had not occurred to me that neither man would be at the fort once I made my way there! *Now what?* my head cries in despair.

"Lieutenant Foster's who you should see," the same soldier says to me. "Follow me. I'll take you to him."

You would think that I would get used to being stared at. It seems that everywhere I go, white or red, I cause the same reaction; people stop, their mouth sometimes drops open in surprise, they stare … I'm never more happy to be back on Willow. Somehow being high up on the back of a horse is always better than looking people eye to eye. We stop at one of the three buildings, and up close I can see that one indeed has more of a business look to it while the other two appear to be more of the home type.

The soldier knocks and we hear, "Enter!" shouted from inside. I think as an afterthought he would have liked me to wait, for he turns to say something to me and seems right startled to find me standing directly behind him. He wipes his heavy boots as best he can clean of mud and wet and walks inside. I stand behind him as he salutes. "Lieutenant Foster, sir," he begins, "as the patrol was riding out this morning the sentry informed us that there was a lone Indian rider approaching."

"Lone rider?" I hear. "Are you sure?"

"Yes, sir," he says, "here she is."

The soldier stands aside and Lieutenant Foster stares at me with surprised eyes, taking in all there is to see about me. I wonder how much of the bruising has faded from my face and neck and know that there is just a small scab on my lip. I know I could use a good wash and when was the last time I combed my hair? I think about my bear skin cape, my permanent marks on my chin and my Indian clothes and I stand a little bit taller. I think it'll work in my favor to look as savage and strong as possible. Shouldn't it?

Lieutenant Foster does the stare and the stop but he keeps his mouth from dropping open in surprise. I wait and let his brain catch up with what his eyes are telling him. He's older, I think as I study him, but not very old. I see lines by his eyes and mouth and gray in his hair. As I look at him I notice that his right hand's missing three fingers and his face has a long puckered scar down the right side. *How did he get his scars I wonder?* I think of my eleven scars on my chest from Weasel's teeth and knife and the rope burn scars on both my wrists. *Does he have memories locked far away that he never, ever opens, too?*

"Thank you, Private Watson, that will be all," he finally manages to say to the solider in front of him while he's still staring at me. I continue to stare back at him as Private Watson leaves and shuts the door.

Lieutenant Foster finally stands and he's one of the tallest men I have ever seen. He just keeps growing and growing and growing from behind his desk and then extends his hand to me. "How do you do, Miss...."

"My name is Elle Graves, late of Ward's Mill, Virginia," I tell him.

His eyes flicker and I know he knows the name. He gives me a formal bow from behind his desk and says, "Lieutenant George Foster, Commander of Fort Winston, Virginia, Second United States Cavalry, Company A, and Ninth Virginia Cavalry, Company D.

"Please Miss Graves," he says and I notice his mouth on the side with the scar moves funny as he talks sometimes, "do sit down," and he gestures toward a seat that faces his small desk. As I sit down he says, "You look a little road weary, can I offer you something?"

"I'd be most obliged for something to eat," I must tell him over the loud rumbling of my stomach, "as I've not had anything since I finished the last of my food yesterday morning."

He studies me again and then finally walks around his desk with the help of a cane, goes to the door and opens it. "Private Russell!" he shouts. "Bring up a tray of hot food and something to drink!" then shuts the door and goes back to his desk and sits down.

I decide to speak first. "You'd think that I'd get used to all the looks I get whether I'm in white or Indian Territory but it never seems to quite stop bothering me."

He absently rubs the scar on his cheek with his maimed hand and says, "I know a little of what you say. Someone always wants to hear the story of my scar and hand." He looks at me then with a pointed look. "I think I'll let you go first, though."

"What have Major Everett and George Maw told you of me?" I ask.

"They provided me with a very detailed account of your rescue and return as well as their perception of your welcome at Ward's Mill, Virginia." He searches through the draws of his desk and draws out a file that I assume must contain information about me. "I do not think either of them will be surprised to find you here when they return from Washington," he says as an afterthought.

So I tell him honestly about my situation with the Coopers. I tell him about Henry and what I thought had happened to him and now what I know about him. I tell him about what Mr. Cooper said he'd do to Henry or me if the debts were not paid and how he talked of something called a *Promissory Note*. I'm honest and tell him about taking the ledger and the discovery of Mr. Cooper's dishonesty and thievery after they'd taken Willow from me. I tell him of Old Man Hobson and taking Willow back and why I felt it was right and not stealing. I even tell him about the deeds we found and how I now hold the deed to my family's property in Ward's Mill although I admit that I don't know what I'd do with it. I don't tell him anything about my time with The Real People of the Maple Forest or where Mr. Cooper's ledger book is. And I don't tell him about my baby.

There's a knock at the door and a soldier brings in a steaming tray of hot stew that smells wonderful. Beside it is a hot steaming mug of coffee. He's surprised to see me but Lieutenant Foster hustles him out before he can stare too long. Lieutenant Foster pours himself a cup of coffee from a pot that sits behind him on the small stove and then gestures to the bowl of steaming food in front of me. "Please, go ahead. Don't wait another minute."

It's venison stew with potatoes and carrots and I don't stop until the bowl's empty. "Thank you," I finally manage to say.

"More?" he asks, but I shake my head 'no'. My stomach's happy for a bit now. "What are your plans now that you're here?" he finally asks me.

"Well, I am hoping that Major Everett would be willing to escort me back to the trading post of William Holland Thomas in Forest City, North Carolina."

Lieutenant Foster wrinkles his brow and looks confused. He looks down at my file and searches through the pages. Finally he asks in puzzlement, "What does William Thomas of Forest City, North Carolina, and you have in common?"

"William Thomas is a good friend of mine and of the Indian people that I consider my family. Once I get to the trading post, it'll be a simple matter for me to be reunited with my husband," and I smile a real smile, the first one in months and months at the thought that I'm finally a small bit closer to getting back to Bright Feather and my life with him.

"HUSBAND?" Lieutenant Foster says. "You claim to have an *Indian* husband?"

I feel the smile slip from my face like butter off a roll hot from the oven as I nod my head ever so slightly, 'yes'.

He looks down at the file and scans through what I can see to be neat tidy script. "This report says nothing of a husband, nothing of any type of family connection. It refers to," he scans the writing carefully, "New Echota, Georgia, Major Everett's aunt and uncle in their capacity as missionaries down there, his offer to escort you home as he was headed back to Fort Winston anyway ..."

He looks at me and I can see an anger that causes his face to get a shade of red that his scar does not. "What *Indian family* do you speak of that he has failed to report about?"

I swallow and take a deep breath and think, *oh no, Oh No, OH NO*, for I've opened up something that was obvious even Major Everett felt was quite wiser to be left closed. I can't close this thing I've opened any more than I can wash the permanent marks off my chin. I try hard to explain, "I didn't return to Ward's Mill, Virginia, because I wanted to. I returned to Ward's Mill, Virginia, to assure that the people I love and now consider my family were not blamed for my abduction. I returned to Ward's Mill to put out any fires that might be burning and cause danger or problem for My People."

Lieutenant Foster, reaches up to massage his scar, a gesture that seems to be a habit he is unaware of. "And who are these people that you love so dearly and you consider your family and," he looks at me and struggles to remain calm, "*your people?*"

"I am Bear," I say, "daughter of One Who Knows of the Elk Clan, mate of Bright Feather of the Wolf Clan, son of War Woman and Great Elk chief of The Real People of the Maple Forest."

"The Real People," he mutters to himself, "The Real People," like he's familiar with the sound of the Indian name but can't place where. At last he seems to remember, "You mean The Cherokee," he finally says.

I nod my head, "That's what the whites call them, yes," I say.

He folds his hands in front of him across the folder on his desk that tells things about me, but I now know *not everything.* "Do you know that the Cherokee are one of only five remaining Indian tribes east of the Mississippi?" he asks me. I shake my head 'no' for I didn't know that.

"Do you know that the government of the United States of America has been tremendously *generous* and *patient* and *fair* with these Indians and despite that they continue to grumble and complain about what they need, what they don't have but should have, what they're entitled to, how they're being constantly put upon by the white settlers?" I don't shake my head this time for I really don't think Lieutenant Foster cares what I know or don't know at this point.

"Do you know what the purpose of Fort Winston is to be? As well as the five forts currently being built in Alabama, the thirteen forts currently being built in Georgia, the eight forts currently being built in Tennessee and the five forts currently being built in North Carolina?" I stare at him waiting for him to continue and fearful at the same time of what I'll hear. He keeps asking me questions that I'm sure he knows I have no answers to.

"Do you know what our new President of the United States, the esteemed President Andrew Jackson's policy is towards the Cherokees east of the Mississippi? Do you know why he was able to win the election primarily from the overwhelming support of the south eastern states of Virginia, Tennessee, North Carolina, South Carolina, Georgia, and Alabama?" I feel a terrible chill all of a sudden like cold water has been poured down the inside of my warm furs and I shiver slightly waiting for Lieutenant Foster to finish talking so that I can go away and hide somewhere, *anywhere.*

He looks at me and I wait for him to tell me the answers to all these questions. He stands and reaches for his hat that's hanging carefully on the peg behind his desk which he settles on his head. "You must rethink your plans, *Miss Graves*," he says pointedly using my white name, "for the policy of President Andrew Jackson and the platform on which he was elected promises *Removal Of All Indians* from *all* lands east of the Mississippi either by their *consent and willingness* or," he gestures around him grandly and smiles broadly and I can see that besides the scar and the fingers, he is missing all the teeth on the top right side of his jaw as well, "*by force* with the aid of thirty newly built forts to assist those Indians who think they'd rather fight. For you see, the United States of America *will* succeed in this endeavor to eliminate all red savages east of the Mississippi. It's just a matter of time to prepare and then follow through on our well laid plans."

He smiles what he tries to be a friendly smile at me. "I'm so happy that you're such an *adaptable* young woman and that with the death of your first family you were able to *adapt* and find comfort with the Indians. That'll set you in good stead now for unfortunately, *you soon will have no Indian family to go home to.*"

He comes around the desk and ever so politely supports me under the elbow to help me stand. "Let's see if we can find you suitable accommodations while you stay here with us, shall we?" and I allow him to lead me out into the fading afternoon twilight. I realize with the greatest of despair that I'm farther away from Bright Feather than I've ever been in my whole life.

In the end, I stay with Lieutenant Foster and his wife Joan and their three children, Lydia, Nate, and Paul. Lieutenant Foster is the only one to have his family present at this early stage of the fort's existence. I'm told by Joan that eventually other wives will come but for this first winter she's the only one. Lydia's younger than me by only two years but towers over me and her mother already. She's the other woman I thought I saw as I watched the fort. Nate and Paul at twelve and ten are as close to being cavalry soldiers as a body can without actually joining. They drill, ride, and work at the fort's continued construction along side the other soldiers. They're tall like their father, too, and aside from being told their true ages cannot be told apart from the other soldiers.

I know that both Joan and Lydia find me and my choice of life style dreadful but they are so starved for the company of another woman that they swallow their disgust and tolerate my company. Lydia must also tolerate sharing her small bed with me and spends each night pressed as tightly to the wall as a body can get. I told all of them that I was more than happy to sleep on the floor with my bearskin but they would not hear of it.

Talk of my Indian life and family is never discussed. Should I mention my time with The Real People in passing to make an observation or correct a misconception it seems as if the entire world stops stock still for a moment, cleans its ears of the filth, and then moves on as if I've not spoken a word. I learn to talk careful like. I can say, "Down south the spring comes much quicker," and that receives a conversational response. Should I say, "In the Maple Forest the winters do not seem so harsh," the world cannot seem to hear.

I'm allowed to send Deer a letter informing him of my change in location *due to unforeseen circumstances* and am encouraged to write another letter to the Department of the Army in Washington requesting the whereabouts of one *Henry Graves*. The second letter, Lieutenant Foster takes an active interest in, instructing me as to the proper wording, telling me what details I should tell and what details I should avoid (yes to former homesteader of Ward's Mill, Virginia, no to being the mate of a Cherokee brave). He tells me who and where to address it to. I'm encouraged to see both letters leave almost immediately with patrols; one that's headed south and one that is headed north. It's somewhat reassuring to me to know that soon those that love and care for me *in the south* will know where I am and how I'm faring. The letter that goes south is a brief note that offers no details other than to say where I am and what date it is. I've no great hope for locating Henry and establishing any kind of life with him. What would an enlisted army soldier do with a long lost sister pregnant with an Indian's child?

After a few weeks as winter slips into spring and the snow is replaced by rain and rivers of mud, talk turns to providing me with some "suitable" clothes. I'm agreeable to this for much to my dismay I find my Indian clothes becoming snug with my growing belly. I don't think that anyone suspects as of yet for I've been careful but I can feel the tightness of the space around my middle and I know that I don't have much time left in these clothes. It's almost the beginning of April and I think of Jane West's small stomach. In private moments I gaze down at the growing mound and I think, *What am I growing in there that I am so much bigger?* There's no doubt in my mind that come the end of May, anyone who doesn't know my secret is either blind or powerful stupid. I'm startled one morning as I lie in bed next to Lydia, trying not to think how much I need to pee for I will wake her with the movement and I feel the strangest feeling in my stomach. I gasp for it feels just like the touch that Bright Feather does on my cheek to give a tender sign only this time *it's in my belly*. I put my hand on my growing stomach and I think, *Hello little one. How are you this morning?*

Miss Joan and Lydia are thrilled when I don't fight the idea of a new wardrobe. There are bolts of cloth in the stock house (the other cabin that eventually will be another home should a family arrive) and in between the pile of chores that are a typical part of running a household with three children, we work on sewing me a new set of clothes. When the time for measurements comes, I put on a grand show of being powerful shy about things. I manage to whisper, "scars from my time down south", and "difficulties I'd rather not have to remember" and I'm afforded great understanding and courtesy. I learn to bat my eyes and look downcast whenever talk involves something that might reveal the true state of me and the baby and Miss Joan and Lydia are happy to cooperate. In the end we sew two petticoats, a camisole, a corset (which I agree to for it may help with the hiding of The Belly), two full over skirts and two over blouses. It's with great sorrow for Miss Joan and Lydia that they do not have extra materials for making proper stockings and there are no extra materials for shoes and I'm barely able to hide my delight. All in all, if I can ignore the agony of the corset, I'm quite happy to at least still be in my silent and comfortable moccasins.

This family's a puzzle to me. I struggle with the two different sides they show to me over the course of my time with them. In some ways, with their obvious hatred of the Indians they are no better than the Coopers and even Old Mr. Hobson and others I have heard speak at Cooper's store who see with their eyes and nothing more. They seem unable to even consider the idea that a 'red savage' is anything but greedy, stupid, and in general, downright evil. *My* only fault seems to be that I'm unable to understand and agree with this. How can a body hate another body just for the way they look? How can a body wish another body *dead or gone* just because they live their life in a different way? Am I so very odd in the way I think? Is there truly no one else like me? Have my experiences over these past few years changed me so much that I can now look at a body and assume *nothing* based on how a body looks? And is hard experience the only teacher to make a person wise?

I do my best to smile and be polite and cooperative. I try extra hard to do all the chores expected of me plus any extra ones I can find. As a result, the other side they show me is always kind and friendly. They don't mind my questions about their family history or life at the fort. Nor do they seem bothered by the additional hassle my presence has brought. They work to include me in all aspects of their family and show a general love and kindness towards each other. When I talk of repaying them for the clothing they've helped me make Miss Joan is stunned by the idea. "Do you realize how much work you save Lydia and me around the house? You're more than deserving of a new set of clothes." In those instances they're so far different from the Coopers that I scarce can see how I would consider such a thing.

I have no one to talk to about all this. But one thing is right certain: every single word and action I feel I must guard. I can't ever be the person I am; the powerful woman I've become. I feel just like I am being pushed backwards instead of forward. I am no longer a blooming plant but instead I am being stuffed back into the seed pod. For the Fosters like me, but only so long as I be the young woman they want me to be. I can't be Bear except in my most smallest snatches of privacy and there are never enough of those. I miss Bright Feather but I miss someone else even more. I miss myself.

On the morning that I see Major Everett and George Maw ride into Fort Winston at the beginning of May as the first flowers bloom, I've once again adjusted, as best as I can, to life in a new place. I worry as Major Everett and George Maw make their way into Lieutenant Foster's office to give their report of their travels. I stand out in the bright sun so they can see me. The fact that Major Everett stops, says something quick like to George Maw and then both men look at me tells me that *one surprise* – that of my presence – is no longer a problem. I hope they see the message that I try to communicate to them with my eyes. *Lieutenant Foster knows more than you told him about me now and it is all my fault. I'm sorry.* For a brief moment the three of us stare at each other across the muddy ground and then they both turn and make their way into their meeting.

They're in there a long time and it's not until the next day that I hear my name from behind as I am working on a pile of laundry in the bright May sun. I turn and see Major Everett standing watching me.

I straighten up and massage the crick in my back. "Welcome home, Major Everett," I say. "I've been waiting a powerful long time for your arrival." I know that Miss Joan and Lydia are just a stone's throw away working on the next load of laundry for me to hang up and I glance in their general direction.

"So I understand, Miss Graves. Would it be suitable for you to go for a walk and talk and finish your chores in a bit?" *Let's talk private where no ears will hear,* his eyes say to me from under the brim of his hat.

"Just a moment and let me tell Miss Joan." Moments later we walk across the wide open area that'll one day be the center of the fort, doing our best to avoid the mud and puddles from the rain the night before.

"I'm sorry," I say in a rush before he can speak. "I hope that I didn't cause you problems with saying things that I didn't know I should've kept quiet."

"You had no way of knowing," he says in response. "I tried to keep my word to you and not let *anyone* know the location of your village. I wrote a very detailed report, but I simply left a few bits out." He shrugs his shoulders. "Until you said something, no one noticed.

"I think it's really just as well," he says after we walk for a bit. "The truth's out there now, no deception and now we must just work on getting you where you should be."

I stop and look at him. "And where's that?"

He smiles and puts his hand under my elbow to keep me walking and to steer me around a massive puddle. "You're not stupid, Miss Graves." He sighs and looks at me quick. "That makes some things easier and some things harder.

"I argued that you should be returned to William Holland Thomas. I know that's what you wish and should you ever be reunited with Bright Feather, that's the place we need to get you to."

I stop walking and interrupt him. "What Lieutenant Foster has told me is true then about the removal of The Real People east of the Mississippi?"

He makes me keep walking. "You must keep moving, you must look cheerful, you must make this look like a polite social call. There are many eyes watching us at this very minute."

I walk again and take some moments to gather my thoughts. I sigh a deep sigh, make myself laugh out loud at nothing in particular and then finally flash him a bright smile. "I'm just about five months pregnant and any day now everyone will know. I want to go back to my husband and my people, Major Everett."

Now it's his turn to stumble, but he recovers quickly and throws back his head pretending to laugh at the funny thing I've told him. "Holy

Christ," he says with a smile to match mine although his eyes look full of panic, "Who knows about the baby?"

"Just the two idiots standing in the middle of this half finished fort," I whisper and laugh again, this time a little more quietly.

He tucks my hand in the crook of his arm and steers me out past the sentry up in the tower out down the road that leads into the forest. We walk only a short distance until we come to a log that can serve as a bench for a seat for the two of us. It's a good spot for we're in view of the sentry and seem to be hiding nothing.

Major Everett takes quite a few moments to gather his thoughts before he begins to speak. "In answer to your earlier question," he says with a sigh, "yes, President Andrew Jackson will propose The Indian Removal Act to the Senate and House of Representatives of the United States of America at the end of this month. He will request the authority to exchange lands with all Indians currently residing in any states or territories east of the Mississippi with lands west of the Mississippi with *or without* their consent or agreement." He looks at me with sad eyes and says, "And as sure as I'm sitting here with you, he will be given that authority. There is no doubt."

"Does that include The Real People of The Maple Forest?" I ask quiet like.

He nods. "They're Indian," he says, "so they'll be removed. The authority given the President will allow him to nullify any existing treaty agreements that are currently in place."

"They're United States Citizens, too," I say to him and watch the look of amazement grow in his eyes.

"What foolishness are you talking about?" he says to me.

"From what I understand, The Real People of the Maple Forest are part of a small group that broke from The Nation of The Real People and accepted the offer of citizenship that was offered to them in the Treaty of 1819."

Major Everett looks at me with stunned eyes and then turns to stare off into the forest and think. "Well, I'll be damned," he finally says after a time, "I'll be damned ..."

But finally he shakes his head. "That won't help you too much at the moment, though," he says after a bit. "Lieutenant Foster is dead set against sending you *south*, but is more inclined to let you wait until you hear from Washington regarding the inquiry you sent about your brother. He has a," he pauses for a moment searching for the right word, "*history* with the Indians that would make it powerful unusual for him to allow you to be returned to them."

I look at him without speaking. You know, I think, I am getting powerful tired of having my life made more difficult by all of these people with stories from their past that seem to interfere with my life right now. I look at Major Everett and give him a mighty fed up glare. Go ahead, let's hear it, my look says to him.

Glancing at the fort, Major Everett takes off his cap and runs his fingers through his hair. "I'll make it a quick story. Lieutenant Foster was captured by the Creek Indians when he was leading a battalion. He was in the army fighting during the Battle of 1812. I don't know exactly all the specifics. He was held prisoner and they tortured him. He'd been knocked unconscious by a rifle butt to the face, that's where the scar and the loss of the teeth happened. But from what I understand they gradually cut his fingers and toes off, bit by bit. He was rescued before they could kill him. When he's in his cups," he looks at me serious like, "which isn't often mind you, he likes to joke that the Injuns thought so highly of him that he was forced to leave a few bits of him behind to keep them company." Major Everett looks at me. "He's a good leader to the men but it's not by chance that the army put him in charge of *this fort* for the purpose it's being constructed for. I can think of few military officers who would be more than happy to oversee the removal of the Indians from this area.

"He told me that you are welcome to stay here at the fort for as long as it takes to find your brother and bring him here to claim you." He looks at me for a moment as though deciding if he should say something else. "He even hinted broadly that perhaps you'd find a man here at the fort and be happy to settle down."

He reaches over and puts his hand on my tightly clasped ones, staring into my eyes that are filled with worry. "I tell you that only so you understand how much he does not understand of what and where you want to be."

"What do I do?" I say to him. This circumstance I am in is getting messier and messier with each passing day!

"Well, in a few more weeks, according to you, you won't have to worry about any more hints of you finding a man here at the fort," he says in an effort to bring a little humor into our conversation I suspect. The exasperated look I give him makes him apologize. "I'm sorry.

"Look, let's wait a few more weeks and see if we do get a quick response from Washington about your brother. In the mean time, I will talk with George Maw and see if he has any suggestions. Is it alright that I tell him of your *situation?*"

Calling it a *situation* doesn't make things sound any better.

A few weeks later as we sit at the breakfast table, me and the Fosters, Paul Foster sees fit to tease me as I bring fresh biscuits to the table. "Miss Elle, you better skip these biscuits, you're getting quite a belly on you!" He laughs and laughs at his joke. I laugh too, to cover the blush that blooms across my face. The conversation continues to swirl around the table and I resume eating my breakfast but as I look up and meet Miss Joan's eyes the look on her face tells me that my secret is out. We clear the breakfast dishes and I do my best to act like everything's normal but my brain works powerful overtime as I consider all the options. It could almost be funny I think. I may not be able to mention my time with the Indians, but how are we going to avoid *this?*

My thoughts are interrupted by the shouts of my name outside. "Miss Elle!" I hear shouted with great excitement. "MISS ELLE! MISS ELLE!! COME QUICK! YOU'R BROTHER IS HERE!" My heart begins to pound and my fingers go numb as one of Miss Joan's good china platters drops to the floor and smashes into a mess of pieces.

Remember the sky that you were born under,
Know each of the star's stories.[20]

~Jo Harjo

Sister

I stand frozen for a long series of moments, my heart hammering in my chest like it's just going to explode. I bend over to start picking up the broken pieces of china that are scattered all over the floor. *"Go,"* I hear said firm and forceful behind me and I look up to meet Miss Joan's eyes. She can't wait to get me and my dirty secret out of her house her looks says. "GO." I stand up and walk out the door.

It's Major Everett who's calling to me still as I walk out the door, shouting his excitement over the good news that's walking right next to him. "Miss Elle, look who's here! Your brother Henry's just arrived from Washington! Can you believe it, Miss Elle? He's here! HE'S HERE!"

I look at the face grinning with delight standing in front of me and I can't believe what my eyes tell me they see. There he stands, done up in his Sunday best with a suit and tie looking nothing like I last saw him and nothing at all like I remember him to be. For standing in front of me is *not* my brother Henry at all, but William Holland Thomas, eyes twinkling with delight and mischief. "Sister dear!" he shouts for all to hear, "What an answer to my prayers it is to see you standing in front of me well and healthy after all this time." He steps forward to embrace me as I collapse into his arms.

I never fade to blackness, really. I'm aware of strong arms lifting me up and bustling me in to sit on the chair at the table still filled with the remains of breakfast. I hear the crunch of Deer's boots as it breaks the china into smaller bits. I hear conversation swirl around me, "Been on business in Washington," "Came as soon as I received the letter," "Can't wait to get her home to our new family home in North Carolina," "All the excitement seems to be too much for her," "Always was a fragile child even when she was little". At that last comment I start to stir and I see him give me a teasing glance. Major Everett hovers on the fringes of the excitement obviously terrified I'll say the wrong thing and cause him even more problems.

I put my hand up to touch his face. "Let me have a look at you, Henry," I say.

Deer squats down grinning broadly in front of me enjoying every moment. "Elle, my sister, after all this time ..." He makes a show of wiping the corners of his eyes as if to catch the tear or two he's shed from pure happiness and joy.

I touch his face and a wave of emotion hits me as I realize all of a sudden that I'm closer to Bright Feather than I have been in more than five months and I begin to cry. Great gulping sobs as I touch his face and hair and finally rest my hands on his broad shoulders. "She always was an emotional mess over things," Deer says to our surrounding audience, reaching into his pocket for a scrap of linen. "Here my dear sister, use this."

He hands me his handkerchief and I can't resist. I blow my nose noisily in it. Pulling myself together I decide to join in on the joke. "It is so good to see you, Henry," I finally manage to say wiping my eyes and blowing my nose again. "Our separation has been hard on you I can see. You look so much *older* and more *tired* it seems." I grin at him, now having as much fun as him. "I hope that you've been able to control that horrible twitch you get in excitable situations."

"We'll have to see, dear sister," he says, "We'll have to see," and I'm crushed in a bone breaking hug as I begin to sob again.

Deer's in his element, talking with Lieutenant Foster, complimenting Miss Joan, and teasing Lydia about her beautiful eyes. The more he talks the more I come to realize that he really *has* been in Washington for he knows even more current information about President Andrew Jackson's Removal Act than Major Everett did. "President Jackson presented the Indian Removal Act before the Senate and the House of Representatives on May 28th, and it was well received by all," he reports.

Lieutenant Foster's in fine spirits over this news and whiskey's shared by him and Deer and Major Everett. He talks about his grand plans of completing Fort Winston by the end of the summer and having it fully manned and operational by fall.

"How long will you be staying here with us, Mr. Graves?" Miss Joan finally asks. She looks at me and I can see her struggle mightily to contain her disgust. "I imagine that Miss Graves is eager to move on with her life and get back to something more settled than this temporary situation."

"First, before I answer your question, I must thank you from the bottom of my heart for the hospitality and kindness you have shown my sister," Deer begins and Miss Joan blushes her acceptance. "I hope you'll not think me terribly rude if I make plans to leave at first light with her though. I've been away from the homestead far too long and must return as soon as possible to see to my crops."

Miss Joan's so pleased by his answer that she insists I help her pack my things right away. I find it most funny that she's just as happy for me to leave as I am.

I cannot sleep. My mind and body are so full of excitement that the thought of going to sleep seems inconceivable for the rest of my life. I lie next to Lydia as she twitches and jumps and mumbles in her sleep and I keep thinking over and over and over again, *I am going home! I will soon see Bright Feather! All this is over at last!* I don't care what situation or circumstances I return to, alls I care about is that I'll be with Bright Feather. At last I think I see a lightening of the night sky and I ease myself out of Lydia's bed and make my way to the necessary house. Knowing it's useless to go back inside, I sit out on the front porch steps and wait for dawn's full light to come.

I hear stirring inside and footsteps and I'm surprised to see Miss Joan sit down next to me with one of the bed quilts wrapped around her. "Will your brother be understanding of the child do you think?" she asks. She looks tired and worried, her eyes red from lack of sleep. Seems as if she's not had much sleep this past night either. I think, once again, about the puzzle of this family. While she can't abide the thought of me having a child by an Indian brave she still worries about me and what the future holds. I think of Henry and wonder if I ever will truly see him in this lifetime and what he will think of me should that happen. Then I look at Miss Joan.

"This child was brought about through great love and was something I wanted very much with my husband, Bright Feather. I long for my husband still, just as I have longed to see my brother. I would hope that both parts of my life will be able to live with the choices I have made so far." I look up to see Deer emerge from Lieutenant Foster's office, stretch and greet the morning and us. "When I last knew my brother he was a hard working, loving … man. I cannot see how he would reject this child of mine."

I reach over and touch her and I feel her stiffen, working hard to not pull away from me. I do not remove my hand and wait until she raises her eyes to meet mine. "I know that you don't approve of the choices I've made and yet you and your family have made every effort to make me feel welcome here in this place. I thank you, my brother thanks you, and my family thanks you." Then I remove my hand and stand up to prepare to leave.

We eat a hearty breakfast and it's funny how fast both Deer and I eat. We're given generous supplies of grain and meat for the trip we take *south* to North Carolina. Major Everett's waiting as we mount up on our horses and comes to bid me good-bye. "I thank you once again for your kindnesses to me," I say to him. "If you're ever in the area, I hope you'll stop by."

"If I'm ever in the area, I hope you'll still be there," Major Everett says back to me very serious like. He looks at Deer as he is checking the supplies on the back of the two pack horses then as he mounts up his own horse. Deer's talking and laughing with Lieutenant Foster and some of the other men all the while he works. "He's a good man to have on your side," Major Everett says, "I have heard things about him in Washington and all of it is good."

"My brother's an amazing man," I say with a smile that's big enough to split my face in two.

We leave finally and once on the trail I can't contain my happiness and excitement. Deer laughs at me for every time he turns around I have a broad smile on my face. Even the baby jumps with delight over the thought of going home. We must make more stops than usual for me to have private moments in the woods and after the third stop, as I return to mount Willow, I find Deer standing silent next to his horse chewing a blade of grass. "How far along are you?" he asks quiet and watches my face closely.

I can't help myself as I smile another big smile, turn sideways and press my skirts close against me to show my growing belly. "Nigh onto five months," I say.

He thinks for a bit and then says, "So you didn't know before you left," almost to himself.

"No," I say puzzled, "why do you think that?"

"One Who Knows told Bright Feather that you were with child when he returned from his first trip to me after you had left." He stares off into the woods, "It always puzzles me how that old woman knows stuff sometimes before everyone else." He mounts his horse and I mount up on Willow. "I'd thought perhaps you'd told One Who Knows before you'd left but didn't tell Bright Feather to keep him from worrying."

I think of One Who Knows' last words to me, I've filled it with important herbs that will be no good to you if your thick skull can't remember what to do with them. At least most of them will smell good when you are sick. I think about the herbs the basket contained: figwort root (good for fevers and anxiety and sleeplessness in pregnant women), red raspberry leaves to brew for tea (good for sore throat and used to strengthen pregnant women and aid in childbirth), wild yam ground up for tea (good for stomach upsets, in particular morning sickness), and minty perilla leaves (good for colds and fevers and also for relief of morning sickness and irritability during pregnancy)[21].   Each and every herb particularly good I remember now for morning sickness, stomach upsets, tiredness and pregnancy woes in general. I shake my head at my thick skull and sigh. I didn't even remember to try smelling them. "Seems she knew even before me," I say to Deer.

"Won't be the last time, either, I suspect," he says. We travel in silence for part of the day, careful I'm sure of where we are and the trickery we have used to get there. We do not speak in the language of The Real People. We behave just as we have pretended to be at Fort Winston: a business man and his long lost sister traveling home.

"I was in Ward's Mill quite a few weeks back," Deer says at last. "On my way to Washington, I promised Bright Feather that I'd stop there. Seems like I missed you by just a few weeks."

"What did you find?" I ask almost afraid to hear what he has to say.

"Those Coopers are a right friendly couple, I must say," he says and I wish I can see his face to see if he's teasing me. "We had a right neighborly conversation until I asked them where Elle Graves was and if I could speak to her."

He turns to look back at me so I can get a good look at his face when he says, "You can imagine my reaction when they told me you were *dead.*"

"Oh ..." I say.

He turns forward. "They went on at length about how you were a thieving, plum crazy, Injun lover and that after you attacked both of them at knife point you ran off into a raging blizzard stark naked."

I have to chuckle at the story that they tell. A wave of pure joy at where I am, who I'm with, and where I'm heading hits me and I know I'm grinning again. "You know," I say casual like, "many parts of that story are quite true."

I see Deer's shoulders shake like he is chuckling and he shakes his head back and forth. "Well, then," he says after a moment, "I'm glad that I said what I said then."

"What did you say?" I ask and I can only just imagine.

"I might have said something along the lines of how I'd hoped that you'd caused them great injury and pain during the attack and that should I find out what they say is true about your death that they'd better be miles and miles away from here for you were not a lover of *one* Injun, but of an entire *village* of blood thirsty, revenge loving Injuns who would like nothing more than to eat a hearty dinner of their cold unfeeling hearts and their big fat asses. I assured them that at my earliest convenience I would inform this village of blood thirsty, revenge - loving Injuns of the story that they had seen fit to tell me. I promised them that they would be hearing from me and or some other not - so - civilized as me in the near future and they should make every effort to prepare." Deer shrugs. "Course, I also pointed out that being prepared and fortified for attack only makes the Injuns angrier and more determined and as far as I was concerned the two of them best get their affairs in order because there wasn't much time left for either of them. Then, I *think* I said I was much obliged for the information, tipped my hat and left.

"I was followed out of the store by some sorry old man who'd heard the whole exchange while soaking up some liquor over in the corner. He volunteered that while it was best to let the Cooper's think what they think, the last time *he* saw you, you were in fine health, in full Injun gear, and heading out on your horse north."

"Old Man Hobson ..." I say quiet to myself.

He looks back at me and winks. "I *had* to get to Washington, Bear, and I liked the sound of the old man's story better than the Cooper's so I went with that one. Nothing prepared me for the letter I was shown by a friend of mine in the Department of the Army though once I got to Washington from one *Elle Graves, late of Ward's Mill, Virginia* inquiring of the whereabouts of her brother Henry Graves currently enlisted in the United States Army." He shrugs, "At least I knew you were alive."

"I discovered many things while I was in Ward's Mill these past months," I say quiet like. "Including the fact that Bear John's surname seems to have been *Cooper.*"

Deer turns once again to look at me and I suspect my sorrowful face convinces him how true my words are. "I'll be damned," he says for lack of anything else.

We stop early that first day out as I am unaccustomed to a full day in the saddle and I am a bit sore from the riding. But when Deer says something about my 'delicate' condition I have to laugh at him.

"Where did you hear something silly like that?" I ask him as I help set up camp and care for the horses. "You should know that I *did* leave the Coopers stark naked in a blizzard and that I *walked* the first part of the way to Fort Winston in that same blizzard. I didn't have Willow until Old Man Hobson put his shotgun away and let me take her back."

As we prepare our meal by the light of the fire, Deer finally says, "Tell me of your time," and so I do. It all comes pouring out and I realize just how hungry I have been to be able to speak freely and just be Bear. I tell him of the Coopers and the Wests and even Old Man Hobson. I tell him of the discovery of Henry being alive and of Bear John being known as "precious Johnny". I tell him of the promissory note that I burned, the ledger that Jane and Ezekiel West have hidden in their straw mattress and of the deed to the Graves homestead I have in my book of hymns.

When I am at last quiet and finished telling my story, Deer says, "Seems trouble, mystery, and disasters follow you in the white world just like they do in the red." He ducks when I throw a rabbit bone at his head.

"Did you know of Lieutenant Foster?" I ask him finally. "You seemed right comfortable with him."

Deer snorts. "There are few people who travel in military circles that do *not* know of Lieutenant George Foster. He is a bit of a legend in some circles: whispered about and spoken of with great awe. As for me seeming comfortable with him, that's one thing that's good about me and the life that I've led. I can be right comfortable in most any situation if it suits me."

I think about Lieutenant Foster and my time spent with him and his family. I think about the different faces he and his family showed. "He reminded me of a dog that has been sorely mistreated by its owners and then rescued," I say as I stare into the fire and remember flashes of my time at the fort. "When the dog gets to his new family, he adjusts well and gets on fine with them but should a stranger come that looks or smells like the first family, the dog is inclined to rip the stranger's throat out as soon as look at him."

Deer hands me a cup of hot tea in my battered tin mug. "You continue to be a good judge of people, Bear," and I think *how good it feels* to hear my name *Bear* spoken. "Foster was a soldier during the War of 1812. I was just a boy then, just adapting to my time in Great Elk's village." He looks at me. "Bright Feather has told you of me."

It is a statement, not a question and I just look at him over the fire. I sense he wants me to tell him what I know so I swallow my sip of tea and say, "I know that you are an orphan like me and that you were adopted into Great Elk's village like me. I know that you were brought in by a hunting party that found you wandering in the woods but that you were never able to remember how you got there or what happened to your family. I know that after a time you struggled with who you were and where you belonged and that you traveled back to the white world on your own. You found some family but never learned the story of how you became an orphan. You chose to live in the white world, get schooling in the white world, and you have ever been a friend of The Real People of The Maple Forest from then until this very moment and beyond."

He studies me for a moment and I can hear the hoot of an owl somewhere out in the dark shadows. It's a beautiful spring evening although a bit chilly and I've my bearskin wrapped around me. He looks at the fire, picks up a stick and pokes the flames to life a bit. "Well, that's the general story, but it isn't exactly accurate." He looks at me, wanting to see my face, I suspect, and says quietly, "Actually, my mother's still alive but she's been insane for almost her entire adult life from what my aunt has told me. It never seemed necessary to say anything different once I found her and saw her condition. She never recognizes me. She lives on the family estate that my aunt and uncle still run and that I'm technically still owner of. Seeing her and the condition she's in is one of the many powerful reasons that made me choose a life other than that of a plantation owner. I couldn't have lived out the rest of my life with her near."

He stirs up the fire again with a stick, sending sparks flying high while I sit there so shocked that I have no voice to speak. He shrugs, "It's true that I never remembered *how* I actually got to be where I was the day the hunting party found me, but I did eventually remember *why*.

"My parents did *not* have a good marriage. Oh, I think my Pa tried, but even the small memories I have of my time at home with the both of them are filled with tension and fear. I think my Pa spent much of his time away, traveling to stay as far away from my Ma as possible." He looks at me then and says, "He was a fine businessman and trader. I think I take after him in that respect."

He takes a sip of his tea. "He left me with my mother and the slaves that ran the estate. I wonder sometimes if he knew just how terribly ill she was or if he thought that she was just unhappy with him and that things were better when he was away." He shakes his head. "I'll never know.

"When he was away, things were definitely *not* better and probably they were worse. I remember hiding under beds and far in the woods to escape her crazy ranting and her anger. She would get so furious ..." He smiles a sad smile at me. "She never called me William, I remember that. She called me 'Martin', my father's name, and any anger she had for him she directed at me when he was away. If she caught me, she would beat me something fierce, I remember that, too. The slaves were as good to me as they could be, especially the big cook, Elishebah. She hid me in the pantry or even under her skirts a time or two, I recall.

"My Pa came home one time as my mother was chasing me across the front lawn, screaming threats at me. I was never so glad to see him in all my life. I remember hiding behind him as he dismounted from his horse as she continued to charge at both of us never once stopping her shouting and yelling." He stops almost seeming to regret the picture he's making in my mind of his mother.

"Sometimes she was peaceful, you know. Sometimes she was quiet and kind and would take me on walks or tell me stories or laugh at my playing. It was just so unpredictable. One minute things would be fine and the next moment the world would be in chaos."

He makes eye contact with me again across the fire as I sit there with my tea going cold in my hands. "She marched right across the lawn that day, eyes blazing. She never hesitated or seemed to register that Pa was standing there now, not me and that was when I truly knew that she was crazy.

"I can remember him talking quiet and low to her. 'Now Amanda, no need to carry on so ...'" Deer's quiet for a minute and he swallows with difficulty and then looks past me into the woods and stares for a bit. "She pulled a knife from her apron pocket and before he could even raise his hand to defend himself she plunged it into his throat. He dropped like a stone. I did eventually remember how I stood there in those first few moments staring at the both of them frozen in place with disbelief. Had I really just watched my mother kill my father?

"She looked at me standing there in shock and as angry as ever said 'Martin ...' then bent over and pulled the knife out of my father's throat."

He makes an effort to smile. "I'm dumb, but I'm not stupid. I ran like hell and kept on running. I got my name 'Deer' for being a fast runner. When I arrived at Great Elk's village with the hunting party I'd been running practically my whole life." He takes his hat off and runs his hands through his hair. "I didn't remember any of what I just told you until I traveled back to the whites, met my aunt and finally saw my mother again." He laughs a bitter laugh. "The first time she saw me after all those years, she said how good it was to see me and called me 'Martin'." He shook his head. "Some things never change it seems."

"It was in Great Elk's village that I learned the meaning of love, security, family, honor, ..." He grows silent. "I did all of my healing and growing to be a man in that place. I owe them my life."

"Why did you ever go back? Why didn't you just stay with The Real People?" I finally have to ask. I think about his mate Possum who struggled with learning to live in the white world as a trader's wife named Mary Thomas. I think about Bright Feather, Beaver, Great Elk and War Woman who are as much a family to Deer as One Who Knows is to me.

Deer gives me a sad smile. "Don't forget, I didn't remember a lot of this until I saw my mother once again. All through my childhood in The Maple Forest I had the same dream over and over and over again of my father calling me, pleading with me to help." He snorts and shakes his head. "I still have it now and then." He tosses the remains of his cold tea into the fire. "I worried maybe, *just maybe*, my father needed me and that's why I finally went back.

"I'm sure One Who Knows knew a big part of the whole situation. She was the one who encouraged me to go back but she cautioned me before I left about preparing myself to face whatever horrors I originally ran away from. She said, 'You are Deer now, of the Real People of the Maple Forest. You must face your past and understand it before you can go on with your future. No matter how dark your past is, remember it is what pushes you towards future greatness.'" He studies me for a moment and then winks at me. "I bet she's said things like that to you, too, hasn't she?" and I nod my head.

"I came back after a season to the village and I just wanted to hide there and never face that darkness again. But my aunt and uncle were kind and eager to help me. They offered to send me to school. My uncle is a lawyer and offered me all the resources and opportunities that were available to him. They were not thrilled with my love of Indians and yet they were appreciative of what they had done for their nephew. It was my uncle who pointed out that equipping me *in the white world* would make me more powerful to help those I loved *in the red.* For a while there I wondered if I'd ever have peace *anywhere.*"

He grins at me. "Possum helped me find my place in life. She helped me understand that I could not abandon either part of me and that I had to find a happy place right in the middle. She was the only one who could show me that, because she struggled, in some ways, harder than I did between both worlds for no other reason than *just for the love of me.*

"I feel a tremendous responsibility towards The Real People of The Maple Forest, Bear. There is nothing I can make right in my white life, but there is *everything* I can make right in my red one."

He chuckles, "We were talking about Lieutenant Foster, weren't we?" he says and he catches me hiding a yawn. "How about I tell you *that story* tomorrow on the trail?"

As we bed down by the fire, it is my turn to chuckle as I hear his quiet snores even before I can fall asleep. I look at Deer fast asleep curled up in his bedroll looking everything like the typical white homesteader. I think about what brought him here and how every single one of us is so much more than what we show on the outside.

As Deer tells me Lieutenant Foster's story the next day, I realize that if what you are on the *inside* is so scarred that it shows on the *outside* then that makes for an even more complicated individual. And a more dangerous one as well, I think.

"Lieutenant Foster's story is best started at The War of 1812. And The War of 1812," Deer begins as we ride out bright and early the next morning after a quick breakfast consisting of the leftover remains of the meal the night before, "was a war unlike any other. Depending on where you were, you fought for totally different things, against totally different enemies." He shrugs his shoulders. "You even fought against ghosts from the past." He's quiet for a minute as he gets his thoughts together.

"Just remember this rule that never, *ever* changes: the French have always hated the English, the English have always hated the French, and the *Americans*, by the early 1800's have big issues with the French *and* the English but cannot openly declare a hatred for either of them for they are busy establishing a new country that needs their trade business." He turns back and looks at me over the two packhorses. "Got that so far?" I smile and nod my head 'yes'.

"Have you heard of the five civilized tribes?" He asks me still staring back at me.

"Lieutenant Foster mentioned them my first day at Fort Winston but I don't rightly remember much at all about that day ..." I say.

He turns forward. "Well the five civilized tribes," Deer continues, "consisted of The Cherokee – our Real People, the Choctaw, the Creek, the Seminole and the Chickasaw. They were called the five *civilized* tribes because these Indians tribes had made some attempts to accept the white ways and it was a back handed compliment to differentiate between tribes out west that had done no such thing and were still actively involved in warfare. Through treaty negotiations with *the five civilized tribes*, the white language, religion, and customs had gradually begun to seep into these tribes making them *civilized*." The tone he uses as he speaks to me says he thinks little of this opinion. He shouts back to me. "Got that so far?" but he doesn't wait for my answer.

"Now remember this rule: the Cherokee have always hated the Creek, the Creek have always hated the Choctaw, the Choctaw have always hated the Chickasaw, and *all of them* have always hated the Seminole." He turns around again to look at me and I can see laughter in his eyes, "Got that so far?" I smile at him and nod my head even as I try to keep all of these rules of hatred straight.

He sighs, turns forward again and says, "Okay, so here's where the problems begin. There were some Americans that felt that some British were helping some Indian tribes for the purpose of war. Then there were some British who felt that some French were helping some Indian tribes for the purpose of war. Then there were some Indians that felt that some whites were helping certain other Indian tribes for the purpose of war ..." Deer waits while all this sinks in. "These problems grew and grew until it got big enough for war to be considered as the only solution.

"America declared war on Britain in June of 1812, just two summers after my arrival at Great Elk's village. I was, near as I can figure, about seven years old by then. I, of course, was unaware of most of the political intrigue between the white governments, but became well aware of the existing hatred between The Real People and the Creeks in the south. So *my* understanding of the War of 1812 had little to do with much beyond the Indian perspective." He hesitates for a moment and then laughs. "Here I'm afraid to tell you, it gets a little complicated, for you see the Creeks within their tribe were divided and fighting amongst themselves, too. Tensions were so bad that there was already a formal distinction between the two groups. There were the Upper Creeks, who called themselves the Red Sticks after the custom of casting red sticks in their council circle to determine when, where, and how to go to war. The Red Sticks believed that anything white was evil. They sought in all ways to maintain the ancient way of their people and rejected anything the whites had to offer.

"There were about one thousand Red Sticks, or Upper Creek warriors plus women and children. They settled at the Tallapoosa River in the state of Alabama along a stretch that the white's called Horseshoe Bend because of its shape. They built, from what I'm told, a massive barricade of dirt and logs that sealed off the bend of the river as a defense. I've heard soldiers who were there and actually saw it, speak of it still with awe to this day.

"Now opposing the Red Sticks, were the Lower Creeks who had managed to put aside their differences with the Cherokee – The Real People. The Lower Creeks, The Real People and more than three thousand United States Army troops commanded by then General Andrew Jackson assembled to fight the Red Sticks." He looks back at me, but now his look is sad. "Got that?" he says. I nod 'yes'.

We ride for a while in silence and I ponder all the different forces: men, women, children, red, white … all meeting up at Horseshoe Bend on the Tallapoosa River in Alabama that day. Every single one of them fighting for what they thought was right and true and for so many different reasons.

"It was a brutal fight," Deer says. "There was tremendous bravery on both sides, both red and white from what I was told. The barricade is so strong that the cannons that Jackson has brought along cannot penetrate it. Some Lower Creek and Cherokee braves actually swam *up the Tallapoosa River* and began the attack from behind. Others, including many American soldiers, led by a tall, wild and crazy *Corporal* George Foster scaled the barricade and attacked from the front. Foster managed to scale the barricade in the heat of the battle and kill many Red Sticks before he was wounded and taken prisoner. The Creek women," he looks at me with a serious face, "as was the custom of the Cherokee women you should know, tortured many of the prisoners as the battle continued around them. I've heard different stories of how he eventually escaped. Some stories say he was rescued by the victorious army. But one I heard, claimed that as he was being tortured - they were cutting his fingers and toes off one by one – he got a hold of one of the women and literally tore her head off with his bare hands. Despite his injuries, he established himself as a fearless leader and continued with great success in his military career – primarily in the constant battle to suppress Indian uprisings. He was a *very good* friend of Andrew Jackson's and his command of Fort Winston is his crowning military achievement, I would think.

"In the end over eight hundred Red Sticks were killed as well as many women and children and they were defeated. The Creeks as a nation signed a treaty with the United States after the battle – Upper *and Lower* – and were forced to give away *all* of their land, over *twenty million acres*. It was a lesson for many to learn as both the losers of the battle *and the victors of the battle*, both the enemies of the United States of America *and the allies of the United States of America* ended up homeless."

We stop for me to have a private moment and drink from a nearby stream. "The Battle of Horseshoe Bend made a tremendous impact for many of those that were there. The *victory* at Horseshoe Bend was a great accomplishment for General Andrew Jackson and a primary reason why he is *President* Jackson today." He looks at me pointedly. "Always remember that we are *all* products of our past, even Presidents and Fort Commanders." He looks at the water flowing past in the stream and says quietly, "And Indian Chiefs as well.

"Great Elk and Dark Cloud fought in the battle of Horseshoe Bend, too, Bear. For the Real People, it was the start of a division that we live with today. Great Elk and Dark Cloud looked at the battle and the results with very different eyes and as a result took their villages in very different directions. For Great Elk, he saw the deception and trickery that he and War Woman had seen before with the whites and their government during the Great War with Britain. He witnessed the unfairness that the Lower Creeks were forced to endure in losing their land all the while they called themselves victors and the United States continued to call them their allies and friends. He saw the treatment of the Lower Creeks and rightly thought, *What will make The Real People different in the future?* He knew that the friendship between *any Indian tribe* and the government of the United States lasted only until more land would be needed.

"Dark Cloud saw the opportunity to advance in prominence within the white culture. He gained the attention of General Andrew Jackson in his fierce and brave fighting. In fact, Jackson told Dark Cloud, 'As long as the sun shines and the grass grows there shall be friendship between us, and the feet of the Cherokee shall be toward the East.[22]' It is a promise that Great Elk remembers in particular each time more land of the Real People is taken away in treaties. Dark Cloud has risen to a level of leadership that with the Old Way of doing things he never could have achieved. And Dark Cloud and Great Elk both came to realize that warfare was no longer the way to succeed against the might of the white army, no matter *what* you believe."

That night as we make camp for the night, Deer makes one more observation about the lasting changes the War of 1812 brought about as we both fall asleep for the night. "There are some things about war and betrayal and the truth of life that can only be experienced first hand and not with just telling words. That's something that Great Elk could not explain to Beaver that night when they disagreed. Sometimes words are not enough to understand the way of things. Sometimes you must experience the fear and sorrow and defeat first hand. It is unfortunate that Beaver will most certainly have to discover much of this for himself."

The days pass and I get comfortable with the rhythm of travel and seem to become happier and happier with each passing day as each step brings us closer to home. Deer explains that we travel to Forest City first for he *has* been away a long time and at the pace we are traveling, he suspects we should be there in ten days or so. From there, he will take me to the Maple Forest and Bright Feather. He chuckles, "I suspect, though, he will be waiting for you in Forest City. Before I left for Washington he and I calculated the time it would take me to travel to Washington, with a stop at Ward's Mill, of course, the time I knew I was going to have to spend there and then the journey back. I am late already by our calculations so I can just imagine his impatience to hear news of you."

"How has he faired while I was away?" I ask at last.

"It's been a hard winter for him," is all Deer will volunteer at first about him when I ask. Yes, he is well. Yes, he has stayed close to the village. "He was packed and ready to travel north to see you and make sure you were safe when the first major winter storm hit." I remember that night, too, when I found out from the Coopers that Henry was alive and looking for me. "Bright Feather told me that was when One Who Knows told him that you were carrying his child and that he could not subject you to travel in the dead of winter or the upset of him getting hurt, jailed or even killed should he be found in white territory. One Who Knows convinced him to wait the season out and that no matter how difficult things may be for you, you were better off *there* dealing with things that needed to be dealt with." He looks at me, shakes his head and chuckles. "She's scary sometimes that old woman, I tell you."

I grin back, "You better be really scared if she ever hears you calling her 'old woman', that's for sure."

He looks around like she may be lurking in the dark shadows somewhere. "You're right, I better be careful."

On the seventh night of the journey I dream of Bright Feather. He cuddles with me in my sleep and places his big warm hand on my belly and delights in the feel of the baby kicking. I feel safe and secure and loved cradled in his arms. It's a wonderful dream. I wake in the morning cold on my pallet to the sound of Deer stirring up the coals of the fire to eat our usual breakfast of leftovers. I try hard to slip back into the dream for just a few moments more but it disappears from my head like the smoke above a fire. At last I open my eyes. I'm surprised at how bright the sun is and I think how Deer will tease me all day about sleeping so late. Then I puzzle at the cluster of late spring flowers I see tied in a bunch just an arm's length from my face. *I'm just a little bit late in returning,* I think to Bright Feather as I look at the flowers, *just a little bit late past the first spring bud.* And then my sleepy mind asks, *Why has Deer brought me flowers?*

There's a sudden wave of hope that's so strong it's painful as I think, *Was the dream real?* There's a length of time that I can't look for the disappointment would be more than I could possibly stand. I reach out and touch the flowers and see hidden in the cluster three feathers: one yellow goldfinch, one red cardinal, and one blue jay and I sit up and pick them up. I turn to look at who is tending the fire and it's Bright Feather and he looks *so beautiful.* He smiles his precious smile at me and I have a moment's panic as I think, *Am I still asleep?*

"Are you real?" I finally ask him. He stands and comes by me and touches my cheek and then his hand reaches down and covers my belly.

"What must I do to convince you that I am?" he asks back.

I search his face and I see relief and worry and tiredness and delight all rolled into one. "Don't disappear," I say thinking of the dreams I've had over the past months and disappointment of realizing the actual way of things. I can't help myself and I touch his face to feel it warm and alive and *real.*

His hand comes up to grasp mine and he brings my palm to his lips and he kisses it and I feel the slightest touch of his tongue. I feel like a body feels when it touches a hot ember by accident and the shock of the pain shoots through your whole body, making your heart pump and your muscles jump, only this feeling is *nothing but delight.* "Never again," I hear him say finally. "Never, ever again will we be separated like this. We will travel together and face our challenges together. Never again will we let life break us apart." It's a promise that I'm happy to make.

I start to laugh and I touch his hair and his arms and his broad chest and finally throw myself into his arms. I kiss his mouth and smell his smell and I taste salty tears, too, and I don't know if they are mine or his. I end up in his lap cradled there and he holds me close while I concentrate on the sights and sounds and smells and feel of him near me again *at last.*

I find we are to spend the day together, just the two of us. Deer has 'gone off to hunt a bit' although he will rejoin us tonight at a point agreed upon by him and Bright Feather. "I have traveled too far into white territory to his liking," Bright Feather says to me while at the same time putting a finger to my lips to quiet any comments I might wish to add about the matter, "and he does not feel it wise that we should be without his help should it be needed." He shrugs, "I can always disappear quickly into the woods should the need arise and you could still just travel with Deer and no one would be the wiser."

The first thing he makes me do is take off all my white clothes so that he can see my belly. He asks me many questions, Have I been well? Have I had much tiredness? Have I been eating enough? How do I feel? Is the baby active? It feels so wonderful to talk about the baby with him and watch the looks of delight on his face. I tell him that I'm quite certain that the baby will be born sometime at the very end of the summer and explain to him the friendship I had with Jane West and her thoughts on babies and such. He examines me all over and I realize he looks for scars or marks of misuse. I assure him with words although he seems to need to be assured with his own eyes more. When I reach for my clothes he makes a noise of disgust and throws them in the fire while I stand helpless and naked watching them burn.

"Great Elk's village will think little of me arriving naked, but I can promise you that any white folk we meet on the way back will be mighty put out," I feel a need to explain to him as I sit back in his lap.

He wraps one arm tight around me while he leans far over to reach for a parcel. "From One Who Knows and Otter," he says by way of explanation and drops it in my lap. "One Who Knows said that *if* you still had your old clothes, and *if* you could still fit in them, no matter what I was to burn anything you were wearing so that you could start fresh." Inside the package is a short summer top, wrap around skirt and moccasins, simply but finely made. The skirt, I can see, is cut fuller for my growing belly. I also find special herbs that Otter uses to clean her hair and body as well as new ties for my hair. "Otter sent those," he murmurs close to my ear. I feel him begin to undo my hair from it's wrapping. He works slow and steady undoing the ties and finally winding them up careful for they are still good to use again. I've wrapped some old strips of cloth close around my braided hair and those he unwinds and finally throws in the fire. Lastly he works at undoing my braid and I feel his fingers touch my back starting lower and then going higher and higher up as the braid becomes undone. Between sitting in the warmth of his lap naked, the tickling of my unbraided hair and the warmth of his breath against my neck, my body is tingling inside and out.

I start to giggle. "I have to pee," I finally confess. "It happens a lot with me lately," I say. We untangle ourselves and he takes my hand and walks me into the woods. We walk for only a short ways and I can hear the river. I go one way into the woods and he heads towards the water carrying my parcel of bits from One Who Knows and Otter.

I find him standing at the edge of the river and he is as naked as me now. Again I must think, *He is so beautiful.* I come up behind him and wrap my arms around his waist and rest my face against his warm back. "I think," I say after a time, "that I can stay like this forever," feeling the warmth of his body against my cheek and breasts and my sticking out belly. I feel the baby kick and I giggle again. He turns around and looks at me. "Not that often I hope," he says thinking I need to pee again. I must tell him about the baby kicking for it is too soon for him to feel those things yet.

The water is cold, cold, cold! I yelp and shout as we wade in but it feels so glorious to wash and be washed. He sits patiently on a rock while I soap up his hair and help him rinse it clean. As he does mine I think, *Who ever would have thought that hair washing could make someone think so much of mating?*

I puzzle over this out loud to Bright Feather as we work on rinsing my hair and as I work to control my shivering from the cold I feel his hot breath on my neck as he kisses it. I sit up and swing my heavy wet hair over my shoulder and feel the icy trickles of the water running down my back and I can see that I am not the only one that thinks of mating when hair washing is done. *That is a good thing I know.*

It's high noon before we break camp and travel on and that's only because we know we must get to the meeting place and find Deer. We are clean and dressed and our hair has been carefully combed and braided each by the other. It seems that there are many odd things that make us think of mating over the course of the morning. I point this out to Bright Feather as we are readying the horses to leave and he grabs me and swings me high and then hugs me tight to him in a fierce hug. "In a lifetime I will not get enough of you," he says and kisses me firmly on the mouth.

Deer has left us the pack horses to bring along and we set off in high spirits. "I must tell Deer that I much prefer watching your back to his," I tell Bright Feather.

I ask of those in the village and he tells me bits and pieces. Otter is well and far along in her pregnancy. Raccoon is well, too, and anxious to begin his teasing of me again. Little Bird is speaking many words and Raccoon has already begun to teach him how to hold a bow and arrow. One Who Knows looks forward to my return to resume teaching me about the herbs.

I think of her giving me the basket and how she knew of my pregnancy even before Bright Feather and I. I ask him what he thought when she told him the news.

He is quiet for a moment and then he says, "I was terrified."

I think of his first mate Black Fox and the baby she died trying to give birth to. I think of my mother, too, and how I was the only mother that Eli ever knew. *Childbirth is the war that women fight*, I think. "I did not realize I was to have a baby for almost three months I guess because I was just too busy trying to not die from missing you," I tell Bright Feather. "By the time I realized, I was so glad for the company of your baby."

"When I argued that I was going to see you in Ward's Mill, One Who Knows told me I had two choices to consider. I could let you be the powerful, capable woman we all knew you could be or I could go off into the dead of winter, drag you and the baby back with me, leave a pile of unfinished business and probably kill all three of us in the process." He shrugs, shakes his head, and finally grunts. "Believe it or not, it was a difficult decision for me."

I can't help it, I have to laugh. "She has a way about her, doesn't she?" I ask. After a few moments, I say, "It was a hard, hard time being away from you and feeling so alone. It was lonelier than even my first time at Great Elk's when I didn't even understand the language." I tell him some of the hardest bits. When I get to Willow's sale I say, "That moment, was the worst time for me, I think. That was when things seemed the very darkest. But all of a sudden I thought of you and the baby and I realized that sometimes when things are the very darkest *maybe, just maybe*, it is because I am just in the shadow of something because things are really *so bright*."

He turns and looks at me with such a tender face it feels almost as if he touches me. "You are good for me for you force me to believe that this life is worth living even when we are in those dark shadows, my mate."

We endure Deer's teasing the entire evening once we finally meet up.

"Could have built an entire white man's cabin in the time you two have been gone."

"I'm glad to see you remember the pack horses since the two of you seem so oblivious to anything but each other."

Deer bends over, at one point and looks close at Bright Feather's neck. "Is that a bite, my brother?" he asks in mock concern. "You seem to have some fresh wounds ..."

It's hard to not giggle which only encourages him. Deer has gone out of his way to prove how long he has been waiting in the planned spot and we eat an enormous dinner of squirrel (three), biscuits (two each), fresh coffee, and some cheese which he insists he had time to prepare right there in the forest while he waited.

"I hope you had time to bake one of Possum's apple pies," I say with my best try at a straight face.

"It's in the oven I had time to build as well," he says.

As we sip our coffee and I snuggle against Bright Feather's side and stare in wonder every now and then that he is *really right there where I can touch him*, Bright Feather says to Deer, "Tell me of Washington."

Deer sighs, deep and low. "I am trying to think of some good news to tell before I tell you all the bad," he says at last and then shakes his head as if to give up. "There isn't very much I'm afraid."

"Major Everett spoke of the removal of all Indian tribes that live east of the Mississippi ..." I say in the silence of the evening.

Deer looks at me with great sorrow. "That is now a *law*," he says to both of us. "The Congress of the United States of America, the part of the government that makes up the laws that give one group of people power over other groups of people, has passed a law that gives President Andrew Jackson the right to move every single Indian west of the Mississippi whether they want to go or not. The law is very specific for I have spent the time in Washington reading it carefully. If you are in a state or just a territory of the United States east of the Mississippi, even if you have a treaty that has made promises to the contrary, and you are part of an Indian tribe or nation, *you will be required to move west of the Mississippi*. They make all the same promises that have been given before: like quality of land, cash for improvements you may have made that will be lost as a result of the move, and free assistance in transport during the removal." Deer puts his head in his hands and his despair can almost be seen rising off of him like hot steam.

He can't look at us it seems as he continues to speak without lifting his head. "Their arguments are amazing. 'It will separate the Indians from immediate contact with white settlements.' 'It will free the Indians from the oppressive power of the states.' 'It will enable the Indians to pursue happiness in their own way and under their styles of governing.' They have even said, 'It will help *save* the Indian who has suffered greatly from the white encroachment and will slow down the lessening of their numbers.' They say they hope that this move will help the Indian Nation gradually, with the help of the United States Government and other *good counsels*, become a less *savage* place and more *civilized* community." Deer then looks at Bright Feather and me and shakes his head in disbelief. "They can even be heard to say that they are not only being *open minded and fair*, they are being down right *generous*.

"They were so confident about the passing of this law," Deer says, "that they have people like Lieutenant Foster *already building forts* specifically for the removal *and containment* process that they plan to begin as soon as possible. I understand that there are *thirty* forts being built across all states that currently have existing Indian populations."

"You said that you had *very little good news*," I finally say in the silence that follows all of Deer's bad news, "but you did not say you had *no* good news. So I think I would like to hear what little good news you *do* have."

"There is only one small thing that seems to offer The Real People of The Maple Forest any hope at all," Deer says quiet like and I see Bright Feather wrinkle his forehead in puzzlement, but like a bright flash of lightning on a hot, dark summer night, I know what it is and I sit up fast.

"The Real People of the Maple Forest are *not* part of an Indian tribe or nation," I say softly and Deer looks at me across the fire sitting suddenly stiff and alert by Bright Feather. "They are citizens of the United States of America..." I say in wonder.

"That's it," Deer says grimly. "Now if I can get anyone important enough to listen to me tell them that." He looks at both of us and says, "It is our only hope."

It is good to see Possum and the children when we arrive at Forest City and the trading post but I'm tired from traveling for over two weeks and eager to get home to the Maple Forest. We spend just two days recovering and then head out bright and early, just Bright Feather and I, for home.

Deer will spend some time getting things in order at the trading post and then travel out, too, to The Maple Forest to talk with Great Elk, War Woman, One Who Knows and the others that regularly sit in the council circle. "We must move fast," is all he will say but we know what he means. I worry that nothing will be fast enough.

As with every visitor to The Real People of the Maple Forest the first to announce them is always the dogs. I think about the first time I arrived here, with Weasel and my fear of them as they barked and barked at me. I remember my worry about being so strange and looking so different. Now I grin at the barking dogs and smiling faces that hurry to add their shouts of greetings to the animal noise and I think, *my family*. I am a daughter here, I am a mate here, I am a sister here and I cannot help myself as the happy tears fall. I can hear Deer saying to me, *It was in Great Elk's village that I learned the meaning of love, security, family, honor ...*" I realize how fortunate I am for I *knew* of love and family and security and honor before I arrived here but to be able to find it again, having lost it all, is still a wonderful and amazing thing.

The crowd that surrounds us is full of welcoming faces and even though my eyes are filled with tears, I'm able to shout greetings to those who call to me. Bright Feather's surrounded by well – wishers, too, and it's Raccoon who comes and lifts me off Willow and gives me a big hug. He holds me at arms length, then and looks down at my belly, acting surprised at it. "Oh NO! Not *another one* like you!" he says in mock horror.

I laugh through my happy tears and wipe my eyes and nose on the end of my saddle blanket. "I plan to teach this baby as many ways as possible to bother Uncle Raccoon."

"I would not have it any other way!" he shouts, eyes dancing with delight.

Heavy with the very soon to be birth of her baby, it takes Otter more time than the others to make her way to greet me. We laugh as we bump bellies and try to find a good way to hug each other tight. We put our hands on each other's stomachs and both say, "Sister," to the other at the same time. That causes us to laugh and cry some more. Raccoon shakes his head and rolls his eyes at us and then reaches to put an arm around his mate for comfort and support.

"Make room for a nasty old lady!" we hear shouted from somewhere in back of the crowd and the crush of people parts to allow One Who Knows to make her way over to me. She looks approvingly at my clothes and touches my belly and nods her head a few times. Gradually the crowd gets silent as she examines and pokes and prods me.

"Don't suppose you even remembered to *sniff* those herbs I sent you," she snarls under her breath. I decide not to answer since we both obviously know the truth of things. She looks me in the eyes then. "You seem healthy enough, eh?" and I nod and smile.

"The great fool told you how he wanted to rush off into the storm just to come and catch a kiss?" and I hear Raccoon stifle a laugh with a quick cough. I glance over at Bright Feather across Willow's back and he has his blank Indian face on.

I smile at One Who Knows. "Ahh, Mother, how I missed your loving and tender words when I was away," and I lean forward and give her a kiss on her wrinkled and weathered cheek.

"Hrumpf," is the best that can be said for the sound she makes as she turns and walks slowly away, back into the crowd. She stops and looks around at everyone who seem to be just waiting for one last word from her. "And *I* missed someone to have around who knows how to show me proper love and respect," she says. "I look forward to a visit from my daughter when all of these *prying eyes* have had their fill of things," and she shuffles off without another word.

Otter and I link arms and waddle off to our huts. We are both filled with news and questions and stories to tell and ask each other and we bump words just like we have bumped bellies as we try to talk at the same times. I look over at Bright Feather as I walk away and he's following me with his eyes. I smile back and his look says, *We are home, my mate, really home!*

Within those first few hours in the village, aside from Little Bird, who's no longer the Little Bird I remember, but an active toddler running around and talking almost as much as Otter and I, it seems little has changed in the village for me to see and I say so.

"Well," says Otter with a delighted grin, "Red Fox and Turtle have joined just this past spring and I think she is already with child! One Who Knows has claimed her for a daughter, too, since she has pointed out that her other worthless daughter is never around to help and care for her anyway." She looks at me and laughs.

I laugh, too, and shake my head. "Turtle has been in her hut longer than I was. At first I thought that I should speak with her and give her some advice, but perhaps it should be the other way around."

It's high summer when I arrive and I fall right back into the rhythm of the work of the village, gardening and gathering. Hunting's no longer on my list, because much to my frustration, the shape of my belly and the way I now stand to support its weight, has made it impossible for me to aim and shoot with any accuracy. "That's as good an excuse as any," Raccoon observes as I speak of my frustrations over dinner one night and I hear Bright Feather grunt.

Deer's expected before summer's end, for those in the council are anxious to question him, having heard all that Bright Feather and I can tell. It's decided in council to send some messengers down to Dark Cloud's village to find out their understanding of the way things are, too. "It cannot hurt," Great Elk says, "to hear their impression of the United States Government's policies as well." Red Fox and two other braves from the village make the trip. I wonder if they will see the same things that I saw when I was there. And then I have a greater worry. Maybe things will be even worse.

In the two months or so that I have been home in The Maple Forest, the idea of hiding my pregnancy is now a joke. While I'm not as big and uncomfortable as Otter, I'm obviously very pregnant to anyone with eyes to see.

Sigh. Or ears to hear me walk, it seems, according to Raccoon. One morning as I'm walking over to their hut to begin morning chores with Otter, I look up to see that Raccoon has his bow and arrow drawn and aimed right at me. "What are you doing?!" I ask in shocked tones.

"Oh, it's just you," he says, putting his bow away. "I thought a buffalo was coming and I was going to be able to feed the village for the rest of the summer and maybe even into the fall ..." Bright Feather shows just how wise he truly is for he knows not to grunt when I tell him of the story.

On one of the hottest days I have known since I have been in The Maple Forest, when the air is so heavy you feel you cannot breath it and when your skin feels permanently sticky and sweaty and when you struggle to remember whether you were really ever, ever truly cool, Otter's baby decides to be born. Both of us, miserable in the heat, have gone down to the river to just sit on the edge and try to stay cool.

As we both sit in the coolness of the stream and let the water flow past us, Otter sighs in contentment. "I am not moving from here," she says with force. "No one can make me and I am too heavy to be lifted by even the strongest of men. I'm staying here until it snows." I giggle at her while Little Bird runs around and splashes on the edge of the water just as delighted as we are to be wet.

"Snow?" I say, pretending to be puzzled and confused. "Snow? What's that?"

In the midst of our talking - Raccoon says he has never known two bodies that can never stop talking about nothing in particular - she gasps and clutches her stomach. "Bear ..." she says. Then she laughs, "I'm going to give birth in this river," she says firmly, "because *nothing* and *no one* is going to make me go back up to that hot, sticky hut!" I stand – with great difficulty mind you! *What a pair we are,* I think to myself, and begin to waddle quickly into the village to get some help. I can still hear her shouting, "Tell them I'm not leaving the water! Tell them I mean it!" I chuckle to myself as I make my way to find Bright Feather or Raccoon.

Raccoon looks startled as I puff into view and with one look at my face, he seems to know. "Otter's time?" he says.

I nod and try to catch my breath as the sweat trickles down the sides of my face and I feel it make rivulets down between my breasts and my back. "She says to tell you that she's going to give birth in the river," I manage to gasp out. "She says that she's not moving and no one is strong enough to lift her."

He snorts and looks at a loss for what to do first. "I think," I say to him as I feel my breath slow and my heart begin to go back to an even rhythm, "you should go to her and wait with her and Little Bird. I can make my way to One Who Knows or at least find someone who will go for me."

He looks grateful at me and then smiles. "I will wait until One Who Knows comes before I try to move her. I'd rather have someone meaner than me do the telling if she needs to be brought to a different place."

He heads off to the river and I make my way towards the center of the village and the hut of One Who Knows. Bright Feather's sitting at War Woman and Great Elk's hut and I'm happy that that's the farthest I need to travel in the heat. I tell them the when and where and who and Bright Feather runs off to find One Who Knows.

"Sit, for a moment," War Woman says and she hands me a gourd full of not too cool water, which tastes good just the same. I tell her how Otter says she plans to give birth in the river and she smiles. "Little Bird was a very quick birth and that is unusual for a first baby. It is very possible that she *will* give birth in the river unless everyone hurries."

Bright Feather soon appears with One Who Knows and her gathering bag that I have given her and a rolled bundle under her arm. She takes one look at me struggling to stand and join them. "If we wait for *her* the baby will be on her second name by the time we get there," and she walks right past me. Bright Feather looks torn as to who he should go with.

"Go," I tell him and wave him away. "I'll make my way at my own pace." One Who Knows is traveling at a good speed and he touches my arm before hurrying after her.

It's War Woman who helps me to stand and walks with me in the end. "Men are useless during births, I'll come along in case another pair of hands is needed." She's in no rush though and her quiet, unhurried manner calms my head and my heart a bit.

"You both will be fine," she says almost reading my thoughts. "Both of you are strong and healthy and have had easy times throughout these pregnancies. Some women are just made for having children and I think that both of you are in that category." I think of my Ma and how she had two babies before the final one killed her. *I hope you are right,* I think and then I push the worries away for *what good will it do me?*

I smile at her in thanks for her kind words.

Everyone's *in* the river by the time we get there, although they have moved to the quieter shallows at the edge. It seems that Otter has gotten her wish and will not be moved to the *hot hut.* Raccoon's now squatting behind Otter in the cool of the water bracing her as she too, squats, while straining and pushing. One Who Knows squats in front of Otter and is talking quietly and firmly giving her instructions. I can see Otter, eyes closed as she thinks, breathing and panting in between the pushes. Bright Feather stands next to One Who Knows, obviously frightened and uncomfortable. He seems to be the official gathering bag holder for he holds it carefully above the water so it will not get wet. Even Little Bird's quiet, his hand in Bright Feather's quietly watching the action.

To me, War Woman says quietly under her breath as we both look at Bright Feather, "See? What did I tell you? Men are no use when babies are born." To One Who Knows she says loudly, "We are here, One Who Knows, is there anything you need?"

For a moment I think that One Who Knows has not heard her but finally she says, "It is good you are here for the only help I have seems to be no better than the furniture we sit on and walls we hang our things on. Quickly pass me the new deer skin that is rolled over there!" she points to the bundle I saw her carrying before. I watch in amazement as I see Otter give another great push and a small dark head emerge at exactly the spot where One Who Knows has her hand. Another quick push and the head is followed quickly by the rest of the baby and a rush of liquid. War Woman's moved swiftly and is now standing ready next to One Who Knows who cleans the baby's face and airways with fresh river water. It begins to wail, a loud angry shout, partly I'm sure because of the cool water being splashed all over it.

One Who Knows hands the baby over to War Woman who bends down to receive it, kneeling in the river, too. One Who Knows works quickly tying the cord with bits of sinew and finally cutting the cord with her knife. War Woman finally stands with the baby and wraps it carefully in the soft deerskin. "Well done," I hear One Who Knows say to Otter over the baby's wails, "your daughter is happy to finally be out in this world." One Who Knows sits down in the water to rest and Raccoon gradually lowers himself and his mate into the cool of the river, too. Otter leans against him, eyes closed in exhaustion, and Raccoon takes his cool, wet hand and wipes her sweat-streaked face.

Raccoon leans over and whispers something private in Otter's ear and she reaches up and wraps her dripping arm around the back of his neck. She's still exhausted, her eyes are still closed, but now she smiles, too.

That night, Bright Feather and I decide to sleep outside under the stars for the hut is just too hot to bear even with the sides open as is done in the summer months. As we make preparations for our beds, Little Bird's curled up asleep close by, exhausted from his busy day and the fun of sleeping at our hut for a change.

"I cannot do it," Bright Feather all of a sudden says to me and I give him a puzzled look.

"Do what?" I say back to him.

"I cannot watch you go through that kind of pain and be unable to help you *and* know that I am the cause." He shakes his head full of despair. "It will drive me mad."

I'm quiet for a bit for I *know* that things with Otter were *very quick* and *very easy* compared to what I've heard and seen before. I don't think that this is the best thing to tell Bright Feather, though. I know he thinks of Black Fox and the baby that never was.

"What does your quiet voice tell you?" I ask him and he looks at me at last.

He snorts, "It tells me you will be fine, but I don't know if it is just my head insisting and shouting louder to be heard."

"War Woman had good words to say to me about how she thought Otter and I were strong and healthy and the type of women that are just made for having children ..." I begin but he interrupts me.

"She's been singing that song to me since the snow was still falling and I hadn't even had a chance to see your belly," he says with surprising frustration.

"Oh," I say at last.

"Losing you is the only thing that I fear in this world," he finally says to me and I feel my heart just about stop to look at him.

I go and sit next to him and finally rest my head on his lap as we sit and enjoy the very brief night breezes. "When we were separated, I had great fear that each day I was away from you would make it harder and harder to get back here, until it would become impossible. The night I realized that I was to have your child, at first I was so happy to no longer be alone, but then I realized that it could be just another piece that would keep me from getting back here. I thought I was in a deep dark pit that I would never get out of. I was truly afraid then."

He sits quiet, listening to me talk. "I finally prayed. I remembered Ma's verse that Henry and I liked, *Thou preparest a table before me in the presence of mine enemies*[23]*:* and I prayed that God would send me someone to cook with. The next day I rode on Willow to Jane and Ezekiel West's house and found not one friend, but two.

"I watched my mother die in childbirth, Bright Feather. Part of the powerful woman that I am is because of that. I didn't understand or know that then, but I sure do know that *now*. I've had moments when the fear of having this baby makes me want to curl up and die rather than face it." I shrug my shoulders. "But what good would that do, I think?" I reach up and touch his face and smile a gentle smile and whisper into his worried face, "*Teach me the measure of my days, Thou Maker of my frame; I would survey life's narrow space, and learn how frail I am. A span is all that we can boast, an inch or two of time; man is but vanity and dust in all his flower and prime.*[24]"

I sit up and put my hand on his arm and he looks at me and I look at him. "Would I have come to this village on my own without Weasel? Would I have been able to withstand some of these hard things in my life so far had my Ma not died and I'd been made to grow up faster than I should have? Would Deer have chosen the way of life that brought him to be alone and lost in the woods that day the hunters found him and brought him back here? The answers to all of those questions is 'no'. One Who Knows says that *Joy never comes without a bit of work to get it*. I think it's even a little more. I think great hardship causes great joy. How can you tell day without night? How can you tell pleasure without pain? How can you know fullness without having felt emptiness?"

I take his face in my hands and I kiss him as I start to cry. "Would I risk my life to have a life with you however brief or however long and know all the joys that go with it? How much sorrow can a person say is worth how much joy? I *cannot* live each day worrying about what bad thing lurks around the next bend. I *can* enjoy each and every moment I have with you and be thankful for just that. I carry *your baby* inside me and just the making and the carrying and the knowing and the sharing with you has been joy enough for me *already*. When the worrying does come and I cannot seem to escape it, I just put it in a place in my head that I leave for when I have someone to cook dinner with – be it enemy or friend or husband."

I kiss him deep and long. I kiss his forehead and he sighs and closes his eyes and I kiss each eyelid, gently like a butterfly's touch. I kiss his strong, tan cheeks and finally his mouth again. "We travel on this path together you and I. There are those that love us and wait ahead, there are those that walk beside us and even those that walk behind us. What joy it has been for me to live in this *garden walled around, chosen and made peculiar ground; a little spot enclosed by grace, out of the world's wide wilderness*[25] ... *with you.* But there was great sorrow and heartache for both of us before we got to this place."

I take his big warm hand and I place it on my very busy belly that is jumping and hopping like a puppy in a sack. "I will whisper to God and talk about all these things and you will listen to the voice in your head that continues to talk loud and clear and tell you that things will be all right. And then we will have this baby and face all the many other things that we must face *together.*"

We walk to the river in the faint moonlight and sit naked in the rushing water, enjoying what has to be the only cool spot in this garden we call home. I think of another verse from my book of Isaac Watts hymns that I have read many times, for it's another one of my favorites and I say it to Bright Feather over the sound of the river's passing; *Let my Beloved come and taste, His pleasant fruits at his own feast, I come, my spouse, I come! he cries, With love and pleasure in his eyes*[26].

There's a point, as the summer tries to melt me with its last burst of burning heat and stickiness, that I decide I'm so uncomfortable with this baby, I would rather go through the pain and trial of the birth than go *one more moment* with this baby inside of me. When I tell this to One Who Knows she snorts and says, "So now you are ready to give birth then." She looks at me with a twinkle in her eye. My back aches whether I'm standing, sitting or lying down. My feet are swollen and painful to walk on. The weight of the baby in my belly seems so great at times that I find it more comfortable to hold my belly in place as if were I to let it go it would just rip right off and fall to the ground. I know things are bad when even Raccoon stops teasing me and looks away as if it is painful to even look at me.

Bright Feather seems delighted with the whole process despite the fear I know hides just below the surface. More than once I have awakened in the night to pee to find him wide awake and watching the movements of my belly. "How can you sleep with all that going on?" he asks me one night in wonder.

As I struggle to get up, like a turtle turned on its back, I grumble, "What choice do I have?"

In the final weeks as we wait for the baby to be born, he seems unconcerned with my moodiness and general lack of good humor. He's patient and kind and loving and a day does not go by that he does not tell me how beautiful I am. Sometimes his cheerful self is almost too much for me to take and I think to myself, *It is a good thing that my knife does not fit around my great big waist now for he has no idea how much danger he is in.* Somehow I manage to keep thoughts of that nature quiet and I just give him pale, tired smiles instead.

Since the birth of Otter and Raccoon's daughter, whom they have been calling Squirrel for the cute little face that she has, the heat has not let up, not one bit. For almost an entire month each day begins hot and sticky and ends hot and sticky, followed by nights that are hot and sticky, too. I have no appetite, just a desire to drink as much water as I can get my hands on. The river develops an appeal for more than just it's cooling ability; I drink it and I pee in it, too.

Finally a morning dawns with a different feel to it, but as I make my way slowly out of the hut, it is not necessarily better. The sky is full of dark gray clouds and there is no sign of the sun. The air still feels heavy and muggy, yet it does seem a shade cooler, although that's probably from the cloud cover. Bright Feather follows me out and gazes at the sky and frowns a bit. "Storm coming," he finally says and as an afterthought it seems he adds, "big one." As if to confirm his prediction a breeze blows up suddenly from the east that sends a blast of dust and leaves flying. Storm or no, the breeze feels *wonderful* and I stand there letting it dry the sticky sweat that seems to be permanently dripping from all parts of my very big body.

Raccoon wanders over and he and Bright Feather make observations about the gathering clouds while I am fully engrossed in *enjoying the breeze.*

"Bear? Are you listening, Bear?" I turn to look at Bright Feather who's purposefully moving about the hearth and walking in and out of the hut. "Raccoon thinks that this is a *very bad* storm and that we should move to better shelter."

"Better shelter?" I ask. "Where's better shelter?"

"There are a series of caves up along the ridge," he says and he tips his head to show the direction because his hands are filled with his preparations. "Just a little way further up from your thinking rock. I'm surprised you never found them in your exploring. Some here in the village wish to stay, but others feel it would be wiser to go. I think we should go."

I feel a slight start of panic. "I can hardly walk to the river let alone climb up higher than my thinking rock! I've never gone any farther than that spot because the climb was so steep just to get there! How do you plan on getting me up there? Will you carry me?" I put my hands on my hips and my enormous belly thrusts out at him making my point. *When was the last time I saw my feet?* I think and I stifle an almost hysterical giggle.

"We'll ride the horses as far as possible and then walk the rest of the way. I'll help you, then, and so will Raccoon." He comes and stands in front of me placing both hands on my shoulders, serious and tall. I look up at him and feel the baby give a hearty kick. *Great,* I think. *I have to pee again.* "One Who Knows will *not* come with us. She cannot make the climb and refuses to be carried," he says slowly to me. "She's chosen to stay with a number of others here. But she agrees that *we* should go to the caves."

We stand staring at each other for a few moments as the breeze blows up again and a wisp of his hair blows across his face. I reach up to catch it and put it behind his ear. I sigh. Another choice that seems to be no choice at all. "I have to pee," I finally say to him, "and then it will only take me a minute to get ready."

He kisses me on the mouth. "Good," he says and goes back to packing our carry baskets.

One Who Knows is waiting by our hut when I return from the woods. She holds a bundle just like the bundle she brought when Otter gave birth as well as a baby board. "Just in case," she says and it's my turn to snort at her.

"I cannot see this time," she says and her face shows her frustration. "I truly do not know if your time will come to have the baby during this storm. I told you once before this special sight is a blessing *and* a curse for it does not always tell me what I want to know. I *do know* that should I travel to the caves it will mean my death, I know that for certainty. I think I will take the risk and stay here with the hopes of seeing my," she hesitates and grins, "*grandchild* in the near future."

She sets the bundle down and now it's her turn to put both hands on my shoulders and look serious at me. Only this time I look *down*. "I am not worried about you during the birth should I be unable to be there with you. *It is not your time, you will not die.* Otter has helped me many times in the village and will know what must be done should you need that kind of help. Remember, *stay calm and listen to your body.* It will tell you most of what you need to know." She embraces me quickly and says, "See you in a few days," before heading off back to her hut.

Bright Feather has the horses packed and ready and helps me up onto Willow's back. He adds One Who Knows' bundle to his saddle and mounts up onto Companion. I insist on wearing my own pack basket on my back and even am able to joke a bit, "It helps balance me with a great weight in the back *and* the front." For a while it feels good to be moving, good to be cool, good to be doing something other than waddling around growing bigger and bigger with each passing moment, but gradually the ache returns to my back and it becomes so uncomfortable that even Bright Feather can see the strain of it as I keep trying to shift to make it easier.

I learn that there are many caves up in the hills. Some are closer but with steeper paths, some are farther but with easier paths. Some are larger and some are smaller, too. Some are well hidden and some are wide open and easy to find. Raccoon, with Little Bird, Otter, with Squirrel in her cradle board, Turtle without Red Fox for he is still south at Dark Cloud's village, Bright Feather and I travel to one cave that from what I can understand is *somewhere in the middle of all of these things.*

As I ride on Willow's back behind Turtle and in front of Bright Feather it becomes increasingly plain to me that these back pains are different than the back pains I have been suffering for the past month or so. They are low and when they grip me, seem to travel all the way around to the front of my stomach, causing the pain to grow in a terrible wave that if I concentrate enough makes them gradually fade away. I push my fear of giving birth back over and over again as it works hard to burst out from the spot in my head where I have it tightly stored. *You cannot have the baby …* *now, … here, … yet,* I say over and over again as each pain arrives and works its misery on me. I gradually become so focused on the passing of each pain I'm no longer aware of the moving or the coolness, just the *not now, not here, not yet.*

I feel Bright Feather's hand on my arm and look down surprised to see him standing next to me his face a miserable mask of worry and fear. "The baby is coming, isn't it?" he says to me at last and I can't help myself as I nod my head in misery and start to cry. He grips my hand tightly for a moment and then reaches up to lift me down and I am caught off guard to be standing instead of sitting when the next pain hits. I stand with Willow behind me and Bright Feather in front of me, him holding me up with my arms around his neck and his arms around me and my great belly.

Otter comes into view, her face very similar to Bright Feather's. I'm conscious of the wind now, no longer a breeze and the faint patter of rain drops splattering every now and then on my face and bare arms. "Bear," Otter says, "tell me what you feel."

I describe the pain to her and we wait, the group of us, for the next pain to come to see how long apart they are. When it comes, I rock myself in Bright Feather's arms and think, *Where can I go to get away from this?*

Otter says to Bright Feather, "The good news is that I do not think that she will be long in bringing this baby into this world, but that is also the bad news, too. She has still some time before she will want to push, but I do not think it will be enough time to get to the cave." She looks at me with sympathy, and brushes escaping bits of hair from my face. She manages a small smile, "You asked for cooler weather, but I bet you never thought to be more specific as to what was sent!" I manage a small smile for her. "You might feel better walking for a bit. It sometimes lessens the pains a small way."

"Let's go," I hear myself say. "We can't have this baby here." It's Turtle who steps forward and takes my basket with a shy but determined smile.

In between the pains, I walk as fast as possible. As far as I can tell, walking does not make them hurt less, but I *am* more comfortable in between them than sitting on Willow. When we get to my thinking rock, I must wait again as another pain comes and this time I feel a great rush of wetness pour down my legs. I shout with anger when Bright Feather picks me up and begins to carry me. "Hush," he says fiercely as I try to argue. "You have done all you can. I can carry you the rest of the way now *and I will.*"

I loop my arms around his neck and we actually move more quickly for he carries me through the pains now and we no longer stop. I hear him mutter in amazement when the first pain rides through for he can feel the pressure I feel now as he holds me tightly against him.

The rains come. It's as if one moment you are standing looking at a waterfall and listening to its roar and the next moment you are under it. It comes in great sheets of wet that soaks us to the skin just like *that*. I hide my face against Bright Feather's shoulder so that I can still breath and not be drowned. I hear One Who Knows say, *Listen to your body, it will tell you most of what you need to know* and I concentrate on the *Stay calm* part for I all of a sudden have a powerful urge to push. I can hear Raccoon shouting something up ahead and I feel Bright Feather's arms tighten around me as he says loudly in my ear over the downpour, "We are here. The cave has been found."

The cave's not large, but it's big enough to fit all of us plus our belongings. I hear the wind and the rain and the murmurs of those around me getting things set. As Bright Feather lowers my feet to the ground I'm gripped by another pain and I cannot help myself as I hold onto him and squat and push, push, *push*. I can hear the panic in his voice as he calls, "Otter!"

What a sight we must be, all of us soaked to the skin, except baby Squirrel who for some unbelievable reason is fast asleep cradled in her babyboard, pretty much dry from the little awning that protects her *usually from the sun*. Bright Feather braces his back against the wall of the cave and I squat and brace myself between his legs. Otter's in front of me, just as One Who Knows was in front of her less than a month ago. She talks loudly over the wind and the crashing rain, "Breath in between the pains, Bear! Slow, easy …" Another pain comes and she says, "Now take one deep breath and push! Push with all your might!" She yells at me, "GET THAT BABY OUT!!" I push and push and I can't help myself and I yell my war cry for it makes me feel just a tiny bit stronger.

"Good!" Otter says and I feel her reach down. "Feel, Bear! Feel your baby!"

I reach down and am amazed what I feel with my hand. It is hard and damp and *it feels enormous!*

"One more push and we should have the head out! That is the hard part," I hear Otter say and the pain comes. "Deep breath!" she reminds me, "Now PUSH!" and that she *does not* need to remind me about.

I feel a burning, hot but not hot pain and some release of the pressure and I can feel Bright Feather grow even tenser than he already is as we hear the crying of a baby, *and it is not Squirrel.* Turtle, without being told, has a gourd full of rainwater and a soft piece of deer skin and as I wait for the next pain, I know they clean the baby's face, as I saw One Who Knows do with Squirrel. Otter looks at me with a great big smile on her face, "*Last time*," she says as I feel the pain begin to build again. "War Woman was right, you and I are made for making babies!" And the last pain comes and I push and I feel a rush of relief as the baby leaves my body.

Even over the sound of the storm outside, the baby's cries are loud and I hear Bright Feather laugh low in my ear. "Someone is *very angry* it seems." He lowers us both slowly and carefully to the floor and I sag against him unable to even lift my head it seems to look at the baby. "You did well, little mother," he says and uses his hand to wipe the wetness that is still trickling down my face from the rain and maybe from some sweat, too.

Otter brings me the baby wrapped in soft deerskin and says, "Here, feed this son of yours before we all go deaf!" Bright Feather helps me lift my wet top up over my head and Otter guides the baby to my breast. I jump as his hungry mouth latches on and look at her with shocked eyes at the pain of it as he starts to eat.

She laughs at the look on my face. "They always seem to forget to tell us about that until it's too late. You will adjust and it will become a pleasurable time for both of you very soon."

The baby nurses hungrily, making funny slurping and grunting noises and I shift a little more to get as comfortable as I can having just given birth on the dirt floor of a cave in the midst of a terrible storm. Although I'm soaking wet and sore, I'm at a comfortable temperature for the first time in weeks and weeks and *the baby is born.* I feel a wonderful rush of relief to realize that *I did it, it's done.* Bright Feather's long legs surround us on both sides and his arms encircle us, too. I see his hand reach out and tentatively touch the top of the baby's dark, wet head.

"He has a lot of hair," he finally says in wonder.

"I guess the storm was one way to keep you from worrying about me too much during the birth," I say with a tired smile.

I hear and feel him grunt behind me. "Did you pray about the weather change *and* that I would not fear for you during the birth? You must be careful how you ask these things, I am thinking!" I can hear the relief in his voice about it being done, too.

"Rest," he says to me. "Go to sleep if you can. I will keep you both safe here in my arms." It's the last thing I remember for a while.

I wake up some time later curled on my side, still between Bright Feather's legs. I feel his warm hand on my back and as I sit up I see the baby nestled in his other arm. The look he gives me, wrapped in a smile of wonderment says, *Look what I've got!!* A fire's burning in the center of the cave and the storm is still raging outside. I can see the rain coming down so hard it makes only the closest things something you can barely see. The few trees I see are being whipped back and forth in a wild dance. *How are those in the village?*, I wonder.

Otter's there, and Turtle, too. "Do you think you can stand?" Otter says. "It would be good to try to get you cleaned and cared for now …"

She and Turtle help me to stand, carefully though for the ceiling of the cave's not high enough for even me to stand upright. I can feel the rush of blood and fluids down my legs. We go to the opening of the cave and stand under an overhang and they help me wash as best as I can with the help of the raging storm and a soft deerskin cloth. We lay my skirt out in the rain to be rinsed and I put on a breech cloth - just like the men - wear between my legs and anchor it around my waist. I have brought another skirt that I put on and a short, cool top like the one that still lies wet beside Bright Feather. I smile at them, "I feel better already!" Otter gives me a hug. "You did well, my sister," she says with a big grin. "*You did well!!*"

Turtle looks at us both. "It seems I will be next," and puts her hand on her tiny stomach. "It is good to have sisters to watch and learn from."

Mother

Our son is hungry all the time and impatient with even the slightest wait. He makes his wishes known loudly and with such force that it causes everyone to scurry and get him to me and my breasts fast. Raccoon observes within the first day of his arrival, as the rains and winds make a powerful sound outside the cave, "Which storm is louder, the one outside or the one inside?" and we all laugh. It seems our son has his first name.

"Storm, son of Bear, daughter of One Who Knows, of the Elk Clan, and Bright Feather, son of War Woman of the Wolf clan and Great Elk, chief of The Real People of the Maple Forest," Bright Feather says to him over my shoulder as he wrestles and slurps and gulps his meal, "It seems you are in control of the situation already."

I look down at him nestled in my arms over the course of those first few hours and days in the cave; sleeping, burping, yawning, screaming, and just staring and I fly back in time to when I cared for Eli as a baby in those early times so many years ago. I've always loved babies. I remember being *so excited* when I realized Ma was to have one, and her saying to me more than once, *You are going to be such a great help to me, Elle.* I think, *Little did we both know.* I remember that Eli was a loud baby, too, just like Storm. I can still hear Pa saying, *Hush now, little man, we're all doing the very best we can!* as he yelled and screamed his fury. Pa, Henry and I took turns juggling, rocking, singing and just holding that screaming mass of tears and stink and as I look down at Storm howling at me to *Hurry up and get me fed!* I catch myself getting teary at all the remembrys.

"What's wrong?" Bright Feather asks and I shake my head and sniffle. "Are you in pain? Is there something I can do?"

He looks so worried that I tell him through my quiet sobs about Eli and my remembrances of a time long gone. "Storm has Eli's eyes," I tell him and I must giggle a little through my tears as I add, "and his scream."

Bright Feather smiles and hugs me tight. I tell all of them in the cave how when Eli was first born I remember trying to deal with all the terrible changes in the midst of having a screaming, always hungry, never happy little one to deal with. "Once he settled down with life," I tell them, "he was the sweetest, most loving little one you ever would want to meet. But those first few months just about did us in, Pa and Henry and I." I think about the process of Ma's death and how that has a very shadowy, hard to remember quality about it, compared to all the bright details I remember about Eli: his vivid blue eyes, his stickin' up black hair, how he'd curl his legs up tight to his stomach just before he let loose with screams that would rattle the windows, how at the height of his fury even his fingers would turn bright red but his knuckles would stay white. They all sit there quiet listening to me talk and sniffle.

"I have only one thing I remember when Beaver was born," Bright Feather says finally. "Otter was born when I was about four or five summers I think," he looks at her and she smiles and shrugs, "so that is not clear, but when Beaver was born I think I was close to nine. I remember, after the first few weeks of his crying and settling in, I offered to return him if they could figure out just where to take him." He grunts. "Great Elk told me that I was more trouble than Beaver was and did I think I should have been returned, too?" He reaches down to stroke Storm's hair as he nurses. "That kept me quiet after that, I will tell you."

I sniffle and wipe my nose on my sleeve and manage a tiny smile. "I am glad they didn't return you."

"Me too," he says.

"I have a memory of *you*," Otter says, smiling at Bright Feather, having listened to our talking and remembering. "I was very little and I'd had a terrible dream that really scared me. I remember lying on my mat and whimpering, too afraid to call out even or ask for help. You must have heard me," she says with great tenderness, "for all of a sudden you reached out your hand and I took it. You never said a word, that I remember, you just held my hand and I fell back to sleep at last."

Raccoon speaks up. "I have a memory of Great Elk and War Woman that still haunts me to this day." He glances at Bright Feather. "Do you remember the time with the horses?" and Bright Feather looks very much like he wishes that he could not but does.

"Yes, I remember," he says at last with much regret.

Raccoon looks at all of us seated with him in the cave eager to hear his story that will fill the time. "Deer, Bright Feather and I were out in the woods." He shrugs. "We were *always* out in the woods, hunting, fishing, fighting, running, riding – if we could get ourselves a horse. There was more than one time that we got into a little bit of mischief."

Bright Feather interrupts, "I spent *all* my time trying to keep the two of you from getting *all* of us in trouble." He shakes his head. "Every single day there was some adventure, some plan, some *trouble,* they were planning ..."

Raccoon looks at all of us and then back at Bright Feather. "He was *no fun* I tell you. *Absolutely no fun."* Bright Feather snorts and shakes his head again.

"We had been exploring in the forest and had traveled the better part of the day a pretty fair distance from the village," Raccoon begins with his story, "I cannot remember what we were originally doing, when we heard horses approach and we hid to see who was coming. It was soldiers of all things! Five of them, mounted on horses, in uniform, weapons shining ... We could not believe our eyes! What were they doing in our part of the forest? Why had they invaded our territory? We were all in such a state of excitement."

"*You two* were in a state," Bright Feather feels a need to correct him. "*I* was of the opinion to fade away quiet and go back and tell the village of their presence."

Raccoon ignores Bright Feather and continues. "We followed them for a good mile or so, practicing our stalking. It was the same summer that Beaver was born, was it not?" He asks Bright Feather who nods his head 'yes'. "It was getting to be nightfall and it was Deer who finally suggests that when they set up camp for the night *perhaps* we could take a few of their horses for our own. The idea of having *our own horses* was more than we had ever imagined. We justified that they did not belong on our land, that they were the enemy."

I look at Bright Feather, amazed at the danger and foolhardiness of the idea. "What did you say to them *then?*" He doesn't answer me, but Raccoon does.

"*He* wanted a horse more than the two of us combined, for he saw himself as a great warrior and hunter. But he wasn't much of one *always on foot."*

I look at Bright Feather and he makes a grand show of studying his son's sleeping form in his arms. When he finally looks up at me, he shrugs his shoulders and says, "Bad influence from bad company."

"We waited until cover of darkness," Raccoon said. "Taking the horses was easier than we imagined. We snuck up while the guard was taking a piss and before he could get his pants done up we were on the backs of three of the most magnificent horses you had ever seen and ridden off into the dark night." He shakes his head in remembrance. "It was a grand thrill, was it not my brother?"

Bright Feather looks at him across the glowing fire and is unable to deny it. "Yes, it was, my brother. It was a grand thrill."

"We had already planned out where we would hide the horses and we reached there before first light. We hobbled them, rubbed them down, fed them and then returned to the village like nothing had happened." He grins. "We had two days of the most glorious fun with those horses, did we not?" he says, his eyes dancing with wonderful memories, and I see that even Bright Feather cannot help himself and he nods his head with a dreamy look on his face. "And on the evening of the second day as we returned to the village you can all guess who was seated at the fire with Great Elk, War Woman, and many other leaders of the village."

"The five soldiers," I whisper, and Bright Feather and Raccoon both nod.

"They were on their way to our village all along, part of a regiment that was assigned with scouting out villages of The Real People and recruiting them to fight in another great war that was about to happen with the British. They were not our enemy, they were not trespassing on our land. They were there with the blessings of the leadership of the Real People and it turns out that one of the soldiers was an elected agent from The Real People. Great Elk and many other men from the village agree to join in the fighting for it was against our greatest Indian enemies the Upper Creeks." *Battle of Horseshoe Bend,* I think in wonder.

"They, of course, spoke of the theft of the horses and told of when and where. They had seen nothing specific but suspected that there were three culprits as only three of their five horses had been stolen."

Raccoon laughs. "I can just imagine the expressions on our faces when we see the soldiers as we enter the village. Deer and Bright Feather must return to their hearth," Raccoon gives a wide grin, "which is the *same hearth* where the soldiers are seated."

"I have never been so afraid in all my life," Bright Feather admits. "Poor Deer, had to step forward and converse with the soldiers, being a white boy in an Indian village. He stuttered and stammered and looked like he was ready to just die right there on the spot. War Woman studied us as we stood there. I could feel her eyes boring right into our brains and seeing all the things we had done in the past three days."

"The next morning," Raccoon continues, "we did not know what to do with ourselves. Do we leave like we always do? Do we go to the horses? Do we stay in the village? We are hovering by the river talking, arguing amongst ourselves as to where we should go and what we should do when Great Elk comes and sits on a rock near the river's edge a little ways away from us.

"Now he looks just as casual as could be sitting there in the morning sun on the rock, and yet the three of us knew that there was nothing casual about it."

Bright Feather looks at Raccoon in the dimness of the cave. "Tell them what your brilliant idea was," and Raccoon looks like he would much rather not.

After a pause, Raccoon says, "I went over after a few moments and told him clearly and with great seriousness that if he was wondering or at all worried that we had nothing to do with the theft of those three horses." Otter cannot help herself and collapses into disbelieving laughter.

Quiet Turtle finally speaks up and asks, "What did he say?"

Raccoon grins at her. "Great Elk looked right at me and said, 'Are you speaking of the three horses you have been hiding over the ridge that you've been riding for the past two days?'" Raccoon looks at Bright Feather. "Were we that obvious do you think?"

Bright Feather shrugs his shoulders. "I think that he did not suspect until the soldiers told him of the theft." I can see his eyes smile a bit. "I think he was absolutely sure only after you spoke to him and told him for sure that we had not done it." I see it is Turtle's turn to stifle a giggle.

Raccoon laughs. "It was Deer that comes forward and says, 'What do we do, Father?' and Great Elk looked at him and said, 'Why, tell the truth, son. Always tell the truth.'

"We went and got the horses and brought them into camp to the soldiers. They were busy sitting in council talking and making plans for the coming weeks. We walked the horses up to them and just stood there not knowing what to do. War Woman and Great Elk did not say a thing. The soldiers were very stern with us. They talked at length about the penalties for horse theft."

"What were they?" Otter asks, for Raccoon doesn't say.

"Hanging," Bright Feather says matter of fact. He looks at Raccoon. "War Woman and Great Elk must have spoken with the soldiers in preparation, do you not think?"

Raccoon shrugs. "All I know was that I never felt inclined to take anything that was not mine ever again.

"When the soldiers left, the three of us were summoned to council and we had to sit before all the village elders and explain ourselves. War Woman said to the three of us, 'Many unhappy shadows will happen in your life that will cause you trouble and strife. You should spend your days trying to *prevent* making unnecessary shadows, not causing more. Acquiring something through honest hard work will always mean more than acquiring something through theft and deception.'"

Bright Feather snorts. "Then we were told that we were responsible for *caring* for all of the horses in camp for the rest of the summer *but forbidden to ride any.*"

"And *I*," Raccoon said, "was required to sit at council each night for the entire summer and listen to *wise and honest words* so that I would learn to speak them myself." He looks at Bright Feather. "Bright Feather and Deer escaped that one because I was the one who had lied to Great Elk."

As the storm outside continues with no sign of stopping, the Storm inside wakes and asks to be fed. Otter and Turtle begin making preparations for the brief evening meal we will share together from what we have carried in our baskets. As they work, we hear Turtle say very quietly, "I have no memories of the woman who gave birth to me nor do I even remember what my first tribe or village was." She looks at Otter, Raccoon and me. "Do you know how I came to be in this village?"

It's something I've puzzled over at times. I remember the night in which I stood in the council circle, *so long ago now it seems!*, unable to understand the language, battered and bruised from my treatment with Weasel, still a pitiful white girl slave. I remember Great Elk speaking with One Who Knows and Weasel and seeing Turtle for the first time and knowing just by the look in her eyes, that she was a slave captive just like me. "I remember the night that you were given to One Who Knows and I was given to Bright Feather," I say to her.

She looks at Bright Feather and he looks back at her. "I was part of the goods you brought back from Deer's trading post just that day, was I not?" He looks at her with his Indian face and I can't see anything.

"My earliest memories are of hunger and fear," she begins as we all settle down to eat our meal and the storm outside rages while the Storm inside gulps and gurgles contentedly. "I have been a slave most of my life and I have never known real freedom until these past few months since I have become the mate of Red Fox and the daughter of One Who Knows."

She looks at Raccoon and then Bright Feather, "The unhappy shadows that War Woman spoke to you of were so great at one point in my life that I did not know that there was such a thing as a sun." She includes all of us as she says, "The earliest family I remember that owned me, Indians like myself, told me that my birth mother gave me to them in trade for an amount of liquor." She looks at each of us, shrugs and says, "I believe that to be true for they had no reason to lie to me."

"Deer offered to take me in trade for some goods at the trading post from my last owners. I think he took pity on me." When he saw Turtle, I know Deer was thinking of Raven, One Who Knows' daughter that was sold into slavery by her husband Weasel. "Bright Feather was there trading and Deer had me travel back to this village with him when he left." She smiles a sweet, shy smile. "One Who Knows was easy to live with compared to some of the others I have had to suffer with in my past." She sighs. "And now look at me!" and she pats her growing belly. She looks at me for she knows that me - of all of us - can understand her next words. "Life can be *so strange*, can it not?"

"You were not brought back to this village as a purchased slave," Bright Feather says quietly but firmly. "I brought you back to this village at Deer's request for the trading post was certainly no place for you. He purchased you to gain your freedom from the family you were with, but you were *never* brought here to continue your slavery. It made sense for you to go and live with One Who Knows and help her and learn our ways as you were both in need of what the other had to give." *I never knew*, I think in wonder as I look first at Turtle and then at my husband.

"I owe Deer my life, I know," Turtle says so quietly you can barely hear her. "I owe One Who Knows my gratitude." She looks at all of us. "And I owe all of you my support and strength and love."

The storm's unlike anyone in the cave can remember. It rains and rains and rains for two full days and nights and all of us work to keep the worry out of the cave about those who have stayed in the village for there's nothing we can do. I worry for Willow, too, although Bright Feather assures me that the horses will be fine. On the morning of the third day as the rain slows down to just a drizzle, all of us cannot wait to get out of the cave and stand and stretch. Only Little Bird has had any fun with the adventure, playing with all of the adults and dancing in the mouth of the cave among the drips that fall from the overhang and in the puddles that collect there, too.

Having finally seen a glimpse of the sun peeking through the breaking clouds, everyone's more than ready to travel back to the village. Traveling down from the cave with our remaining supplies, and me with the comfortable weight of Storm in his cradleboard on my back, we're unprepared for the destruction we see as we travel down out of the mouth of the cave. Massive trees are uprooted and lay on the forest floor as if some giant has come and had fun for the day tearing them up and dropping them where ever he chose. The horses are nowhere to be seen, however, all agree that they did not expect them to be where they had been hastily left. "They will have traveled back to the village, I suspect," Bright Feather tells me.

When we reach the place we call home, we stand at the edge of what was once Great Elk's village and there's not one hut standing. Turtle beside me whimpers in fear and we both take the other's hand for comfort.

Raccoon and Bright Feather begin searching the destruction looking for signs of those who stayed behind. We're unsure how many have truly stayed in the end and how many went to the caves. Bright Feather and Raccoon search each and every hearth and destroyed hut calling and searching but not one person is found dead or alive. Otter, Turtle and I busy ourselves with starting a fire and then searching through our respective home sites looking for things worth salvaging.

Gradually people return and it's with shouts of relief and gladness that each is welcomed. Slowly, the village comes back to life with fires and sounds and smells. By nightfall, as the village gathers at the council circle, the only ones missing, besides Red Fox and the two braves who have traveled south to Dark Cloud's village are Great Elk, One Who Knows, and War Woman.

That night, as we sleep under the stars, Bright Feather, Storm and I, we worry about those that are missing even as we are thankful for what we do have. It's not until the following night after a full day of working to rebuild shelters, gather crops that can be saved and retrieve belongings scattered throughout the forest do Great Elk, One Who Knows, and War Woman walk casually into the midst of us.

They seem as glad to see us as we are to see them, but each within his or her own style. War Woman informs Otter and me that the moment we rode out for the caves, One Who Knows looked at her and said, "What are we waiting for, let us go!!"

War Woman said, "I looked at her puzzled and said, 'I thought you did not wish to go to the caves …' She looked at me with great impatience and said, 'I didn't want to go to a cave that had two tiny children, two crabby pregnant women, and two know-it-all men. If you had listened carefully, you would have known that I *never* said that I did not want to go to the shelter of a cave, it was just a specific one I refused.'" War Woman chuckles in remembrance. "At our hearth was her basket already packed, which she carried herself to a cave a fair hike from here. It was a bit wet but we managed just fine."

One Who Knows, after examining her hearth and inspecting the damage of her precious herbs, comes to examine her grandson. She holds him tenderly in her arms and over the course of long moments counts his toes and fingers, examines his belly for all the proper signs of healing and even touches and manipulates his privates. She looks up at Bright Feather and me with the same fierce look everyone's familiar with and opens her mouth to make a flip comment, but instead seems frozen for a moment unable to speak. Slowly her mouth closes and she takes a great swallow as we watch in great amazement as the tears fill her eyes and spill over her wrinkled old cheeks. When she finally finds words to speak, all she can manage is, "He is magnificent…" while she goes back to looking at him, touching the curve of his nose and the slope of his forehead.

"We will call him Storm *Eli*," I hear Bright Feather say to One Who Knows as he gives me a sweet look and it's my turn to join her at a little bit of crying.

At council that night, with a full village present, we discuss the damage of the storm and how it will affect us this winter. Crops were either already harvested or ready to be. Many have been working all day to salvage those that were damaged in storage and those that are still in the field and can be retrieved. We have lost much, but have managed to save much, too. Not all the horses have been found, including Companion and Willow, but many have been and all the dogs have returned. I try not to worry as no one else seems to. Tomorrow, Bright Feather promises me that he will search for the rest of the horses with the other men.

A new location is discussed for the village before all of the rebuilding is done. I discover that every seven years the village is relocated to give the land a chance to regenerate and recover from our presence. Another spot someone remembers from many years ago is talked about. In fact, this village that I have always known as my Indian home is the location that the village moved to only a few summers before my capture. It's decided that it makes wise sense to make the most of our circumstances and start fresh at an altogether new place.

The place where we will travel to I discover is where One Who Knows was actually born and many in the village call it "One Who Knows' Place". I'll always think of this spot I've known for these years as "Storm's Place" I realize as we pack the next day in preparation to leave. I look up to see Bright Feather coming out of the woods. He is leading Companion and one other horse and I am disappointed to see no Willow. My face must show my concern for as he comes close to me, he touches my cheek and says, "Can you whistle?"

I don't have time to though as Raccoon emerges from the woods behind him with Willow and three other horses. She has a great gash on her leg and is favoring it. One Who Knows comes and helps us as we clean it and dress it with herbs and salve that she carries in her bag. The smell of the ointment reminds me of the time after Dark Cloud's village. "You cannot ride her until this heals," One Who Knows says and I nod my head.

"Will she be all right?" I ask as I pet her muzzle and smell her good horse smell.

"She will be the first horse that Storm will ride on," she assures me.

The new village location's along the same river that I have always lived nearby since my time with The Real People, just a two days easy hike east and north a bit. I watch these people, *my people*, and realize as I watch them laughing and talking and singing as we travel why I have felt so quickly a part of them. In just a matter of days, the entire destruction of their village has been turned around as a new adventure and an exciting new beginning. I think about Bright Feather's words to me at a time that seems so long ago, *You are someone who despite all the things that have happened to you can still find joy in life.* And I realize, *my people are like that, too.*

We stretch out throughout the forest as we hike, an amazing mix of tall, short, young, old, loud, quiet, and I feel a wonderful sense of belonging and happiness as I feel Storm give a contented sigh behind me in his cradleboard. "Shadows only show when the sun is so bright," I say to myself and *of course* who's nearby to hear me talking to myself but Raccoon.

"Does motherhood make you talk to yourself?" he asks with a great grin on his face.

"No," I say flip like, "but the search for smart company does sometimes."

"Hmm," he says and we fall into easy step. He is carrying an enormous pack on his back as well as leading two horses piled high with things. No one rides, for the horses are too important to carry things.

"Do you know much of the place we travel to?" I ask him and he nods his head yes.

"I have never lived there, that I remember anyway, but it is an area that I have hunted and it is well known in our history."

"Tell me!" I say, eager to hear a story.

"This river," he points to the one that I have drunk from, bathed in, and that Otter has given birth in, "that we have lived by for so long we simply call '*The River That We Are Always By*' flows from *The Ambush Place* and it's beginning headwaters are called *Where The Spaniard Is In The Water.*"

He grins at me when I laugh at the names. "We travel closer towards *The Ambush Place* and I think that is good for us, given what we fear is coming in the future." I feel the laughs grow quiet in my throat all of a sudden, well aware of where we have come from and where we head to.

"The Ambush Place is named in memory of a battle between The Real People and The Shawnee which took place long ago." I think of Deer and his naming of *the five civilized tribes* and I know that the *Shawnee* were not listed as one of them. "It was a tremendous battle. The Shawnee had sent a large party to invade our territory and The Real People had hidden along the gap which has many large rocks and caves as well as being heavily forested." He smiles at me, but it's a different smile from his teasing one and I feel the goose skin creep up my arms and through my scalp for its fierceness. "The Real People killed every single Shawnee *except one.*"

"Why did one survive?" I ask, foolish in the ways of war.

"Why to go and tell his people of the defeat, the fear, and the massacre, of course," he says matter of fact and I think, *oh, of course.*

"What does the Spaniard in the water have to do with things?" I ask.

"Nothing, with this story," Raccoon says. "But The Ambush Place has been successful in more than one battle you see. The Spaniards were the first whites to arrive, before the British, before the French. Stories tell of them arriving in great ships, with great armor, and with great greed. They wanted nothing but *gold*, something that we did not have, but they did not believe us and they enslaved many unsuspecting Real People – and others I suspect – to look for this gold. They brought sickness and death with them in great numbers and the only good Spaniard I have ever heard of was *a dead one.*"

We walk through the woods for a bit in silence and I think, Is there any place and any people that has only happiness and joy in their lives?

"The Ambush Place," Raccoon says, "was a place that the Spaniards found death from The Real People just as the Shawnees did. One Spaniard in particular found death in the water at the base of the gap where The River That We Are Always By finds its beginnings. *A good place for a Spaniard,"* he grins at me with his sinister smile and I think, *I am glad you consider me your sister!*

At the new spot, each family chooses a hearth spot that suits them. Great Elk and War Woman's hearth are at the center for it'll once again be the spot for council meetings and all other hearths fan out from there. I remember my first impression of the village, arriving as a captive slave with Weasel and thinking how the village looked like a great wagon wheel. It's decided that a large hut will be built with Raccoon, Otter, Little Bird, Squirrel, Bright Feather, Storm, Turtle, Red Fox, and myself in one as a true extended family. It makes much sense as Red Fox is still not back from his travels south to Dark Cloud's village and Bright Feather and Raccoon can work quickly and efficiently together to construct our new hut.

Otter, Turtle and I go to find One Who Knows. Both Bright Feather and Raccoon know that we go to ask her to set up her hearth with us, although I must stifle a giggle at the pained look that Raccoon wears as a result.

"You do the talking," Otter says to me and Turtle nods her head vigorously.

"But you have lived longer with her!" I say to Turtle, unwilling to bear the burden and suffer the probable scars of the conversation to come.

Turtle says as she shakes her head 'no', "You are the *only one in the village* that speaks to her as you do and that she seems to still tolerate in the process." "We did very well living together as long as we did because I am *quiet and cooperative and unassuming.*"

Otter giggles. "You are many things, Bear, but you are *not any of those.*"

One Who Knows is sitting at War Woman and Great Elk's hut tending the fire. She's calm and seemingly unconcerned with the noise and activity around her as trees are cut down and stripped of branches, as holes are dug for poles, as ground is cleared and hearth spots are staked out. There's a peaceful, yet productive feeling throughout the area as everyone works hard to get things the way they need to be.

We sit with her and wait for her to look up and acknowledge us, none of us brave enough to start the fight. She gradually raises her eyes and looks at each one of us and then snorts in disgust at us. "What a group," we hear her murmur under her breath as she goes back to preparing a meal.

"You seem well from the traveling, Mother," I begin, deciding at some point that the silence around the fire has become more tense then the coming conversation. She ignores me and my foolish talking.

"We would have you live with us, Mother, in our hut. All three families plan to be together and your daughters would have their Mother live with them." She stops her meal preparations to look at each one of us for moments. She studies our faces and I feel her, as she stares into my eyes, probe into my head to read my thoughts. It's a most disturbing feeling.

"All right," she says, at last and now it's time for the three of us to sit there stunned at the ease of it all. I can't see the twinkle of mischief in her eyes, but I can just imagine it as she says, "But first, send Raccoon and Bright Feather to convince me as well," and then she looks up at us and she smiles her wicked smile and I have to laugh.

"Very well, Mother," I say as we stand to go. "We will send them to speak with you as well."

Bright Feather's silent at the prospect of going to see One Who Knows and invite her to live at our new hearth, but Raccoon is beside himself. "Why? Why must we go and invite her when you have already done that? She will take one look at my face and know that I am not excited about the prospect of living with her sharp tongue cutting me to pieces at every turn."

"Perhaps," I hear myself say, "she is not excited about the prospect of living with your teasing tongue and all it's joking comments at every turn. I, for one, think it will be quite fun to watch the two of you over the long winter that is to come."

"Me, too," says Turtle and Otter in between giggles. Bright Feather grunts.

In the end, a compromise of sorts is reached between One Who Knows and the men that pleases everyone. One Who Knows will have her single hut built right next to our large family one. That way she will not have to suffer the hands of curious children disturbing her herbs, the constant wit of Raccoon's tongue and yet will still be part of the everyday life of our hearth.

We find that we work well together as a group to establish a home hearth and begin the seemingly endless preparations for the winter that will come all too quickly.

Within those first two weeks after our arrival at our new village site of *One Who Knows' Place* in the Maple Forest, our village settles in and falls into the rhythm familiar to us all. As the second week comes to a close and we adjust to the changes of living in a large family hut, Bright Feather and Raccoon put the finishing touches on our shelter. Turtle, Otter with Squirrel on her back, me with Storm riding happily behind me and Little Bird running through the woods in front of us, head out into the forest to collect wood, late berries, nuts and herbs. We're talking and laughing and enjoying the beautiful early fall day when we all stop and listen to the oddest sound we have ever heard. Little Bird comes and holds Turtle's hand as the sound gets closer and closer to us and a real fear begins to go through the group.

"What is it? Do I hear *bells*?" says Otter to me at last as we listen and listen. It's a strange but oddly familiar sound and I look at Turtle who seems to mirror the same look that I think must be on my face.

"I think it is *cows*," I say at last, disbelieving even as I say it.

"I think *goats*, too," says Turtle more familiar with the ways of things outside this village than Otter is.

And out of the brush and through the trees burst not one, not two, but *five* large cows, mooing and clanking from the bells around their necks. The cows are followed by a grinning Deer, and his oldest son, James, *Red Bird*, and Eliza, *Sleeping Rabbit*, all mounted on horses. Behind Deer, roped, is an enormous bull, horns and nose ring included. Eliza and James have behind them six goats, five females and one male each with their own bells as well. Five more pack horses follow behind loaded down with all manner of things and I can hear the hysterical angry squawks from penned chickens. The sound's deafening in contrast to the earlier silence of the forest: animals, bells, shouts of greetings, Storm's inconvenient sudden screams of hunger, and over all of it, Eliza *Sleeping Rabbit's* questions. But it's wonderful just the same.

"What Ho!" Deer shouts, surprised to see us this far east and I can see the delight on his face as he sees the baby board strapped to my back. I'm not so sure he's pleased to hear the screams anymore then any of the rest of us are, but he's polite enough not to say. Over all the noise, he shouts to me, "It seems that there is a new mother in the village, eh?" And I nod, smile and turn my back so he can see the screaming mass of fury attached to my back. "Powerful voice," he says by way of a compliment, I suspect.

In the end, Turtle stays with me, Storm and Eliza, or *Sleeping Rabbit,* we are reminded to call her, while Otter, Squirrel, Little Bird – in front of Deer on his horse, James, and all the animals travel on to the village. I nurse Storm and answer Sleeping Rabbit's many questions and get answers to a few myself. Turtle, ever silent, smiles at me over Sleeping Rabbit's head, happy to listen to all the chatter.

I learn that the storm delayed their arrival by a good two weeks, but everyone recognizes how fortunate it is that the storm came *before* rather then *during* their trek here. The cows and goats were purchased with monies that Deer has secured from the tribal funds he has been able to get a share of.

"Pa thought that it might be a good source of food and income to the village and that was *before* the storm! We figure, if your supplies were destroyed in the storm, the worst thing you can do is eat all of the animals before the spring! Pa says that Red Bird and I can stay for a few weeks and help you care for the animals until you get accustomed to them in the village."

She asks questions about the baby and is thrilled with the offer of wearing the baby board on the side of her horse as we make our way back to the village. I attach it to her saddle and within moments, Storm's fast asleep with a full belly rocked to sleep by the motion of the horse's movements.

As we enter the village, noisy with shouted greetings and cows and goats and chicken's squawking and bells, I hear even more loud noise as Turtle screams and runs from my side. She throws herself into the arms of Red Fox and he lifts her high with shouts of delight and welcome. I think there will be a party tonight!

Red Fox, and the two braves he traveled with to Dark Cloud's village, Young Wolf and Spring Frog return with one more familiar face that I'm sure I'm not the only one surprised to see. It's Beaver, handsome and fierce, looking much the way he did when we last saw him except for the white man's rifle I see added to his collection of weapons on him and his horse. *It's powerful amazing*, I think to myself, *that they all arrive at the same time to talk about the same concerns. How different will their ideas be this time?*

It's decided that no difficult discussions will be spoken of this first night when *all sons* are present to celebrate the end of the summer and the start of the fall. A little bit late, and without the usual bounty of harvested crops, The Green Corn Ceremony is still one of the highlights of the year. As we gather around the fire, enjoying family and full bellies, War Woman rises to tell the story.

"Grandmother Selu was raising a small boy," she begins as the fire crackles and Storm and Squirrel slurp the last of the evening's food. "His parents were away on a long trip that took them far away from these smoky blue mountains for many moons. Each day, the Little Boy went into the planting field as Grandmother prepared the hard ground to plant corn, beans, and squash. She would rake the ground with a stick to soften it. Sometimes she would call to the worms in the earth to be helpers for the seeds to rest in soft soil for growing. Little Boy would watch her do the medicine magic as she sang an old song, one that had been lost with the passing of the moons. Each evening they went back to their hearth, where she boiled or roasted corn for the evening meal.

"Often Little Boy went to gather kindling for the fire while Grandmother Selu said that she had to go to the corn basket for corn to cook. She always said, 'Little Boy, you gather the wood for the fire, and I will collect the corn from the storage basket.' He was told to stay away from the basket where the corn was kept because of a snake that fed on fallen corn around the basket. It seemed strange to him that he never saw Grandmother Selu carry corn from the field to the storage basket, but she always had beans in a basket and squash from the planning field. She always brought the corn back to their hearth in a long apron, which she then wore over her dress while she prepared the food for their evening meal.

"One day, near the time when the Sun was at rest and darkness was near, Little Boy decided to follow Grandmother Selu and hid in the high bushes near the storage basket. To his amazement, she did not even open the basket but just rubbed her hands as she held the apron open. Golden yellow corn would appear in her apron! Little Boy was so surprised that he immediately said, 'Grandmother Selu, how did you do that?'

"Startled, she turned to him with a look of stars in her eyes and said that now she would have to go away forever. He suddenly felt sad. Grandmother Selu fixed the corn for their evening meal, and later she held him, explaining that some things are not to be seen. The next morning, when Little Boy awoke to the bright morning light, his aunt was there to stay with him. Grandmother Selu was never to be seen again, but in the fields were rows and rows of golden yellow corn ready to be picked from the large stalks.

"As Little Boy harvested the corn, he sang the song he remembered hearing her sing as she planted the corn, which The Real People call *Selu*.

"Corn is considered sacred by The Real People," War Woman says to those of us sitting silent and listening. "Life is focused on survival and this Green Corn Ceremony celebrates and gives thanks for this food of life. We remember Grandmother Selu, who gave her life for the sons and daughters of The Real People to have corn for survival, as long as they worked diligently to plant and grow corn in the fields each summer."

She raises her arms and sings,

"O Great One,
Thank you for the Spirit of the Wind,
It stirs our spirit and sends messages to our hearts.
I thank you for the spirit of Mother Earth,
As I listen to the drum beat,
I hear the heart beat that gives us life.

O Great One,
I thank you for the Ancestors and the teachings,
That guide our way of life here on Mother Earth.
I will forever hold sacred the pipe of peace,
And I will share the tobacco for prayer,
As I give thanks to the elders and the Ancient Fire.

O Great One,
I give thanks to the way of The Real People. "[28]

I look down at Storm sleeping in my arms, a dribble of milk caught in the pool of his mouth against his fat cheek, and I think, *I am a mother now.* Will I ever be a grandmother? I wonder. I look at One Who Knows and War Woman and Otter. I look at Turtle snuggled close to Red Fox, so happy to have him home. I look at the faces of the women that sit around this circle, young and old, and I am proud to be a part of this powerful group of women.

The next night around the Council fire, celebration takes a distant place as we must discuss the realities of the white and red worlds that press at our borders and remind me that *our garden walled round* has walls made of only words and paper.

Great Elk begins the discussions expressing pleasure to have all of his sons present and tells how all of us are eager to hear what news there is to hear, *good or bad*. He expresses his hope that we will gain strength from the different things we know and the different opinions we share and the different paths we walk. He asks Red Fox to speak first.

Red Fox smiles shyly at the group but speaks with confidence. "I was in Dark Cloud's village much longer than we thought I would be. When I first arrived, I was warmly welcomed and they were happy to hear the news that I brought." He smiles and looks at Deer, Bright Feather and me. "It is amazing that this small village, separated from so much of the world seems often to be at the front of the line when it comes to news and information from the outside world. That is a good thing, of that I am certain.

"My words were greatly doubted when I told them of Deer and Bear's discoveries north. Beaver will confirm their disbelief, just as he will confirm *his belief* in the truth of my words." It's a respectful and wise move, I see, that Red Fox has done, bringing Beaver into the discussion of the circle so early by the mention of his name.

"Red Fox speaks the truth," Beaver says, "his words were listened to, but not believed by anyone but me. At first."

Red Fox continued. "Within the first week, however, messengers from Washington, those who were present, I imagine, for the very vote that Deer was present for and that Bright Feather and Bear told us of, arrived at the village and reported things just as I had told them." He looks sad. "Then they believed me."

Red Fox looks at Great Elk, War Woman, and says with great concern in his voice, "There is great controversy within the leadership of The Nation of The Real People. This division has reached such a level of hatred that there are those of one position who wish the deaths of those who take the opposite position. It can only mean disaster for all of The

Real People." He seems at a loss for words and looks at Beaver for help. "Again, Beaver will confirm my words and add to them."

Beaver speaks. "I have returned to this village with Red Fox, for many reasons. First, I am eager to see my brothers and sisters. I wish to see that you are all well and assure you that I, too, am in good health. I have taken a mate and am the proud father of a strong son born at the start of this summer." There are happy murmurs that float around the circle, in and out of the dark and light of the fire. I think, *I hope you have found happiness there, Beaver.*

"I have also returned to this village to share with you what I have learned and now know as fact about The Nation of The Real People. Red Fox has witnessed these things. I have *lived* with them." He looks at Red Fox and then Great Elk. "May I have permission to speak and tell you these things?" Both men nod.

"What Deer has told us in times past of The Nation of The Real People is all true. Dark Cloud, seeks very much to run his village and The Nation like the white government with red skin. I cannot discredit anything that Deer has said and I must give my apologies before this council for any insult I may have caused him in my anger and behavior at the last time I sat here in this council circle." Deer nods his head, Beaver's apology is accepted. I can see approval on Great Elk, War Woman, and One Who Knows' faces as well.

"What is interesting to know, however," Beaver continues, "is that Dark Cloud is not the *elected* leader of The Nation of The Real People. He holds great power and is well thought of by some, especially within the walls of the white government in Washington, but within the hearths of those who call themselves The Nation of The Real People, he is trusted and considered a leader by only a small few. Within the white world, he calls himself *Major Ridge* – a military title to commemorate his great past battle victories - and he has embraced so much of the white world and its ways and beliefs that few feel that he operates any longer for the *best interests of The Nation of The Real People.*

"Within The Nation of The Real People, the *chosen leader*, the one who has been elected within the accepted ways of the tribe now is *John Ross.*" He looks at War Woman and One Who Knows, "No women are allowed to be considered or to cast a vote. He is part white to look at but he has a passion for the welfare of The Real People that makes him full red. Between these two men - Major Ridge and John Ross - is such a fierce hatred that only death would be a satisfactory end. Both of these men, reside in this village, we have known to be Dark Cloud's for these many years, and what is now called, New Echota, Georgia by the whites." Beaver looks at me. "It would seem, during your time in Great Elk's village, that John Ross was in Washington trying to secure treaty promised monies, lands, and supplies. That is why you never met him." I nod. *Would John Ross' presence have made a difference for me during my time there?* I wonder. I will never know.

Great Elk speaks. "We know much of Dark Cloud, tell us of this John Ross."

Beaver looks across at Deer. "Do you know of him?"

Deer nods, "I have met him," is all he will say and I think that he waits carefully for his turn and also to hear what Beaver will say.

"He is a good leader," Beaver finally says. "I respect him, too, and feel that if The Real People are going to survive and keep *any* of their Old Ways and tribal lands, it is only John Ross who will make sure it happens. It is difficult to fight a battle *and win* when you have two powerful enemies to watch, however, and the United States Government and *Major Ridge* are about as powerful as they can be."

Beaver looks at me again. "You were right about the village. It is nothing like it is here. I remember you saying that *nothing is as it seems* and that is a good description." He looks at the rest of the council. "No one's words are to be taken as they are said, no one's actions are to be accepted as they appear."

"Have you come home to us here in The Maple Forest, then?" War Woman asks him.

"My mother," he says with great respect, "it is good to see you and hear your voice these past two days. But I must tell you no, that I will return to New Echota. I feel a responsibility there. I believe that my purpose still lies with The Nation of The Real People and the struggles they face.

"I hope that my presence will help John Ross and will hinder Dark Cloud. I have left my mate and family to travel here to make certain that The Real People of The Maple Forest know the truth of things.

"I wish that the difficulties you have heard spoken here in this circle - between the United States Government and two men who would be leaders of The Real People - were the only problems that we face, but that is not true. Besides this United States Government law that seeks to force all of us west, that I am sure Deer will tell us of in detail, there is another battle that must be fought that causes just as great concern. You must understand that this is as great a threat as any other. The whites of the state of Georgia, on which some of The Real People's land rests, have become greedy. Many of these whites are in positions to make laws of their own that also greatly affect us. Already they have passed laws that make it illegal for The Real People to make agreements with whites and speak in their council meetings concerning grievances. The Real People are helpless against their greed and violence.

"Things that have been promised in past treaties regarding land rights and protection have already been revoked. White settlers have invaded hearths and villages of The Real People and stolen their land and their homes and possessions. With these new laws there is *nothing* that can be done by The Nation of The Real People. Although the state, North Carolina, that The Maple Forest rests in does not have laws such as those that Georgia has made, I fear that soon it will.

"I return to New Echota because I must protect my family. I return because I must fight for the rights of my people. I return because *it is my duty.*"

Bright Feather asks Beaver, "Do you still intend to fight with weapons other than words?"

Beaver does not answer his brother right away. The two men stare at each other across the council fire's flickering flames for long moments. Finally, Beaver says very carefully, "I will fight with *everything I can.* There are many who think the same as I do."

When will things change? I think about the greedy whites and I think about the rifle I saw strapped to Beaver's saddle. The battle for land and things never, ever seems to end.

It is Beaver who looks at Deer. "Tell us what you agree with and disagree with in regard to what I have said."

Deer shrugs. "That is easy to do. I agree with everything you have said up until your last statement. I still cannot agree with you that The Real People will ever be able to succeed with violence. The time for guns and battles and killing is long past. You may kill a few whites and have a moment's glory in the feel of sweet revenge, but you have not been to Washington, you have not been to some of the forts that I have been to and seen the might and strength that sits lazily in the summer sun like a sleeping panther. Any white blood you shed will cause more sorrow, death, and destruction than you could ever imagine for all of those who call themselves The Real People."

Deer looks at Beaver and then at those around the council circle. "May I speak now?"

"We have waited many weeks to hear what you have to tell us, Deer," War Woman says with one of her fierce, unblinking looks.

"I assume that Bright Feather and Bear have told you what I have told them about Washington. I know that Bear will have described to you Fort Winston that is being built." Those around the council nod their heads.

Deer sighs. "I agree with Beaver about John Ross. He is a good man and The Nation of The Real People could have no better leader. Unfortunately, it is the thoughts and beliefs of Dark Cloud, also known as Major Ridge, that are the way of things in Washington and what they want to hear.

"Washington is an interesting place," he says slowly, seeming to struggle to find the right words to paint the best picture. "It is a place that, like it or not, holds great power even right here in this council circle. To travel there and walk the wide streets and see the grand buildings, you begin to understand the forces that came together to create it. Here is what you must understand about the white world in general and Washington in particular: you are only powerful in Washington if you can find someone who will listen to you who is a little bit more powerful than you are. And *that* someone's power is simply measured by who with more power will listen to them. John Ross and Major Ridge are both powerful within The Real People. But it is Major Ridge, I fear, who in the end will find the open doors into the President's office; the place that holds the greatest authority.

He makes eye contact with many of those around the council circle. "Over eleven years ago you made the decision to separate yourselves from The Nation of The Real People and request citizenship with the United States of America in the state of North Carolina. You did this not to choose a side, but to achieve the right to remain *separate and apart* and live the way you have always wanted to live. *I still think it was the right decision.* Now, more than ever, you must seek to separate yourselves from The Real People who look to John Ross *or* Dark Cloud as leaders."

Deer looks at Beaver across the fire with great sadness. "I fear that you will get your fight and that many lives will be lost. And after the fight is over, those of you that are left alive will be picked up and carted across the Mississippi River to the new lands you are to live on *whether you like it or not.* There is not any doubt in my mind that those of you that claim to be an Indian tribe east of the Mississippi River, whether you are Cherokee,

Choctaw, Chickasaw, Creek or Seminole will not have a tree to claim your own in a few short years time.

"For those of you here in the Maple Forest, you too must prepare as if for war. You must live your life as you have always done, preparing for winter and hunting and surviving. But in addition, I must encourage you to begin to make preparations to go into hiding. Gather supplies, stock up on things that may be stored and kept for future needs. I fear that as the hostilities grow between The Nation of The Real People and The United States Government, many will be unable to distinguish – at first glance – the differences within this village and any other Indian village. *That is my job to do* as your agent and your son. There is a time coming of great danger and fear and hardship that I will do my best to ease as much as I possibly can."

He laughs a laugh that holds no humor. "That is why I have brought you these animals. We cannot always rely on the success of your hunts anymore. You cannot risk a lean winter that will weaken you and put you at any further risk. You must embrace some of these white customs for the sake of survival as an investment in the future. You must learn to care for these cattle, chickens and goats as they will help you survive. Butcher them if you must for food or raise them to sell for profit."

Deer looks at me. "Bear will know how to care for them." He smiles at me. "Do you still remember?" And I nod. "She will show you how to get products from them and how to prepare them should you decide to eat them for survival. You must begin to stock pile supplies should you need to leave this village in haste and you must choose and prepare safe places to hide." He looks so fearful for a moment. "I know that time will come, I just cannot tell how soon.

"I have heard of the laws that Georgia has passed." He looks at Beaver. "I heard of those laws when I was in *Washington*, and I know for a fact that they will not be stopped by the President or the United States Government there. The mind of the State of Georgia is the same mind that is in Washington."

To all of us around the circle, he says, "I am hopeful that North Carolina, who recognized the promises made in the Treaty of 1819, acknowledged their mistakes in not keeping the designated land available for you, honored their responsibilities and have paid out real cash money in reparation will not follow in those sorry footsteps made by the state of Georgia. But we cannot be careless, even for a moment.

"There are important meetings to come. Those that are held in Washington, I will be a part of. But those that are held in Dark Cloud's village in New Echota, Georgia, at the place that is considered the capital of The Nation of The Real People you must attend." He looks directly at Great Elk and War Woman. "Not all of you, but a strong representation of this village. There are some that sit around this council circle," he looks at me and, briefly, at Bright Feather, that speak the languages of both the white and the red world. Those people are your strongest warriors now. You must establish your presence; do not let *anyone* make decisions about this village without your say so."

Deer looks at each and every face around the council fire and then says, "I have finished speaking."

Finally, Beaver speaks. "Deer and I may disagree over the course of action that is best taken, however, we are both unified in our concern over the welfare of this village. When I last spoke in this council, it was with anger that I now regret. It was important for me to return to you and establish once and for all with this council that whatever we both decide and whatever direction that we both travel, our goals will always be identical: the safety and preservation of The Real People of The Maple Forest. Perhaps between both of these different paths, we may be successful in the end. I wish only harmony between us and will not leave again until I am certain that I have achieved that."

Deer leaves within a few days needing to get back to the trading post but, as Sleeping Rabbit has told us, leaves both of his children behind to help with the care of the new animals for those first few weeks. Things get busier still as work has begun on a pen to corral the bull, while the cows are left to wander the village and the nearby forest and fields. We grow accustomed to the clank of the bells, although One Who Knows has some choice words about the racket on more than one occasion. The goats must also be penned for they seem inclined to eat just about anything and James worries that they'll not see the end of the first week before they are all killed one after another by the furious villagers. The chickens set up roost in all manner of places throughout the village.

Beaver stays in the village with us for two full weeks, well into the start of fall. He visits each hearth and helps build shelters and hunt to replenish our winter's stock. He's as serious and strong about what's the right path for The Real People as he always has been and yet he seems to carry a new purpose as well. It's almost as if, I tell Bright Feather in the privacy of the night as we snuggle together in our corner of our new large hut, that he's been searching all his life for something he knows he *must find* and he's finally found it. While he still talks of battles and weapons and violence, and seems committed to achieve the path he feels is right *at all costs,* he seems more content with the way of things. I wonder out loud if it's maybe because he has found more like-minded people like him for support. Maybe it's because he's closer to the action and can see more clearly what must be done. Maybe it's because he's finally decided just what course of action he must take and is actually doing it.

Bright Feather nuzzles my neck and offers another reason. "Maybe," he says as he causes shivers to run up and down my spine, "he has found a good woman to love at last."

I'm not inclined to disagree with him at the moment.

Fall rolls into winter and I'm happy for the fierce breath of the season that will slow down white man and red man alike in all this talk of land and laws and who's right and who's wrong. Winter rolls into spring and I'm pressed down by the heavy rains that are like tears of a worried mother about her children. The harmony that's so precious to us here in this center of the world of The Real People of The Maple Forest believe their village to be isn't as smooth or certain as it once was. Spring rolls into summer again and I watch riders travel out to gather the latest news from Dark Cloud's village and Deer's trading post. We'll do as Deer tells us and work to not be caught by surprise.

I watch Storm go from an infant to a baby to an active crawling mass of delightful trouble. I watch Red Fox and Turtle welcome a baby daughter, Laughs Much, and finally enjoy an early summer visit with Sleeping Rabbit and we sew her an Indian tunic with real rabbit fur just as I promised her so long ago. I wander the woods with One Who Knows and work hard to remember all she can pack into my thick skull about herbs and such. When the heat of the summer wraps itself around all of us, I remember the time a year ago when I was *not* a mother, *but almost.* I look down at the sturdy little man at my feet, clinging to my skirt and taking his first steps to the delight of the extended family around him.

I think of the fears that all of us have just close below the surface; fears of soldiers and broken promises and worries of the future. I know of the preparations we've worked hard to do and still continue to work hard toward; of caves well supplied and provisions carefully stored. The puzzle of my life that I once thought, so foolishly, was all finished is now, I realize, just a small part of a huge, never ending scene. There's The Maple Forest part that's almost complete thanks to my listening at council fires and Deer and Bright Feather's patience with my many, many questions.

The Ward's Mill part has many parts filled in, but so many pieces are still missing. What of the Wests? Are they safe and well? Do they still have Mr. Cooper's ledger book hidden in their mattress? What of the Coopers? Do they still hold power over so many of the farmers in the area like a rabid dog guarding its pile of bones? A big part of me hopes they tremble with fear as often as possible of me and my village of 'red savage' friends.

My heart skips a beat and my stomach clenches as I think *What of my brother Henry?* Is he well? Is he safe? Does he worry for me? Miss me? Is he part of this battle to remove all Indian tribes east of the Mississippi? For the truth of things is, if he's still in the army, *how could he not be?* Which makes me sigh and think of Miss Joan's question, *"Will your brother be understanding of the child do you think?"* I snort to myself as I work to wash a struggling toddler boy and think a better question is, What will your brother think of your pink skin? Will I someday find my brother only to loose him once again simply because of the choices I've made about the course of my life?

I sigh as I watch Storm wrestle from my grasp and run on fat toddler legs to Bright Feather who's walking slowly towards us. I battle with the big wave of worry that threatens to pull me down about all my missing puzzle pieces. What of this village that's my home? And my people? What of my husband and son? And mother and friends? Do I have what I need to go to a council circle filled with white and red faces who'll hate me just because of the way I look? Will I be able to speak my mind and heart in such a way to keep all those I love and care for safe?

For I am just a ...

But I stop my self. I'll not finish that sentence for it's not true. I'm not a "just" anything. I am many things. I am Bear, daughter of One Who Knows of Elk Clan of The Real People of The Maple Forest. I am also known by some as Elle Graves, late of Ward's Mill, Virginia. I am a powerful woman who has survived a mighty big pile of difficult surprises and heart - breaking sorrows so far. I am a mate of a man who encourages my many questions, listens to my thoughts and concerns, and loves me with an abiding love. I am a mother of a fine son and I will work hard to grow him into a fine man. I am a sister to many who are inclined to tolerate my pink self. And I am many more things I suspect ... But I remind myself with firm words that I am *not* nor will I ever be "just" anything For to use that word about myself only serves to make me less that I can be.

My two men approach me; one with a serious face full of love and one with twinkling eyes filled with mischief. My husband and I have survived fear, worry, death, separation, hatred, and sorrows no body should have to ever face. I sigh a deep sigh. I suspect that there are still a pile of shadows we still are yet to fight our way through. But we'll do it together, side by side and hand in hand.

I step forward and Bright Feather wraps me in a warm embrace as Storm tangles himself between our legs. I take a deep breath and make myself squint my eyes towards the sun rather then the shadows, *for that is the way it must always be.*

Citizen

For those of us at One Who Knows' Place in The Maple Forest, it's almost easy to forget the world outside our garden walled around wrapped up as we are with the business of life being mothers, fathers, daughters, sons, sisters, brothers, leaders, and friends. The crops, those we grow and those that grow wild in our wood, begin to make their early appearance. We look forward to the gift they will give us with their bounty that'll keep us fed through the coming winter and chase away the season of starving that every early springtime brings. For the women, the tending of our fields and the foraging in the forests is a time for laughter and gossip besides the hard work of it all. Work is always easier with a friend at your side.

It rarely happens to me but every now and then my white self makes a surprise visit in my head and I find myself watching the world I live in and call home with something akin to wonder and just a bit of amazement. It's like unexpected lamplight late on a dark, moonless night. I suppose it ain't that unusual given that I lived my first fourteen years of life as the only daughter of Andrew and Elizabeth Graves. The white part of me still carries Pa's wise words in my head and still remembers the music of my little brother Eli's laughter. The *little* white girl in me still has moments when it misses the comfort of Ma's prayers. I think about my brother, Henry. Where is he? Is he well? Is he safe? At one point in my life I thought he was dead, too, only to discover that not to be so. Now I worry again for his safety. The only thing that I know of my brother is that he joined the Army. After Pa and Eli were killed. After I was taken. After the farm was lost. After he had nothing left.

I wonder sometimes if Ma, Pa, and Eli can see me? For the Real People, to mention someone who has passed on to the spirit world is never done. What if they hear you and return? The red world I live in lives only for the day we are in. We never speak of the past or the people that are no longer with us and we do not worry for the future. If we keep things right and orderly *now* then all things will be as they should be.

But I do worry. I guess that's the white part of me. And I suspect that Great Elk, the leader of our tribe, and his mate, War Woman, work to keep things *right and orderly* now in the village because they know just how wrong things can become. Safe as we are in our little village that my mate, Bright Feather, and I like to call our *garden walled around*, there are those who would do us great harm. Red and White. Aside from our regular visits with Deer – whether it's us going to him or him coming to us – we hear little of the outside world. But visits to Deer and his family at their Trading Post give us all a glimpse of this world and not a speck of it's pretty. It's a world that we cannot truly put aside and forget, for to do that would mean nothing but bad things for us. I wonder sometimes, is that why Deer and I – both with white faces but red hearts - were brought here to be a part of this village? Maybe that's what Reverend Wilder and Miss Rebecca meant when they said to me so long ago, "Perhaps we can teach The Real People how to survive in a white world *and* teach The Real People of God's Great Love and Faithfulness ..." Perhaps this white God of Great Love and Faithfulness looked at these people that have become *my people* and thought, "Maybe I'll send them down a bit of help." It's a puzzle to me, though, how one white trader and one almost eighteen year old girl is going to make much difference.

But that's my white head talking. Thankfully, it makes appearances only on the odd occasion. For the red part of me knows what a powerful woman I've become. I'm a mate, a mother, a daughter, a sister, and a friend. I can hunt and ride and even hold my own with a knife. I can start a fire from scratch, track a deer through the bush and have survived on my own in the wilderness *in the winter pregnant with my son, Storm*. I've been in a passel of right difficult circumstances and managed to keep a clear and level head (along with what some would call a smart lip). I've discovered as my Indian mother One Who Knows has told me (although she would be quick to tell you that some things take a while to get into my thick skull) that I was always a powerful woman, even before I knew it. I'm Bear, daughter of One Who Knows, of the Elk clan of the Real People of the Maple Forest and the mate of Bright Feather, son of War Woman of the Wolf clan and

Great Elk, chief of the Real People of the Maple Forest. And mighty proud of it.

Our village is like a bear trap in the autumn woods. Covered with the beautiful colors that the trees change into just before their winter's sleep, a bear trap is mighty harmless unless you make the mistake of stepping into it. On the surface, we are a quiet Indian village situated in The Maple Forest in a place the whites would call Virginia. Quiet that is as long as you don't think about the collection of caves that are carefully readied and prepared and continually restocked and supplied. Things are fine as long as you don't notice the stock of new rifles that a number of the braves in our village now proudly count as part of their weapon's collection (including Bright Feather, Raccoon and Red Fox) and you don't count the large accumulation of arrows that are carefully maintained as well. And there's nothing to worry about as long as you don't listen too closely to discussions each night at the council circle, with or without Deer present, about the various governments of the white people that continually try to knock at our paper treaty walls and test their strength.

At the end of the spring, in the second summer after my son Storm's birth, we are invited, via a messenger from Dark Cloud's village, to travel to a meeting which will be attended by all those red and white who have interests – *good or bad* – in The Real People and the land they claim to be theirs. We suspect, as we discuss things in the council circle over many nights, that the invitation is specifically at Beaver's insistence. Having left the Maple Forest unhappy with choices made by those in the council, he has chosen a different path. *We walk a different path to get to the same place.* As a whole, The Nation of The Real People seems to have enough on their minds without concerning themselves with our band that has chosen to no longer be a part of their mighty struggles. Contact with Beaver, Bright Feather's brother, over the past two years has consisted almost completely of indirect messages from those who have had dealings with him. It's our job to sort through and find the truth of the things we hear.

From Deer we know that things in the state of Georgia have only gotten worse for The Nation of The Real People. I'm amazed to read an advertisement that he has secured from a traveler that advertises the Georgia Land Lottery – land belonging to The Real People. It promises land lots, rich and fertile, varying in size from 40 acre gold lots, with no guarantee of profit, to large 490 acre spreads, with minimal water access. Applicants interested in participating in the seven drawings which are to be held in variously listed locations across the state had to be white, males over 18, or widows or orphans.

I sit in the council circle and listen to the discussion about the reasons we should or should not attend the meeting. At last, I organize my thoughts enough to say something. It's unusual for me to talk at council circle times. It's not that I'm frightened or feel unwelcome to do so, it's more that until now, the council circle has been a great learning time for me and I've been content with that. I now am comfortable with the workings of the village and those who make the decisions. I now am familiar with the personalities around the fire and the sometimes strong opinions that hold up that individual. I now find that while I've always had my own opinions and beliefs, I now have a pile of experience to back them all up and I know that I've earned the respect of many people in the village and they're ready to listen to me.

"I think that there is no other choice but to go to New Echota," I say finally after the last person has expressed an opinion.

War Woman looks across at me and she seems almost to have an expression that says, *At last*. "Why do you feel that is so, Bear?"

I've already thought of my reasons, so I speak right away. "To stay here in the village, perhaps hoping that we will be forgotten in all the arguing, is as unlikely as one being able to forget a tick silently but fiercely embedded in your skin. Sooner or later the tick's presence is so annoying you must dig it out no matter how deeply it is embedded.

"Also, in desperate times, people do desperate things. My presence here in this village is proof enough of that. I do not want to be sitting here silently and tensely waiting for The Nation of The Real People and The Government of the United States to settle their disagreements with each other, uninformed and unprepared. You are listening to someone who more than once over the course of her life has been used by others as a weapon, a pawn, and even as bait. I was innocent and uninformed in most cases and yet more than once my life was put in grave danger simply because I was in the wrong place at the wrong time. Should The Nation of The Real People or the Government of the United States get truly desperate, don't for one moment think that they will not look in our direction.

"Why wait? I say we show our strength, our intelligence, and our unity by making a show at this meeting. In doing so, they will remember not only that we are smart and capable, but they will also see that we are different from the others. We do not need to show them everything, but perhaps, like a rattler shakes his tail in warning before he strikes, we can make enough noise to make them think twice should they look at us and decide we are in the right place at the wrong time.

"And the opportunity to study our enemies with our own eyes will carry more weight then *any* words of *any* person could." I look around the circle at the serious faces listening to my words and suppress the urge to giggle all of a sudden that *my* words should carry *any* weight with this experienced group of elders. I shrug instead and flash them a smile, "I am finished speaking."

It's decided that a delegation from our village will travel to New Echota, Georgia. I'm chosen to go for my language skills and that automatically includes Storm for he's still nursing and Bright Feather for we will hold fast to our promise, *Never, ever again will we be separated. We will travel together and face our challenges together. Never again will we let life break us apart.* I'm surprised to learn that Great Elk will travel with us too, as well as the two braves that originally traveled with Red Fox, Young Wolf and Spring Frog. I study the group around the fire and think, *Our strength and our intelligence* and yet am pleased to know how much strength and intelligence still wait behind to care for and defend our village.

We travel out one hot, summer day not more than a week after the decision. Storm is beside himself with excitement shouting and calling and waving to anyone who will return the enthusiasm. I'm excited about the journey, too, I realize as I have time to think over the course of the nine days we travel. I go to this place not as a captive this time, but of my own free will as a mate, daughter, mother, and sister of The Real People of the Maple Forest. I realize that even my white skin is no longer something to cause me fear, for I now know that my white life as Elle Graves is safely settled and stored away like all of my other memories of Ma, Pa, Eli and Henry in my Hope Chest spot in my head. I look forward to seeing Miss Rebecca and Reverend Wilder and wonder, will Major Everett be there if the Army will be present? I wonder how I will be received by Dark Cloud this time and will his behavior toward me be filled with hatred for the role he knows I must have played in the death of one of his sons? I remember New Echota and its very odd mix of red and white and wonder what changes three years will have brought?

It seems that New Echota has made the most of the three years since I was last there. As we ride into town down the wide main street, I recognize the large building that had been the school, meeting place and church all in one and the two small wooden buildings that had been the

Wilders' and Dark Cloud's home. But even those buildings have gone through great change.

The large building now bearss a sign that says, 'New Echota Council House and Supreme Court'. The Wilder's small cabin is now obviously a general store and Dark Cloud's home is now a printing office, 'Home of the Cherokee Phoenix Newspaper.' The Mission School and what must be the dreamed of dormitory building that could sleep many is in full use. Standing next to the school is an obvious church, tall wooden spire included. There are so many people walking about town that our arrival causes no particular notice at all. The realities of the way things are gradually sinks in. *No one* comes and goes in Great Elk's village without note.

There are soldiers everywhere. While the large fields of crops are no longer as visible as they once were due to all the new buildings, I can see a vast encampment of white army tents just on the outskirts of town. The field I can see, far off in the distance, has a large white home standing proudly amidst the growing produce. As I watch the press of people it's hard to tell who there are the most of: Indian, white, or soldiers.

"Do you have any suggestion where to go?" I hear Bright Feather murmur close to me and I realize that we all are sitting in awe of what we see. As I scan the village – no, I correct myself, *This is not a village, it's a town!*, I spy a familiar figure coming out of the mission school, turning to walk the road away from the city. Wide as she is tall, with her basket of school books held in her arm, Rebecca Wilder is one person that seems to have changed little at first glance.

"We will go to the Council House," Great Elk says, and I realize he's perhaps more familiar with the *town* than I am from what Young Wolf and Spring Frog have told him. "Do you join us?"

I nod my head in the direction of Miss Rebecca's departing wide back. "That is someone I know from my time last here. I would like to go speak with her." I smile at Bright Feather and Storm sitting looking at me with the same curious expression and I feel a rush of love that makes me breathless for a moment.

"That is Miss Rebecca," Bright Feather says, having heard all my stories and descriptions from my time here before. He looks at his father and the other two braves. "We will join you later." They nod and ride off.

My first glance at her makes me think that little has changed, but as I draw closer it seems that the spring in her step and the same breathless enthusiasm and energy has dimmed a bit. When I'm close enough, I dismount Willow and walk holding onto the reins.

"Miss Rebecca?" I say at last, and even the fact that she seems unaware of my approaching presence does not seem in character I realize.

In those first few moments as she turns and looks at me, I know that she does not recognize me. Have I changed so much I wonder as I allow her to study me, a white woman who looks very, *very* much like a savage Indian maid? My permanent chin marks are new, my hair is longer, but my dress and horse are the same. Even my shape has returned to my former premotherhood size. She looks unafraid but still unsure.

"It's Bear, Miss Rebecca. I stayed with you and Reverend Wilder a few years back ..." at the mention of Reverend Wilder's name she seems to become more alert and at last her eyes truly focus on me and I know that at last she remembers me.

"Bear ..." and a slow smile spreads across her face. "Oh forgive me, Bear, for not recognizing you and greeting you right away!" And then the full force of her greeting settles on me as I'm pulled into a crushing, sweat-damp hug. After a few moments, she pulls back. As she wipes tears away with a crumpled handkerchief she draws out from her sleeve, she looks around, "Why are you here, Bear ...?"

I look to Bright Feather and a wriggling Storm only a short distance away. "I come with my mate and son and the chief of my village, who is also my mate's father, to attend the meetings that it seems everyone else is here to attend as well." I smile at the noise and confusion that seems to be in all directions and she, too, looks around at the bustling town, seeming to look at it almost with the same wonder as I am.

"Your mate? Your son?" she looks all around at first not seeming to comprehend that my mate and son could be the fierce Indian brave sitting proudly on his horse holding the squirming Indian baby with silky black hair and big dark eyes. At my glance, Bright Feather slowly begins riding toward us.

"May I introduce you, Miss Rebecca, to my mate, Bright Feather, son of War Woman of the Wolf clan, son of Great Elk, chief of the Real People of the Maple Forest." Bright Feather stops Companion and nods his head respectfully.

I feel Miss Rebecca start, when he says to her in clear, perfect English, "How do you do, Miss Rebecca?"

"GET DOWN," Storm says in Indian, but whose meaning is clear to everyone as he squirms to get out of Bright Feather's arms. I reach up and take him.

"And this is my son, Storm Eli," I say and grin a proud mother's grin.

"GET DOWN," Storm says again and wriggles out of my arms to begin exploring wherever his feet will take him.

Miss Rebecca studies the three of us for a brief moment. She can't resist and bends down to Storm's level. "Well hello," she says to us, but clearly enchanted with Storm who immediately toddles over to her and begins inspecting her basket. "Welcome to New Echota," she says as she reaches up to tenderly touch Storm's head bent in concentration over the treasures he's searching for. She looks to me and then to Bright Feather as he dismounts from Companion. "Our cabin is down the road from here. Won't you come along and enjoy some refreshments?"

"We would be delighted," I say.

I hear Bright Feather say to Storm, "Come, let's help Miss Rebecca carry her basket back to her place," and I feel compelled to link my arm in hers and begin walking.

The new cabin that Miss Rebecca calls home is just a short walking distance from the new mission school and dormitory. It's not much larger, but she explains that it was quieter than being in the center of town. "As the town grew, it became obvious that the old cabin could be used for business purposes and we could enjoy a bit more quiet and privacy away from the hustle and bustle." She serves Bright Feather and me a cool glass of apple cider and offers Storm some early strawberries. He sits happily at my feet making a terrific mess of himself and her clean floor. "The town is not always so busy as you see it today. When big meetings are not scheduled, things are much more quiet." She studies me for a moment. "But probably busier than you remember."

She's much more quiet I think as I study her. I remember that breathless energy that she and Reverend Wilder had when I was last here. "Tell me of the school," I say.

Flashes of her excited old self flash to the surface as she talks. "Oh, the school is just magnificent! It was just being built when you were last here, wasn't it?" She asks me and I nod, 'yes'. "James has worked tirelessly to promote the importance of spiritual salvation and literacy among the Cherokee. He has been friends for many years with a brilliant young Cherokee man named Pig's Foot and -"

I can't help myself. *"Pig's Foot?"* I interrupt. "He's named Pig's Foot?"

"I have heard of him," Bright Feather speaks for the first time and he speaks in English as a courtesy to Miss Rebecca. "His name is because he was born with feet that look like those of a pig." He says all this as if it makes perfect sense to him and as I look at him he shrugs his shoulders. "He's the one that writes talking leaves."

"Talking leaves?" I say now as I look at both of them.

Miss Rebecca can't help herself and she smiles and laughs a small laugh. "Many whites call Pig's Foot, 'George Gist', but I know he has always preferred his Indian name and so I call him by it." She looks at me with a little twinkle in her eye. "I'd prefer George Gist though!

"The talking leaves that Bright Feather speaks of is the Cherokee language in written form." She frowns at me. "You have not heard of it?" I must shake my head 'no'. She stands up and goes beside the bed and picks up a newspaper and hands it to me. *Half* of it I can read, for it's written in English. The other half *has* to be the language of the Real People for I realize as I stare at the unfamiliar shapes that it looks exactly to my eyes what the sounds sounded like to my ears in the first months as a captive; a tangled unintelligible mess.

"You knew of this?" I ask Bright Feather.

"Deer spoke of it one of the last times I saw him, although neither of us has had the chance to see the actual writing. Deer feels that it is a great progressive step for The Nation of The Real People as a means of communication." He looks at Miss Rebecca. "I understand that it is very easy to learn by anyone who already speaks the language."

She nods her head enthusiastically. "Yes, here, look!" Bright Feather leans over my shoulder as we look at the paper and she speaks the sounds and points to the shapes that correspond. She no longer struggles with the words as she did the last time I saw her. It's amazing to me to see the language before me on a written page. "There are eighty six symbols that must be learned and once they are mastered, you are virtually able to read almost immediately.

"James was very passionate about the newspaper and is good friends with the editor, Elias Boudinot. They've known each other since college times up north. James felt that if he could achieve a level of literacy within the tribe, then he could spread God's Word to them as well. He has been actively working on translating major portions of the Bible into Cherokee. The newspaper has been a grand success these past years. The first issue was February 28, 1828," she says with great pride. As I go to hand the paper back to her she says, "Please, keep it."

"Between the newspaper, the church, the school, the translating, the building, and," she chuckles, "at times he serves even as the local doctor, James was busier than five men! The Cherokee call him Messenger, you know. He was very proud to receive that name ..." She grows silent and seems at a loss for words for a moment. Gradually, her face crumples and she begins to cry great gulping sobs. Bright Feather and I look at each other. Storm, all red and sticky from the strawberries, stands up and toddles over to Miss Rebecca and I cringe at the strawberry stains that are added to the pattern of her skirt.

"Lady cry?" Storm asks. "Lady sad?" She sniffles and searches for her handkerchief again. She smiles down at Storm's concerned face and touches the top of his silky head and cups his fat cheek in her palm. She then takes a deep breath as she meets first my and then Bright Feather's concerned faces.

He's dead, my mind flashes all of a sudden and I feel a great sorrow for the loss of this good man and for this loving woman who is left to travel on the path of this life without him. "I'm sorry for your loss," I say to her but the words feel empty and useless as I hear them.

She realizes the conclusions we have come to and waves her hand as she blows her nose. "He's not dead," she finally says to us. "but he may as well be. He's been sentenced to four years of hard labor at the Georgia State Penitentiary" As Bright Feather and I exchange shocked looks she says, "I miss him *so,*" and she dissolves into loud sobs again.

I decide, reminded of my comforting times at Jane West's home, to make Miss Rebecca a cup of tea while she makes every effort to pull herself together. As she sips on her tea and Storm has an afternoon snack courtesy of my breasts, the story gradually is told.

"Georgia and the United States Government want to be rid of all Indians east of the Mississippi," she begins. "The Georgia state legislature officially adopted a policy of forcible Indian removal right after President Jackson passed the Indian Removal Act more than two years ago." She looks at us with sad eyes. "This year, Georgia began a Land Lottery in which *white* would-be settlers, pay a small fee for the opportunity to take a chance and draw a parcel of land *free for the taking.* It's not free for the taking, it's Indian land. Land owned and settled by the Cherokees. The state has already passed laws that say no Indian can cause a white man to be brought to court and no legal documents can be considered valid if signed by an Indian. Those Indians whose land will be drawn in the lottery cannot even defend themselves when the new owners arrive to take possession." She looks out the window and says very quietly, "Leave on your own or we'll make you leave. That's the choice.

"Georgia has been incensed for a long time that the Cherokees have written their own constitution and set up their own form of government." She smiles a proud smile. "The Nation of the Cherokee have become quite a force to be reckoned with you see; establishing a government modeled after the white man, developing a written language, electing powerful leaders. Now add in the fact that *gold* has been discovered on Cherokee lands! Not only are there whites who have no land and want some, now there are whites who already have some land, but want some *with gold in it.* For the Georgia Government, success of the Cherokees and the establishment of their own government was tantamount to the Cherokees dismissing Georgia and their authority." She shrugs. "Which I guess they were.

"When Georgia passed a law requiring all whites – missionaries included – to get a license to work on Native American lands, that was the last straw for James. You see," she explains, "in requesting from the white government the permission to operate on Indian lands, the hierarchy of authority is clearly established. In other words, if Indians cannot give permission as to who or what is occurring on their lands, then obviously the land in reality is not theirs after all."

Miss Rebecca smiles a tired smile and looks at me. "You can imagine James' reaction to all of this. Oh, the fury!! We prayed and prayed as to what to do and were very gratified when our very own mission board took a strong stance *against* the state and federal policies. James and a number of other missionaries in the area drafted an official resolution of protest against the laws of the Georgia state assembly and published them right up the road at our very own printing office. In it James, *of course,* refuted the authority of the state to require permission of whites to continue working and living on Cherokee lands. In his opinion, which I share, he had already received the permission from the Cherokee leaders and would not seek permission elsewhere." Lost in thought, she says softly, "Twelve brave men of the cloth signed that document."

She's quiet for many moments, and I stand and carefully lay a sleeping Storm on Miss Rebecca's bed in the corner. "The militia arrived not long after the resolution was published and arrested James and all the others who had signed the protest."

She sighs a world weary tired sigh. "It was a quick trial. All of the men were sentenced to four years of hard labor. Their lawyers appealed and brought the case to the State Supreme Court and did such a wonderful job, that we actually won! The Supreme Court of the State of Georgia ruled that the Cherokee Nation was independent and all dealings with them fell under the federal jurisdiction that had been originally established."

I look at Bright Feather and he looks at me, unable to understand the way of things. "Then why is Reverend Wilder still in prison?" I ask puzzled.

"The governor of Georgia *and* President Andrew Jackson chose to ignore the Supreme Court's rulings. All but two of the men charged *have* been released. I suspect, because James is so eloquent and forceful with his words, that they chose to keep him imprisoned rather than setting him free to continue talking and writing inflammatory newspaper articles. James has been in the penitentiary doing hard labor for over a year now. I have not seen him since last fall."

She sits at the table and looks out the small window of her cabin. "I had a terrible time in those early months. I couldn't even seem to get out of bed. I laid there," she looks at Storm's sleeping form and smiles, " and thought, I shall just lie here until I die."

She gets up and collects the cups which she carries over to the wash basin. "What kind of example would *that* have been? I thought of you, then, Bear. I remembered those months you were here and all of a sudden I knew how you had felt to be separated from those you loved and cared for. I understood the feeling of powerlessness and the frustrations of just wanting to make everything right again. It was bitter medicine to swallow some of the words I had so glibly told you ..." She turns and looks at me. "I agonized over whether I had ever provided you any true comfort while you were here, not really understanding what you were going through. At some point, I realized that after this time of trial, I would be better able to minister to those suffering from loneliness and despair and heartache. I knew that I would be better in the end for all of this sorrow and that to just lie here and let everything fade away was a travesty to all the hard work and answered prayers that James and I had experienced.

"That made me realize that *we know that all things work together for good to them that love God, to them who are the called according to His purpose.*[30] I lay there in that bed and thought of the love that James and I shared, and the many blessings that Our Wonderful Lord had bestowed upon us, and I looked at all of the tremendous things that James and I had accomplished by God's faithful grace and mercy. There was no doubt in my mind that I was one of those *who had been called according to His purpose*. So I got out of bed, made sure I always had a handkerchief ready for when the tears come, and went back to teaching and working here in town. I pray for James and his health and state of mind *every single moment that I can spare*. I know he does the same for me. Just because I can't hold his hand does not mean that he is outside of my embrace.

"While you are in town, you will stay here," she says to Bright Feather and I in a tone that does not offer any discussion on the matter. "Bright Feather, I suggest you make your way into town and establish your presence here with Dark Cloud and the other leaders. Bear and I will get dinner started."

I look at Bright Feather and grin. I guess he's been told. He stands and says, "I thank you for your kindnesses to Bear when she was here last. You said that you worried that you had not provided her any true comfort while she was here. She has told me of the time she spent with you and Reverend Wilder. She spoke with great love and respect of the two of you. We have talked many nights of the things you shared with her, of this God that you can talk to even in just your thoughts and who had such a great love for all of us that He was willing to sacrifice His son for us." He looks at Storm sleeping peacefully on her bed and places a hand on my shoulder. "You can be assured that Bear's time here with you and your husband *was* full of comfort and peace, strong enough to follow her home to our village and still work within our home and hearth even up to this day. Sometimes the greatest gifts one person can give another is nothing the eye can see." He gives her a gift of one of his rare smiles and quotes Isaac Watts, *Yet, Lord, thy saints on earth may reap, some profit by the good we do; these are the company I keep, these are the choicest friends I know.[31]*"

I laugh at Miss Rebecca as she sits there in stunned silence, looking at this fierce Indian savage quoting to her Christian hymns in perfect English. At last, she manages, "Was that Isaac Watts you just quoted to me?!"

Bright Feather nods. "Bear has taught me English to speak and Isaac Watts has taught me English to read." He touches my cheek and walks out the door saying over his shoulder, "We will be back in time to eat with you."

Once he leaves, she looks at me and finally said. "You taught James and I things, too, while you were here. You taught us to appreciate the culture of the Indians and to understand that it is just as greatly involved and important to them as ours is to us. You taught us that we must approach them as intellectual equals rather than uncivilized savages. I learned from you something that every successful missionary must know and understand, but that we are rarely taught during our schooling and preparations: Everyone on this vast earth is part of God's great design and plan without consideration to race or nationality or even gender. We are all just at different spots along the way. Once I stopped thinking that only I had something valuable to teach them, and realized that it should be more importantly an equal sharing between us, I was accepted and felt a part of this wonderful Nation. Just like you now, Bear, I am a little more pink than white I think." She laughs as she looks down at herself. "But all my pink is on the inside."

I insist on sharing some of the food we have brought along in our pack. There's dried venison and some herbs that One Who Knows has insisted I bring along to cook with or to trade. Miss Rebecca and I set about preparing a meal for the six of us, plus Storm. Over dinner, she asks me many questions and I fill her in on my time with The Real People of The Maple Forest. It feels good to tell her *everything* now and not have to be careful to guard my words. I tell her of my first capture and my early time in Great Elk's village. I tell her of my second capture and how it was that I arrived at her doorstep three years ago. I tell her of my time with the Coopers and my fears of giving birth and how quickly my prayers were answered. I tell her of Major Everett's many kindnesses and my time at Fort Winston. I do not tell her of my time with Weasel and my rescue by Bright Feather and Raccoon and she does not ask. Some things are just better left unsaid.

"Alexander was to be here for this meeting," she says. "but he has once again traveled to the Georgia Penitentiary to discuss James' release. He has done everything in his power to secure James' release and is greatly frustrated at his lack of success. Poor boy, he has had almost as much trouble with this as I have."

Great Elk tells us, and I translate for Miss Rebecca, as we all talk over dinner, that our arrival here is a great surprise, but we are not unwelcome. In another two weeks time, at a time when the corn is to reach it's highest height, a meeting is to be held in which all parties will discuss the path that The Nation of The Real People should take. At that time, all people who have any opinions will be given the opportunity to speak and a decision will be proposed and voted on.

Bright Feather, Storm and I set up camp in a nearby grassy meadow behind Miss Rebecca's place. We politely decline her hospitable invitation to sleep in her cabin. The heat, cramped quarters, and Storm all combine to make it a most unappealing prospect. She seems content with our close proximity and the apparent ease in which we seem to adjust to this temporary outdoor life. *Little does she know*, I think to myself. Great Elk, Young Wolf and Spring Frog find places elsewhere in the town to stay.

Beaver is nowhere to be seen. Careful questions reveal that although he's well known, he's not someone that's considered a permanent inhabitant of the town. Bright Feather and I are not surprised at this and we discuss among ourselves whether he will even be present for the meeting in two weeks.

"I cannot see Beaver attending council meetings here very regularly," he says. "Knowing his opinions, they are even too far in the direction of the Old Ways for even John Ross." I must agree.

My first encounter with Dark Cloud, in my opinion, goes well. The five of us attend an evening council meeting a few nights after our arrival. Miss Rebecca, as taken with Storm as he is with her, has agreed to care for him while we go. I sit between Bright Feather, Great Elk, Young Wolf and Spring Frog and I enjoy the feeling of peace and security that seems to flow through my body seated between these fierce Indian braves. *You cannot harm me*, my thoughts sing over and over again as Dark Cloud makes every effort to ignore my presence.

The feel of the council meeting is different than it was last time I was there. There's a clear division between the two leaders, Dark Cloud and this John Ross we have heard about. John Ross is not anything like I would have expected. He looks nothing like any Indian I've ever seen; short in stature and without the slightest bit of Indian features anywhere, from the top of his head to the tip of his toes. Sitting near Dark Cloud around the large meeting table, his tiny size, compared to Dark Cloud's looming presence, could almost be funny. But what he lacks in size is more than made up for when you hear him speak. I'm mesmerized by the way he handles each and every person and topic that's brought up. This is a man that's intelligent, shrewd, and focused. I cannot imagine *anything* stopping him in his quest to secure what is best for his people. This council meeting is filled with tension and anger. I think of children fighting: No you did not! Did to! Did not! John Ross handles things well, however, for those who acknowledge Dark Cloud as the preferred leader, there's only so much he can do.

Dark Cloud, in contrast to John Ross, seems the same sly, self assured person. Although all present, except ourselves, are in proper white man clothes, Dark Cloud's heritage as an Indian leader, chief, and brave seems to seep out of him from every pore. He seems to communicate that he knows a secret and that he has all the answers and he's not going to tell it to anyone until he's good and ready. The division between the groups is evident at almost every level; where people sit, how people speak to each other; and what opinions come out of each person's mouth. If only these two forces could work together rather than apart, I think to myself.

I distinguish *Elias* whom Miss Rebecca has referred to and who must be the editor of the tribe newspaper. When he speaks, he does it with care and choice words. He seems one of the few in the meeting that has not chosen to be part of one side or the other. Bright Feather points out Young Snake, Weasel's brother and the one who I remember Deer saying was present with the military when they took the census of the tribes back in 1818. He, of all the people in the council meeting that night, is the only one who makes direct eye contact with me. It's the only time I feel a bit frightened.

There are soldiers present at the council meeting. Important ones, I suspect for they have ribbons and buttons and all manner of fancy bits on their uniforms and seem to carry themselves with a certain air that makes you want to sit up straight and look serious. More than once I know they glance at me, the odd white girl surrounded by Indian braves, but try very hard to not let me see that they do.

We fall into a routine and by the end of the second week, I regularly spend mornings with Miss Rebecca in the school helping her with her teaching responsibilities while Bright Feather cares for Storm. In the afternoon, while Miss Rebecca deals with the many aspects of her and Reverend Wilder's other responsibilities in the town, we are left to our own plans. I'm unsure whether word has been spread regarding me and my history or that the town is just so busy and full with all manner of people from all walks of life that no one thinks much of a white woman in Indian dress. No one seems to take much notice of me and that suits me just fine. We visit the General Store on occasion and Miss Rebecca insists that we have a tour of the newspaper office, but we do not have the opportunity to meet Mr. Elias Boudinot. I do avoid the areas that seem to attract the most soldiers and find a private space to bathe and do my domestic chores like collecting water and cleaning clothes. Still, the high activity of the place keeps me careful and I work hard to draw as little attention to myself as possible. Aside from the occasional council meetings we attend (unlike Great Elk who attends them every night), we decide to keep quiet and out of the main view of things as much as possible.

Walking home, after my school time with Miss Rebecca one hot early afternoon, my thoughts are interrupted by the sounds of horses approaching. The jangle of metal and loud laughter and voices can only mean one thing: soldiers. I move to the side of the road, keep my head down and pick up my pace.

"Well, lookie what we have here!" I hear and I keep *walking just a bit faster.*

"Ain't this the white woman that seems to prefer dressin' and livin' like an Injun squaw?"

"That's her. Even got herself an *Injun husband* and *Injun brat* by him, too, I hear."

"That's disgusting. Tain't natural. It revolts me to just think about it."

"Can't rightly tell though with her head down and such. Hey, Injun squaw! Do ya speak English? Be respectful to your *superiors* and look at me when I'm talking to you. Let's have a look at you so we can do introductions proper like."

What do I do? my mind thinks. Ignore them, keep walking.

"Hey! Now that ain't polite now is it? We're trying to have a neighborly conversation and she's just being plain rude. Stop her, Jimmy." My path is suddenly blocked by an enormous horse. I stare at the shiny boots and the blue uniform trousers. I take a deep breath. I stand there and wait.

"What's a matter, girly?" A voice says to me full of amusement and fun and *unkindness*. "Why won't you have a neighborly chit-chat with us here by the side of the road? We're just trying to have a *conversation* with you. You gave up your white life it seems, don't tell me you can't no longer speak the white language? Why have you chosen the Injun way of life over the white one anyway? Never found a white man to keep you happy I suspect …" There's snickering laughter. "Why, just spend a few moments with me and I'll show you what you're missing and change your mind back right quick …" More laughter.

I take stock of things. There are four of them, all on horses. I'm unarmed except for my knife in its sheath strapped to my belt. I'm a distance from the town, almost to Miss Rebecca's house which I know is probably empty. Even if Bright Feather is there, can he and I deal with four soldiers armed with serious weapons and filled with trouble on their minds? And then I have an awful thought. *This is Georgia,* where Indians have no rights and cannot even defend themselves in court. I must *not* go to Miss Rebecca's, *especially* if Bright Feather is there for if there's trouble, he will surely suffer the most for it. I'm a fast runner, but would be unable to outrun even the slowest of horses and I know I cannot make it back to town before they would catch me. That leaves the woods ...

They're to my immediate left for I've stepped to the side of the road to allow the soldiers to pass. It's not dense underbrush which is good for me should I choose to run into it, but is also good for any one chasing me on foot or on horseback.

"Cat got your tongue, squaw?" I hear in an impatient tone and one of the soldiers dismounts and begins walking towards me. I know, that once I'm in their grasp, I'm not strong enough to escape. I've been there before. Before he has time to take one more step towards me or I've time to think one more thought, I drop my basket of books and things and take off into the forest at a full run.

They seem delighted by my move. They laugh and whoop and shout like this is what they had planned all along. Three crash their horses into the woods after me while the one on foot follows close behind. I tear through the woods, my mind, heart, and legs racing. I reach for my knife and pull it out of its sheath.

A river runs behind Miss Rebecca's property and it's where I hike to each morning to wash and gather water for our camp. I feel the ground slope down gradual as I run and I know that we are approaching it. Branches slap my face and tear at my skirt. I loose one moccasin. I run as fast as I can through the branches and bushes and rough ground. I listen to the soldiers shout instructions to each other and try to adjust my path accordingly. When I finally fall I'm almost more angry at myself and my clumsiness then I am at the soldiers.

Breathing heavy, clutching my knife, I manage to stand as they surround me. The soldier on foot is the last one to arrive, but he's grinning.

As he takes in great gulps of air, he surveys the wild forest all around us and looks me right in the eye. "Couldn't of chosen a better spot, myself. Right private and *secluded*," and I realize with great dread that he's right. I hear the other soldiers dismounting from their horses and slowly begin walking toward me, closing in.

Now what? my brain says to me again. Beaver taught me how to use a knife in a fight, but he neglected to instruct me as to what to do when the fight involves *four soldiers.*

They all jump me at once and I'm disgusted that I do not even have the chance to draw the blood of one of them. The knife is knocked from my fingers and rough hands grab me by my arms and long braid and there's great laughter and fun as if this is some planned celebration.

"Hold her arms!"

"Careful! I hear squaws bite something fierce."

"Ow! Christ! Someone grab her feet! She just kicked me."

"Where's that knife of hers? Make sure it's out of reach."

Before I know it I'm on my back, with one soldier kneeling on my braid and holding both of my arms. Two other soldiers both hold my legs. The fourth soldier, the one who did all the running, kneels between my legs and lifts my skirt. "Now let's just see if things *down here* have changed any."

The laughter now is different. And a trembling starts to run through me, full of fear and helplessness. *Oh Bright Feather!* I think, *Not again! Terrible trouble does seem to follow me wherever I go!*

I feel myself exposed and the laughter goes away for a moment as the one who's pulled up my skirt says, "Nope, seems like things are *just fine* down here," and I see him reach down to start undoing his trousers. "I'm first boys, I did the most work. Now you hold her tight. We don't want my rhythm to get interrupted or anything ..."

As the nervous, tense laughter travels around the circle of those holding me down, I can't help myself as I look up at the one looming over me, sitting on my hair and holding my arms. His face is flushed with the chase and more so, with the prospect of what is to come. He licks his lips nervously. He's not looking at me, he's looking at the place where all the action is about to happen; between my legs. He must feel me looking at him and he briefly glances at my face.

We stare into each other's eyes for that brief moment and I think clear as a bell, *Why hello, Henry, my brother, imagine meeting you here.*

The shock on his face, quickly replaces his flush of excitement and he lets go of my arms and jumps away from me like he has just uncovered a rattlesnake. I sit up fast and without even thinking grab forward at the soldier who is still working on getting his trousers open. I grab him by the hair and pull him toward me with all my might. All chaos erupts as he topples forward and they begin shouting and cursing and I work very hard to remove the soldier's ear with my teeth.

The soldier, whose ear I hold between my teeth, is tangled and trapped, fighting to free his arms pinned beneath his own body while I work at holding him down with my free arms and concentrate on making my teeth meet. His screams are horrible and the two soldiers still holding my legs seem confused at the turn of events and can't seem to decide whether they should let go of me or not.

It's my brother Henry, that recovers his senses enough to scream, "LET GO OF HER FOR GOD'S SAKE!!" and I feel my legs released. Then I hear Henry, shouting in my ear, "Elle! Elle! FOR CHRISTS' SAKE! WHAT ARE YOU DOING?!! *LET GO.*"

I do finally let go, and the soldiers who had held my legs, help their still screaming comrade to his feet. "SHE BIT MY EAR OFF!" he screams, clutching the side of his head as blood trickles down his neck and between his fingers. "The *Injun whore* BIT MY EAR OFF!" He looks at me with tremendous fury and I know I'm closer to death than I've been in a long time.

"Actually," I say, as I wipe my mouth of his blood and spit out a rather large piece of his ear into my hand, "I only bit *part* of it off, not *all* of it." I toss the piece of ear at him and it lands with a quiet *thump* at his feet.

As he makes a lunge for me, Henry steps fast between us and puts his hand out to stop further movement. "Get a hold of yourself, Steven," he says. "Pull your self together and listen to me! *She's my sister.*" That seems to stop the rest of them in their tracks. The three of them stare at me in disbelief.

"You *said* that she was *dead* and that the *Injuns* killed her," says one of them with two missing front teeth as he continues to stand and hold his bloody friend.

"Obviously, I got it a bit wrong," I hear Henry say. I straighten my top and do my best to rearrange my skirt. I walk over to where I see my knife laying and pick it up and put it back in its sheath. I'm still breathing heavy and suddenly feel light headed and dizzy. *Great,* I think as I sit down on the ground for a minute and put my head in my hands, *now I'll faint.* I feel the prickly feeling my breasts get when my milk lets down and feel the trickle of milk dribble down my belly.

Moments pass and no one, including me, seems to know what to do. Missing Ear pulls himself together enough to button up his pants. I hear the horses munching clover they find on the forest floor. Gradually my blood slows to a quiet enough pace that I can hear the river flowing in the distance. At last I look up and the four of them are looking at me, seeming to wait to see what I'll say or do next. I'm at a loss for words, too, but *only I've drawn blood*, I think, so I feel better for it.

I look at Henry standing with his friends. *How old must he be now?* I wonder. *Twenty - two at least*, I think, for I know him to be four years older than me. With nothing better to say, I address my brother standing tall and grown up in his military uniform. "How have these past years treated you, my brother? I hope the friends you have here are not the best you have to show for yourself."

He looks across the patch of forest at me and I'm surprised to see loathing and disgust as he answers back, "The years seem to have treated me kinder than they have *you, my sister*, since I've not sunk so low as to be an *Injun whore*."

Oh, a tired voice in my head says to me, *so that's the way it's going to be.*

I stand up and take a moment to test my head and my strength. I'm happy that there's no dizziness anymore. "So good to see you, too," I say to Henry and walk off into the forest in the direction of the river.

I take a long time to get back to Miss Rebecca's field and our little camp sight. My thoughts keep me company as I work my way down the river. I walk in the river as it's cooling and I know I leave no trail. It being high summer the river is low so the going is easy and refreshing. I listen carefully to the forest and see if it tells me that I'm being followed, but it seems that I'm alone at last.

My mind plays tricks on me and it seems that a bird calling in the tree says over and over again, "HenREE! HenREE!" I cannot believe what has happened to me over the space of just a few very, very long moments. Twice the tears build up behind my eyes and I fight them back. What good are they to me? Will they change the bruises and scratches I feel all over my body including between my legs? Will they change the look of loathing and disgust I saw on my brother's face? Will they change the awful set of events that I fear will come into play when Bright Feather and Great Elk hear what has happened?

As I near the spot in the river at Miss Rebecca's where I only this morning washed out a top of mine and gave Storm a quick bath, I decide that perhaps the best course of action might be to say nothing at all. I decide that maybe, the chase and attack and appearance of my brother is better left as an awful memory only in my own head. Surely the soldiers will say nothing. That leaves only me. But as I hike up the slope that leads to the place that we call our temporary home, I know that that'll not be possible, for not only do I see Bright Feather, mounted on Companion, but

I see Miss Rebecca crying, Great Elk, Young Wolf, Spring Frog, and two cavalry soldiers all mounted and obviously ready for action. And toddling at their feet is Storm, carrying the basket I dropped in the road just before I ran into the woods.

The relief I see on Bright Feather's face cannot be put into words. He seems at one moment to be stiff, alert, and ready for battle and with the sight of me, in moments, almost unable to stay seated on Companion. In fact, he slides off quickly at the sound of my voice and the sight of me and runs the distance to me. It's almost slow motion as I watch him coming toward me and I know that what he sees does not calm his fears; I'm scratched and bleeding, my skirt is torn in many places, and as an afterthought I wonder, *Have I washed Missing Ear's blood off my mouth?*

"Bear ..." is all he can gasp out before he grabs me and crushes me to him. "We were just going out to hunt for you ..." He pulls back and holds me at arm's length. "Are you well? Are you injured?" He touches my mouth and the dried blood. "You are bleeding ..."

"No," I say to him, "it's not my blood there. I'm alright but I need to sit down." *And I need to feed Storm,* I think as my breasts tingle again.

It's no use, I must tell them the entire story, down to the attack and finally seeing my brother as one of the men holding me down. I assure them, fearful of Bright Feather's reaction, that Missing Ear is far more injured then I am. Miss Rebecca, all the while I talk, tends to my scrapes and cuts and provides me with a clean cloth to wipe my face. The soldiers, two cavalry officers who had just happened to be talking with Miss Rebecca when Bright Feather came tearing up the road with Storm and my dropped basket, stand silent in the background as I talk.

As I finish, one finally speaks. "We will need to know the name of your brother, Miss, er ..." he finishes lamely.

"I'm called 'Bear'," I say quietly. I hesitate, unsure if I want things taken any further.

"And your brother's name, Miss, er, Bear?" he says.

"My brother's name is Henry Graves," I say at last. "Missing Ear should be quite easy to find. I also heard the names Steven and Jimmy."

"Thank you," the soldier says. "There will, of course, be an investigation. We will need you to come to the officer's tent to give a statement. Would tomorrow be convenient?"

I sigh a great tired sigh. The prospect of traveling to the soldier part of the town, never an appealing one, now seems more than I can possibly even consider. I reach down and lift Storm into my lap and kiss the top of his downy head and enjoy the warmth of his body close to mine. He seems to be of the same mind as me and begins to make the motions to pull my top up and have a quick bit to eat.

It's Miss Rebecca who speaks up. "We'll do our best," she says at last, "but perhaps it might be the day after tomorrow, eh Bear?"

I nod my head. "I'd like to feed my baby, now," I say and don't wait as I begin shifting my top. It's amazing how fast some men will run at the prospect of watching a woman nurse her baby.

Bright Feather and I talk that night in the safety of our temporary shelter as Storm snores his quiet little baby snores in the corner. It's then that the tears come as I tell him of Henry's look of disgust and loathing and of him calling me an *Injun whore*. As I lay there beside Bright Feather, all the disappointments come crashing down on me, with the realization that things will never be as I had hoped they would be should I have found my brother. I remember Joan Foster and her barely hidden disgust to discover that I was pregnant with an Indian's child. I remember her question to me when she thought that Deer was my brother, *Will your brother be understanding of the child do you think?* and my confident answer to her, *When I last knew my brother he was a hard working, loving … man. I cannot see how he would reject this child of mine.* I think about how wrong I was and cry a little bit more.

Finally, Bright Feather says quiet in my ear, "Would you have changed anything about the way your life is now if you could?"

I think about all the things that have happened to me over my life, good and bad that have brought me here to be in this quiet space with a man that loves me and a healthy, happy baby besides. I think of the friends I have, white and red, and those that are my family. "No," I finally say to Bright Feather, "there is nothing I would change."

"Perhaps Henry cannot say that," he says back and for the first time I must look at the world through Henry's eyes. Loss of his entire family, failure to keep his family farm, unable to help his sister captured by savages, alone, frightened, surrounded now by strangers in the military – the only option to a penniless young man I would think. Could I have developed such a hate as he seems to have? What type of person would I be? Who could know? I feel the anger and the very large disappointment slowly fade and be replaced with great sorrow and pity for him. *My life is so much better than his and he will never know or understand that.*

I sigh and snuggle closer to Bright Feather and I feel him relax against me, knowing that my thoughts are easier in my head. "Thank you," I say at last out loud and then I wonder, *Who am I saying that to?* I realize that it's a prayer, for the difference between my life and Henry's can only be through this *mercy* that Isaac Watts writes about all the time in his songs. *Thy mercy stretches o'er my head, the shadow of thy wings; my heart rejoices in thine aid, my tongue awakes and sings[32].*

Two days later, with Bright Feather by my side and Storm in front of me in the saddle, we travel to the military tent that contains the commanding officer. We have decided that I'll do all the talking and Bright Feather will observe. Our secret of his ability to speak the white word seems one better left kept between just us. As we ride through the town, past the general store and the newspaper office, I've a wave of homesickness for One Who Knows Place in the Maple Forest that takes my breath away. I look at Bright Feather riding straight and serious next to me and am never so glad to see him within arm's reach. He glances over at me and quick as a flash winks at me. *I love you,* I think to him.

"I am First Lieutenant William Dawes," the officer says to me as I'm escorted into his tent. "Thank you for coming," and he ruffles through the papers on the table that serves as his desk until he finds one that he's looking for.

"Ah yes. We need to take a statement from you which is your version of the events which transpired on," he refers to the papers in front of him, "Friday, August 12, 1832."

So I tell him of my walking back from the mission school, hearing the four soldier horses approaching, the comments, the chase, the attack, this discovery of my brother, the final comments and my departure. I even go so far as to tell him that I'd decided to say nothing, fearful of how my mate would react but that proved impossible.

Can I identify my attackers? I'm asked like I've just described to him the pattern of footprints that an annoying raccoon has left behind.

"One is named Henry Graves," I say, growing somewhat impatient at his manner. "I also heard the names 'Steven' and 'Jimmy' and of course, there is the one who is missing part of an ear," I finish sure that he has heard the account that I've told earlier to the other soldiers at Miss Rebecca's house.

First Lieutenant William Dawes looks up at me sitting across from him holding my baby and looking Indian, but relatively innocent, I suspect. "Missing part of an ear?" he asks puzzled.

"Yes," I say ever so politely. "I bit it off."

"Oh ... hmmm, I see," he says and goes back to scribbling his notes.

The entire visit takes very little time and then we are politely but firmly dismissed. I feel a spark of anger as things resume within the tent as if we have already left.

"Excuse me," I say after a moment. "What will happen now?"

First Lieutenant Dawes looks at me confused at my meaning and my continual presence it seems. "Why, we will question the officers involved and should their stories match yours they will receive suitable punishment."

"And what if the stories do not match?" I ask feeling the growing sparks of anger grow high in my chest.

"My dear Miss ..." he looks down at the papers he has already set aside and obviously forgotten, "Miss *Graves*," he says clearly dismissing my Indian name in favor of my white one. "Army soldiers under my command never, ever lie."

The anger grows bright and hot in me. I stand, handing Storm to Bright Feather. "I *see*," I hear myself say in angry but carefully controlled tones. "But the words of a white woman who has taken up with an Indian brave would *always be suspect* it seems."

His face assumes a careful blank look as I continue. "It also makes perfect sense that I'm in the habit of *biting someone's ear off* in the course of normal polite conversation." I look around the tent at the soldiers now standing carefully alert watching me and my Indian mate and baby. "It is *so reassuring* to know that the United States Government and its army are protecting the interests of its *citizens*."

I turn to walk out of the tent with Bright Feather behind me and I hear First Lieutenant Dawes say, "Your citizenship and the rights and privileges that go with it are no longer at the top of my priority list from the moment you *married* your Indian brave there and aligned yourself with the *Nation of the Cherokees* rather than the United States of America." He does not suspect, I realize, that Bright Feather understands him as he has been quiet through this entire visit.

I turn and smile at First Lieutenant Dawes and he seems puzzled by my reaction. "My Pa told me one time that it is unfair and downright unkind to expect more than a body is capable of. My life so far has taught me that there are many different kinds of people: brutal, loving, idiot, smart, hateful, and kind. I will give you some sound advice, but all things considered what I've heard and seen so far from you, I doubt that you will take it: *things are not always what they seem*."

Three days later, the great council meeting that we have traveled all this way for convenes. Because the crowd is so tremendous, it's held outdoors in front of the council house. As part of the crowd, we find space to sit as best we can in the shelter of trees to escape the bright summer sun. We search and search the crowd but there's no sign of Beaver that any of us can see. The meeting begins at high noon and will go all day and into the night. Those that speak stand on the front steps of the Council House. We listen to the military speak, offering a sum of money – *three million, two hundred and fifty thousand dollars* – that is so large that my head cannot even understand it. We hear the promises that have been made many times before: assistance in travel, safety, and assurances of defense from future white invasions by the military. I look at First Lieutenant Dawes and the other officers as he speaks and I think, *Do you realize how often these people have heard these things and how often your promises have not been kept?*

Tensions increase as the temperature rises. Having heard all the proposals the military can offer, Young Snakes stands and speaks favorably of this treaty. He argues strongly for the decision that'll give up all claims to land east of the Mississippi and move the entire Nation of The Real People west. He's well spoken and obviously educated. And he's called by the white name *John Ridge* when he's introduced. I watch closely the look on John Ross' face as Young Snake gives his eloquent speech. As Young Snake names those leaders who favor the treaty, it's only *Elias Boudinot's* name that causes Ross to look pained. Even the name *Andrew Ross*, whom Great Elk confirms is John Ross' brother when I ask does not cause a reaction. Dark Cloud sits silent through all the discussions. It's powerful obvious which son has been chosen to be his successor.

In the late afternoon, John Ross stands and addresses the council. After such a long day of speech after speech, some have fallen fast asleep in the heat, lulled by the endless drone of the voices, the heat and the flies. But as John Ross stands to speak, you can feel the shift in the mood. It seems as if everyone takes a mental splash of cold water and prepares to listen to the best and final show.

John Ross stands for many moments, looking through the crowd, acknowledging his supporters with subtle nods, staring pointedly at his critics unblinkingly, and respectfully bowing to the military officers present. When he begins to speak, there's not a sound to be heard in the vast crowd, and small though he is, his voice is powerful, strong and sure. "It is known to all of us, that the history of the Cherokee Nation up to the present, has been one of repeated, continued, unavailing struggle. The cruel policy of

Georgia, on the part of that State, has been one of unparalleled aggravated acts of oppression upon the Nation. The Cherokee Nation is depending implicitly on the good faith of the American Government. Believing that the Government prides itself as it does upon its justice and humanity, we must trust that it would not disregard the plight of our Nation, but would eventually interpose to prevent it from being disregarded and trampled into the dust by the State of Georgia. We further shall appeal to the Executive, Legislative and Judiciary Departments of this United States Government for redress of all wrongs committed and security against injuries apprehended.

"In defiance of Acts of Congress, decisions of the Supreme Court, and of solemn treaties, Georgia has gone on to despoil the Nation of their laws and Government and impose upon them laws the most obnoxious. Georgia has distributed lands unbought to her own citizens by lottery. Lastly she has driven our people out to hunger and perish in the wild forests through use of armed bands of her citizens who are now parading proudly through Cherokee lands.

"All those who share a love and concern for the Nation are deeply affected with this deplorable condition of The Real People. It is our responsibility to remind those who still rest upon the comforts and enjoyments of life which have been so profusely scattered around us that hundreds of Our People, many of whom are women and children, may now be homeless wanderers, suffering with cold and hunger, for no crime, but, *because they did not love their Country less.*

"The crisis of the fate of the Cherokee people, seems to be rapidly approaching – and the time has come when they must be relieved of their sufferings. Being fully convinced in our own judgment that we could not prosper as well any where else as upon this native land, the Cherokees will and shall decline all offers extended them for purchase or trade of these sacred lands which we have and always will call *ours*. We must be fully determined against a removal to Arkansas.

"A delegation must, with great haste, be sent to his Excellency, President Andrew Jackson, to most respectfully and earnestly ask to be informed, upon what terms will the President negotiate for a final termination of these sufferings put upon us by this State of Georgia. We must be able to reassure our people that they may repose in peace and comfort on the land of their nativity, under the enjoyment of such rights and privileges as belongs to free men.

"The will of the Cherokee people will be expressed and their wishes will be carried to Washington. The Treaties entered into between us and the United States Government are very strong and will protect us in our right of soil. United together and of one mind, there is no danger of our rights being taken from us.[33]

"I am finished speaking."

Silence follows John Ross' talking for many moments and then finally a lone person begins to clap. Gradually more and more join in and the square in front of the Council House seems to fill with the sounds of enthusiastic agreement. Voices are added to hands, shouts, whistles, war whoops. I study the expressions on all those who carry importance in this meeting: First Lieutenant William Dawes, Dark Cloud, Young Snake and even John Ross. I find it amazing that all have the same carefully controlled blank expression.

A vote is called and it's overwhelmingly decided that any treaty supporting removal across the Mississippi should be rejected. There are just eight who vote for the removal acceptance: Elias Boudinot, Young Snake, and John Ross' brother Andrew among the group. Those in our group are surprised to see that Dark Cloud is not part of that group, however.

As the crowd disburses, I'm called and I turn to see First Lieutenant Dawes as he makes his way towards us against the press of bodies. He removes his hat respectfully, "Miss Graves," he says. He turns to look at Bright Feather who shows a fierce unresponsive face and he nods briefly. Bright Feather does not respond in word or movement, just continues to stare at him.

"First Lieutenant Dawes," I say by way of answer. I chose not to make conversation easy as I've no desire to have one.

Still with his hat in his hand, First Lieutenant Dawes says to me, "I wanted you to know that I spoke with all four soldiers and they are most sincerely sorry for any fright they may have caused you with their mischief. Seems you misunderstood their humor, interpreting it for harm, when they only meant some tomfoolery. I have reprimanded them severely for causing you any upset and they have assured me that in the future they will be more careful with *who* and *how* they speak to those who may not have the same take on their fun."

We stare at each other for a moment. "Do you have any children, First Lieutenant?" I ask and I watch him struggle to shift his head to this path of the conversation.

"Why yes, yes I do, Miss Graves. I am the proud father of two daughters, Sarah, age 13, and Anna, age 12," he says and he seems to relax some at what seems to now be a pleasant social conversation.

"It will be my greatest hope that both of your daughters might find the *harmless intentions* of these four soldiers or any of the remainder of your fine company of *truthful* militia, within the scope of their sense of humor and good fun. Far be it for your men to suffer for the lack of enough suitable women to *enjoy their type of wit.*"

Bright Feather's hand tightens on my arm and we turn to depart into the still milling crowd.

"Miss Graves!" I hear and I turn to see First Lieutenant Dawes standing still where we have left him. We stop and I look at him, waiting. "Why did your husband and those in your party not vote tonight in this important council decision?"

I look at him. I realize that he truly believes his men and truly *does not* believe me. He shows no anger over my comment that wishes both his precious daughters to experience the same brutal treatment that I've experienced. I realize that the comment I made to him the other day about *things not always being the way they seem* has made no mark on him whatsoever. *Can't teach a cow to drive a plow, Elle,* I hear Pa say. I've a strong desire to just walk away from this soldier, empty of smarts or the ability, it seems, to acquire any, but I fight against it. "Why did you not vote, First Lieutenant?"

He frowns. "Why, the vote was not opened to United States Citizens, it was open only to those who consider themselves members of the Nation of the Cherokee."

I see Great Elk emerge from the crowd. He sees us and makes his way towards us. I cannot help myself as I look up at Bright Feather and he looks at me. He reaches out and touches my cheek. I walk slowly back to First Lieutenant Dawes, still standing waiting for an answer from me. We reach him just as Great Elk does.

"My name is *Bear*," I say to him loud and clear over the noise of the talking and laughter of the disbursing crowd. "I am the daughter of One Who Knows of the Elk Clan. This is my mate, Bright Feather, son of War Woman of the Wolf Clan and this is Great Elk, my mate's father and chief of the Real People of The Maple Forest. All of the people of my village are *citizens of the United States of America.* We could not vote tonight for the same reason that you could not.

"But do you know what I think? I think that you will not believe this white woman who has chosen to love and live with an Indian brave and his people. Her words will always be *suspect,* especially when judged by someone who can only see the *outside* of a person and never anything deeper."

We leave him then, standing confused and no smarter in the crowd out in front of the council house.

All of us are eager to leave New Echota, Georgia and preparations begin the next day. Miss Rebecca does a powerful reenactment of my last departure, sobbing loudly. "At least your skirts will be clean after we go," and that causes her to laugh through her tears, for there has not been one day since our arrival that she has not carried some dirty, sticky mark of Storm's love and affection somewhere on her.

"Your visit has been so good for me, Bear," she says at last. "I do not know what the future holds for either of us, but it is certainly better for our time spent together, isn't it?"

I answer her with a tight embrace. "I need to ask a favor of you," I say to her in our last moments. "Would you seek out my brother, Henry Graves, and give him this?" and I hand her the deed that I took back from Cornelius Cooper over two years ago. "It is the deed to our family farm. He thought he had lost it to unpaid debt, but he was mistaken. When he finishes his time with the army, I would like him to know that there is something for him to go back to."

Bright Feather comes up to stand beside me. I cannot hear him, silent as he is, but I see her look up and I know. "It is a decision that we both feel is best," he says to Miss Rebecca. "It should not be ours, but his."

"I will do as you *both* wish, then," she says. She reaches out to Bright Feather and takes both of his dark strong hands in her plump white one's. "This thing you have with Bear, this love and cherishing, is a gift from the Almighty. It is *rare* and *precious* and something few people understand." She smiles a sad smile. "James and I share it, too. *Set me as a seal upon thine heart, as a seal upon thine arm; for love is strong as death; jealousy is cruel as the grave; the coals thereof are coals of fire, which hath a most vehement flame. Many waters cannot quench love, neither can the floods drown it; if a man would give all the substance of his house for love, it would utterly be condemned*[34] I believe God gives this great gift to couples that He knows will be of great positive change in this world. You and Bear are such a couple and I am pleased to know you.

"You will be in my prayers at all times, and just like my James, though you will not be close enough to touch, I can still hold you in that precious embrace." She hugs Bright Feather and it's a unique sight to see the two of them standing there.

"Now go, *quickly,* before I cause such a flood with these tears of mine that you will be unable to depart for the downpour!"

We wave and wave until we round the bend and then hurry to the place we call *home.*

Guard well your spare moments.
They are like uncut diamonds.
Discard them and their value will never be known.
Improve them and they will become the
brightest gems in a useful life.[35]

~Ralph Waldo Emerson

Trader

We celebrate the Green Corn Ceremony a few weeks after our return from New Echota. It's good to be home and pretend that things are fine and safe. It's easy to do as we enjoy a fine harvest and share the fellowship of those we call family and friend around the council fire. It's with great delight that we enjoy the company of Deer, his mate Possum and their three children, too. Possum has not been to the village to see her family since before Richard, *Small Turtle's* birth and there are many tears of happiness from her mother and sisters and old friends.

It's the following night after all the festivities, however, that Deer proposes a startling idea to the council circle that causes everyone to think so hard you can almost hear it with your ears. "I would like to open up a trading post here in the Maple Forest, right here by One Who Knows' Place," he says and murmurs begin around the circle and he adds quickly, "Please listen to my reasoning before you make a decision one way or the other.

"First, trading posts, owned by whites are rarely set up on Indian land." He makes a face. "It is usually a mutual sentiment: the Indians don't trust the whites and the whites don't trust the Indians. Were we to set up an Indian post on your territory, a mutual level of trust would be visible for all to see. We would further cement the truth that this is not Indian land, but that this is land owned by citizens of the United States.

"Second, I would establish a trading post here, in my name, but I would expect you as a village to run it. I can't be in two places at one time. We would use my funds to start it, but I would consider you the owners and would expect you to keep any profits made. It is my hope that it may bring income into the village *and* should times get rough, you may take whatever you need from its stores. You could sell goods made here in the village whether it is woven products, animal products, herbs, and even the growing products you are beginning to accumulate from the cows, goats, sheep and chickens. The maple syrup you produce is consistently the best I have ever tasted in my whole life."

He grins at us. "I don't think you realize that as a village you are time and again more productive than any other village that I deal with. Whether it is with your planting or harvesting, hunting and fishing, or now," he gestures as a cow lows loudly in the background, "with the domestic animals I brought you a few years back. I think that once people see the quality of the things that you have to trade, and recognize the honesty with which you deal, you could turn a fair profit."

He looks around at the faces staring thoughtfully at him. "Now I know it has *never* been the way of this village to desire money or possessions. The concept of wealth and power is not something The Real People have ever sought. The Old Way does not look to the future, but only lives for today. Even the language of The Real People does not have words that talk of anything but the here and now. *But*, it has always been the desire of this village to keep the land they have always claimed as theirs. In that respect, money has been a good thing for us. I have secured monies from the United States that has been due you from past treaties and that you have never received but should have. I have secured monies from the state of North Carolina which has been given to you in trade, rather than the land that you were promised. *I am buying land with that money.* I am thinking and operating in the white world like a white man, but my goals are for my red family and their values and wishes. Profits from the trading post could keep you more supplied during the lean times *and* perhaps buy more land to call your own.

"Third, I see it as an excellent bridge to establish another piece of uniqueness between The Real People of The Maple Forest and The Nation of The Real People. It shows a level of confidence and even bravery to embark on this endeavor, when others are simply preparing to do battle just to keep their land. I believe it will make others look at you with a different understanding.

"I am finished speaking," he says. He sits back and waits for the discussions and questions to begin. Raccoon is the first to speak.

"It would bring strangers and even whites into our village boundaries," he says and Deer nods.

"Yes, Raccoon, it would," Deer agrees. "Further more, I would encourage us to eventually build and maintain a road that would make it more accessible to get here. You must understand this: *if* you are going to stay *here*, you will gradually *in all directions* be surrounded by whites. While we fight to establish and maintain our boundaries, I see no reason why you cannot begin to establish some link with these neighbors that *are never going to go away* and will just become more numerous with every passing year. Rather than wait and fight with them over the level of contact *they* may wish to set up, let's begin to establish a level of contact that is *satisfactory* to us. Make the first step.

"These whites that are our neighbors are not even thinking about doing business with you; they're still trying to figure out just exactly what you are. Are you enemy or are you neighbor? Do you have a valid claim or are you just being stubborn? Are you part of The Nation or part of the United States? While they're still scratching their heads in confusion, let's get on with it and make some productive moves that can only benefit you."

"What type of trading post do you propose?" Great Elk asks.

Deer shrugs. "It should be one that the whole village is in agreement on. I'm sure you will not allow liquor. I'm sure you will not deal in slaves." He looks sad at some of the shocked faces that go around the circle. "Yes, I'm sorry to tell you that that is quite common." I look at Red Fox across the circle from me and he gives me a sweet smile. *Another shadow that has brought sunshine,* I think of him and Turtle and their daughter, Laughs Much.

"How you run the trading post is something you need to discuss and perhaps even add to as the business grows. It can be a typical trading post that everyone is familiar with or it could be one that is as unique as you are. There are no rules."

"What benefit will the road be to us?" War Woman asks.

"Well, the trading post would be a permanent structure. The trees we use to build it could be the start of the road that travels to it. Products would not always be brought on just horseback. Wagons would bring things in to you, too. Maybe that is a choice you wish to make, but in giving no wagon access, you will restrict the type of trading you will be able to do."

For the next few days, the trading post is the only thing discussed and thought about. Great Elk has made it clear that he does not want to divide the village over this issue. I'm proud to be a part of this village that talks and thinks without making quick decisions.

Finally, some three days later, the night comes to decide upon the course we will take. Because everyone has spent so much time talking and thinking, the vote is quick and while some do not voice an opinion one way or another, there are no formal disagreements. It's decided that a trading post will be established, with more decisions to come as to what exactly it will have to offer, who will run it and how it will be run. The building of a formal road will not be discussed until the trading post is established and the changes it brings to our village can be carefully studied and discussed. It's much easier to make a trading post disappear than a road.

Deer seems pleased with the decision and privately tells Bright Feather and I that there's really only one couple suitable to run it – us. "You are the only two that speak both the white and red languages fluently. There is no other choice. Add to it the fact that you can both read, too, makes it even more decisive. Does anyone know that you speak the language?" he asks Bright Feather.

Bright Feather makes an odd face at both of us. "Great Elk and War Woman both know. I did not tell them specifically, but they spoke to me early in the spring and said that if I was foolish enough to have lived with Bear all this time and was still unable to understand or speak the white language, then I was very unwise." He looks at Deer. "They shared the same opinion as you, of it being a good weapon to hold in secrecy from all but the closest in our group. I told them they should have no concern." He grunts and looks at Deer suspiciously. "I was surprised to learn that it seems they know quite a bit of the white language as well. How do you think that could be so?"

Deer looks at both of us with his careful Indian face. "I'd have no way of knowing," is all he says at first and then he does a quiet chuckle. "Let's just say that perhaps my encouraging you to learn from Bear was not an original idea. I was not this wise all on my own to start with. Great Elk took the time to learn basic English from me many years ago knowing that it would never hurt to have that knowledge. I just thought the same could apply to you, Bright Feather, and that's why I suggested it. I've had some powerful teachers over the course of my life here in this village. I've learned much of my smarts through example."

He looks at both of us. "Think about the running of the trading post and decide if that is what you wish to do. It is a great responsibility. Just the fact that Possum has not been here in these many years is proof of what I say. I had to move heaven and earth to get someone willing to run the post in Forest City just so that all of us could come out here and visit with you as a family. It would be easier for you, I would think, because you would have the entire village to fall back on, unlike us who have only the immediate family to rely on." He looks at us with a funny grin. "And who knows how many are here in this village that we don't know about who also can speak those difficult white words? Eh?"

Before Deer leaves, he makes suggestions for the size and arrangement of the trading post. He sketches ideas in the dirt and the men discuss supplies; what we have and what we need to get. Many take an active interest in the plans and I'm surprised to hear how many have had contact with the white world and have observed the building structures they have entered. Even I make some suggestions based on my time at the Coopers and what I remember worked and didn't work. The building will be a permanent structure, unlike any other that the village has ever built, including a necessary house and a small private room off the back which will not be open to customers. I remember my Pa's root cellar and how helpful it was in the winter to keep vegetables and such and make the suggestion that we build one of those, too.

Locations are discussed and a place is finally decided a safe distance east from the village. Stakes are set to mark out boundaries of the structures and where the root cellar is to be dug. One Who Knows' Place will not be visible in any way from the store, but it will be just a short hike away. It's hoped that the structure will be completed by the start of spring and Deer will make every effort to get the word out from his store's location about the new one opening up. I'm amazed that some of his customers travel such a great distance to get to him that our store will cut their travel time in half.

"I will be back within the month with as many axes and other building supplies as I can lay my hands on." He pats the list on which he has carefully recorded all the things that'll be needed as soon as possible. "If the winter is kind, I should be able to come back and forth a few times, before I bring the major first supplies with me to stock the store just when spring begins." He smiles a brilliant smile. "I think we're in business?"

As the fall paints its colors on the trees, it seems that every single person in the village has more things than they can possibly do. Gathering, hunting, replenishing hidden supplies, *in addition to* the frenzied activity of felling trees, stripping tree trunks, making notched logs for the building, digging foundations and root cellars before the ground freezes …

It's Red Fox and the two braves, Young Wolf and Spring Frog, who Deer traveled with to Dark Cloud's village, also known as New

Echota, who take over the directions of the building. It's with great relief on Deer's part to find out that their time spent there was primarily helping with some of the buildings we saw during our last visit. Even Bright Feather has some skill with building, having helped Deer build the trading post in Forest City. Raccoon, the one with no building experience at all, is put in charge of the root cellar. I try not to giggle as each night he comes home to our hearth tired, aching, and covered in dirt from his work.

And so the fall slips into winter and the winter is kind to us, such that Deer travels to see us two more times to supervise the building and help however he can. We are far ahead of schedule and before the snow begins to melt, for we do get some, he arrives with his first stock of supplies. He brings axes and horse bits, pitchforks, hoes, plows, and two enormous iron kettles that weigh more than my sturdy son who is approaching his third summer. Three weeks later, I giggle watching my Indian friends and family sort through things he brings on his second trip: bolts of bright cotton and shiny ribbons, a teapot and cups, woolen shawls, candles and lamp stands. On his last trip, he's to bring foodstuffs like tea and coffee, pepper and salt, rice and molasses. And when he does finally arrive, besides the food, he brings our first customer: my brother, Henry.

I know, before I even see Henry, that things are different simply by the way that Deer is riding his horse as he enters the village. He usually has a comfortable easy ride from a lifetime in the saddle. But as he rides into One Who Knows' Place that late afternoon, he seems to have a pile of sharp thorns stuck in his pants. He looks stiff and pained and mighty uncomfortable.

Raccoon notices, too, and shouts in good natured fun, "Deer! Seems to me that you've traveled once too many times to us over the course of this winter. You look mighty saddle sore, if I do say so myself!" I feel the laughter die in my throat and the smile disappear from my face as Deer looks in our direction and Henry rides stiff and tense into view. I stand there quietly beside Raccoon, not knowing what to say or do. Henry seems to have the same feeling.

Raccoon's manner changes instantly at the presence of a stranger in the village. The way that Henry stares at me causes Raccoon to look down at me standing stiff and silent beside him. As I meet his questioning eyes, I watch him put the missing pieces in the proper order. Raccoon has heard about my chase in the woods of New Echota and the discovery of my brother. We may not look alike, but no two people could be so uncomfortable in each other's presence than my brother and me. *Ah ha,* his look says to me as he raises one eyebrow, *so we get to meet the brother at last.* I watch him change from teasing trickster to fierce unwelcoming savage.

"Who is this stranger you bring to our village?" Raccoon says in a loud and unwelcome tone. While I would be almost certain that Henry cannot understand the conversation, it seems that Raccoon will take no chances. I study my brother as he sits on his horse. He looks like he would rather be anywhere else in the world than where he is right at that moment. He's in his military uniform and even his horse has the look of a soldier about it in the style of it's saddle, the cut of it's mane and tail, and the brand that I see on its black flank.

Great Elk and War Woman, almost always the first to greet all who enter our village, come forward to welcome Deer. Great Elk, never having met Henry, does not know who he is, but *anyone* could sense Henry's discomfort and tension.

Deer dismounts and as Henry follows suit, he says to Great Elk and War Woman, "Greetings my mother and father, it is so good to be home again and have the opportunity to be in your company. I have brought supplies for the store, which I have already unloaded. May I present to you, Corporal Henry Graves of the United States Army. He has requested I escort him here to your village and perform the proper introductions. He is here because he seeks someone who lives in this village." Deer follows the proper way of things and saves important business until the evening council circle.

Does Great Elk recognize the name? I wonder to myself.

"Welcome to our village, Corporal Graves," Great Elk says. "It is not always that we have visitors, but as the store reaches its final stage of completion, it seems that we will have to become more accustomed to that. Will you join us for our evening meal?"

Deer translates and I hear Henry say stiff and formal, "Yes, thank you for the offer."

"It would be wise to have all your sons present tonight for the evening meal," Deer says to Great Elk and War Woman, who glances at me and then Henry with knowing eyes.

As War Woman stands looking across at me frozen and unsure, she says, "Will you, Bright Feather and Storm join us for our evening meal tonight, Bear?" I nod my head 'yes' unable to find any words.

Deer is unable to speak privately with us before the meal, so we enter the circle of the hearth, Bright Feather, Storm and I, uncertain as to the purpose of Henry's visit. Neither one of us can even venture a guess why my brother would make the trek out here to see me, when he made his opinion of me so obvious the last time he saw me. When we arrive to eat, the conversation is working through fits and starts with the help of Deer's translating.

Storm, never one to be shy of even the strangest of strangers, walks right over to Henry and says, "Who are you?"

"Storm," I say to him, "give the proper greeting."

Having continued to live up to his name, *Storm* Eli is never that quick to be inclined to follow *anyone's* directions. He studies Henry, who studies him right back, and finally decides to take the easy path this evening, "Welcome to the village of The Real People of The Maple Forest," he says.

I look at Henry. "He welcomes you to the village of The Real People of The Maple Forest," I say to my brother in English.

"Oh. Can he speak English?" Henry asks me.

"No," I say and I sense his disapproval across the fire.

"We are glad to have you join us for our evening meal," War Woman says and Deer translates. "Corporal Graves has brought us precious gifts of tea, coffee, and sugar. I hope that the evening meal will leave no one unsatisfied."

The meal progresses with conversation flowing primarily about the store and the new supplies that Deer has brought. This latest shipment, which contains foodstuffs, will be the last of the start supplies. As we talk, Deer does the quiet translating to Henry, as I'm seated on the opposite side of the fire. We talk about costs and the methods we will use to record credits and debits. Deer tells us of the latest news since his last visit only three weeks ago.

"I hope what I have heard turns out to not be true," Deer says with great concern in his voice, "but I understand that when John Ross returned from his trip to Washington to meet with the President – he was there the entire winter – that his home had been taken over by whites who had won his property in the land lottery. His mate, who was very ill, and their two children were being held virtual prisoners in two rooms of their home."

Deer says in a disgusted voice, "He traveled all the way to Washington to tell the President under no circumstances will The Real People sell their land *for any price* and returned to find that he has no personal property to call his own anymore." I sit there and imagine us returning to One Who Knows' Place to find it overrun with strangers, while Otter, Little Bird and Squirrel are held prisoners, sick and frightened. It's a thought too disturbing to hold in my head for long.

"Those I know who have connections in Washington say that President Jackson is so eager to commence the removal process, that he is ready to try desperate measures. That could only mean forced military action in my mind. It's becoming a fearful time, *for all of us.*"

This conversation has not been translated for Henry. I watch his expression as we talk and his face shows anger and frustration at being excluded. I'm quite sure he does not speak the language of the Real People. War Woman glances at me and then looks at Henry. *Prepare yourself*, her look tells me and I do. "Corporal Graves," she says to him and Deer speaks quietly, translating to him, "whom in our village do you seek?"

"I've come to bring my sister home," Henry says and I think that that's the very last thing I expected him to say. I realize that for those around this small family group, what he has said is no surprise to anyone and that's a small comfort. I feel Bright Feather's leg muscle go tense against my arm. I watch Deer's face, guarded and rigid.

"I tried that once," I say with distaste, "it was not a good idea."

"You returned without my knowledge or my protection," Henry says to me from across the fire and Deer's voice translates for the others. I find that my mind waits to hear Deer's words rather than my brother's.

"I've experienced your protection once just recently and I would prefer to avoid it for the rest of my life," I say with a voice that was sharper than I intended.

"I did not know that it was you!" he says defensively.

"That does not change the person you have become!" I throw back.

The silence stretches into long moments. *I'll kill him*, I think to myself, *before I let him take me back with him.* It's a stunning thought, I realize but I know it to be true.

"What do you offer your sister that would make her leave this life she has here with us, Corporal Graves?" War Woman asks. "Do you intend to encourage her to bring her mate and her child with her?"

"And the new child that I carry and that will be born in late fall," I blurt to the group. This secret thing that has been between just Bright Feather and me these short few weeks must now be thrown out for all to know. I want Henry to realize that this life of mine is not just something that can be washed away with strong soap or abandoned just by riding a horse east.

I feel a strong sense of satisfaction as I watch him process the enormity of the fact that I'm pregnant *again* with another Indian baby. I hear him call me *Indian whore* again in my head and I think, *Why are you really here?*

"From here I travel to Ward's Mill, Virginia." So he will go home to claim the family property and reestablish himself. Miss Rebecca has kept her promise and given him the deed of property that we left with her. He looks at me across the fire and I suddenly understand why he is here. *Responsibility.* I can hear Pa saying, *A man is judged by the responsibilities he keeps.* Henry Graves, Corporal in the United States Army, feels a responsibility for his poor, abducted, Injun lovin', sister. *Now that he's got his farm back by her anyway.*

"My sister," He never calls me by my name, I think, He can't stand to call me by my Indian name and is not brave enough to call me by my white one in this company. He continues, "can live on our family farm while I finish my duty. When my tour is completed," he shrugs, "we can go from there."

What foolishness is this? I think and say, "I appreciate the confidence you have in me, but I sincerely doubt I can run a farm all on my own. Having experienced the *hospitality* of a majority of the neighbors, I doubt they'd be inclined to help me out much," I struggle to keep my temper and try to distract myself with Storm's antics as he wanders around the fire and takes turns crawling into different adult's laps.

Henry glares at me. "I've communicated with *neighbors* in Ward's Mill and I understand that there are tenants living on the property," he explains to me and seems to be struggling with his temper as much as I am. "The cabin was repaired and a room has been added onto the cabin and it can be yours." He looks at me with some impatience. "You practically ran the place when you were eight, you can certainly do it again now that you are grown."

He takes a deep breath, trying to calm the tempers he and I seem to be building. "I've gone out of my way to seek you out. I traveled to Mr. Thomas' trading post because I was told he was a trader that had knowledge and connections with a number of tribes in the area. I had learned from Mrs. Wilder in New Echota these names and locations. Mr. Thomas was willing," he looks at Deer for a brief moment, "although I would not say *eager* to help me locate you and speak with you. I've two more years of duty with my army responsibilities and I've requested a transfer to Fort Winston in Virginia. From Ward's Mill, I travel there to assume my post."

Deer looks at me across the circle at his words, *Fort Winston*, and the full impact of it all settles on my head. My 'brother', a successful businessman with *property in Forest City* came and retrieved me from Fort Winston almost *three years ago* and now my *brother* will return there within the month, completely different and completely uninformed as an enlisted soldier. How will the knowledge of our deception be received, as it will most assuredly be discovered? What would be the impact for Major Everett, Deer, and even myself and this village? Our deception will be out, a damaging thing to all involved. *So that's why Deer brought him here,* I realize, *he had no choice.* My mind thinks fast and furious and I feel like I'm dancing bare foot around burning hot coals.

The words just flow out of my mouth. "You have no responsibilities toward me, Henry. I'm safe, happy, and *where I want to be.* It was my *choice* to return to Ward's Mill over three years ago. I did it not knowing you were alive, *not because I wanted to,* but for the sole purpose of establishing that this village had *no role* in my abduction. I learned that you were alive some time later and of the financial difficulties you had faced through no fault of your own. Very soon after that, I was forced to flee from the Coopers for I feared for my safety and that of my baby." I shrug, not happy to be reliving these memories and eager to finish the story. "I came about the deed by accident, but by then I knew it was rightfully ours so I kept it."

I look at Deer across the circle and he meets my gaze with his unblinking stare. *What do we say and not say?* I think to him. I remember the story of Deer, Raccoon, Bright Feather and the horses and the advice Great Elk gave to Deer about what they should do, *Why tell the truth, son, tell the truth.*

To Henry I say, "I lived in Fort Winston for part of the winter when I was pregnant with Storm. I stayed with Lieutenant Foster and his family. Major Everett is the nephew of Miss Rebecca and Reverend James Wilder and he was the one who escorted me from this village to Ward's Mill."

I look back at Deer and give him a loving smile. I remember seeing my 'brother' standing there grinning at me that day and the relief and joy to see not Henry's face, but his. "I sent two letters during my time there. One to Washington, requesting information about you and your whereabouts and one to Deer telling him where I was." I look at Henry. "I wanted to *go home.* I wanted to be with *my family.* I wanted to return to those *that I love.* I wanted to *come back here,* to The Maple Forest.

"Deer showed up at the fort, having not received the letter I sent *him*, but having seen the letter I sent to Washington *about you*. He pretended to be you and secured my release and brought me back here."

I put my hand on Bright Feather's tense thigh and I see Henry stiffen to see the intimate touch. I smile at Storm curled up fast asleep in Great Elk's embrace. "I will not go back with you, Henry. I'm pleased that you will be able to reclaim the farm in Ward's Mill and perhaps restart your life once your time in the army is done. And you need to know the way of things in Fort Winston before you arrive and any confusion or trouble sets in. I apologize only for that but I do not regret it for one moment."

Henry looks at me and then finally says through stiff lips, "What if I insist that you return with me?"

"That day in the woods, you called me an Injun whore. I know I will always be that in your mind. It is important for you to know that Bright Feather, my mate, and I gave you the deed to the property because we wanted you to have it. It was a joint decision. We realized what a difficult time you have had in these past years and wanted you to have something to go to once your time in the army was done. We do not want the property. We do not want that life."

Henry looks at Bright Feather's face that's carved from stone. Then he looks back at me. "*Joint decision? We?* You speak almost as if you *pity me* and have given me *charity!*

"I've spent the last four years of my life first trying to find you and then trying to come to terms with the fact that you must be dead! I joined the army because I was told that there was extensive Indian contact and I thought at first that I could find you, but eventually I hoped only for revenge. And what do I finally find?! I find you dressed like an Injun, living like an Injun, and calling these Injun your family that you love!!

"These Injuns *killed Pa!*" He shouts at me and my brain registers that Deer is no longer translating the angry words he is now shouting at me. "They took so much of his scalp that they *cut the top of his skull off and left his brains for me to clean up!!* And they did the same with Eli, only *they cut his hands off first to stop him fighting!!* I came home to them dead, the house just about burned down and you nowhere to be found. I've spent four years agonizing over your safety and your rescue and what do I see when I finally find you?" I listen to his horrible words and the sorrow and grief I have felt over Pa and Eli is torn open like a new wound. I put those awful pictures in my head that I do not want there and know it will take much hard work to store them away.

Through stiff lips I force out, "You find me flat on my back in the process of being raped by you and your friends." Henry looks at me, breathing hard and fighting back tears it seems. I find I *do* pity him. My life has been so much better than his, but I'll never be able to convince him of it. *Not now, anyway*, my head says.

I talk quietly, remembering those first months and being so homesick and frightened here in Great Elk's village. "It was hard those first months for me, too, Henry. I prayed that you and Pa and Eli were safe and alive. There was a time when death for me would have been a relief." I look up to him and feel tears trickle down my cheeks. "When I found out that all three of you had been killed, I just thought the grief would swallow me right up for a time.

"But these people we sit with today, *they are not the ones we both can hate together.* Those that have caused us such great sorrow and turmoil in our life are dead. *The revenge has been met.* Look around this circle at these faces, Henry. Make every effort possible to see past the red skin. These people in this circle have loved me, cared for me, and made me feel like a friend, sister, and daughter. They have brought happiness back into my life that could have been nothing but sorrow. They deserve your gratitude, not your hatred."

I can't help the images that crash around in my head of Pa laying on the ground and little Eli lying next to him. I cannot help myself and I think about Eli's hand in mine and that feeling of love and trust and I put my own hand to my mouth to stifle the moans and to fight the sickness that all of a sudden seems to overwhelm me. I choke back the tears and the vomit and feel the shelter of Bright Feather's arms as he pulls me into a comforting embrace and at last lifts me up and carries me away to the darkness and security of the corner of our hut. He lays down beside me holding me close as I cry and try to wash the pictures from my mind. I concentrate on the reality of him and his love and finally let the escape of sleep take me away.

I sleep late the next morning and even after I'm awake I lay and listen to the sounds of the hearth and the village around us. I think about Pa and Eli again and think about the paths of life and the choices and the *not* choices we face. The early weeks of this pregnancy seem to be much easier than my pregnancy with Storm and aside from an occasional feeling of sickness – that never amounts to much – and some lingering tiredness, I feel strong and well. I think the changes between the pregnancies must be because I'm safe and secure with those I love this time around.

I finally rise from bed at the insistence of a very cute and handsome little man who can't figure out why Momma is still in bed. All the morning chores are close to being finished and a warm bowl of stew is waiting for me by the fire. I find I like living in this big hut with all these capable women and I joke with Otter and Turtle that maybe I'll just start sleeping late every morning. It's Turtle who gives me a smile and says with a dreamy voice, "Maybe we could all do it and take turns …" That makes us all laugh.

I'm anxious to see what supplies Deer has brought and Storm and I make our way to the trading post. It does not cause such a start for me anymore as it comes into view. I found that the early days when the building was taking shape caused my heart to pound with fear on occasion. Seeing a white man's building in the middle of my Indian village home took some getting used to.

All the preparations have been completed and those that are involved in the building have been released to other responsibilities now. Raccoon's Cellar, as we call the root cellar, is wide and spacious but empty. I stand at the opening and try to imagine it full of our summer's harvest, ready for trade and winter eating. Storm likes this place because it seems to be a secret world to hide in and he laughs and giggles while I examine the final shelves and solid door that has just been recently added.

Inside the store, I examine the piles of supplies that have been carefully placed just inside the door for me to sort through. It seems as if *everyone* in the village has naturally assumed that I will take over the major running of the store, primarily because of my language abilities. Consequently, I've begun to think of this place as *mine*. The first shipment of things was unloaded and stored willy-nilly all over the place much to my frustration! I had everyone chuckling behind my back as I moved and shifted and rearranged things more to my liking. Now, things are just left in a pile for me to sort through and put away and that suits me just fine.

"How are you today?" I hear a male voice say behind me and I do not need to turn around to know that it's Deer.

I do though and give him a smile and a chance to see my face. "I am fine," I say.

"There was no way for me to make yesterday easier," he begins and I walk over to him and give him a hug.

"There is no need for you to apologize," I tell him. "Where is he now?"

"He's made camp just outside the village, and the last I knew, Bright Feather and Raccoon were going to go and invite him to go fishing with them."

I look at Deer to see if he's teasing. *"He went with Bright Feather and Raccoon to fish?"* I repeat, watching for the twinkle.

"Yup, at least they were going to extend the invitation."

I think on this for a moment and try as I might I just can't put the three of them, Henry, Bright Feather and Raccoon, laughing and having a fun 'ole time down by the river spending a day of fishing. "Might there be something more than fishing going on do you think?"

Deer shrugs his shoulders. "Not that I was made aware of. Hey, Little Man!" he greets a grinning Storm who squeals with delight as he's swung high up over Deer's head. "Are you busy helping here with the store?"

He sets Storm down and kneels down to his level. "James has sent you a gift," he says and from out of his pocket he pulls a carved likeness of a horse, a cow, and a chicken. "He says he will send you more next time."

Storm is enchanted with the figures and I'm impressed with their detail. "They are wonderful," I say. "Did he do those himself?"

Deer nods proudly. "Yes, he's got quite a talent for it. Now if I could get him to do his chores with as much enthusiasm as he does his carving, then we'll all be just fine." He looks over at Storm now lying on his stomach on the floor of the store playing with the pieces and then Deer looks at me and grins. *"Just wait!*

"He showed up at the store in Forest City about two weeks ago," Deer says and I know he speaks of Henry. "I tried to put him off, tried to be vague, but when he said the words *Fort Winston,* I knew the path I had to follow. You did right to tell him the truth. There really was no other choice."

I tell him about the story I've heard of Deer and Raccoon and Bright Feather and the horses and I have to laugh when he makes the same pained look I remember on Bright Feather's face. He nods his head in recollection and quotes Great Elk, "Tell the truth son. Always tell the truth."

We stand silently for a moment, watching Storm play on the floor. "Your brother's full of pain, anger, hate and feelings of failure ..." He snorts. "Being in the army is not the best place to put someone suffering from one, let alone all four of those emotions," he says. "I'm inclined to believe him because he's made himself perfectly clear that he really doesn't give a hoot what *anyone* thinks of him anymore; that the incident with you in the woods at New Echota is not something he was ever party to before. He was quite put out to find out I knew of it. I told him so he would know how close we are. I can't speak for the rest of the group, but from what I can figure from our casual conversation, he seems to have few close friends. He seems quite eager to get to Fort Winston and be closer to what he considers home.

"He reminds me of Turtle, of all people, when he first walked into the store. Silent, cautious, and closed ... Only spoke with me because he *had to*. Only answered questions that suited him to answer and that he felt would get him what he needed. Made the most of his military uniform and insisted on wearing it at all times, almost like it is the only thing that is holding him together. *Maybe it is*," Deer says very quietly.

"Anyway, I finally agreed to escort him here, given the condition that he told me specifically why he was looking for you. When he said it was to bring you home, it took all my strength to not laugh out loud. I knew that you would never go back with him and if he forced you, he'd end up dead." He looks at me right in the eye. "I told him that, too.

"So nothing you said to him last night should have been much of a surprise, although I suspect it was still painful to hear."

"Do you think he will say anything at Fort Winston?" I ask.

"To what end? What good would it benefit him to admit that he is the *real* Henry Graves as opposed to simply *another* Henry Graves? He probably wouldn't be inclined to talk about you much, anyway," he says with an arch of his eyebrow, "even if you *did* go home with him."

Late that afternoon, as we begin to prepare the evening meal, I go to the edge of the village to the place where Henry is camped. I know from Bright Feather that the offer to fish was politely but firmly declined and from the best of my knowledge my brother has been here, isolated on his own, the entire day. He's not by his sleeping roll and hearth, but I can see him sitting further on, near the river's edge.

I sit down near him on a boulder and stare at the water as it flows by. I say after a time, "We call this *The River That We Are Always By*," and then say the Indian word slow and careful, "*Oconaluftee*."

Without looking at me he says, "I don't need no lessons in being Injun."

A burst of anger makes me stand right quick and say to his stiff back, "Maybe not, but you could sure use a lesson in being *polite*," and I start to walk away.

As I begin to trudge into the woods I feel all of a sudden as if Ma, Pa, and Eli are standing right there with us in the forest and I imagine them looking *so powerful sad*. The feeling makes me stop and I struggle to settle my temper down to a level that'll let me speak civil again. "Is this the way it will be between us, Henry?" I say to him at last without bothering to turn around and face him.

He doesn't answer me for so long that I decide that his silence is his answer. Finally, though, he says so quietly that I can barely hear it over the river, "I've spent so long hating them, Elle, and I just can't change overnight."

The pity comes again, like a first heavy snow and it snuffs out the last of my anger. I remember a time, not so long ago really, where there was a mighty big difference in my head between a body with white skin and a savage with red. I remember how long it took me to change my head and my heart and become as pink as I am at this very moment. "If you're inclined, we'd like you to join us at our hearth this evening. Before you leave, I would like you to see and meet those that I call my family now and who mean so much to me." He does not say anything and I begin to walk away.

"Thank you for the deed," he says at last to my back.

"You will never stop hating them until you start to know them," I say without turning around. "I'm sure I don't need to remind you how thick my skull is when I'm set on a particular thought. Anger, hatred, and getting revenge are tastes I still remember right well. But I much prefer the flavors that I've been chewing on these past few years." I make my way back to the village and I realize that my brother and I have not looked at each other's face once.

Storm calls Henry, *Bluebird*, because of his uniform I suspect. As we sit and eat our evening meal, it's Storm that shouts, "Bluebird is here!" and jumps up in excitement to greet him. *How can you not see that love?* I think as Henry is drawn into the bright flickering lights of our fire by Storm's chattering excitement.

Henry sits awkwardly down in a space near me and Storm. "This is my brother, Corporal Henry Graves," I tell the group. "Storm has named him Bluebird, though." There are welcoming smiles and I tell Henry his Indian name.

"Bluebird?" he says and I nod and smile. A moment passes. "Tell me the word for it in Indian," Henry says with eyes just for me. When I do, he looks at Storm and repeats it to him. Storm rewards him with a bright smile and walks over to show him his carvings from James.

I slowly work my way around the group and do the introductions. For each person I try to tell Henry something about them to help him keep the name and the face in his head. I've flashes as I look at each one of them, seeing them with Henry's eyes as opposed to my familiar ones.

"This is my mother, One Who Knows," I say and she makes no effort to show kindness or welcome. *What else would I expect?* I chuckle to myself. "She is a healer in our tribe which is good because her words can be sharp enough to sometimes almost cut you in two."

When I translate that she's quick to respond, "That is because the majority of people in this camp are so dumb, only sharp words and big sticks can penetrate their thick skulls." Amid the laughter of the group, I translate her response to Henry who maintains a careful face.

"This is my sister, Turtle," I say and she gives Henry a shy smile. "She is the daughter of One Who Knows, too, and is married to Red Fox. Their daughter, Laughs Much, was born the spring after Storm. I am an excellent shot with a bow and arrow because of Red Fox and my bow and quiver are the finest in all the village." Red Fox and I exchange fond glances.

"This is my sister, Otter," I say. "She is the daughter of War Woman and is married to Raccoon. Their son is named Little Bird and their daughter is named Squirrel." I look across at all of them and I think of my first days when I was at Bright Feather's hut, alone and frightened, still not even knowing the language. I think of that first bath and I smile at her with great tenderness. "It is because of Otter that I came to love this village. She showed me kindness and love and patience. And it was with Raccoon," here he gives me a look that says, *And just what will you tell him about me?* and I grin at him, "that I learned to hunt. I made my first kill hunting with Raccoon," I say proudly.

"Father," says Little Bird, who is listening carefully to all that's being said, "isn't that the deer you said was blind and deaf and dumb?" As the group dissolves into laughter, and I attempt to translate this to Henry, I hear Little Bird puzzle out loud, "I was always amazed that a deer could be such a thing …" which makes everyone laugh all the harder.

I must tell Henry the whole story of my "dogged" persistence and Raccoon's eventual giving in. I feel compelled to be honest about my constant questions and how Raccoon was often the brunt of many of them in those early days. Henry, at last must look across the fire at Raccoon who says and I translate, "She has a way about her," and gives a decidedly painful look.

Henry looks down at his hands clasped in front of him and then to Raccoon and then back at me. Finally Henry says very quietly, "My Pa used to say that she could make a body more tired with her questions than a full day's plowing," and the group collapses into laughter again for they have heard me tell that already. Henry doesn't join in with the laughter but as the conversations and the meal progresses looses his tense, uncomfortable way a bit.

At last I put my hand on Bright Feather's arm. "This is my mate, Bright Feather. He's the son of War Woman and Great Elk. I owe him my life and I give him my love." I weave my hands together in the sturdy bridge that One Who Knows showed me many summers ago. "We are strongest when we are together, a bridge that cannot be broken." Bright Feather and Henry exchange looks across the fire, sizing each other up as politely as is possible in a situation like this.

"And this is our son," I say looking down at the now sleeping form curled up in my lap and then looking up to watch Henry's face, "Storm *Eli*."

I see the name register on Henry's face as he looks at Storm sleeping peacefully. Finally Henry says, "I've watched you in the camp with him today. It reminds me of how you were so good and patient with Eli all the time." He looks across the fire at me and all of a sudden it seems that everything fades away but just him and I. "You were a good mother then and you are a good mother now." I fight the tears that crowd up behind my eyes.

"I will leave tomorrow," he says at last.

"Will you carry a message for me?" I ask quickly and Henry looks across at me and nods.

"Ezekiel and Jane West were kind to me when I was there. Would you tell them I send my greetings and that I've a son and am expecting another child? Will you tell them that we are well?" and I look at Bright Feather and smile.

I'm surprised to watch a frown cross Henry's face as if he's been posed a problem that he cannot solve. He stands at last and says, "I'll be right back." When he returns, he carries with him a letter that he removes from the opened envelope and scans quickly down to the bottom of the page. "I thought so," he mumbles to himself. "Here," he says, "I guess you should read this."

I take the letter and bend forward so that I can read it by the flickering firelight.

26th November, 1832

Dear Mr. Graves,

It is with pleasure we received your letter, dated 27th, August 1832, requesting information on your family's property located near Weirs Creek, here in Ward's Mill, Virginia.

My wife and I have made every effort to keep a watchful eye on your interests here. To that end have secured tenants to repair the home (it has been rebuilt with an extension as the current tenants have six children) and manage the farm. We have charged what we feel to be a fair rent for the property and homestead and have been keeping a careful record of your accounts here at the store in anticipation of your eventual return.

The present agreement with the tenant is whatever profits he can secure above and beyond the set rent he may keep free and clear for himself and his family's needs. I am pleased to report that these past few years have been very productive and I believe that you will be as pleased as he is were you to see the actual accountings.

We have charged no fee for this service but are simply happy to provide you with some solid foundation for your inevitable future return as well as a tidy sum of money for any future needs.

In closing, I offer apologies have I overstepped my bounds by opening your letter addressed to "Cornelius Cooper, General Store Proprietor". Both Cornelius and Naomi Cooper have been gone from this town for a number of years and no one is certain of their present whereabouts. As I and my wife are the current proprietors of both the general store and the mill, we thought it acceptable to open, read, and respond to your letter.

We wish you God's Grace and Guidance and a speedy and safe return at some point in the near future.

Sincerely,

Ezekiel West, Proprietor

Ward's Mill General Store and Mill

I laugh out loud when I read the closing signature and hug the letter to my chest. "Oh, Henry!" I say to him, "this is *good news!* Thank you for sharing this with me!" I then tell those in the group, all who are familiar with my time in Ward's Mill, the wonderful turn of events.

I smile at Henry, "So when you have finished your time with the army, you will have a home and farm to go back to, and even some money as well! There are worse ways to start off!"

He looks at me with serious eyes across the fire. "I will not ask you to come back with me again," he says, "but will you understand that I will always have a place for you, too?"

I shift a little with the heavy weight of the little man in my lap and I look down at his sleeping form, content and relaxed. "I understand," I say, *but I could never leave this*, my eyes tell him across the fires, *NEVER*.

He stands to leave. With care he goes around the circle and makes eye contact with each and every face that I've introduced to him as my family. "Thank you for your hospitality," he says and I carefully translate. "I am glad to have met you." He puts his hat on and walks away into the night. In the morning he's gone before first light.

Over the next weeks and months, word spreads that there's a new trading post at One Who Knows' Place in the Maple Forest of the Real People. Those first early days, it's with frightened beating heart that I come running to the shouts of my name, more than once, only to discover that someone has come to do business and I'm not at my post, but rather gardening, washing clothes, cooking, gathering in the forest, or tending to Storm. Raccoon, tired of hearing my name shouted, takes one of the huge iron kettles and one of the iron hoes and sets it outside the store. From then on, when I hear "CLANG, CLANG, CLANG" ringing through the forest, I know where to go without such a fright. *I'll have to buy a bell with some of our first profits*, I think with a giggle as I walk to the store amidst the racket.

The village relaxes as the store seems to bring no real dangers or problems just new faces to meet and greet. I suspect that many who visit the store are unaware as to the exact location of the village and that suits all of us just fine. Perhaps the most stunning thing of all, with the opening of the trading post is that I receive *a letter* one day carried by a customer. The envelope is dirty and rumpled and bears the marks of many hands that have carried it on its travels. As I look at it in my hand, I wonder at it and what it says:

> *To Be Delivered to The White Woman Known as Bear*
> *Proprietress of The Trading Post*
> *One Who Knows' Place*
> *Maple Forest*
> *North Carolina*

I do not open it right away. I can't imagine who would be writing to me and I spend the rest of the day with it tucked in my belt, floating back and forth between excitement and dread. At last, Otter threatens me with bodily harm as I wonder about it aloud *again* as we prepare the evening meal.

"Open the letter, Bear!" she says in frustration and waves a stick of kindling at me like she plans to hit me with it. "Has it not gotten worse, the worry of the not knowing? Surely whatever is inside could not be anything worse than this!"

I smile at her and chuckle at my silliness. "I've never received a letter," I say to her by way of apology and explanation.

"*Neither have I,*" Otter says to me in a tone that tells me what a fool she thinks I am. "Open it." So I do.

20th June 1833

My Dearest Bear,

It is my most earnest prayer that this letter finds you, Bright Feather, your son, Storm, and your unborn child well and healthy. We received with much delight all the news that your brother, Henry, had to share with us and he was most patient with my seemingly endless questions as to your welfare and current situation. As soon as I realized that there was a formal location, Your Trading Post, I knew immediately that correspondence between the two of us could be a reality.

As I write this, our daughter, Rachel, born just three years ago today (my how the time flies!) is a horrible sticky mess sitting on my floor eating some early summer peaches we have just picked. Whenever I hunger for peaches, I think of you arriving in that snowstorm with the jar of some in hand! She is a delightful happy child and we treasure every moment with her. Her infant brother, Matthew, born the 9th of February just this year (in the midst of a horrible blizzard!!) is thriving as well. We are a growing family!

I am happy to say that Ezekiel and I are doing fine. Henry says he shared with you our letter to him so the fact that we are now proprietors of the General Store and Mill should be no surprise to you. We now have tenants working and caring for the property you knew as our home when you were here and we now permanently reside at the store. We have added a bit on the back as the quarters were just too cramped for all four of us.

The reasons <u>why</u> this change in our circumstances has come about should not be too difficult to figure out. Your sudden disappearance from Ward's Mill caused quite a stir once the rains came, the snows melted, and the Coopers were able to spread the word. Words of "theft", "insanity", and "attempted murder" were thrown about. It seems that with each telling you grew and grew in might and terror. When they began to speak of swearing a warrant out for your arrest, Ezekiel took it upon himself to pay the Cooper's a private visit. What was specifically discussed I do not know, but we can both imagine, can we not?

Not long after Ezekiel's talk with them, Mr. Hobson informed us that a stranger came into the store asking for you and when the Coopers spoke at length about you and your crimes and state of mind, this stranger threatened them with all manners of horrors from wild and vengeful Indians. It was immediately after that, that the Coopers packed and left for parts unknown, leaving no forwarding address.

As I was the daughter of the former mill owner and experienced with business life and we had been left in possession of the Cooper's Ledger – which we offered to burn and allow everyone to "start fresh" - it was unanimously agreed that we should take over the running of the general store and mill. Since that time, we have discovered the deeds to the mill still in my parents' name, making us the legal owners. As for the general store, we have decided to make it something of a cooperative effort, with everyone sharing in it's profits and losses while we run it in the day to day. Even Mr. Hobson has been active – and not just in the liquor corner!! I think, should you ever visit our fair town again, you would find things very different.

We had a good visit with your brother. He carries with him many demons, I fear. He spoke politely of you and the visit he had just had and yet the sadness that surrounds him seems to be something he can barely stand for the weight of it all. He seemed pleased with what we have done with the farm and Ezekiel rode out with him the day he went to visit and meet the tenants. I think it is a relief to know that at least that is something he need not worry about.

News is not abundant here, but we do hear some things and word is never good regarding the Indians. We hear regular news about the impending availability of land for homesteading following the removal of the Indians. Ezekiel and I worry for you and your people. There is a heavy presence of military here now with Fort Winston in full operation and we fear it can only mean sadness and danger for you.

We keep all of you in our prayers and desire only security and happiness for you. I would be most delighted to receive personal news from you via word of mouth or letter.

Yours most sincerely,

Your friend,

Jane West

I enjoy so much the reading of it that when I finish it, I read it through again lost in the news, most of it happy. When I finally have finished reading it for the third time, I look up to see all members of my hut sitting quietly and concerned, having decided that the letter can only be bad news.

I grin at them, "Mostly good news and the bad is mostly things that we know regarding the military and the desire to take away our land." Over the evening meal, I read the letter a fourth time, translating for them all and interrupting to tell added details as needed here and there. Dinner is over and it's full night by the time we have all finished enjoying my very first letter.

That night in our corner of the hut, Bright Feather and I snuggle together and talk privately between ourselves. He asks, "Will you write back to Jane West?"

"With what?" I say and make as if to look around the hut for a quill and ink.

He props himself up on one elbow and does what is his latest habit, which is to rest his big hand on my ever growing belly and see if he can feel the movement I feel all the time. He adds a puzzled look though, "There are writing supplies at the trading post, are there not?" Then he looks excited at me, "I felt that!"

I giggle because most of the time when he says that, there has been nothing really to feel, just like this time. His looks of disappointment are so great sometimes when I tell him the truth, that I've taken to letting him have his fun no matter how different the reality of it all is. "Do you think it is all right for me to use those supplies to write personal letters?"

He frowns at me as if he cannot understand what I'm saying. "Bear, you have put many days into the trading post, while still meeting all your other responsibilities within this hearth. *Plus*, you have just entertained *all of us* this evening with the sharing of your letter. Added to all of that is the benefit we could receive from getting any additional news from the outside. I think you should write to Miss Rebecca, too. It never occurred to any of us, even Deer, that the permanent structure of the trading post would also mean news from the outside world in the way of letters."

The idea of receiving *more letters* gets my heart racing and he grunts at me. "I can see your mind working already," and he leans over and kisses the hollow of my neck and travels down between my breasts and I find that letters take a distant second to other thoughts now crowding my head.

He studies me in the dusty twilight. "I do not have such fear about you having this baby. Do you?"

"No," I say, "this time I am just eager to get to know him or her, having had such fun with Storm as we do. Do you care if it is a boy or a girl?"

"I would enjoy having another powerful woman in my life, I think," he says and kisses me long and slow and sweet. I wrap my arms around his neck and enjoy the pressure of his body as he leans across me and my belly to kiss me more. The baby gives a hard kick at the unwelcome pressure, I suspect, but Bright Feather is too preoccupied with other things now to notice. So am I.

As the final months of my pregnancy settle in and I remember the weight and the pressure and the pulling and the cramping I must stay closer to the trading post. Raccoon makes the observation that I'd just as well sleep there, since I've gotten so slow it takes me twice as long to get there and back anyway. Even Storm grows impatient with my slowness and often runs ahead of me to greet the customers with smiles and chatter before I waddle into view. At last I no longer go back and forth as the CLANG, CLANG, CLANG summons me, but sit quiet and still on the steps all day doing work that I've carried with me or someone has brought me to keep me busy.

With delight I watch Raccoon's Cellar fill with our own village vegetables as well as produce we have accepted in trade. I enjoy watching the entries in our ledger grow, for fall and harvest is our busiest time yet. I write a letter to Miss Rebecca and one to Jane West and send them off with willing customers going in the right directions. The trees turn their bright colors and then shed them in a brilliant display that for once I seem able to sit long enough to really enjoy.

And finally one day, I know it's my time. It comes upon me so quick that I know I dare not try to make it back to the village in time. Storm for once, has stayed with Otter and Turtle, preferring the company of the other children and having grown absolutely frustrated with my unwillingness to go for even short exploring walks in the woods. I feel the pain grip me and I remember, more than three years ago, One Who Knows and Otter's careful instructions, "Breathe slowly, concentrate on your body and listen to what it tells you …"

I laugh at myself as my head thinks, *My body says it's time to have this baby!!* I finally go over to the great large kettle with the iron hoe sitting in it and, in between pains, I CLANG, CLANG, CLANG, for someone to come. I struggle to remember where Bright Feather has gone for the day and I finally remember that he has gone to do some late autumn hunting. It seems to take a long time before I hear someone calling my name, having finally realized that *no one* should be clanging since I'm always here now. I hear the running footsteps and know it's Bright Feather before I even see his concerned face. He takes one look at me and I do not need to say any words, but I do think, *Just in time!*

And so our daughter is born on the floor of the trading post. Attended by her father, welcomed by her mother, she screeches her intentions to the two of us with great force and fury. "I must say," Bright Feather says as he ties the cord with new twine, cuts the cord with his knife, wraps the baby with soft clean new cloths, and brings me clear, cold water in a new tin cup, "that were I to ever have the opportunity to choose where you were to give birth again *in the future*, a fully stocked trading post is *much better* than a cave."

"Hmm, me too," I say but I'm sleepy and tired and quite comfortable propped up on a few sacks of grain nursing our finally silent little girl. I look down at her and am amazed to see blue eyes peeking at me and much fairer skin then Storm's.

"She's beautiful," he says to me and I close my eyes and listen to him moving around in the store. I hear pounding footsteps on the front steps and the last thing I hear before I drift off to sleep is Bright Feather's voice saying, "Welcome! Come see and greet my beautiful daughter!!"

Our daughter goes for a number of weeks without a name. Not for laziness on our part, just for lack of one that seems to fit her. We are in no hurry, just waiting for the time when it will settle on her gently like a curious butterfly looking for a sweet flower.

From the moment we walk back to the village that first day with the baby, One Who Knows is so taken with this granddaughter that she seems to not be able to get enough of her. She's always holding her, rocking her, singing to her and I suspect if it were possible, she would be nursing her, too. It seems that only One Who Knows can ease her belly when it's aching; only One Who Knows can comfort her when she cannot seem to fall asleep; and only One Who Knows can coax a smile from her. It only makes sense to all of us when it's One Who Knows who finally finds her name.

As she hands her to me one afternoon to feed her, she gives me a rare smile and a contented sigh. "She makes me feel young again, I feel like there are many good things to hope for with her here now." Our eyes lock and then we both smile and say at the same time, "Hope".

"*Hope*, daughter of Bear, of the village of One Who Knows' Place, of the Real People of the Maple Forest," One Who Knows whispers to her as she slurps contented at her meal, "we welcome you with love."

Later as Bright Feather sits holding Hope while Storm and I wade and splash in the chilly river, Bright Feather says, "Tell me the name of your mother that gave birth to you."

I look at him across the expanse of rushing water and say, "Elizabeth."

He looks down at Hope and says, "She shall have the name Hope Elizabeth then, to join both of your lives like we have done with Storm Eli." I nod and smile at this wise man that I call my mate.

Winter comes early and stays late. Poor spring has fits and starts and battles with winter for many weeks before she finally wins her place. Summer comes hot and fierce and seems to want to make as great an impact as winter has. Customers return to the trading post and we enjoy another good year. We hear disturbing reports about forced, military assisted removals from a number of areas in Georgia and it concerns me greatly that I never receive any answer from my letter to Miss Rebecca.

As another year slips by I watch my son learn to ride a horse and Willow is patient with his eager attempts to make her a swift-as-lightning war pony. Red Fox is more than pleased to begin Storm's instructions in making a bow and arrows and within a short time he's practicing his shots. I watch Hope go from infant to crawler to toddler and her bond with One Who Knows does not diminish, but seems to grow. Hope develops the same, unblinking, unencouraging expression that One Who Knows has and nothing is more disturbing than trying to converse with *either one of them* when the other is present. Although her eyes darken to a unique dark gray, rather than blue, they're always startling to me in a world of only brown eyes. Bright Feather grunts when I make this observation, "My world is not full of only brown eyes," he says, "My world is *only* one pair of green ones," and I ponder the ways of hearts and how they never seem to stop growing fuller with each day.

In the early months of winter, just after Hope begins her third year, Deer visits and there's such an air of tension about him that he does not joke or smile his entire visit. He insists on seeing the caves and how they're prepared and urges greater stocks and even suggests that we begin to do trial treks to the caves – day and night. He insists we develop a warning call or signal that'll notify the village to *drop everything and run for safety*. He cautions hunters and trappers and even the women who gather far into the woods to never assume that the village is a safe place to enter *unless we see and hear it to be so*. He tells us of a treaty, rejected by both John Ross and amazingly John Ridge, that requires all of the Real People to move west, and promises money for schools, money for those who have fought in wars, money for improvements that have been made on land that must be given up, free transportation, blankets, kettles, rifles, medicines, wagons, and *four million five hundred thousand dollars*.

Then he tells us of *another treaty*, signed on December 29, 1835 and considered official and final, by twenty Real People leaders, including Major Ridge, Elias Boudinot, John Ridge, and Andrew Ross, that gives up *all* of The Real People's territory east of the Mississippi for five million dollars. It contains all the usual promises, but it's not signed by *any one of the elected Real People officers* of the Nation.

"How can that be official then?" Great Elk says with great puzzlement. "What is the use of elections and officers and signatures and treaties if all can be ignored in the face of strong opposition?"

Deer looks utterly defeated. "John Ross is still fighting for the majority of the Real People who do not want to leave. This 'treaty', called The Treaty of New Echota, is a blatant deception, secured through lies and threats and greed." He looks at all of us around the circle, "And it will mean the downfall of The Nation of The Real People of the east."

Sitting with all of us around the evening fire, Deer says, "The United States Government has no more patience. I hear this wherever I go and with whomever I speak, whether it is a government authority in Washington or a farmer bringing his produce to trade. *The Indians are as good as gone*. President Jackson was elected with the promise that the Indians would be removed west. He is in his second term of office and is passionate that this promise will be kept before his term is up. Every soldier I talk with seems to simply be waiting for the order to begin the round up."

"What do you mean 'round up'?" War Woman asks.

Deer looks at her. "Thirty forts have been built surrounding the land currently claimed by the Indians. You can call them forts or you can call them *containment centers* meant to hold *by force* Indians that have been rounded up *by force* to be shipped west *by force*.

"*It is only a matter of time now.* It is no longer a matter of *if.* I continue to make every effort to establish you as separate from The Nation of The Real People. I continue to make every effort to get those in places of power to acknowledge your citizenship and the promises made to us so many years ago. I have traveled again to Washington to talk with anyone in power who will listen to me and I have traveled to Raleigh, the state capital of North Carolina and talked with government officials in power there, too. Our paper walls are still there, I work to keep them strong and sure every opportunity I get.

He sighs and looks at all of us around the council circle. "Things are very bad in Georgia. The *Georgia Guard*, the state army, has begun to regularly drive entire villages away from their homes, farms, and businesses. They often wait until the women and children are alone. There's great alarm and fear throughout most of the Real People communities in Georgia. John Ross heads the *Anti Treaty* Party, while John Ridge heads the *Treaty* Party. Each sent a delegation to Washington earlier this year. Only Ridge's party was received by the President. Ross' party couldn't even get in the door.

Deer puts his head in his hands. "Anyone who thinks that this will not be a tragedy *and* a travesty is mad."

Mid pleasures and palaces though we may roam,
Be it ever so humble, there's no place like home;
A charm from the sky seems to hallow us there,
Which, seek through the world, is ne'er met with elsewhere.[36]

~John Howard Payne

Fugitive

In the middle of one early spring night, we are summoned to do a practice run and hide in the caves. There are those who do not want to do this and grumble about the waste of time and energy, but those of us close to Deer cannot escape the feeling of dread and worry he has left behind in the village, even after his departure.

"We will do this," Great Elk says firmly over the council fire, "for the loss of an occasional night's sleep is worth the life of one person that may be saved because of the practice. We have entrusted our life's path with Deer and his guidance, we will not disregard his advice now."

And so, by the light of a bright spring moon, we make our way through the cold night taking care not to slip on the frost covered ground. The children always think it's a marvelous adventure and I must smile at my Storm running ahead with his bow and arrow strapped to his back. Hope rides on my side in a sling I often carry her in when I gather in the woods. She's tiny in size but big in spirit, making every effort to keep up with her brother. Bright Feather carries both sets of bows and arrows plus his rifle and ammunition. But I marvel at other groups I see departing in different directions, complaining about the loss of sleep *again* with nothing on their backs but a fur blanket against the nighttime cold.

Each cave is unique and secret. Our group has never been to another's cave and no one but our group has seen or known where ours is. Each family is instructed to move with haste and speed to the cave they have been maintaining these past years. I worry about others who have not been as vigilant with their supplies as we have been. It seems that there are some who prefer to operate with the idea that if they never really think about it or believe that this will come, it simply *will not*.

Within a short time our small group is on our own in the forest. Our cave will have all of those from our hearth, including One Who Knows, as well as Young Wolf and his new mate, Sweet Maple, and Spring Frog. Each family has carefully maintained the supplies, rotating them to keep them fresh and helping to keep the cave at a suitable level to live. There are other creatures who would appreciate our food supply efforts and wish to move in and must be continually discouraged!

It's Raccoon who calls a halt to our hike with his question, "Where is One Who Knows?"

In the confusion of the drill, those of us with children have been too busy with our own problems and a grip of guilt invades my heart. One Who Knows is always one of the loudest of those who complains about the drills. Although she rarely draws attention to herself and her pains, we know that it's a struggle each morning for her to get up and out of her pallet, let alone do it twice in one night with a long hike in between. "I bet she hoped she would be forgotten and is home chuckling over the fact that she is still warm in her bed," Raccoon says with frustration and a bit of envy I think.

"I will go back for her," he says with conviction and I suspect he has the attitude *If I'm going to be miserable, so are you, too.*

Otter looks at him in the moonlight and places her hand on his arm. "Be kind and gentle, Raccoon."

He bends over and kisses her. "Don't worry, I won't get close enough to get bit."

Our cave is large enough for us to all comfortably lie down. The ceiling is high enough to stand, *in most spots anyway*, and we have done our best to anticipate our needs should we have to go there in haste. Baskets of food, necessary tools, weaponry, furs and deerskins, and even some additional supplies from the trading post are now carefully stored in the back darkness of the cave. Those of us who come to the cave on a regular basis never take the same path twice in a row. The entrance is my favorite for it's well hidden.

As we hike, I remember the first time Bright Feather and Raccoon showed us the cave. We had hiked up as a group, those from our newly built home and hearth as well as Young Wolf and Spring Frog. Only One Who Knows stayed behind. "The cave entrance, although it cannot be seen, would be visible from where we stand," Bright Feather said to us. He looks at Raccoon. "Whoever can find the opening, Raccoon and I will do all of their chores for a full day. Go and see if you can find it!"

No one was more determined than Otter, Turtle and I. We hunted and scoured the area. We sent Little Bird crawling underneath the bushes and scrambling up over the boulders nearby. Finally though, we all admitted defeat. No one, not even the men, were able to find the opening. But when we looked to find Bright Feather and Raccoon, they were nowhere to be seen. It was as if they had disappeared into the air! We called and called them and then at last, we heard faint bird calls coming from the boulders that we had helped Little Bird crawl up just moments before.

In the dark shadows of two enormous boulders and shaded by the dense brush of a massive evergreen tree, we finally found an opening large enough for even the men to fit through. The cave was wondrous big, dry, and flickering with a lamp that Raccoon and Bright Feather had lit.

"How did you ever find this?" Red Fox said in wonder as he wandered around the entire space.

"Hunting," said Raccoon. "Bright Feather and I found this years ago when we were still young and foolish and could spend days away from the village hunting and causing trouble." He walks over and shows crude pictures scratched in the walls. "We were stalking a killer … *raccoon*," he says with a grin, "and just when we were certain that we had him cornered, he disappeared!"

He looks at Bright Feather, standing casual against the wall. "We had a bet and had I been able to catch the raccoon, I would have won *for once*. I was determined to find that raccoon, *which I did,*" he finishes smugly and wiggles the raccoon tail hanging from his hair, "and, we found this cave!"

For this drill, we are just to walk there and back, with another one planned in the future when we are to sleep the night. I think Great Elk worries, as I do, that some families have done nothing in preparation, despite all the warnings. While all were in agreement when we first began these plans more than five years ago, the tension and need has been dulled by the everyday responsibilities of life. People are busy enough without having to worry about some never used cave up in the hills they are supposed to keep stocked and always ready.

When I voice my concern with Great Elk, he says to me, "Bear, I can only tell them what I think is right and make a good example. A good chief knows he cannot *make* his people do anything." I've never thought of it that way.

We wait for a time, expecting Raccoon and One Who Knows, but as time passes we decide, as we are all growing tired, that we should make our way back without them. As we reach the boundaries of our village, I can see that many are back before us. But it's the sounds of wailing songs of mourning that make me run, for I know for certain who they sing for.

For a second time in my life, my mother has died.

As her daughters, Turtle and I have the responsibility of preparing One Who Knows body for its travel to the next life. We wash and comb her hair and clothe her in a new deerskin tunic. I wonder at how tiny and frail she seems and realize that true strength certainly does come from within. Turtle and I are silent as we work, but I know that her thoughts must be the same as mine, filled with memories of this fierce Old woman that we owe so much of our happiness in life to. I see her standing looking at me with her fierce look the night I stared down Weasel outside her hut when I was a slave. I hear her words to me, *You were always a powerful woman even before you knew it.* I remember her tears of joy at Storm's birth and I treasure the strong bond she has had with Hope. I find myself almost chuckling at her unwillingness to suffer fools or make accommodations for idiots. *I am far to old to worry about what people will think of me or my words. I speak only truth and those who hear can decide to listen or not.* I'm proud to be her daughter. I feel the tears come and Turtle and I sniffle and work with our memories and our tears.

While we do these responsibilities and shed our tears, Bright Feather and Red Fox dig a grave in a spot we have chosen in the forest along one of her favorite gathering routes. Her body is placed, head facing east, curled as a baby is cradled in its mother's womb. I put her gathering bag and some herbs I know to be special: dandelion for the tea she loved so much, branches of fresh red cedar for it was what she loved to make her bed upon and spearmint for the leaves she loved to chew and that was what she often smelled of. Turtle covers her with a finely woven blanket patterned with symbols of love and security. We place baskets of corn and dried berries for food along the way before she reaches the next place along this path that's the journey of life. Storm places one of his arrows with her for protection and Hope must be convinced that *she cannot go now too, she must wait for a time.*

You are with your daughters Raven and Black Fox, now, I think, and I take comfort in knowing that she will not be lonely for she's rich, with the love of many powerful women that she calls her daughters, both in this life and the next one to come.

In the middle part of the summer, a party of five, three soldiers and two government officials, arrive in our village with the express purpose of counting our numbers. This census, whose purpose is *"to determine the size and scope of the Cherokee nation on the eve of its removal to more suitable land west of the Mississippi River"* has a frightening quality to it. These strangers that invade our borders, have no fear of us, disregard what information we have to tell them, and are high and mighty in their dealing with us. There are *no* representatives of The Nation of The Real People present, no appointed agents and no translators with them. Had I not been present to explain their purpose, I cannot imagine how their visit would have been interpreted. The communication is clear: *Discussions are over, actions are what we are concerned with now.*

"What if we refuse to leave our land?" Great Elk asks at one point during their three day stay and I translate the conversation carefully.

The officer in charge, a Lieutenant Miller, stares at Great Elk for a few moments before answering. "Sir," he says. "You will leave *this state's land* with or without government assistance, *but you will leave.* There is no discussion of this matter. Those who make any effort to avoid removal, will be arrested and charged with trespassing, which has a penalty that carries lengthy jail time."

He looks at all of us and speaks in a tone that questions our intelligence and our common sense, "Fertile lands west of the Mississippi seem far more attractive to me than a cold, dark jail cell.

"The New Echota Treaty, signed by representatives of the Cherokee Nation and ratified by the United States Congress guarantees removal of *all Old Nation Cherokees* by May 23, 1838. President Jackson has issued a proclamation that the United States no longer recognizes the existence of any government among the Old Nation Cherokees and any resistance to removal will be put down *with force* by the Army."

"May I ask what today's date is?" I ask, having no real way to know the passing of time other than watching my children grow before my eyes.

Lieutenant Miller looks at me for a long time and I feel his eyes travel from my bare feet crossed in front of me all the way up to the colorful collection of feathers I still keep woven in my hair. I stare back at him. *You are my enemy,* my eyes tell him, even if I'm careful not to say it with my mouth.

"Today's date is," he turns and speaks quietly to one of the nonmilitary assistants sitting next to him, "Wednesday, July 11th, 1836." He studies me for a moment longer. "Do you know that according to the census we are taking, that there are some two hundred whites intermarried within the Cherokee nation?"

"It is reassuring to me to know that I am not the *only* white who can make wise choices," I say with hatred.

"It should *not* be reassuring," he says to me with equal dislike, "to know that of the roughly sixteen thousand Cherokees currently living east of the Mississippi, in less than three years there will be *none*. You have my guarantee of that."

"When will the removal process begin?" War Woman says, glancing at me in caution as she asks her question.

"The removal process is *on going* and has been for this entire year. Since there are very few wagons *or* major roads throughout this territory, military detachments are working their way gradually to each and every settlement providing encouragement and assistance as needed. Some support has been welcome and the process has gone smoothly." I look at the faces of those seated with Lieutenant Miller and I can tell that he lies and leaves out much of the truth of things.

"Those here in this village, can either make their way, as soon as they are ready to depart, to Fort Payne, just west of here across the North Carolina border into Tennessee, or they can *wait for a military escort.*"

After their departure, we discuss among our hearth that perhaps their visit is good for us in a way. There has been a new passionate interest in the caves and the possible safety they may provide and I'm relieved to see many families making the preparations that we have already done.

The fall harvest is productive again and our trading post does a brisk business. Even Deer has remarked that it has exceeded his expectations. One early winter afternoon, I'm busy at work taking an inventory of new and existing stock. I find I get a great satisfaction out of keeping things organized and watching the numbers tell the same story that any eye can see; *business is good.* Hope is my regular partner at the store. I smile to myself and think, *Hope is my regular partner everywhere.* She's quiet and shy and will speak only with the closest members of our hearth. Even Great Elk and War Woman must work very hard to coax the briefest of conversations out of her. What time she does not spend in chatter with me at the trading post, she fills with observation and is a quick learner with just about anything we show or explain to her. She misses One Who Know greatly and has grown even quieter and more withdrawn since her death. While Storm often travels with Bright Feather or Raccoon or any other man who will show him the manly pursuits of hunting, fishing, trapping, building, wrestling, or stalking, Hope is now my companion to almost every place I go. When I call her Shadow, she gives me her shy sweet smile. Alone on our own, whether we are gathering, cooking, or working in the trading post, our conversations are lengthy and involved. Sometimes I see her, this tiny mite of a thing just three years old, and I think she's already an old soul inside a child's body.

She's quick enough that with her time spent in the trading post, she has picked up a large part of the white language. Unlike Storm, who cannot sit still for the moment it takes to explain things, Hope has quietly absorbed everything she has heard like a dry piece of ground soaks up a summer shower. She remembers voices, too. Her favorite spot is hiding at my feet behind the counter listening to all that's going on but not having to speak or interact with the strangers that troop through. It's a true compliment to the customers when she emerges from her hiding spot to speak with them and they always seem to know it.

As I work on the inventory, we practice our counting and at her request, we work in both languages. As I listen to her sing song voice saying clearly, "One, two, three, four ..." she stops and looks at me funny. "Bad bluebirds are coming," and she scuttles back behind a big sack of seed, so that only the tips of her bare toes are visible under the counter.

"What ... ?" I say to her and then listen, for suddenly I too hear the sound of horses. *Many horses.* "Hope," I say quick like without looking at her and standing watching the door for the soldiers I know that'll enter at any moment. *"Do not come out of hiding,* no matter what you hear, until someone calls your name. *Do you understand?"*

"Yes, Momma," she says, "and I will be oh so quiet like a mouse, too."

The solders ride in and I wish very much that I could give some signal to warn the village, but that's impossible. Bright Feather, Raccoon, Red Fox, Little Bird and Storm have gone hunting over the ridge today, hopeful to get some winter fat deer or elk for our stores. I can see many soldiers outside, remaining mounted, but five dismount and come into the store.

"Welcome, Gentlemen," I say in a voice that I hope to be calm and casual. "What business do you have here at The Trading Post at One Who Knows' Place in the Maple Forest?"

The man in charge, a towering red head with full beard and mustache says, "Good day to you. We represent the First United States Cavalry, Company B, stationed at Fort Payne, Tennessee. By order of the

President of the United States, Andrew Jackson, we are here to assist in your removal and departure from these ceded lands in anticipation of your move west."

"Your name sir?" I ask him.

"Begging your pardon, ma'am.   My name is Sergeant Peter McTavish."

My heart is pumping so hard and so fiercely I worry that it will explode right out of my chest. I know that *any time* that I can stall this group of soldiers will allow more time for everyone to run and hide. I'm almost certain, *but not positive*, that I saw Squirrel's face appear and then quickly disappear along the trail that leads to the village. She often brings me and Hope a late noon meal if we do not make it back to the village to eat. I look at Sergeant McTavish. "I was unaware that the removal policy proposed by President Jackson was for the removal of *United States Citizens*. Surely the documentation you carry makes a distinction between tribal and nontribal peoples."

He's prepared for this argument I can see for he looks neither puzzled nor flustered. "The United States Army is aware of the current attempts by various villages throughout this ceded territory to make rash claims based on the misguided attempts to remain. *No claims will be discussed unless said claimants have made their way to the appointed locations of processing and departure.* This village is scheduled to be escorted to Fort Payne, Tennessee.

"Should you have a desire to speak with those in authority, once you have reached Fort Payne, that can be arranged. But for now, my orders are simply to remove *all Indian personnel* from the designated areas I have on my map.

"We leave at dawn. Let me escort you back to the village so you can collect your things."

"I am expected to pack all of my belongings in less than a day?!" I say in a voice that sounds even to me like it's close to tears. "Surely you are making a very poor joke!"

"Ma'am, the order of removal was signed and put into law over *five years ago*. The United States Government has patiently negotiated with The Cherokee Nation to secure acceptable conditions for both sides and a treaty has been signed and ratified that has been accepted by both parties. Whether *your people* have made the proper effort to inform you of the time schedules for departure or not, *we leave at dawn*."

He makes a move to step behind the counter, but fearful of Hope's discovery, I step out and allow my arm to be firmly grasped. I'm escorted out of the trading post and into the cool, early winter afternoon.

"Please, let me lock up properly," I say and he releases my arm as I fumble with the lock and key. *I love you, Hope. Do not be frightened. Mommy will be back!* I drop the key once and must bend to retrieve it and my fingers are shaking as I insert the key in the padlock and securely lock my daughter inside and alone.

"Which way to the village?" Sergeant McTavish asks me and I've a moment of indecision about what to do. Do I speak? Do I stay silent? I opt to take the middle road and take them on a long, winding round about way to the village along the river rather then the quick direct route through the forest. I breathe a sigh of sheer relief as we enter a village filled with wandering cows and chickens, bleating goats and smoking fires and *not one person as far as the eye can see.*

"Damn," someone says.

McTavish looks at me, "Someone will come and rescue her. Tie her and leave her in the center of the camp." He looks to the officers standing near him. "Send out search parties in all directions to scour the surrounding forest – quickly – for they've only just left. See? The fires are still burning. And speaking of fires, burn the village. We'll stay the night by the warmth of the *fires,*" and he grins an evil smile at me, "and see what big fish we catch with this *white bait.*"

While I sit tied in the center of the village, staked against a tree, they search each and every hearth, ripping through baskets and tossing belongings left and right. I'm silent; worried about Hope, prayerful that the rest have made it to the caves and thoughtful about what I do next. I sit there and watch them burn each hut once they're satisfied there's nothing of value to take and keep my courage and spirits up as I watch different patrols return with no Indian faces with them.

It's a moonless, cold autumn night and I shiver, tied and unable to move and get the blood flowing into my arms. Worse yet it has begun to rain, a hard, cold downpour that soaks me to the skin and makes me even colder. I shift my legs, trying to ease some cramping and I hear booted footsteps approaching. It's McTavish.

"Getting a bit uncomfortable?" he asks and I choose not to answer or even look at him.

He reaches down and I feel him untie my wrists, leaving one wrist firmly tied with a rawhide strip and gripped in his gloved hand. "Figure you could use a moment of privacy in the woods, although I'll have to come along to make sure it doesn't turn into a party."

I stand and feel sharp prickly pain in my one hand for it has begun to go numb. I rub my wrists and shift my shoulders feeling the pain as the blood begins to flow and wake up parts that have gone to sleep. "Come along," he says and we walk out to the edge of the village where the forest tree line begins.

All around us are soldiers. There must be close to thirty I count. Many are asleep, snoring loudly, hunched against trees with woolen blankets and hats propped on their head to shield them from the rain. Others sit around campfires talking quietly amongst themselves, seemingly unconcerned with the pelting wetness. My brain says, *This is your only chance! You leave at dawn. You must be quiet and you must be quick.* But how?, I wonder. How can I escape this man that holds on to me like I'm a leashed farm animal?

In the shelter of the trees, the rain is not so loud or so heavy. The few remaining stubborn autumn leaves above us provide some shelter. I *do* have to pee. I hike up my tunic, squat and pee, too busy thinking to be embarrassed at my situation. There's a snap of a twig over the rain and we both hear it. McTavish comes instantly alert, raising his rifle and jerking me to standing before I've a chance to finish my business. I stumble in the dark, trying to get my wet tunic down and listening as carefully as my captor is.

In a flash, there's an arm around McTavish and a knife at his throat. White words with a heavy Indian accent say, "Drop your gun. My knife cuts your throat and we will be gone before others know what happens."

McTavish drops his gun and I whip my hand away with all my might to get free. When McTavish holds on tight to my leash, the voice says, "Loose her," and I'm suddenly free.

In Indian, the voice says to me, "RUN, BEAR!!" and I do not wait one moment, but run with all my might into the rainy wet night. I head first to the trading post to get my baby. I run fast, but careful, unsure what is happening behind me and knowing full well, that once the alarm is sounded, the forest will come alive with angry soldiers. *And once I have my baby*, I will not be able to run as fast.

My heart stops when I get to the trading post for they have searched this place, too. I put my hand to my mouth to keep from crying out. My carefully placed lock is still there but the door hangs to the side. I see bags of flour cut and spilled white against the dark wet ground. And I smell smoke. I run across the open expanse and crawl into the dark inside, slipping and falling on broken jars of maple syrup spilled all over the floor.

"*HOPE!*" I cry out in a desperate whisper. "HOPE!! Are you here?! It's Momma! Come quick! We must run!"

"Momma, the bad bluebirds made a mess," she says to me matter of factly and I jump at the sound of her voice so close to me in the darkness.

With a glad cry of relief, I scoop her up and run to the door, taking moments to listen and be happy to hear only the hard rain. "We must run quickly to the cave, Hope. Hang on tight to Momma." And I dash out into the pouring rain, glad for its cover despite it's cold.

I take the risk and run the most direct route to the cave. I know my tracks will be washed away with the sound of the heavy rain and will cover the sound of my running feet. When I'm close to the cave entrance, Hope and I stop and sit quiet for a long time, listening for any sounds of soldiers. It's quiet.

We are greeted with glad cries when we enter the cave. It's pitch dark inside, for a fire cannot be risked. "Who is here?" I ask and listen to the names Otter rattles off in a quiet whisper. "Turtle and Laughs Much, Young Wolf and Little Bird, Spring Frog, Squirrel and I."

We are given a blanket and I wrap a shivering Hope and I in it. My mind thinks of those who are missing: Bright Feather, Raccoon, Red Fox, Little Bird and Storm. "Where were they hunting, do you know?"

"The far ridge north and east of here. We had spotted elk tracks and they were headed in that direction," Young Wolf says.

"The soldiers come from Fort Payne," I tell them, north and *west* of here.

"How many soldiers are there?" Spring Frog asks.

"At least thirty, I think. Many went out to search the surrounding forests and I am unsure how many there were to start with. No one was brought back to the village that I know."

"That is good," Otter says. "See Squirrel? Your warning helped everyone get away safely."

"I thought I saw her little face," I say.

"I came to the clearing just after the soldiers arrived," Squirrel says. "I hid and tried to count but there were too many. I ran back as quick as I could to tell everyone."

"You did a fine job," I say.

We lay quiet in the cave, too tired and worried to talk, listening to the sounds of the rain outside. We pass the rest of the night and all of the next day huddled with each other, worrying for those in our cave that are missing and for those in other caves that we don't know about. I tell them of my release and they press me to try and recognize the voice of my rescuer. I puzzle over it in my head and I cannot figure out who it could have been. "He knew me, for he called me by name," is all I know for sure.

"It all happened so quickly, in the dark, with the rain ..." I say in frustration.

"Who among us besides you can speak the white language?" Otter wonders out loud. I think *Bright Feather, Great Elk, War Woman* are the three I know for certain. "Can Raccoon?" I ask Otter.

I see her shake her head in the dim light. "No, just a few words good for trading. I don't think he could have spoken even the brief few things you heard. Besides," she says, "where is he if it was him?"

Exactly, I think. *Where is he whoever he is?* If it was Bright Feather or Raccoon, and *they were not hurt or captured* they would have come to the cave by now, wouldn't they have?

The waiting and the not knowing are almost physically painful. We eat some of the stores of food we have and fall into fitful sleep. Late into the night we hear not one but two people entering the dark shelter of our cave. "Who is it?" I hear Turtle whisper.

"Mother! It is Storm and I!" I hear Little Bird's voice say and break with emotion.

Both of us worried mothers scramble forward in the darkness and clutch our boys to our chests. Storm is wet and shivering from cold and fright I suspect and I wrap him in the warmth of my body and my blanket. His solid form comforts me even as my mouth asks the question, "Where are your fathers?"

Storm starts to cry, great gulping sounds that I muffle against my chest with the blanket while I rock him in comfort. He may be a big boy, but he cries like a baby in my arms. I hear Little Bird's voice tremble, too, as he says, "They hid us away and let themselves be seen by the soldiers to distract them. We watched as they ran and were chased and finally captured. Red Fox, too."

The despair and grief swallow me like a cold, deep spot in the river where I cannot touch. *Now what?* I think.

In the end, we stay in the cave for three full days after Little Bird and Storm's return. They speak of a tall, red headed soldier that was part of the capture party and I know they must speak of McTavish and our men must be taken to Fort Payne, Tennessee. Before all of us emerge, Young Wolf and Spring Frog venture down to see the way of things while the rest of us stay and try to amuse the children.

When we finally return to the village, under assurances that the soldiers are long gone, there's really nothing to return to. As we search the different hearths and huts, there's little to salvage; the destruction is greater than the great storm so many summers ago. The trading post has some things that we can salvage – we are interested only in food. It seems that the attempt to burn it down was discouraged by the rain. I'm overwhelmed by the thought that had it not rained, my daughter would be captured or dead and I must sit quiet for a moment and work hard to put the fear away where it will not swallow me up whole.

Gradually, those from the village creep cautiously back. We sorrow to know that it seems two families from two separate caves were discovered and captured. One cave, close enough to another one, had to sit quiet and listen while their family and friends were dragged terrified and screaming away with the soldiers at gunpoint.

We erect temporary shelters and post nighttime guards should the soldiers return. We discuss our choices about rebuilding, supplies, and other immediate survival issues.

We discuss who my rescuer was again and puzzle over the mystery. No body has been found in the woods where I was released, so we know that McTavish didn't kill him. But as all those from our village return that can, no one claims my thanks. The mystery seems to remain unsolved until Beaver walks into our sorry village two nights later amid glad shouts. Then I know who I must thank.

"I came to warn you, but I was too late," he says with sorrow. "I thought I could get here before the soldiers. We had been traveling and came upon another camp of soldiers discussing loud and clear their path and the path of others. When I heard the direction that one was headed, I knew it had to be here. When I arrived, I saw the village in flames and only Bear as a captive. I was relieved to see no others, though."

He listens to the tally of those that have been captured. "I should have killed him when I had the chance ..." he says quietly to himself. He looks at all of us. "The soldiers will be back, but not for a while. They are too busy elsewhere. How are your supplies for the winter?"

We tell him of our caves and supplies. He tells us not to rebuild the village before winter but to live in the caves and we agree. We will butcher the cows and the rest of the farm animals for food since we will be unable to care for them over the winter from the caves anyway.

He looks at me. "And what do you do?"

I feel like I'm in a dark fog. "Me?" I say to him. "What about me?"

"You are the only one of us who can secure the release of those captured. You are the only one who can walk into the white world and walk out without a fight. What is your plan?"

I look at Storm sitting next to me with wide eyes and I look at Hope curled up in my lap and never separate from me since 'the bad bluebirds' came. I look at Beaver and those around the circle and I realize that *everyone* knows what I've only just discovered. "I go to Fort Payne, Tennessee," I say. I wait a moment and then say, "But first I go to Forest City and get Deer."

The hardest thing I've ever had to do in my whole life is leave Hope sobbing and screaming in Turtle's arms. First she looses One Who Knows, then she looses Bright Feather, Raccoon, and Red Fox, and now she looses me. She wails her sorrow and her fury while Storm stands stoic and quiet with tears trickling down his brown cheeks, my bear claw necklace around his neck and his hand in Great Elk's.

I've taken time with both of them privately. Storm is torn from wanting to be the little boy he is and keep his Momma safe right by him and wanting to be the little man he is and not cry or cling or show worry. He at least can understand *a little* that Momma will come back. "I go to bring Father and Raccoon and Red Fox and any of the others that I can home. See my skin, Storm? I can be white *or* red and that makes me very powerful." He nods solemnly and hands me one of his precious arrows to go in my quiver. Hope would crawl right up my nose if I would let her and as I speak to her she grips me tighter and tighter with her tiny hands. I suspect she sometimes knows things before they happen – One Who Knows' gift – like the day she knew the "bad bluebirds were coming" before I could even hear or see them. I talk to her in the most reassuring way I can, while I tie each one of my feathers, my robin one, and my blue, red and yellow ones from my bunch of welcome home flowers so long ago in her dark hair. "You will keep these for me, but *only until I come back for them*. Understand?" She's solemn and will not talk to me. "I love you, Hope. You are my heart. I will come back to you."

The day the soldiers came, the village horses were widely scattered. Some have returned, but others have not and we suspect they have been "removed" as well. Willow *and* Companion are amongst those that have not returned and I ride a sturdy horse from one of the hearths that no longer needs it. Beaver will travel with me for a way and then we will separate. He's mysterious in his plans and it seems as much for *our* safety as well as his.

We ride hard and fast as possible through the forest. A normal trek to Deer's can take five full days, but we travel light and by the third night on the trail, we know that I'm a day's ride from Forest City. We have spoken little, too caught up in our own thoughts and concerns, while always listening for trouble in the form of soldiers. As we bed down that night, Beaver says to me, "I will go south tomorrow. Are you sure of the way?"

I review with him what I remember and he's satisfied. "What of your mate and son?" I must ask him.

He stares at the dark forest. "They are in hiding, but when last I saw them they were well. My mate awaits the birth of another child that should be born any time now." He looks at me. "I had intended to come north to The Maple Forest to see if it would be safer for them here. But it seems that no place is safe right now."

I've no words of comfort for him.

In the morning we part ways. I feel as if I want to say something to him but the words don't seem to form in my head. At last I say simply, "Thank you."

In many ways he's so much Bright Feather's brother; unsmiling, serious, always trying to be strong. "You are a powerful ally for our people, Bear. You do not show fear and you think quick in difficult situations. If anyone can secure the release of those captured, you and Deer can. I am glad that you are both on our side." He nods his head briefly and rides away.

I arrive at Forest City late that fourth day, tired and saddle sore. It has been a while since I traveled so much and so far by horse. It's Possum who greets me and must listen to my sad story. And it's Possum who must tell me the awful news that Deer is not here. He's in Washington and she does not expect him back for another three weeks *at least, weather permitting* until after the first of the New Year.

It's then that I cry the tears that up until this time I've kept carefully stored away, fearful that once I let them begin I would never be able to stop. I cry myself dry until there are no more tears inside of me and then fall into dreamless sleep, curled up by the fire wrapped in my bearskin.

In the morning I feel hollow. I miss Bright Feather, I miss my children, and I miss my home. It's Possum who gets me moving though. "You have three weeks. Let's make the most of your time then. What supplies do you carry with you?" When I show her she makes a disgusted noise. "It is *winter*, Bear. You will be traveling *over the Great Smokey Mountains* to get to Tennessee. You do not have the proper clothes or equipment to survive a winter dressed and prepared as you are."

I look at her with hollow eyes and she looks back at me. "I have more equipment than any of those that were taken," I say and she puts a reassuring hand on my arm.

"Come," she says, "let us make some preparations." We spend three weeks sewing and packing and thinking and repacking. I do my best to talk and converse with the children and help Possum around the house and trading post. I practice with my knife and my bow and arrow to fill the time and sharpen my out of use skills. I do my best not to go mad with the waiting and the not knowing and the ache of missing those that I love.

With the start of my fourth week there, I begin a ritual where I walk every day far up the road to the top of the hill and scan the lower valley searching for Deer. The first weeks I worked hard at trying to make my mind blank, trying not to think of Bright Feather and the others, cold, wounded, imprisoned, perhaps already part of a transport west. That succeeded only in making all of the horrible thoughts I refused to think of *awake* invade my sleep at night causing nightmares that woke all of us with my screams. On the walks, I began to do my quiet whisper prayers I did as a child with Ma. I have conversations with this God who I'm told loves us so much and I share with Him my worry and my anguish over my mate, friends, family and children. I cry a little, I shout a little, and I feel better a lot. My nights are more peaceful, too.

Deer arrives home at the start of the fifth week, weary but victorious, for he has secured government recognition for the rights of The Real People of The Maple Forest of One Who Knows' Place in of all places, the hated New Echota Treaty. He sits at the kitchen table, still with his hat and boots and coat on and reads to us his battered copy of the New Echota Treaty, *Article 12:*

"ARTICLE 12: Those individuals and families of the Cherokee nation that are averse to a removal to the Cherokee country west of the Mississippi and are desirous to become citizens of the States where they reside and such as are qualified to take care of themselves and their property shall be entitled to receive their due portion of all the personal benefits accruing under this treaty for their claims, improvements and per capita; as soon as an appropriation is made for this treaty. Such heads of Cherokee families as are desirous to reside within the States of North Carolina, Tennessee, and Alabama subject to the laws of the same; and who are qualified or calculated to become useful citizens shall be entitled, on the certificate of the commissioners to a preemption right to one hundred and sixty acres of land or one quarter section at the minimum congress price...³'" He looks at Possum and I with a triumphant smile.

"I had the 1819 document, that listed all of the families that took citizenship *then*. I had this treaty that offered citizenship *now*." He looks at me, "And I had documented proof of the success of the trading post that has been in operation and *self supporting* for over three years."

He waves another piece of paper at us. "NOW I have an official document listing all of the original families and signed by the Secretary of War, Lewis Cass, stating that you are *exempt from the removal process*.

He sighs a weary sigh and says, "So let me change my clothes, repack, and we can be off."

"You can change your clothes and kiss your mate and children," I say, "but we've already packed for you."

Deer stands up, sweeps his hat off his head and grins at Possum, "Pucker up woman, *I'm home!!*"

We leave early the next morning after a hearty breakfast. If the weather holds, Deer tells me it will take us two full weeks to reach Fort Payne. *Seven weeks*, I think to myself. *Will they still be there?* I cannot let my mind think past that awful question. *I cannot.*

The snow is heavy as we cross over the Great Smokey Mountains and I worry night and day about all of those captured from our village and the lack of warm clothes and supplies. *Will the army provide them with things?* When I ask Deer this question he will not meet my eyes and says he does not know for sure. I understand the truth of things.

There's one final complication I must contend with as we travel those two plus weeks in the winter cold and snow. I'm almost certain that I'm pregnant again. The signs are all there, similar more to the first time I was pregnant with Storm rather than the second time I was pregnant with Hope. It makes sense in my head, as this time, like the first, I'm dealing with many worries, separated from Bright Feather, and traveling in cold and snow. I struggle with tiredness and a constant impending feeling of sickness. There are times that I'm so hungry that I think I could eat my horse, but once the food is in front of me I'd just as soon vomit as eat it. I decide this is best just mine to know, but there are few secrets on the trail and at last Deer asks me, "How far along are you?"

We sit at another meal that I just cannot manage to choke down. Up until the moment the bowl is in my hand, I'm ready to eat *anything*, but there's something about the smell of hot, fresh rabbit stew that makes my stomach roll and flip at the sight and smell of it. I take a deep breath and swallow. "I suspect a little more than two months. If things go as the other two, I should be better in a week or two." I make a face at him. "Not the best time for this, I know."

Deer shrugs. "If we all waited until it was the perfect time to have a child, there would be no more babies." He grins at me a tired but loving smile. "It *is* a rather awkward time, your mate captured by evil soldiers, your village burned to the ground and you traveling out in the wilderness in the dead of winter." He shrugs again, "But that's just one man's opinion."

I manage a tired laugh that rolls into a yawn. "How is it you can always get a laugh out of me even in the bleakest of circumstances?"

"*If* you can stay awake long enough," he says as I stifle another yawn.

When we are, by our calculations, a day away from Fort Payne, over dinner we discuss our plans. "First," Deer says to me, "you must prepare yourself for *anything*. I expect the conditions to be deplorable. There will be sickness and hunger and drunkenness. Under no circumstances are you to leave my side for *any reason*." He looks at me intensely. "You are *not safe* with the soldiers *or* the Indians. The impression you have of Indians and the way of life they embrace and lead is unique *even among other Indians*. Do you understand me?"

I nod my head. "What will you do?"

He shrugs his shoulders. "What I do best," he says with a grim smile. "Dance the dance that keeps us alive and kicking. You do your best to keep in step."

Fort Payne is nestled in a picturesque valley along the banks of the Tennessee River. Similar to Fort Winston, it's constructed entirely of felled trees with towers in each of its four corners. I think that perhaps it's somewhat larger than Fort Winston, although never having seen it completed I'm not certain. As we approach the closed gates, an overwhelming terror washes over me at what I might see and hear in the minutes to come. In starts in my cramped, empty stomach and creeps up to my lungs and out to my cold red hands and lastly to my exhausted mind. I imagine Bright Feather injured, tortured, dead or almost worse, *not here*, *never here* or *already removed west.* I feel the breath in my lungs stop flowing, I feel the heart in my chest beat faster and I hear the ringing in my ears grow louder. As we reach the point where we stop the horses and shout to the sentry to be allowed in, I look at Deer and say, "I'm so sorry, my brother, you'll have to dance this first dance all by yourself ..." and the blackness overtakes me.

I wake unsure who I am, where I am, or what I'm doing. I lay there listening to the sounds around me and I hear a presence as well as smell a wood fire and some food that makes me think of Ma and home. I open my eyes and I'm in a dimly lit room and next to me is a tray of biscuits and a china cup full of tea. As I turn my head, the straw ticking makes an awful racket and the presence in the room materializes as a young woman, my age or perhaps a bit younger. She comes closer to my bed and sits down at a stool and I realize that she *is* younger, perhaps fifteen or so.

"Can you drink some warm tea?" she asks and I sit up and mumble my thanks. *Where is Deer?* I think. *So much for us never being separated.*

"Where am I and where is my brother?" I ask for we have decided to maintain the farce that has gotten us such success in the past.

"Your brother is with my father, the commanding officer of this fort," she says to me. My name is Linda Scott," she says staring at me with intense curiosity.

"I must go to my brother," I say holding my head and struggling to remember who I am and what I'm doing here.

"Your brother said I was to tell you to 'lie quiet and still and he would be back moments after you awoke if not sooner' and that 'you had his loving word on it'," she says concentrating to get the message exact.

"Hmpf," I say, "guess I've been told."

"Please, have something to eat," she says, and despite myself the plain biscuits look appealing and I take one and start eating it. "Your brother says you've been feeling right poorly the last few days on the trail and that some plain broth and biscuits might be the best thing for you. Shall I fetch the broth now that you're awake?"

Might as well make the most of it, I think. "Yes please," I say at last.

"Might I be so bold as to ask you a question?" she asks and she seems about ready to explode.

"Go right ahead," I tell her.

"Are those marks on your face *really truly Injun marks* and *do they really never come off?* And did you do them yourself?" Her eyes are big and wide and I realize I must be about as interesting as a fully grown grizzly bear laying here in this bed.

"Yes, they're permanent and yes they're Indian, but no, I did not do them myself, although I asked for them to be done."

"Oh ..." is all she can say and she scuttles out the door to fetch the broth. I stand and make my way to the window and am frustrated to see that it's full dark and I cannot see a thing outside. I sit back on the bed as I hear her approaching.

"Here, ma'am," she says and I thank her for her kindness.

"Can you speak Injun?" she says and I nod my head as I sip the broth. It's good in my stomach. I eat another biscuit.

"Have you lived with the Injuns?" she asks and I begin to ponder just how much I tell and don't tell. *What's the difference?* my mind thinks.

"Yes, I live with them *now*," I say. "May I ask *you* a question?" I ask just as politely, making the most of this possible source of information.

"Why sure," she says, "go right ahead."

"How many Indians are here right now?"

She seems to think on it for a bit. "They come and go all the time," she says and my heart sinks, "but I'd say right now there are close to three hundred."

Three hundred in this tiny fort?! I think. "Where do they go from here?" I ask.

"Oh, the only ones that go *right now* are the ones that die," she says matter of factly. "The whole big group of them won't go west until the ice thaws on the river and we can ship them north on the packet boats. That won't be until the end of February, in another week or so I suspect at the earliest." *Maybe we are not too late then*, I think.

I hear footsteps outside and Deer enters looking grim but not defeated. He gives me an arch of his eyebrow and a wink. "You were right, sir, she's eaten all of the broth and most of the biscuits!" Linda Scott says to Deer.

Deer looks at me and his eyes say, *Are you okay?*

"I'm sorry for all the commotion, my brother, but I am fine and ready for whatever we need to do next," and I stand as if I'm ready to go into battle.

"Well, I hope you haven't spoiled your appetite, for we're to get ready to go to dinner at the commander's cabin inside the hour. *If* you're up to it of course."

Commander's cabin. Dinner. I look down at my filthy hands and clothes. "I will be fine as soon as I'm given a chance to wash up," I say.

"I thought you'd say that. A soldier is bringing you in your packs. I'll be back to get you in a bit then," and he turns and leaves me alone again with Linda.

She bustles around heating some water, getting me a soap and towel, offering me a comb, and lastly bringing in my packs once they have been delivered. Her curiosity is almost like something alive with us in the room. "What is this?" I say as I lift a separate parcel.

She shrugs, "Your brother said it was something for you he found in his pack."

I open it and inside is a beautiful Indian tunic, embroidered and fringed in great detail. It's old, I can see by the faint fading of the colors here and there but the quality is not diminished by it. There are moccasins, too, these having obviously been worn before.

"Oh, it's so beautiful!" Linda exclaims and she gently touches the details on the dress and the shoes. "It looks like a wedding dress almost," and all of a sudden I know that it must have been Possum's dress when she married Deer. I can hear her saying to me, *We must plan for all eventualities* and *I* thought it was only to do with practical things like frostbite, starvation, and injury. Leave it to Possum to prepare me for *dinner at the Commander's cabin*, too.

I comb and rewrap my hair and wash myself as best as I can standing in a room with a pan full of water, a bar of lye soap and one washcloth. *But I certainly look better than when I started.* Even Linda seems impressed when I emerge from the room out into the family living space proper. I see that she has combed her hair and has her winter cape on ready to go.

There's a knock at the door and Deer stands there smiling at me. But I've a distinct feeling he's not seeing *me* in this pretty tunic, but a stubborn Indian maid he fell in love with many years ago. "Madam," he says to me as he bows deep and proper and then offers me his arm, "shall we dine?"

The air is frigid without my fur lined trousers and bear cape and Deer puts his arm around me to give me warmth and steer me along on the slippery path. Behind us Linda follows, commenting about the cold and the snow.

Under my breath, I ask, "Are they here?"

The most Deer can say to me grips my stomach with dread, "Yes, *if* they are still alive."

Commander Winfield Scott, Major General in the United States of America's Army is a tall, thin, imposing man. He looks down at me over his large beaked nose and then bows properly with great flourish. His great shock of white hair is carefully combed and I detect a scent of cologne. "Mistress Graves," he says in a voice that seems too large in the enclosure of the room, "welcome to Fort Payne. I do hope that you are feeling better than when you first arrived."

I stare at him and get the distinct feeling he's used to almost everyone he speaks to being overwhelmed by his presence, his manner and his power. *The dance has begun*, my head thinks for I will be none of those things. "Commander Scott," I say in as clear and strong a voice as I can manage, "thank you for this wonderful hospitality! I am feeling *much better* having had the fortune to be under the care and company of your lovely daughter, Linda," and I smile at him a brilliant smile.

We size each other up, I think, in those first few minutes and he takes in my Indian *and* my white selves. You can almost hear the adjustments he makes in his brain as he recalculates the tiny Injun loving woman in front of him. "Excellent, *excellent!* Come let us dine! I am famished."

I'm seated to his right and Deer to his left. Linda is seated next to me and there are five other officers seated around the table besides us. There are no other women present at the table and I find it most disturbing to have a glass of wine poured for me by a young Indian girl servant. Deer catches my eye across the table and I hear him say to me again, *You must prepare yourself for anything.* I must admit that when he'd said that to me over the open fire, was it just last night?, that I didn't think it meant eating venison, potatoes and cherry pie off china plates, drinking wine from crystal goblets, and wearing the fine Indian tunic Possum wore at their wedding!

The food's good and for once my stomach cooperates and I'm able to eat. Perhaps the broth and biscuits were a good start after all. I sip the wine carefully, wanting to keep my wits sharp. Conversation revolves around the river, the ice, the boats, the impending departures and certain *situations*.

"It is the fourth time the situation has occurred," an officer with a long drooping mustache says. "Indians have been rounded up, and no matter how many guards we have posted, in the morning some *if not all* of the captives have escaped. Guards are tied and gagged, often with their own clothing or equipment and *no one* can give any description or explanation for it!"

"We have questioned some of the Indians from the villages in which these situations have occurred and no one can provide us with any information."

"Except for the name," one of the officers says. *"Charly.* Who ever heard of an Indian called *Charly?"* he says with disgust. He looks around the table at all of those present. "If that Indian's real name is Charly, then I'm wearing my wife's petticoat." One of the other officers raises one eyebrow and makes to look under the table, to the laughter and delight of the others present, including Linda.

"It happened to McTavish *twice,*" I hear one of the officers at the end of the table say and there's muffled laughter. "He's got quite a vendetta out against Charly as a result." He chuckles and says, "I think I'd rather have an angry grizzly bear after me then McTavish. That Charly better watch his back at all times!" I look at Deer across the table and will him to know my thoughts. *Charly?* I think, *Charly?* If they say it happened twice to McTavish, one of those times has to have been my escape and I know only that Beaver was the one who gained my freedom. He meets my stare calm and cool, *Just keep dancing,* his eyes tell me.

"We *must* get things moving with the first opportunity!" Commander Scott says, "There will be other shipments arriving as soon as the winter breaks and I want us to be fully operational when they do. We have got less than two years to move over sixteen thousand Cherokees and I have given the President my word that this *can* and *will* be done!"

"The packet boats are still north, stuck in ice flows," one of the officers seems compelled to explain. "It took a dreadfully long time to navigate up the river with the last shipment and the weather caused innumerable delays. Our soldiers have suffered in these conditions and much of the cargo has sustained damage due to exposure to the elements and resulting illnesses."

I look across at Deer for I must find a face that I can try to gain some strength in. The words *shipments* and *cargo* are hard to listen to when they could be referring to those that I love and care about.

"Why the great rush to do things *now* when weather conditions are so difficult?" I ask and Commander Scott smiles a polite smile.

"Shipping Indians west, is a little bit like having a baby, my dear. If you wait for the perfect time, it will never happen. We have had to deal with tremendous difficulties here in this fort and in forts all over the country: illness, drunkenness, brawls, fornication, attempted escape ..." He shakes his head, "No, containment has been a bad thing all around and all of us are in agreement that the sooner we get the Cherokees and all other remaining Indian tribes west of the Mississippi, all will be happier.

"I have admonished my soldiers to use every possible kindness in carrying out the difficult task of removal. Yet these Indians, despite repeated warnings, arrive ill prepared and angry. What is the army expected to do? Feed and clothe sixteen thousand people who have already received millions of dollars, free land, free transportation, plus additional cash in hand for everything from past military service to whether they've built a necessary house as an improvement on their land?" There are chuckles around the table and I glance at Deer quickly before I look back at Commander Scott who places a firm, warm hand on my own stiff, cold one. "My dear, *we are the United States Army* not a missionary society. We must draw the difficult line at some point and say enough is enough. The government and, I must add, the leadership of the Cherokee Nation, has spoken."

He smiles at me, eager to make his point and have me smile back in understanding, but I stare at him cold as a stone. "So we have situations like we have here at this fort. Some Indians have arrived unwilling and unprepared and that, I'm afraid, is *their own choice*. Like a disobedient child that must be taught the proper lesson, we must maintain the kind but firm hand that all good parents have. Some lessons are harder to learn than others, I'm afraid."

He removes his hand from mine, realizing that he has not found an ally or a convert to his way of thinking. "But enough of this difficult talk! I understand that you are searching for someone! Is that so? Major Sinclair is in charge of the roster of those here at camp, why don't you tell him who you are looking for?"

I look at Deer and he nods at me. "I have explained to Commander Scott your situation and have showed him all the necessary documents proving the mistaken removal of some of your family with the first main sweep of the area. He has been most apologetic for any misguided actions on the part of his officers and is more than willing to help us secure their release should they be here."

I look at Commander Scott and he gives me a smile that says, *See? I'm not all that bad.* I look at Major Sinclair who is a short round officer with round spectacles perched on the end of his nose. "How have you recorded the identities of those you have present?" I ask.

"Well, some have volunteered their names," he looks at his comrades and rolls his eyes as they chuckle, "which is difficult in and of itself. Others have either been unable to understand what we require from them, or unwilling, and in that case I have recorded a brief note of any distinguishing features, a broad description of the location from where they were removed from as well as the officer who was in charge of the round up."

"I see," I say. "Well, perhaps you would be so kind as to let me look at your records, for I can provide you with names, descriptions, locations *and* the name of the officer in charge of the round up: *Sergeant McTavish.*

"Let's make a plan to do that tomorrow, shall we? McTavish is not present here at the fort at this time, he is busy continuing the removal process, but I have all the records we would need to locate those individuals you seek. I'll include the death rosters as well just in case." Major Sinclair gives me a friendly smile across the table while I struggle to maintain my frozen one. *If I have to read through the death rosters,* I think as I struggle to calm my flipping stomach, *I know I'll vomit all over them.*

It's too strange for me to sleep in Commander Scott's cabin, in his daughter's room and bed, and enjoy his gracious hospitality, while Bright Feather, Raccoon, Red Fox and two other families from the Maple Forest are freezing to death outside. I toss and turn most of the night, aching with the need to go outside in the freezing cold and dark and scream their names until I find them alive and well. *This dance is too hard,* I think to myself.

Smiling Major Sinclair arrives as promised first thing in the morning, followed by Deer who looks as if he got as much sleep as I did and we sit at Commander Scott's kitchen table, sipping tea, going over the pages and pages of documents. Linda has lost some interest in all of this and no longer hovers with her fascinated presence.

McTavish has been very successful with his round ups. There are pages and pages of documents listing those he has brought in, written in Major Sinclair's neat, legible handwriting. It's almost comical when I find myself on one of the lists. *"1 white woman – escaped"* is listed in the area marked "Western North Carolina. My heart beats as I scan down the list of names after mine and at last I see who I so desperately seek:

Male, facial marks 3 stripes each cheek and chin

Male, facial marks across forehead and down nose

Male, no facial marks, scar on right cheek

"I've found them," I say and the first time I say it my voice does not work and I must repeat it.

"Oh, good," Major Sinclair says, "now just let me cross reference with the death list. No sense wasting our time searching through the masses if there's nothing to find, right?"

At that moment, I feel almost like a snap in my head and I wish to plunge my knife in this man's throat and there's *nothing* that'll stop me. I feel my hand reaching for my weapon and Deer must see my intent for he says, "Elle! Let's take a moment to catch a breath of fresh air while Major Sinclair checks that last list," and he grabs my weapon hand and pulls me to my feet.

We stand out in the bitter cold and I'm so angry that I do not even feel it. I lean against the rough logs and hear Deer from far away say, "Take a deep breath, Bear, you cannot loose it now, we are *too close*. We have been successful because we have been proper white folks, not because we have been Indian savages. All will be destroyed if you kill that God damned idiot inside." His coarse language makes me realize just how raw he is as well and I feel my anger ebb and I take a shaky breath. "Good," he says to me as he watches me calm a slight bit.

"Now look over there, Elle," he says fierce and hard to me, "do you see the fencing? Three hundred men, women, and children are over there. Take a breath, Elle, can you smell the stench? Those are the captives you smell. Can you walk through the piles of miserable humanity, stepping over those dead and dying or crying out for your help and ignore them while you search for the few that we can secure freedom for? Can you keep your temper as you are escorted by soldiers that will say and behave in ways that will make you want to kill them, too? And will you be able to stand the hatred that will be directed to you from those you walk amongst that only see your white skin?

I swallow hard and take a deep breath and I *can* smell the stench. I look at Deer and he and I exchange looks that flash between hatred and horror, despair and determination. "Yes," I say, "I can do it."

He looks at me and says, "I know you can."

"Oh, good news!" Major Sinclair says as he opens the door to find us outside. "It seems that I have found *two of the men you seek!* According to my records they are in the west corner containment area. Shall we go?"

"Only two?" I say through wooden lips.

"Yes," he says to me with a slight flash of regret it seems, "one is listed on the death roster." Deer goes inside to get my bearskin cape, for he feels that I've begun to shiver and he wraps it around my shoulders. He takes my hand and hooks it into the corner of his arm and says to me, "We'll hold each other up, okay?" and does not wait for my answer, but leads me down the steps following Major Sinclair.

How can one people hate another people so much that they cannot see the suffering and cruelty and horror that I see as I walk among the bodies on the frozen ground at my feet? The west containment center holds about seventy five people in an area that seems only slightly larger than Commander Scott's home. We have a soldier escort us there, but he stands stoically at the unlocked gate and does not enter. Neither does Major Sinclair, who says, "I will wait here with the lists to confirm who you take out."

At the last minute, before I step in, I say to him, "You understand that there were two full families taken besides the three men we seek. Should we see any of those familiar faces we will bring them out, too."

"Yes, yes, I understand," he says. "We just need to confirm and make note on my lists here." As an afterthought, he adds as we walk away from him, "Should you find who you are looking for, the most likely place to bring them is the stables," he gestures, "over there." *Certainly not the commander's cabin or anywhere else that civilized people go,* his expression says to us.

There's no need for military protection from the people within this space for they barely have energy to breathe, let alone attack someone. Some are huddled under blankets, almost all are coughing or sniffling. The stench of unwashed bodies, sickness, and, most surprising to me, liquor, hit us like some physical force as we step inside and hear the gate click shut behind us.

"Move quickly," Deer says, "I do not know how long they will tolerate us in here and if things start to stir with trouble, that will be it for us."

"I'll take this side," I say to him and set off.

There are some that I must bend down and speak to for I cannot see their faces huddled as they are for warmth or due to illness. Some are unconscious from alcohol, splayed out without an apparent care in the world. Deer is right and many of them look at me with hatred, although they have little energy to do anything else. Towards the back, against the end wall, I hear my name called and I look into the fever bright eyes of Red Fox. "Deer!" I shout, and I hear him scrambling over legs and bodies to get to me.

"Red Fox, where are the others?" I say touching his hot face and willing him to answer me.

"Shall we practice shooting now?" he says to me and smiles and I realize that he does not know what is real and what is not.

"Red Fox, we have come to take you home. Where is Bright Feather and Raccoon? Where are the other families from our village?"

Deer bends down beside me and quickly touches his arms and legs to see if there are any great injuries, I realize. "Look close by," he says to me, "they would have made every effort to stay together. The rest we seek cannot be far."

I find Bright Feather feverish as well and fast asleep, laying against the wall two men down from Red Fox. He has been badly beaten and he holds his arm cradled against him. I begin to cry for many reasons, but mostly for Major Sinclair's words, *One is listed on the death roster* and I know that I will not find Raccoon. "Bright Feather! *Bright Feather!*" I speak to him and touch his face that's bruised and cut in many places. I will him to wake up and not be dead before me. He opens his eyes and blinks once, twice, and through my tears I see him mouth the word, "Bear," but no sound comes out.

"I am here, to take you home," I say and now the tears are pouring down my face with sorrow and with joy and with horror and with fury. "Are there others here from our village, Bright Feather? Are there others? You must help us find them; we do not have much time!"

He struggles to focus on my words and my face. I turn to Deer who seems to be at as much a loss as I am, "What do we do?"

Deer looks at me. "How many were in each family that was taken?" he asks.

"There were five adults, three men and two women, and two children, both girls in the one cave and four adults, two men and two women and three children – two boys and a girl - in the other cave. Are you thinking what I am thinking?"

He nods his head. "They all would not have survived and we have little chance of finding them. The containment list and the death list that I looked at" he looks at my startled expression, "*yes, I looked*, was not detailed enough for us to ever know who was from the Maple Forest that died or who is still captive. So few gave their names ..." he says in frustration. "Look around, choose anyone who looks healthy enough to make the trek – if you can find any – and who understands with little explanation that they must pretend to be a part of your village *immediately* to gain their freedom." He stands up and looks around. "That one over there seems like he can walk on his own," he points to a brave seated and staring at us.

"Have you heard us speaking?" Deer asks him across the small space of the containment area.

The brave looks at us and blinks, "Yes."

"Are you fit to walk on your own?"

"Yes."

"Can you become a member of the Real People of The Maple Forest *now?*"

"Yes," he says.

"Then come," Deer says. He bends down and bodily lifts Red Fox. "Christ," he says, "he weighs *nothing.*"

"Bright Feather," I say, "Can you stand? I will help you ..." and I come close to him and take his arm to help him stand.

I feel a hand, cold as ice, grip my ankle and I look down at the sorrowful face of a woman. "I am fit to walk on my own and I can become a member of the Real People of the Maple Forest, *my baby and I,*" and I see that she has an infant wrapped in a tattered fur and clutched to her chest.

I look at Deer and he says grimly, "Bring her."

"Come along," I say, "but I cannot help you for I must help my mate."

I get Bright Feather to stand and he leans heavily against me. "Arm ..." he says.

"Yes, I know, I see it, I will be careful. Come now ..."

"OPEN THE DOOR," Deer shouts to the outside guard and the gate swings open.

"Oh, good," I hear Major Sinclair say, "I see you've found a few!" like we have just gone berry picking in the late summer.

I ignore him and head to the stables, knowing full well that Bright Feather will probably not be able to make it there with only my help and I'm not inclined to stand here and chit chat until he drops. Ten steps from the stable door, he stumbles and it takes all my strength to keep him upright. The woman with the baby comes to the other side of him and between the two of us we get him to the stable and the first empty stall we find. Deer comes in right behind us and lays a shivering Red Fox beside Bright Feather. "You stay with all of them while I go see what supplies I can get from the *charitable United States Army*" he says with great sarcasm and he's gone.

Deer returns with blankets and Linda, carrying a tray with mugs of steaming hot tea. "Can we have some of your delicious broth?" I ask and give her the most pleasant, friendliest smile I can manage. I'm not surprised to see her curiosity in full bloom again.

"Why sure!" she says and she runs off.

While Deer helps Red Fox, I tend to Bright Feather. The brave and the woman silently sip their hot tea and sit in the far back of the stall wrapped in blankets that Deer has handed them.

"His arm is broken," I say to Deer, "can we get some bandages to set it do you think?"

"I asked if there was a company doctor, but Linda says he won't treat Indians," Deer says grimly.

After I've fed Bright Feather his tea and he has swallowed as much broth as I can get down him, and after I've made sure that he's as warm as I can manage in this freezing cold stable, I stand and look at Deer. "I'm going to see the doctor."

He looks at me and I see just the hint of a smile hidden behind the grief, worry and tiredness. "I thought you would be. His place is two buildings down from Commander Scott's home toward the main gate."

I trudge across the fort square, past curious eyes, around the wagons and horses and the business of life, walk right up to the door that says, 'Doctor Tucker' and I pound as hard as my fury will let me.

I'm not a big woman and to meet a man that I look *down on* is an amazing thing. My first thought is, *No wonder he won't treat Indians, they probably scare him to death*, and I instantly take a different path than I planned.

I look down at the curious bespectacled face in front of me and burst into tears. "Oh please, kind sir!" I say between my wrenching sobs. "You must be the good doctor I was told would be able to help me! We've only just arrived here to the fort yesterday, and I find that my beloved husband is deathly ill with fever. More disturbing his arm is broken and needs to be set. My good friend, who is as close as a brother is also terribly ill with fever, and *I just don't know what to do!*" I collapse into a nearby chair and sob into my hands.

"Please! Madam! I'll be more than happy to treat your husband and friend. We must get them here immediately so that I can give them the proper treatment they desire."

I lift my tearstained face out of my hands (careful to keep my chin marks covered though) and say, "Shall I have them brought here? They've fallen terribly ill in the stable."

"The *stable!* Good God, let's get them here as quickly as possible where it is warm and comfortable and I can care for them properly!" He rushes to the door and shouts to two young soldiers walking across the square. "Private Russell! Private Mead! Assist this woman immediately to get her sick husband and friend here to the infirmary! On the double!"

"Yes sir!" they shout.

"Oh thank you! *Thank you,*" I say between renewed sobs of gratitude as I rush out the door.

I trudge back across the square with Private Russell and Private Mead following close behind. Once inside the stable, they seem at a loss as to what to do. Deer stands as we enter and I say, "The good doctor has urged us to get both Red Fox and Bright Feather to his infirmary immediately, although he is unaware of a number of specific details." I look at Private Russell and Private Mead. "My husband is too ill to walk, you'll have to help me carry him. Mr. Thomas can assist you with Red Fox."

At their hesitation, Deer looks at them both. "Is there a problem, men?"

"Er, no sir, I guess not sir. It's just that, well you see …"

"Yes?" I say.

They look at each other for a moment and shrug. "Nothing," they finally say.

In other circumstances, the expression on Dr. Tucker's face could be funny. I see him watching intently for our arrival, then squinting curiously as we get closer, then looking horrified as he realizes that not one, not two, but *four* red savage (for the woman and the brave will not leave our sides) are headed in the direction of his infirmary *at his express orders.*

I talk quick as we make our way up the steps. "Oh, Dr. Tucker, thank you so much. I just don't know what I would do without your help!" He has two cots made up and Deer and I do not hesitate but carefully put both Bright Feather and Red Fox down on the clean sheets. "Both are running high fevers and I believe my husband's right arm is broken." I look at him earnestly. "Where do we start?"

Dr. Tucker looks at my tear stained face, Deer's fierce one, Bright Feather and Red Fox's unconscious ones, Indian Brave and Indian Woman's blank ones, and the two private's curious ones. "Well, first, you two get *out.* I've got no room to work with all of you crowding in here," he says to the privates who scurry out. "Those two," he gestures towards the newest members of the village of One Who Knows' Place in The Maple

Forest, "if they are not ill, have them go sit quiet by the fire and tell them to *NOT TOUCH ANYTHING.* You," he says to me "let's begin to wash his cuts and scrapes and get that arm set, and you," he says to Deer, "you better start talking damn quick about what the hell I'm doing with four Injuns in my infirmary. And start giving each of them sips of water - as they'll take it - while you're talking."

Doctor Tucker listens to Deer's words and seems unimpressed by them. He seems more concerned with the fact that citizens of the United States or no, there are *four red savages* in his infirmary and there's nothing he seems to be able to do about it.

He makes one comment at the end of the first day about perhaps finding more suitable accommodations for *my husband* and *friend* elsewhere in the fort. I stretch my tired legs and walk over to him and stand close enough that he must look up into my fierce, angry eyes. "*NO,*" I say, "*they will stay here.*"

I do not threaten him, *really,* but I stand there and continue to look at him, unblinkingly, until he finally clears his throat and licks his lips nervously and says, "Right, well, there really aren't many other places to take them *anyway.*" He looks at the two Indian statues that decorate either side of his fireplace. "You *will* do something with *the baby,* though," he says in a pointed voice and walks out.

I'm puzzled by his comment and then it hits me with a powerful force. In a whole day I've *never* heard the baby cry, I've *never* seen the woman feed the baby, I've *never* seen the woman do anything with the infant but clutch it to her chest, wrapped in its filthy fur rag and I realize, *the baby is dead.*

The two Indians have not moved from the spot I've told them to sit. I've given them portions of food and drink as it's brought, but have been too busy caring for Bright Feather and Red Fox to deal with anything else. Now I look at her and her eyes meet mine and I think of Raccoon and those still outside within the cold containment areas and my head says, *The sorrow is too great for me to bear ...*

I walk over to her and I feel the tears pool in my eyes and trickle down my face and I touch the woman's head and now warm cheek and she starts to tremble and rock back and forth clutching her baby tighter to her breast.

The woman looks at me with pleading eyes. "It was so cold ... and my milk would not come any more. She cried and cried but finally I was able to comfort her and *shhhh,* now she is asleep ...!"

"May I hold her?" I ask, and she hesitates a moment before she puts the baby in my arms. I open the blanket and see this beautiful doll in my arms, peacefully asleep and cold and hard as a stone. "She is lovely," I say, "so peaceful ..." I look at the woman through my tears. "She will never be hungry any more, or cold or frightened or sick. You have let her go to a safe place where she can run and play and laugh and wait for you to join her." I put my hand to my ear. "Listen? Can you hear her sweet laughter? Look. Can you see how peaceful and content she is?"

The woman looks at me and then at the baby's face and begins to rock back and forth again. "She is dead ..." she says at last and starts to cry soft soundless tears that trickle down her face and drop onto the empty arms in her lap.

Deer has come in at some point I realize and he's standing quietly behind me as I kneel in front of the woman, holding her child. He squats down so that she must focus on him, too. "My name is Deer, I am son of War Woman, of the Wolf Clan, son of Great Elk, Chief of the Real People of the Maple Forest. I would be honored if you would let me care for your child and find a safe place for her to rest."

She looks at me and I give her a reassuring nod and then to Deer and finally nods through her tears. As Deer carries the baby out of the infirmary, she begins to sing quietly to herself a song of mourning for her baby girl who has gone on to the next world.

I do not leave Bright Feather or Red Fox's side, except for necessary trips, day or night for three days. Deer comes and goes as business calls within the fort, Linda Scott visits now and then when her curiosity makes it required, and Doctor Tucker avoids his infirmary as best he can once he has given me basic instructions on how to care for them. We set Bright Feather's arm, and clean his cuts. I'm constantly feeding or tending to one or the other while Indian Woman and Indian Brave sit stoically watching me.

On the third day, Red Fox looks at me with clear eyes and I know that his fever has broken. I give him water to sip and more of Linda's constant supply of broth. I sit by his cot and touch his cool forehead. We do not speak for a very long time, but he watches me tend to Bright Feather and looks around the place where he is.

Finally, I give him information about things I know. "It has been almost eight weeks since you were captured. Deer and I arrived here just about a week ago. When I left our village, Turtle and Laughs Much were safe and well, living in our cave. Little Bird and Storm made it back safely and were able to tell us what happened with you. Besides those that were taken with you that day, two caves of families were discovered and taken away, too."

"Do not search for them for you will not find them," he says to me in a voice hollow with sorrow and we both grow silent again with our grief. He looks at Bright Feather. "How is he?"

"He still sleeps and has a fever, but today he is more peaceful that he has been and I think that is good."

Red Fox stares at the ceiling of the infirmary and tears trickle down the sides of his face. "He spoke up for us, all of us. He spoke loud and clear in the white language and told the soldiers what he thought of them. They beat him for it and to make him silent."

I look at the silent, sleeping form of my mate and can just imagine him speaking quiet and strong like he spoke to Major Everett that day they took me back to Ward's Mill, Virginia. I can hear Major Everett's amused voice, *"Well, we had a right polite conversation, him and I. In perfect English I might add and he very polite like told me that if anything were to happen to you before you are returned to him he would hold me personally responsible and hunt me down and kill me."* I look at Red Fox, "He does have a way with words …"

I've taken to sleeping, curled on my bearskin, between the two cots so I can be close should anyone need me. In my sleep during the fourth night, I feel the gentle brush of fingers smoothing my hair from my face and I look up at Bright Feather's tired face looking down at me over the edge of the cot.

"I knew you would come," he says to me at last.

"Well, we have that promise, you know," I say and I sit up to look closer into his beautiful brown eyes.

"Is Red Fox well?" he asks and looks across at his sleeping form.

"Yes, his fever cleared this afternoon and I spoke with him a bit. He is tired and needs more rest, but he is well."

He lays back on the cot and drapes his bandaged broken arm across his eyes. He's silent and I touch the top of his head and the clenched fist so close to my face. He takes a deep ragged breath and then I know that he's crying. "I did my best but it was not enough," he whispers through his tears, "I tried to find the sunshine at the edge of the darkness, but it was *nowhere to be found.* I could not save him," he says and sobs rack his body there on the small cot, *"There was nothing I could do …"*

I lay across his chest and my sorrow joins with his. In the darkness of the night, he puts his good arm around me and holds me tight and we mourn together for our beloved brother, Raccoon.

Hunter

"How soon do you think they will be fit to travel?" Deer asks me by the end of a full week at Fort Payne, as we sit quiet near the fire while Bright Feather and Red Fox sleep. "I do not know how much longer Doctor Tucker will tolerate our takeover of his infirmary," he says with a bitter tone, "and personally, I do not think I can stand it here much longer myself."

"Both Bright Feather and Red Fox were up and walking about today, but I can't imagine them being strong enough to travel any distance for some time." I look at Deer for I've thought of something that's a concern. "What will we do for horses? I did not think of that on our way here, I had too many other things on my mind."

He studies me for a moment and then finally says, "Have you looked in the corral outside at all?"

I've walked past it many times over the course of the week, but have always been so focused on other things, that looking at horses *or anything else for that matter* is far from my mind. "No," I say.

He leans back and says, "Go take a walk and have a look."

My curiosity gets the better of me so I pull on my bearskin and walk out into the frigid cold. I wander over to the corral, ignoring the stares from the soldiers and stand looking at the horses. All of a sudden I start with surprise for there's none other than Companion calmly chewing on some grain in amongst the other military horses. He wears a military brand and his mane and tail have been cut in military fashion, but it's Companion just the same. I search and search and must put my hand to my mouth to keep from crying out for there's Willow, too, looking healthy, if decidedly more *white* and *military* than when I last saw her. The soldiers cast glances at me, but something makes me be quiet and push down the urge to whistle to my horse to come and let me pet and talk to her.

When I go back inside, Deer says, "Have a good walk?" casual like to me.

"Can we get them back?" I ask.

"Well, while you have been nursing Bright Feather and Red Fox back to health, I have been busy *talking* shall we say. I have pointed out a number of things, such as *denial of rights, invasion of private property, theft, kidnapping, murder…* I've got a pile of lawyer books at home that I've been reading in all my spare time and it seems that maybe some of it has finally paid off. While all the conversations have always been polite and civil, they no longer seem as happy to have welcomed you and I into their fort as they did in the beginning. I think it would please everyone if you and I and our four *friends* just disappeared and never returned.

"To that end, I have made a list of supplies that we will need to travel back, including food, clothing, and *horses*. Now, I'm sure we'll end up with the sorriest horses they can come up with, but it is mighty convenient, as far as I'm concerned, that both Willow and Companion are sound trained. The fact that they're branded and now broken to be military horses makes it difficult for us to prove previous ownership, *except* for the fact that those two horses will come when you summon them." He looks at me sideways, "We'll save that piece of information, though, for when we *really* need it."

To keep the peace, we make the offer to move out of the infirmary, as soon as we are provided with the necessary supplies to leave. Although Bright Feather and Red Fox are still very weak, with proper supplies we know we can camp outside and survive. Our plans are to leave the fort as soon as possible and travel home, but to also travel slow and easy to give Bright Feather and Red Fox time to gain their strength.

Indian Brave's name is Double Arrow and he's from territory south of here. He speaks little of himself and, according to Bright Feather and Red Fox, the only reason he's in such good health is that he had only arrived within the last few weeks to the Fort. Indian Woman's name is Mary. Her story, as best as I can understand it, is that she was raised and educated in one of the mission schools that had been established by people such as Rebecca and Reverend James Wilder. Her village was nearby the fort in Tennessee and had been completely converted to Christianity at the time of the soldier's arrival. To my surprise she informs me that she can speak and read English as well as the language of the Real People. She does not speak of her mate which leads me to my own sad conclusions.

We explain to them of One Who Knows' Place and of the choices our village made many years ago. I can see that Double Arrow is disturbed to hear that we *are not* members of The Nation of The Real People, but rather citizens of the United States and hence the reason for the successful releases. For Mary, the attitude seems far more accepting. Perhaps it's because her upbringing has been more a mix of the two cultures than even ours has been.

As best as I can calculate, we prepare to depart Fort Payne, Tennessee, roughly nine very, very long weeks from when the *bad bluebirds* first came into The Maple Forest. Deer is right and the horses we have been provided with are perhaps the sorriest example of horseflesh I've ever had the pain to see.

Seeing us off, is Major Sinclair, the keeper of the lists. "I know that the United States Army is *not* a missionary society," Deer says, "but I had no idea that it *did* consider itself humorous. Have the soldiers laid bets as to how far we will get before our sick and injured are carrying the horses rather then the other way around?"

Major Sinclair does his best to look affronted at the implication. "My dear Mr. Thomas, this is a *military outpost* which depends *solely* on the strength and capability of its finely trained military horses. Look around you, do you see any horses that we should be able to spare?"

My heart skips a beat, for the corral so full of horses just the other day is nigh onto being empty. Where are Willow and Companion? My panicked eyes search the square. And then I see them both, saddled and in the process of being mounted and ridden out of the fort. "Not all your horses are finely trained military ones," I hear Deer growl under his breath. "I would venture a guess that half of these before us are stolen from the Indians you have caged like animals in this very fort."

"How *dare* you!" says Major Sinclair. "You have just called us thieves and you have *no proof whatsoever* to what you claim."

I can't help myself and just as a soldier is about to mount Willow, I let loose a piercing whistle. Up goes her head and with what *I* think to be a very happy gait, she trots over to my welcoming embrace. "Major Sinclair, I would like to introduce you to my horse, Willow, taken from my village on the same day that my husband, family and friends were abducted by soldiers from this fort."

"Many horses are trained to sound commands," Major Sinclair says with a voice unimpressed by what he has seen. As the soldier that was about to mount Willow walks across the square toward us to retrieve her, Sinclair shouts to him, "Call the horse back with a whistle."

The soldier stops, puckers, and lets loose a loud piercing sound. Good ole Willow doesn't even look up. Relief floods me as I look at Major Sinclair, grin a wide grin and say, *"That's the hard part!"*

As the other soldiers mount their horses, Major Sinclair can barely contain his anger. "Well, fine then. It seems *somehow* one lone Indian horse has managed to become a part of our stables, but that in no way gives you the right to accuse-," his words are cut off by Bright Feather behind me as he whistles a high piercing sound followed by three quick hoots. Companion rears up on his hind legs, unseating the unsuspecting soldier and then trots over to join Willow in our circle. I look at Major Sinclair, standing beside me with his mouth hanging open and say, "And that's even harder."

In the end, we leave Fort Payne, with what we arrived with, plus, one mate and friend on the mend, one brave named Double Arrow, one Indian woman named Mary, two horses of quality by the name of Willow and Companion and four horses of questionable age and ability. In addition, we have supplies for winter travel including food and clothing. Most important of all, though, is one document signed by Winfield Scott, Major General in the United States of America's Army and Commander of Fort Payne, Tennessee, acknowledging the release of four mistakenly captured *citizens of the United States* from One Who Knows Village of the Maple Forest, North Carolina, and authorizing the possession of six military horses.

We travel back very slow and steady. Some days we stop early and many days we start late. But rather than the trek being too hard on Bright Feather and Red Fox, both seem to be better and better each day as we put distance between our small party and the fort. We spend three days, hunkered down in a makeshift shelter just after we cross over the mountain range patiently waiting out a fierce snow storm. Double Arrow shows an amazing skill for hunting and manages to take down a deer, much to our delight. Although the deer is thin from the long winter, he's food just the same and we are thankful.

One night over dinner, Deer asks me to retell him about McTavish's capture of me and my escape. He presses me to remember even the smallest details and I try as best as I can.

Deer listens to my retelling and pokes up the fire with a nearby piece of kindling. I'm snuggled next to Bright Feather, enjoying his warmth and the fire's. I seem to feel the cold more than ever lately. "McTavish is a formidable enemy," he says after a while. "Do you know that he is fluent in the language of the Real People?"

"How is that?" I ask.

It's Bright Feather that answers. "He lived with them for a time. Apparently he didn't have a good visit though," he finishes with sarcasm.

"The story I heard," Deer tells us, "is that he spent time with The Real People as an older boy, perhaps ten or eleven. His parents had settled on what was Indian Territory and when the Indians retaliated, both his parents ended up dead and he ended up a captive. I'm guessing he was adopted into the tribe after a time, but when the opportunity presented itself, he killed a number of the Indians in the village and escaped home to tell the tale. Eventually he joined the army and was just a *perfect* candidate to head a removal party."

Deer looks at me. "They joked at the dinner you were present at about McTavish's desire to achieve revenge with this *Charly* and the troubles Charly continues to plague him with. You of all people may be able to understand some of the emotions McTavish has towards settling scores and such. I would think the last thing he would tolerate would be an *Indian* that causes him trouble and difficulty while he travels this chosen path of his. The way you tell your story, your rescuer – this same Charly - called you *by name*, Bear. McTavish does not strike me as the type that would miss such a detail. He may not have put all the pieces together yet, but my guess is that sooner or later McTavish must realize that if *Charly* knows *your name, you* most assuredly must know *his*.

"It is another reason I decided it was best for us to leave Fort Payne as soon as we did. We were unbelievably fortunate that McTavish was not present during the time we were there."

"So it isn't over," I say in a tired voice.

It's Double Arrow that says across the fire, "It will *never* be over." He looks at Deer. "How is it you know of this *Charly?*" He looks at me. "And why does Charly know your name?"

Deer and I exchange glances across the fire, wondering what we tell and what we don't. "Why do you ask?" I must finally say to Double Arrow.

"Many from my village are free because of him.," he says. "Soldiers came into our village weeks ago and told us that we had to leave the place we have always called home. Our village was not a large one, but they treated all of us as prisoners and encouraged us to listen to them with the muzzles of their guns. We were allowed to take only what we could carry on our backs. On the trail to Fort Payne, we were never left alone or unguarded. Four days outside of the Fort, in the middle of the night, a small band of braves came silently into our camp, surprising the soldiers, tying them up and telling us to flee. The leader told us to go in different directions, but to *not go back south to our village*. We hid in the forest for many days. I do not know where many of my family and friends are for we separated as he told us." He looks at me and then Deer. "I was recaptured again and brought to the fort only a few days before you came. I ran away from those who I was with, to try and keep the others from being caught. The soldiers saw me running and followed." He gives a satisfied smile. "I ran long enough so that we were far away from the others before I allowed them to catch me.

"I know this name "Charly" because that is what I heard someone in his band call him."

Deer and I exchange glances. "Charly freed me too," I finally tell Double Arrow, "but in my village I was the only one that was captured. He must have heard me tell McTavish my name, I guess." I see Deer nod ever so slightly, acknowledging the story and the bit of information I've revealed. I think to myself, *How many other people are free because of Beaver's daring and bravery?*

Bright Feather and I have had not one moment of private time between us since I found him unconscious and close to death in the west corner containment area. As he healed, Red Fox was always within arm's reach as well as Double Arrow and Mary, no more than three steps away. On the trail, I hover close by as he rides Companion, but so does everyone else. I've not had a moment to talk to him about the baby, although he has asked endless questions about Storm and Hope and talks in front of others are filled with plans for when we get home to the children.

For me, I wait with great enthusiasm for that magic moment in time when I feel normal at last, but unfortunately that time has not come. I think back and try to recall when my last woman's monthly time happened and cannot quite remember. I've battled furiously against the tiredness and on two occasions I've forced myself to eat even when I didn't want to, in a misguided attempt to keep my strength up. The results weren't favorable and I've given up that route. With more people on the trail, things are not so focused as it was between just Deer and I and I suspect that no one is the wiser. I tell myself that when the right time presents itself, I will tell my secret. So I bide my time to tell him about the baby.

For Bright Feather, I know his arm pains him and he battles a recovering exhaustion greater than my pregnant tiredness. I suspect that ribs may have been hurt or broken, too, for he favors his bad arm in a way that always protects his right side as well. Mounting Companion is a painful process that's done with absolutely no help at all, thank you very much. I know he's haunted by Raccoon's death, for he's more quiet and withdrawn than I've known him to be in a long time. He cries out in his sleep at times, and the most unusual thing of all is that he often shouts in English, *"No! You cannot do that! Stop!"* He reminds me of the Bright Feather I first knew, who spent his winters in the forest and was known as One Who Is Always Alone. I know that's how he deals with his grief and I struggle between allowing him to heal slowly on his own inside and out and wanting to help him in any way I can think of.

Now you would think that me, of all people, would no longer be surprised when life takes an unexpected turn, but I still seem to be regularly caught unawares. As we ride the trail five days after we left Fort Payne (with three days hunkered down by snow), I feel the distinctively uncomfortable feeling that I've felt only twice before in my life - right before I gave birth. *Why that's impossible*, my mind says to me, *you are only nine or ten weeks along. You cannot be feeling the feelings you feel before you give birth!* and so I ignore the aches and twinges and general discomfort. When we stop at noon for a time to rest and eat and give Bright Feather and Red Fox time to rest a bit, I'm completely dismayed to find bright red blood mixed in with my pee and trickling down my leg.

I stare down at the blood red and yellow snow and think stupidly, *Now what?* The pains seem to intensify as I stand there and I'm uncertain what to say or do as I make my way slowly back to the group. *Pardon me, it seems that I am having a bit of a problem ...?*

As I come upon the group, all in various stages of rest, I make eye contact with Deer first, who stands in concern, by the look on my face. One after another they turn to look at me as I stand there feeling the blood trickle down between my legs. Bright Feather stands and walks to me, a concerned look on his face. "Bear? Are you well?"

"I've been meaning to tell you something, and I've been waiting for just the right time," I begin, "but now it seems too late, actually." I can't help myself and I begin to cry as another pain grips me and he reaches out to me. "We were to have another baby, but that seems to not be so anymore ..."

It's quiet Mary who comes forward and begins to give directions to the men who scurry this way and that. A hasty camp is made and a fire is built. She talks quiet and reassuringly to me. "You loose the baby," she says after she examines the blood that continues to flow from me. "It is a sorrowful thing, *I know*," and her eyes fill with tears. She struggles with a tremulous smile, "But there is always tomorrow and a new day, is there not?" and the two of us look in each other's eyes and become sisters right there in the cold and snow and wildness of the forest. She knows of medicine and herbs and tells me what I should be feeling and what I *should not*. We determine after much discussion that the loss of the baby will be the way of things, but it seems that no additional things are happening to cause me, or a worried Bright Feather, any more concern. I ponder the way of things, that of those we rescued from Fort Payne one is a strong capable hunter and one is skilled in the way of medicine.

"Why did you not say anything to me in the Fort when I nursed Bright Feather and Red Fox?" I ask her over the course of the two days we stay so I can rest.

"Why?" she asks most puzzled. "You did a fine job and have quite a skill yourself in care and healing. I needed to watch that fool that calls himself a doctor more than I needed to watch you." That makes me chuckle a bit.

By the third day, the pains are still there, but less, and I'm all of a sudden *so eager* to get back to my home and children I cannot stand another moment being still. At my insistence, I think I say something like, "Well you can all stay, but *I'm leaving*," we strike camp and make our way east to familiar territory and faces. A trip that should have taken just seven days, takes us close to two weeks and even Willow seems to hurry the last bit, eager to get *home*.

The first face we see, well not a *face*, really, for it's just a streak of hair and feathers, is Hope's, closely followed by Turtle's terrified one racing through the woods after her charge. When Turtle sees that it's us, she relaxes and stands on the edge of the clearing where we are as I jump down from Willow and accept the wild running package that crashes into my arms. Red Fox dismounts and walks towards her and she begins to laugh and sob with relief and joy, and then she's running into his arms, too.

We enter the village, Bright Feather with Hope riding in front of him on Companion and me walking beside them leading Willow. Red Fox holds Turtle's hand, Deer leads all of the pack horses, and Double Arrow and Mary hang hesitantly in the background. As decided, the huts have not been rebuilt, but there are many in the village place working. I search the faces for my sister, Otter, but she's not to be found. It's War Woman who, after embracing both Bright Feather and I tightly in welcome says, "She is at the river."

I do not think in the many years I've been in this village I've *ever* seen Otter sitting doing *nothing*. Her hands are always busy, her mouth is always laughing or talking or saying wise things. She has a loving, powerful energy that I've been fortunate to experience since the first morning so long ago when she walked out of the mists and I noticed her *kind eyes*. Bright Feather and I find her seated quietly at the riverside doing nothing and I know, before I even speak with her or see her face that she knows. As I walk toward her, she looks at me and her eyes tell me of her grief.

I walk to her and sit beside her there at the river's edge and she puts her head on my shoulder, as if it's too heavy for her to hold up any more. I put my arms around her and I rock her like she was my precious child and we hold on to each other and grieve.

"I dreamed a dream," she tells me quietly, "he came and said goodbye to me. He spoke of each of his children and of his love for me." The sobs come from a place deep inside her and I feel helpless to stop her pain. "I have already sung the mourning song," she says and I rock her some more. We stay like that for a long time.

At last she looks up at Bright Feather standing stiff and silent beside us both, tears quietly trickling down his face as he looks across the river to the forest edge and beyond. She reaches up to take his hand and he grasps hers tightly. "You know of this sorrow I feel, you know of my loss," and he looks down at her with a look that almost breaks my heart. "You were a best friend, you were a loving brother, and you were *not* responsible. Whenever there is sorrow nearby you, my brother, you always seem to want to claim the cause." She stands up and he embraces her fiercely. "I am glad that you were with him, for that was as it should be," and as I see his shoulders shake with his crying, I go and put my arms around both of them. I do not know how long we three stand there at the edge of *The River That We Are Always By*, holding each other up, while we grieve.

Although Deer is anxious to get home to his family, we spend three nights discussing plans for the future of this village. While the caves have saved our lives, it's obvious to all that it has been a long, difficult winter. It's the first time for me that I think that Great Elk *looks old* and I realize that he and War Woman have taken One Who Knows' place as the oldest members now. I realize that for the two of them, this past winter has been most hard; their village has been in hiding, their son has been captured and imprisoned, the other son has been involved with activities that seem to have made him a hunted individual and their beloved son-in-law has been killed, making their daughter a widow with two children. This weight of leadership that the two of them carry seems, at last, to have become something that's almost too heavy for them to bear.

I look at Bright Feather seated next to me, wrapped in his furs, looking more like himself than I've seen him in many, many days and I think *will you be the next chief?* The enormity of it crashes down on me. I look across at Deer, sitting serious and intense, talking about what he thinks will be the best way to deal with things now, and in the immediate future. I realize that despite what he has said to me in the past, about him becoming chief among us, *It is not my calling...of that I am quite certain,* I realize that he would be a very good choice for a chief. I think of Beaver and worry about this battle of might and wits and hate that has begun between him and this soldier named McTavish. It can only lead to death I know.

"There is no doubt in my mind," Deer says, "that you must get the trading post up and running as soon as possible. It was not the treaties that assured your exemption from the removal process, it was the fact that your village was self supporting and independent from the assistance of The Nation of The Real People and The United States Government." He looks at me, "That should be your very first priority now that you are back. Take stock of what you need and let me know as soon as possible how I can help with supplies." I nod at him.

"Perhaps it is time for the road," Great Elk says and everyone is quiet for a moment. "And perhaps, it is time for us to build more permanent structures like the trading post to live in. It has not escaped my thoughts that the only structure that survived the soldiers was the sturdy one built with logs." He smiles a tired, rare smile, "Perhaps these old bones of mine might enjoy a softer mattress and a sturdier roof over my head in my final years ..."

Deer nods his head. "That is something everyone should consider. The village should be rebuilt, come the spring, in one manner or another, for to leave it fallow like this any longer will send a message that it is not a village at all, in the white man's eyes. As the road is built, the logs could be used to make homes for those who wish."

Deer stretches and yawns. "I leave tomorrow. I miss my mate and children. I have been away from them for this entire winter."

Great Elk looks at him. "We owe you a debt of gratitude that can never be repaid."

Deer is quick to answer. "You owe me *nothing*. I am the man that you see before you, because of the love and patience and support that this village invested in me when I was no more than a scrawny, scared, orphan white boy. I owe you my life and my protection for as long as I can manage it. It is one of the few things that makes me proud to be who I have become."

So the village rebuilds gradually from the start of spring, through the summer, and into the fall. There's not a moment that there are not ten things for each person to do. There's the gardening and gathering and hunting and fishing that feeds us and prepares us for the winters. We repair and restock the trading post and business trickles back by way of Deer's advertising in Forest City and word of mouth. There are those that rebuild their huts to be exactly how they have always been built and there are those who decide to build more permanent structures. Our hearth's decision is not ours to make, but seems to be a choice of the children: Little Bird (who now calls himself Swift Feet), Storm, Squirrel, Laughs Much, and even little Hope. It's their desire to have a permanent structure.

Swift Feet, who has taken it upon himself to be the man of his family now, is the one who puts it best, "I want what is safe and most excellent for us and this permanent structure is it." He and Storm work along side the men as they build first one small cabin for War Woman and Great Elk and Mary (who has been invited to live with them and help in the many chores of a home), and then another larger one for Bright Feather, me, Otter, and the children. Turtle, pregnant with their second child, and Red Fox decide to wait until the next year for a permanent building, *if ever*.

Time passes and I marvel at the changes that come about. Our stores grow, and farm animals such as chickens, cows, goats and even sheep are replaced by a late spring delivery from Deer, James, and Sleeping Rabbit. Turtle and Red Fox, welcome a son, Tall Elm, to their hearth. By the first snow, our village is rebuilt, looking decidedly different than it has ever looked before. And the start of a road, still unfinished, stretches deep into the forest towards the white world, that we must now call our friends and neighbors and forget that they have been our enemies.

A surprise, but not an unwelcome one, arrives in our village at the very earliest part of spring of the next year. I've just begun to prepare for business to pick up in the trading post and at first I think that man that darkens my door is a customer I've dealt with in the past. It takes me a few moments to recognize him without his military uniform, beneath the beard and long hair, but the friendly smile soon helps me see it to be no other than Major Alexander Everett, of the second United States Cavalry, Company A.

"Major Everett!" I exclaim, "welcome to our trading post!"

"Please, just call me Alexander," he says and he removes his hat and runs his fingers through his long hair. "I am no longer in the military and prefer to go by the title my mother gave me many years ago," he says with a smile.

"Alexander, it is then," I say. "Come back to the village with me, I was just closing up here."

He keeps me company as I do my final bits and lock up, and then walks along side me, leading his horse and pack horse, as we make our way to the village. He asks me about the trading post and all those names and faces that he remembers from so long ago. He's amazed at the progress we have accomplished in the few short years since he was here: the trading post, the under construction road, and the few permanent homes. But my greatest delight is watching the expression on his face as we sit down to dinner and I introduce him to Storm, who is now approaching his eighth summer. He's a tall boy, strong and sure, never shy, but like his father, never one for many words. He has, much to his delight and pride, had his first big kill just this past fall, and it was my turn to tease him about it being deaf and blind and dumb. He greets Alexander Everett with no words and masks his surprise well when Alexander greets him in his native tongue.

"It is a pleasure to meet you, Storm." Alexander says to him. "I knew your mother before you were born and the fine strong man I see you becoming is no surprise to me."

"Why Alexander!" I shout in delight. "Well done!"

He smiles at me, but I see dark shadows in his eyes, "I made it a point to learn the Indian's language, as we had so much contact with them. It did not help them much though," he says.

"It is a pleasure to meet you too, Mr. Everett," Storm says to him. "Both my mother and father have spoken highly of you and often use you as an example of a white person that knows how to keep his word."

I must laugh at that, but then see fit to apologize. Alexander will hear none of it, "It is a proud accomplishment for me to know *that* is how I am remembered in *this* Indian village," and I see the shadows pass by again.

Though we live in a proper wood frame house now, and though we sleep on wood frame beds filled with mattresses made of straw (although mine *always* must have a fur covering for I cannot stand the awful noise the straw makes), and though I've a stone hearth in which Otter and I do a majority of our cooking now from the big iron cauldron that used to sit outside the trading post, we still regularly eat as we did in old, outside around the open hearth fire of Turtle, Red Fox, and Laughs Much. When the weather is quite miserable is the only time we crowd into the shelter of our wood home to eat. We enjoy a fine meal outside that night for Alexander has brought gifts of different food stuffs for us to enjoy. War Woman, Great Elk, and Mary join us, too, and there's fun and laughter and it's just a good time.

"I was wondering," he says towards the end of the evening, "if I would be allowed to stay for a while here with you. Since I have resigned my commission with the army, I have no place in particular I *must* go and I thought perhaps, now that I hear of all the work you have to do with the road and perhaps more permanent homes you wish to build, that you could use an extra pair of hands.

"I have left the army because I could no longer be a part of what they are doing. I carry in my pack my honorable discharge and pay for my service that is not in gold but is in the form of a land deed for a piece of *Indian reclaimed land*. My Aunt Rebecca and Uncle James have made the choice to follow the Cherokees west to their new place, but I have made no choice at all as to where I will settle."

Alexander Everett looks at us around the fire. "I have no place that I wish to go, no place that I can call my home. I have been wandering these past months from town to town searching for *something*, although I do not know what and it is only since I have been *here*, that I have felt a contentment, a peace. I will not ask you to give me an answer now, here, in front of me. Please take your time to discuss it amongst yourselves and I will be more than happy to abide by whatever is the decision of this fine village."

He smiles at us. "Now, if you'll excuse me, it's been a long day riding in the saddle. My belly is full and happy and I look forward to my bed."

As he stands to leave, it's War Woman who speaks to him. "Alexander Everett, we do not need to discuss anything privately among ourselves. You have always been a man of your word and have been highly thought of by everyone in this village. Our daughter, Bear, owes her life to you and your kindnesses and there are many who owe you their gratitude as well. Should you wish to remain with us, you are most welcome."

He makes eye contact with those around the circle. "I'm much obliged then," he says. After a moment he smiles at us. "It's good to be home, then."

The next day, Alexander joins me as Hope and I gather water at the frigid river's edge. "Good day, Bear. Good day, Hope," he says with a smile.

"Good day, Alexander," I say and look down at Hope and then back at him. Over her head, I shrug my shoulders and give him a look that says, *Good luck!*

"Hope," he says, and he sits down on a nearby boulder, "I was wondering what your thoughts are on my living here in the village for a time," and I can see that he really does want to know her opinion. Still shy and quiet as she approaches her fifth summer, I do not know if she will even speak with him.

She studies him with great intensity and I see him struggle to maintain a serious face and not chuckle. "You were a bad bluebird once," she says.

He thinks, trying to understand the "bad bluebird" reference I can see and I wonder if I join this conversation or keep my mouth shut.

"When you say 'bad bluebird' you mean a soldier I would guess," he says to her and she nods solemnly.

I go to open my mouth and his look silences me. "Yes," he says after a time, "I was. I came into villages such as this on my big horse, with other soldiers and we forced those people to leave their homes and travel with us, frightened and afraid, to big walled places we call 'forts'."

"My father was in such a place," she says and he looks at me startled across the top of her head. I look back at him and nod my head. *We should probably have a long talk soon*, my look says to him.

He reaches down and picks up a pebble from the river and turns it over in his hands. "My father was a bluebird, Hope, but he was not a bad one. He did many things that helped to make this nation great and I was proud of him and wanted to be just like him." He looks at her. "Can you understand those feelings?"

Hope sighs a great sigh and sits down on another boulder close by and I, too, decide to sit down for this might be very interesting to watch and hear. "I think I know what you speak of," she says, "I am proud of my mother, too, and want to be just like her when I grow up, but it will be hard for me I think. You see my mother is both white and red and that makes her very powerful. Sometimes I wonder just what I am meant to be when I am older? Mother was white and became red. I am very red, but I wonder will I grow up to be white?

"Mother lives like an Indian, but sometimes she must be a white person. That is how she got my father out of the fort. I can speak both ways of talking. Will I need to be able to do things like that, too?"

I look at Alexander over the top of her head with surprised eyes. She and I have never spoken of these things.

"The world is changing, Hope," Alexander says to her after a time. "Not necessarily all bad, but not necessarily all good either. I became a bluebird to be just like my father, but I realized after a time that what I was doing was nothing like the good he did and at last I had to make my own choices and choose a new path that I could call mine. I'm sure you will have to do that too."

"I suppose so," she says after a moment of pondering his words. "Mother says that your uncle is in prison. She says he chose to go to prison and for what he believed in, rather than to do things that he knew were wrong."

"You speak of my Uncle James," Alexander says. "He was in prison for four years because he would not agree with certain things other white men said about how your people should be treated. Sometimes the right choices are the hardest. That's the tough part of life."

"My Uncle Beaver makes choices like that, too," she says and I cannot believe what I'm hearing. Hope and I speak occasionally of Beaver, but never of anything specific, and she has met him just once.

"I can tell you because of who you are now," she says to him in serious tones. "He fights the bad bluebirds and he faces the tough-part-hard-choices that will mean good for some and sorrow for others. I have met him once when my father was at the fort. He told me that my name 'Hope' was good, for he could see good things were to come of me." She picks up a stone, like Alexander is still holding and rolling about in his hand. "Is your Uncle James still in prison now?" she asks.

Alexander shakes his head. "No, he is west of the Mississippi now, in a place called Oklahoma. He chose to go there and make ready when he and my aunt realized that so many of your people must move there to live. My Aunt Rebecca and he are called missionaries. Do you know what that is?" I get the feeling that neither one of them have any thought of me sitting quietly listening to their talking anymore.

"Mother says that missionaries are people who go to tell other people about God. Mother says that God is a great strong being that no one has ever seen, who is so powerful and so strong that He can hear your tiniest whisper, even if you say it just in your head or your heart." I think I must be more careful what I let her hear and see, for she has remembered everything, it seems, that I've ever said or done.

"And what do you think of that, Hope?" Alexander asks with a very curious look.

"This God had a son and his name was Jesus," Hope says. "Mary has told me many stories about God and Jesus for she went many years to a Mission School. I think it is right, you know, that all people take responsibility for their actions." She lowers her voice to a whisper, "Storm got in trouble for taking a knife from the trading post and Mother made him work to pay for it. She said just because you want something and it's there for the taking, doesn't mean you can just have it. Storm wasn't so happy about all of that.

"But Mary says that this Jesus took the responsibility for all of the bad things we do. 'Course, we have to speak to Him private like and let Him know we're sorry for all of that and everything. Mary says that we need to think long and hard about ourselves and our lives and then decide, Do we want to live a life that will be a pleasure to God or not?"

"I've done that," says Alexander, and Hope looks fascinated.

"You *have?*" she says.

"Yup, I did that long ago. Wasn't much older than you, I think. I listened to what my Aunt Rebecca told me, and it just made sense to me, you know? It's not complicated or involved. I just said a quiet whisper prayer, like you and your Ma call it, and I asked Jesus to take over my life for me. It's helped me a lot, especially with some of these very tough-part-hard-choices I've had to make recently."

"Well, I think it's a good idea," Hope says at last and stands up and drops her rock in the river with a solid *thunk!*

Alexander looks a bit puzzled. "Good idea?" he asks.

"Yes," she says rather impatiently I think. "You asked me what my thoughts were about you staying here in the village for a while and I think it's a good idea." She walks over to him and touches his bearded cheek. "You bring joy and light with you, and will find some here for yourself as well I think." She turns to me, "Race you home, Mother!" and darts off into the forest.

"Well, well," Alexander says and he watches her race off up the forest path while absently touching the cheek that still shows the wet handprint of her small palm, "that was one of the most amazing conversations I've had in a long time."

"You're telling *me*," I say as I watch my daughter disappear around the bend.

At the start of a surprise spring snowstorm, an Indian woman and her two children come into our village. She appears out of the forest almost as if she's a ghost come back to life. Strapped to her back is a baby and walking beside her is a young boy about Storm's age. He wears a pack of supplies on his back. The woman and the boy look *lost* is the best word I can think of as I look at them. And sorrowful. It's War Woman who approaches them, speaks with them, and with a glad cry embraces them and brings them to her and Great Elk's hearth.

Her name is Martha and she's Beaver's mate. Her children, the baby Fern and the boy, Still Waters are quiet and watchful. We learn that they have been hiding within a day's hike of our village for over a week, fearful of soldiers who have been following them and deciding when is the best time for them to enter. The snow was a good thing, for it covers their tracks and is what helps them decide to come to us at last. Beaver will not enter the village. For our protection, as well as his family's, he still hides.

"I go to him," Bright Feather says, and in answer to my concerned look he says, "I will go and hunt, Bear, *he* will find *me*." He takes an unusual amount of food with him for a day's hunt, as well as some warm furs and such things that Martha tells us will be welcome. As Bright Feather kisses me goodbye, he says quietly to my ears only, "It will be good for him to know that the family is here safe as well."

In the shelter of our home, we feed them and give them warm, dry clothes. The baby, just over a year old, reminds me of Hope, with her solemn eyes and tiny frame. Hope is enchanted with this little miniature version of herself and carries her all over the house, cooing and whispering quietly to her. The boy, Still Waters, is quiet and watchful. He and Storm, who has returned from fishing, eye each other across the room, each taking stock of the other. I cannot help myself, but I feel that there's an impending sense of doom and disaster that they bring with them, and I struggle to be cheerful and welcoming. Aside from basic answers to polite questions, not much is said and by the time it turns dark and the evening meal is finished and cleared away, no one is the wiser as to the state of things. I stare at their sleeping forms on the floor near our hearth fire, bundled in their furs and I think, *What is your story?* and *Is it as interesting as mine?*

Bright Feather returns late in the night, well after everyone has gone to sleep, except me, of course, who sits wide awake by the fire willing the sound of his footsteps on the front porch. *I'm getting too old for this,* I think and then quietly chuckle at the thought. I'm twenty - three by my best count, just this past fall.

"Come," he says to me, "we must go to War Woman and Great Elk's hut," and I follow him without hesitation. It's no surprise that they, too, are awake, waiting.

"He has killed McTavish and two other soldiers," Bright Feather says without introduction. "One soldier did escape; he was on a swift horse and Beaver and his companions have no horses. Beaver is certain that his crime and his description will be carried back to Fort Payne. That was three weeks ago. He seeks to get his family settled and safe and we have talked of many different plans, including one to travel north as swiftly as possible, maybe to Canada."

"Did you tell him what Deer thought about McTavish and the fact that Charly knew my name?" I ask.

"Yes, I did, and that disturbed him greatly." Bright Feather looks at me and then to War Woman and Great Elk. "Beaver feels very strongly that Deer should be summoned. He believes that the military will come here to this village, even regardless of what I've just told him, because there is still great distrust of this Indian village that has escaped capture. He fears that the soldiers will come here once again and seek to take us all away, using him or any number of other excuses. He feels we are in great danger based on the things he has heard and seen watching the soldier camps. So I leave tonight to go get Deer," he looks at me pointedly, "on my own."

It's not how I want it to be, and neither does he, but it makes sense. He can travel faster as one, than as two, and I can be more help here. Especially if the soldiers come before Bright Feather and Deer return. I say nothing to him, but my eyes make every effort to say, *I'm a powerful woman, you know.* He reaches out and takes my hand.

Great Elk looks at both of us. "I am getting old," he says at last in the flickering light of their hearth, "and I would talk with the two of you about the future of this village. I would tell you my thoughts *now* and leave the two of you to think these things over for a time. It is something that should be said maybe sooner or maybe later, but I will say it *now* just the same.

"I have three sons and one daughter that have made me a *great man*. Greater than any accomplishments I could remember or even dream of. They have chosen fine spouses to love and have given me grandchildren that make me walk tall and proud. There is not one wish that has not been granted to me in regard to my mate and the children we have shared between us. I have enjoyed every happiness. May every chief have the same difficulties I have faced in having three sons that are strong and wise and capable of leading such that the choice of who is to succeed him is such a difficult one to make!

"Beaver has chosen a path that has brought him far from this village. *He is the son of my youth* for he reminds me of my idealism and belief that I was going to make the difference. While his concern and dedication for us has not diminished, his purpose and direction has made him choose a path that *leads away* from us, rather than to us. It is an honorable path, one that I believe was part of him and who he was from the moment of his birth. It is right that he has fulfilled his destiny. Some people make a great impact over the course of an entire life, and some people make a great impact in the flash of an instant, like a bolt of lightning. Beaver has saved many lives and we may never know how great his deeds truly are. We know already of the many people he has helped with his bravery and sacrifice. I look at two of them here. The role of chief, however, is not one that Beaver can assume.

"You, my son," he says to Bright Feather, "have chosen a path that loops in many directions from this village but always leads back to *here*. *You are the son of my heart* for you are most like me; you love fiercely and you are loyal to death. I look at this strong young woman next to you and I *remember*," he looks at War Woman with a tenderness I've never seen him display before and then looks back to Bright Feather. "You have a love of this village and a love of our Old Ways that continues to serve us well to this moment and beyond. Yet, you recognize that in order to survive, sometimes you must make hard choices and changes to secure a better life for those you love and care about. You are a son that has made me proud in everything you have done or said. The role of chief is one that you could assume and do just as well as you have done everything else in your life." He reaches out to hold War Woman's hand, "But it will steal from places most precious to you that you should not have violated and I am loath to have that burden and sorrow with you for the rest of your life."

He sighs and smiles a fond smile. "Deer is a lightning strike. He is a presence in this village because of a series of violent storms. Just like a leaf can end up sitting gently and delicately at the opening of your hut after a raging downpour, he became a part of this village through no plan or design of anyone but the wind and the rain. He has struggled his entire life - and he will never stop - to find a definitive spot in the white world or the red. *He will never find it.* A wise person takes his weakness and their struggles and makes the most of them and *he has done that,* although I do not know if he realizes that yet." He shrugs his shoulders and looks at War Woman again briefly. "Maybe he never will. He has secured a life in both worlds, one that is successful and respected. *He is the son of my destiny.* When next he comes to this village, I will give him the greatest challenge of his life for I will ask him to assume the position of chief here when I am no longer able. He has the love of our ways that is as permanently a part of him as his white skin and yet he has the foresight and know how to keep this village alive, together and successful in the turbulent years to come."

Great Elk reaches out his hand and places it on Bright Feather's clasped ones. "Travel swift and sure to Deer. Beaver is right; Deer needs to be here now."

The next day, Great Elk informs the village of the way of things with Bright Feather having already left to summon Deer. He cautions them about the soldiers and the ever present fear that they may return. He reminds them to maintain their caves and caution their children and prepare themselves for every eventuality. It's decided by all that Martha and the children should be hidden away in one of the caves for safety immediately. Desperate people do desperate things and the opportunity for the army to acquire Charly's family is a weapon we do not wish for them to have. We take them to our cave, for it's the most spacious and it's still, because of our hearth's ever present worry and need to be prepared, stocked and kept at the ready. We arrange a method of delivering supplies and a way of communication, so that we can keep in touch with each other without having much contact. And we all hope that Deer and Bright Feather will arrive before the soldiers do.

It takes nine days for Deer and Bright Feather to return to the village and in that time, the snow has melted quickly away and spring has decided it's here to stay. Those in the village all take an active interest in delivering supplies up to the cave, many still not knowing its exact location, but simply knowing a specific spot in which to drop off things. No supplies are ever left in the same place twice and only on a few brief occasions are words exchanged.

Over dinner the first night of Deer and Bright Feather's arrival home, Great Elk discusses with the village his wishes for the succession of chief. He speaks eloquently and with great pride and love about each of his sons and there's no one who wishes to argue with the wisdom of his words. Privately to just Bright Feather and I, Deer tells us that Possum has been aware of these plans for almost five years. "An *Old woman*," he looks pointedly at me when he uses the reference, "told her that she should not worry about seeing her friends and family again, that sometime in the near future, she would return to live permanently as the *mate of the next chief*. I told Possum that they were *both crazy* if they believed such a statement. You should have seen the look I got from her when Bright Feather told me of Great Elk's wishes that first night he arrived."

Deer is pleased to have Alexander in our midst. He welcomes the availability of a mind that understands the United State's military one. Alexander makes a most comical face, however. "I am *here*," he points out with a sweep of his arms, "because I *could not* understand the military mind. I don't know what help I can be for you, but I will try."

Deer dismisses this.   "There is little possibility that Major Alexander Everett's military history from Fort Winston, Virginia, will have traveled as far as Fort Payne, Tennessee. The United States Army has too many other things on its mind right now, unfortunately. Your presence here in this village of United States citizens, along with your honorable discharge papers," here Deer pauses and looks inquiringly at Alexander who nods his head 'yes', "can only support our continual stance that this is not a tribal village full of only Cherokee Indians."

Deer looks at Bright Feather. "I want to see and speak with Beaver."

Bright Feather nods. "He waits until you are here. He wishes the village and his family to be safe. He is in *The Place Of The Sun*," he says and Deer nods with obvious understanding.

Bright Feather looks at me. "Beaver thinks highly of you and has specifically asked that you come with us when we travel to see him. Can you make arrangements to come along?" I nod my head.

Spring is here in full bloom it seems. I find it amazing that only two weeks ago it snowed and now the trees are in full bud and everything seems to be eager to burst with life. *The Place of the Sun* is a full day's ride, mostly north of our village into an area that I do not think I've ever traveled. It leads high into the blue misty mountains and as we ride, things look a little less like spring, because we travel high up where it's cool and winter has still not yet decided to give up the fight. As we journey I think, *was it only just a little more than a year ago that we traveled, broken and battered back from Fort Payne across these very same mountains?*

We reach a point where the going is too steep for the horses and we hobble them and let them graze. The rest of the way we climb on foot. The going gets very rocky and there are fewer large trees and more short squat shrubs and great boulders. The hard work of the climb makes me sweat and I welcome the cool stiff breeze that blows all the time. "We are here," I hear Bright Feather say to me at last and I know why this is called *The Place of The Sun.* As I look to the west at the sun, it rides low and begins a glorious sunset. As I work to grab hold of the loose bits of hair blown about my face by the strong wind, I look to the east and know that should I sit patiently all night I would see the sun when she makes her way around the earth and begins a new day.

"*The Place of The Sun,*" I say quietly to Bright Feather and smile my understanding of the name.

"For many, many, many years, it has been a sacred place where The Real People believe that you can communicate with those that have gone on before us to The Spirit World," he says over the rush of the wind. "It is often where people go to make difficult decisions, to prepare for battle, or to prepare for the possibility of their death."

I look up at Bright Feather and feel once again like I did long ago, when I knew that a puzzle was being built, but I didn't quite know what the picture would reveal. I sense that he understands things that I do not even know to ask about. He looks tired and determined. He touches my cheek, "I am glad you are here."

I reach out and touch his face, starting at his forehead and down past his eyes and wind blown cheek. He closes his eyes and sighs a deep, world-weary sound. He catches my hand just as it would slip off his face and draws my palm to his mouth and kisses it. "We are each other's strength," he says just loud enough to be heard over the wind.

Beaver does not seem surprised to see us. He sits quietly facing the beautiful sunset, calm and unhurried, like it was the front porch of his home and we are expected guests arriving for a party. He stands as we approach and embraces first Bright Feather, then Deer and finally me. "Come," he says and makes his way down a bit out of the wind.

There are three other braves with him and no names are exchanged. One brave has only a scalp lock, a style in which the hair is completely removed from the head except for the long tail that hangs out the back. His face and arms are heavily marked in a permanent fashion and he's perhaps the fiercest and most frightening Indian I've ever seen. He eyes me up and down and I stare right back at him and think, *You may be Beaver's partner in battle, but I'm his sister.* He does not scare me and even makes me a little bit mad with his glances. The second brave I meet nods a polite greeting. For this brave I note the fact that he has not one, but two rifles strapped to his back plus his knife at his waist. He wears all of them comfortably like they were his skin and I've no doubt that he's *never* without them. The third brave, should I see him on the street, I would expect him to look down on me for my Indian permanent marks and dress. He wears buckskin clothes that a white trapper would wear and seems to not have a trace of Indian blood in him. I think of John Ross and myself and remember that it is what's inside that counts.

There are no formalities or pleasantries exchanged. Deer simply says, "Speak to me."

Beaver says, "There are a number of us that have been tracking the army as it rounds up those of our people to send west. They speak of advance warning, kindness, free transportation, assistance, and safe passage. I see brutality, murder, rape, and terror. They pen them in the camps where they die from exposure, disease, and starvation. They separate mates from wives, children from mothers, and they simply shoot the old or ill that are too slow to keep up. They fill the men with liquor and terrorize the women. They even steal what little amounts of money or possessions our people manage to bring with them." Beaver gestures to the three sitting silently beside him. "We watch, we bide our time, and when the opportunity is right, *sometimes,*" he looks at me, "we are able to set a few free.

"We have been careful to cause no blood shed, realizing that to do so would step up the level of their fury and need for revenge." He looks at Deer. "I remember your words about paper walls and how you have said, *The time for guns and battles and killing is long past.* I understand the wisdom of your words and made every effort to work within that way of thinking." He shrugs. "It worked for a time, but it became obvious to us as we watched *Red Hair,* that the time for different action was fast approaching. When he captured a number of our band, including most of the women and children, *and he knew who he had,* there was no doubt in my mind that he must be killed." He looks at the three of us. "It was a choice between our families or a few soldiers. There was no difficulty in the decision."

"Our only fault," says Scalp Lock, "is that one escaped. He was injured, but I do not think it was life threatening. He will return to the fort, of that I am sure."

"Bright Feather has told you my thoughts," Deer says to Beaver.

He nods. "Yes, I remember the night I rescued Bear. I did call her by name." He looks at me and for a moment we are both back in that cold, rainy, dark forest. "She did not know who I was then, though, I was sure of it." I nod that he's right.

"I have spoken little with anyone about that time, except with Deer and Bright Feather. There are those in the village that know, though," I say. Beaver nods at this.

Deer speaks low and serious. "In the Maple Forest we have a man that knows the way of the military. He agrees with you that despite whether they realize your connection to our village or not, the army will come to us in their search for you. He says, as you have told Bright Feather, that it will be a choice between you or the village and that there will be no one who will be able to stop the army in its quest to find the murderer of three soldiers. The past crimes of the soldiers towards Indians will have no concern. He says just as Bear was a liability at one point by her presence among us, now your freedom is a liability for us as well."

The pieces of the puzzle fall into place and I think again how desperate people will do desperate things. Our connection with Beaver does not matter. We are guilty by association simply by the reality of skin color. They will use the death of the three soldiers to remove our village in The Maple Forest and no piece of paper will be able to protect us from it. I feel a terror wash through me. Why are we here? Why are we not all running? Why are we all not hiding? Why have we left our loved ones alone in the village while we come and have this chit chat here in this *Place of the Sun*?!!

In a panic I look from one face to another, Deer, Bright Feather, Beaver, Scalp Lock, Weapons, and White Face. They all seem calm and peaceful and *resigned*. And then I know. Then I realize why Martha and the children look so lost, what Bright Feather and Beaver must have discussed already and why Deer was summoned to be present with us. These men before me will not run or hide or travel north to Canada. These men will turn themselves in and make the peace. They are here at *The Place of the Sun* to make preparations for the *end of their lives*. I struggle with tears, curling my fist into tight balls and biting the inside of my mouth to cause me pain in another place beside my heart. I taste blood.

Beaver and the three others will follow us after our departure and hide out in the cave we took shelter in at Storm's Place in the Maple Forest. We will wait for the soldiers, tense and certain of their eventual arrival and once again be strong, because we are prepared and have already chosen a path. It's discussed that the presence of Alexander Everett, William Holland Thomas, and myself will be a powerful white deterrent when the army firsts appears and that we must stand our ground and use our paper walls as a first line of defense. We know it will not be successful. Then we will begin to negotiate and it's after a time then as I listen to them talk, that I must leave the circle and walk to the top of the mountain to *the place of the moon* and shed a river of tears, for I cannot bear to hear anymore the things that they discuss and plan.

I sit, wrapped in my bearskin, all night and wait as the sun begins to rise. I sense a presence behind me which then sits next to me. It's Beaver and we watch the sunrise together. "There is great power in the witnessing of a sunrise, you know," he says at last. "East is the direction of beginnings," and I think of the four permanent chin marks on my face. "The sun is all powerful. It gives us life with the growing of our food and helps us survive during the cold winter months. This direction focuses on preparing for the future and securing protection for your family or tribe." He sighs a deep sigh. "The lessons from the direction of the East are to accept all that comes to you and then choose what is comfortable for you. You should always be connected with the circle of close friends and family for protection, but then always keep yourself free for choice."

He reaches out his hand and takes my hand and holds them both up in front of us and I squint against the brightness of the sun as it rises in the sky. "Red is the color of the direction of the east and the color of our people, Bear. Red is the color of life, the power color of the female who leads the family, the color of fire, and *the color of war*. The spirit of the east is the bird, a hawk or eagle. The Real People believe that a feather lying in your path is a message that something special will come to you. Bright Feather told me long ago of the time in the forest when the robin's feather was in your hair. That was a positive omen, for it marked your direction of life and foretold great leadership responsibilities in your future.[39]

He squeezes my hand and lets it go. "The direction of the east is my direction, Bear, and it is yours, too."

I put my head down on my arms, which are folded across my bent knees and feel the tears flow again. I cannot carry this sorrow; I fear that it will choke me to death. Beaver says quietly, over the wind, "Do not grieve for me, Bear. It is a privilege to be able to choose the time and way of your death. White men don't understand that and it will be a gift they will unknowingly give us in their passionate desire to achieve revenge.

"I have a request of you," he says to me and I must lift my tear stained face to his and look at his calm, handsome one. "That is why I told Bright Feather that you were to come with them when they came here. *You* of all people know what it is to lose ones you love in violent circumstances. *You* of all people know what it is like to be in the presence of strangers while you grieve. *You* of all people know what it is like to fight to make a place for yourself and find your true path that will give you happiness and peace. You of all people know how to make brightness out of dark.

"Martha," he hesitates, searching for words, "has known little peace or joy with me. You must teach her all that you know about being a powerful woman. My destiny did not include much time for me to be a mate and a father. When the time is right - you will know it - will you tell her she was my one joy in life? Will you tell her that I remember every second I spent with her?" He searches my face and I brush the tears that cloud my vision away impatiently, and only nod to him, fearful that I've no voice.

He takes a deep breath. "My son, Still Waters ... will you tell him that my only regrets for anything I have done in my life were about the times I lost with him? And can you impress upon him that while I would not ever wish to change any of the choices I have made in my life, will you tell him they were many, many, times more difficult than anyone warned me they would be?" He pauses for a moment and squints at the sunrise now lighting up the valley before us.

"I have only seen the baby twice," Beaver says with a sigh. "She does not know me and cries when I try to hold her. She is beautiful, though, is she not?" And I nod again through my tears. "I met your Hope only once ..." he looks at me. "She has the gift of sight, doesn't she?"

"I think so," I say over the wind.

"Martha was not raised in the Old Ways. She does not know the joy of being a powerful woman." He looks at me, "I know what a gift it is to be educated and loved by a powerful woman. I would wish that you would teach Fern to be the strong, powerful woman that I know you will teach Hope to be. And I would have you tell her that I wished that for her, too," he says.

Beaver sits by me for moments and I think of this man that has loved his people more than his own life and I feel the tears begin to flow again for the sadness of it all. Finally, he gets up and walks away and leaves me with my sorrow.

Bright Feather comes a little while later and brings me something to eat. He looks as I do, grieved almost to death. I lean my head against his shoulder and he says, "It is a privilege that Beaver wanted you to carry words of his back to those he loves. Eat up, you will need your strength, for we leave shortly."

We do not say good-bye. Bright Feather and Deer are simply beside me suddenly and they begin to make their way down. The horses wait for us and we unhobble them and travel the path home. We are silent in our thoughts and in our sorrow and we arrive just before the evening meal time, exhausted from worry, grief, and sheer tiredness. Bright Feather and Deer go to Great Elk's cabin. I go to sleep.

We have two days to prepare before the soldiers arrive. There's a party of fifty I count, headed by none other than Major General Winfield Scott. The soldiers casually form a ring around the village with their horses and weapons. *A human fence of bad bluebirds,* I think to myself. General Scott and two other officers approach the small group of us that have been hand picked to sit at the council circle when they arrive. As he begins to speak, he speaks in English, with no translation. Deer, Bright Feather and I sit stoically silent as he talks. He seems unconcerned that a majority of the people sitting around the council circle cannot understand what he has to say. No longer in charge of one fort, Major General Scott informs us he's now in charge of an entire army of some seven thousand army and state troops and in full command of the removal of all Cherokees to west of the Mississippi. Furthermore, he has been placed in this position by none other than new President Martin Van Buren. He wastes no time providing us with numbers and specific details of his power. The threat is obvious, if unspoken. The signed piece of paper *we* have from Lewis Cass, the *old* Secretary of War, holds no power over this military man hand picked by the *new* white president to round up all Cherokees by the treaty deadline. And should we wish to fight about it, he has fifty armed soldiers to start the fight and many thousands more to finish it.

Deer, answering to the name William Holland Thomas, wears his Indian face well. He briefly summarizes for all of those around the circle what General Scott has said. He shows no concern or worry and simply asks in the language of the Real People, "Congratulations on your promotion, sir, but, why are you here?"

The expressions on the three officers is one of annoyance. "We are well aware that a number of you around this fire can speak both languages," Scott says with great impatience." He makes eye contact with me, Bright Feather and Deer in particular. We stare at him, with such intense dislike and silence that he's finally forced to ask, "We are in need for someone to translate this conversation for both sides. Is one of you willing?" Deer glances at me, and it becomes my job. I translate Deer's comment, "Congratulations on your promotion, sir, but, why are you here?"

Aside from that one dinner at Fort Payne, I've never had anything more than intermittent contact with General Scott. I look at him across the fire and am amazed to realize that he looks as commanding and powerful across an Indian hearth as he does at a table set with fine china and crystal. It's not the setting that makes this man. "We seek the Indian known by many as 'Charly' who is responsible for the murder of three United States Army soldiers. We have reason to believe that this village will know of his whereabouts."

"And why is that?" Great Elk asks. I'm kept busy translating.

"By our best estimate, Charly is responsible for the escape of some fifty - two individuals who were slated for removal west," General Scott begins and I think, *fifty-two!!* He looks at me, "*You,* being one of them." I choose to say nothing and work hard at my Indian face while I continue to translate.

"What is distinctive about your escape," General Scott says to me, "is that you are the only individual he called by name, and you are the only instance in which only one individual was targeted for escape. It was Sergeant McTavish's express belief that you knew this Charly personally. Had we been aware of Sergeant McTavish's theories, we would not have been so quick to release your husband and friend, nor would we have been so quick to allow you to leave Fort Payne." Another time when Deer was right about the way of things, I realize.

"I will not waste my breath asking you for information on him." He looks at all of us around the circle. "I will not waste my time speaking with each one of you. Nor will I make an effort to force information from you about this Charly. I will simply tell you that you have two choices to consider: either I have possession of this Charly and his three companions in exactly two days or this village will be removed to Fort Payne *under suspicion of harboring a fugitive* and *aiding and abetting known criminals.* Once at Fort Payne, each and every one of you, *men, women, and children* will be questioned extensively to determine the information we seek. And then, of course, you will be removed west of the Mississippi with the remaining Cherokees already in the process of relocation."

In the silence of the people around the circle, the fire crackles and the birds above us call to each other noisily as I wait for whose words I will translate next. The threat joins us at the council fire like a living breathing person. I think, *Hello death and sorrow, why are you here again so soon?* Great Elk finally asks, "What if we are able to produce this Charly? What assurances do we have that you will not remove this village anyway?"

General Scott looks across at Great Elk for a moment and then says, "You have no assurance but my word. That is all I can offer you."

"You can offer more than that," Deer says low and quiet. Sometimes Deer speaks in English and sometimes Deer speaks in the language of the Real People. This he speaks in English, so I tell the others what he says using the same low and quiet voice that carries as much force as shouting.

"Such as?" General Scott counters with raised eyebrows.

"How about offering a small detachment of soldiers to travel with a party of our braves to go out and hunt for this Charly together? How about offering assurances that should we be able to help you find this Charly, that should he or his companions have family with him that you would not harm them? How about offering the opportunity for any of the family members that should they wish it, they may reside in this village rather than face the further trauma of removal?" With each question, Deer pauses and lets me translate for those around the fire.

"Why would I bother to do such things?" General Scott says to Deer.

"Time and prestige," Deer shrugs casual like and says. "You gain precious time. You maintain your valuable prestige. Look around you General. This is not a small village. Look around you, General. This is not an easily intimidated village. Look around you, General. Your threats could backfire on you and you could end up with quite a fight on your hands *and* still no Charly.

"I'll offer *you* two choices," Deer says in a voice filled with strength and menace. "You and your soldiers may choose to leave this village at daylight, except for a detachment of ten men, yourself included if you wish. A group of individuals from our village will join you in a search to find this Charly. *If* we find him and his companions, you will promise safety to all family members that may be with them. Or you can choose to wait out the two days you have given us and see how stubborn and difficult an entire village of red United States citizens can be. I have finished speaking."

"That is good, for I have heard enough," Scott says impatiently when I finish translating Deer's words. "This detachment of ten men, which *will* include me, will travel with your group in the morning to search for this Charly. You will lose one day because of your demands, and should this Charly and his cohorts not be in our custody by nightfall tomorrow, the soldiers that do leave at daybreak *will return* with the full attachment of *five hundred* that camp just three days ride from here. At that time they will level this village and *burn the forest*. I will not be foolish enough to expect to find any of you here, for I know you have places in which you hide quite efficiently, but I will dedicate the rest of my military career into removing this village either by bodily force or through hunting and execution. *There will be no Indians in this forest*, of that I will make certain.

"And there is one more thing you must offer for me to agree," Scott says and as I repeat his words, I feel a chill start in the center of my stomach and spread outward to my already cold hands. "When we find this Charly and his companions, it will not be a military execution squad, it will be a *Cherokee execution squad* that completes the task. I will not be a party to creating martyrs. Whoever you send from your party, make sure they are good marksmen or good with a rope."

I struggle with the translation of the last few sentences, faltering on the words and Scott glances across at me, seemingly disappointed at my lack of control. "All in a day's work," he says low to me without emotion.

I do not know how many of us, red or white, sleep that night. It cannot be many. In the morning, bleary eyed and already exhausted, we watch a major portion of the army ride out with only a small party, ten in total, remaining behind. I could rejoice in our small victory were it not for the reality that we have guaranteed Beaver's execution by our own people.

A party from our village prepares to ride out with the soldiers. I watch Bright Feather, Red Fox, Deer, Alexander Everett, and War Woman mount up on their horses. In the distance, I see Double Arrow and five other braves also preparing to ride out. Of all of them, it's War Woman that causes me to sorrow the most. *I know what a gift it is to be educated and loved by a powerful woman*, I hear Beaver say to me. Great Elk stands stoically alone looking old and used up. I see Otter walk and stand near him. Soon Swift Feet, Squirrel, Turtle, with Tall Elm on her back, Laughs Much, Storm, and Hope join him. I watch Hope slip her hand into his and he's no longer by himself, but held up by a wall of powerful women and their children.

I walk over to Bright Feather sitting like a rock on Companion. We have spoken at length late into the night and have shed our tears together over this awful thing that must be done. I know that at *The Place of the Sun* Beaver talked at length of not wanting to be brought back as a prisoner to Fort Payne or any other white man's place. Bright Feather, of all people, understood his wishes in this. Beaver wished fervently to die and be buried *in the Maple Forest* where his spirit would remain. I know, too, that they talked of methods of execution and Beaver wished to die by firing squad as opposed to being hung. "I have watched both," he said "and to choke off the breath is such a bad way to die." Other things that were discussed I couldn't stand to hear and that was when I'd walked away to sit at *the place of the moon* all night.

I agonize with Bright Feather as I stand there touching his thigh of stone, for I know that Beaver has asked him specifically to be part of the execution squad should that be a choice. It's one thing to kill someone out of hate. That all of a sudden seems so powerful easy to me. *But to kill someone out of love?* That's something I cannot find the strength to understand, let alone do. I come and lay a hand on his hard thigh and I feel it stiffen and twitch, but he does not look down at me for I know the tears would spill out. I tie carefully to his belt a bag of corn kernels. "I give you these sacred seeds of life to sprinkle at the right time," I tell him as he continues to look straight ahead. "Were an Old woman here, she would have made sure you had such a thing as you go on this difficult mission." I pause a moment and then say as I rest my face against his leg, "*God, my supporter and my hope, my help for ever near, Thine arm of mercy held me up, when sinking in despair,*[40]" I say it for only Bright Feather to hear.

It's Deer who says behind me loud enough for all those nearby to hear, "As I walk the trail of life in the fear of the wind and rain, Grant O Great Spirit that I may always walk like a man.[41]" He urges his horse forward past the soldiers and into the forest. No words are spoken by anyone as they ride out of the village.

Survivor

We are The Real People of the Maple Forest and the center of the world rests right here where we live and walk and breath. We believe that as long as the world is in balance, life is good: good crops, good health, good weather. It's the Real People's job to make sure that the world is always good. A wrong must always be made right, a bad deed must always be punished, and a slight must always be revenged.

But the world is not in balance the summer that follows the execution of Beaver and his companions and it seems as if just like us, it's barely able to carry on. We face a spring and summer in which almost no rain falls. We watch our crops make every effort to grow and slowly wither and die. The river slips lower and lower such that to lie down in its very center doesn't even cover your face. The lack of rain affects business at the trading post. No one has crops or produce to trade. The worry for the winter grows big and large in our midst and it fights for time in my dreams between the sorrow and grief of those we love and miss so very much.

Great Elk develops a cough that no herb Mary or I know of can help and seems to begin to disappear before our eyes, loosing strength and alertness and in the hottest of days, he still wraps himself in his robe and complains of the cold. Hope takes it upon herself to spend much time with him in their cabin and there are nights when she sleeps there as well. When I speak with her about this, worrying how his death will affect her – for we all know it rushes towards us, she brushes off my concern. "Mother," she says, "Great Elk will travel on soon. He goes to be with those we love and miss already! I reassure him that they are waiting for him and that very shortly all will be well with him when he is at last in their company again. He tells me grand stories that I have never heard and I fetch him hot tea and fix his wrap when it slips. War Woman says that I am good company and that I can stay as long as I wish." She leans over and whispers in a know-it-all voice, "And we *both* know that should she wish me to leave, I would know that! Besides, Mary tells grand stories, too, from what she has learned in the mission school and I don't want to miss any of those either!" So I become accustomed to doing my chores without my chattering shadow that I've grown most used to by my side.

Deer travels home to Forest City and begins preparations to move his entire family back here to the Maple Forest and assume the role of chief. It's something that'll probably take him almost until next spring to accomplish, with all the responsibilities he has. We begin to build a home for him in anticipation of his arrival. A sturdy home is also built for Beaver's mate Martha and her children, Still Waters and Fern, as well as one for Red Fox, Turtle, Laughs Much and Tall Elm. We continue to work on the road and it now stretches so far into the forest that you must walk for almost a full day before you reach the end. Sometimes I go and stand at the beginning of that long gash in the forest and I think, *What will this road bring to us - more sorrow or joy?*

We are never more grateful for the farm animals we have, for successful hunting seems to be more and more a thing of the past and magical tales told over the hearth fires late at night. We build a smoke house to cure our meats in preparation for the winter to come and many of the women and men begin to wear the white man's clothing in some form or another for there are no animal skins to cure and use anymore. Even I must look with fond regret at my old bearskin and realize that perhaps this winter a coat made of heavy wool might be what I wear.

I watch Otter with her children as they adjust to life without Raccoon. I see the sorrow in her kind eyes often when she thinks she's alone or at times when I know that Raccoon would have made a teasing observation. She's still young and full of life and love and I wonder; will she ever love another? I watch Martha struggle with the many things that she must deal with; new faces, new place, and new customs all alone without the man she loved. As I look at her, I see Beaver's wise observations, for even though she's an Indian, she's like me in many ways when I first arrived here in The Maple Forest. I make tentative offers of friendship to her and they're greeted first with suspicion, next with curiosity, and last with welcome. I make tentative overtures to the children as well, in particular Fern, and watch with pleasure as Hope draws her into her privileged circle of love and companionship. Storm and Still Waters have much in common and along with Swift Feet become the mischievous boys of the village that try everyone's patience and remind us of the delights of youth. As the hot dry spring moves into a hot dry summer, I keep Beaver's words carefully in my heart, waiting for the right moment to gift them to those he loved so very much.

Our village, always very industrious, is continually willing to try new and different things that solve our needs. There are those that work well with the animals and those that work well with the products that come from them; leather, wool, and food such as butter, cheese and milk. There are those that have taken well to the many construction responsibilities and have developed such skill and confidence that they even redesign and improve on the tools to make their efforts more efficient. There are those who still embrace much of the Old Ways and continue to hunt and fish and gather the best that they can. There are those who have a gift with gardening and go so far as to not only plant those crops that we do every year, but venture to plant wild plants nearby and encourage their growth like strawberries, blackberries, and gooseberries that'll perhaps do better in the drought. There are those who have the gift of sewing and between my rusty experience and their talent, we manage to sew a majority of the clothing needs within the village using the white man's materials and style. Even Mary, eager to find a place in the village, volunteers to begin to teach the children to read and to write. Using the precious copy of the *Cherokee Phoenix* that Miss Rebecca gave me so many years ago she works faithfully to teach all those interested – children and adult - how to read and write in the language of The Real People. She also works to teach, anyone who will take the time to listen, the language of the whites. In the process, she teaches many stories of the white God to our village one way or another, which is what she desired to do most all along, I suspect.

Bright Feather returned home with the village party five full days after they departed with the soldiers in search of Beaver and his companions. They're as silent on their return as they were on their departure. Over the months that pass he carries his sorrow with him over the death of Beaver and the ever-present misery of Raccoon's death like dark feathers woven into his hair. His nightmares have never gone away but have intensified and I worry over the heartache he carries. Many, many weeks pass before he finally speaks to me of these things, almost as if in finally voicing these thoughts out loud, he hopes to rid the awful images from his head. In the endless dry heat of the summer, we have taken to walking slowly and carefully down the slippery center of *The River That We*

Are Always By each evening, in the cool of the nighttime, listening to the buzz of the mosquitoes and watching the fireflies search for a mate. Sometimes we walk the whole time without speaking a word, just gaining strength from the other.

"Hope has told me today that my sorrow needs to be put away," Bright Feather finally says to me suddenly as we walk and splash one night.

I must chuckle quietly at this. "She makes my life easy, as I just need to stand next to her and she always manages to deliver all the hard things that need to be said, while I just have to listen and agree."

"So you think it is time for me to put my sorrow away, too," he says quietly.

I'm silent for a time, getting my thoughts just right. "I miss them, too," I say with a sigh. "I miss jokes no longer told, and stories no longer spun, and insults no longer thrown." I chuckle again, "I hear the words in my head all the time and I bite them back, because I feel they're not my place to say and that the words still belong to others." I take Bright Feather's hand in mine. "Do you still hear your voice speak to you?"

He does not answer right away and I think about myself and say, "I hear so many voices now, it is almost like I have a crowd in my head all jostling for a chance to speak." I chuckle again, "Sometimes it's hard for me to get a word in edgewise."

"My voice has been silent for a long time," he says to me at last. "It went away at just the time when I would no longer miss it, when I was busy listening to Storm's many questions and Hope's wonderful laughter, and your words of love and encouragement." I feel him shrug his shoulders, "My voice was always simply trying to get me back to a place where I could find love and joy again."

We walk for a time and then Bright Feather finally says, "I cannot escape the sorrow, Bear. It follows me wherever I go. It is there in the places I have traveled with those that have gone on before me. It is there in the faces of the children I see every day. It is there in the faces of the women I share my hearth and my village with.

"I hear screams of pain and torture in my dreams. I see life flowing from a chest that should be whole and strong. I see military horses trampling over broken bodies of those I love and mixing with kernels of corn that I have strewn over graves, that even in death the soldiers cannot keep themselves from desecrating. I ride in the woods and still turn to tell something to someone who is no longer there. I wonder how different life would be for Martha, Otter and their children. *I feel guilty for living.*"

I think about his words and what to say to him. "Your sorrow is something you wear like the feathers in your hair. Everyone can see it and for me I can even feel it. I do not think that any of those that we miss so much wanted you to grieve so long and so hard for them. That must grieve them, don't you think?" He looks at me silently.

I smile in remembrance. "Hope told me a Bible verse she learned from Mary the other day," and I struggle to remember the exact words, "*O Lord, my God, I cried unto thee, and thou has healed me, For His anger endureth but a moment; in His favor is life; weeping may endure for a night, but joy cometh in the morning*[43]. She says that is Mary's favorite verse and that she says it all the time." We stop at a spot we sometimes do, a grassy bank that's shaded by a large weeping willow tree. I sit down; he follows. I look over at him in the moonlight, "I have had much sorrow in my life, but I must watch for the joy as much as possible, for otherwise I would just sit down and die. You seem caught in the middle, unable to escape it and yet unable to accept it either. When I met you, you spent all of your time running, because of the sorrow that chased you. Now, because you have me and Storm and Hope, you cannot run, so you carry it around you like a horse strapped to your back.

"You say you cannot escape your sorrow and I see you struggling with it every day. I think, What can I do or say?" I shrug my shoulders. "I can be here when you seek me out, I can listen when you choose to talk, and I can love you no matter what. That's the best I can do."

Bright Feather reaches out across to me in the moonlight and smoothes his hand down the back of my head and all the way down my braid. It's a tender, loving gesture I've grown to love, one that communicates his love and desire for me more than words can say. I feel him wrap his hand in the base of my braid and slowly wind it around his palm like you do when you want to make sure you have as tight a grip on a rope as you can possibly have and he leans over and kisses me deep and long and lovely.

"And what about you?" he says to me after the kiss. "Do you remember the sorrows from me when you look at me?"

"YOU?" I ask in stunned silence. "What sorrows have you brought me? What have you brought into my life that is anything other than joy?"

I watch as the weight of the sorrow settles back on him and he slowly unwinds his hand from my braid, draws his knees up and rests his chin there. He sighs a most sorrowful sound. "You lost the baby because of me," he says at last.

Even I'm startled by the force of my emotion as I answer, "What foolishness are you speaking of?! Did you cause the soldiers to come into our village? Did you cause yourself to be captured and imprisoned? Did you cause whatever things that happened in my body to happen? *Did you cause the winter time?!* It is one thing for me to watch you suffer for the things that you have had to bear, Bright Feather, it is another thing for me to watch you suffer for the things *that you had no control over!*"

I can't help myself and I stand and begin to pace back and forth at the end of the river that should be wet but is dry and dusty with drought. "It is hard enough for me to fight this sorrow you carry for things that you have had to experience and see and be a part of, Bright Feather, but it is impossible for me to fight these things that have no basis in fact."

"You have not conceived since that time," he says to me quietly.

"*So?* Are you saying that I have not conceived another child because I am so angry or so sorrowful with you *I have kept it from happening?* Do you hear what foolishness you are saying to me?! *Maybe* it might be because we have had soldiers and sickness and drought and work and children and planning and *just plain living* keeping us so busy that it hasn't happened!"

I'm filled with fury over the helplessness of things all of a sudden and I cannot stop myself as I continue to rant and shout, walking back and forth along the riverbank. "But wait! Perhaps you have been the cause all of the sorrow and disaster in *everyone's* lives. Let me think," I stop and put my finger to my chin. "Is it your fault that the soldiers are here causing such terror and chaos among our people? Has it been your fault all along that my family is dead? It is your fault that Reverend Wilder was unfairly imprisoned for four years? Did you cause that horrible storm that destroyed the village so many years ago? Wait, let's make a complete list!" I put both hands on my hips and face him. "Bright Feather, you cannot …" but I stop for his face is now down in the cradle of his arms and his shoulders are shaking with sobs. All the anger flows out of me and I walk to the riverside and sit down beside him and put my arms around him to comfort him.

But something is terribly wrong as I get close to him, for what I hear is not sobs but … *laughter?* He lifts his face to me and struggles to control himself, wiping his streaming eyes with the back of his hands. "All these years," he says to me, "it took all these years for you to finally lose your temper with me." He grabs me and flips me over on my back while

I'm still too stunned to speak. *I have never heard his laughter,* I think. "I love you *so,*" he says to me and kisses me.

He touches my cheek with a tender caress and the look of love he gives me causes me to just about melt. "So let me be sure that I understand what you are saying. You have *not* been having a child purposely because you are upset with me?" and I look deep into his beautiful brown eyes as he gazes down at me.

"Actually," I say to him after a time, "in trying to keep up with my past history, I have just been waiting for the *worst possible time* to get pregnant *again.* It's a gift I seem to have you know."

"Ahhh," he says, "*Now* I understand," and he kisses me again and is in no hurry at all to stop. "And I can stop feeling guilty about drought and famine, and storms, and war and other acts of sorrow and disaster that seem to follow me wherever I go?"

"Deer *has* already accused *me* of many of those things," I feel I must be truthful about that to him.

We stare at each other for a very long time there in the moonlight by the too dry riverbank. I want so much to know what he sees and thinks as he looks at me, but those are not for me to know. Finally he says, "So I guess it *is* time for me to put my sorrow away then."

"And it is time for you to begin to accept responsibility for *only the things* you have responsibility for," I say fiercely. I take his face in my hands and say very carefully and gently, "and you have not caused this sickness that Great Elk struggles with either that will very shortly take him to his next path of life." Clouds drift across Bright Feather's eyes as I say this, but I hold his face tight between my hands, "There is nothing we can do, but make his last moments of time with us *happy and filled with love and laughter.* Let *that* be your responsibility, Bright Feather. Watch Hope, she is working hard at that now." I draw him down to me and kiss him again and we lay entangled in each other's arms for some time, peaceful for the first time in what seems to be a long time.

After a time he says, "I will insist on claiming responsibility for one thing," and I feel his hand touch me in private secret places that only he has ever touched. I agree with him on that.

Fall comes early because of the drought. The trees seem to say, "Enough already, I will go to sleep and try again next year." With the fall comes the rains, but it's too late to save most of our crops. I watch in dismay as the leaves turn colors and begin to fall and the harvest we have is frightening in its scarcity. I try not to think, *but then I must,* about the winter we face that begins with us already hungry and unprepared. We harvest what we can, we gather what we can, we hunt what we can, and we slaughter those animals we know we must and hunker down for a winter dance with starvation in this world that lacks so much balance and harmony.

I do have an occasional customer at the trading post, mostly trappers, and one brings me, of all things a letter, late in the fall, from none other than Miss Rebecca Wilder. Alexander, who has shown no signs of leaving, but has become a permanent fixture in our village, has worked on the construction of many of the homes within the village, including his own version of an Indian hut. He's well liked by all and I chuckle as he's a regular guest at various huts – including ours - for meals, having mastered the skill of never having to cook anything for himself. I wonder if he knows he's the focus of several matchmaking schemes. That night, I invite him to eat with *us*, so that we can share the letter together.

August 27, 1838
Monday
Tahlequah Mission School
Tahlequah, Oklahoma
My Dearest Bear,

It was with great delight that I <u>finally</u> received your letter dated August 3, 1833. I do hope that this letter arrives sooner to you than yours did to me! I also hope that this letter finds you and your family and dear loved ones and friends healthy and happy and safe. It has been so long since we have exchanged words, I scarce know where to start. I guess I should start at the wisest point, the beginning.

James was released from prison in the spring of 1835 and we immediately determined that the Lord's Will was for us to travel to Oklahoma and prepare for the inevitable arrival of our Beloved Cherokee Brothers and Sisters. While they continued to fight the battle of words and might, we upheld them in prayer and made preparations for whatever the Good Lord would send our way.

There is no one, however, who could have prepared us for what we have witnessed and experienced over these past years and I cannot adequately communicate the devastation and despair we see daily. We have been experiencing a severe drought this summer, making removal by boat – the preferred method of transport – virtually impossible. Mr. John Ross secured wagons, horses, and oxen from General Winfield Scott, the military officer in charge of The Removal, and the permission to wait until the drought abated. But consequently, many of our dear ones are still being held in the sweltering camp prisons throughout this terrible heat. Those that have made the trip and survived to tell the tale, speak of sickness, death, misery, and unspeakable brutality at the hands of the military. It is truly a trail that is awash with tears. We have heard tell of thousands who have died along the trail west! This most sorry episode of American history overwhelms me and is a true reflection of both the United States Government and the Public's character.

I do not know what level of information you receive, however, better too much, than not enough? It is with mixed emotions I write and tell you of the assassinations of Major Ridge, his son, John, and Elias Boudinot. The ill will that many Cherokees felt towards these men that orchestrated the New Echota Treaty and the subsequent forced removal of an entire nation of people could not be forgotten or set aside. James believes that the old Cherokee clan "law of blood" – revenge for our way of thinking – is the impetus behind these apparent executions. The two of us struggle with Our Lord's admonition to turn the other cheek, while we watch daily as these pitiful masses of humanity are dropped literally at our doorstep by a blind, deaf, and unfeeling army.

I had received some early communication from my dear nephew, Alexander, regarding the criminal acts being perpetrated on the Cherokees and his despair over his connection with it. My last communication with him spoke of his decision to resign his commission from the military and seek to repair some of the hurt and damage he was unable to prevent. Do not be surprised should he appear in your midst, as your strength and fine example, of a young woman who has made the most of difficult circumstances, has impressed him greatly.

James and I have grand plans for a new church and mission school, hence my optimistic return address at the top of this letter. I was most sorrowful when our mission school and church building were burned down by Georgia militia. But we have already a large congregation that meets Sundays and Wednesdays for worship and I have more children than I know what to do with to teach. I have begun to train some to be teachers in the hopes that I can meet all the educational needs that I face here.

Bear, I have just read through this letter to you and am dismayed at the pages of bad news it carries to you! What must you think of me? Please be assured that James and I are well and healthy and busier than ever. The Lord continues to work His Grace and Patience and Guidance with both of us and we delight in the clear direction that He constantly shows us. Would we have been able to move west and leave our beautiful church and school in Georgia? Would we have been able to minister to the <u>entire Cherokee Nation</u> had we not moved here to Oklahoma? Would I have been as strong and independent as James says he found on his return from prison had I not had those four long years to grow in that direction? Would James have had the time to translate an entire book of Christian hymns as well as the four gospels of the New Testament, had he not had the years in prison to do so? We continue to allow the Lord to make us, each and every moment, a beacon of Light and Love in this dark and troubled world we live in.

I remember our last visit and how good it was for me to see you and your husband, Bright Feather, and your lovely son, Storm. (Does he still love strawberries so much?) I think about the unborn child you spoke of in your letter and can imagine you with a beautiful daughter or another strong fine son. You have touched my life twice, just for a brief moment in time, but with great impact. The Lord does not always allow us to see what a blessing we are to others, but you must know that you have been a great blessing to me. I pray that you and your people are healthy and well and safe. I pray that the hardships that come your way make you stronger, but do not break you. I pray that the Light of God's Love continues to shine in you. I pray that you stay close to Him in your thoughts and prayers and life's direction.

With great love and fondness,

Rebecca Wilder

The Lord bless thee, and keep thee; the Lord make His face shine upon thee, and be gracious unto thee, the Lord lift up His countenance upon thee, and give thee peace.[44]

"We will have to write her a letter together, so that she can get an update on the both of us," Alexander says with a smile when I finish reading the letter aloud. "It is good to know that they are safe and busy and that those that go west have them to welcome them. That is some small comfort to the grief and despair that I know so many are facing."

I ponder the way of things and the deaths of Dark Cloud and Young Snake, and even the gifted Elias Boudinot, who had such a passion for the *Cherokee Phoenix* newspaper. I think of the strife within the Real People and how it's our job to make sure that the world is always good. How can that be if we are fighting amongst ourselves to the point of death? I think of the difficult spring and summer we have had and think with dread again towards the winter we must face. I feel like a lone leaf trapped in a rapidly flowing river, who must some how make it to shore and still its spinning world. *Help us* ...

Winter brings death with its first snowfall. I hear the song of mourning being sung and I step out into the first flakes of snow. Great Elk, chief, warrior, father, mate, and friend, has gone on to a better place, one that does not have sickness or cold or hunger. As we prepare for his burial, I think about the wide road his life has cut in this forest of life. It's a *good road*, up steep hills, across turbulent rivers and even directly through a number of tall mountains. He has forged on in the face of war and sickness and decisions so difficult, that a weaker individual would have just given up and walked away. I look at the legacy of what he leaves behind in the form of this remarkable village, this *Garden Walled Around* and I hear myself say a quiet whisper prayer as we conduct his burial and sing songs of his greatness and of his passing, *Let me leave behind only a small portion of what he has done and I will be satisfied.*

The winter hits, and true to form, when times couldn't be more difficult or complicated, I suspect that I'm pregnant again. *At least,* I think to myself with an attempt at humor, *I know that things are as bad as they can be.* Bright Feather can say nothing but happy words for, I remind him with an arch of my eyebrows that this one is, after all, *his responsibility.* If all goes smoothly, a new baby will be added to our hearth in the spring. Hope is *delighted* and talks with great enthusiasm about this impending new addition. I look at her and think, *Oh to be a child who has no cares or worries.* Even Storm shows interest in the prospect of the new brother or sister that'll come. Occasional waves of sickness come and go, but I'm more tired and more hungry than I've *ever* been with any of the other pregnancies and struggle greatly. It's almost as if my body and my mind know that the food is scarce and must be carefully doled out to last the winter and as a result wants to eat *everything in sight.*

Deer comes to us just before the full brunt of the winter settles in on top of us. He brings some precious bags of grain and some other foodstuffs, but not as much as he would like for the drought has affected him and his customers as well. "It is my plan to be here with the start of spring," he says and I recognize his serious face and concerned eyes as those of the responsibilities a chief must face. I hear Great Elk saying to both Bright Feather and me, *It will steal from places most precious to you that you should not have violated and I am loath to have that burden and sorrow with you for the rest of your life,* and I understand.

I've been hungry before, but never to the point where it saps your strength and seems to consume all your waking thoughts. I watch my mate grow thin before my eyes and those of our village lie and say they're not hungry so that the young and old and *pregnant* can have a few more mouthfuls. The majority of our village food stuffs are kept in the trading post under lock and key. I know, too, of a secret store in our cave that we have put away for when times reach a desperate state. Spring can be the *season of starvation* while you watch your crops grow and wait until you can eat them. It's during this winter of hunger that I realize what a truly powerful woman I am, for in my pregnant state I believe I could sit and eat the entire place clean of food - given the opportunity - *but I do not.* With Alexander Everett's assistance, I dole out portions each day to family representatives who come for their share. We work side by side, he growing gaunt with hunger and both of us watching my stomach grow to what seems to be enormous proportions. It has been six full years since I gave birth on this very floor, I remind myself, and yet I do not remember being unable to reach my feet and get things down from shelves so early on with the other pregnancies.

Otter comes one day to collect her portion of food for the day and exchange a few words with us. It seems none of us has much energy to talk or laugh much, and after she receives her portion and has left, I find myself staring at Alexander Everett for a long while.

"What?" he says after a time.

"You have not developed the skill of the Indian face," I say after a time and struggle to lower myself down into a chair.

"Oh?" He says again and his struggling attempts to look blank make me laugh a rare laugh.

"You gave Otter a double portion," I said to him finally.

"I give her mine at times," he says finally. "Your pregnant and hungry state has made you not as swift as you should be. I've been doing that for the last few weeks."

I stare at him for a long time and will my thoughts to enter his head and his heart. I find it's quite easy. "You are in love with her," I finally say in wonder.

He looks at me with what appears to be pride, "*How could you not be?*" he says at last.

"Does she know?" I ask him.

He sighs a deep sigh and begins straightening and organizing things that do not need his attention. I watch and observe, glad to think of things other than my stomach and the gaunt looks of hunger on those that I love and care about.

"I think she does," he says at last.

"You *think* she does?" I say.

"We have not spoken of it," he says and then snorts. "We have not spoken of much *actually*. It seems that I am incapable of coherent conversation whenever she is around."

I laugh, "Oh, she knows then."

His head snaps around to look at me. "Why do you say that?"

"Blubbering idiocy is always the first sign of love," I say to him with a twinkle in my eyes, "all women know to watch for it."

He laughs then and sits down and does his familiar gesture of running his fingers through his mop of hair. "I don't know what is the proper way to proceed …"

"Well, you've done the first steps," I say.

"What's that?!" he says stunned.

I fly back in time to the handsome young brave's words as he spoke to me across a fire many years ago, *Can it possibly be ten?*, and hear myself repeat his words, "Well, the overtures can come from either side, but often it is the woman and she begins to spend time with whoever she is interested in. She accepts gifts from him and does kindnesses for him in return, and at some point they choose to set up a hut together."

The look on his face makes me smile at him. I see him thinking so hard I can almost hear wheels turning in his head. Finally he says, "Otter has invited me to share her hearth many times since I have been here, and she is even the one who has sewed these clothes I wear," he looks down as if seeing them for the first time, despite their obvious age and careful mending.

"And she's accepted your gifts of food that you have obviously been giving her," I say. "Sounds like you two are almost married." And I have to laugh again at the look on his face.

We both jump guiltily as someone walks into the trading post and who of all people is it, but Otter. "I forgot to ask …" she starts to say and then looks back and forth at Alexander's bright red face and my smirk.

A speedy and graceful exit are impossible for me, but I do my best. I struggle to stand. "Otter, of the Wolf clan, of One Who Knows' Place, in The Maple Forest of the Real People," I say and she looks at me like I've absolutely lost my mind, "may I formally introduce to you, Mr. Alexander Everett, also of One Who Knows' Place, in the Maple Forest of the Real

People?" She looks over at his face, completely puzzled, as he stands there: a beet red bumbling idiot. They look at each other for a brief few moments and then she gives him a sweet smile that says, *Oh, hello, Alexander,* and slowly sits down in a vacant chair. As I step out into the cold and shut the door with a careful click, I hear the hesitant starts of a conversation between the two of them.

I've taken to talking whisper prayers on my journeys to and from the trading post, remembering the peace they brought me while I waited for Deer to return from Washington and while I prepared to travel to Fort Payne. I search for peace again this winter amidst the hunger and the strife and the uncertainty of the pregnancy and am drawn back to that time, when I found a moment of calm in the center of a great storm. I feel that this loving God must not always like to just hear requests and complaints from me and have begun to list things I'm thankful for, too. Kind of like a balanced trade off, at least in my way of thinking. So while my stomach rumbles with hunger and the baby does such forceful flip flops in my stomach that I fear I will lose my balance and topple over, I say, "Thank you, O Great and Loving God, for Alexander Everett and Otter, of the Wolf clan. This village needs some happy distraction in the midst of these hard times."

We manage to make our stores last until almost the end of winter and look to the welcome signal that the grip of winter has begun to lose its hold. We have reached a critical state in the village, however, and have had to bring down the stores from the caves, and I fear we cannot last until the first early crops of summer. Hunting is scarce and the last of the meats from the smoke house and the vegetables from the root cellar have been eaten. Each day hunters go out in search of something, *anything,* but disappointment is usually the only thing they return with.

"I go to Deer," Bright Feather says to me one evening, "to seek his advice. If possible, I will travel to wherever he sends me in the hopes of securing food for us to make it to the first harvests." He looks at me, for he will most certainly not make it back in time for the birth of the baby, something both of us are loathe to have happen.

I sigh, a tired, discouraged sound it seems to me. "There is no choice, is there? To sit here is to just wait for death to claim its first victim. Who will you take with you?"

"I think that I will ask Alexander to go," Bright Feather says and I nod in agreement. "He may be able to gain access to places that I cannot."

And so, the village waves them off two days later, down our unfinished road that stretches toward the white world *and food* I hope.

I've grown so uncomfortable with the pregnancy, that no position is comfortable for more than a short while. As I shift and grunt and haul my enormous self into a different position one evening, Otter studies me in my discomfort and then says, "Come lay on your bed, Bear, and let me look at something." The bed is not any more or less comfortable than any other place, so I waddle over to the crunchy straw mattress covered with my bearskin and slowly and carefully lower myself down.

We pull up my tunic and she puts her hands on my belly and feels and thinks. Gradually her face develops a most puzzled frown. "Bear, give me your hand. Do you feel here? This is the baby's head, is it not?" I reach to my left side and place my hand on the large hard mass that bulges hard and firm.

"Yes, that must be the head," I say.

"Then what's this?" she says to me and puts my right hand on an identical mound bulging out from my right side. I place my hand on the hard mass and then feel the movements I've grown so accustomed to and the left mass disappears, but the right one stays still.

I look at her with startled and surprised eyes and then dawning realization and finally terror, as she looks at me with a knowing look. "TWO," is all she says and all of a sudden everything makes sense to me. There are two babies fighting and growing inside of me, not just one, *no wonder I'm so huge.* My next thought is, *Good thing Bright Feather is not here right now to begin his worrying.*

The village is thrilled with the news that I carry twins. "A good omen." "A sign of new beginnings." "A special gift from the spirits." "A restoration of balance." All I can think of is *TWO.* I'm overwhelmed with the prospect of giving birth to two babies and caring for two infants when I was unsure if I had enough strength for *one*, given our difficult winter.

It's War Woman who visits me in those early days of shock as I come to terms with what is inside this enormous belly of mine. "I bring you a gift," she says and we exchange glances, for I know from the way she speaks that the gift is not from her. "This was made for you more than three summers ago and was to be kept for you until you needed it." Her face is carefully blank and I take the bundled package from her. The outside cover is a smooth deerskin, cured the old way, soft and lovely with its suppleness. Inside is a second skin, just as lovely. As I open the second cover, I look down in my lap at not one, but *two* of One Who Knows birthing bundles and many precious herbs for me, as well as for the babies. My head registers the fact that *three years ago* she knew that one day I would give birth to twins. *Thank you, my mother*, I think to her.

I take a deep breath and I touch them carefully. I feel an immediate peace descend on me. You are tiny to look at but strong like a stone inside. There is much difficulty as well as joy to come for both of you. Joy never comes without a bit of work to get it. The wise words tumble around in my head, crashing into the worry and sending it scurrying away. "Thank you for this," I finally say to War Woman.

"I thought perhaps this was the right moment to give these things to you, before the worry pulled you over the edge," she says to me wisely.

I manage a small smile. *"Just in time,"* I say to her.

Bright Feather and Alexander are gone one week, two weeks, three weeks and I know that my time cannot be far off, although spring is not really here yet and I know it's early for the babies to arrive. "Babies that come in twos often come sooner," Otter says.

I want to ask her, "Do babies that come in twos have as great a chance at survival?" but I choose not to ask, for I really do not want to hear the answer.

The day I go into labor, is the first day that seems to me to have the smell of spring in the air. I rise early, as the ever present need to pee seems to be all consuming for me these days and have just enough time to take a breath, before I feel wetness pouring down my legs. I feel the terror grip me and do battle with it with a quiet whisper prayer.

Thank you for the spring smell today, O Great and Loving God, I say, Please let me greet Bright Feather with two healthy babies upon his return.

Like Hope's birth, the pains are fast and furious once they start. "*OTTER*!! MARY!!" I hear myself calling and people come hurrying from all directions with my cries.

"The Babies!! The Babies!" I hear people shouting and scurrying and in between pains I've time to think, *Hello! Will someone please help me?"*

It's War Woman who appears at my side, and with surprising strength helps me up the stairs to her hut's porch to sit down. "This is a quieter place than your hut," she says and I don't disagree as I sit on their small porch and watch all the action unfold as I breathe deeply between each pain.

There's much activity and it seems as if the *whole village* wants to be in on the action. Hope appears at my side, her wide excited eyes seeming to fill her entire thin face.   Otter appears, breathless, having run from wherever she was summoned, with Mary close behind her.   They're all business, shouting orders, making preparations and I must marvel at the humor of it all, for *at last,* it seems that I will have a birth not in a cave and not on the floor of a trading post, but in a *bed.*   If it weren't for the starvation and the fact that there are two babies instead of one, it might be quite *normal.*

The first baby, a boy, is born without much fuss or bother or fanfare and it's War Woman who receives and welcomes him while I keep working.   The second baby, however, seems to already wish to be unique, for despite my continual pains and work, he or she does not appear.   I labor for the rest of the afternoon and feel exhaustion drag me down deeper and deeper into its dark pit.   I catch a look on Otter's face and feel the thread of fear begin to weave its web as I see her worried expression as she looks across at Mary.

"Otter," I manage to say between pains, "speak to me and tell me something you know."

She sits on the bed beside me and wipes a cool cloth across my forehead and offers me cool water to drink.   "The baby is turned wrong," she says, " and will not turn into the proper position to be born."

Hope, ever present and practical, says, "Why don't you turn the baby yourself?"

I look at Otter, as another pain grips me, "Yes," I gasp out as I breath short breaths and look up to concentrate on the cracked wood patterns in the ceiling, "why don't you?"

With Otter pushing on the outside, Hope reaching with her small hand on the inside, Mary praying all around us and me bearing down with the very last bits of my strength, the second baby is born to glad shouts and relieved cries.   I hear that it's another boy, just before I fall into exhaustion's blackness.

It's dark but not quiet when I open my eyes to the angry shouts of not one, but *two* screaming babies.   Mary props me up, and I'm handed two very hungry young men who latch on to me with much force and power.   "I always hate that first time," I mumble to myself, as I adjust to the sweet discomfort of nursing.   I look down at my two littlest men and study first one and then the other.   Mary tells me that sometimes babies born at the same time look exactly alike, but I see that my two are very different even in these early few minutes.   Around me are War Woman, Otter, Mary and Hope standing looking tired but proud.   I see Turtle in the background and

I can hear the quiet hum of what sounds like the entire village within shouting range just outside the door.

"Well done," I say with a tired smile to those around my bed. *"We did it."*

The babies are two weeks old and I think, although I'm not absolutely sure, that I've had approximately *one* night's sleep total since they were born. I seem to always be trying to sleep and yet always seem to be shaken awake by some apologetic person. In different circumstances, others could help feed the babies or I know that we could use goat or cow milk, but I'm the *only person* in the village that's healthy enough to nurse and has sufficient milk and we have eaten all the goats and cows that we have had over the course of the winter.

I receive a regular meal still, although I suspect that that's no longer the case with many in the village. When I mention this, War Woman says in a stern voice, "We are a *family* and we help those who need it most. You will eat this food so that you can feed our babies." I do not miss the term "our" babies and I eat the food I'm brought so that I can feed these babies that belong to us all. I'm not surprised that War Woman has taken to caring for Easy One, while Otter has taken to caring for Difficult One, those being the names I tend to call each of the babies in my head, for they have no real names yet.

After feeding both of the babies, for once at the same time, Otter says, "Go! Hide! Go find a quiet place to lie down and sleep where no one will disturb you and you cannot be found. If the babies cry, we can keep them happy for a bit until you wake." I look hesitantly at her through bleary eyes. "GO," she says with a voice that she tries to make sound fierce and frightening. *Raccoon used to do that and wasn't any more frightening than you are,* my tired mind thinks. I walk away towards the trading post.

I curl up in the trading post on some calico material that seems to be one of the only things left that we have not eaten and sleep a dreamless sleep. I wake to achingly painful full breasts and the irony of the fact that, but for the pain, I probably could have slept much longer. I step out onto the front porch of the trading post and see a startled Bright Feather riding past.

As I think on it later, I can imagine how I must have looked. Dark circles under my eyes, groggy with sleep *and* the terrible lack of it, decidedly *not pregnant* and without the ever present babyboard and baby that any new mother would *never* be without. Bright Feather looks at me and takes all this in and I watch his face as he struggles to maintain his composure and not howl his sorrow. He quickly dismounts from Companion and rushes to my side, eyes full of pain and despair. He grips my shoulders and bends close to look into my groggy eyes. "I did not make it back in time!" he says to me, before I've a chance to truly register that he's really back. "I am so sorry, Bear, *so very, very sorry* that I was not here with you -," As he speaks to me, I hear in the distance, the distinctive howls of Difficult One getting progressively louder and louder.

Bright Feather stops and looks toward the direction of the village. "What is that *sound?*" he says to me in puzzlement.

I manage a tired smile at him and touch his cheek that still hovers so close to me. "Your son," I say, "and by the sounds of him, he's *furious* with hunger."

"My son?" Bright Feather says as he straightens up and looks in the direction of the enraged screams. I see Otter come hurrying down the path with the same desperate look that everyone eventually gets, once they've held Difficult One for a period when he's decided he's hungry and I'm not quick enough with my breast.

Otter is so intent on finding *me* and *my breasts* that she gives Bright Feather only a passing greeting, as she practically runs the last few steps. "I'm sorry, Bear, I kept him happy as long as I could, but I am afraid he'll explode with this screaming if I wait any longer ..." She looks at me with apology. "War Woman's on her way, too ..."

At her words we hear a distinctively similar screeching coming from the direction of the village and I sit down on the steps of the trading post and quickly lift my top to give us all a bit of peace and quiet. Bright Feather cannot process all of this and looks to me and the baby and to Otter and then looks in complete puzzlement towards the village and then back to me. "What is *that* sound?" he asks as we hear the distinctive screams growing louder and louder.

"That's your *other* son," I say to him and even Otter must laugh at the look on his face.

War Woman hurries into view with our second screaming son and behaves much the same way that Otter did in her drive to reach me and my breasts. "He has a strong voice that's for sure," she says with grandmotherly pride.

Bright Feather must sit down, for it's all too much for him to absorb. "Here then," Otter tells him, "move closer so that she can lean against you," and she shows him how to sit close so I can rest my arm against him while I hold both babies as I feed them. War Woman has already sat on my other side and I rest my other arm against her.

When he finally looks at me, I smile a tired smile. "Welcome home," I finally say, "it is good to have you here at last," and I rest my head against his shoulder.

"TWO?" Bright Feather finally says to all of us and we all nod our heads. "When?"

"Two weeks ago," I say. "This one," I gesture with a nod of my head to the one on my right that Otter has brought me first, "was the difficult one, and this one," I gesture to the one on my left that War Woman has brought, "was the easy one. You'll have to ask Hope for the details since she's been telling the tale of the birth to anyone who will listen."

"Two," is all he can seem to say, "two sons ..."

"Where is Alexander?" Otter asks tentatively.

Bright Feather, still having trouble processing what his eyes and ears have told him, gestures toward the road. "He travels with the wagon," he says, "I grew so terribly impatient the closer we got to the village, that he encouraged me to ride ahead with the pack horses and tell everyone of our success."

"Success?" says War Woman and she lifts her head almost as if to sniff for the food that is supposedly on the way. "Deer knew where there was food?"

"We never went to Deer," Bright Feather said. "It made no sense, since we knew he was struggling just as we were at the start of the winter. We went to Ward's Mill."

I lift my tired head off his shoulder and now it's my turn to look absolutely stunned at the news he has to give me. "You went to *Ward's Mill, Virginia?*"

He smiles a small smile as he looks deep into my eyes, delighting in the chance to give *me* a pleasant surprise as well, "Yes," he says, "we've been to *Ward's Mill, Virginia,* and we have food – lots of it, for they have suffered no drought this past summer. We have letters and one ridiculously heavy *Hope Chest* from your brother, Henry."

"Ma's Hope Chest?" I say to him in stunned surprise and I feel tears fill my eyes and he nods at me.

"You have Ma's Hope Chest?" I say again in amazement.

"Is that all you can say?" he says with a pleased smile and touches my cheek.

It was Alexander's idea to travel to Ward's Mill, although it took quite a bit of arguing to convince Bright Feather of the right of it. "I had been there on my travels through from Fort Winston," Alexander said, "and I knew that things were different than they had been the last time I had been there." He looks pointedly at me. "I finally made Bright Feather realize that if things were so bad with us, they couldn't be much better with Deer and we would lose precious time traveling north or south once we confirmed that."

We sit around the campfire and for the first time in months and months, we have eaten our fill. I look in amazement at the wagon load of food and supplies in the distance that still must be unloaded and the piles of supplies that have been lifted off the pack horses for eventual sorting and storage. I must keep blinking to see that it's all truly real. Bright Feather has a similar expression to mine, I believe, although his is in regard to his two new sons, which he holds alternately with much delight and wonder. Even grown up Storm, who struggles between the dance of being a man and still a boy, cannot conceal his fascination with the whole thing and sits beside Bright Feather, alternately touching Difficult One's tiny feet and hands.

"What do you call them?" Bright Feather asks me quiet like and I must have a flash of embarrassment for a moment, for he looks curious at me and says, "What?"

"I call the one that War Woman is holding Easy One and the one that you are holding Difficult One," and I laugh quietly to myself. "It is time to find a better name for each though, I am thinking."

"I have a suggestion!" Hope says and I smile at her across the fire where she sits close beside War Woman. She's never far from one or both of the babies.

"What is that, Hope?" Bright Feather says to her, filled with curiosity.

"Well," Hope says, "Mary tells a wondrous story of a boy who is the youngest of *twelve sons*. Even though he is the youngest, God chooses him to go on to greatness; when he is still small, he kills a mountain lion and a giant! He goes on to become a magnificent fighter, a great king and does wondrous things for his people and God loves him very much. His name was David, which Mary says means 'beloved'. I would call this one," and she gestures to Easy One that War Woman holds, "*David Beaver,*" and she smiles a brilliant smile across the fire at her father and I, "since you have given all of us two names, a red one and a white one."

I see even War Woman start at the name and look down at Hope's shining head, which is now bent over in concentration as she coos and plays with the baby.

I look at Bright Feather and then back to Hope. "Do you have a name for the other baby, Hope?"

"No," she says, "but Storm does, although he is too shy to say."

Poor Storm. All eyes turn to him and he looks like he would like to be anyplace else but *here.* "What name do you have, son?" Bright Feather asks him quietly.

He looks first at Hope who meets his fierce stare with little concern and then at me and then Bright Feather, and then finally down at the baby in front of him. "I have listened to many of Mary's stories, too," he starts, hesitant to speak to the group of us who are looking at him intently. "She tells a story of a man named *Joshua,* who did not show fear in even the most impossible times, but simply did what the Great Spirit God told him," and he looks at all of us in wonder, *"and he succeeded,* even when times were bleak and hopeless. He fought a battle where his army simply marched around the fort and the walls, well, they just *fell flat."* He smiles a sad smile. "There are those that we love and miss, who I think would have found a joke in a battle such as that. I think of these times we have faced as a village and as a people. I think of those that have gone before us and how much we all miss them. I think, *if only we had a Joshua,* maybe we would be *just fine."* He looks at all of us a little self conscious, but confident nonetheless and then he looks at Otter and sits up a little straighter and says, "I would call this baby, *Joshua Raccoon. "*

There are very few adults with dry eyes in those first moments. I watch Alexander quietly reach for Otter's hand and hold it in his own. I watch War Woman as she focuses intently on the baby in her lap for a moment and then take a shaky breath and lift her head to proudly face us all. I look at those around the circle that I love and care for so much and then I look at Bright Feather and smile.

"David Beaver and Joshua Raccoon. Those names sound perfect," he says at last. "I think I speak for many around this circle when I say that nothing sounds more right."

I've two letters that I read that night to those of us around the hearth circle. One from Jane West, whose careful penmanship I recognize, and one that Alexander and Bright Feather tell me is from my brother, Henry. I choose to read Jane's letter first.

March, 1840

Ward's Mill General Store
Ward's Mill, Virginia

Dearest Bear,

I write this letter to you in Great Haste for Bright Feather literally stands over me waiting to leave to return to you and your precious village.

I hope that the supplies we send to you will be adequate to sustain your village until the first summer harvest. I felt it important to let you know that the various things that have been sent to you have been a <u>town effort</u> and in particular you should know that the wagon, the team of horses, the two sacks of grain and the side of beef are from none other than Mr. Daniel Hobson, a grumpy but apparently grateful old man who lives down the road a piece and who's acquaintance you made once some time ago.

Please know that you are in our prayers continually. I am sure that you are as busy as I am but I would be so appreciative to hear word from you so that I would know how things are with all of you. I need to know what specific things I should continue to speak to Our Most Gracious and Loving Lord about in my daily communications with Him.

Sincerely and with Great Love,

Jane West

Post Script: I thought you would enjoy the sketch that I've enclosed. I drew it last fall during our harvest festival.

There's a second piece of paper enclosed and I draw it out from behind my letter. It's a detailed drawing of none other than my brother, sitting casually on a grassy slope in profile, with his arm draped protectively around a young woman, who looks vaguely familiar to me. Seated on his lap is *Eli*, as I remember him to be, at about the age of three. They all sit in rapt attention, casual and comfortable with each other and the world, it seems. As I stare at the picture long enough, I take in the details that Jane has carefully included; the woman's loving hand on Henry's thigh and her long hair that has tangled itself in with Henry's in the soft breeze. The boy, who could be Eli, clutches a carved toy in his hand and I realize he's wearing Henry's hat, for it's far too big for him and pushed back from his face.   My vision blurs with annoying tears and I brush them away impatiently while I carefully touch the beautiful drawing I hold in my hands. In Jane's careful script, at the bottom of the page it says, *The Graves, October, 1839, Ward's Mill Harvest Festival.*

"What is it Mother?" Storm asks in concern.

I sniff a sniffle and say with a shaky voice, "It is my brother, and his wife and his son," and I turn the picture around for all to see and there are ooohs and aaahs at the drawing.

"You'd best read the other letter, now," Alexander says with a smile. I draw out the other envelope and this one has careful script from one who is not so accustomed to writing much. *"The Sister of Henry Graves, Maple Forest Trading Post"* it says and then, below, as an afterthought perhaps it says, *"Elle Graves"*, and then finally, *"Bear"*. I smile to myself as I open it up.

March, 1840
Ward's Mill, Virginia
Dear Sister,

It is my most powerful hope that this letter and the supplies we send you reach your village in time. We have been most blessed with the harvest of last summer and so we were happy to have food that we could send you.

I write by the light of the lamp for it is late as I have spent most of the day and night dealing with lambing time here at the farm. My wife, Lydia, has been most forceful in insisting that I write you a letter to go with the supplies we send and this is the first chance I have had. She sends her regards to you and says I am to tell that she was known to you as Lydia Foster during your time at Fort Winston. She found it most curious that there seemed to be so many Graves spending time at and visiting Fort Winston and that was the start of the first words that we spoke. One thing led to another and now here we are married nigh onto four years and our son, Andrew, will be three come this Christmas time.

Elle, (Here this is scratched out) Bear, if I cannot find the right words to speak I surely cannot find the right words to write now. I am now a husband, a father, a friend, and a farmer and I seem to do them all well enough. But I fear that I have failed miserably as a brother. It seems everywhere I go, you have been there before me in far more difficult times and yet you always seem to leave a good memory. I find people who disagree with you, people who question whether you are right in the head, and people who love you fiercely and yet all of them have only good things to say about you and who you are. Words cannot tell my sorrow at things I have said and done to cause you grief and pain, but I will say them anyway (Lydia says that it will be good for you to read).

I am sorry.

I am proud to call you my sister.

Your brother,

Henry Graves

P.S. Lydia and I wish you to have the Hope Chest. It is another joint decision that I think will bring about happiness.

The next day Hope and I go through the Hope Chest (I have to explain to her that it's not hers simply because it bears her name) in the privacy of our cabin while Joshua Raccoon and David Beaver slumber behind us on the bed with full bellies. I struggle with the memories in my own carefully stored away hope chest in my head that contain many pictures with as much detail as Jane West's drawings. Inside we find a beautiful lace wrap that I suspect was my Ma's when she married Pa. There's the family Bible with names carefully written that go all the way back to a time when the family lived in a world across the ocean. There are locks of hair carefully wrapped in an embroidered handkerchief that I remember Pa telling me were from Henry's first haircut. There's a corn husk doll that stirs vague memories of a time before I had to grow up *fast* …

I must sit for a time in the midst of our searching to still my head, heart, and emotions for I fear that I will burst with the strength of all my feelings. Bright Feather comes in at some point and sits beside me on the floor leaning against the bed, looking at the babies and staying close. I know he has sensed my distress *and* my delight with the many things that have happened over the course of these last few days. When we have reached the bottom of the chest, Hope, scurries out of the room to other adventures leaving Bright Feather and me alone, until someone gets hungry anyway.

"Are you all right?" he asks me quietly and I'm at a loss for words for a long time and just sit there amidst the touchable memories of my old life. I cannot even nod my head. I just look at him.

He lifts the sketch of Henry, Lydia, and Andrew and stares at it for a time. "I saw a picture of you when I was in Ward's Mill," he says to me at last and I start and look at him. The only picture I've ever known there to be of me was the poor sketch on the notice announcing my missing. "You are fast asleep, cheeks rosy from the cold, dressed in your furs and curled up on your bearskin. You looked to me like a powerful and brave Indian maid, although I could see your beautiful white features and I knew you were no longer a maid, but that you were already pregnant with Storm by that time. Jane West told me that you were asleep on her floor when she did the sketch." I remember the second time I visited them, after I'd fled the Coopers and before I made my way to Fort Winston. I remember the fear and the loneliness. I remember, too, the freedom and the confidence in myself that I'd rediscovered at last.

Bright Feather looks at me. "Henry has it hanging in his home," he says. "I stared at it for a long time when I first saw it, willing you to stay strong and sure and know that we would be back to you soon. Henry said that Jane gave it to him sometime after he moved back home to Ward's Mill." He looks at me and pauses and we stare at each other for long moments talking our love and happiness with our eyes. "He thanked me for the farm, Bear, and he thanked me for the care of you." I slide over across the floor and bury my face in his neck, take a deep smell of him and convince myself that he's here and all of this is *truly real*. He shifts a bit to draw me closer within his embrace and we sit like that for what seems to be a lovely long time.

He picks up the Bible and leafs through the pages, randomly searching. He stops and reads for a bit. Finally, he reads out loud to me, "*Rejoice in the Lord always; and again I say, Rejoice. Let your moderation be known unto all men. The Lord is at hand. Be careful for nothing; but in everything by prayer and supplication with thanksgiving let your requests be made known unto God. And the peace of God, which passeth all understanding, shall keep your hearts and minds through Christ Jesus. Finally, brethren, whatsoever things are true, whatsoever things are honest, whatsoever things are just, whatsoever things are pure, whatsoever things are lovely, whatsoever things are of good report, if there be any virtue, and if there be any praise, think on these things. Those things, which ye have both learned, and received, and heard, and seen in me, do: and the God of peace shall be with you.*[45] "

He kisses the top of my head and sighs a contented sigh. As the babies begin to stir behind us and as we hear Hope and Storm's thunderous bare feet clambering up the front steps, I hear him say, "This is a wise book," of the great family Bible that still rests in his lap, "for it tells me to do what I have already found gives me peace and happiness: I think of you in my thoughts, I love you in my heart, and I am thankful to this great God for you with my lips. Here we are: a powerful woman, a man who is no longer always alone, surrounded by all these blessings in our *garden walled around* us."

Hush! my dear, lie still and slumber;
Holy angels guard thy bed!
Heav'nly blessings without number
Gently falling on thy head.[46]

~Isaac Watts

Old Woman

There are some who hear my story and say, "My goodness! You lived a whole lifetime before you were even old enough to be called an adult!" I guess, for some that might be true. But I think the way of my life was always meant to be as full and complicated as it was, because I lived *two* lives really, not one, being both *red* and *white*. The story certainly does not end at the time when the babies were so small and we were still just a struggling village, but I grow weary with the telling now and it's as good a place as any to stop. After all, it's an old woman's prerogative to do what she wants; that's one of the benefits of having to suffer aching joints and endure the stupidity of youth.

I heard a young child the other day in our town call me "Old Woman" when they thought I wasn't listening. I may not be so quick on my feet anymore and I may have a face like a dried apple, but I've got hearing as sharp as a hawk's and I let that child have an earful of sharp words that are probably still causing him a bit of pain.

As I listened to the words that came flying out of my mouth, I had to stop and finally chuckle at the way of it all, for I realize I've become the sharp tongued old woman of the village. I remember what One Who Knows told me so very, very long ago - that sharp tongued old woman who went before me. As I'm throwing my words at that smart-aleck boy, I all of a sudden remember One Who Knows and it catches me up short and I just started laughing and laughing at the way of things on this path we call life. That fool boy went running off and I'm sure he's calling me *Crazy* Old Woman now. Let him.

I would be remiss to not tell you of the joining of Alexander and Otter and the subsequent birth of three children. Or of the election of

William Holland Thomas to the North Carolina senate, which brought recognition and great prosperity to our village, that has become a fine town (with even a railroad path traveling through). And the final official acknowledgement of our small band of Real People as being residents of the state of North Carolina and the country of the United States *with all rights and privileges afforded thereto.* As I speak to you, our tribe, known as the Real People of The Maple Forest, or The Boundary of One Who Knows' Land, lays claim to more than *fifty - six thousand acres*, all thanks to the dedication and persistence of our friend, brother, and chief, Deer.

It would be nice to tell you that things were smooth and easy for the rest of my life and there are only good things to hint about and briefly tell. But that would mean we must forget the great battle between the states that began in 1861 and went on for four long and terrible years. And we would have to forget the terrible plague of small pox that killed many in our village in 1865. Or even of the steady decline of our dear and beloved chief, Deer, who slowly followed the way of his mother and slipped into madness in the later years of his life.

I attended his funeral just a few weeks ago. For Deer, I sang the mourning song and insisted on placing kernels of corn in his grave. For William Holland Thomas there was much fanfare and speech making and even the firing of many guns to honor him. It was a good thing I'd a seat close up to the front, for the crowds that came to pay tribute to him – red and white – were great. He's the very last of those original people who welcomed and loved me in those early years when I first came to the village, a terrified captive white girl, and who helped me become the powerful Indian woman I am now. As I sat there, at a place of honor besides his family, and listened to the words of the preacher man extol his virtues, I heard the whispers of those wondering who the strange little old white woman was with the Indian tattoos and the colorful feathers still tied in her hair. These foolish young ones think that with gray hair and wrinkles comes deafness and stupidity. It suits me fine for them to think such things, for they reveal their secrets and their weaknesses, too. "Captive", "Mate", "Sister", "Bear", "Elle Graves", and "Old Woman" were but a few of the titles I heard given me and I thought to myself, *Why, they've missed a few, actually.*

It will not be long before I'm able to join all those loved ones who have gone on before me. Old age can be a curse and a blessing, I think. The desire to see your children, grandchildren, and in my case, great grandchildren and great-great grandchildren grow to be accomplished adults can be a delight. But to watch those you love go before you to the next world leaves one feeling lonely and tired at times. The voices still talk to me in my head, only now I often let them do the talking for me. The voice of One Who Knows cannot suffer fools with any patience; the voice of Raccoon still cannot resist to give an observation on the ridiculousness of life and the voice of Beaver speaks through me and tells those who will sit and listen, of the stories that must be remembered and treasured so that the Old Ways are not lost.

The voice of my beloved Bright Feather I keep just for myself and share with no one. He walks beside me all the time, for we made a promise to each other many years ago that whoever went first on this path of life would stay and wait and walk with the one left behind. He visits me in my dreams and speaks to me when sorrows are too great for only me to handle, and he smiles his sweet smiles of delight when happiness dances past me. I can still feel his gentle touch of love on my cheek with the whisper of the wind and it's he who always makes sure there's a colorful feather to be found for me to weave into my white gray hair.

I've been so many things over the course of this life's path and I've learned so many things about myself, others, and this world we live in. Hope, not a spry young little girl anymore, but a wise outspoken leader of our town, said to me, "Put your white face on, Mother, and tell the story of our people that your red face will not speak of. There are many who need to know the story. They need to know the wise lessons you have learned about perseverance, trust, love and faith. *If you do not tell it, no one will ever know.*"

It's the story of belief in one's self and the realization that my Pa was right when he said to me so very, very long ago, that life is truly *what you make of it.* It's a story of family: mothers, fathers, sisters and brothers and the understanding that it's not blood that truly joins you or the color of your skin, but the decision of your head and your heart that you are a family and to love and support one another no matter what comes your way. It's the story of love between a man and a woman and the discovery that true love delights with all the joys of life making them greater. It comforts in all the sorrows of life, making them easier to bear. And it's the story of God, who shows perfect patience, perfect love and perfect faithfulness and *hath loved us and hath given us everlasting consolation and good hope through grace* and who *comforts our hearts and establishes us in every good work and word.*[47]

This is my story. You hold it in your hands.

Black earth wear earth.
Remember the plants, trees, animal life who all have their
Tribes, their families, their histories, too.
Talk to them. Listen to them. They are alive poems.
Remember the wind. Remember her voice
She knows the Origin of this universe.
Remember that you are all people and that all people
Are you.[48]

~Jo Harjo

Actual Facts

Every historical fiction novel has a little bit of fact and a lot a bit of fiction. For me as a reader I always have a strong curiosity as to which is which. Believe it or not, I had close to seventy pages typed of the story of the fictional Elle Graves who becomes known as Bear before I knew *who, what, where,* or even *when* she was captured. Not until she began to understand the language and talk with Otter did I finally place her in history. I knew I wanted only three things: that she be captured by a tribe that was *matrilineal* (all family heritage is traced through the woman rather than *patrilineal* like we are in our society), that she be somewhere on the east coast of the United States - an area I was most familiar with, and that the story have a happy ending. Little did I know how difficult that would prove to be.

The history of the Native American Indians is about as bleak a story as you'd care to read. Starting with DeSoto's arrival in 1540 and following up through the arrival of the English, Spanish and French, by the early 1700's, it is estimated that nearly half the Native American population had died from small pox and other "white men" diseases and vices (slavery, greed, alcoholism…). Whole tribes simply ceased to exist. Add in the French and Indian War (1754-1761), the Revolutionary War (1776-1783), the War of 1812 (1812-1816) *including* the fierce battle between the Upper Creeks also known as the Red Sticks and the Lower Creeks, who joined with the Cherokees, *and* then General Andrew Jackson and the Civil War (1861-1865), *what's an author to do?*

The Cherokees called themselves *The Principal People* and from the moment I read Chief Ostenaco's documented quote, *"Where are your women?"* spoken to British representatives who had come to negotiate with him back in the early 1700's, I knew I'd found my tribe.[49] By the early 1800's, the Cherokee Nation was a stellar example of success, with a population of approximately 17,000 men, women, and children and land boundaries encompassing the north eastern corner of Alabama, north western corner of Georgia, a small western tip of North Carolina and a small eastern tip of Tennessee.   In 1820, the Old Nation Cherokees reorganized the tribal system and adopted a republican form of government that was modeled after the United States Government: they had a national council consisting of an upper and lower house, a council president, thirty two representatives who were elected by the people, laws, a judicial system, a superior court, a Cherokee Light Horse militia, and an established capital, New Echota, Georgia. They even collected taxes.[50]   They developed a written language by 1821 invented by an Indian man who went by the name of Sequoyah ("Pig's Foot") or George Gist, wrote their own constitution and even published their own bilingual newspaper called *The Cherokee Phoenix,* with the first issue dated February, 1828, and Elias Boudinot as the original editor. The Cherokees became successful in business, politics and life in general and it was reported that a vast majority of the Cherokee people were literate as well.

The story of the Cherokee Nation versus the United States of America is one no author could make up. It has murder, deception, intrigue, betrayal, infighting, and assassinations. And it is a tragic example of a people who began to fight amongst itself and in some cases became their own worst enemies. During the 1820's, as the Cherokee nation shifted from the Old Way matrilineal structure of family to the newly adopted patrilineal structure of the whites, a number of significant figures were produced that would greatly influence the fate of the Cherokee Nation: John Ross, Major Ridge, his schooled son John Ridge, and Elias Boudinot, among others. These men "were men of intellect and ability who could see into and debate issues on a level with the best of minds."[51]   The unfortunate part of the story is that they did not agree with each other on the best course for the Cherokee Nation, causing it to eventually crumble in on itself.

The divisions within its own ranks of leadership, coupled with the pressures exerted on the Nation by determined state governments, most notably being the state of Georgia, who was a fierce opponent of Cherokee interests, and the pressure of their greatest foe, the United State's own President Andrew Jackson, who "skirted U.S. laws and manipulated a fallacious treaty against the Cherokees"[52] forced the Cherokee Nation into its darkest hour. In the end, the Cherokees were no match for the greed and might of the United States and her people.

Georgia welcomed the election of hard nosed Andrew Jackson and did, shortly after his election, pass a series of laws that stole the Cherokee's rights, gold, land, and anything else promised in past treaties. Brave Cherokee missionaries, who were currently living in Cherokee country when Georgia passed these laws, refused to swear their allegiance to the state and were indeed imprisoned. In particular, Dr. Samuel A. Worcester and Elizur Butler, were arrested, put in prison garb and assigned to hard labor with criminals.[53] Tried and convicted, on appeal they won their case when the Supreme Court ruled that the Cherokee nation was independent and all dealings with them fell under federal jurisdiction. However, the ruling was ignored by then Governor Gilmer of Georgia and President Andrew Jackson and the men were held in prison for almost four years. [54]

There is a fascinating paper trail that can be followed and is available ron the Internet. Every Indian treaty ever written is available at the Okalahoma State University Library, Bureau of Indian Affairs: Laws and Treaties. You can read the promises made, see the names of those who wrote their signature or mark, and you can feel the frustration the Indian leaders must have felt as they signed treaty after treaty after treaty and simply lost more and more land. Andrew Jackson proposed the Indian Removal Act in May of 1830. His First Annual Message to Congress dated December 8, 1830, is chilling in its false concern and flowery words of reassurance and goodwill. When he speaks of "separating the Indians from immediate contact with the settlements of whites; freeing them from the power of the States; enabling them to pursue happiness in their own way and under their own rude institutions, retarding the progress of decay which is lessening their numbers and perhaps cause them gradually, under the protection of the Government and through the influence of good counsels, to cast off their savage habits and become an interesting, civilized, and Christian community"[55], I could almost be like Bear and vomit. Surely his quote, "Build a fire under them. When it gets hot enough, they'll move,"[56] is a much more honest picture of his true sentiment on the subject!

Major General Winfield Scott, placed in charge of the entire removal process by new President Martin Van Buren in 1837, is given some seven thousand army and state troops and ordered to remove the Cherokees by the treaty deadline of May of 1838. While publicly he told his soldiers to use "every possible kindness" in carrying out the task, it became "an orgy of nefarious behavior by the army."[57] While the public press of the day was virtually silent, personal journals and letters of missionaries and even brave army officers tell a far sinister tale.

Major William M. Davis, on March 5, 1836, wrote to then Secretary of War Lewis Cass, "that paper containing the articles entered into at New Echota, in December last, called a treaty, is no treaty at all, because is was not sanctioned by the great body of the Cherokee people, and made without their consent or participation in it, pro or con; and I here solemnly declare to you, without hesitation, that, upon a reference of this treaty to the Cherokee people, it would be instantly rejected by more than nine-tenths of them."[58]

During the removal process, there was indeed such a severe drought that many of the rivers were too low for boat travel.[59] I despaired when I read the history of the Trail of Tears, which departed with its first group of wagons on October 1, 1838, when *sixteen thousand* men, women and children of the Cherokee tribe were forcibly removed west of the Mississippi. Conservative estimates list the death toll at over *four thousand.* While the documents of the Indian leaders of the times are heartbreaking, it was the quotes from actual journals of missionaries, such as Evan Jones who wrote on June 16, 1838, that struck a cord with me, "The Cherokees are nearly all prisoners. They have been dragged from their houses, and encamped at the forts and military posts, all over the Cherokee nation. In Georgia, especially, multitudes were allowed no time to take anything with them, except the clothes they had on. Well-furnished houses were left prey to plunderers, who, like hungry wolves, follow in the trail of the captors. These wretches rifle in the houses and strip the helpless, unoffending owners of all they have on earth."[60]

Another missionary, Daniel S. Butrick wrote of a deaf and dumb man who was shot and killed when he failed to obey a soldier's command; of fathers seized away from their homes and not permitted to return to their wives and children; of mothers dragged away leaving behind children who were still hiding in fear in the forest; and of virtually all the Cherokees being forced to leave behind all of their worldly possessions – clothes, cattle, horses, furniture, bedding, pots and pans – everything except the clothing they wore. Buttrick wrote in his journal on May 31, "A little before sunset a company of about two hundred Cherokees were driven into our camp. The day had been rainy, and of course all, men, women, and children, were dripping wet, with no change of clothing, and scarcely a blanket fit to cover them. Mothers brought their dear little babes to our fire, and stripped off their only covering to dry, their little lips, blue and trembling with cold.[61]

The history of the Western Cherokees versus the Eastern Cherokees divides permanently with the completion of the Great Removal of 1838-1839. The census taken in 1835 on the eve of the Old Nation Cherokee's removal west gave a total population of 16, 542. Nearly half the females were under the age of sixteen and half the males were under the age of eighteen and within the tribe were *two hundred and one* intermarried whites.[62] John Ross continued to be a powerful advocating force for the Western Cherokee his entire life and signed the Treaty of 1866 on July 19th, just two weeks before he died on August 1st. As for Major Ridge, John Ridge, and Elias Boudinot, they were brutally executed by a never identified chosen group of men for the part they played in the New Echota Treaty and the removal of the Cherokees west of the Mississippi. It is doubted that John Ross ever knew of the secret meeting held on June 21, 1835, in which twelve names were drawn and execution squads were sent to carry out the old Cherokee clan "law of blood".[63]

Missionary Samuel Worcester, after his release, did travel immediately to Oklahoma with his wife and become a part of the Western Cherokees. It is largely through his endeavors that the Cherokee translations of the Bible, as well as hymnbooks, almanacs and other printed documents were made available. By 1851, there was both the Cherokee Male Seminary and the Cherokee Female Seminary, two large brick and stone buildings that concentrated on occupational skills, formal learning, cultural advancement, and the classic arts. The Cherokee Nation steadily rose like a phoenix from the ashes and once again established themselves as the most advanced Indian tribe in America.[64]

As I researched through all of this sorry history, I felt truly greatly discouraged and seriously doubted whether my "happy ending" goal could be accomplished. At one point in my frustrations to find a safe place in history for Bear and those I planned to have her love and care about, my husband said, *"Just make it all up why don't you?!"* But in the end, it was my decision that a *good* historical fiction novel could not twist the truth of things so much that the reader comes out misinformed. And then I found the name *William Holland Thomas* and I knew I had found a place for Bear to be.

William Holland Thomas, *was* adopted by a chief named Drowning Bear or *Yonaguska,* if you're more inclined toward the Cherokee. I found at least one reference that puzzled over Thomas' insistence of calling himself an orphan, despite the fact that his mother lived on family property and was a "continual influence".[65] He was a trader, he was a self taught lawyer, he was a politician serving in the North Carolina Senate from 1848-1861, he was the chief of the Eastern Cherokees, from 1839-1867. The Civil War, in which he and his own battalion of Cherokee braves fought for the Confederate side, sapped him of his money and his sanity. Eventually, creditors foreclosed on his property, attempting to sell all of his land holdings to settle his debts. Despite insane ravings in and out of court and arbitration, he remained steadfastly committed and coherent on one point: *the land belonged to the Cherokees.* He did marry and have three children (two boys and a girl), and he did, unfortunately, die in the Dorothea Dix Hospital insane at the age of about 92. He truly was *the savior of the Eastern Cherokee Nation.*

This small band of Cherokees that William Holland Thomas was adopted into, did take the option for citizenship. The Treaty of 1819 lists the names of those Cherokees who made what must have been a most difficult decision to sever their connections with the Cherokee Nation and choose the frightening path of citizenship with the United States. I think of the confidence they had to have had in Thomas to make such a decision and the weight of the responsibility he carried on his shoulders as the result of it. This area became known as the *Qualla Boundary,* named after an old woman named "Polly" ("Qualla" was the best they could pronounce "Polly") and who was well thought of in the village.

The story of Charly, or *Tsali,* as the Cherokees called him, is wreathed in legend and actual facts are scant. Depending on who you are inclined to speak to, Cherokee or white, Tsali was either a murdering fugitive of justice or he was a hero who sacrificed his life for the assured security of his family and that of the Eastern Cherokees. The facts I found that both sides agreed on were that Tsali was a Cherokee, who killed a number of soldiers in the struggles during the great removal time, that William Holland Thomas assisted in Tsali's capture thereby securing permission for the Eastern Band of Cherokees to stay in Western North Carolina, and that Tsali was executed by a Cherokee firing squad. The Cherokee perform a reenactment of Tsali's story called *Unto These Hills* at the Oconaluftee Indian Village near Bryson, North Carolina for a major part of each year.

Situated by the *Oconaluftee River*, (from the Cherokee work *egwanul'ti* meaning "by the river"), the Qualla Boundary, Indiantown, the Oconaluftee Indians or the Eastern Band of the Cherokee Nation were described by an author who visited them in 1848. "About three-fourths of the entire population can read in their own language, and though the majority of them understand English, a very few can speak the language. They practice, to a considerable extent, the science of agriculture, and have acquired such a knowledge of the mechanic arts as answers them for all ordinary purposes, for they manufacture their own clothing, their own ploughs, and other farm utensils, their own axes, and even their own guns.

"Their women are no longer treated as slaves, but as equals; the men labor in the fields and their views are devoted entirely to household employment. They keep the same domestic animals that are kept by their white neighbors, and cultivate all the common grains of the country. They are probably as temperate as any other class of people on the face of the earth, honest in their business intercourse, moral in their thoughts, words, and deeds, and distinguished for their faithfulness in performing the duties of religion.

"They are chiefly Methodists and Baptists, and have regularly ordained ministers, who preach to them on every Sabbath, and they have also abandoned many of their more senseless superstitions. They have their own court and try their criminals themselves. They keep in order the public roads leading through their settlement. By a law of the state they have the right to vote, but seldom exercise that right, as they do not like the idea of being identified with any of the political parties. Except on festive days, they dress after the manner of the white man, but far more picturesquely. The live in small log houses of their own construction, and have everything they need or desire in the way of food.

"They are in fact, the happiest community that I have yet met within this southern country."[66]

The Cherokee who embrace the Old Way do not focus on time, wealth, or power. In fact, their language makes no reference to the future or the past, but just focuses on the present, today.[67] As you read the history of the Eastern Cherokee, it is a stunning example of a people who were committed to surviving *at all costs*. They bent when the wind was too strong, but they never broke. They looked carefully into the future and recognized their strengths and their weaknesses and consequently made wise choices for survival that others could or would not see. I see no conflict between the Old Way of the Cherokee and choices that were made back in the early 1800's by the Qualla Indians, who became the Eastern Band of the Cherokees, so that their Old Way of life could be preserved.

Today, the Eastern Band of the Cherokees, sits on fifty-six thousand acres of land in western North Carolina and has a population of over seven thousand individuals.[68] In the end, the land was placed in federal trust, communally owned by the Eastern Band of the Cherokees. Unlike the Oklahoma Cherokees, whose tribal government was dissolved by the Dawes Act and Jerome Commission, the Eastern Band of the Cherokees still continue their own legislative form of government today. They elect a principal chief, who serves a four-year term and presides over a legislature compromising two representatives elected from each of five town districts.[69] Their principal source of revenue is tourism, but there is still significant investment in other businesses both large and small. A wonderful book I stumbled on, *Footsteps of the Cherokees, A Guide To The Eastern Homelands of the Cherokee Nation*, helped me - as I sat at my computer - feel what it must have felt like for Bear as she tromped through the woods and experienced the beauty of the North Carolina forest wilderness. At last I found a safe place to put her that could have a happy ending.

They are The Cherokee, The Principal People, the Ani-Yun-wiya.

You can't judge a man by his color
you can't see the savage within
but the deeds that he may do to his brothers
will reveal the true hearts of men70.

Acknowledgements

Personally, the entire process of this book, from the initial idea (a very vivid image of a frightened white girl being very gently touched on the cheek by a fierce Indian brave) to the final, *real* possibility that this could be published has been nothing short of a miracle. I could write pages about all the wonderful coincidences (some that gave me goose bumps) that occurred during the writing, but the book is too long already. Suffice it to say that I could *not* have done this on my own.

There is a strong Christian message in this story and that is not by chance. Had the book arrived, packaged with a nice neat bow on my front step, God could not have shown me more clearly what He wanted to do. While I did not want to cram any of this "God stuff" down reluctant throats, I cannot escape the very essence of what I strive to be; "a woman after God's own heart". No one's life is perfect; there is great sorrow we must face, things rarely work out just as we'd hoped they would, and disappointments are a dime a dozen. But I don't believe you go through this life alone and so my story *must* reflect that.

From the very first time I hesitantly said, "I think I'm writing a book…" (said with great wonder and trepidation) family and friends have encouraged and championed me. To Mom, Marylynn, who read it and said, "Best Seller" (in her best Mom's voice), to Dad, Herb, who gets teary when he talks about his girls (and the good things they get up to), to Wendy who carried the 500 pound binder with her on her two week vacation to Cape Cod *and read it*, to Aunt Evie and Debbie Francis who, between the two of them sent me close to *fifty pages* of corrections and will remain forever as the world's best proofreaders, to my sister, Amy, who after reading all 700 plus pages was furious because the last chapter was "so short", to my wonderful husband, David, who dealt with no dinners, unfolded laundry, and a general lack of care and attention and kept saying, "just tell me when I can retire", to my son, Ian, who said, "If you get famous, do you think I could get to meet J.K. Rowling?", to my daughter, Gracie, who upon opening and reading yet another rejection letter said, "Well...at least she said she liked it before she sent it back to you. She didn't have to do that, you know", to my youngest son, Luke, who when I said I was going to miss him when he went off to kindergarten said, "Don't worry, you'll just have more time to work at your computer", to my friend, Linda who has been so patient – and yet *so certain*, waiting for me to get famous so that she can get on television (Hi, Regis!), to Pam Frueh the world's best editor who seems to be able to get inside my head and make changes and suggestions that still match my style and goal (I really appreciate you even if I groan when I get the hundreds of changes...!) and to my Bible Study ladies who are all powerful women each in their own right and wonderful role models for me to follow: Patti, Beth, Melony, Kate, Jen, Jenn, Maria, Judy, and Kim, and to Laury Vaden, artist extraordinaire who brought the face of Bear to life with her talent and has tirelessly and patiently designed for me The Best Book Covers In The World ... For want of better words: THANK YOU.

Sue McG

Cast of Characters

The People of the Maple Forest

- ❖ **Bear** – Elle Grave's Indian name
- ❖ **Bright Feather** – Indian brave who joins with Bear
- ❖ **Deer** – adopted son of War Woman, also known as William Holland Thomas
- ❖ **Raccoon** – Indian brave, mate of Otter
- ❖ **Otter** – Indian woman, daughter of War Woman, mate of Raccoon
- ❖ **Little Bird** – Raccoon and Otter's son
- ❖ **Squirrel** – Raccoon and Otter's daughter
- ❖ **Great Elk** – Chief of the Indians of the Maple Forest
- ❖ **War Woman** – Mate of Great Elk
- ❖ **Cloud** – Indian brave
- ❖ **Red Fox** – Indian brave
- ❖ **Beaver** – Indian brave
- ❖ **One Who Knows** – Indian woman, village healer
- ❖ **Double Arrow** – Indian brave rescued from Fort Payne, Tennessee
- ❖ **Mary** – Indian woman rescued from Fort Payne, Tennessee
- ❖ **Turtle** – Indian woman, daughter of One Who Knows, mate of Red Fox
- ❖ **Martha** – Beaver's mate
- ❖ **Still Waters** – Beaver's son
- ❖ **Fern** – Beaver's daughter
- ❖ **Storm Eli** – Bear and Bright Feather's son
- ❖ **Hope Elizabeth** – Bear and Bright Feather's daughter

The People of New Echota, Georgia

- ❖ **Dark Cloud** – Chief, known in the white world as Major Ridge
- ❖ **John Ross** – Elected leader of the entire nation of Real People
- ❖ **Weasel** – Indian brave
- ❖ **Elias Boudinot** – Indian brave, editor of Cherokee Newspaper *The Cherokee Phoenix*
- ❖ **Sequoia** – Also known as Pig's Foot, invented the written language of the Cherokee
- ❖ **Reverend James Wilder** – Missionary to the Real People, based in New Echota, Georgia, called The Messenger by the Indians
- ❖ **Rebecca Wilder** – James Wilder's wife

❖ **Martin DuBois** – French trader

The People of Ward's Mill, Virginia
❖ **Elle Graves** – daughter of Andrew and Elizabeth Graves
❖ **Andrew Graves** – Elle's Father
❖ **Elizabeth Graves** – Elle's Mother
❖ **Henry Graves** – Elle's brother, four years older
❖ **Eli Graves** – Elle's younger brother, eight years younger
❖ **Cornelius Cooper** – Proprietor of Cooper's General Store
❖ **Naomi Cooper** – Cornelius Cooper's wife
❖ **Johnny Cooper** – Cornelius and Naomi Cooper's son
❖ **Ezekiel West** – resident of Ward's Mill, Virginia
❖ **Jane West** – Ezekiel West's wife
❖ **Daniel Hobson** – resident of Ward's Mill, Virgina

The People of Forest City, North Carolina
❖ **William Holland Thomas** – Proprietor of Trading Post in Forest City, North Carolina, also known as Deer of The Maple Forest
❖ **Possum** – of the Turkey clan of The Real People of The Maple Forest, Deer's mate, also known as Mary Thomas
❖ **James, Red Bird** – Deer and Possum's eldest son
❖ **Eliza, Sleeping Rabbit** – Deer and Possum's daughter
❖ **Richard, Small Turtle** – Deer and Possum's youngest son

The People of Fort Winston, Virginia
❖ **Alexander Everett** – Major, Second United States Cavalry, Division of the Army, Company A. based in Fort Winston, Virginia
❖ **George Maw** – Alexander Everett's interpreter
❖ **Lieutenant George Foster** - Commander of Fort Winston, Virginia, Second United States Cavalry, Company A, and Ninth Virginia Cavalry, Company D
❖ **Joan Foster** – Wife of Lieutenant Foster
❖ **Lydia Foster** – daughter of George and Joan Foster
❖ **Nate Foster** – son of George and Joan Foster
❖ **Paul Foster** – son of George and Joan Foster

The People of Fort Payne, Tennessee
❖ **Sergeant Peter McTavish** - First United States Cavalry, Company B, stationed at Fort Payne, Tennessee

- ❖ **Commander Winfield Scott** - Major General in the United States of America's Army, stationed at Fort Payne, Tennessee
- ❖ **Linda Scott** – Commander Scott's daughter

Book Timeline

Black type = actual facts

BOLD CAPITAL TYPE = NOVEL STORYLINE

BOOK CHAPTER

Date	Event
1540	DeSoto explores.
1684	England makes treaty with Cherokees.
1738	Smallpox arrives in South Carolina and ½ of nation dies in one year from small pox.
1754-1761	French and Indian War (Cherokees side with British.)
1763	Proclamation of 1763 a royal decree of George III of Britain, which prohibits colonists from settling west of the Appalachian Mountains and reserves this area for Indians.
1775	Cherokees sell what will become Kentucky to English.
1776-1783	Revolutionary War (Cherokees side with British.)
6/25/1788	Virginia becomes the 10th state of the USA.
4/30/1789	George Washington elected as President.
3/4/1801	Thomas Jefferson elected as President.
1802	**BIRTH OF BRIGHT FEATHER.**
1802	William Holland Thomas born.
1807	**MARRIAGE OF ELLE'S PARENTS: ANDREW AND ELIZABETH GRAVES.**
3/4/1809	James Madison elected as President.
1809	Sequoyah begins work on a Cherokee alphabet.
1809	Cherokees set up a central government that acts for the whole tribe and models the white style of government.
1810	**HENRY GRAVES'S BIRTH.**
1810	**WILLIAM HOLLAND THOMAS IS FOUND AND ADOPTED BY GREAT ELK'S VILLAGE.**
6/1812-12/1814	War of 1812
3/27/1814	The Battle of Horseshoe Bend
10/1814	**ELLE GRAVE'S BIRTH**
1817	**WILLIAM THOMAS, KNOWN AS DEER, RETURNS TO THE WHITES IN SEARCH OF HIS WHITE FAMILY.**
1817	**ELLE'S FAMILY MOVES TO HOMESTEAD IN FAR WESTERN VIRGINIA; WARD'S MILL.**

7/8/1817	Treaty of 1817, ratified Dec. 26, 1817.
Spring 1818	**WEASEL OF DARK CLOUD'S VILLAGE MARRIES ONE WHO KNOWS' OLDER DAUGHTER; RAVEN, OF GREAT ELK'S VILLAGE.**
6/6/1818	Census taken of all Cherokee.
2/27/1819	Treaty, Proclaimed Mar 10, 1819, tribal lands given up, offer of citizenship made, small number of Indians in North Carolina near the Oconaluftee River take the option for citizenship.
1820	**BRIGHT FEATHER MARRIES ONE WHO KNOWS YOUNGER DAUGHTER, BLACK FOX.**
1821	Cherokee Written` Language, Sequoyah develops a system of 86 symbols that stand for Cherokee syllables.
1821	William Holland Thomas establishes trading post near Indian Territory.
1822	**DISAPPEARANCE OF ONE WHO KNOWS OLDEST DAUGHTER, RAVEN.**
1822	**DEATH OF BRIGHT FEATHER'S MATE, BLACK FOX, AND UNBORN SON.**
1822	**ELLE'S MOTHER'S DEATH, ELI GRAVES'S BIRTH.**

BOOK I

3/22/1828		*CAPTIVE*
Late summer 1828		*BEAR*
2/1828	Cherokees print a bilingual newspaper, ***The Cherokee Phoenix*** with Elias Boudinot as editor.	
5/6/1828	**Treaty**, proclaimed May 28, 1828.	
Early spring 1829		*POWERFUL WOMAN*
Late summer -Early fall, 1829		*MATE*
		LISTENER

BOOK II

Winter 1829-1830		*ELLE GRAVES*
		GUEST
February 1830		*JOURNEYWOMAN*
		SISTER

5/30/1830	President Andrew Jackson's **Removal Act**
Late Summer 1830	🔲 *MOTHER*
1830	**Georgia,** shortly after Jackson's election, passes a series of laws against the Cherokees.
1832-1833	**Georgia Land Lottery**
Today	🔲 *ACTUAL FACTS*

BOOK III

7/1832	🔲 *CITIZEN*
1833	🔲 *TRADER*
1835-1837	🔲 *FUGITIVE*
12/29/1835	**New Echota Treaty,** proclaimed May 23, 1836. Major John Ridge, leader of a group of Cherokees in Georgia and of mixed blood, signs a treaty agreeing to move west for 5 million dollars and 13 million acres in the west.
3/8/1836	**Led by Chief John Ross,** 16,000 Cherokees do not want the treaty. They go to Washington with a petition, but President Jackson does not even look at the paper, as he no longer recognizes the government of the Cherokee Nation.
5/23/1836	**U.S. Congress** legalizes the New Echota Treaty.
Spring, 1837	**Martin Van Buren** elected as President.
Spring, 1837	🔲 *HUNTER*
1838	**Gen. Winfield Scott** is given command of 7,000 army and state troops charged with removing the Cherokee Nation.
1838-1839	17,000 Cherokees are forced to leave their homelands and travel west. 4,000 die on the trip. "**The Trail of Tears.**" This band becomes known as the Western Cherokees.
1839	🔲 **SURVIVOR**
1839	**William Holland Thomas** made chief of Eastern Cherokees.
1861-1865	Civil War
1866	**North Carolina** recognizes the Cherokees of the Qualla band as permanent residents of the state.
1866	**Smallpox epidemic** decimates the tribe.
1867	**William Holland Thomas** resigns as chief of Cherokees.
1867	William Holland Thomas **is declared insane.**

1893	▩	*OLD WOMAN*
Today	▩	*ACTUAL FACTS*
Today	Known as the **Qualla Boundary, Cherokee, NC,** is home to the Eastern Band of the Cherokee Nation. Covering over 56,000 acres the Qualla Boundary and Cherokee, NC, is nestled in The Great Smoky Mountains.	

Family Tree

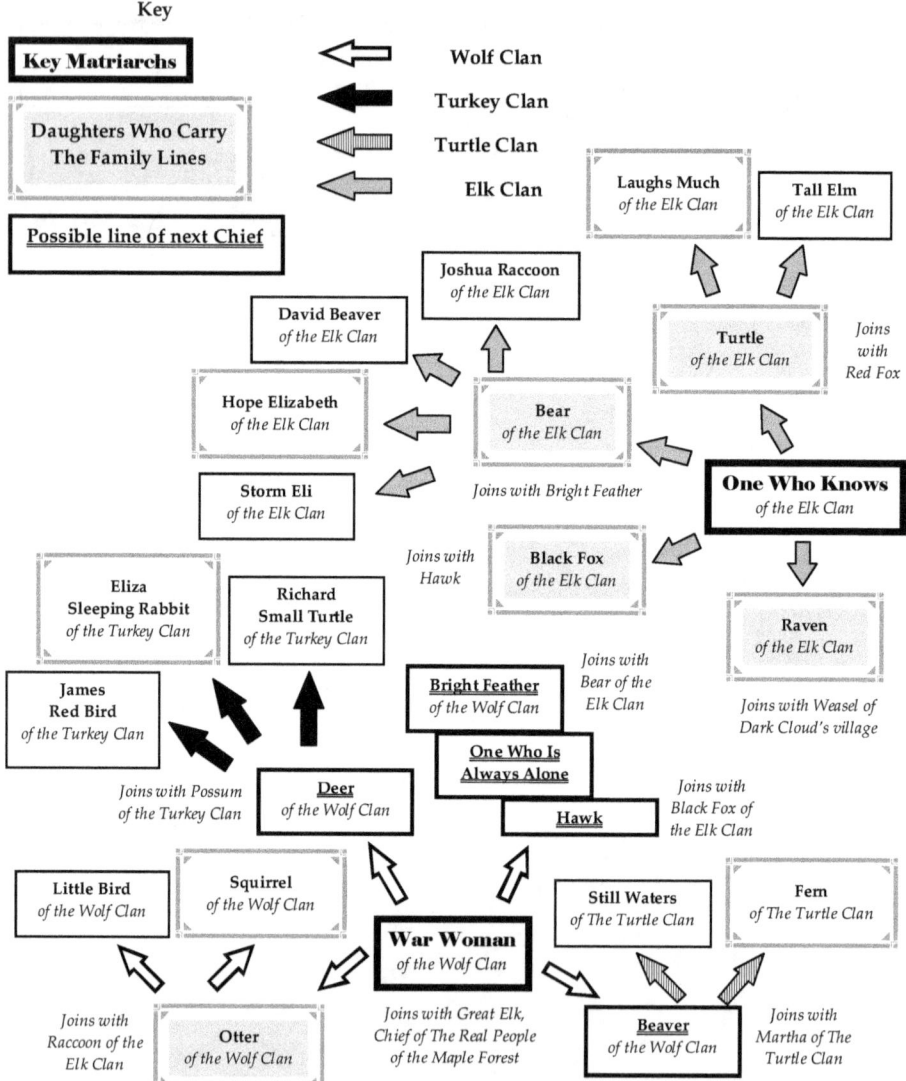

Key

Key Matriarchs	Wolf Clan
Daughters Who Carry The Family Lines	Turkey Clan
	Turtle Clan
Possible line of next Chief	Elk Clan

Laughs Much
of the Elk Clan

Tall Elm
of the Elk Clan

Joshua Raccoon
of the Elk Clan

Turtle
of the Elk Clan

Joins with Red Fox

David Beaver
of the Elk Clan

Hope Elizabeth
of the Elk Clan

Bear
of the Elk Clan

One Who Knows
of the Elk Clan

Storm Eli
of the Elk Clan

Joins with Bright Feather

Black Fox
of the Elk Clan

Joins with Hawk

Raven
of the Elk Clan

Eliza Sleeping Rabbit
of the Turkey Clan

Richard Small Turtle
of the Turkey Clan

Joins with Bear of the Elk Clan

Joins with Weasel of Dark Cloud's village

James Red Bird
of the Turkey Clan

Bright Feather
of the Wolf Clan

One Who Is Always Alone

Joins with Possum of the Turkey Clan

Deer
of the Wolf Clan

Hawk

Joins with Black Fox of the Elk Clan

Little Bird
of the Wolf Clan

Squirrel
of the Wolf Clan

Still Waters
of The Turtle Clan

Fern
of The Turtle Clan

War Woman
of the Wolf Clan

Joins with Raccoon of the Elk Clan

Otter
of the Wolf Clan

Joins with Great Elk, Chief of The Real People of the Maple Forest

Beaver
of the Wolf Clan

Joins with Martha of The Turtle Clan

North Carolina Today

Counties: Swain, Graham, Jackson
Population: 13,400
State Recognition: 1889
Federal Recognition: 1868

"The Eastern Band of Cherokee descended from the Cherokee who in the late 1830s remained in the mountains of North Carolina rather than be forced into Oklahoma along the infamous Trail of Tears. These thousand or so tribal members lived along the Oconaluftee River, some hiding out. The Cherokee eventually gained the Qualla Boundary reservation, the 56,572-acre site where the tribe resides today. The Cherokee are the only indigenous people in America to have their own written language, developed by Sequoyah.

The Eastern Band of Cherokee is the only federally recognized tribe in North Carolina and the only tribe living on land held in trust. The tribe actively promotes tourism on the boundary, with cultural activities, events, and an outdoor drama. In addition, the Cherokee sell traditional arts and crafts such as baskets, pottery, beadwork, stone carvings, and wood carvings. The tribe's involvement in many business ventures helps ensure its livelihood."[71]

About The Author

Susan McGeown is a wife, mother, daughter, sister, friend, aunt, uncle (don't ask), teacher, author ... but, most importantly, a "woman after God's own heart." Living in Bridgewater, New Jersey, with her husband of over twenty years and their three children, writing stories is just about the best way she can imagine spending her free time. Each of Sue's stories champions those emotions nearest and dearest to her: faith, joy, hope and love.

Philippians 1:20-21

For I fully expect and hope that I will never be ashamed, but that I will continue to be bold for Christ, as I have been in the past. And I trust that my life will bring honor to Christ, whether I live or die. For to me, living means living for Christ, and dying is even better.

Footnotes

Portions in the book that tell of stories from the Cherokee: Beaver's story of the Ceremony of Life, One Who Knows story of The Beginning of Time, Bright Feather's story of the Four Sacred Directions, and War Woman's story of Grandmother Corn and the song that she sings are based on the descriptions of these stories given in the book <u>Meditations with The Cherokee, Prayers, Songs, and Stories of Healing and Harmony</u>, by J.T. Garret, Ed.D., Bear and Company Publishers, Rochester, Vermont, 2001.

---

[1] Henry David Thoreau

[2] *The Cherokees, A First Americans Book*, By Virginia Driving Hawk Sneve, Holiday House, New York, 1996, p. 4

[3] Sir Thomas Overby, *The Wife*, December, 1613, Stationers' Register

[4] *The Cherokees, A First Americans Book*, By Virginia Driving Hawk Sneve, Holiday House, New York, 1996, p. 28

[5] *Women in American Indian Society*, By Rayna Green, Chelsea House Publishers, New York, 1992, p. 32-33

[6] Psalm 23:4, King James Version

[7] Jeremiah 29:11-14, King James Version

[8] Lloyd Carl Owle, Cherokee Poet,
http://www.homestead.com/spirithorse/mp.html

[9] Psalm 23:5-6, King James Version

[10] Cherokee Expression

[11] "Teach Me The Measure Of My Days", Isaac Watts, 1674-1748

[12] Lamentations 3:22-25, King James Version

[13] "We Are A Garden Walled Around", Isaac Watts, 1674-1748

[14] from a Cherokee Sacred Formula quoted in <u>A Bare Unpainted Table,</u> By Gladys Cardiff, New Issues Press, Western Michigan University, 1999, p. 33

[15] From a poem entitled "Remember Me", Copyright 1989 Renee Womble

[16] 'Twas The Watches of the Night, Isaac Watts, 1674-1748

[17] God My Supporter and My Hope, Isaac Watts, 1674-148

[18] Psalm 23:5, King James Version

[19] From a speech given May 26, 1826, by Elias Boudinot, at the First Presbyterian Church in Philadelphia

[20] "Remember" By Joy Harjo (Creek) *Women in American Indian Society*, By Rayna Green, Chelsea House Publishers, New York, 1992p. 100

[21] <u>Eastern/Central Medicinal Plants and Herbs,</u> Peterson Field Guide, By Steven Foster and James A. Duke, National Audubon Society, Houghton Mifflin Company, New York, 2000

[22] Spoken by General Andrew Jackson to Cherokee chief Junaluska on March 27, 1814 at the end of the Battle of Horseshoe Bend in Alabama.

[23] Psalm 23:5, King James Version

[24] "Teach Me The Measure of My Days", Isaac Watts, 1674-1748

[25] "We Are A Garden Walled Around", Isaac Watts, 1674-1748

[26] "We Are A Garden Walled Around", Isaac Watts, 1674-1748

[27] "Remember" By Joy Harjo (Creek) *Women in American Indian Society*, By Rayna Green, Chelsea House Publishers, New York, 1992p. 100

[28] Meditations with The Cherokee, Prayers, Songs, and Stories of Healing and Harmony, by J.T. Garret, Ed.D., Bear and Company Publishers, Rochester, Vermont, 2001, p. 124

[29] The Cherokees, By Virginia Driving Hawk Sneve, Holiday House, New York, 1996, p. 22

[30] Romans 8:28, King James Version

[31] Preserve Me Lord, In Time of Need, Isaac Watts, 1674-1748

[32] 'Twas In the Watches of the Night, Isaac Watts, 1674-1748

[33] John Ross' speech is an amalgamation of three separate written documents: Papers of John Ross, Volume I, page 166, John Ross' letter to President Andrew Jackson, dated January 23, 1835 and John Ross' letter to Secretary of War, Lewis Cass, dated February 29, 1836. They are not direct quotes as tenses were changed to fit the text.

[34] Song of Solomon 8:6-7, King James Version

[35] Ralph Waldo Emerson

[36] Home Sweet Home, By John Howard Payne, composition date approximately 1823

[37] Treaty with the Cherokee, Dated December 29, 1835, Article 12

[38] The Brother's Cry Written by Carl Towns ©1998 Abiel Publishing, BMI

[39] Meditations with The Cherokee, Prayers, Songs, and Stories of Healing and Harmony, by J.T. Garret, Ed.D., Bear and Company Publishers, Rochester, Vermont, 2001, p. 26-27

[40] God My Supporter and My Hope, Isaac Watts, 1674-148

[41] Unknown author, Old Cherokee Prayer

[42] *The Cherokees*, By Virginia Driving Hawk Sneve, Holiday House, New York, 1996, p.6

[43] Psalm 30:2, 5, King James Version

[44] Numbers 27:13-14, King James Version

[45] Philippians 4:5-9, King James Version

[46] Watt's Cradle Song, Isaac Watts, 1674-1748

[47] 2 Thessalonians 2:16-16, King James Version

[48] "Remember" By Joy Harjo (Creek) *Women in American Indian Society*, By Rayna Green, Chelsea House Publishers, New York, 1992p.

[49] The Cherokees, By Virginia Driving Hawk Sneve, Holiday House, New York, 1996, p. 22

[50] The Cherokees and Their Chiefs, by Stanley W. Hoig, University of Arkansas Press, Fayetteville, Arkansas, 1998, p. 121

[51] The Cherokees and Their Chiefs, by Stanley W. Hoig, University of Arkansas Press, Fayetteville, Arkansas, 1998, p. 124

[52] The Cherokees and Their Chiefs, by Stanley W. Hoig, University of Arkansas Press, Fayetteville, Arkansas, 1998, p. 145

[53] The Cherokees and Their Chiefs, by Stanley W. Hoig, University of Arkansas Press, Fayetteville, Arkansas, 1998, p. 148

[54] About North Georgia, Internet site:
http://ngeorgia.com/people/worcester.html

[55] President Andrew Jackson's Case for The Removal Act, First Annual Message to Congress, 8th December, 1830.

[56] President Andrew Jackson, in 1829 *The Cherokees*, By Virginia Driving Hawk Sneve, Holiday House, New York, 1996, p. 22

[57] The Cherokees and Their Chiefs, by Stanley W. Hoig, University of Arkansas Press, Fayetteville, Arkansas, 1998, p.166-167

[58] The Cherokees and Their Chiefs, by Stanley W. Hoig, University of Arkansas Press, Fayetteville, Arkansas, 1998, p. 167, quoted from the *Baptist Missionary Magazine 18* (September 1838), p. 155, quoted from the *Daily National Intelligencer*, May 22, 1838.

[59] The Cherokees and Their Chiefs, by Stanley W. Hoig, University of Arkansas Press, Fayetteville, Arkansas, 1998, p. 167, quoted from the Baptist Missionary Magazine 18 (September 1838): 169

[60] The Cherokees and Their Chiefs, by Stanley W. Hoig, University of Arkansas Press, Fayetteville, Arkansas, 1998, p. 167, quoted from the *Baptist Missionary Magazine 18* (September 1838): 236

[61] The Cherokees and Their Chiefs, by Stanley W. Hoig, University of Arkansas Press, Fayetteville, Arkansas, 1998, p. 167, quoted from *The Butrick Journal*, Oklahoma Historical Society, Archives and Manuscripts Division

[62] The Cherokees and Their Chiefs, by Stanley W. Hoig, University of Arkansas Press, Fayetteville, Arkansas, 1998, p. 167, quoted from the *Baptist Missionary Magazine 18* (September 1838) p. 163.

[63] The Cherokees and Their Chiefs, by Stanley W. Hoig, University of Arkansas Press, Fayetteville, Arkansas, 1998, p. 167, quoted from the *Baptist Missionary Magazine 18* (September 1838), p. 192-193.

[64] The Cherokees and Their Chiefs, by Stanley W. Hoig, University of Arkansas Press, Fayetteville, Arkansas, 1998, p. 167, quoted from the *Baptist Missionary Magazine 18* (September 1838), p. 205-207

[65] "Haywood man devoted his life to the Cherokee". By Kathy N. Ross

[66] An author named Lanman, who visited the Eastern Band in 1848.

[67] Meditations with The Cherokee, Prayers, Songs, and Stories of Healing and Harmony, by J.T. Garret, Ed.D., Bear and Company Publishers, Rochester, Vermont, 2001, p. xiii-xiv

[68] Footsteps of the Cherokees, A Guide to the Eastern Homelands of the Cherokee Nation, by Vicki Rozema, John F. Blair, Publisher, Winston-Salem, North Carolina, 1995, p. 62

[69] The Cherokees and Their Chiefs, by Stanley W. Hoig, University of Arkansas Press, Fayetteville, Arkansas, 1998, p. 167, quoted from the *Baptist Missionary Magazine 18* (September 1838), p. 268

[70] Written by Carl Towns(©1998) Abiel Publishing, BMI)

[71] http://ncmuseumofhistory.org/workshops/ai/Session1.htm